A Fortunate Age

a novel

JOANNA SMITH RAKOFF

Scribner

NEW YORK   LONDON   TORONTO   SYDNEY

SCRIBNER

A Division of Simon & Schuster, Inc.
1230 Avenue of the Americas
New York, NY 10020

First Scribner hardcover edition April 2009

SCRIBNER and design are trademarks of
The Gale Group, Inc., used under license
by Simon & Schuster, Inc., the publisher of this work.

For information about special discounts for bulk purchases, please contact Simon & Schuster Special Sales at 1-800-456-6798 or business@simonandschuster.com.

Designed by Kyoko Watanabe
Text set in Bembo

Manufactured in the United States of America

10   9   8   7   6   5   4   3   2   1

Library of Congress Control Number: 200824808

ISBN-13: 978-1-4165-9077-4
ISBN-10: 1-4165-9077-3

For Evan

What she was clear upon was, that she did not wish to lead the same sort of life as ordinary young ladies did; but what she was not clear upon was, how she should set about leading any other. . . .

—GEORGE ELIOT, *DANIEL DERONDA*

A Fortunate Age

one

On a gray October day in 1998, Lillian Roth found herself walking down the stone-floored aisle of Temple Emanu-El, clad in a gown of dark ivory satin and flanked by her thin, smiling parents, who had flown into New York from Los Angeles a mere seven days earlier, still in mild shock that their obstreperous daughter was submitting to the ancient rite of marriage. The synagogue's vaulted ceiling spinning above her, she took small, self-conscious steps toward the bima, where a serious-faced young man named William Hayes—saddled with the improbable nickname of Tuck—waited for her in an unfamiliar black suit, purchased two days earlier by his mother, who'd deemed the gray suit selected by Lil and Tuck inappropriate for an evening affair.

Four years and four months prior, Lillian had graduated from Oberlin College with honors in English (just plain honors, she often reminded herself in the years that followed, not *highest* honors, like her friend Sadie Peregrine, or even *high* honors, like their departmental nemesis, Caitlin Green). At her commencement brunch, dressed in another frock of dark ivory, she'd made a scene, feverishly arguing with her father about the purpose of marriage in the modern age. "It's an outmoded institution," she'd insisted, her dark brows moving closer together. The brunch, sponsored by the college, was held in a dank tent on Wilder Bowl, and the Moët was flowing perhaps a bit too freely. Lil had already spilled several sips down her dress. "Read *any* modern thinker—" Struggling to come up with a specific name, she looked to her friends, her "crowd," as her father annoyingly called them—Sadie, Beth Bernstein, Emily Kaplan, Tal Morgenthal, and Dave Kohane—who sat around and opposite her, surrounded by their own parents, faces flushed proud. "They all say so."

The adults grinned serenely (*smugly*, to Lil's mind) and tilted their heads toward her, in gestures of intense patience. "You want a certain sense of *security*," suggested Sadie's mother, Rose, with whom Lil was a great favorite, having been brought home to the Peregrine town house for numerous Thanksgivings and spring breaks and even one summer, which Lil recalled as two months of unbridled bliss. "At a certain point, you want to *belong* to something, to a family."

Dave's mother leaned across the table toward Lil, her long red hair falling into the remains of her omelet. "I remember saying the exact same thing when I was your age."

"*Mom,*" Dave moaned.

"Really?" said Lil, biting bits of dried lipstick off her lower lip. "I really don't think I'm going to change my mind." Her elders shared a dark glance. "I mean, is there *any* reason why people should get married?" Lil's father raised his wiry black brows, white threads extending from them like antennae, and let a gust of air out through his nose, from which hairs, white and black, also poked, mortifyingly. Twenty-odd years in Los Angeles had done nothing to weaken his Brooklyn accent.

"Taxes," he grumbled. "You get some tax breaks if you're married."

"*Barry,*" cried Lil's mother, giving his arm a push.

Lil rolled her eyes. "Then why," she asked, "do I always hear people complaining about the 'marriage penalty'?"

Those five friends now sat in the synagogue's front benches—soon they would be called to the bima to take part in the ceremony—the girls zipped and laced and strapped into evening dresses, which they'd carried uptown in plastic garment bags and hung up to steam in the guest bathroom at the Peregrine town house, almost thirty blocks north of Emanu-El. They'd emerged from the 6 train at Eighty-sixth Street in the early morning to the sights of this strange and hectic neighborhood: blonde moms in jogging suits pushing goggle-eyed babies in old-fashioned prams; fancy grocers and chemists; matrons with pageboys, in dated suits and low-heeled pumps, and even, in some cases, neat fabric gloves. Such things proved exotic to these girls, who were just discovering the city from the vantage point of its more downtrodden, Bohemian outposts: Williamsburg, Carroll Gardens, the grimy fringes of the Lower East Side. All neighborhoods that now command impressive rents, but were then regarded as vaguely suspect and marginally safe, particularly by the parents of the young persons in question.

Not that they cared ("Mom, it's *fine!*"). They lived where they could afford to live without the dreaded parental supplementation: in run-down tenements on narrow Brooklyn blocks, illegal sublets found through friends of friends (who could afford a broker's fee?), or rickety apartments in crumbling back-houses, let by landlords who'd never heard the word "code" in their miserly lives and who insisted on installing everything—from stoves to toilets—themselves, despite their inability to read English-language instruction manuals. According to Lil, Emily's apartment, on an increasingly expensive block in Williamsburg, had almost exploded a year prior, when the landlady used water piping rather than gas piping in the flat's little wall heater. "The gas just *ate through* the pipes," Lil had told Beth, breathlessly, over the phone. "She got home from work and there was gas puddled all over the floor. The fumes were so strong she could smell them on the street. Brooklyn Gas told her that if she'd worked an hour later, the place would have blown." Emily had stayed with Lil, at her place on Bedford, for nearly a week before things were straightened out.

And though Emily and Sadie worked in midtown and Lil attended Columbia, they met at bars in the East Village, coffee shops on the Lower East Side, and restaurants in Brooklyn, which Sadie Peregrine had, for a year or two after college, until the joke became old and a little embarrassing, called "the Far East," as she'd never visited the borough in her youth, never mind that her mother had grown up in Greenpoint, in a railroad apartment above Sadie's grandfather's optician shop (though she behaved, as Sadie liked to say, relishing the cliché, as though she were to the manor born).

Thus, the Upper East Side—where Sadie herself was born and raised, as were several generations of Peregrines before her—was alien territory to the other girls, save for the occasional trip to some doctor or other or, of course, to the Peregrine house, where they were occasionally brought round for dinner or Sunday breakfast with the dwindling Peregrine clan. Said neighborhood struck them as utterly outside the realm of *their* New York (the *real* New York, Emily privately thought, though she would never say so in front of Sadie), it being primarily inhabited by persons of some degree of wealth or those who aspire to it. Which is not to say that these girls—and their male counterparts, Dave and Tal—did not come from money, for, in a way, they did. With their shining hair and bright, clear eyes, they, all of them, were the dewy flowers of the upper middle class and, as such, were raised in needlessly large houses with a surplus of bathrooms and foodstuffs in the fridge, with every convenience, every luxury, every desire met. Their high school classmates—the superstudents of Scarsdale (Beth), Brookline (Tal), Sherman Oaks (Lil), and so on—were starting residencies at Mt. Sinai or on the partner track at Debevoise; they were, perhaps, even living in the blank residential towers of the East Nineties (despised by Sadie's parents for blocking their view), biding time before making their escapes to Westchester or Long Island or even (dread!) New Jersey.

But this group, our group, wanted nothing to do with money, the whiff of which had, they thought, spoiled their brash bourgeois parents and aunts and uncles, all of whom were, inevitably, doctors or lawyers or businessmen or sometimes teachers, and none of whom had read *Sentimental Education* or could identify the term "deconstruction" or made regular visits to the theater, except, perhaps, to see musicals or Neil Simon comedies. They—the adults—were too corrupted, too swayed and jaded by the difficulties and practicalities of adulthood, by the banal labyrinths of health insurance and Roth IRAs, by the relative safety of Volvo versus Saab versus Subaru, or flat Scottish cashmere versus the newer, softer, fluffier—but possibly less durable—stuff, imported from Nepal, that Neiman's is carrying lately. Their children were interested in art, though they wouldn't have ever put it like that. They had read *Sentimental Education*—Dave in the original French—and directed Ionesco and Genet plays. They went to the Whitney Biennial and visited the new galleries in Chelsea and Williamsburg and twice attended the Lucian Freud retrospective at the Met, but scorned anything to do with Picasso or Seurat or Monet or—*my God*—the pre-Raphaelites. They kept up with not just *The New Yorker* but *Harper's* and *The Atlantic* and even, for spurts of time, *The New York Review of Books,* and lately, *Lingua Franca* and *Salon* and various little magazines, though they agreed that the heyday of such ventures had passed decades earlier (what they wouldn't have given to be transported back to those early days of *The Partisan Review,* arguing Trotsky with Lionel Trilling and Mary McCarthy). They joked about Derrida and Lacan and Heidegger and Hume and Spinoza and New Criticism, and went to Shakespeare in the Park, and to see the RSC at BAM, and to movement-oriented stage adaptations of *Anna Karenina* at La Mama, and to Goddard, Fellini, Pasolini, Lubitsch, Bergman, and, of course, Woody Allen festivals at Film Forum.

Or, at least, they had done so—read their classics, favored black-and-whites in repertory—for four long years. Now, at twenty-six, as they struggled to make rent on their grimy apartments, as they bathed in chipped bathtubs, which in Emily's case—poor Emily being the most impoverished of the group—also served as a kitchen sink, they were starting to feel a little tired, a little sick of the nights in cafés typing on their laptops, the endless drinks dates because who could afford to eat dinner out. Lately, they were starting to look upon their parents' houses, the green of their lawns, the comfortable lives of their youth, with a bit more kindness.

And then—entirely without warning—Lil announced that she was getting married, married to a man she'd met in her doctoral program, a man none of them knew well, if *at all,* though they'd glimpsed him at parties over the past year, Lil's first at Columbia. He was older, at least thirty, and had an aura of glamour about him, which the girls attributed as much to his large, masculine features as to his polite, disaffected air. There was, Sadie remarked, a bit too much James Dean about him. He'd studied poetry, like Lil, before dropping out to take a job at a new magazine, supposedly a cross between *Spy* and *The New Yorker,* but focused on business, or technology, or both. Lil spoke as if this was a great opportunity for him, but her friends weren't convinced.

As was the practice of those of their class and generation, she'd introduced him, at first, as her "friend," and they'd pretended for some months that there was nothing more to the story. So well did this pretense work that they'd barely adjusted to the idea that Tuck was her "boyfriend" when he became her "fiancé"—though thankfully she refrained from using that term. It was impossible for them to imagine Lil married, in part because it was impossible to imagine any of them married. They knew no married people of their own age. And so, when Lil called her friends, one by one, and told them, in the hushed tones required by her summer job—an internship at a poetry organization, where she was largely responsible for answering the phones—that not only was she getting married but also that she would have an *actual* wedding, with a white dress and a rabbi and maybe even a veil and a bouquet (though definitely no bridesmaids in matching dresses, that much she could promise), she waited, tensely, for the jibes, the disapproval. But they were so shocked, her friends, that none—not even Dave, not even Beth—could think of anything to say, other than "Wow!" and "Lil, that's *great!*" and "I can't wait to meet him, *really* meet him."

Two weeks later, the couple got in Lil's beat-up Accord and drove down to visit Tuck's family in Atlanta, where his mother—hair elaborately dyed and streaked an unnatural auburn, nails manicured to a high sheen— outfitted Lil with an alarmingly large diamond, tucked inside an elaborate Victorian setting, for which she apologized. "Those old settings don't show off the stone at all," she said, her lipsticked mouth pulling down at the corners. "But it's *at least* three carats." The ring had belonged to Tuck's grandmother, his mother's mother, and possibly her mother before that, no one knew for sure. It was exactly Lil's size and precisely her style, the girls told Lil, though in fact the ring instilled in them an odd mix of anxiety and admiration, aesthetic interest and adolescent annoyance. It was so *large,* so "important" looking (in the words of Rose Peregrine, who agreed that she should have the stone reset), so unequivocally grown-up. Were it not a family heirloom, according to Emily, it would be horribly uncool.

Beth, meanwhile, felt that it quite possibly defied the feminist principles they'd mastered—or, she'd thought, internalized—in college. The ring claimed Lil as somebody's chattel, some man's prize. "You're wearing an engagement ring?" Beth whispered into the phone one hot night in August, incredulous. She was still in Milwaukee, working on her doctorate. In September, once she'd finished teaching summer session—two sections of Feminist Approaches to Twentieth Century Advertising— she'd move to New York to teach at the New School and write the second half of her dissertation, which she couldn't do without a semester or two of research at the Museum of Television and Radio, a need that neatly coincided with her absolute desperation for her friends and her mounting disgust with freezing, boring Milwaukee. That is, *if* she could get everything straightened out with her teaching credits. She'd been sure she had enough, but in June—after she'd accepted the job at the New School—she'd received a note saying no, she was one credit shy. Maddening. And embarrassing. She said nothing of all this to Lil. "A *real* engagement ring?" she asked, peevishly, instead. "Like, a *diamond*?"

"Yeah," said Lil, sighing. "His mom gave it to us. It means a lot to her that I wear it, so I feel like I have to."

"Oh," said Beth. "I guess I didn't think you were the sort of person who would wear an engagement ring. But it makes sense, I guess." Lil, she thought, was moving in this new and strange direction, becoming someone other than the girl she'd roomed with in college, the girl who'd earnestly churned out papers critiquing the phallocentric focus of Harold Bloom's critical work on Zora Neale Hurston's *Their Eyes Were Watching God.* "But you don't feel weird, wearing this big *rock* on your hand? It doesn't make you feel like your mom or something? Or like one of those girls we went to high school with? It doesn't make you feel"—she paused here, unsure of what she meant—"like you're someone you're not?"

In fact, it did. Lil understood now why jewels were once considered amulets, investing their wearers with supernatural powers. With the large diamond glinting on her left hand, she felt herself to be a new and different Lil, one capable of doing anything, going anywhere. At night, she and Tuck drank brandy out of tumblers and talked about writing novels and making documentaries and moving to Romania. By day, whispering furtively into her office phone, she negotiated with caterers and jazz quartets and the Sisterhood of Temple Emanu-El, the Peregrines' synagogue, and the only venue Lil considered acceptable for the ceremony, despite the fact that she was not, of course, a member, nor was she from the sort of family that belonged to Emanu-El, with fortunes in banking, real estate in the vicinity of Park, and rarefied German lineage. Her grandfather had sold black bread from a cart on Orchard Street and her father was a plastic surgeon who catered to the faces of Hollywood's third tier, preferred pastrami from Langer's to sushi, and on Fridays brought home prune danish from Fairfax, where the Orthodox lived in large pink houses. But Lil had Rose Peregrine—secretary of the Sisterhood, member of every possible committee, and the preschool's board of directors—and thus, by July, Lil had a date in the Beth-El Chapel, and by September a dress, heavy and autumnal, from the sample rack at Kleinfeld, where she'd journeyed alone, taking perhaps too much pleasure in the fuss the saleswomen made over her small waist. As the month wore on and the hot, humid weather continued unabated, she began to wonder if she should have gone with her second choice: a dead-white ballerina dress, with delicate off-the-shoulder sleeves and a full tulle dancing skirt. But she kept such fears to herself, for Sadie and Emily were irritated that they hadn't been invited on the buying trip. In fact, she avoided talking about the wedding whenever possible, as her friends, she was realizing, were, despite their alleged enthusiasm, a bit, well, weirded out by it. Beth grew silent when Lil told her, gleefully, that Tuck had found them a new apartment, a loft big enough to hold the reception. Dave got crabby when she recounted the talents of the jazz band they'd enlisted—a bunch of NYU students—for a cut rate. He'd just dropped out of Eastman, moved back to New York, and joined a band himself, though not the sort of band that played at weddings, of course.

"They'll probably suck," he said.

"No, they're great," she assured him. "We heard them play at Aggie's."

"*Aggie's,*" said Dave. "Whatever."

Only Tal seemed, however vaguely, to approve of the nuptials in general, and Lil's plans specifically. After college he'd broken from his parents almost completely—they still barely spoke—but he'd never quite shaken their conservative bent, at least toward things like marriage and family. He smiled at babies in the park and had, on occasional Sundays, been caught reading the "Vows" column. "It's sweet," he said. "Especially the old people."

But as the day approached, the girls began to grow excited. This wedding—which had seemed some elaborate game of make-believe, some goofy lark—was really, actually, truly going to take place. Lil was going to walk down the aisle in a big dress, with a fluffy veil and maybe even a bouquet (her mother and Rose Peregrine were insisting, offering to pay), *get married,* and become Lillian Roth-Hayes.

"It sounds like a bank, doesn't it?" Dave said the night before the wedding, after the rehearsal dinner, as they sat around Tal's big apartment on Union drinking beer, their toes picking at the frills of mismatched linoleum that emerged from the floor. Lil and Tuck had gone home to bed. Beth was, at that moment, stranded in Pittsburgh. She'd had to stay in Milwaukee later than she'd anticipated, and Lil was pretty put out that she'd cut it so close and missed the dinner ("She couldn't have flown in *yesterday?*").

"No, a law firm," insisted Emily, who had temped at many such firms. "I can totally see the letterhead."

"A midlevel brand of dress shirt," suggested Sadie.

"It sounds pretty great, actually," said Tal. His friends looked at one another, unsure if he was kidding. "I like it. It's kind of regal." He wrinkled his nose with self-deprecation. "Or British."

"Sort of," said Sadie, prodding his corduroyed thigh with her foot.

"It's nice," he said. "You guys—" He shook his head. "It's *nice* that they're combining their names." And they all grew silent, ashamed, looking down their noses into their sweating bottles of beer, for the truth was, they agreed. Some of their mothers—feminists, children of the 1960s—had kept their own names, even if just professionally, which the girls thought dry and unromantic. They had all been thinking, separately, that when they married (*if* they married), they would do as Lil did and hyphenate, or turn their original family names into middle names.

The next morning, at promptly nine o'clock, Emily arrived at the Peregrine house on East Ninety-second, breathless and apologetic, her dress stuffed into a crumpled grocery bag, followed a few minutes later by Beth, pale hair rising statically from her head, her plump, freckled face arranged in an expression of mild agony. Rose had insisted they meet at this early hour, at her house, to "strategize," though they'd simply have to journey downtown on errands and then over to Brooklyn to help set up the loft for the reception, and then *back* uptown to dress for the wedding.

"You look exhausted," Rose told Beth, once she'd seated the girls at her kitchen table, a massive slab of scarred oak, and placed cups of coffee in front of them. "You just got in last night?"

Beth nodded. "Midnight." She took a tentative sip of her coffee. "I *am* exhausted. It took me two hours to get here this morning."

"*Two hours?*" Rose cried. "You took the train in? You're staying at your parents'?"

Beth shook her head.

"She's in Astoria," Emily explained. Beth was subletting an apartment from a CUNY prof, an alum of her program who was in Finland on a Fulbright. When she'd signed the sublease, she'd thought, of course, that she'd be arriving in the city at the start of September—the start of the fall semester, her favorite time of year—but there'd been that problem with her credits, which she'd worked out, sort of, by teaching the first section of a "special topics" class. Now her credits were in order, but she had—most likely, it wasn't entirely clear—lost her New School job, at least for the fall. And paid double rent for a month, which she could ill afford. But she was in New York. That was all that mattered.

"Astoria?" repeated Rose. "*Queens?*"

"Ye—"

"Isn't it all *Greek* there?"

"Not anymore," Emily told her, spooning a scant bit of sugar into her coffee. "There's a big Middle Eastern community, too. There's this great Egyptian restaurant on—"

"You're living in Astoria, *Queens?*" Rose repeated, frowning at Beth and cocking her head suspiciously, as though the girls were playing some sort of practical joke on her.

Beth nodded.

"We told her not to take it," Emily told Rose, giving Beth a little smile. "But she didn't listen."

"*Well,*" said Rose, pulling out a chair and sitting down on Emily's right. "It's all the same." She shrugged. "I don't understand why *you* girls insist on living way out in Brooklyn."

"Because it's cheap," Emily said, then turned to Beth. "How's the place?"

"Fine, I guess. Pretty big."

In fact, she'd barely examined the place. She'd gotten in so late and risen so early, nervous about finding her way to the Peregrines', and preoccupied with the wedding—or not so much the wedding itself as the fact that she would soon find herself face-to-face with Dave Kohane, whom she'd managed to avoid for the four years since they'd departed for their respective grad programs, she to Milwaukee and he to Rochester, at which point he'd dumped her, in a strangely passive manner. Or not "dumped" her—she hated that term—but allowed their couplehood to peter out, for reasons she'd never understood.

"Okay," said Rose, clapping her hands together, "let me get my list. We've got to get started." She glanced pointedly at the clock on the stove. "Beth, do you want to wake Sadie and Lil? They'll be *thrilled* to see you."

"*I'm up,*" came a gravelly contralto from the stairwell. Still in the old blue pajamas she'd worn in college, when they'd all shared a crumbling house behind the art museum, her curls flattened by sleep, Sadie padded into the kitchen, trailed by George, the Peregrines' ancient orange cat, and gave Beth a silent, enervated hug. She had her own little apartment in Cobble Hill, but she'd spent the night at her parents', as was her occasional wont. With a yawn, she glanced at the kitchen clock. She was a small girl, with a long-waisted figure that gave the illusion of height. Her dark, glossy hair and waxily opaque, vellum-hued skin came from her mother, Rose, a woman of Italianate good looks, as did her curious, formal way of speaking. But her hooded eyes and her bearing were pure Peregrine—as Rose often reminded her, in moments of anger. "Sadie," said Rose, an edge rising in her voice, "we've got to get started. Did you wake up Lil?"

Sadie poured herself a cup of coffee before answering. "She's at home," she said finally, with another, larger yawn.

"At *home?*" Rose asked in alarm.

"She was supposed to stay here last night," Sadie told Beth. "Tradition. You know. Spending the night before the wedding apart from Tuck." Beth nodded. "But she couldn't *bear* to be apart from him. Even for one night."

"Oh," said Rose, pursing her lips. "Well, then what's the plan?"

Sadie took a long sip of coffee and made a face at Emily. "She has an appointment for a facial at ten—"

"At Arden's," said Rose.

"No," Sadie told her. "She decided to go to some place in Soho."

Rose emitted a sigh of deep disappointment and pressed her fingers lightly to her temples. "All right. So—"

"So, we'll go get the flowers and meet her in Brooklyn," said Sadie. "At the apartment. Her parents are already there."

"All right," Rose acquiesced. "We have to be back here by three, the latest, to get dressed."

"It won't take us that long to get ready," said Sadie. "We don't have to be at the synagogue until six, right?"

"I'm not talking about *you*," snapped Rose. "I'm talking about Lil. The *bride*." She shook her head at Emily and Beth. "And," she added, "I have a manicure at three thirty. So let's go, girls."

And off they went: to Chelsea, with a big wad of cash, to pick up flowers—short-stemmed roses, monstrous tulips, assorted odd lacy things—then to Lil and Tuck's new loft, on what turned out to be a grim stretch of Bushwick, where Beth and Emily found Lil's mother, Elaine, directing a team of volunteers—various Roth cousins, some of Lil's childhood friends—who were stringing tulle and candles around the room, wrapping fairy lights around the loft's fat beams, and rinsing the old milk glass vases in the kitchen's small sink. Lil's father stood behind a small card table, manning a platter of deli meats and chewing open-mouthed on a corned beef sandwich. "Better get to work," he said, with a wink. "Elaine's on the rampage." The girls trimmed the stems off hundreds of flowers, filled the vases with tepid water, and cobbled together what Rose called "French bouquets." "You don't think those look sloppy?" asked Elaine, squinting at a drooping tulip. "I would have been happy to pay for arrangements." But Lil hadn't wanted arrangements, just as she hadn't wanted to be married in a hall on Long Island, despite her mother's insistence that it would be "so much easier."

At lunchtime Tal and Dave arrived to set up the sound system and help with any heavy lifting. Some friends of Tuck's—a slender couple with a tiny baby in a sling—dropped off case after case of beer and wine and champagne. They were followed by another couple—smiling, with Southern accents—who carried in the cake, covered all over with bright buttercream flowers. The florist came by with white cardboard boxes containing wrist corsages for the mothers, rosebuds for the girls' dresses and the mens' jackets, and Lil's bouquet, which was paler than the other flowers and round in shape, so beautiful and perfect that Beth, against her will, said, "Oh!" and drew in her breath. A widowed cousin of Elaine's showed up, already dressed for the wedding in a pink silk suit, and tied floppy white bows on the vases. Then Lil called, saying she'd been delayed and would meet them at the Peregrines', and the band swooped in, setting up yards of equipment in a corner; then suddenly the caterers were bustling about, loudly creaking open long tables for the buffet, which would be in Lil and Tuck's bedroom, at the rear of the apartment ("It used to be a meat locker," Elaine kept telling anyone who passed within arm's reach of her), and it was *time,* Rose said. "Girls, we need to go *now.*"

"We do, we do," agreed Elaine. As they gathered at the door, they stopped for a moment and surveyed the room: its pillars shrouded in tulle and twinkly lights, dozens of white-covered tables scattered over the worn oak floor, generous bouquets at their centers.

"It's beautiful," said Beth.

"It is," said Emily.

"It's fine," sighed Elaine, smoothing her crisp blonde hair. It had once been black, like Lil's, but over the years had grown lighter and lighter. She wore it straight, with long bangs that covered her eyebrows, a trick, Lil said, to hide the wrinkles in her forehead, wrinkles she was forever asking Lil's father to "fix," much as his partner had "fixed" Lil's nose between her junior and senior years of high school. "I still don't see what was wrong with Leonard's of Great Neck," she sighed, raising her thin brows. "It would have been so much easier."

"Come on," said Rose. "It's after two."

They took the train, for there were no cabs to be found in Lil's desolate section of Brooklyn, three stops in on the L, and Elaine smiled delightedly, saying, "I haven't been on a subway in *years.* It's so clean!"

"Giuliani," the girls said, smirking.

"Too bad he's a fascist," Emily told her. They emerged, once again, at the corner of Eighty-sixth and Lex, in boisterous spirits, practically running to the Peregrine house. There, spread across the Peregrines' four bathrooms, they showered and shaved their legs, the widowed cousin making dour remarks about the time, did they know (yes, they knew) they had to be at the shul by six at the latest? Quickly, they smoothed makeup onto their faces, fingered their hair into waves and ringlets, and pulled on stockings and variations on the wispy, girlish dresses popular that year. So dressed, they turned to Lil, who had spent the day alone, receiving the ministrations of various Eastern European women, and who now emerged from the third-floor bathroom to greet them clad in Sadie's old striped robe, a foggy look on her face, which—they all noticed—appeared a bit too pink, particularly around the edges of her nose. "She should have gone to Arden's," Rose whispered to Sadie, who squeezed her mother's arm in warning. Elaine rushed over to her daughter. "You're all red," she said, inspecting her face. "You're going to *have* to wear foundation."

"*Okay,* Mom." Lil seemed to shrink a bit in her mother's presence, her eyes widening with what Sadie thought were tears. But then Lil caught sight of her friends and smiled, unsure of whom to greet first, and cried,

"Beth! Oh my God! You look beautiful! I love your dress! Are you wearing *lipstick*? It looks great!" Before Beth could answer, Lil had embraced her in a warm, perfumed hug. "It's so good to see you. We thought you'd never get here. We missed you last night." And with that, she launched into a thousand questions: How was Beth's apartment? Did she like Queens? Were Dave and Tal coming over, as well, or would they meet them at the synagogue? Was Sadie wearing her hair up or down? How were the flowers? Had her eyebrows turned out even? And could they please keep old cousin Paula away from her? Who had brought her back here anyway? Everyone knew she was a complete nuisance.

Somehow, they managed to coax Lil into Sadie's room—unchanged since Sadie's childhood, with its green and white toile coverlet and curtains—and sit her down at the dressing table. Much discussion ensued over whether Lil should dress or have her makeup applied first, until Elaine and Rose decided the matter: Lil should dress first, then a large cloth would be draped over her as Emily applied her makeup. ("*Overdo* it," Elaine hissed at Emily in the hallway, laying a tan, bare arm conspiratorially on Emily's back, the beading along the edge of her turquoise dress scraping Emily's pale shoulder. "We don't want her to look pasty.") Lil pulled on scant tulle underwear—a gift from Sadie—and a long-lined bra, then attached stockings to the bra's dangling garters, slapping away Cousin Paula's attempts at help. "This is so porn star," said Emily. "I know, this thing makes my boobs huge," Lil intoned, with a wry smile, fastening around her waist a glaring white crinoline, and, finally—thus trussed and plumped—slipping the heavy dress over her head, to the oohs and aahs of the girls, and a grimace from Cousin Paula.

"You wouldn't really call that dress white, would you, Elaine?" Paula asked. "It's almost *gold,* isn't it?" She stopped to scrutinize the heavy satin between thumb and forefinger. "Is it *actually* a wedding dress?"

"It's white," snapped Lil. "Mom, can you button me up?"

The sky clouded over, threatening rain, and Tal and Dave arrived, looking absurdly old and handsome, transformed by their black suits and glossy ties. Lil rushed up to hug them, though they seemed slightly afraid of her, in her thick lipstick and big, costumey dress, her black hair pulled back from her face in a heavy bun. "Lil, you look beautiful," whispered Dave, as if apologizing for his stiff embrace. Tal smiled, took her hands, and pulled her an arm's length away. "Gorgeous," he said.

"Okay, kids," called Rose, with a clap of her manicured hands, "I hate to break this up, but we need to get going. Start heading for the door."

Moments later, it seemed to Lil, she arrived at the rabbi's study, where Tuck was waiting for her by a diamond-paned window, his mother fussing with his tie. "*Mom,*" he said, grinning brilliantly at Lil, so brilliantly that her irritation and anxiety fell away, and she laughed with relief at the sight of him. "Oh my God," he said when she came into full view. It was all she could do not to wrap her arms around him and press her face to his cheek, which still showed the strokes of the razor. "Shall we get started?" said the rabbi, and they signed the wedding contract—Tuck squeezing her hand—then she was walking down the aisle, bits of whispers and coughs and laughter wafting uneasily toward her, her mother on her right, smelling faintly of White Shoulders and Max Factor pressed powder, her father on her left, baldpate glowing. Both of them were, to her surprise, smiling. They were happy, she realized, or at least happier than she'd expected they'd be about this marriage to a boy they'd met but once. Not that she'd cared; she'd long ago realized that nothing she did could truly please her parents. "But that's how young people do it, Barry," her mother had insisted back in May, when she'd given them the news. "Tuck's thirty, mom," Lil had said impatiently. "We're not that young." But now, as she walked down the aisle, with a hundred sets of eyes uncomfortably focused on her slow progress, she felt, really, much as she had on the first day of kindergarten, dressed in her stiff, unfamiliar uniform, unsure of what awaited her. Her mother, for once, was right.

•

Standing in a crowd around the chuppa—two poles held by Tal and Dave, two held by friends of Tuck's—the girls, at first, felt faintly uncomfortable, looking out at the rows of people before them, unable to fidget or fuss with their hair. Then, slowly, they began to relax, whispering mildly to one another. They held little white cards in their hands, inscribed with the blessings each would recite at the appointed moment. None of them was familiar with this bit of ritual—even Tal, whose mother ran a kosher catering business and who'd actually gone to Hebrew school—but then, they weren't familiar with any sort of wedding custom: this was the first wedding they'd attended as grown-ups.

One by one they stepped up and read their blessings, which were strangely simple—"Blessed are You, Adonai, our God, King of the universe, Creator of Human Beings" and "Blessed are You, Adonai, our God, King of the universe, Who has created everything for Your glory"—and somber, and even, Dave said later, *generic,* just your basic prayers, praising God, nothing about marriage specifically, until Tal, handing his chuppa pole to Emily, stepped up to the bima and read, in his calm, mesmerizing way, his cheeks blaring red at the center, his dark eyes fixed on the guests in the pews below:

> *Gladden the beloved companions as You gladdened Your creatures in the garden of Eden. Blessed are You, Adonai, Who gladdens groom and bride.*

The synagogue, which had seemed quiet before, fell into a deep, stunned silence, contemplating the groom and bride before them. *She's really doing this,* thought Beth. *She's a* bride. And her heart began to beat faster, so much faster that she nearly missed her cue to step up to the bima herself and read her poem, a short thing by Linda Pastan, which had seemed appropriately unsentimental when she'd chosen it, but as she read, the words—all simple, all arranged in plain, declarative sentences, rather like, she realized, the Seven Blessings—began to accrue, taking hold of her in an unexpected way. Her voice wavered, and as she reached the last line—"Because everything is ordained / I said *yes*"—she broke into a small sob. Mortified, she stood, frozen, swallowing back tears, staring out at the people in the pews, the rows and rows of white-haired ladies, the assorted young people, some of whom she knew and some of whom she didn't. Some were crying a bit, as well, including her friends standing around the chuppa. Including Dave, who smiled ruefully at her. They hadn't yet spoken, had merely nodded at each other across Sadie's bedroom, the girls forming a shield around her.

Moments later, Tuck stepped heavily on the glass, grabbed Lil around the waist, and kissed her roughly, lifting her up off the ground. "Mazel tov," shouted Dr. Roth in his loud, rheumy voice. And the crowd began clapping and shouting. Quickly, the moment passed, and a flock of old ladies began moving slowly down the aisles, holding one another's arms and peering around them through thick, oversized lenses. These were Lil's elderly aunts—her great-aunts, really, but since neither of her parents had siblings, she called them her aunts. There were twelve or fourteen or twenty of them, and they all had thrilling Jazz Age names like Fritzi and Ruby and Ella and Minna, and had so long outlived their husbands that, Lil said, it was hard to remember they'd ever had them. Lil herself was named after one—the youngest on the Roth side and Dr. Roth's favorite, who'd died tragically in a boating accident somewhere in the Catskills, when Dr. Roth was a teen. Her mother had wanted to name her Jessica.

Outside, a cool evening wind tossed around the first fallen leaves. The air smelled faintly of wood smoke, from the fireplace of some nearby brownstone, Sadie knew. A fleet of town cars ordered by Dr. Roth—Lil had thought everyone could just take the subway—stood at the curb, waiting to ferry guests to Williamsburg. The conventional part of the wedding was over. The unconventional would now begin: instead of a sit-down dinner, with carefully contrived seating charts, guests would sit wherever they liked and eat the fried chicken, ribs, sautéed greens, pickled beets, macaroni and cheese, mashed potatoes, and corn bread laid out on long tables in the back bedroom. "It's all served room temperature, like a picnic," Lil had told them that afternoon, ignoring Rose and Elaine's shared sigh.

The trees along Fifth formed a dark outline against the darkening sky, and the synagogue's doorman guided the guests into the polished, snub-nosed cars, which glided off down the avenue, streetlights stringing a long chain behind them. Beth, Emily, and Sadie walked through the synagogue's oversized doors, Dave and Tal close on their heels. They breathed in the smoky air and turned to one another, smiling.

"That was beautiful, wasn't it?" said Beth brightly, reluctantly pulling her old brown raincoat over her thin dress, a maroon satin she'd purchased at Milwaukee's one good shop, Dave maddeningly in mind. A week before, she thought it beautiful, perfect, magical, but the moment she zipped it up, at Sadie's, she saw that it was wrong, *horribly* wrong—nothing like the sleek, fitted things the other girls wore—with its childish row of buttons down the front, its prim little collar, its empire waist and tie at the back, the sort of style they'd worn in college, over engineer boots and tights.

"You did good," said Emily, elbowing Beth. "Not a dry eye in the house."

"We better get down there," Beth said, flushing with embarrassment and flinging her hand south, in what she thought to be the general direction of Brooklyn.

"Definitely," said Sadie.

But, it seemed, there were no more town cars left. Dr. Roth hadn't ordered quite enough, or perhaps there were more guests than he'd accounted for.

"It's those friends of Tuck's," said Sadie, shaking her head. She had, in the end, worn her hair down. "They just *showed up!*"

"What?" asked Beth. "They weren't invited?"

"No," Emily told her, eyebrows raised. "You didn't hear about this?"

"They're a band," Sadie explained. "I can't remember what they're called, and they're in town for the weekend, staying with that couple, Tuck's friends from Atlanta—"

"Not the people with the baby," clarified Emily. "The others. The woman has a Southern accent—"

"And she told them that they should just come along."

"Does Tuck even know them?" marveled Beth.

Emily nodded. "They were friends in high school."

"Oh," said Beth. This didn't seem so terrible. Though, she supposed, to Rose Peregrine it was more terrible than terrible. From time to time Sadie vehemently agreed with her mother, to her friends' surprise.

"They just *showed up*," she said now, shrugging her shoulders furiously into her shiny mass of curls. "With their *girlfriends*. You saw those girls, right, in the fifties dresses?"

"*Crazy*," said Emily, smiling at Beth.

"It *is*," said Sadie, settling her mouth in an angry line.

"Hey," said Tal, touching his long fingers to Sadie's arm. "I'll get us a cab."

"We'll need two."

"Then I'll get us two."

"Okay." Sadie appeared chastened, cowed. She looked up at Tal through her lashes. "Thank you."

"What band?" Dave asked.

Sadie looked at him and sighed.

"What?" he said, holding up his hands in a gesture of exaggerated innocence. "There are a lot of good bands coming out of Atlanta right now." But Sadie already had her arm stretched up and out into the night sky, her face eclipsed by the yellow lights of an oncoming cab.

•

The *Times* and the *Voice* and *Time Out* and *New York* had all declared Lil and Tuck's neighborhood—a section of Williamsburg east of the BQE and generally referred to as Graham Avenue, for the L stop that serviced it—the next spot for artists and writers, which meant, of course, that it would really be the next spot for whoever could afford the newly inflated rents and newly opened bistros. But Lil and Tuck's block—a treeless stretch of Bushwick Avenue, punctuated with twisted subway grates—

radiated a forcible menace after dark. "Isn't that a gang tag?" asked Tal, pointing at a swath of graffiti on the steel gate of a bait shop.

They stood on the curb, poised to enter the loft, from which emanated a few tentative strains of Coltrane, a hundred chatting voices, and the faint odor of cigarette smoke.

"Crips," confirmed Dave. Since moving back to Brooklyn a few months earlier, Dave had come to consider himself an aficionado of street culture, to the amusement of his friends.

"Yes, Dave, the Crips operate all the bait-and-tackle shops in Greater Brooklyn," murmured Sadie, furtively running lipstick over her mouth without the aid of a mirror.

"Um, I'm sorry," said Dave, "but aren't you the person who visited this borough for the first time at some point during our *junior* year of *college*. And aren't you the person who had to ask Emily for directions to *Prospect Park*—"

Emily held up her hands like a conductor. "Enough, peoples. We're going in."

Inside, they found themselves packed into a throng of ancients: the white-headed aunts, innumerable thin, tan ladies in dramatic evening gowns (leopard-print chiffon, yellow sari silk shot through with gold) and slim-cut suits, a half dozen corpulent, balding men possessed of a vaguely mafiosi demeanor, scads of professorial types in bow ties and wire glasses ("Columbia people," whispered Sadie knowingly, though Emily, who was from the South, suspected they were Tuck's Atlanta relatives). As they pushed their way back to the bar—set up in Lil and Tuck's second bedroom, a luxury afforded by Tuck's new job—the crowd grew progressively younger: First, baby boomers, the women in rough-weave shifts. Then, Tuck's thirtyish friends: the baby people, drinking Perrier; the band guys, in threadbare suits and skinny ties, and their girls, hair cut in retro bobs; a troupe of handsome preppy types, indistinguishable from one another in their dark suits and pale blue shirts. And finally, their own friends, the corollary members of their little group, like Maya Decker, who'd flown in from Houston, where she was dancing with a big modern company, and Abe Hausman, who was back at Oberlin, strangely, on some new philosophy postdoc, and Robin Wilde, Lil's freshman-year roommate, whom they all found a little quiet and dull ("but *sweet*," Beth was always quick to add).

"Hello, hello," they said to these people, "oh my God, how *are* you?" and grabbed drinks from passing trays: glasses of Lillet and orange, which the girls thought fabulously original and such a *Lil* thing to do, forcing a hundred-odd guests to drink an obscure and archaic aperitif that no one but Lil—or, they supposed, Sadie, from whom she'd probably cribbed the idea—would think to order. They were tremendously interested in cocktails, having gone off beer in the years since college, and they were learning how to make proper sidecars and Manhattans and French 77s, they told Maya and Abe gaily. Dave had become a *master* martini maker, his technique cribbed from an oft-watched episode of *M*A*S*H* in which Hawkeye explains how to obtain the proper dryness. "You've got to really *stuff* the shaker with ice," said Dave. He was disturbed to be talking about such idiotic things with people he hadn't seen in years, and as a result, he found himself taking an increasingly emphatic tone. "You pour the vermouth over the ice, then you pour it out through the strainer, so the ice cubes are just *coated* with vermouth. And then you add the gin. Ideally Bombay Sapphire." Sadie made a face. "Gin. Bleh. Vodka's much cleaner." Maya Decker nodded gravely.

They made their way into the main part of the loft, now lit by the glow of hundreds of tiny candles—votives clustered on the table, around the "French bouquets," which looked wild and lovely in the dim, rustic room, with its oak-planked floor. Beth sat down at a central table, with Sadie and Emily, and rested her hot forehead on Emily's bare, freckled shoulder. "I think they're about to do the toast," she said wearily. "The waiters are coming around with champagne."

"Or something that looks like champagne," said Dave, coming up behind the girls, "but most definitely is *not*."

"Dave, shut up," said Sadie, not unkindly, as Tuck stood on a chair and tinked a fork against his flute. The room quieted and the girls rose and moved, with the other guests, toward the open space at the center of the room. "This," said Tuck, clearing his throat, "is the happiest day of my life, as most of you realize. And so I want to start things off by making a toast to my wife, Lillian Roth-*Hayes* . . ."

This was the first chance that Beth had, really, to examine Tuck. She could tell from his speech that he was kind and intelligent, if a bit self-absorbed. But he was also well-spoken and well built, though short, with broad shoulders and a narrow waist. His face, she thought, was crudely striking, his eyes so big and sad, like a silent film star's. Like, she thought, Buster Keaton.

"Tuck was born to wear a suit," said Emily.

"I suppose," sighed Sadie. "I'm going to get a refill."

"He usually wears glasses, doesn't he?" Emily frowned and squinted.

"I don't know," said Beth absently, watching Sadie make her way across the crowded room, her long curls vibrating against her shoulders. She wore a simple dress of slate-blue taffeta, with a fitted bodice and a square neck.

"She hates him," said Emily, jutting her head in Sadie's direction.

"Hmmm," murmured Beth uncomfortably. This was not the time, she thought, to fill her in on everyone's feeling about Tuck, who was now recounting how he and Lil had first met, a story that, Beth was surprised to discover, she hadn't heard from Lil. "We should probably listen," she told Emily, and turned toward Tuck, who still held his hand in the air, his jacket raffishly unbuttoned, a sheen of sweat on his forehead. "I was standing on the steps of Low Library," he said, "when the most beautiful woman I'd ever seen came up to me and asked if I could direct her to the business school. And I thought, 'Well, I guess I'll never see *her* again.'" Flicks of laughter rose from the crowd. "MBA students don't tend to date scruffy poetry scholars. So you can imagine my surprise when, a few hours later, this gorgeous creature walks into my Yeats seminar." Lil, at Tuck's side, smiled and shrugged, embarrassed and pleased, her face flushed from champagne. "Turns out, she already knew something it took me two years to discover. The business school cafeteria sells the only decent coffee on campus. And she was a scruffy poetry scholar like me."

From the crowd came shouts and claps and calls of "Woo-hoo" and "Here here" and "Mazel tov," and Tuck thrust his arm higher, above his head, and shouted, "But we clean up pretty well, don't we?" causing the volume of clapping to surge and the clinking of glasses to commence. "To Lillian Roth-*Hayes,*" he cried, slipping his arm around her waist and tossing back his champagne. Lil's grin had grown so large it looked, to Beth, almost painful. She'd never seen Lil this happy.

Emily smiled. "That was sweet," she said.

"It was," said Beth, dipping her head closer to Emily's, which smelled, wonderfully, of peppermint. Like Sadie, she wore a close-fitting dress—from the sixties, Beth thought—and the vivid blue-green of the satin contrasted sharply with her red hair. "You like him, don't you?"

Emily shrugged. "I do," she said. "Though I really don't know him. But I think I *get* it."

"Yeah," said Beth. "I think I do, too."

Lillian's father had started speaking, though the chatter threatened to overtake his husky voice. Across the room, Sadie had reached an impasse by the threshold to the second bedroom. She stood under a small orange light fixture, talking to Tal, who bent his tall frame over to whisper in her ear, causing her to laugh prettily, throwing her head back and raising her thin shoulders. Her dress, Beth thought, was perfect. "Who's the dark beauty?" a voice whispered in Beth's ear, an unmistakably English voice. Beth whipped around. One of the Columbia guys stood behind her, smiling sardonically. He appeared to be somewhat older than she and wore his hair in an odd, archaic style, parted deeply on the side, so it fell across his expansive, bulbous forehead in thick clumps. His suit—unlike that of his cohorts—was an olive green color, which Beth thought rather ugly. His face, however, was quite handsome, in a manner so common and dull that Beth generally discounted it: dark eyes, square jaw, ruddy skin, the protuberant sort of nose that looked good on certain men. With his jacket unbuttoned and his hands slouched in his pockets, he had the louche, disaffected air of the corrupt second son on a *Masterpiece Theatre* adaptation of an Edwardian novel. The skin around his eyes was white with fatigue. *A grad student's eyes,* she thought. "Which one?" she asked, though she knew which one. "The woman over there? In blue?" She gestured toward Sadie. The man nodded. "Sadie Peregrine," she told him. "She's Lil's friend from school. Have you not met her?"

"I think I have, actually, but not when she's been wearing a dress," said the man, giving Beth a long, appraising glance, then turning his eyes back to Sadie, who was talking rapidly at Tal, her hands flying in all directions. "Women should always wear dresses."

"Yes," said Beth, feeling the blood rush to her face. "And they shouldn't own property or vote."

"Exactly," said the man. "You read my mind." He sipped silently at his drink, raising his eyebrows with pleasure. "And you don't like her, Sadie Peregrine."

"No!" cried Beth. "Oh my God, no! Why would you say that? She's one of my best friends." She paused, feeling that she was rambling, though she hadn't said much at all, really.

"I see," the man said, annoyingly, as though he was trying to make her feel she was blathering. "So then you know which of those fools is her boyfriend."

Dave, she saw, had joined Sadie and Tal. "Oh, neither," she said, laughing. "Those are our friends Dave and Tal. From Oberlin. We all, you know, went to Oberlin together."

"Dave and *Tal*," the man said ruminatively. "From Oberlin. Of course." What this meant, she had no idea, but it led her to a horrible thought: Sadie and Dave. *No,* she thought, *impossible.*

"I'm Will," the man said finally. "Will Chase." He put out his hand to Beth and she shook it lightly.

"Another William," she said.

He stared blankly.

"Like Tuck. Tuck's real name—"

"Oh, right. Yes, of course." He sipped loudly at his drink and ran his eyes around the room. "And *you,* it seems, are part of the Oberlin mafia."

Beth laughed. "I guess. Except I didn't know there was an Oberlin mafia."

"Oh, yes. Of course. The city's overrun with your kind. It's a well-known fact. Scheming Oberlin grads dominate the publishing industry, hold all the important positions in the more *humanistic* subjects at major universities, and so on." Beth smiled. This *was* sort of true. "Oh, and you *must* know this," he went on, "they control the waste disposal industry."

"I thought the waste disposal industry was all, you know, Harvard men," said Beth, sipping at the dregs of her drink. She was thirsty, but the journey back to the bar for water seemed far too long, too arduous.

"Oh, no. Don't be naive. It's Oberlin, all the way."

"Really?" said Beth, warily allowing herself to smile. British men, from her experience, were better at chitchat than their American counterparts, but ultimately unable (or unwilling) to drop the witticisms in favor of real conversation. She had dated a Welshman in Milwaukee who'd proved a cruel companion in the end. And yet she sometimes still thought of him with longing. "How would you know? You're clearly not one, or I'd know you."

"Well, that's simply untrue. I left *university*"—he hit all four syllables, mocking the American habit of saying "college," though Beth had no idea what, exactly, made one term more proper than the other—"in 1988, when you were still playing with dolls." Beth started to protest—she'd been sixteen in 1988!—but he held up his hand and shook his head no. "I could easily have come and gone before you even arrived."

Beth smiled. "But you didn't." She was beginning to feel the effects of her two drinks. "You're a friend of Tuck's?" she said. "From Columbia?"

"Pretty much," he said, rocking back on his heels.

"What's your field?" she asked, pleased that she'd correctly assessed him.

"I work for the *Journal,*" he said.

"The *Journal*," she repeated slowly, wondering which journal he meant.

"Sorry. *The Wall Street Journal*."

"Oh," she said, growing hot. She'd been wrong. "And here I thought you were some kind of pathetic grad student like Lil and Tuck, scribbling away on"—she searched her mind for a suitably obscure author—"Aphra Behn."

"Aphra Behn! *Lovely!* Well, yes, you're quite right. I was. I was indeed. But I had an epiphany of sorts . . ." He paused, a bitter smile on his wide mouth. "Academia is the biggest racket of all. And if I'm going to be involved in a racket, I may as well make some money, and the world will have to go without my monograph on Defoe. Terribly sad, I know." Distantly, Beth heard Lil making her toast to Tuck.

"So you're a reporter?"

"Hmmm." He drained his glass of champagne and placed it on the table behind them. "Technology. But the business end. Start-ups. You know. I'm interviewing all these *CEOs,* analyzing the *viability* of corporate strategies, all that."

"Oh, interesting," Beth murmured, slipping a shard of ice under her tongue. She knew nothing about business but that it was boring—though an acceptable profession for men of her parents' generation, like Sadie's father, except Sadie's father was closer in age to Beth's grandfather, who still worked two days a week, filling cavities and making crowns alongside Beth's father, at their practice on Popham Road. Interesting people of her own age were writing novels or making films or acting, or perhaps organizing Wal-Mart workers into unions, like Meredith Weiss, who'd signed up with the AFL-CIO after college. Beth would never marry some sort of lawyer or doctor, like her mom and all her mom's friends, and she knew Sadie and Emily—and, clearly, Lil—wouldn't either. "It sounds interesting," she said.

"It is. It really is. This is *such* a cool time to be immersed in the world of commerce. Everything is changing so quickly, old models being thrown out, new ones being tested. Seventeen-year-olds making billions. And destroying the infrastructure of corporate giants. It's the only revolution our generation will ever see. And it just happens to be economic."

"I see," said Beth, troubled. "And was it you who convinced Tuck to drop out of the program and work for that magazine?"

"Well, it *is* possible I planted the seed in his head," he told her, placing his hand on her arm as if to steer her somewhere—but there was nowhere to go; they were locked in on all sides. "And I told him, yes, about the job. *And* put in a good word for him with the editor. He's a brilliant writer, Tuck. Really."

"Really?" said Beth, relieved to hear this.

"Yes, really. And *Boom Time* is a cool magazine. All eyes are on it, you know?"

Beth nodded, though she didn't really know anything about it.

"Do you know Ed? Ed Slikowski?"

"Er, no—"

"The editor . . ."

Beth was mystified by this question. How or why on earth would she know the editor of Tuck's magazine, which she'd never even heard of. "Um, I don't think so. Did he go to Oberlin?"

Will shook his head, a sly smile playing at the corners of his mouth. "Caltech. Then MIT." He gave her a strange look, his head cocked to one side. "You've really not heard of him."

"No."

"He's kind of famous." Beth didn't know what to say. It was beginning to strike her that she and her friends had been living in parallel universes these four years. She'd not realized that an editor of a magazine could be famous. "When *Boom Time* launched, the *Times* magazine did a cover story on him."

"Oh," said Beth. "I guess I've, you know, been in Milwaukee." She could, of course, have subscribed to the *Times* in Milwaukee, she realized as she said this. "I just got back," she said dumbly, waiting for him to explain. "So, who is he exactly?"

"He's one of those wunderkinds." Will rolled his eyes. "He started this usenet board"—this Beth understood; she was on various pop culture listservs—"on start-ups. A few years ago. He was a grad student at MIT. Artificial intelligence. Did a lot of stuff at the Media Lab. And it became this big thing. These VC guys—"

"Vee cee guys?"

"Venture capital—"

"Oh, right." Beth had no idea what this meant, but she nodded and smiled.

"He was scooping all the business mags and these VC guys were all over it. They think he's a visionary. So one of them gave him money to start a magazine."

"Wow," said Beth. "Just like that."

"Just like that." Will smiled. "Do you want to meet him? He's over there, talking to your friend Sadie." Indeed, a third man now stood in Sadie's thrall, a shiny fringe of black hair falling over eyes that Beth could see, even from this distance, were the palest, coldest blue—wolf eyes. He was thin and wore his beard full, like a seventies rock star or an Amish farmer, and his feet, below a well-cut suit, were clad in Converse One Stars. "In the gray Armani." Will shoved his hands in the pockets of his pants and let out a guffaw, like a bark. "*Boom Time* is a *heavily financed* venture. Even a lowly staff writer like Tuck commands the kind of salary that can pay the rent on"—he waved his hands toward the loft's high ceiling— "a place big enough to hold a wedding." Beth nodded and smiled. It hadn't occurred to her that the rent might be steep. The neighborhood— well, the brief glimpse she'd caught of it—struck her as bleak: low, off-kilter houses covered in vinyl siding or roofing tile, with no sign of people living behind their facades but the glare of the television; cracked, weed-sprouted sidewalks; a profusion of nail salons and dollar stores. At least Queens, from the little she'd seen of it, had trees.

"And where do you live?" she asked, harboring a vague hope that he was her neighbor in Astoria. He seemed the type to scorn the trendy, the voguish.

"In sorry seconds," he replied, with a smirk, then removed his hands from his pockets and buttoned his drab jacket, as though preparing for departure. "Tuck's old apartment on Havemeyer," he told her, with a sigh, running his eyes around the room.

"Havemeyer?" she asked.

"Williamsburg," he said, with a smile that, she thought, might be construed as condescending. "West of here. Closer to Bedford."

"Oh," she said, reluctant to ask what or where Bedford was.

With his chin, he gestured toward Sadie and her circle. "I think one of your friends is going to make a toast." Indeed, Tal had stepped forward and raised his hand, which held not a glass of champagne but a bottle of beer. Sadie, her eye on him, patted her hands together in a halfhearted clap and whispered in Dave's ear.

"Our sophomore year, Lil and I worked at WOBC," began Tal, causing the chatter to cease. He was not handsome, not to Beth at least, with his broad brows and sharp nose, and yet he had grown, in the years since college, very *attractive*. The tone of his voice, Beth thought, had become somehow more patrician, more precise, over the years. He was an actor and suddenly everything had started happening for him: skits on *Conan*, a play at Circle in the Square, a screenplay sold (for some dumb teen comedy, but still). "We had a two to five slot." He grinned. "That's two to five *a.m.*"

"I remember that," Beth told Will. "Lil and I were roommates that year. She always woke me up coming in."

"Needless to say, this was the *least* coveted slot on the schedule," Tal continued. From across the room, Beth heard Lil's laugh. "But we loved it, because we got to run around the student union in the middle of the night."

"*Which was actually kind of creepy,*" Lil called, sparking a wave of laughter.

"It was," Tal agreed, with a smile. "But it was also really fun. And we got to do whatever we wanted." He paused. "Because no one was listening." More laughter. "We played these obscure public service announcements about checking your kids' heads for lice and helping old ladies cross the street. And we sang along with Marlene Dietrich. I think our only listeners were Obies pulling all-nighters, total nutcases, and teenagers in Shaker Heights, who thought that listening to WOBC at three in the morning constituted a major act of rebellion." Titters and claps. "All of them were completely in love with Lil—or Lil's voice. They'd call in with really bad requests and try to keep her on the phone. If I answered, they'd hang up." He took a long sip of his beer. "And this is my point, I guess. That now, Tuck is the only person in the world who gets to hear Lil's voice at three in the morning. And he's a lucky, lucky man."

"The luckiest," Tuck shouted, pulling Lil close to him with one arm.

"Wow," said Will, with a bit of a grimace.

"He's right," said Beth, with a shrug.

"I'm sure," said Will, but his smile suggested otherwise. "Shall we attempt to get another drink? It seems like the speechifying is over for the time being."

Slowly, they made their way through the crowd.

"What are you doing in Cincinnati?" he asked as they shuffled, his arm on her elbow.

"Milwaukee," said Beth. "Popular culture. Like, you know, cultural studies. American studies."

"Well," he said, in a manner that was, yes, she was sure now, slightly condescending. "That's pretty general. You're doing—or did—a master's?"

She shook her head and stopped. They had managed to move about six feet. She was too tired to go any farther. "Doctorate. I'm ABD. Writing my dissertation right now. But here. In New York."

He raised his pale, bushy eyebrows. "On what? Popular culture?" He snorted. "I can't even imagine."

"*Dark Shadows,*" said Beth quickly. She was used to this sort of response. "You probably haven't heard of it. Though it aired, I guess, in Europe, too."

"A television show?"

"From the sixties. A soap opera," she explained. "Which makes it sound bad, but it's *amazing.*" She drew in a breath and launched into her prepared speech for those who had not yet been initiated into the cult. "I mean, it's *crazy.* It started off as kind of a normal soap, you know, about this rich family in a small town, but then"—she shook her head and flung her freckled hands around, to indicate chaos—"a ghost appears, and then this character turns out to be a phoenix—"

"A *phoenix*? The mythological bird that rises from the ashes?"

"Yes! This, like, perky blonde woman—it turns out that she's actually a phoenix! And then—and this is when things get really amazing—this ancient vampire arrives. Barnabas. I know it sounds weird, but the sixties were a really strange time for TV. There were all these shows with supernatural elements. *The Addams Family. The Mun—*"

"Barnabas the vampire," Will suddenly cried with delight. "I have an uncle Barnabas up in Skipton who could pass for a vampire. He's about a thousand years old. Long, yellow nails. Do you think he was the prototype?"

"Could be," said Beth.

"Brilliant. That sounds *absolutely brilliant.* I must see it."

Around them, guests filed into the back room, returning with plates of fried chicken and glowing magenta beets. "Beth," called Emily, waving from a few feet away. "You want to get something to eat?"

"Sure," murmured Beth. "Will, nice to meet you. I'm sure I'll see you later." She held out her hand to him, again, but he was already walking forward, across the room, toward Sadie.

Holding the bones between their fingertips, the girls ate chicken, chatting with the aunts and an elegant friend of Lil's mom, her hair in a high chignon, who asked them questions like "Do you girls go to nightclubs?" Lil wandered around the room, stopping briefly at their table. "Lil, it's *perfect!*" they told her, before her mother pulled her away to talk to this relative or that one. Soon, the old aunts made their departure, swarming Tuck with thin white check-holders, and the band contingent deposited themselves at Beth and Emily's table. They were nice, really:

three guys with modified shags and two girls, a severe blonde and a stocky brunette, her eyebrows plucked and drawn in with pencil. Both girls wore the kinds of dresses the group favored in college—Atomic Age frocks, with fitted bodices, full skirts, and bold patterns, in drab green or mustard yellow. They all agreed that Lil—her makeup now faded—had never looked more beautiful. "And more *herself*," cried Beth.

As they ate the last bit of mashed potato and contemplated the corner of the room reserved for dancing, Tuck grabbed the microphone and announced that it was time to cut the cake. The guests headed, en masse, to the back room, where the cake—enormous and round, with its bright blossoms sprouting off the sides and top—presided, like a pasha, on top of a raised platform. Lil and Tuck were ushered through the crowd and Lil picked up a long silver knife, which Sadie, against her will, recognized as Tiffany's Shell & Thread pattern, with the little scallop on the end. *That's a nice present,* she thought, then shuddered, for her mother, she knew, was thinking the exact same thing. Lil brandished it over her head, like a samurai, then sunk it deep into the cake, extricating a sliver, placing it on a plate, and scooping a bit into Tuck's mouth.

"I can't believe they're doing this," whispered Dave, dourly, to Beth. It was the first thing he'd said to her all evening. Somehow, she'd ended up next to him in the throng. It was a relief, actually, to get this bit out of the way, the awkward first conversation. Inwardly, she smiled. *He* had spoken to her first.

"I know," said Beth, though she wasn't as bothered by this particular bit of wedding drivel as she'd expected. She knew, also, that Lil's mom had thrown a fit when Lil suggested cutting the cutely-feeding-each-other-cake bit.

"What's next?" asked Dave. "Is Tuck going to, like, take off the garter with his teeth?"

"I doubt it." Beth grabbed a piece of cake from a passing tray. Sliced open, the cake looked even more rich: a layer of deep, eggy vanilla, then chocolate buttercream, then a layer of deep chocolate.

"Isn't this incredible?" she heard Sadie say, her low voice sharpened by drink. It wasn't actually—the cake was overly dense and crumbly—but Beth ate it anyway and deposited her little plate on the now bare buffet table.

"You know, I haven't been avoiding you all night," Dave said. Beth nodded gaily, attempting to indicate that she hadn't given a moment's thought to whether or not he might have been staying out of her way. "I just thought that we, you know, needed to talk. That we would be alone later." Beth nodded again. Why he would think such a thing was beyond her, but it sent a shudder through her limbs.

"Hey," she said, without knowing exactly what she planned to tell him. "Why don't we dance?"

The band had started up a rendition of "They All Laughed." On the dance floor, they found both Dave's parents and Sadie's parents, the former self-consciously attempting a modified hustle, the latter smartly executing a neat fox-trot. They were members of an older generation, the Peregrines, having had Sadie quite late in life, and their clothes and habits spoke of an earlier, more storied era. The group tended to align themselves more with the Peregrines' generation—with their big band music and their cocktails before dinner—than with the one that followed, the boomers, with their Simon & Garfunkel and their marijuana after dinner. Rose Peregrine, for example, *dressed* to go shopping, ordered all her groceries in from a small shop around the corner, and visited her hairdresser twice weekly. This evening, she wore a fitted suit in dove gray shantung—the color not far off from that of her hair—with a high standup collar, and a thick row of complicated beadwork running down the jacket's front. But Dave's mom—in a long, shapeless navy blue shift, white threads springing from her red hair—looked nice, too, Beth thought.

"They're such dorks," said Dave, waving at his mother.

"I like them," said Beth.

"Yeah, well, they like you." He grinned down at her. "But you're a dork, too."

"Right," said Beth, willing herself to have a sense of humor. She'd spent five minutes with Dave and already he'd stung her. Had she actually been looking forward to seeing him? No, she hadn't. Actually.

Over his shoulder, she watched Lil's aunts stream out the front door, blowing kisses and waving royally.

"My mother," she told Dave, "would love this wedding. The loft. All the candles. The little kids running around." Her mother believed young people raised during the Bush and Reagan administrations were too conservative and complacent. Rebellion, Beth's mother believed, was healthy. She'd encouraged Beth to experiment—offering her wine with supper, tokes of the occasional joint, taking her to see Bergman and Bertolucci films when she outgrew *Snow White* and *Bambi*. Beth wondered what her mother would have to say about her dancing with Dave. For two years, she'd slyly refrained from commenting on him, but once they'd broken up, she'd blurted, "Oh, honey, he wasn't for you."

"Lil didn't invite them?" Dave asked.

"She did. But they already had tickets to California. It's Jason's fall break. His *last* fall break." Her brother was a senior at Stanford, studying things she admired but barely comprehended: computers and politics.

"Right."

A song or two later the room was half empty, the older generations gone home. The band finished their set and stood chatting, ties loosened, with Tuck's friends from Atlanta. Quietly, the caterers began moving crates of cutlery and dishes out to their truck, and Lil and Tuck sat down at a table, white wine in her hand, whiskey in his. The group slunk into chairs around them, Beth both relieved and disappointed to be out of Dave's arms, Sadie prying herself away from that awful Will Chase, with his idiotic ideas about the "New Economy" (her father said it was all a load of bunk, none of these websites were going to make any money, not from selling pet food in bulk or books or anything), and his smug, overconfident air. Tuck's friends—the band guys and their girlfriends; the Southern couple, and the couple with the baby; various Columbians and coworkers in suits, among them Will Chase, his tie loosened, his jacket off; and Ed Slikowski, his long, pale face eager and earnest—gathered around them, sprawling their legs out and draping their elbows on the tables. The photographer, a journalist friend of Tuck's who was shooting the wedding as his gift to the couple, came by and snapped his camera at them, cracking, "Oh *yeah,* there's the album cover. Hot."

The girls weren't exactly sure what to do. It was just getting on midnight—still early—and had this been a normal party, they might have helped Lil and Tuck clean up, then gone out for a drink at a nearby bar. But the caterers would be cleaning everything up. "Should we see if everyone wants to go to Galapagos?" Emily whispered to Dave. The bartender there was an actor Emily knew from voice class, and would certainly grant them a round of free drinks or a bottle of champagne. "Or is it too far a walk?" The dark-haired band girl conferred with her friends, then came over and squatted behind Emily and Dave, her arms hooked companionably over the backs of their chairs. "Hey, we were thinking, if you guys want, we could go to Irving Plaza. Guided by Voices is playing and we have, like, VIP passes. We can definitely get you all in. Bob"—she pointed to a small, bucktoothed man with extraordinarily greasy hair—"toured with them last year. Lil could go in her dress. It's cool."

Before Dave or Emily could say anything, Sadie was standing on a chair, the toes of her silk pumps primly touching, the last trace of her peevish mood vanished. She tinked a fork on a dirty champagne flute, the imprint of someone's coral lips adorning its edge. "Okay, everyone," she said, tossing her arms open wide in a gesture of mock theatricality. Sadie was quiet—reserved rather than shy, like Beth—but lapsed, with drink, into fits of irony-fueled giddiness. "It is time for Lil to throw the bouquet. All the ladies must gather *here*." She pointed to an open space near the door. Nobody moved.

"Oh, come on, Sadie, they did the cake-eating thing," Dave protested, tugging on a hank of his hair. "They don't need to do this." Emily kicked him under the table. "Don't be a spoilsport," said Tal. "You know you want the bouquet."

"I know *I* want the bouquet," said Ed Slikowski.

"Everyone up." From her perch, Sadie gazed imperiously down at Dave. "Lil, *up*."

Wearily, Lil rose, leaving her round-toed pumps at the base of her chair. Without them, she appeared to crumple in on herself, like a doll, her dress trailing sadly on the floor. She walked to the fridge at the back of the loft's great room and removed a box. "Throwaway bouquet," she explained, holding a small bunch of roses aloft. "My mom ordered it. It's so you can keep your real bouquet." Dave rolled his eyes.

"Okay, on the count of three," Sadie shouted, jumping down unsteadily from the chair. "One. Two." The band girls scrambled up, and the others—giving each other looks of forbearance—followed suit. "*Three*." Lil, her back turned, tossed the roses into the air. The bouquet arced up sharply, then dropped directly toward Sadie herself, who tilted her neat profile up in the air, making her hands into a basket for her dubious prize; but as the flowers reached her waiting arms, the smaller band girl, the blonde, jumped directly in front of her, knocking her to the floor, and snatching the bouquet with one outstretched fist. The heavier band girl rushed over to her friend and hugged her, their outsized joy rather undermining their hipstery aspirations. The band guys raised their fists in mock salute and shouted, "*Yeah*. Way to go, Taylor. All *right*."

As one, the group glared at Taylor and then turned toward Sadie, whose yellowy skin had gone rather white, though she smiled, forcibly, as she rose from the scarred wood floor. Carefully, she made her way back to her seat, at Tal's right. He tucked an arm around her shoulder. Her hair, in large, loose ringlets—wilder and heavier than Lil's smooth, glossy waves—sprung up around her long face. Had her eyes, Beth wondered, always been so large, so shadowed? Up close, in the flickering light, she had the aspect of a serious child—a child from a Dutch painting, prematurely aged by the rigors and politics of court. How could *Taylor* have caught the bouquet, Beth thought, angrily. Taylor, who wasn't even *invited*. The evening had soured for her. Was it bad luck, she thought, for a stranger to catch the bouquet? Did this bode poorly for Lil's marriage? No, no, of course not. Across the table, Lil leaned heavily against Tuck's shoulder, her eyes drooping with fatigue.

"It's time," said Sadie, meeting the eyes, pair by pair, of her friends, "for all of us to go." And so they gathered their coats and shawls and bags, pecked Lil and Tuck on the cheek, and offered a final congratulations.

Outside, the air had turned cold, wintery, the harvest moon hanging low in the black sky, orange and unreal, like a painted set. The girls shivered in their thin coats and shawls. Dave offered his cigarettes around, pulling one from the pack with his lips, then lighting one for Sadie. They began walking west, toward Bedford, the populated part of Williamsburg. "That was really fun, wasn't it?" sighed Sadie. The others nodded their assent and quickened their step, for the air was growing cooler, it seemed, each moment, as they drew closer and closer to the river. Instinctively, they huddled together as they crossed under the BQE overpass, a desolate, graffiti-covered tunnel, the girls stepping gingerly in their delicate shoes to avoid the broken beer bottles and black, desiccated banana peels that lay at their feet in scant piles.

"I'm so tired," said Beth, with a shiver, her voice echoing in the dank little hollow. A quick wind picked up scraps of trash—plastic grocery bags, candy wrappers—and swirled them in their direction, the fruit scent of rotting garbage filling their mouths. "Maybe we should just go home."

"We can't go home yet," Will Chase shouted from behind them. "Be strong, Beth Bernstein, there is liquor to be drunk."

"First round's on me," called Ed Slikowski, who was half jogging down the street. "Let's drink to the love!" he shouted.

Emily looked at Beth. "It's freezing," she whispered. "Maybe you're right."

But then they were back under the cover of the city's black, monolithic sky. There were, Beth saw, no stars. Not one. The wind died down—

or perhaps it had been a product of the tunnel—and the air cleared, smelling now of leaves and gasoline and a thousand other things coming from the thousands and thousands of cars and houses and people and dogs and cats that surrounded them.

"We're almost there," said Sadie. And it was true, they were only a few long blocks from the water—with their next step, the orderly lights of the Manhattan skyline, beaming across the river, began, slowly, to enter their line of vision.

two

As Beth followed Will Chase down the dim hallway leading to his apartment, a peculiar notion insinuated itself into her brain. Some months earlier, Lil had walked down this same corridor with Tuck, to do, perhaps, the same things she might now do with Will. Not that she had decided she was going to do *anything* with Will—she still wasn't even sure if she liked or hated him. And not that she knew whether he actually wanted to do anything with her. An hour earlier, as they'd finished dinner, at a dark Mediterranean restaurant with walls of bright mosaic, he'd asked if she had "plans for the rest of the evening." She was rather taken aback by this question, seeing as it was eleven o'clock on a Wednesday night—four days after Lil's wedding. What exactly might she have planned at such an hour?

"Well," she said, smiling, "I *am* supposed to meet some friends at the Tunnel, but that's not until four. So I guess you're stuck with me for, oh"—quick look at her watch—"another four, five hours."

"Would you like to take a stroll, then? The weather's gorgeous. And the moon is out." Somehow, the clipped tones of his voice managed to drain whatever romantic potential Beth might have wanted to associate with words like "moon" and "stroll." Alarmingly, he stuck his head under the table. She snapped her legs closed. "You're not wearing ridiculous shoes, are you?" She gestured toward her boots—calf-covering things with low square heels, which she'd bought the day before at a loud shop on Eighth Street—and they ventured off down Berry Street, then west, toward the river, where he showed her a giant mound of glass—blue, clear, a thousand shades of green—glinting in the white moonlight. "Is it for recycling?" she asked, hating the studenty tone of her voice.

"Don't know," he said, shoving his hands in his pockets and rolling back on his heels. "But it's gorgeous, isn't it?"

They walked for blocks among Williamsburg's low houses, which were certainly *not* gorgeous, she thought, with their vinyl siding and creaky metal awnings, decrepit warehouses with flat, narrow banks of windows, garbage on the street. Why did her friends want to live here, in this ugly place? But maybe there were parts that were nicer, the streets lined with soothing brownstones, like where Dave had grown up. When Emily and Lil and Tal had talked about living in Brooklyn, she'd pictured Dave's parents' apartment—preposterously narrow, lined with bookcases, wedding cake moldings—and their shady, quiet block, with its tall stone stoops, the onyx facade of the funeral home on the corner.

"I think Emily lives near here," she said, stopping at a dark corner and peering down the street they were about to cross. "North Eighth Street, I think. That's her street."

"Do you want to stop in?" Will asked, in such a way that the question sounded rhetorical.

"No, no, no." Beth flushed, feeling suddenly stupid, though not exactly sure why. Was it such a banal thing to mention that her friend lived nearby? Was that what he was implying? "I just . . . she's probably not home." She studied the buildings around her, with what she hoped appeared to be cool, anthropological interest: a barely lit bar, the restaurant in which they'd eaten—somehow they'd doubled back and she'd not realized it—and a lawn on which the Virgin Mary stood, hands clasped in prayer, a sky-blue plaster shell at her back. Was Lil and Tuck's place near here, too? It was hard to tell.

"Then would you like to come to my place?" asked Will. "For a nightcap?"

"Um, sure," said Beth. She wasn't necessarily enjoying herself, but she wasn't yet ready to give up on the *possibility* of enjoying herself. And she was flattered. He'd seemed only half interested in her all evening, inspecting the coterie of pretty women at the restaurant's bar (all of them somehow *sharper* than she), while she, perhaps, talked too long about her family ("My mother is the best!") and Astoria ("Lil said there wasn't any place even to get a cup of coffee, and she was right") and the classes she'd taught that summer ("I totally overloaded the syllabus") and Dave, whom she'd not meant to talk about, but of course, *did* ("It was just so weird to see him"). But then there they were, passing under the slender trees of Havemeyer Street—just beginning to shed their spade-shaped leaves—and into the glaring light of his building's bare, ugly lobby. He twisted open a battered tin mailbox and extracted a sheaf of envelopes and flyers, then guided her up a flight of stairs and down a short hallway to a shiny new steel door. The door, it turned out, opened directly into the apartment's sitting room, a sparsely decorated space, with a neat white couch on one wall, a fussy little chair facing it, and a square kitchen table in the far corner. To her left, she saw a small bedroom, the mere glimpse of which made her flush. And around a corner, a tiny kitchen—really just a walled-in section of the living room—with plants on dusty shelves bolted across the windows.

Will went into the kitchen and emerged with a bottle of dark liquor in one hand, two unmatched tumblers in the other. "Remy, okay?" She nodded, though she wasn't sure what it was. She rarely drank; she couldn't, couldn't smoke either, due to what her mother half jokingly called her "delicate constitution." She'd spent her junior year of high school in bed with a bout of mono, like some sort of Victorian spinster. "Sit, sit." He gestured toward the futon, placing the glasses on the little table and unscrewing the bottle's cap. She sat, straightening her skirt around her and crossing her legs, fighting the urge to take off her new boots, which were pinching her toes.

"Most of this furniture was Tuck's actually," he said, handing her a squat tumbler. "He decided he wanted to start *afresh* with Lil, so he left it here. He has good taste." He shrugged. "And I don't have any. So I'm happy with his hand-me-downs." He had a habit of pronouncing certain words—clichéd phrases—as though they had quotes around them. Beth was beginning to find this affectation a little annoying, in part because she was so familiar with it. Her friends in grad school had all done the same. This was the fate of academics the world over: to view even the most harmless phrases as dangerous clichés. She was guilty of it herself.

She took a tentative sip of her drink, coughing a little from its fumes, and immediately began to feel warm all over. "You didn't have any furniture of your own?" He shook his head, swallowing. "Not much. I'm not good with stuff." For the first time that evening, she felt she had his whole attention—but she was now having trouble focusing on him. To her right, above Will's head, several rows of mounted shelves held well-thumbed books—she could spot no fiction published since the First World War—in front of which, at various intervals, stood an army of garishly colored children's toys: a plastic dinosaur, a Kewpie doll, and a Lego tower. After four years around pop culture grad students, this didn't strike her as all that strange. She knew forty-year-olds with complete collections of original-issue *Star Wars* action figures or Strawberry Shortcake dolls still in the original packaging.

"You have some toys," she said, smiling.

"Yes, yes," he agreed, nodding a bit too energetically. "Yes, I do."

"Is there a story behind them?"

"Well, yes, yes, there is. They belong to my son, Sam."

"Oh." Beth grinned stiffly. "Wow."

He turned his palms upward, smiling. "I know, it's rather a shock, isn't it?"

"No, no, of course not."

"No, it is, you mustn't be overly polite about it. I'm the Englishman, right?" he said, smiling broadly—sadly, actually—and his particular beauty hit her with a thud. For a moment, she was certain she'd never been so attracted to a man.

"Okay," she said, drawing out the word. "I won't. Promise. No politeness from me. How old is he, Sam?"

"Four," he said, leaning back on the couch and crossing his legs at the knee. "He started prekindergarten last month. It's a *big deal*. He has a backpack."

"I can imagine," she said, taking another inventory of the toys on the shelves. There was a Barbie, naked, her long legs jutting from the shelf. No gender hang-ups, Beth thought.

Will followed her glance. "It's a game we play. He stands on the couch and lines up everything on the shelves. Hours of entertainment."

Beth nodded, suddenly impatient. "So does Sam have a mother?"

"No," Will replied. "No, he doesn't. It's quite an amazing story. He was hatched from an egg."

"That *is* amazing. Does he look at all like, I don't know, a chicken?"

"No, he's a perfectly normal little boy. Quite blond, though, now that you mention it, a bit chickenlike, isn't it? So maybe there is a bit of chicken blood somewhere in there. That *would* explain the egg thing."

"So, he doesn't live with you?"

"Well, it's funny. We don't actually have any firm custody arrangements—me and the egg, that is—so, for now, Sam stays here about half the time. Usually on weekends. Which is why I made our *assignation*"—a sardonic smile—"for a Wednesday. Otherwise I'd have done the proper thing and asked you out for a Saturday night. But Sam will definitely be with me this Saturday."

"And the rest of the time he lives with a broken egg."

Will laughed a true, unguarded laugh, his first of the evening. "Well, yes, that's actually a pretty accurate description." He bunched up his mouth, a not unattractive gesture. "Shall I put some music on?" Before she could answer, he'd risen and turned his back to her, shuffling through a pile of CDs on the mounted shelves. "Yes, well. Sam's mother is actually kind of a *nutcase*. She is, as you've probably guessed, my wife."

"Your wife?" said Beth, in a voice that sounded, to her, like a squeak.

"Yes. I'd *like* to say ex-wife, but we're not quite divorced yet. Almost there, though."

Beth stared at him.

"I know, I know," he said. "It's not some line. We've been separated for a long time. Since Sam was a baby."

Then why aren't you divorced yet, she wanted to ask, but couldn't bring herself to, for this would imply that she cared—though, of course, why would he have told her all this, if he didn't *want* her to care. But then, he hadn't. He'd said nothing until there was no way for him *not* to say something.

"Listen," he was saying now, "let's stop talking about this. Why don't you take off your blouse?"

Beth laughed. "What?"

He looked at her intently for a moment, then glanced down at the jewel case in his hands. "Take your blouse off."

"Um, Will . . ." She laughed again.

"Beth." His back was to her once again. She heard the tray of the CD player slide out and watched him slot in a CD, the silver disc shooting bits of light at her.

A quivery heat, pulsating and uncomfortable, was developing between her legs. He turned and looked at her, crossing his arms across his chest. Unsure exactly of what she planned to do, she rose from the futon. There was no reason to obey him. But was there a reason *not* to? For a moment she looked at him, then—almost to escape the glare of his eyes—she slowly began to untuck the tails of her shirt, which was black and made of a thin, shiny cotton, in the style of a men's dress shirt. It, too, was new. She unbuttoned the cuffs, the sleeves falling over her hands, then, gaining speed, unbuttoned the mother-of-pearl discs on the front placket. Will held out his hand and, after a minute, Beth—realizing his meaning— handed over the shirt, which he laid over the almost feminine chair, gingerly, taking care not to crease it. She stood in front of him, her freckled breasts propped up by a plain black cotton bra, a demi cup. He hadn't pressed play on the CD player, she realized, and the apartment felt strangely silent, no street noise creeping in, no sounds from the apartments above or below. He gestured toward her skirt—her favorite, a velveteen A-line, in brownish maroon, that fell just below her knees—with an open palm. But this seemed too much. Her breasts, she knew, were her best feature. Until recently, she'd liked her thighs, which were long and smooth and white, and her narrow knees and flat calves. But at Sadie's, as the girls dressed before the wedding, she'd become acutely conscious of their flaccidness. Her friends—who had once scorned exercise and, moreover, the conscious pursuit of thinness; who had taken the Women and Body Image ExCo class—had become sleek, muscled creatures. Emily, in particular, once pleasantly curvy, now had the solid, ridged legs of a chorus girl, though, Beth supposed, she *was* a chorus girl, of sorts.

Will finished off his drink, with a low rattle of ice, and placed the glass on the shelf behind him, next to a wild-haired troll doll and a worn-looking Raggedy Ann. "Take off your skirt," he said, gesturing again. What could she say? What reason could she give him? She had started this and she couldn't stop. She should have said no in the first place. She should have left in a flurry of moral outrage. She should have kissed him and shut him up.

"I," she started to say, but the sound didn't really come out. A muscle in his jaw twitched. He nodded at her, as if to say *Go on, now, silly girl.* Before she could think better of it, she unhooked the fastenings on her skirt and stepped out of it, bending carefully at the waist and knee. He took that from her as well, folding it neatly, and smirking slightly at the label. "BCBG. That's hilarious." She smiled at him blankly. "Do you know what it means?" She shook her head. "*Bon chic bon genre.* It's a term for a certain sort of Parisian young person. Kind of like calling someone a hipster or a *yuppie* or a Sloane Ranger. But there's no real equivalent in English." She nodded. The throbbing between her legs continued, and her heart thunked loudly below her breasts, but a certain calm was settling over her. "Take off your bra," he said, as she'd known he would. This time, she didn't hesitate. She reached behind her and undid the hooks and eyes, slid the straps off her shoulders, and handed him the bra. Her breasts hung heavily, loosely on her chest. In junior high she'd wanted to have them reduced—the horror of gym class. Without waiting for him to tell her to do so, she stepped out of her underwear—plain, black cotton—and found herself standing naked but for her high boots, like a girl in *Playboy,* in front of a man she barely knew, a man who, she had an inkling, was not interested in the sort of relationship she was accustomed to, would not even tell her that he loved her, as a manner of courtesy, as had Glyn, the Welshman she'd dated on and off in Milwaukee, who was, honestly, an asshole, as were, she'd found, all men with an overhealthy interest in *Star Trek.* "Why don't you come here," he said now, gesturing toward himself. He'd placed the rest of her clothing over the back of one of the wooden chairs at the table, a small action that she found stupidly reassuring as she crossed the room—taking care not to move too fast and cause her body to ripple unduly—and sat down next to him, a bit too stiffly, unsure of what to do with her arms or her breasts or the small pouch of her stomach, until she busied herself with—at last, *thankfully*— unzipping her punishing boots and stripping off her thin black socks. As she did so, he stroked her hair—paternally, she couldn't help thinking now, knowing about Sam—and said, "You're lovely."

"Oh," she said foolishly, pressing her face into his chest, which smelled of tobacco and laundry detergent and sweat and something else she knew but couldn't name, all of which was too much for her, and so she turned herself from him and pressed her back against his side, her legs curled on the couch. His feet were still stubbornly set on the wood floor, legs uncrossed now. "Oh," he said, too, his breath close in her ear, ragged and short, his hands now running lightly over her body, reaching down and unbending her legs, stretching them long on the couch, stroking up the bone of her shin, over her knee, along her thigh, a brief visit between her legs, then up over her stomach, her ribs, and onto her breasts. As his hand—large, alarmingly masculine, a father's hand, with gold hairs sprouting off its edges—cupped her nipple, she realized, with alarm, that his other hand (Left? Right? She'd lost all sense of orientation) had moved from her hair to her mouth, smelling more strongly of the elusive scent she'd detected earlier, peppermint, a bit anti-septic, vaguely loamy—it came on her slowly—Dr. Bronner's, the all-purpose liquid soap that she'd used in college. They'd bought it in large bottles at the health food co-op in Harkness. Supposedly, you could dilute it and use it as mouthwash, but she never had—could never fig-ure out the ratio of soap to water—and as this thought slipped and faded into the hills of her mind, she felt her body come unnervingly alive. Her mouth opened and released a moan that seemed to come from someone else, or from somewhere behind her, and released moist par-ticles into the palm of his hand. His other hand still circled her one breast, then, without warning, slipped away from it and scrambled behind him on the futon for something.

She shifted, stretched one hip down, then the other, and felt her spine release with a small, ladylike pop, along with a decidedly more animalis-tic throbbing between her legs. *Oh God,* she thought senselessly. Her head now rested in his lap. Then his hand was leaving her mouth—she'd closed her eyes at some point—and something soft and cushy was being tied around it. She wasn't sure she wanted this—scarf? gag?—and moved her head from side to side to indicate her ambiguous feelings about the device. But she was unable—or unwilling—to speak and break the spell, for she didn't want things to end, didn't want him to stop touching her. It was all fine so long as she kept her eyes closed. As though from a distance—from behind the lens of a camera, perhaps—she saw herself lying naked on the couch, him fully dressed, his slightly scratchy wool trousers against her cheek, and again thought of *Playboy*. Was that her only pornographic reference model? *Yes,* she thought, *yes it wa*s. As a kid, she'd stolen a copy from her father's nightstand and hid it under her bed. Her pose now reminded her of the black-and-white comics scattered, *New Yorker*–style, throughout the magazine, in which large-bosomed girls lay naked, just as she was, their heads lolling in men's laps.

No, she didn't want it to end, so she didn't say no. Nor did she open her eyes. Instead, she moved her head and moaned slightly, this time consciously, which made him pull the cloth tighter, then reach down and pinch her nipple, forcefully—something she'd always hated, squirmed away from, but which sent a hot shot through her midsection, and caused her to arch her upper back into his hand, which he promptly moved to the scarf, fastening it firmly. She writhed, unsure of what message she was sending by doing so (and equally unsure of what message she *wanted* to send). Again, he reached back, lifting her head slightly as he did so, this time placing a similar fabric on her forehead, no, down, over her closed eyes, quickly pulling it tight and tying it. She offered no resistance this time, though she felt both more frightened and more excited, almost inconceivably so. But as his touch turned more gentle—removing her head from his lap and placing it carefully on a small, hard pillow—and her mind stopped racing, she became fraught with the foolishness of her immediate situation: she had gone home with a man she barely knew, a man with a wife and child (Where? Who knew? Lil; she would ask her tomorrow), whom he had *neglected* to mention until moments before instructing her to strip. What kind of person did something like that? What else was he not telling her? Were there bodies beneath his floorboards?

Here she was: naked, gagged, and blindfolded, like something out of a movie (a porno? She'd never seen one), or something more risqué than *Playboy*—*Hustler,* perhaps, or *Screw*. Of course, this wasn't a movie, this was real life, *her* life, and this man—this virtual stranger—could kill her or rape her or, or, do anything with her that he liked. What did she know about him? Nothing, really, but that he was Tuck's friend and she barely knew Tuck—really, she didn't know Tuck at all. A warm trickle of something leaked down from inside her, cooling her thigh. *Oh God,* she thought again, *oh God.* She felt his hands part her legs, just slightly. She could feel the soft, dense hairs of his thighs rubbing against the back of her own. He was kneeling on the futon, beneath her legs. And he'd removed his pants. His hands, again, moved up her legs, inside her thighs, which were now embarrassingly moist. She moved to close them, making awful "uhhh-unnn" sounds, like a sheep. "No, no," he said, firmly holding them apart, and placed his hand there, then slid a finger back. What was he doing? His finger, wet, slipped in behind, then another finger.

Oh God, she thought, not *this,* she'd never thought of this, never conceived of it as an option, though she'd read about it, of course, most memorably (*indelibly,* she supposed) in Martin Amis's *London Fields,* where the main character—Nicola Six, who really isn't very much like a real person, but more like a man's masturbatory fantasy, but that's kind of the point, she supposed, kind of what the book is about, kind of what *all* Martin Amis books are about—can't get enough of it and her doctor, Nicola Six's doctor, that is, tells her it's okay, as long as she does it first in the proper place, second in the *other* place, where one of Will's fingers now moved gently, as it's not healthy to do it the opposite way, a girl could wind up with all sorts of infections and things. And then there was Lucy, a strange girl from her grad program (writing her dissertation on BBC adaptations of Austen), with whom she'd made a brief attempt at friendship—a Brit, like Will—and Glyn. One night, two-odd years back, the three of them had gone for drinks at the Gasthaus, and Lucy had started in on the sexual ineptitude of British men. One boyfriend, a cyclist whom she'd otherwise adored, was only capable of doing it . . . *this* way, "in the arse," Lucy had said, laughing.

"Well, clearly he was a fag," Glyn had said.

"No," Lucy shrieked, "he wasn't! He wasn't. He just had problems."

Glyn shrugged and swilled his Guinness. "What did it feel like?" he asked, trying to pass this off as a casual question. "Did you like it?"

"Hmmm." Lucy considered, pushing a bony hand into her blonde, wiry hair. Affecting intense interest in the menu board, Beth had avoided her friends' eyes and pressed her legs together to stop the throbbing that had started up between them. "It felt a bit like going to the loo, if you know what I mean," she said. "It felt like there was something inside me that wasn't supposed to be there, and my body was trying to push it out."

Her thin, serious face broke into a smile. "But I also quite liked it, in a way, doing the *taboo* thing, you know? It *added* something."

That night, Beth had expected Glyn to want to try it. Instead, he'd fallen dead asleep—no, passed out—on her tattered couch. She wasn't sure whether to be relieved or disappointed. And now here she was, doing the taboo thing, or on the verge of it, not sure if it would be more sordid or less, for the fact of her being in New York, with someone she barely knew. Her mind raced, health center pamphlets flashing before her eyes like a grammar school slide show: AIDS, HIV, herpes, burst blood vessels, intestinal blockage, something in *Story of O* about being "rent" by this activity, if the man's . . . organ . . . was too large, rending meaning, she assumed, ripping, though perhaps it was something worse.

But no, these were just his fingers—*for now*—and they felt strange, not necessarily painful. She could see what Lucy meant, about having something unnatural inside you. Her muscles contracted. And yet there was also this feeling—she fought against it—of his fingers being too small, too *sad*, of wanting *more*. Her body rocked, without her intending it to do so. And she felt his body—large, that smell of peppermint and tobacco and maybe shaving cream—hovering over hers, the corner of a worn T-shirt, a brush of boxer short. "Have you done this before?" he asked. His voice, she realized, was low and extraordinarily pleasant. She would not, she thought, have discovered this if not for the blindfold and the gag. It was true what they say about sensory deprivation—block off one sense and it heightens the others. Like Hellen Keller. She shook her head no, rather wildly, fearing he might misunderstand. "I didn't think so," he said, moving his fingers more deeply inside her. His other elbow (left? right?) rested on the futon, just next to her ribs. Now he moved this hand to her breast again, clamping down on it. Hot and swollen—prickly, almost as if she were getting her period—from all this touching, her breasts seemed to be acting of their own accord, divorced from their owner.

He was holding his body off of her, perhaps not wanting to crush her with his weight, but she wanted to feel his weight on top of her, the smell of him, his body obliterating the thoughts and anxieties of her own, shutting down the system. Instead, he shifted her in one smooth motion and lay down next to her, on his side, his mouth at her ear. "I don't want to hurt you," he said. As one, her muscles went limp at this declaration. She had nothing to worry about. Lil or Emily would never worry in a situation like this. They would strip off their clothes and stand boldly before

Will, hips tucked back to lengthen their legs, as models did. Sadie, she thought, would never *be* in a situation like this.

Then she remembered how they'd met—"Who's the dark beauty?"—and shuddered. It had been four days since the wedding, four nights. Perhaps Sadie had been here one of those nights. Perhaps Sadie *had* been in a situation *exactly* like this. No, she'd seemed utterly uninterested in—annoyed by, even—Will at the bar after the wedding and she'd left early with Tal. "Are they?" Beth had asked Emily. "Who knows," Emily had told her, with a roll of her eyes. "He follows her around. She won't talk about it. You know how she is." Beth did. They all, rather, followed Sadie around. Beth couldn't blame Will for wanting her, but what bothered her was the thought that he might have treated Sadie differently. Hung on her every word in the restaurant. Been unable to take his eyes from her.

This line of thought was pointless, she told herself firmly, willing her mind back into the moment. Will, she thought, had admired Sadie, but recognized in Beth a sensual—*darkly* sensual—nature she'd always suspected lay dormant, unrecognized by her few, inept lovers. *Yes,* she thought, *yes.* He was stroking her now, back and front, his breath hot in her ear, and she was, she *was* going to come, but she couldn't, shouldn't, *would not* with this *stranger* watching her—and she unable to see him—witnessing whatever contortions and contractions of her body, whatever ugliness she might possess at such a moment. She fought it, willed it away, twisting her hips and shutting her legs. "Stop," he said firmly, like a schoolteacher, keeping his hand between her legs. "You're being very, very bad." *Oh God, oh God, this is a terrible cliché,* she thought, almost against her will (why, why, why could she not simply experience things, without comment?), *from a thousand pornos.* She tried to remember the names of the classic ones, *Deep Throat, Behind the Green Door,* which she'd heard about—grad students liked to joke about them, to use puns on the titles in their papers ("Behind the Greek Door: The Frat House as Metaphor in Contemporary American Film")—but never seen, though pretended she had on numerous occasions, *Debbie Does Dallas, Anal Invaders, Electric Blue.* The ridiculous titles, the list of them, calmed her and she thrashed her legs against his.

"You need to stop," he said. His voice now closer, speaking directly into her ear. "You're being a very bad girl. If you don't stop, I shall have to bind your hands." And at that, at those words, uttered in Will's crisp Oxbridge accent, her body released in a thousand different directions, waves of hot and cold shooting through her—her low cries spilling, fuzzed, through the scarf. She pushed him, his hands, away from her, *off of her*—it was unbearable, too much—but he refused to move the front one, holding her against him by the pubic bone, feeling, no doubt, the mortifying waves running through her, her mouth clenched tight so as not to scream. Slowly, she became aware that he was close to her now, his front pressed to her back, and she could feel him, hard, against her. She reached behind her to touch him, thinking this the proper, appropriate thing to do, though part of her wished he would simply *leave,* but he grabbed her hand and said "No," again in that firm tone. Then he gathered her other hand into his left one—the arm attached to it cushioning her head—and ran his right along her stomach. "Did you like that?" he asked. She nodded. "You did?" She nodded. "Tell me." But she didn't want to speak, not yet. "Yes," she said, her mouth straining against the thick fabric. "I thought so. You're a very bad girl, Miss *Scars*dale." Why did this sound dirtier, more appalling—but also somehow more *manageable,* more *expected*—coming from an Englishman?

As her body calmed itself, cooled by a stream of air from the kitchen window, her mind grew rapidly more awake, shaking off the fug of wine and food, so that she felt more alert than she had in days, weeks—bizarrely, grimly awake, her mind jumping from one thing to the next. Should she have danced with Dave at the wedding? Why had they not talked, as he'd said they would? And why was she wasting time worrying about all this— three whole days already—when she needed to get to work on her research? Tomorrow, she *must* go into the Museum of Television and Radio and get herself set up for the next phase. No, no, tomorrow she needed to call Gail Bronfman, at the New School, and settle things with her job, if she had a job, which she knew she probably didn't, but she couldn't quite admit defeat. It was all so humiliating—not just that she'd screwed things up with her credits, but that she'd handled everything wrong. "But I can be there by the first week in October," she'd told Gail Bronfman (this was how she thought of her, not as "Gail" or "Dr. Bronfman," but as "Gail Bronfman"). "So, if someone could sub for me for the first few classes—"

"*Sub* for you," the woman had shrieked. "This isn't elementary school. These are *your* classes. Your syllabus. Your students. You need to be there."

"I know. But I can't—they won't—" At this point, shouting commenced on Gail Bronfman's end of the line.

"I'm just going to have to find someone else for the fall. A week before classes begin. What a treat. Thanks. You've made my day." Beth asked, sensibly (she thought), if she could simply begin teaching in the spring semester—if they could simply change the start date of her contract. "We'll see. Call me when you get to New York" was Gail Bronfman's response, followed by a loud click and silence.

She willed her mind away from this conversation—which she'd shared with no one but her advisor—and toward Will, who was also, for now, a secret. She'd rather easily managed not to tell any of her friends that she would be seeing him—in part because she had a suspicion that they would warn her away, and in part because, she realized only now, she didn't want Dave to know about it, though she knew that was stupid, but she felt some dumb need—what was it?—to maintain the illusion that they might, if they wanted to, pick up exactly where they'd left off, four-odd years ago, at commencement, before he'd told her, in that mumbled, half-angry, Dave way, that he thought when they went off to grad school they should see other people. She didn't know anything of his "other people"—her friends had been very good about keeping silent on this subject—and nor did he, as far as she knew, know anything about hers, so perhaps they could simply pretend there hadn't been any—just as there had been no horrible, humid summer, while they waited to leave for their respective programs and spent countless silent hours wandering around the streets outside his parents' apartment, drinking beer in barely air-conditioned bars, and fumbling awkwardly, gingerly, in his narrow childhood bed, which barely fit in his closet-sized room, Beth on the verge of tears each time they finished, each time she had to put on her clothes and board the subway to Grand Central, then the train back to Scarsdale, then her green Accord through the village and the curving streets back to her parents' mock Tudor. *Dave,* she thought. The memory of that terrible summer—when she knew she'd lost him, yet continued to pretend she hadn't, and he (worse) allowed her to—somehow reminded her, more than had anything else in recent years, of how she had loved him. Will, suddenly, seemed—in his not being Dave—even more alien than previously. *Oh my God,* she thought, *why am I here? What did I just do?*

Just then, Will's hand dropped heavily to the futon, releasing her wrists. He was, she realized, *sleeping.* Ripping the loosened cloth off her eyes and mouth, she turned to face him. Weren't men supposed to fall asleep after orgasm? Had he, somehow, without her knowing it, reached . . . climax?

By rubbing against her? She glanced down at his boxer shorts, which were plain white. They appeared clean and dry. Tentatively, she reached a hand out and touched their front. At this, Will started awake, taking hold of her hand. "No touching, Scarsdale." She must've looked stricken, for he released his grip on her, smiled, and pushed her bangs to one side of her forehead. "*Beth*. Sorry. I just think it's funny. I always thought Scarsdale was a mythological place. Like Xanadu. Where rich Jews go to die or some such thing." Beth rolled her eyes. "I mean, dating a Jewish girl from Scarsdale is a bit like dating a WASP from Greenwich, isn't it?"

Beth sat up and looked around for her clothing. "I don't know," she said. "I don't really think of things in those terms." This was absurd, this kind of talk. She'd hated growing up in Scarsdale, hated every second of it, couldn't wait to get out, and now this, this *lecher*—this person who was possibly some sort of pervert or, at the very least, an unscrupulous libertine—had decided to nickname her *Scarsdale,* as though she were some sort of metonym for conventional, conservative, upper-middle-class Jewry. And he clearly knew nothing about Scarsdale, for if he did, he'd know she was nothing—*nothing*—like the girls there, with their perma-manicures, their carefully highlighted hair, their spots on the soccer team, their stupid, *stupid* outfits from Great Stuff, their obnoxious accents, their middlebrow aspirations, their cruel cliquishness, and their moronic sorority membership ("Dee Phi Eee! At U Mish!"). These were the girls who had mocked her from, seemingly, birth. And now, eight years after she'd left the place for good, someone was mistaking her for one of them, simply by virtue of . . . *what?*

She shot him a slit-eyed glance as she climbed over his body, off the futon, and began to gather her clothes. He watched her, idly. Then, as she made her way by him, toward the bathroom, he grabbed her calf. "Let me *go,*" she cried, wrenching her leg. But he held on, swinging his legs around so he was sitting, his head level with her stomach, and climbing his hand up her body as he stood, towering over her, she in her bare feet. "Beth, Beth," he began. "I'm sorry. Don't be so sensitive. I can be a bit of a cad." Beth was afraid to speak, certain the tears—her famous, dreaded tears—would begin to flow at the first word. She pulled away from him. "You don't know anything about me," she said, voice wavering. "You shouldn't make generalizations like that. If you knew *anything* about *Scarsdale,* you'd know I'm nothing like the girls there." He smiled without showing his teeth. "Maybe you are in ways you don't know." This was too much, too, too much. Her stomach clenched with rage. Suddenly, out of nowhere, she was screaming, "Fuck you, fuck you, fuck you," her voice ragged and shrill. She stormed into the bathroom.

Slumped against the door, the tears finally came—prickly relief—and she turned quickly to lock the nicked brass handle, trying to quiet herself. In a moment, to her surprise, she felt calm. She would wash her face and leave and never see this person—this monster—again. She splashed water on her cheeks, rubbed herself dry with a plush white towel, peed quietly, and swished yellow Listerine in her mouth. Gingerly, she stepped into her underpants and bra, her breasts still achy, pulled on her blouse, and stepped into her skirt. Glancing tentatively into the mirror, she smoothed her hair with a plastic comb she found on the counter, tucking the front pieces behind her ears. She was ready. She unlocked the door, opened it, and stepped out into the front room, her swollen lips pressed together with grim determination. Will was not there, but her boots were neatly lined up by the door, her socks tucked inside. She picked them up, sat down on the couch, and slipped them both on, closing the boots' long zippers up over the sides of her calves. As she stood to leave, her hand hovering by the doorknob, Will appeared in the bedroom doorway, fully dressed—wool trousers, blue shirt, sleeves rolled to the elbow, white undershirt peeking out below his collar. Blond hairs curved out over the undershirt's ribbed neck, filling in the hollow at the base of his throat. "Oh, hello," he said. "You're Lil's friend Beth, aren't you? We met the other night at the wedding. You were wearing the most stunning dress. I'm sure I'm not the first to remark on it. You were easily the loveliest girl there. All the old codgers were *checking you out*. I noticed you the minute you walked in, with that ginger-haired girl, what's her name. Redheads. Never cared for them, myself." She smiled, against her will. "So," he said, smiling back at her, "what brings you to the neighborhood?" She sighed inwardly. "Well, I'm thinking about moving here," she found herself saying, in a voice she knew to be soft, seductive, "so I thought I'd take a look around." He held out his hand to her. "I see. Well, I happen to be an expert on the area." Now he had stepped closer and taken her hand. "Perhaps you might allow me to . . ." Now he trailed off, pulling her in close to him, untucking the back of her blouse from her skirt, holding his mouth in close to her neck. "Show you around."

•

Later, much later, they lay in his bed, a futon laid out on the floor like Lil and Tuck's. Again, he held her from behind, he half dressed, she entirely undressed. Again, he'd refused to let her touch him. She slipped out of his light, sleepy grip and turned to face him, inspecting the blue circles under his eyes, the creases that ran between the folds of his nose and the corners of his mouth. "Hey," she said gently, trying for a joking tone. "Hey, London." He smiled and yawned. "Miss Bernstein, you know perfectly well I'm from Oxford." He opened his eyes and looked at her. "You want to know why . . . why, all this?" She nodded. "Well. It's not pretty." He paused, smiling sarcastically. "I'm *impotent*." Again, he spat out the word as though it had quotes around it. She started to protest. "No, no, no. I know what you're thinking but you need to trust me on this one. I know what I'm talking about, m'dear. There are things you simply don't know about." Beth nodded. She had felt him . . . but perhaps there were many forms of impotence, perhaps some men could maintain the initial . . . erection, but couldn't complete the . . . act. But then why— well . . . hadn't he been intending to enter her *the other way*? Perhaps not. Perhaps when he asked if she'd "done this before" he was referring to the blindfold, the gag. Or to sex with strangers, in general.

"Is it—" she began. "Does it have something to do with your wife?" she asked, knowing, as the words came out of her mouth, that it was the wrong thing to say.

He laughed, almost a bark. "Yes, yes, it's quite tragic, actually. My wife cheated on me—a regular *slag,* as the lads would say. She used me, it seems, as a free ticket to New York, then, once ensconced in this fabled city, threw herself at every man who crossed her path—and now—" A face of exaggerated pain. "I cannot bring myself to commit the *act of love* with another woman, so *scarred* am I by her actions. She has displaced the very foundations of my manhood."

He was telling the truth, of course, despite his overdramatic tones. She wondered if, perhaps, he had, earlier, wanted to *try* to make love to her, in the proper way, but was worried that he couldn't carry through till the end. This, she thought firmly, *must* be what had happened. She said nothing. "I don't know how long this will last." He dropped his tone of mock gaiety. "It's been three years since the egg and I split up. That's a long time. It could be forever. But as long as you want to come round here, I'm happy to have you. Though *obviously* I'm never going to be some sort of boyfriend in the way you're used to. I'm never going to be Tuck." Again, she tried to protest, to explain that she didn't even know Tuck. "I've tried that route and it didn't work. I'm not cut out for that sort of thing, the everyday stuff, the oh-you-look-pretty-today and how-was-work-honey. I just can't do it. And I don't go to dinner parties or gallery openings or lectures by visiting professors or any sort of poetry reading or family gathering. I travel frequently for stories and absolutely refuse to call home during my trips. In other words, I simply don't *do* obligations anymore. I'm done. And that's never, *ever* going to change." She stared at him, jaw dangling. Was he for real? This speech seemed like something cribbed from a movie. Or, actually, a Martin Amis novel. "Though the other thing, well, it could get better." She nodded. "Okay," he said, more a question than a statement.

"Okay," she whispered, smiling. "I'm going to go to the bathroom." He pointed her to a robe of smooth blue flannel, hanging inside his small closet. Tripping on its long hem, she walked, again, through the sitting room to the tiny bathroom.

In the mirror, she looked closely at her brown eyes. She was, she thought, glad she'd stayed—glad Will had dropped his posturing and summoned her back (with, of course, another bit of posturing, but still)—but felt herself succumbing to vague unease, the causes of which eluded her. If she was honest with herself, she knew what he meant about Scarsdale. He thought, deep down, she wanted to get married—like Lil—to have children and move uptown or, of course, back to Scarsdale. Nothing, she thought gleefully, could be further from the truth. She was in New York, after four years in *Milwaukee,* all she wanted was to have fun, to do the things her friends had been doing for four years: to date mysterious men, to eat ethnic food in obscure restaurants and drink old-fashioned cocktails in hotel bars, to see foreign films in downtown theaters, to walk down the street anonymously. He was entirely wrong about her, imagining her to be a closeted bourgeois. Well, she would show him, she thought, narrowing her eyes at the mirror, in imitation of a film vamp. There was no way—*no way*—she would fall in love with him—how could she? His being a perverted know-it-all—but she would return here, to his apartment, until she grew tired of him. While seeing other people, of course. And, *of course,* he was full of shit, anyway, about not wanting or being able to do everyday things. He had extraordinarily expensive sheets—pale green sateen—for someone who wasn't "good with things." Perhaps, she thought with a shiver as she slipped out of his robe and lay down beside him, they'd been a wedding gift.

three

Four days after her encounter with Will Chase—for this was how she had started to think of it, as an *encounter,* rather like happening upon a bear in the woods—Beth arrived at a point of panic. Despite his countercultural pose—his alleged objection to monogamy—she'd expected him to give her a call. But he had not, and now, the following Sunday, she was headed back to the very same restaurant at which she'd dined with him to have breakfast with Emily, whose apartment was, indeed, around the corner, on North Eighth Street, just as Beth had thought.

On Thursday, when they'd made their plans, Beth had declined to mention that she'd been there already, even as Emily laboriously gave Beth directions, shouting into her cell phone from some busy corner ("You're near the G, right? You can take the G to the L"). Her brain was already leaping ahead, wondering if she should call Will and tell him that she would be in his neighborhood and could, if he liked, stop by after breakfast. Sam, of course, would be with him, but did that really matter? Beth loved children—though she had very little experience of them—and she had already formed a picture of Sam as a tiny version of Will: large black eyes, a precociously inquisitive manner, blond wavy hair like Little Lord Fauntleroy. It was strange, she thought, that he'd not offered to show her a photo of the boy. Strange, too, that he'd told her very little, really, about himself, even as she blathered on and on. As the days passed—and the phone, just like in some stupid movie, refused to ring—she grew increasingly curious and speculative. Lil, she knew, would have all the information, being an expert extractor of personal histories, but she couldn't bear the nerve-racking scrutiny that would accompany Lil's involvement. She knew exactly what Lil would say: that Will pursued Beth rather than Sadie (though, Beth supposed, he might have pursued *both*) because Beth was more approachable. Lil had a way of saying things—a certain false gentleness to her voice, an overenthusiastic insistence that no, those pants do *not* make you look fat—that made her true, more unpleasant meaning utterly plain.

But what she dreaded more was Lil speaking to Will about her, feeding into whatever ideas he had about her as a predictable little bourgeois. "Has she taken you out to her house yet? Oh my God, you have to get her to take you out! It's *huge*. Her mother *literally could not clean it herself*." Lil being Lil, she didn't want to know that Beth's grandfather built the place in the 1920s, when Scarsdale was still a sleepy village and land there not necessarily expensive, and that the structure had started off much smaller, with space for the first Dr. Bernstein's office added during the Depression. But Lil preferred to perpetuate this fiction of the Bernsteins as part of some sort of Scarsdalian elite, in possession of infinite sums of cash, when, in fact, her family was certainly not among the wealthiest inhabitants of the town. Her mother drove a Volvo, her father a Toyota. They didn't belong to a country club, nor did they, by rote, spend Christmas on one of the various islands named after saints. But Lil—like Will— seemed transfixed by this weird popular mythology that had lately sprung up around Scarsdale, believing it to be a Jewish version of Cheever country, populated by polo-shirted, bob-nosed, golf-playing all-Americans. In fact, the opposite was true: in Beth's lifetime, the town had become a haven for the tackily affluent. Women whose wrists sagged under the weight of eighty-carat tennis bracelets. Men who squeezed their bulk behind the wheels of tiny German cars. And their cruel, vapid children, trained to seek out weakness in their peers. Beth had sought refuge from them as soon as she could, along with the other hippies, Goths, math geeks, violin prodigies, and so on, in the town's "A school," where her mother taught. But even this odd institution—with its freaky, depressed student body—struck Lil as vaguely glamorous, peopled with misunderstood millionaires.

Emily, she knew, would regard the Will situation somewhat more sympathetically. She had done some curious things, sexually speaking, though Beth only had a vague sense of what these things were, as Emily tended to keep the specifics to herself, speaking in goofy euphemisms and referring to her boyfriends in code—"Method Actor," "Big Law"—to prohibit the group from taking seriously her involvement with them. In college she'd hung around with a group of attractive dilettantes, a subset of the theater crowd, who favored self-consciously risqué gear—velvet hot pants, fishnet stockings, dog collars—and devoted much time to the organization and execution of "sex parties" or "orgy nights," in their off-campus Victorians, which they painted purple or black and named "Whore House" or "House of the Little Death." Their academic activities tended to consist of large-scale productions of Grand Guignol plays or public performance art projects involving nudity, like that of Sebastian Beckmann, who'd shaved off all his body hair and spent three days in a glass box in the middle of Tappan Square; or Seth Morris, who'd made a plaster cast of his penis, from which he manufactured a hundred bronze members, and "planted" them in the garden outside the Conservatory; or Emily herself, who, famously, baked a coffin made of bread (using ovens and flour at the group's co-op, Tank), then *ate* her way out of it.

Emily still saw some of these people in New York—most had traded their fishnets and capes for jobs in graphic design or script supervision, but a few performed in burlesque shows at the Slipper Room or worked as strippers (ironically, of course)—and had made the acquaintance of any number of equally flamboyant types: actors and directors and other theatrical folk. She seemed to date an awful lot of men. Though *where* she met these men was a mystery, Lil said, since she spent much of her time hanging around with men who most definitely and exclusively preferred *other men*.

But Emily was, actually, intensely sensible—she was the only one of their friends who actually balanced her checkbook—with a puritanical streak that emerged at unexpected moments, sending all but Tal into shamed fits of petulance. Beth could imagine Emily's response to Will. "This sounds like *bad news*. The wife? The kid?" Beth's stomach clenched. She knew it sounded like bad news.

On Friday, as her lunch with Emily drew near, she woke with the intention of making the dreaded phone call to Gail Bronfman and straightening out the situation with the New School, if indeed it could be straightened out. The longer she waited, she knew, the less likely it was that they could use her, if not for her original position, then for something else—adjunct, she supposed—or, at the very least, for a January opening, if by chance there was one. She secretly hoped that the woman would crow with delight upon hearing Beth's voice. "Oh, no, we simply couldn't find anyone as great as you, so we held your classes until you arrived." Or "Oh, Beth, I'm so glad you called. The person we hired to replace you simply *won't* do. We've had to let her go. Can you take over next week?"

But she knew that this would be unlikely. After that disastrous conversation, back in August, her perpetually helpful, overly avuncular advisor, Dr. Ham (as he was known, being saddled with the name of Hamburger, a source of much amusement to him), had tried to smooth things over for her. He and Gail were friends from grad school, which was how Beth had landed the job in the first place. There was no reason, he thought, that Beth couldn't show up a few weeks late for the fall semester. A week later, he'd called her back to his office, beetlish brows twitching with displeasure. "Listen, kid, she's not backing down on this. She says she's already hired someone else."

Beth felt the familiar sting of tears. "Hired someone else just for the fall?" she asked. "Or for the whole year?"

Dr. Ham smiled. "I'm not sure. It was hard to hear, what with all the yelling."

Her face must have belied her feelings—it always did—because Dr. Ham stood up and raised his hands in the air, like a preacher. "For God's sake, don't worry about Gail frigging Bronfman," he barked. "You met her. She's four feet tall. You could take her." Beth forced a smile, for Dr. Ham's sake. He'd received tenure in the glorious early days of cultural studies and didn't quite understand how hard it was out there. "Just go in to see her when you get to New York, like she said. Suck up a little. Ask if you can help her with research. Talk to her about Barnabas. She's way into vampires; I think she did a paper on *Blacula* a few years ago at the PCA—"

"She did," Beth said. "It was pretty good. Kind of reductive."

"There you go!" enthused Dr. Ham. "Just give her that Beth Bernstein charm."

But Beth did not feel charm to be her province. And perhaps the only thing she feared, at this particular moment, more than Gail Bronfman—who, despite her lack of height, had the sort of brisk, overcaffeinated conversational style that reduced Beth's normally low voice to a whisper—was confrontation itself. And so, on Friday morning, she decided that before she called the woman, she should make a complete to-do list, so as to feel a bit more in control of her time, and after completing said list, she was relieved to see that there were any number of tasks that she could, and *should,* tick off before picking up the phone, errands that absolutely needed to be run before the weekend, such as having her hair trimmed, and picking up some new clothing, and getting a facial. Quickly, she took the train to Soho, where these processes depleted both her savings and the rest of her day, but were, she thought, necessary to her psychological welfare. If she didn't call Will, she decided, fate would reward her, by sending him across her path on Sunday. She would be crossing the street, dressed in a brown poplin shirtdress she'd seen in the window of a large, glassy store on Broadway, and look so ravishing—skin glowing, hair shining—that he would instantly regret not calling and invite her over for supper with Sam.

When Sunday morning finally arrived, Beth arose ragged and tired, having barely slept the night before, and dressed carefully, in threadbare jeans and a close-fitting black sweater, the only bits of her Milwaukee wardrobe that now seemed even vaguely acceptable (the brown shirt-dress, if purchased, would have finished her savings), and took the two trains to Williamsburg, emerging from the station's darkness into an impossibly gorgeous, sunny day. *If only,* she thought, *it had been like this for Lil's wedding.* She found Emily seated on a bench outside the place, swinging her legs, her mouth plugged by a blue lollipop. "The hostess just came out and gave us these," she said, pointing to the lurid candy. "There's a wait. But they'll bring us coffee if we want."

"Oh, good," said Beth, sitting down beside her.

"Yeh, if I don't have some coffee I'm going to die. I got home at, like, four last night."

"Oh no," cried Beth. "You should have called. We could have met later. I feel terrible. You must be exhaus—"

"No, no, no," said Emily, shaking her head. Her red hair needed, Beth thought, a washing: it frizzed out around her small head, struggling to escape from the microscopic, rhinestone-crusted barrettes that held a few strands back from her forehead. "I've got rehearsal at noon. I had to get up anyway. And I wanted to see you. I can't believe you've been here a week already. Things are just crazy."

"I know."

"This show is killing me. I think the director is losing his mind. He wants us there, like, twenty-four hours a day. We're all exhausted."

"Is he allowed to do that? Aren't there, like, union rules?"

"It's a non-Equity show. We're getting paid shit. And he can do what-ever he wants. If Equity finds out, I'm dead."

"Ohhhhhh," said Beth, nodding with what she hoped appeared to be understanding. She knew that Emily had "made Equity" last year and that this was a big deal, that Emily's career should be taking off (for this was how Emily had explained it). She wasn't quite sure if it actually *was* or not—with Tal, she could see him on TV—but Emily always seemed to be in rehearsal. They had barely spoken in the last year or so.

"What play is it?" she asked.

"It's actually amazing. I shouldn't complain. I think it's going to be big—or something's going to happen with it. It's, you know, an ensem-ble thing about people, friends, in the East Village. Sort of satirical. The writing is just *amazing.*"

"That sounds great," said Beth, truthfully.

Emily waved her hand, as if to dismiss her previous enthusiasm. "It's okay." She did, indeed, look very, very tired, the thin flesh under her bluish eyes—really a strange, unearthly shade of aqua—tinged gray with lack of sleep, worry lines tracing a faint script across her forehead. "*Anyway*," she said breathlessly. "How's the place? Do you hate Queens? Did you have any trouble getting here?"

Beth opened her mouth, then closed it. "Actually, I was here the other night," she confessed, with a twisted smile. "For dinner." Emily frowned, as though she couldn't believe Beth could find her way to the neighborhood without explicit directions from Emily herself.

"You were in Williamsburg?"

Beth nodded, folding her mouth down into an ashamed grimace.

"Why didn't you call me?"

"I was on a 'date,'" she said, smiling, for some reason, with embarrassment. She and her friends didn't go out on dates. "With that guy from the wedding."

Emily widened her eyes. "Beth, holy shit. That really hot guy? The blond guy? What's his name? I didn't talk to him at all."

"Will," said Beth. "Will Chase. You think he's, um, hot?" She heard herself pronouncing this word with quotes around it.

"*That* was Will Chase," cried Emily, pulling the lollipop out of her mouth with a childish *pop*. "Wow. *Wow*. That's not how I pictured him."

"You've heard about him?" asked Beth, her heart thunking. This was not the reaction she'd expected. But then, of course Emily had heard about Will. He was a close friend of Lil and Tuck's.

"I think Lil was kind of into him before she met Tuck," Emily was saying.

"*What?*" Beth's heart now seemed to have dislodged itself from its surrounding tissue and begun jumping, freely, around the inside of her rib cage. "Really?"

Emily nodded. "She makes him out to be kind of a romantic figure."

"How so?" asked Beth.

"Well, I'm sure you know."

Beth shook her head. "I don't know that much about him."

And so Emily explained: He'd been a journalist in London, it seemed, before coming to the States to do his Ph.D. He was, Emily thought, a bit of a hotshot at some British paper or other, writing unusually harsh and learned book reviews or, possibly, interviewing terrorists. "Something like that," Emily said. "I think maybe he was trying to write—or wrote?—a novel or something. There was some trouble—maybe no one wanted to publish it? Or maybe someone did and it got really bad reviews?" The difference between these two scenarios was so huge, Beth couldn't believe that Emily didn't recall which it was. It had to be the former. If Will had published a novel, surely he'd have mentioned it. "And he went to Stanford," Emily was saying, "on a Fulbright, I think, to do comp lit. Maybe not a Fulbright. *Some* big-deal fellowship—"

"He was at Stanford!" Beth cried. Her brother was a senior at this exact school. "Recently? When Jason was there? Not that they'd have met." She busied herself with unpeeling her lollipop, in an attempt to slow the thoughts dashing around inside her head. *Stanford*. She'd *been* at Stanford—on the actual campus, in the main library—four or five times in the last few years. She could have walked right by him. "Who did he study with there? I know a few people in English—"

"I don't know," interrupted Emily, who was wearied, Beth knew, by her friends' infatuation with academia. Emily's mother was a professor, and there was nothing terribly exciting about it, she often reminded Beth and Lil. Lots of committee meetings. "But I guess he hated Stanford. You know. He's from *London*." Beth thought it would be inelegant to correct her. He was, of course, from Oxford. She knew this much, at least. "And it's Palo Alto. Everyone is, like, blond and jogging and they think he's insane for smoking or whatever." Beth nodded. On her visits she always wound up feeling pale and enervated in comparison to those around her, including her hale, athletic brother. "Anyway, he starts hanging at this particular bar."

A pretty waitress, her bare arms tattooed with small Hebrew script, handed them chipped mugs of coffee and set a pitcher of cream on the asphalt in front of Beth. "Here you go," she said. "It should just be a few minutes."

Emily peered sadly into the creamer. "I bet this isn't skim milk," she said.

"No," confirmed Beth. "It's half-and-half." She sloshed some into her coffee and passed the pitcher to Emily, who made a face and set it back down on the ground so quickly it nearly toppled. "So," said Beth.

Emily swallowed some coffee and sighed. "So," she said. "He gets to know this cute bartender, who *you know* has her eye on him. Here's this guy, he looks like a fucking J. Crew model—"

"He *doesn't*," Beth protested weakly.

"He does," said Emily, in a tone that made it clear this wasn't necessarily a positive attribute. "So they become, like, friends and he tells her that he's always dreamed of living in New York—like every other person in the world—and that he has this idea that maybe he'll apply to transfer to Columbia."

"But if he was here on a Fulbright," Beth prodded, "then how could he? It doesn't work that way. You have a host institution—"

Just then, the waitress poked her head out. "Emily?" she called. "We're ready for you." The girls picked up their cups and followed her—Beth shaky with anticipation and utterly without appetite—inside to a small table by the front window.

"So what happened," asked Beth as soon as they were alone again, her heart threatening to jump out of her mouth. *What had happened? What could possibly have happened?*

"Well," said Emily. "The bartender was like, 'Let's go.'"

"Let's go where?" asked Beth.

"To New York."

"Wait," said Beth, slowly. "She said, 'Let's go to New York,' meaning 'Let's go to New York *together*.'"

"Yup," said Emily.

"But they barely knew each other."

"I know."

"I don't get it," said Beth. "What happened?"

"He married her. And dropped out of Stanford."

Beth stared at Emily in amazement. Nobody would do that. Nobody would drop out of one of the *top Ph.D. programs in the country*—so what if it was in some dull California suburb? So what if you didn't love it?—to move to New York with someone he barely knew.

"You're kidding," she said finally. "He dropped out of *Stanford*."

Before Emily could answer, a series of short bleeps issued forth from the brown corduroy coat Beth remembered from college; they'd purchased it, together, at Mini-Mart, marveling over its full fur collar. "That's Sadie," she said, fumbling for the source of the noise. "*Shit*," she muttered, "where the fu—*oh*," and drew, finally, a shiny, oblong wand from her right-hand pocket, its keypad glowing blue. "Sades," she said. "We're at Oznot's." Uncomfortably, Beth looked around, certain Emily was breaking some unwritten code of deportment, but no, no one was paying them any attention at all. Two tables down, in fact, a couple sat, facing each other, talking away into their own separate phones. "Okay, cool.

We'll see you then. Cool deal." She held the thing up to Beth. "Sadie's coming," she said.

"Cool," said Beth, though she didn't quite want Sadie to intrude upon them just yet. For a moment, they sat in silence, contemplating their coffee. "So," said Beth quietly, in an effort to hide the urgency with which she *needed* to hear the end of Will's story. Why hadn't he told her any of this? And she, telling him everything. Why had she been so open, so transparent?

"So, right, okay," began Emily, leaning in toward Beth. "They come to New York and she's decided she's married a millionaire, not, like, some grad student living on a fellowship."

"But why?" asked Beth. "She knew he was a grad student."

"Because it turned out she was poor. Like *really* poor. Not, you know, middle-class pretend poor. She was from, like, East Palo Alto. So to her all the Stanford kids seemed rich."

"They are."

"Well, yeah."

"So she burned through all his money," said Beth stonily. She suddenly had an idea where this was going, though she wished, somehow, that she didn't, that she'd never mentioned any of it, that she'd kept Will all to herself for a little while longer, that she'd let him tell her all this, in his own way, his own time. She felt, somehow, dirty.

Emily nodded. "Yeah. And then some. She took out all these credit cards in his name. Racked up like a zillion dollars in debt. He couldn't even make the minimum payments. Had to declare bankruptcy."

"Oh my God," whispered Beth. This was more than she'd imagined, and different. "He said she was a slut. I thought she cheated on him."

"Well." Emily sighed. "I guess. She did that, too."

Silently, the waitress slid their food in front of them, Beth's eggs staring, woozily, up at her. Why had she chosen these lurid, viscous things? She felt an urge to order the waitress, Garbo-style, to take them away, get them out of her sight. Emily, she was dismayed to see, had already tucked into her pale, glossy omelet.

"That looks good," Beth said dully.

"Egg whites," she said. "You can have some."

Beth shook her head, concentrating her attention on her toast, which was thin and spread with a foamy layer of butter. This she could eat, taking small, deliberate, symmetrical bites. How, why, had this woman treated Will so horribly? And yet, how—*why*—had Will had a child with her?

"It's crazy, right," Emily said finally, examining her own slice of toast, "about Sadie and Tal."

"What?" asked Beth, trying to extract herself from the increasingly furious loop in her brain—shifting restlessly from sympathy to blame—and return herself to Emily.

"After the wedding. They—" Emily smiled.

Beth suddenly understood Emily's meaning. "Oh my God!" she cried, as a pang shot through her, which she quickly identified as jealousy. Not that she had wanted Tal, other than in the way they all had, vaguely, in college, at one point or another. Though there *had* been a period, sophomore year, when she and Tal had spent all their time together. The others were all off on their own—Dave dating some annoying girl from Great Neck, Sadie taking too many credits and studying round the clock, Lil frantically in love with a lanky philosophy major—and she and Tal were left with each other. She'd run lights on the student production of *True West*—he'd played Austin—and they'd walked home together each night from Little Theater, tracing the edge of Tappan Square, sometimes parting ways at Keep, where she shared a room with Lil, sometimes going further to East, where he'd wrangled a grim, cinder-block single, and where they ate pretzels and listened to Bob Mould. She'd even slept on his extra mattress some nights, when she knew Lil and her boyfriend had overtaken their room, and she had wondered, hadn't she, what would happen if Tal were to kiss her, half expecting him to simply because she was there, half dismayed that he didn't, if only because it would have proved her desirability, half relieved that they could remain uncomplicated friends. But that time had passed quickly. And the following fall, she and Dave, well, became she and Dave. But she had always thought that she and Tal had an understanding. They were the quiet ones, the good ones. Tal would be wonderful and generous to Sadie. No one, she thought sickly, would ever love her like that. Dave hadn't, Will wouldn't.

"I know!" Emily widened her eyes and shook her head. "It's just weird. Though he's always wanted her, right?"

Beth nodded. "I can't believe Sadie didn't tell me." Beth suddenly felt the full force of her absence—they had all been living their lives without her, moving forward, falling in love, *getting married,* while she had largely stayed in place: another college town, another series of papers.

"Yeah." Emily shrugged. "Apparently, they're, like, picking out baby names. She hasn't been home all week."

"I guess," said Beth, feeling that she needed to comfort Emily and herself without actually explicitly appearing to do so. There was something that bothered her about this. Everything changing just as she came back. And Sadie, who had always been so stridently alone—so *unfettered*—attaching herself to someone else, to *Tal*. But there was something else, something else that seemed faintly wrong, faintly *disappointing*: this vague feeling that Tal just seemed too easy for Sadie, too uncomplicated. It was not—Beth struggled to untangle her thoughts—that Tal himself wasn't sufficiently complicated—he was—but that his worship of Sadie seemed destined to outweigh whatever feelings she might have for him. They'd always imagined Sadie with someone strange and mysterious, someone sleek and unfamiliar. "I guess you go to a wedding, it sort of makes you want to get married."

"Yeah," agreed Emily. "I wonder if she's bringing him with her."

In silence, they contemplated their eggs.

"So, what happened," Beth finally asked, "to Will's wife? They had a baby."

"Right." Emily speared a mushroom and sniffed it. "You should ask Lil to tell you the whole story. But I guess he left her. Then it turned out she was pregnant. And he went back."

"But how did he know the baby was his? If he'd left? And if she was cheating on him?"

Emily shook her head and looked at Beth with something akin to pity. "That came later. And the dates worked out. Also, according to Lil, he looks exactly like Will. Have you met him? The kid? What's his name?"

"Sam," said Beth, cold with disappointment. "No. I haven't met him."

"Well, Lil says he's great. And the mother is a nightmare. She's an actress, of course. That's why she wanted to come to New York. She actually managed to get a manager, which is more than I can say—"

"Is that like an agent?" asked Beth.

Emily shook her head. "Kind of, but not really. It's a new thing, kind of like a middleman. A manager basically gets you an agent."

"Oh," said Beth. "That makes sense."

Emily sighed. "Actually, it doesn't. It's completely stupid."

"What happened to her?" If she was, somehow, *famous* now, Beth would not be able to cope.

"Nothing. She did a Wisk commercial a few years ago. Lil thought it was hilarious."

"Did you see it?" *Is she pretty?* Beth wanted to ask.

"No. I don't have a television."

"How do you *live*?" Beth asked, laughing.

"It's rough," said Emily. "But I have a support group."

Beth looked toward the door—no sign of Sadie. She did not, she decided, want to hear what Sadie—a giddy, happy Sadie—had to say about any of this. No. "So, how," she asked Emily, "did it end? How did he leave her? With a baby?"

"He didn't," said Emily. "She left him."

"*No.*"

"And the baby," Emily added.

"And *the baby*?" Beth repeated.

Over the dregs of their coffee, Beth came to the point—the question she'd meant to pose right away, before she knew that Emily was in possession of a wealth of knowledge about Will. "Have you ever slept with a man who says he's impotent?" she asked, briskly ignoring the various contradictions and impossibilities in this question.

"Well," Emily began, fiddling with the collar of her shirt. "Yes. I have. I mean, I was with this guy for a while who couldn't, you know . . ." Her voice trailed off. "You know about that whole thing." Beth shook her head. "Really? I'm sure I mentioned that guy to you. Pellegrino Bongwater?"

"*What?*"

"Pellegrino Bongwater," Emily said sardonically, but she was mocking herself as much as the guy in question. This was why Beth loved Emily. "He was a writer for *Conan*. Does this ring a bell?"

"Not yet," said Beth. "Did I ever meet him?"

Emily chewed thoughtfully. "Maybe. He was very tan? And he wore, like, sweater vests?"

Beth shook her head again.

"Anyway, he was poached for some new audio-streaming television thing. They offered him like a million dollars or something." She rolled her eyes, then peered at something behind Beth's head and waved broadly.

"Hello, hello, hello," cried Sadie, squeezing Beth's shoulders from behind and planting a cool, soap-scented kiss on her cheek. "Can I pull up a chair? Do you think there's room?" There wasn't—the next table was uncomfortably close and its inhabitants looked annoyed at the prospect of Sadie encroaching on their territory—but the waitress grabbed a seat from across the room and gave Sadie a smile. "I'll need to scoot behind you," she warned.

"Of course," Sadie told her, shrugging off her coat, a nubby tweed. "Thanks so much. Really. And I'd be so grateful for a cup of coffee when you have a chance." She arched her narrow back against the bentwood chair, squared her shoulders, then looked from Emily to Beth and back again. "So," she said, raising her dark brows, "have you guys talked to Lil?"

Emily and Beth shook their heads.

"She's completely freaking out. Tuck's magazine was sold to some big conglomerate." She picked up the coffee that was placed in front of her and took a delicate sip, tendrils of steam rising in front of her nose. "Well, not *big*. But big-ish. She thinks they're going to fire Tuck."

"Why?" asked Beth.

"He's the newest hire," Sadie said, with a shrug. "And he's not really a reporter." She put down her coffee and smiled. "So what's with Will Chase?"

"Um, nothing," said Beth. "How did you know?" *What's with you and Tal?* she wanted to ask, but somehow she didn't ask such things of Sadie.

"Lillian *Roth-Hayes* told me." Sadie smiled and shrugged.

"*Nothing?*" asked Emily.

"The *famous* Will Chase!" Sadie went on, undeterred, her smile widening to include her teeth. "Did he tell you his tale of woe?"

"Sadie's not so keen on him," said Emily, returning Sadie's grin.

"Oh," said Beth, at once relieved and mortified.

"He's fine," said Sadie primly, her smile turning into a little moue. Emily and Beth exchanged a glance. They knew there would be more. Sadie pressed her lips together and folded her long fingers in her lap. "He's just such a know-it-all," she said quickly. "And he just never asks about anything other than—" She stopped and smiled again, her lips tightly closed. It was, Beth thought, a pretty expression. "I'm going to shut up." A pause. "I suppose, maybe, he seems like a jerk to me, because *he* doesn't like *me*. He seems like the sort of guy who, if he's interested in you, can be *completely* charming, right?" Emily and Beth nodded. "How was it? Was he nice?"

"He was great," said Beth, looking into her coffee cup. "I had, just, a really wonderful time."

"That's great," said Sadie. "And you heard about the wife and the little boy and all that."

"Actually he didn't talk much about it," admitted Beth.

"Hmmm," murmured Sadie, maddeningly.

"Em was just telling me the whole saga."

"Oh?" Sadie brightened at the prospect of a story. "What part are you up to?"

"We're done," answered Emily. "We've moved on to"—she paused and gave Sadie a look of mock seriousness—"Pellegrino Bongwater."

"Oh my God," cried Sadie, clapping her hands with delight. "I'd forgotten all about him!" She turned to Beth. "You've missed so much! He was this *ridiculous* guy who was just *always* tan—"

"Like, George Hamilton tan," Emily added.

"Where did he work, Emily? At some start-up?" Emily nodded. "And what was his story? All they did at his office was smoke pot. Out of this enormous bong, right?"

"Yep. An enormous *cobra-shaped* bong. And he was convinced that they would get cancer or something if they used tap water in it. *That's* how much pot he'd smoked. He was permanently paranoid. So he insisted on filling it with Pellegrino water. The refrigerators at his office were, like, stocked with it, so what did he care? I mean he wasn't paying for it." Beth laughed. "And he could not," Emily said, adopting a mock formal tone, "get. It. Up."

Sadie turned to Emily, her mouth widened into an O. "I didn't know that," she said. Emily shrugged.

"Was it because of the pot?" asked Beth.

"I assume," Emily told her. "But he was a fucked-up guy. And he was just kind of weird about women. I don't know that he'd ever actually *had* sex." She gave Beth a hard look. "But why do you ask? Is it Will? Because it sounds like he could be seriously messed up about women. I mean, considering . . ."

Sadie had swiveled around in her chair, searching for the waitress; discussions of sex made her uncomfortable. "Ask what?" she said, distracted. "What did Beth ask?"

"Yeah, you're right," said Beth, ignoring Sadie's question. She'd lost track of how many times the waitress had refilled their cups, and her hands were beginning to shake from the caffeine.

"Because of what happened with his wife," said Sadie sharply.

"I know," said Beth. "She was just so awful to him."

"Well, not just that," said Emily, her voice also taking on an edge. She's had too much coffee, Beth thought. "*Because* he had a wife. *That* wife. What kind of person marries someone he's never even had dinner with, never spent any time alone with? Other than in bed?"

"A messed-up person," said Beth, turning her eyes to the window.

Dozens of people now waited for a table. They really should leave and give theirs up. It wasn't fair to the waitress. They would have to leave a huge tip.

"No," said Sadie. "No. A hopeless romantic."

•

The next morning Beth awoke to find that the mild anxiety of the past few days had been supplanted by a feeling that could only be described as dread. It was Monday. All her friends were heading off to work or school, while she was alone in this large, silent, grown-up apartment, surrounded by the belongings of some stranger—his mod furniture, his shelves of Douglas Coupland books—in the middle of a neighborhood in which she knew no one, many train stops from everyone and everything she cared about. And it seemed to her now that there was something *demoralizing* about living in Queens, wasn't there? As though one had given up on any semblance of hipness, as though one had simply relinquished all hopes of participating in the world of art and culture and commerce. She'd parted with most of her savings to live in this place, in New York, through May: the two months rent and the security deposit had come to more than two thousand dollars, a large percentage of her teaching stipend. And here she was, with nothing to do, nowhere to be, no one to see.

No one, that was, except Gail Bronfman. At nine o'clock, she swallowed the dregs of her coffee, put the cup in the sink, sat down at the desk in the bedroom—the notes for her dissertation, spread over five white legal pads, neatly piled in its left-hand corner—and dialed the woman's number, thinking, *She won't be there at nine o'clock on a Monday. I'll leave a message.* Instead, she was greeted with a chirpy "Hello-oh."

"Gail," she replied, attempting to sound confident and cheerful though the name stuck in her mouth. "It's Beth Bernstein." She rushed on before the woman could say anything. "I just arrived in New York and thought I'd just, um, call and check in with you. I was thinking maybe I could come in and talk to you sometime this week. I just, you know, feel awful about, about what happened and I'd love to be able to make it up to you. And also to explain it all to you, because I don't know if you ever got the whole story. It was just"—she paused here, feeling she was, perhaps, going off in the wrong direction, focusing on the past, rather than the brilliant, happy future, in which she and Gail Bronfman swapped war stories in the faculty lounge—"a ridiculous situation. I know, also, that you would be such a great resource for me, for my dissertation, that we have some overlapping interests, and I'd love to work with you while I'm here, in whatever way I can."

The woman said nothing. "I mean," Beth continued on, "I hate to think that this stupid mix-up with my credits has damaged what could—I mean, has ruined—"

"*Beth,*" Gail Bronfman said finally, in a sharp voice, hitting hard the final digraph, "from what I understand, from what you yourself told me last month, there was no *mix-up*. It's your responsibility to keep track of your credits. And you didn't."

It was Beth's turn to remain silent. In all her ruminations on the subject, this particular explanation had not occurred to her. She'd viewed herself as the incontrovertible victim of a stupid bureaucratic glitch. Or, no, maybe not. Maybe, perhaps, *possibly,* deep down she'd known it was her fault, but hadn't wanted to admit it.

"Now," the woman continued, "you're a bright girl and, from what we've heard, an excellent teacher. And we were all quite taken with your chapters." These were the first two chapters of her dissertation. Beth's heart began to boom below her ribs. It was all going to be okay. All would be forgiven. "We'd love to have you join us in the spring, but I just don't know if it's going to be possible. You put us in a very difficult situation. We had to scramble to find someone to fill your place. And *he* had to scramble to prepare for classes, but he's working out very nicely. And as you might expect, we offered him the same contract we offered you, which runs through the spring semester."

Tears popped into Beth's eyes and a thickness overtook her throat. She would not, she knew, be able to speak. Mercifully, Gail Bronfman had more to say.

"We might be able to take you on as an adjunct, though you'd be teaching intro classes and the pay would be considerably less. And you'd have no benefits. But we won't know until January."

"That would be great," cried Beth in a strangled voice. "Really, that would be fine. That would be great."

"Okay," said Gail Bronfman, her tone softening. "Well, we'll keep in touch. You might also be able to pick up a composition class. I can put you in touch with Bob Deangelis, in the English department."

"Oh, thank you," said Beth, with perhaps too much passion. "Thank you. That would be wonderful."

She hung up the phone, thinking, *That went well. Everything will be fine.* But slowly, as she wandered restlessly through the three rooms of her borrowed apartment, the sick dread returned. Adjuncts were the lowest of the low. She didn't want to be an adjunct. And once you started adjuncting there was no way out. You were stuck in the adjunct lane *forever,* unless you published a book or did something spectacular, which you didn't do, because you didn't have any time or connections, *because you were an adjunct,* and had to teach way too many classes to make a living. And she had to have benefits. Her inhalers alone would cost hundreds per month.

But she had no other options. It was October, obviously too late to apply for full-time teaching jobs for the current year, unless, by some chance, someone was going on sabbatical or maternity leave in the spring. But that was a long shot. All she could do was try for jobs for the following fall—do the interview circuit at the PCA in March, just as she'd done the previous year—and beg the other city schools for some spring classes. Or, of course, she could finish up her research in the next three months, find a sub-subletter for the apartment, and go back to Milwaukee in January, but that seemed, somehow, impossible, her life there already a distant dream. "How did this happen," she said aloud. "Oh my God." Before her thoughts could go any further—toward self-pity or anxiety—she threw on her clothing from the day before, slipped her feet into her scuffed brown clogs, and ran down the four flights of stairs.

Breathless, she pushed through the lobby's ornate glass door and walked around the corner to the closest commercial strip, a decrepit block consisting of a Laundromat, a wood-paneled pizzeria perpetually filled with teenage boys in puffy jackets, and a sporadically-in-business candy store, stocked with Necco Wafers, Mallo Cups, yellowed cellophane bags of circus peanuts, and assorted other off-brand sweets, all of which appeared to have been manufactured in some bygone era, before the advent of Hershey's and M&M's. Her friends had been right to warn her away from the neighborhood. Even the closest grocery store was blocks and blocks away, blocks that felt extraordinarily long when lugging home a half gallon of milk and a can of peeled plum tomatoes. She briefly contemplated the pizza place before settling on the candy store. Therein, she spent a happy few minutes poking at dusty cellophane packages of wax lips and thumbing through outdated copies of *People,* until a low, smoke-addled voice from the front of the shop interrupted her reverie. "Can I help you, miss?" Startled, Beth dropped her magazine back onto the rack and walked over to the counter, where a diminutive person—a dwarf, she realized, *a dwarf*—of indeterminate gender peered at her from behind thick corrective lenses. "Yes," she found herself saying, "I'll have a pack of Lucky Strike Lights," though she didn't smoke and never had, other than the occasional nervous puff at a party. And yet, as she walked the two blocks home she began confidently, instinctively, tapping the cigarette pack against her palm, before realizing why: Dave. She stopped dead at the corner of Forty-eighth Street and Thirtieth Avenue, where a fig tree had spilled overripe fruit over a row of parked cars. *Fuck,* she thought. *Dave.* For a few days now, she'd managed not to think about him in anything but abstract terms. Now, the full extent of his Dave-ness—the over-whelming reality of his existence, just miles away from her, in Brooklyn—hit her sickly. Would Emily or Sadie or Lil tell him that she'd gone out with Will? Possibly. Yes, very possibly, thinking that he should know that she wasn't hung up on him, that she hadn't come here because she was still in love with him, or, at least, that any lingering infatuation hadn't *con-tributed* to her decision to move here, or that she hadn't even been think-ing, *Hey, I'm moving to New York. Maybe Dave and I will get back together.* But all of this, of course, was true, or sort of true. She didn't know if she wanted him back, but she wanted him to want *her* back. And she wanted him to think of her as his and his alone, as the girl who'd loved him fully and purely four years earlier.

Oh my God, what is wrong with me, she thought, stomping up the stairs to the apartment and snapping open the deadbolt. *He's such an asshole.* And, yet, a part of her—she saw it now—thrilled to think of the hold he still had on her, that there was some vast repository of feeling within her, largely untapped during her four years in Milwaukee, when she'd spent unthinkable amounts of time alone. Hands shaking, she ripped off her jeans and sweater and bra and shrugged on an old blue T-shirt and a pair of faded flannel pajama bottoms, pulled directly out of her suitcase, and slipped back between the cool, rumpled sheets. Since her arrival in New York, she'd been sleeping endlessly, ten, eleven hours a night. Oversleep-ing, she'd read, was a sign of depression, but she didn't *feel* depressed. Still, she could see herself through her mother's eyes, lolling around in bed all day, unable to summon the energy even to make herself breakfast. "I'm *not* depressed," she said aloud, "I'm just hungry." And for the second time that day, she tossed back the covers, pulled on her clothes, and threaded her arms into her old suede jacket, her new cigarettes still buried, thrillingly, in the ripped left-hand pocket. *Lucky Strikes,* she thought, vaguely disgusted with herself, her index finger tracing the packet's slick edge. That was Dave, too, of course. Heart lurching, she clopped down the stairs again and strode out into the bright sun, and quickly walked two blocks south to the Twin Donut, where she bought a paper cup of watery coffee, a copy of the *Times,* and a chocolate cruller. Thus armed, she returned, again, to her building, smiling cheerily at the old ladies taking up their posts on the sidewalk as she pulled open the heavy glass door. This was what normal people did in the morning: Read the paper. Ate doughnuts. But she was not, she reminded herself, a normal person. She was alone. Jobless. Friendless. Abandoned. In Queens.

Fuck, fuck, fuck, she thought, running up the stairs, though she knew she shouldn't, not without her inhaler in hand. *Fuck Will. Fuck Dave. Fuck Emily for telling me all that about Will. Fuck Sadie for being so fucking judgmental. And fuck fucking Gail Bronfman.* A thought rose, skittishly, to the surface of her brain, slowly taking shape as she sat down at the kitchen table, her breath coming in sharp, jagged bursts, and peeled the plastic wrap off her cigarette pack. She was, she thought, incapable of trusting her instincts. She'd disliked Will when she first began talking to him— though, of course, she found him attractive—but out of politeness she'd ignored her initial impression and given him a chance. And she'd been right, hadn't she? Yes, he was a cad and an asshole. He'd been wronged by his wife, sure, but that didn't give him the right to be such a freak with Beth; that didn't make it okay that he hadn't called her. And besides, Sadie was right, he'd *chosen* to marry someone he barely knew, someone clearly untrustworthy and unstable. What did that say? That Beth should have steered clear of him from the start.

But the weird thing was: the same held true for her other friends, her *best* friends. She'd been skeptical of them—each and every one—at first. Only Sadie had she loved from the start: her large green eyes, the thick French notebooks in which she'd jotted thoughtfully throughout Haskell's Intro to Jewish Studies. Lil had struck her as gawky and overloquacious. Tal, quiet and remote. Emily, silly and way too cool. Dave she'd *hated* for the first year she knew him. During their two English classes together—101 (Approaches to Literature) and 200 (Introduction to Drama)—he was one of those guys who *had* to argue every point, thinking himself hilarious and brilliant. The worst of it was that others actually bought his act: he had a little following, who backed him up when he began harping on relativism and laughed at his acid jokes, tipping back on their chairs, knees against the seminar table.

It was at the end of that year, her freshman year, that he walked up to her one day, as she sat on Wilder Bowl with Sadie and Lil, the three of them reading fresh copies of *Below the Belt*—the editor was handing them out to everyone on the Bowl—and said, "You hate me, don't you?"

"Um," said Beth, unconvincingly. "No."

"Beth, meet Dave, a classic narcissist," said Sadie. "He believes we're sitting here talking about how much we hate him. When in fact we've never even uttered his name aloud."

Dave smirked. "Beth and I know each other. We're in Goldstein's Intro to Drama together. She hates me. I can tell. She gives me nasty glances every time I open my mouth. But hey—that's fine. I'm hatable."

Lil rolled her eyes. "I'm sure Beth doesn't hate you. Beth doesn't hate anyone." Beth felt her blood hop and jump, anger slitting along her spine. People always said that about her: Beth is so nice. Beth loves everyone. Beth whistles cheerfully to the birds who land on her windowsill each morning.

"Um, I hate lots of people," she'd said, surprising herself. "You're right." She nodded at Dave. "You kind of drive me crazy in class." Dave laughed—a loud squawk—and plopped down next to her.

"Aha!" he said. "My plan has worked!"

That night, she found herself in his room, listening, alternatively, to Xenakis and Public Enemy, fiercely debating the merits of *Long Day's Journey into Night* ("boring melodrama," Dave insisted, no matter how passionately Beth attempted to explain why melodrama could be *good* sometimes). She spent much of the following year in a variation of that situation: sitting around Dave's room listening to music and arguing or driving off in his dented brown Tercel, Sadie and Lil sometimes in tow (Emily and Tal always in rehearsal), in search of the Lorain Dairy Queen or the art theater in Cleveland. The others deferred to Beth—letting her sit in the front, always, where she and Dave might speak softly to each other. Other men avoided her, for she seemed to bear Dave's imprint. He was always, in some way, around her: picking her up from class, meeting her for dinner at Tank (though he himself ate at Keep that year), reading at a table in the snack bar at the exact time she liked to pick up her mail. But he was not, most definitely, her boyfriend. He never even flirted with her in the way he did with Lil or Sadie.

Moreover, much of his time—when not at work, or practicing—was taken up with anxious attachments to other women, women Beth and the others regarded with suspicion, all of them tiny and doll-like, with sleek dark hair and upscale Bohemian wardrobes: tattered jeans, halters made from sari fabric, low-heeled suede boots. Often they wore studs, microscopic diamonds or small flowers, of a vaguely South Asian style, in their little noses, which, Beth knew (and Lil, the expert, confirmed), had become more little by way of the surgeon's knife. And generally they were tan in the manner of girls from the wealthier parts of Long Island or, of course, Beth's despised hometown: a glossy, rich Caribbean brown. There was a sameness to these girls, a moneyed handsomeness enhanced by a deep-felt security in their own beauty. Dave, mercifully, rarely spoke of these women and when he did, he complained: Claudia had a Long Island accent, Alex was too clingy ("She can't sleep alone"), Whitney was too bossy and, to his horror, cheated on him with a scruffy-headed Kurt Cobain type, the lead singer of a popular campus band with which Dave occasionally played ("*Whitney,*" Lil scoffed, "her name is *Whitney,* Dave").

Three days after returning to school for their junior year, he appeared outside the house Sadie, Emily, Lil, and Beth had rented, on the little road behind the art museum. They hadn't yet hung curtains—or, the sheets of theatrical fabric, stolen from Hall Auditorium's costume shop, that would eventually serve as curtains—and Beth, unpacking books in her second-floor room, saw him gazing up in her direction and knew that something had changed, not just in him but in herself. The next day, as they walked home from the gym after registration, it began to rain and they ducked under a tree, where, somehow, he managed to pull her close to him and, after much fumbling with cheeks and noses, kiss her, a sensation at once deeply, perfectly right, and strangely, frighteningly, utterly wrong. He had, he told her late that night, as they lay in her bed, wanted to kiss her from the moment he saw her sitting in the lounge of Talcott—a turreted, Victorian dorm—reading *The Mysteries of Pittsburgh* while waiting for their English class to begin. "You looked like Holly Hobbie," he told her. "Um, is that a compliment?" she asked, laughing. "Of course," he said, too quickly. "You have those beautiful, full lips"—his voice quavered uncomfortably on this compliment—"and your freckles . . ." She wanted to believe him—about everything—but she wasn't sure she did. A niggling voice told her that he'd settled for her.

A year later, Dave left his battered journal—an old black sketch-book—open on her desk and she peeked inside. "There's something too pliant and languorous about her," he explained, with the aid, Beth thought, of a thesaurus. "There's something that bothers me about her. It's as though she's too vulnerable. Too soft. With those plump cheeks, like a kid. And yet, I wonder if this is what attracted me to her in the first place." Reading his misgivings gave her a strange sense of relief. She'd been right all along—she wasn't crazy. For some reason, after she and Dave became boyfriend and girlfriend—rather than simply *friends*—she had lost her ability to question him, to call him on his bullshit, to engage him in any sort of real discussion. She became increasingly afraid of him, she realized now, sipping her too-sweet coffee, or afraid of *losing* him. Why? And how had she never realized this before, in all the hours she'd spent dissecting their romance?

She placed a cigarette in her mouth, fumbling a bit with the pack (how *did* you get one out, they were packed in so tightly), lit it from the stove, and inhaled deeply. A pleasant little hum started up between her ears. She exhaled, giggling slightly. She hadn't coughed, like a priss in a teen movie, like her friends would have expected. No, like *Dave* would have expected. He'd loved to see her as a bumbling, frail child. And she'd played into that, hadn't she? She had, in a way, *become* that person—too soft, too vulnerable—so as not to disappoint him.

After the cigarette, the coffee, the cruller, Beth's panic subsided and was replaced by a dull, faraway ache behind her eyes and a restless twitch in her fingers. When the phone rang, her heart leapt and she jumped up to answer it, then thought better of it and slumped down in her chair again. Her parents had returned from California the night before and it was most likely her mother, asking when they might expect her for a visit. She missed her mother and was looking forward to sitting down and talking to her—in theory. Just now, the gulf between them seemed too, too wide. How could she tell her about Will? About her lost job? Her wrecked finances? The mess she'd seemingly made of everything. The mere thought of going home increased the throbbing in her head: she couldn't bear to picture the train, the quaint train station, the sloping lawns scattered now with rust-colored leaves, the ice cream shop in Scarsdale Village. The phone rang twice more and she heard her own voice—annoyingly breathy and a tad nasal—say, "Hi, this is Beth. I'm not home—" then ran into the next room and held her thumb to the volume button until she was left in a silence so welcome that she began, giddily, to laugh.

four

In December, Tuck lost his job at *Boom Time*. He was certain, Lil said, to find a similar job, and quick, at a similar magazine, like *Fast Company* or *Bubble Economy,* or *Salon* or *Slate* or *Feed,* or a portal like Yahoo! or Google, which was where the real money was, or even at an ad agency or branding firm or something.

"Could Tuck really do that?" asked Beth. It was difficult to imagine anyone she knew working in advertising, a soulless, ethically dodgy industry, which she'd taught her students in Milwaukee to dissect.

"Totally. The new companies operate on a different business model," Lil told her, missing the point. They were shivering their way through bowls of crab bisque at the Grey Dog, with Sadie and Emily, on the first Saturday of the New Year. "They're not looking for MBAs or whatever. They just want smart people who have new, exciting ideas." Her friends nodded dutifully, their cheeks still reddened with cold. "I mean, I'm not *excited* that he was fired, but I guess, it's like: if you're going to be fired once in your life, this is probably the time."

"You're so right," said Beth, leaning in toward Lil. "Will keeps wondering if he should go to a dot-com."

"Would he do that?" asked Sadie, blotting her nose with an oversized handkerchief. "He seems so entrenched in the *Journal.*" Sadie's mother disliked the *Journal*'s politics—despite appearances, she was a staunch Democrat—and sniffed disapprovingly when she caught James Peregrine reading it.

Beth shrugged. "His friend Ben just got a job at this new site, Law.com, and he's making like a zillion dollars."

"What is it? A magazine?"

Again, Beth shrugged. "I'm not sure. They haven't launched yet. Apparently, Ben has, like, nothing to do. He writes freelance pieces all day." She blew, halfheartedly, on a spoonful of soup. "It's just so weird. Jason tells us the most crazy stories about Stanford—"

"That's where the guys who started Yahoo! are from, right?" interrupted Lil. "Weren't they Stanford students?"

"Mmm-hmmm," said Beth, "but Jason says there are so many start-ups that there aren't enough people to staff them. So they're recruiting freshmen. So, like, these eighteen-year-old guys are dropping out of school and making these huge salaries. Jason says they come back to campus for parties, and they're like driving Maseratis."

Emily gave a low laugh. "Can you imagine?" she said. "Weren't we all, like, eating ramen when we were eighteen?"

"Beans and rice," Lil corrected. "At Fairchild."

"Oh, right," said Emily, cocking her head to one side. "That's *now*. That I'm eating ramen. I can't afford beans and rice."

"Me, either," said Beth. She was still waiting to hear from Gail Bronfman—as well as the Gail Bronfmans of NYU, Hunter, Brooklyn College, and Baruch—about teaching in the spring semester, which was starting soon, so soon that she was sure nothing would come through and she would have to—well, she didn't know. Work as an SAT tutor. Copyedit. Temp. Ask her parents for money. Or, as Will kept suggesting, write for magazines. She'd just, with an introduction from him, sent on a brief section of her dissertation, on the annual *Dark Shadows* conference in Pasadena, to an editor at *Salon*—and to her shock had received a brief, kind note saying they'd like to run it. She'd been debating the right time to tell her friends. If she mentioned it before the piece was thoroughly, truly, completely published, she worried she might jinx the whole affair, causing it to disappear into thin air. Now, with this bad news about Tuck, she thought she might not tell them at all. For she knew Lil. Lil would take it as an affront: Beth infringing on Tuck's territory.

"Well, so are we," said Lil. "I kind of love ramen, actually. Though it's so bad for you."

"Maybe Tuck's next job will be *better*," suggested Emily.

A too-bright smile appeared on Lil's face. "I was thinking the exact same thing! *Salon* would be great, wouldn't it? He's perfect for them."

Her friends nodded. "Yes, definitely," Beth agreed. No, she would say nothing about her piece. "I can't believe they fired him right before Christmas. They could have waited until after the holidays, at least. It just seems so cruel."

"I know! It was awful." Lil had barely touched her soup. "Everyone else in the world was buying presents and, like, flying to the Bahamas, and we were afraid to buy coffee."

"That sucks," agreed Emily.

"I know," cried Lil, pushing a heavy lock of hair behind her ear. "The worst thing, though, was that we were completely paralyzed, because all the magazines pretty much *shut down* between Thanksgiving and New Year's. Nobody does any hiring."

Sadie, who had remained quiet all this time, neatly sipping her soup from the side of her spoon, now sighed heavily. "Of course," she said, in such a way that it wasn't clear whether she meant *of course* no one does any hiring around the holidays, what kind of fool would think otherwise, or *of course* Lil and Tuck had been dealt a wretched hand by fate, or *of course* Tuck *believed* himself to have been dealt a wretched hand by fate, when in fact he had clearly, obviously, *of course,* brought about his own bad fortune by being an egotistical ass.

Lil chose to believe the first. She nodded seriously at Sadie. "So there was no way he could even begin looking until last week. I think it was driving him crazy, feeling like there was nothing he could do."

All of this was, of course, exactly what Tuck had told her, a week or so prior, when she'd timidly asked how the job search was going. "Lil, come on," he'd said. "They'll think I'm an idiot if I send out my résumé now." He was lying on their couch—a low velvet thing they'd purchased at Ugly Luggage for $350—reading *Wired,* its lurid orange and silver spine glaring at her. Eighteen months earlier, when she'd first met him, Tuck had carried around battered volumes of poetry—Frank O'Hara, John Ashbery, Randall Jarrell—in an old army surplus bag. Now he professed himself incapable of focusing on the minutiae of verse. He read magazines and watched television.

"It's my *job,*" he told her when she commented on this change in his habits, over Thanksgiving weekend, which they'd spent alone at their apartment, eating a miniature turkey Lil had carefully roasted according to instructions in *The Silver Palate Cookbook.* They couldn't afford to fly to L.A. or Atlanta—the wedding and rent had eaten up all their cash. "I'm writing about mass culture, about popular culture, not *poetry,* Lil. I need to know what's going on." Yes, Lil said, she understood that his job necessitated a certain immersion in the more banal aspects of contemporary life—though of course he seemed no longer to consider such things banal—but did he always have to be "working"? Couldn't he read poetry on the weekends? "Lil," he said, sighing brusquely. "I know it's hard for you to understand. Since you were, you know, born in a bookstore." He cracked a smile—that gorgeous, rare smile of his, which she couldn't resist returning—and ran his hand proprietarily over her hair, a thrilling feeling. "But once you leave academia, it just starts to seem pretty irrelevant. It's hard to get lost in a novel when you know it's all a lie and what's going on in the real world—the stuff I'm writing about for the magazine—is so exciting. And poetry is like . . ." He raised his hands up in a gesture of surrender. "No one actually reads poetry. We just fool ourselves into thinking it's important."

"It *is* important!" cried Lil. Over the summer, she'd worked at the poetry organization down in Soho, answering phones. And hundreds of people had called *each and every day* with questions about matters related to poetry. Tuck didn't understand that poetry could save a person's life, had saved *her* life, because she *wasn't* born in a bookstore. She was from *L.A.* Her parents sat in front of the television each night and talked about the price of gas. She wouldn't have made it through middle school without Frank O'Hara, high school without Plath. "Tuck, it is. How can you say that?"

"Lil, it's *not*. Business is important. Money is important. Jobs. Economics. People's day-to-day concerns. Poetry is a luxury."

Lil felt certain he was wrong, but couldn't articulate why and, thus, left the matter alone, eyeing Tuck nervously when he snapped on the television and tuned the channel to some moronic sitcom, which, only a short time earlier, he and Will Chase would have declared a vicious assault on art. Perhaps she *was* born in a bookstore, at least in the sense that she'd learned much about life from novels. But so had Beth and Sadie. And, for that matter, Will Chase, who'd done the whole Svengali thing: married some idiot, thinking he'd turn her into an intellectual. That's the big difference, she thought, between novels—or movies—and life. In real life, people don't actually change.

"So what happened," Sadie asked her. "I thought Ed loved Tuck."

"He did," Beth confirmed. She and Will regularly got together with Ed, which put her in the uncomfortable position of possibly knowing more about the situation at *Boom Time* than did Lil and Tuck. "He *does*. *He* didn't fire Tuck. He's horrified by the whole thing."

"Ed has no control anymore," Lil explained, resting her cheek on her fist. "*You* know. They said everything would be the same." She turned to Emily. "The First Media people."

"I know," said Emily.

"But it wasn't." The girls nodded, lips pursed, eyes wide with concern. They'd heard about this in the fall. How the suits at First Media—or "Worst Media," as the *Boom Time* staff took to calling them—after insisting that they wanted to maintain the magazine's "voice" and "magic," had fired Ed's young section editors and replaced them with warhorses from the trades, tabloids, and glossies, who had, in turn, done away with the magazine's structure and practices, under dictate from First Media's balding CEO. The new regime required employees to arrive by nine clad in "business casual" attire (no jeans, flip-flops, sneakers, Hawaiian-print shirts, or T-shirts with logos or writing on them; no hats, unless necessary for the practice of one's religion). No longer could Tuck roll in at eleven, send out for coffee and breakfast, chat with Ed for half an hour (in lieu of a staff meeting), and get to work around noon. Nor could his friend Jonathan, who had a baby and a house in Nyack, arrive at eight and leave at four, to give his wife a bit of a break (even if he'd won a Pulitzer for his reporting on the Gulf War). Nor could any of them, Ed included, while away an hour in the chill-out room, tossing around story ideas while reclining on plush bean bags, sipping slushies, or playing a round or two of Ms. Pac-Man or Frogger. First Media had moved the magazine from their loft at Broadway and Houston into the company's anonymous corporate headquarters—acid green burlap cubicles, industrial carpeting—at Forty-first and Third.

"Maybe it's not such a bad thing," Beth suggested. "He was really unhappy, wasn't he?"

"He was," Lil admitted. And he wasn't alone. Jonathan, whom Tuck worshipped, had taken a job at the culture desk of the *Times*. Others left for *Boom Time*'s imitators, none of which had been taken over by larger corporations (yet). Ed locked himself in his small new office all day, allegedly reading copy and writing an eternally unfinished piece about web-based film distribution, but really, Tuck suspected, succumbing, in his own odd way, to despair: obsessively posting to tech listservs and typing screeds for his old usenet board and playing some creepy fantasy game involving orcs and elves. "He could barely get out of bed in the morning, in the end. I sort of knew this was going to happen. He was late— like, an *hour* late—every day. I told you, right, about the ID cards." The "Slikowskers"—as the original staffers had taken to calling themselves— had so much trouble getting to work on time that the company had installed a swipe card system. In order to get in—or out—of their offices, they had to swipe their IDs. Hours were tallied each week, with particular emphasis on lunch breaks, which could be no more than a half hour. Which was kind of absurd, seeing as under Ed's regime, they'd happily worked twelve-hour days.

"Yeah, it was completely fascist," said Emily. "Remember in school they tried to do that to the dorm cleaners? There was a huge protest."

"I think they did it anyway," said Sadie, picking up one of the small, hard rolls that had accompanied their soup. They loved this café—with its purposefully unhip New England clam-shack decor—and had recently decided that they also loved its neighborhood, the tiny streets south and west of Sixth Avenue—Bedford, Carmine, Downing. "Is that why he was fired? Because he was late?"

Lil shook her head. "He got something wrong in a piece. That story about anarchists. Like, the web allows them to organize without, you know, having a central organizing body. Did you guys read it? In the December issue?"

Sadie and Beth nodded. "Will loved it," Beth told her.

"Oh my God, he was reporting it for months." Lil sighed and shook her head. "He talked to, like, a hundred people. And this one guy, he'd asked to be anonymous and Tuck used his name." Beth looked down at her bowl. She knew, from Will, that this wasn't nothing. "The guy complained. He's, like, threatening to sue."

"Wow," said Emily.

"I know," said Lil. "But the thing is they were *looking* to get rid of Tuck. Or that's what he thinks. That they knew they could replace him with a twenty-two-year-old—who they could pay, like, a third of his salary."

"It's probably true," said Sadie, breaking off a piece of roll.

"His boss was just *on* him all the time." Tuck despised this woman, a severe, slate-haired middle-management type in her fifties, who didn't, according to Tuck, get *Boom Time* at all. Lil had met her, just once, and trusted that this was true, but also suspected that the woman sensed Tuck's resentment and disdain—and behaved accordingly. Tuck believed she was both jealous of him—for being young and successful—and bizarrely attracted to him. She bothered him about obscure grammatical matters, complained about his lateness, and made not-so-subtle—inappropriate, really—comments about his failure to shave on certain mornings. "I don't know if I ever told you guys this, but back in November, one night he left early to meet me at your play, Em, and she made this big deal about it. I guess he sort of made it out to be my fault and she said, 'Your wife is demanding, isn't she? Journalism is for the unattached and ambitious.'"

"Who is she?" asked Sadie. "Rosalind Russell in *His Girl Friday*?"

"I know, right." Emily laughed. "That's crazy."

"Wasn't she, like, the copy chief at *Seventeen*?" asked Beth. "Or that's what Will said."

Lil nodded. "But she never would have gotten there if she hadn't been *unattached and ambitious,*" she said, smiling wickedly. The truth was, Lil sometimes wondered if Tuck wasn't making some of this stuff up, skewing his stories so that he seemed the victim. Tuck had terrible problems with authority. It was why, she knew, he'd never become a true star at Columbia. He didn't *get* that he had to wend his way into the good graces of his superiors. He hated schmoozing with professors at cocktail parties and readings. He never went to office hours or engaged his advisors in lively discussions of current scholarship or even sought advice from them. Everyone knew academics—toiling away in their nichey salt mines, publishing papers in *Eighteenth Century Studies* or *Gender and Hegemony*—wanted to feel needed and appreciated and *worshipped* by their students. But Tuck made them feel the opposite: unnecessary and outmoded. Which, Lil had to admit, many of them *were.* But still. It was as though he was determined to lead life in the most difficult way possible, out of some misguided sense of integrity.

He talked constantly of the new regime and the small rebellions planned and enacted by the Slikowskers. Lil listened patiently and sympathetically, but she thought she, in Tuck's place, might change her habits and adjust her thinking to meet the demands of the new people, who were, after all, simply doing their job, the best they knew how. They were trying to make the magazine operate more like other magazines. Was there anything really so wrong with that?

"The whole thing is so depressing," lamented Beth. "Ed is just a wreck. He really regrets selling."

"Then why did he do it?" asked Sadie.

"He needed money," said Lil.

"His backers were freaking out," Beth explained. "They're these software guys. They don't get that magazines don't make money overnight. They were threatening to pull the plug."

"Especially magazines run by people who have no idea how to run magazines," said Sadie. Lil gave her a dark look, through lowered lids, for Ed's lack of magazine experience was—as everyone knew—what had made *Boom Time* great. Ed was a visionary, a genius. At sixteen, he'd earned a modicum of fame for hacking into his high school's computer system and rearranging students' schedules, so that uptight AP physics students wound up in health class with dull-minded jocks and cheerleaders. The school's guidance counselors quickly remedied the prank, but not before Ed's goal—a *Breakfast Club*-style commingling of social groups—had been realized and, moreover, reporters had flocked to Pasadena, wanting to interview the techno-socialist. He'd wound up a human-interest item, in the pages of *People* and *Time* and *USA Today,* cheerfully opining on the vicious social structure of the modern high school and the democratizing power of the home computer. Most magazines, he'd told Lil when she'd first met him, were written by "corporate whores and yuppie porn slaves" and filled with "glorified ad copy and assorted insipid drivel." The world was ready for stories that explored popular culture—for that was what technology was becoming, wasn't it?—without sycophantic references to demi-celebrities and barely concealed product placement. He'd decided to run *Boom Time* as if it were "the first magazine to walk the earth."

The *Times* mag, in their profile, had run a photo of him at sixteen, in a green Atari T-shirt and too-long jeans, his elbow resting on a boxy Mac Plus, his cheeks, even then, covered with a dense, inky growth. Lil had loved this photo, for reasons she couldn't explain, and she'd blushed and stammered when next she saw Ed, remembering how she'd lingered over it. The real Ed was somewhat less approachable. He always greeted Lil like an old friend, but he spoke so passionately and forthrightly and earnestly that it perpetually caught her off guard. "What do you think about this impeachment madness?" he'd asked the last time she saw him, in November, before Tuck was fired. "It's crazy," she'd said, stupidly, realizing that her thoughts didn't go much deeper than that. By all rights, he should consider her an idiot. But he didn't seem to, which made her even more uncomfortable, for this made her the recipient of his charity.

"I think he's going to leave," Beth told them.

"And do what?" asked Lil skeptically.

"Go back to MIT, finish his Ph.D., work in the Media Lab."

"How could he go back?" asked Lil. She seemed almost angry. The girls looked at one another. "To *Boston*? To school? After running his own magazine?"

Beth shrugged. "He's been talking about making a movie. With Jonathan. About this company they wrote about last year. They own the rights. I think he's working on the screenplay."

"A *movie*?" cried Lil. Her friends looked away, embarrassed by this display of emotion. Why should it matter to her if Ed left *Boom Time*? Though, of course, Sadie thought, she felt betrayed. Ed could leave, could go off and do whatever he liked, could rise from the ashes of his success, but Tuck had been forced out, demoralized.

"Would Tuck go back to Columbia?" she asked.

Lil shook her head furiously. "No, never. He thinks it's all bullshit now." She smiled, a bit wanly. "And I suppose it is." They had talked of this too long and her head was beginning to ache with all that she couldn't say. Namely, the figures that kept appearing before her eyes, the money they owed ($1,500 for rent, for December *and* January; $400 for Tuck's student loans; a frighteningly high figure in credit card bills, since they'd paid for much of their wedding with plastic, rather than cede control to Lil's parents). And the terrifying notion, which she tried to push out of her mind, that Tuck was somehow not the person she'd thought he was, someone very different from the man who'd come home from work each night during the hot summer of their engagement, peeled off his clothes, and carried her to bed, murmuring "You're too far away" if she so much as rolled out of his arms. Everything she did, everything she said seemed to be wrong, and *had* been wrong since sometime in the fall, a few weeks after the wedding. But certainly it had been worse since the day Tuck was fired.

She'd been standing at the stove, browning meat for Bolognese and panicking about a rash of late papers she needed to grade, when she heard the lock turn in the loft's heavy front door. It couldn't be Tuck, she thought, as it was just getting on six o'clock and he never left work before seven or, usually, eight. But it *was* Tuck. She knew what he had to tell her even before he'd shut the door. "Hey," she said, taking care to keep her tone light.

"Hello," he responded jauntily, locking the door and rushing over to her. "Hey," he said, and kissed her neck, wrapping his arms around her from behind, so that she could smell the faint odor of his sweat and cigarettes and something else, something sweet and slightly sickening. "You look beautiful."

"Hey," she said again, stirring the meat and half turning to face him. Strands of graying hair fell lankly over his forehead—he was long overdue for a haircut—and the lids of his eyes were crepey, worn. "Is everything okay?"

"Why wouldn't it be?" he asked, narrowing his eyes. "Why do you always expect the worst?"

"I don't," she said softly, willing herself not to get angry. She had so many papers to grade. She couldn't fight with him tonight. "I don't, sweetheart, really."

"Well, you're right," he said, swiping his hair back and letting his lips go slack. "Those fuckers," he said, gripping her arm. "Those *fuckers*."

"Who, Tuck?" she asked, though she knew who, but maybe, maybe he was talking about something else.

"Who do you think, Lil?" he shouted. His face was slick with sweat, though it was cold out, and that faint sweetness was, she realized, whiskey. *Oh God,* she thought, *he didn't really stop at a bar on his way home.* "Those fucking corporate bastards. They've been out to get me from the start, just waiting for me to make a mistake, looking for an excuse to fire me."

"What?" she asked, pouring tomatoes into the meat. "What happened? Please just *tell* me."

"I was fired, Lil. What do you think?" He dropped into a kitchen chair, rested his elbows on the table, and dropped his head into his hands.

"Why don't you take off your coat?" she said, trying to quell her anxiety. "Why don't you let me run you a bath and fix you a cup of tea? You can just relax and I'll finish making dinner. And then we can talk." She turned the heat down on her sauce, wiped her hands on a dish towel, and ignited the flame under the teakettle.

"I'm not," said Tuck, his eyes following her movements in a way that made her freeze, both literally and metaphorically, "a five-year-old, Lil, so don't treat me like one."

"Tuck, I wasn't—"

"I've. Just. Been. *Fired,*" he said. "I've just been completely humiliated." He circled his hands in front of his face, as though words couldn't capture the full measure of his fury and degradation. When he spoke again, his voice was a notch higher. "A cup of *tea,* Lil? Herbal tea, right? Because it's too late to have any caffeine. I'd be *up all night* and that would be just *frightful.*" He grasped his cheeks in an expression of mock horror. "Thanks, but I don't want any *tea.* I'd like a drink and if you had any *compassion,* you'd join me."

Lil, by this point, had flattened herself against the counter and averted her eyes from his. "No, thanks, not right now," she said, though she was thinking, *Why did I bother to make dinner? I could have been grading my L&R papers.* "I'm okay. If you're not going to take a bath—"

"Lil, what is *wrong* with you?" Tuck shouted, banging his fist down on top of the kitchen counter. Lil opened her mouth but said nothing. *Was* there something wrong with her? *Did* she lack compassion? "You think this is all my fault, don't you?" His voice was lower now, ragged from shouting. "Well, you're wrong. They were itching to fire someone, to make someone an example, and it just happened to be me. I *happened* to be the asshole who got stuck slaving for that pathetic bitch. And you can't, you can't have a drink with me, like a normal human being? What is *wrong* with you? Why do you always blame *me*?"

At this, Lil burst into tears, for he was right, he was right, he was always right. Deep down, she did blame him. "I'm sorry," she said, through sobs. "I didn't know how bad it was for you. I'm so sorry. It's just, I have so much to do. I'm so tired. I have like fifty papers to grade and I made dinner—"

But it was too late. He was beyond consolation, possessed by some sort of wild, rigid fury. "I didn't *ask* you to make dinner," he screamed. "What is *wrong* with you? If you have papers to grade, *grade them*. Don't make dinner."

"But we have to eat," she said, or shouted, for she was angry now, too. What was wrong with *him*? Why did he always act as though everything was *her* fault? "What would we eat for dinner if I didn't cook?" Didn't he see that this was the point of being married? To eat dinner together, to make a life together, out of small things.

"Why do you have to be such a bitch?" he asked, grabbing a bottle of scotch, uncapping it—keeping his eyes on her, as if daring her to react—and tipping a slug of liquid into his throat, then exhaling dramatically, like a movie outlaw. "Why?" he asked. "I don't get it." And the sad, quiet way in which he asked this question—as though he really wanted to know the answer; and as though an answer were truly possible, as if she might say, "Well, Tuck, you see, I received this special training from an institute in Uzbekistan"—stung her more, somehow, than all his shouting and sarcasm, for she could see that he really meant it. He really thought she was being purposefully unkind, undermining, castrating, whatever. But she could not answer, and so she watched, fighting more tears as he wiped his lips with his hand, and stalked heavily into the bedroom, closing the door behind him with a resonant thud.

"So, is this why you didn't go away for Christmas?" Sadie asked her. Emily had gone up to the counter to get them coffee and a cookie.

Lil nodded. She'd seen Sadie at New Year's—the Peregrines' annual party—and not said a word.

"Were your parents upset?" asked Beth. Will, to all of their shock, had taken her home for Christmas. Sam had been with his mother's family, in California.

"Not really." Lil smiled. "You know they hate the holidays." Lil's parents both reviled Christmas and rejected Hanukkah, which they viewed as an invented holiday and "too much fuss." Still, Lil and Tuck had planned to visit them in December—spending the twenty-fifth, as per one of the Roths' few traditions, at the Golden Panda on Melrose—and then head to Atlanta, for a few days with Tuck's mom, over New Year's. But they'd waited to buy their tickets, which they thought they'd pay for with Tuck's bonus, rumored to be handed out in cash on the twenty-third. But fate— or Tuck's boss—had intervened three days before that date and there had been no bonus, which meant there had been no trip. And though her parents weren't terribly upset, they were baffled that Lil canceled so late. "Are the tickets refundable?" her father asked. "Um, we don't actually have tickets," Lil told him. "How were you planning on getting here?" he asked gruffly. Her father would have made the arrangements back in September, perhaps cashing in some of his many frequent-flier miles. He would have planned the whole trip long before Thanksgiving, from car rentals to guidebooks to restaurants. This was part of it, Tuck's inability to *plan*. He was, it seemed, incapable of thinking beyond the next five minutes. When he was hungry, he wanted to eat immediately. Or, as with his job, if he wanted to sleep, he simply slept. He was a child. And she'd thought him, when they met, so grown-up, so different from Dave and Tal and the other men she knew, who all seemed spindly and adolescent by comparison.

"I think I was more disappointed than they were," she said, dropping an irregular lump of brown sugar into her coffee. It was true. Her parents, typically, seemed more annoyed at the inconvenience of her canceling than disappointed that they wouldn't get to see their only child at the holidays. But then Lil hadn't been particularly looking forward to seeing them, either. Her visits home always devolved into arguments—"What are you going to do with a Ph.D.? Work in a coffee shop?"—which ended with Lil slamming the door to her childhood room and hiding therein for hours, thumbing through old copies of *Sassy*, just as she had in adolescence. As a child she'd wondered if she was adopted—a fantasy she now recognized as commonplace and clichéd—and that her real parents, quiet and dignified, might swoop in and save her from the Roths, who in turn existed in a state of rankled perplexity at their bookish daughter. (Did she really not want a nose job? Did she really not want to spend Saturday at the Beverly Center?) She wasn't sure, in retrospect, why she'd wanted to go home, other than to show Tuck off, to show them that she'd succeeded, if not in the way they'd wanted her to. "I was really needing to get out of the city."

"But you got to go to Rose Peregrine's fabulous partay," said Emily.

She'd gone down to North Carolina for the holidays. "You guys were, like, doing lines off the coffee table, right?"

"Of course," said Sadie. "But we stopped when the hookers arrived. They get so greedy."

"It was fun?" asked Beth earnestly.

"It was fun," Lil confirmed. In fact, it was the promise of the party that had sustained her, in a way, on that awful night, while Tuck stayed locked in their room and she finished dinner—boiled the penne, compiled a pale, perfect salad that she knew would not be eaten, at least not that night. Tuck would find another job, a better job, she told herself, as she peeled cucumber and tore apart the cool leaves of a Boston lettuce. Or, if he didn't, she would convince him to go back to Columbia, which would, in a way, be better. They would have less money—much less—but he would become Tuck again, the man who could spend hours talking about the prosody of Gerard Manley Hopkins and why Charles Simic was a fraud, which she would infinitely prefer to a fifteen-hundred-square-foot loft and a trip home to L.A. And it would be fun to be in New York over the holidays. They could do New York things, touristy things—the storefronts of Fifth Avenue, the skating rink in Central Park—and, for the first time, attend the Peregrines' party, which, to Lil, had taken on a sort of mythic status. She envisioned the Peregrine place lit gauzily by candles, flowers springing from oversized vases, chattering masses of Peregrines dressed in black.

But when she pictured herself among her beloved Peregrines, she saw herself alone. She could easily imagine the party, like others she'd attended, but more festive, more fancy. She would wear the navy wool sheath she'd just found at Beacon's Closet, a Dior from the sixties, which was surely worth more than she'd paid for it, and sip prosecco from a slender flute, her back warmed from the parlor fire as she chatted with Rose Peregrine or Sadie's aunt Minnie, whom she loved, a cranky old socialist. She tried to insert Tuck into the picture, to no avail. Though she *could,* without effort, imagine arguing with him about going to the party. She had seen it happen countless times. He would agree to go, then, when the night arrived, say, "Where is it again? All the way up *there*? Isn't it just going to be a lot of old people?" And then there would be the assertions that the Peregrines hated him, *everyone* hated him, everyone was against him, even those whom he'd met for all of a moment. And on and on, so that it would come as a relief when he said, at last, that she should just go alone.

Oh God, she'd thought, putting down her knife. Before her lay the remains of a red pepper, its delicate seeds clinging to the counter. *This is bad.* And an impulse came over her: to take off her white chef's apron and walk out the door, to go to Emily's or, really, Sadie's. Sadie could make sense of all this. But Sadie was always with Tal now. Lil had barely seen her since the wedding. And she didn't want to talk to Tal, nor did she want to talk to Tal and Sadie together, a smugly happy couple, offering advice to their troubled friend. How could they understand anyway? In choosing each other they'd taken the easy route, the path of common understanding. There would be no arguments of this sort between them. They knew each other completely.

Just then, the phone emitted its shrill digital chirp, a sound Lil hated, and she rushed back to the study—they didn't yet have a phone in the kitchen—certain that Sadie was on the other end, that she'd summoned her with her thoughts. By the time she'd arrived at her desk, the ringing had stopped. Tuck must have picked it up in the bedroom. She heard faint murmuring through the closed door, then Tuck's boisterous laugh. "Hey, honey," he called. "Lillian? Are you there?"

"I'm here," she said, in a small, choked voice. She wasn't prepared to face him. Tuck opened the bedroom door with one long arm and smiled at her, the portable phone cradled under his left ear.

"Hello," he said, softly, with a crooked smile. "It's Rob. He's wondering if we want to come over and have a drink with him and Caitlin."

"I don't know," said Lil, the words sounding wobbly and wrong to her. "I don't really feel like going out right now. And I've already made dinner."

"No, later. After dinner. Maybe at nine or nine thirty. Caitlin's not even home yet."

"They don't want to come here?" Lil desperately did not want to go out, did not want to walk through the cold wind on Metropolitan all the way to the Green-Golds' dingy flat. But she knew she should agree. This was Tuck's way of apologizing. "We still have all that leftover wine from the wedding."

"No, they want us to come there. Caitlin's really tired. Today's her heavy day: three classes. And Rob's baked a pie."

"Okay," whispered Lil, forcing herself to smile. Rob's pies were disgusting. "That sounds great. I'm going to go check on the pasta."

"Okay, I'll have a quick shower." He turned back to the phone. "You still there, Robby?" Lil shut the door and went back to the kitchen.

Lil always forgot about Rob and Caitlin in cataloging her friends, as they didn't fit neatly into any particular category, and yet she and Tuck generally regarded the fact of the couple's existence as a happy accident, a sign that the Roth-Hayes were meant—if not *fated*—to be together. Rob Gold was a childhood friend of Tuck's, who'd dropped out of Bard to trek through Asia, then resurfaced a few years later in Portland, Oregon, living in a squat and heading up some sort of anarchist group. It was he who had tipped Tuck off to the story that had gotten him in so much trouble.

Lil, meanwhile, knew Caitlin Green from Oberlin. Like Lil and Sadie and Beth, Caitlin had studied English—the four of them, in fact, were the only women selected for the Honors seminar their senior year. Her parents taught biology at Haverford or Swarthmore, someplace Quaker, and her early and prolonged exposure to academe had lent her a too-warm sense of her own intellectual superiority and sophistication, which, in turn, led her to regard her fellow students with unconcealed disdain. She adopted a world-weary pose in all her classes, even the Honors seminar, resting her round cheek on one black-nailed fist, sighing whenever someone asked a question she found particularly elementary, and periodically trying to catch the professor's eye, so the two might commiserate over these sad products of the American education system, who didn't fully grasp Bataille's concept of sovereignty. Her field of specialty was "queer theory" and she habitually accused professors and peers alike of "unconscious gender bias" and such, when not organizing rallies for the LGB union and "students of color," though she herself was neither gay nor visibly *ethnic*. If questioned, she said that she was bisexual and that Jews were "the original persons of color."

In college, Lil had hated Caitlin, particularly after she launched a campaign against George Wadsworth, Lil and Sadie's advisor, whom she considered dangerously misogynistic ("Why," she shouted, on Tappan Square, "are there only four women in Honors English?"), but she seemed to have changed, matured, in the ensuing years, during which she'd met and married Rob, who was slight, and odd, and serious. His latest project was a nonprofit aimed at curbing the prison industry, which Lil had not really seen as "burgeoning" and "sinister" until Rob explained it all to her— that prisons were now run by private companies, which had, of course, a profit motive for getting as many people as possible behind bars. A week after their wedding, she and Tuck had run into the couple on Bedford and discovered the coincidence of their mutual acquaintance. Caitlin had lost weight. She was now gaunt (but still, Lil noted, *wide-hipped*) and her eyes were smeary with dark circles, which lent her face a hollow, exhausted look that, Lil decided, was strangely sexy, as though Caitlin had traveled many places and done many things.

"Will you guys be okay?" Beth asked as they finished their coffee. They were both restless and reluctant to step out into the cold. "Did he get severance?"

"He did," said Lil. "But it's getting hard. We just have to find ways to cut back."

"I'm sure Caitlin Green can help with that," said Sadie. The Green-Golds lived like monks, making do with almost nothing, in a dingy rail-road apartment they'd cordoned off into small, nooklike rooms, subsisting on various grains and nuts and legumes, and riding their bikes around the city rather than taking the train or a taxi.

Lil rolled her eyes. "I know. We went over there the night Tuck was fired."

Her friends let out a chorus of groans.

"I was a wreck. And I was stupidly honest with her." She paused, unsure if she should speak honestly again. "I told her our apartment was too expensive and that this was going to push us over the edge."

"What did she say?" asked Sadie. "That you should become vegan?"

"Yes!" marveled Lil. Sadie shrugged. "She's just *too much*. She was like"—Lil adopted Caitlin's ripe vowels—"'It's unbelievable how much you can drop on cow pus alone.'"

"Cow pus?" queried Beth, her mouth bunched in revulsion.

"Milk," Emily told her.

"And I told her I *love* milk. I just can't imagine giving it up. And she said, 'Dairy cows are raped, like, twelve times a day.'"

"Even the organic ones?" asked Beth skeptically.

"That's exactly what I said," cried Lil, turning her palms upward. "She says even the organic ones." Lil sighed. "They only spend forty dollars a week on food."

"Well, that's not hard when all you eat is beans and rice," said Emily.

"True," said Sadie, with a roll of her eyes. But Lil felt there was something admirable about such frugality, though in Rob and Caitlin's case, it seemed slightly histrionic, because Rob was rich. Truly rich. His father owned half of Atlanta and all of Richmond. Their apartment was studded with heavy bureaus and thick rugs and oils of long-nosed ancestors filched from his great-grandfather's Rhinebeck "cottage." It was all a game to them. They could live on nothing but get married on Baldhead Island. They could eat beans but buy Hindu Kush.

This should have made their choices seem *more* heroic—they had simply opted out of conspicuous consumption—but for Lil it only made them seem less so, a childish pretense, their convictions mere self-righteousness. And Tuck's infatuation all the more galling, particularly when he held Lil up to their model for comparison—and, of course, found her lacking. "Everything is in its place," Tuck liked to say, almost angrily, after visiting the Green-Golds. "Their apartment is small, but they've made the best of it. They use every bit of space." Or "They don't have piles of shoes and books lying around. Did you see Caitlin's desk? There was nothing on it." Lil's own desk, at any given time, was covered in mounds of papers—Xeroxed articles, drafts of her own papers, student essays, coupons, receipts, Post-it notes with scrawled reminders on them, gum and candy wrappers, dog-eared legal pads containing her copious notes for her dissertation proposal, grocery lists, to-do lists, recipes clipped from the Dining In section.

"I would have run out of there screaming," said Emily.

"I did, kind of." Lil pressed the heels of her hands into her eyes. "I was so tired, I just felt like I couldn't stay awake another minute. It was kind of crazy. I told them I had to go home, I had all these papers to grade, but Caitlin, of course, was like, 'I have papers to grade, too. We can go to the L tomorrow and just plow through them.'"

"As if you can't grade papers alone," said Beth, contemplating the remains of their cookie. "That's just weird."

"I know! It was *too much*"—she paused, unsure whether her friends would think her actions deranged—"and I just kind of *left*."

"You didn't say good-bye?" asked Sadie, starting to laugh.

"I couldn't! I just had to get out of there."

"Wow," said Emily. "Good for you."

What she didn't tell them was that Tuck had come running after her, furious, shouting her name down the block. At the corner of Marcy he'd caught up with her and made to grab her arm. "Don't touch me," she'd shouted, in a voice she didn't recognize, low and tear-choked. "Don't talk to me like that," he'd shouted back. "I'm your husband. Do you not love me anymore? Because it doesn't seem like it." But before she could answer, an electronic ring pierced the air between them: her new cell phone, obtained for her, against her wishes, by Tuck, who'd become umbilically attached to his own since starting at *Boom Time*. She fished it out of her pocket and pressed the talk button. "Hello?" she said, the word emerging more as a question.

"Hey!" came Sadie's voice, hollow and distant, with a slight echo. "My long-lost friend. Is this the only way to reach you? You're never at home."

"Hey," said Lil, stunned with relief. "I was going to call you earlier."

Who is it? mouthed Tuck.

"Really?" said Sadie, her voice rising with curiosity. "Why didn't you?"

Tuck's angry mien was breaking, senselessly, into a smile.

I love you, he mouthed, and pulled her to him, lifting her off the ground like a child, the cold air slapping against her cheeks. "Hang up," he shouted.

"What's going on?" asked Sadie. "Who is that?"

"Nothing," Lil shouted, squealing a bit as Tuck began to spin her around. "No one."

five

L il and Tuck were having a party. It was to be their first big party in the loft—other than the wedding—which they'd now been living in for the better part of a year and which was, everyone agreed, absolutely *made* for parties. And now, after five dark months, they had a reason to celebrate: Tuck was writing a book.

It was Sadie who'd engineered the project from start to finish. One blustery day in March she'd called Lil and said, without her characteristic preliminaries, "Listen, I have an idea." Why, Sadie posited, didn't Tuck write a book about Ed Slikowski, or maybe not directly about Ed Slikowski, maybe a kind of first-person narrative nonfiction, six-months-at-the-world's-hottest-magazine sort of thing. "Kind of Gay Talese–ish." Sadie, who was still slaving away as an editorial assistant (none of them could understand why she hadn't been promoted, or jumped to another publisher, or written her own book), could put Tuck in touch with an agent who did that sort of thing. Tuck would have to write a proposal and some sample chapters—that was it—which the agent would then send to editors, one of whom (undoubtedly, Sadie said) would give Tuck a contract. He'd then have a year (or maybe six months, if they wanted to get the thing out quickly to capitalize on Ed's current, though waning, fame) to write the book itself.

And—to Lil's shock—that was exactly what happened. Even more amazing was the fact that Sadie herself was to be Tuck's editor. Her geriatric boss had allowed Sadie to acquire the book in her own name, which made it her first real acquisition, to use the publishing parlance. So they were celebrating for her, too, really.

Lil had almost died when she heard the amount of Tuck's advance: $30,000, but then Tuck's agent—a pudgy, goggle-eyed fellow who bore the odd name of Kapklein, with whom Sadie had worked, a zillion years ago, at Random House—explained that it was actually pretty modest. And, worse, that Tuck wouldn't receive a check for that amount at the outset. A third would arrive upon the signing of the contract (still being worked over by Kapklein "so they don't screw you over"), another third upon the completion of the manuscript, and a final third on publication of the book, with Kapklein's fifteen percent commission deducted from each installment. But Kapklein wasn't worried about the small advance, because, he said, Sadie's house, the elegant, literary division of a huge publishing conglomerate, would lavish Tuck with "real, old-fashioned editorial attention" and the reputation of the publisher would add "luster" to the book, ensuring that it would be reviewed in all the right places, and so on. "And besides," Kapklein told Tuck and Lil and an uncomfortable Sadie, when they went out for a celebratory drink, "There's film potential here, too."

But the money part didn't really matter so much. The point was: Tuck was really a writer now. In a year or so, his book would be displayed in the window of the Union Square Barnes & Noble and reviewed in the *Times*. He'd have no trouble getting freelance work—in fact, magazines would *ask* him to write for them—and they'd travel around the world, on interesting, important assignments. On the subway, she'd see people bent over Tuck's book and restrain herself from saying, "That's my husband." All of this was more important than their immediate financial crisis, which the first chunk of Tuck's advance would only barely resolve. And the happy prospect of Tuck's success went a good ways toward deflecting her worries about her own research, which had been giving her trouble lately, since Tuck had started staying at home.

In point of fact, it wasn't the research itself that was giving her trouble. She could happily spend hours poring over source materials. But she seemed to have lost the ability to write, or, rather, to formulate her own ideas. When she sat down at her old enamel desk, her mind went everywhere but to Mina Loy—whom she was writing about for her modern poetry seminar, though in truth she found Loy's life more interesting than her poetry—and she caught herself examining her cuticles, wondering if she ought to run out and spend seven dollars on a cheap manicure, or what she should wear the following night to one of Sadie's book parties, or whether she should get her hair trimmed or continue to grow out the last cut, with its overzealous layering. And it wasn't just her dissertation proposal: she'd taken incompletes in two of her three spring classes, due to the fact that she had been, frighteningly enough, truly *unable* to write her final papers for them. Her professors had been kind and accommodating, but made it clear that she had to get the papers in soon, and start thinking seriously about her orals.

The problem was, she thought, as she put wine in the fridge to chill for the party, that Tuck's unhappiness over these months had cast a pall over their home, which had affected her. But soon he would be productive again—sitting in the study and writing, happily, at his old scarred desk, catty-corner from hers. She would get back to her own work. She would churn out her two papers by the end of June and then start reading for her orals. She still burned with shame about the incompletes and she'd told no one, not even Tuck.

The party was a success. A horde of Slikowskers—many of them still employed, unhappily, by *Boom Time*—raced manically around the loft, making blue drinks in the blender, beaming one another software from their Palm Pilots, and crowding, puppylike, around Ed Slikowski himself, who had stationed himself by one of the big front windows. He'd cut his hair and shaved his beard, so that his eyes loomed even larger and paler, sunk deep within the hollows above his cheekbones. "Hello," she'd cried when he arrived, giving him an awkward hug.

"Lillian, what's going on?" he asked, handing her a bottle of champagne.

"Well, the *book,* I guess," she said, as the Slikowskers encroached on them. "I'd better put this in the fridge."

"Yeah, it's great for Tuck," said Ed. "I feel like hell about what happened. Like I should have protected him more."

"No, no," said Lil, though she did wonder if Ed had done all he could to save Tuck. "It was inevitable, I think."

"Yeah," agreed Ed, shaking his head. "It was. That place is cancer now. It's really depressing." He'd left the magazine, just as Beth had predicted, back in April, and done the predictable: traveled through Nepal, then Vietnam, then home to California to visit his mother. "But it was good while it lasted, right?"

Lil nodded. "It must be hard," she said, with a sudden flash of insight. "After you created it. To see things change so much. To lose control."

Ed shrugged. "Yeah," he said. "But, you know, I was sick of it anyway, really. It's hard to be the boss. Signing off on every single thing. And all those deadlines."

"I know," murmured Lil, her mind returning uncomfortably to her incompletes. "Let me introduce you to some people . . ."

Everyone had come out: Her few friends from Columbia—a trio of tiny dark-haired women—smoked fiendishly in a corner, and made husky conversation with Tuck's friends from Columbia, glowering, bearded men of South Asian and Irish and Soviet-Jewish extraction, in rumpled shirts and khakis, from whose mouths frequently issued terms like "Marxist" and "hegemony" and "fascist" and "post-structural fallacy." Caitlin and Rob stood by the bar with Tuck's college friends and a little troupe of publishing people from Tuck's agency.

And for the first time since the wedding the entire group came, all of them bearing news. Emily's play—the dark, satirical thing she'd done in the fall—had been picked up for a respected off-Broadway theater. Dave's band was opening for a *big* band in a few weeks, at Irving Plaza. "Who?" asked Tal. Dave gave them a wry smile.

"Don't laugh," he said, "Reynold Marks."

"*Reynold Marks,*" marveled Tal. "Wow."

"Isn't Reynold Marks, like, a complete tool?" asked Emily.

"He's actually really nice," said Dave, his jaw tensing. "It's his fans who are tools."

"But you've only played, like, once," said Lil, wrinkling her brow, "haven't you? Have you done other shows and not invited us?"

Dave shook his head. "He saw us when we played at Mercury Lounge. It's crazy."

"That's amazing," said Sadie, with a wide, close-mouthed grin. They could see she wanted to say something more.

"What?" asked Dave, irritably.

"Nothing," she said, wrapping her arms around Tal. "Tell them," she said to him. Tal shook his head. "He's got the lead in a big movie."

"It's not a *big* movie," said Tal, grimacing. "It's just a movie."

"It's a John Cusack movie," Sadie explained. "Directed by that guy who did *Se7en.*"

"That sounds big," said Dave.

"That's great," Emily said, but the rest could see she was rattled.

"It's stupid," said Tal, running his hands over his face. He looked, they all thought, tired and distracted.

"It's *not,*" said Sadie, twining her fingers in his. "It's a thriller. It's good."

"So, you're, like, going to L.A.?" asked Dave.

"For this, yeah," Tal nodded. "In three weeks." Silently, they were all asking, *Will you stay? Will you bring Sadie with you?* Or, more accurately, *Will Sadie come with you?*

And then Beth, her cheeks flushed, said, "I have news, too." They all turned to look at her and she awkwardly held out her hand. "I'm getting married."

"To Will?" asked Dave.

Beth's face paled. "Of course to Will."

"But you just met," said Lil.

"We met in October," said Beth, her voice halting and choked. "That was eight months ago." She took a deep breath. "You and Tuck had only known each other nine months when you got engaged."

"You did the calculations," said Dave, smirking.

Beth's face began to crumple, her liquid features drawing closer together, at its center, as if for protection. They had all seen this before. "I knew you wouldn't be happy," she sobbed. "I know you don't like him." For a moment they watched, in silence, as the tears began to flow, then Tal stepped forward and wrapped his arms around Beth.

"Beth, don't be crazy," he said, in his soft, firm voice.

"Seriously, we're thrilled," Sadie chimed in, rubbing her friend's back. "Will is *great*. And he loves you. This is *great*. Dave was just teasing you."

"I was just teasing," said Dave, with a barely audible sigh.

And then they were upon her, with a thousand questions: Had they picked a date for the wedding? Had she told her parents? Would Sam come and live with them? Would they stay in Tuck's old apartment? And, wait, where *was* Will?

"He's in San José, reporting on that big merger," she explained, still hiccuping. "He had to fly out yesterday. He was really sad to miss the party. He's so happy for Tuck."

"You have a kind of *bridal glow,*" Lil told her, and it was true. Her cheeks were rosy (with blush, but no matter), her lips dewily glossed, her thin, sandy hair piled dramatically atop her head, a smallish diamond glittering on her left hand. Once she recovered from her tears—apologizing, as she always did—she swayed lightly to the music, wound her way back and forth from the kitchen, saying hello to everyone she passed, the skirt of her blue dress swishing around her knees. She sipped scotch from a tumbler, cigarette dangling from her hand, chatting gamely with the various members of Dave's band, who showed up near ten with a six-pack of Schlitz and prowled the place shyly in a pack, and Kapklein, who peered owlishly at her over the tops of his wire-rim glasses.

They had all promised Lil that they would stay until midnight when a band—that is, *the band,* the band that had crashed Lil's wedding—would play. "They opened for Beulah last night," Lil confided, "at Bowery Ballroom."

"Yeah," Dave confirmed. "They're getting a lot of play on college radio."

"Do you like them?" asked Lil, in such a way that there was only one appropriate answer.

"They're okay," he conceded. "They're very tight. I'm just not loving that produced eighties sort of sound." He shrugged. "But everyone's doing it. It's cool."

Soon after, Lil began to worry that *she* wouldn't be able to make it to midnight, much less beyond. She installed herself on the couch with a glass of wine and one of Kapklein's colleagues, an extraordinarily tall young man with dun-colored hair, a mildly self-satisfied expression, and the skittish air of a greyhound. His name was Tom Satville and he was quick to tell Lil that he himself was not just an agent, but a writer, too.

"Iowa," he explained. "Fiction. I'm finishing up a novel."

"Wow," said Lil. "How do you have time?"

He took off his glasses, revealing small, round brown eyes, with deep maroon smudges under them. "I don't sleep much."

"Oh." Lil nodded. "I wish I could do that. I'd get so much more done. Tuck is like you. He can stay up all night working." In fact, though he often stayed up all night, she wasn't sure he was actually working. The television often seemed to be on.

Tom Satville smiled in a way that made her slightly uncomfortable. "Yeah, well, you kind of have to be like that these days. The workday is getting longer and longer. We're just a small agency and nobody leaves before seven. Nobody takes lunch . . ." This was clearly a favorite subject of his.

"Yes," she said, "that's partly what Tuck's book is about—"

"That's what my novel is about, too. It's set in an office, an ad agency—"

"At *Boom Time,* it was like, the staffers *lived there*. Tuck kind of loved it, though."

"But you didn't?" he asked in a husky voice, draping his arm across the back of the couch on which they sat. She pulled her skirt down over her knees.

"I don't know," she said. "I liked that he loved what he was doing. He was so excited about it." She remembered those evenings, the previous summer, when he'd call her as he left his office, the sun just setting, the air cooling, and say, "Meet me for dinner." She'd shower quickly and pull on a sundress, run the ten blocks to Oznot's, where they'd sit in the garden and drink Lillet—this was why she'd served it at the wedding, because of those happy nights—and eat thin slices of lamb. Each day there'd been a new story, a new triumph, just as when they'd first met, the previous fall, and spent hours at Aggie's, drinking bourbon and reciting lines of Wright and Lowell and Berryman. That all seemed so long ago, and she and Tuck so young. "I guess I missed him," she told Tom Satville. "We'd, you know, been in school together. So I'd seen him all day, every day."

"And you're still in school?"

"Mmm-hmmm." Across the room, Tuck's friend Gary appeared to be shoving bananas down his pants. "The sad thing is, I'm one of those people who became an English major because I wanted to sit around and read novels. Whereas Tuck loves the hard stuff. He actually gets deconstruction and all that. It was all so easy for him."

"Was he bored?" asked Tom Satville, his hand sliding lower, to her shoulder. She'd thought, somehow, that men didn't hit on married women.

"Maybe," said Lil.

"People like to be challenged," he told her. "Especially intelligent people."

"True." This explanation pleased her, as it would allow her to give up her suspicion that Tuck was, simply, a failure, a person who lacked the drive and discipline to finish his degree, who had opted out at the first opportunity. *Stop, stop,* she told herself. Why would she be thinking this now on the night of his triumph? What was wrong with her? "I think also some people just can't deal with the hypocrisies of academia. It's like, they love books so much that dissecting them grows kind of *tiresome*. Like my friend Sadie." She pointed across the room, where her friend, in a belted dress of dull gray silk, stood talking to Ed Slikowski, their dark heads bobbing toward each other. "Have you met her?"

He placed his glasses back on his face and peered toward the kitchen— not the direction she'd pointed—scrutinizing the throng of women attempting to uncork a bottle of champagne. "No, I don't think so."

"She's Tuck's editor," said Lil. "Sadie Peregrine."

"Oh, right! Yes. Sadie Peregrine. I've never met her, I don't think—"

"She was the star of our department—"

"So you know her from—"

"Oberlin." Lil tried to catch Sadie's eye, but she was nodding enthusiastically at Ed Slikowski. "Everyone thought she would go to grad school. Her thesis won the big award. Her advisor wanted her to send it to *The Atlantic*."

"What did she write on?" Lil hadn't thought about this in ages. It was so embarrassing, how stupid she'd been, how unsophisticated. She had *not* been the star, but she could have been, she was sure of it, if she'd had parents like Sadie's, if she'd gone to Dalton. Her own children—if and when she had them—would be raised in New York, without television; they would go to St. Ann's, like Dave, where they could take yoga instead of gym.

"Dawn Powell. The Ohio novels."

"Oh, *brilliant,*" said Tom Satville, dipping his head in delight. He had, Lil thought, a faint British accent. "Most undergrads write on Plath or Dickens."

"I know," cried Lil, declining to mention that *she'd* written on Plath, though obscure Plath—the early landscape poems, really quite Audenesque, not "Daddy" and all that.

"Which one is Sadie, again?" the agent asked brightly. "I can't believe we haven't met. She's Delores Rosenzweig's assistant, right?"

"Sadie, come here," Lil called loudly, by way of an answer. "We're talking about you. Sadie." With visible reluctance, Sadie pulled herself away from Ed Slikowksi, who held in his hands, Lil saw now, a bowl of the spiced nuts Sadie loved. "Sadie, this is Tom Satville. He works with Kapklein."

"Oh, hello," said Sadie, with a nod of her neat head. She knew Lil wanted her to say something brisk and professional, like, "Sadie Peregrine. I'm Tuck's editor." That was, of course, why Lil had called her over here, to instigate a frenzied professional discussion of the sort Lil disproportionately loved. Under normal circumstances, Sadie had no aversion to shop talk, but she was not in the mood for it tonight. This whole party—the huge deal Lil was making about Tuck's contract, before he'd even signed the thing—made her nervous, for it only underscored the extent to which Tuck's fate—and, by extension, Lil's fate—lay in Sadie's hands, a power she wasn't quite sure she wanted, in part because, as of now, she didn't have very much power, still being a serf in Delores Rosenzweig's increasingly ineffectual fiefdom. An influential serf, sure, since Delores had largely checked out lately, to the extent that Sadie was essentially doing her job for her, but a serf nonetheless, with a whimsical and strange and anxious ruler, who often reneged on agreements and meted out unfair and illogical criticism or punishments.

There was promise of escape, though. The previous week, Sadie had been summoned for a talk with Val, her publisher, who had congratulated her on finding Tuck's book—"Delores would have never even looked at that New Economy stuff"—and told her that as of July 1, she would be an associate editor (not *assistant* but *associate,* which meant a sort of double promotion) overseeing a new series of novels by writers under the age of thirty-five called "Fast-Forward Fiction," a title clearly devised by a team of marketers who still listened to their Creedence Clearwater Revival or whatever on cassette tape. "If you can sit tight for a few more weeks, we'll make it official," said Val, with a tight smile. "It's not official?" asked Sadie. Val shook her head. "It is. We just haven't told Delores yet. So, please, not a word to anyone. We don't want Delores to hear about it from anyone other than me." "Of course," Sadie told her, "I completely understand." And she did—no one wanted to upset Delores—but she also *didn't.* Why must they all be, perpetually, in Delores's thrall? And, more important, if Delores put up a fight—as she might, for she'd certainly realized how dependent she was on Sadie—would they retract the promotion? This didn't seem out of the question.

Sadie glanced at Lil, who looked anxious and weary, despite her constant proclamations of joy about Tuck's book. The joy, Sadie thought, had been a bit too long coming, which was why Sadie had concocted her little plan. Though she'd failed to take into account the fact that she'd now have to work closely with Tuck, about whom she was still a bit too ambivalent. Sometimes she found him funny and charming, with a sly, satirical eye, and she wondered why she'd wasted so much energy disliking him. Just as often, though, she was disgusted by his overabundance of pride, which his dismissal from *Boom Time* had exacerbated rather than cured. Sadie didn't doubt his affection for Lil, but she found something unnerving in his need to marry her immediately, and in the way, now, he made such a big show of her being his *wife*—his arm always draped heavily around her—never mind that he was eternally abandoning her, refusing to come with her on New Year's Eve or, now, allowing her to be cornered by this smarmy guy, with his thin, reptilian lips and his ersatz British affectations (a tweed jacket in *June*?), who was now blathering to Lil about the decline of the novel, but peering at Sadie expectantly, an ironic smile twitching at his jowls. He reminded Sadie of some sort of desert mole, with his dark, tiny eyes, blinking behind microscopic, rimless spectacles, his skin nearly the same colorless brown as his hair.

"So you worked with Kappy at Random House?" he asked, turning to her.

"I did," she said, offering him, unthinkingly, a small grin. He was, she thought, the sort of fellow who would be easy to win over and hard to dismiss. Better to get away quick. Toward the back of the loft, she spotted Tal, leaning against the kitchen counter and glumly sipping a beer. He'd been acting strangely since Thursday, when his agent had given him the good news. In fact, he hadn't wanted to come tonight. "You go by yourself," he'd told her. "You haven't seen any of them in ages." It was true. She had been spending all her time with Tal. She hated to admit it—hated to think what it might signify about herself—but she couldn't stand to be apart from him. At work, as she drafted letters and thumbed through manuscripts and checked on contracts and answered the phone, a low buzz, a sort of vibration, enveloped her body—she imagined it as a circle of wavy lines, the sort that connote electrocution in the old Warner Bros. cartoons—rising in volume and intensity as the day progressed, so that by six o'clock, her need to see him, to feel him and smell him, was as physical and unignorable as the need to breathe or sneeze. It wasn't sex exactly. But she wasn't sure *what* it was.

"Will you excuse me for just a moment?" she said, rattling the ice cubes in her plastic cup. "I'm afraid it's time to—"

"Her entire family talks like that," Lil said.

"No, they don't," she said, giving them a small wave and turning toward the kitchen. *Here it comes,* she thought. And, yes, a moment later, Lil's voice came at her.

"They're kind of an old New York family, but in the Jewish way. Like in Laurie Colwin?"

Sadie's family was a favorite topic with Lil, who imagined the Peregrines to be terribly special and genteel and charming, playing chess on long winter nights, arguing about subjects intellectual, engaging in quaint customs at the holidays. To some extent this was true—or *sort of* true—but that didn't necessarily make them fun, and regardless, Sadie disliked having her life read back to her, transmogrified into mythology. But that was Lil, making myths out of accidents, deciding that, say, the sidecar was "*our* drink" or Von was "*our* bar" or even determining that their little circle of friends constituted a "set" (a word she appeared to have gleaned from *Gatsby*), when in reality they were just a bunch of people who were friends in college (though equally friends with other people, like Maya Decker and Abe Hausman) and had ended up living together, and thus grown close. But to Lil, the very groupness of their little group was as important as the individual friendships that comprised it. Sadie knew, of course, the reason for this: that Lil felt herself an alien in her own brash family and, thus, sought a sort of hysterical comfort in her friends—not to mention Sadie's own family. And Lil's parents, from the little Sadie had seen of them, were indeed a bit horrible, but then so were Sadie's own. Lil just never saw that side of them, never saw the ways in which Rose could be cruel and controlling, and James silent and remote.

By raising the volume on her "excuse me's," and pushing aggressively on the elbow of a young man whose muttonchop sideburns curled fiendishly toward each other, Sadie managed to make it to the kitchen area, where she wove in and out of the various bodies opening and closing and drinking from bottles of wine and beer and liquor, and, at last, wrapped her arms around Tal's narrow waist and looked up into his face. It was an odd face. The mouth too wide. The nose long, sharp, like one of Picasso's women. The whole thing just slightly too compressed, too small for his long body. He would never be a leading man, though it wasn't clear to her—even after all the years she'd known him, the long nights talking, the dark walks around campus, years back—if he wanted to be. His latest round of headshots, she supposed, supplied the answer: a three-quarter view, which minimized the slope of his nose, his dark eyes gazing stormily at the camera from lowered lids. "It's your George Clooney shot," she'd told him. "My agent picked it," he'd said with a shrug.

"Hey," he said to her now, flatly. Who knew how long he'd been standing here on his own, half crushed against the counter, waiting for her or Dave to come rescue him from abject boredom.

"Are you okay?" she asked.

"Yeah, yeah." He untwined her arms from him, put his bottle down on the counter, and stretched his arms up over his head, yawning. "Dave and I were talking about getting something to eat."

"You don't want to see the band?" To her left they were setting up, laying out a complicated network of wires and amps.

He shook his head. "They suck."

"Okay." Though she wasn't sure she needed one, she began making herself another drink: fresh ice, slosh of bourbon, cherry juice. "Are you heading out now?"

"Soon." He turned to face her. "Do you want to come with us?"

She took a sip. Too sweet. "You guys should do your guy thing. Drink beer. Eat hamburgers. Talk about football."

"I think it's baseball season." He turned to face her, hunching over the counter.

"I'm impressed that you know that."

"Well, I'm not sure, actually." He smiled.

"Okay," she said, sighing. Against her will, she felt wounded by this small abandonment. *Stupid, stupid,* she thought. She saw him almost every night. But in a couple of weeks he'd be in L.A. and she had a suspicion he wouldn't be coming back.

"I'll see you tomorrow?" he asked.

"No," she said, perhaps too curtly. "I have brunch. Then I've got to work."

From behind her, Lil and Tom Satville materialized, grabbing tall bottles of wine and sniffing them.

"A gewürztraminer," Tom Satville cried.

"Sadie brought that," Lil responded, clapping her hands and shooting Sadie a look of amazement, which Sadie chose to ignore. "Is it one of your dad's?" Lil pressed.

"No." Sadie caught Tal's eye. "It's from the wine shop on Court Street. The one that looks kind of ghetto. With the bulletproof glass." She turned to Tom Satville. "Have you met Tal?"

"Sadie's dad collects wine and sometimes he gives us his castoffs," Lil confided. "Her parents are *amazing.*"

"Amazing," said Tal, nodding.

Lil ignored him. "Tell Tom about your mother," she instructed.

"What about my mother?" she asked, though she knew full well what Lil wanted—tales of the wacky Peregrine clan, straight from the annals of Salinger. Why don't we talk about *your* family, she sometimes wanted to say, for she knew Lil had funny stories about her father's practice—the aging porn star who wanted to up her cup size to J (Dr. Roth had refused, saying breasts of such magnitude would be disproportionate to her height—five two); the lingerie model who'd asked for fat to be sucked from her pubic area, because it "puffed out too much" (on this, he had obliged)—and her general rearing in Los Angeles, a city of vast mystery and fascination to New Yorkers. "My mother's really not that interesting," she said, with a yawn.

Lil rolled her eyes. "*Sadie,*" she complained, shaking her head. "Sadie's mother is the most amazing woman. She's actually *from* Greenpoint! She grew up there, in the fifties."

"The forties, actually," said Sadie, smiling at Tal, who shook his head. He didn't share Lil's adoration of her mother, which came as something of a relief to Sadie.

"The forties?" said Tom Satville skeptically. "She must have had you late in life."

"She was forty-two," confirmed Sadie. "It was scandalous at the time. Everyone used to think my dad was my grandfather."

"You must have older siblings," the man said, rather presumptuously, she thought. She was used to this question, and yet it always bothered her. The funny thing was, now it was perfectly normal for people to have kids in their forties. And yet everyone always acted like it was just *bizarre* that her parents were two generations removed. "Are you one of many?"

"I have a brother. A half brother." She refrained from mentioning that this brother was dead. For this, in fact, was how her parents had met: Her father's child from his first marriage, a boy named Ellison, arrived at the Dalton infirmary—where her mother, widowed by the Korean War, doled out aspirin and bismuth—complaining of a headache. Thirty hours later he was dead of meningitis. Or something like it. Sadie wasn't exactly clear on this, the disease itself. She'd never asked and neither of her parents had ever volunteered the grim particulars, not even Ellison's age at his death. Her father's first marriage hadn't survived the tragedy. The story came to her from her aunt Dora, her father's sister, after Sadie happened upon some photos in a drawer (a beautiful boy, with her own deep-set eyes), and was later confirmed by her cousin Bab, in London. Sadie herself hated mentioning this brother, for what did she have to say about him but that he was dead. She hadn't known him, nor had her parents told her anything about him—and yet it seemed somehow dishonest to say she had no siblings.

"But the thing about Sadie's mom," Lil went on, though it seemed to Sadie that Tom Satville was not particularly interested in hearing about Sadie's mother, of all people, "is that she's *brilliant*. When she was young she looked like Joan Fontaine. Do you remember her? From Hitchcock? Vivian Leigh's sister. And she's still gorgeous now."

"She is," confirmed Tal. "She's like something from a different era."

"She *is*," Sadie clarified, "from a different era."

"She doesn't watch TV."

"She watches a little," said Sadie. "She loved *St. Elsewhere*."

"And she was really into the first season of *Survivor*," said Tal.

"She *was*?" cried Lil, a look of horror on her face.

"No," Sadie assured her. "No."

"Oh," said Lil, turning to Tom. "Sadie had, like, a storybook childhood." This was, of course, how Rose liked to characterize Sadie's early years.

"Which means," said Sadie, who had now resigned herself to playing the role Lil had chosen for her, "I had no friends. All the other kids thought I was weird."

"Can you believe it?" Lil asked.

"I can't," said Tom Satville, shoving his hands in the pockets of his corduroy pants and rocking back on his heels.

"Oh, it's true," said Tal. "She was a major dork. I've seen the pictures."

"I'm afraid so," said Sadie. "My mother would throw birthday parties for me and invite my whole class. And the kids would come and bring these big, expensive presents and then whisper 'You *smell*' as soon as my mother left the room."

"Poor little rich girl," said Tal, stroking her palm.

"You don't know my pain," said Sadie.

"Why did they hate you so much?" asked Tom Satville.

"I was weird," said Sadie dispassionately. "I was fat. My mother dressed me like it was the fifties." Her mother had also prohibited her from watching any television, except *Sesame Street* and *Masterpiece Theatre* and, moreover, striven to give Sadie a "women's education" in the style of the class Rose had made her own—albeit one, as Tal had said, of a far-bygone era. Sadie took lessons in piano, painting, dance, gymnastics, tennis, skiing, singing, and golf. She rode in Central Park and skated at Wollman Rink. She learned to sew and knit and bake. She took Saturday classes at the Met, where she picked up the difference between a Manet and a Monet, and Sunday classes at the Museum of Natural History, where she studied dinosaur bones and the earliest forms of humanoid life. She learned to throw pots from a married pair of potters, with a kiln in the basement of their Ninetieth Street brownstone. With the city parks commissioner—a tan, wiry fellow, who lived around the corner and played squash with James Peregrine—she studied different sorts of trees and shrubs and plants and birds. At eight, she dissected a cow's eyeball in an after-school biology tutorial, and drafted illustrated storybooks in the manner of Edward Gorey, with titles like "The Girl and the Monster" and "Penguin Have Sharp Teeth." She refused to drink soda or eat sugared cereals or packaged cakes and went through a period of vegetarianism in her tenth year. She was an excellent student, but never the *top* student, which her mother took as a sign of success ("Sadie has interests *outside* of school") and her teachers took as a sign of boredom, since she was always finishing her work ahead of the other students and withdrawing a thick book from the woody interior of her desk, or sketching complicated William Morris–like patterns on filmy sheets of onionskin with a set of calligraphic pens and colored inks. All of this, of course, was why she'd had no friends. She hated now to think of her childhood—at least the part lived at school, outside the safety and comfort of home.

"What does she do, your mother?" asked Tom Satville.

"She's on a bunch of committees. Hadassah. The temple sisterhood. That kind of thing. She throws parties. Fund-raisers." She smiled. "And she shops. That's mainly what she does."

"And she *reads*," corrected Lil. "She's read everything. She reads like, ten books a week."

Sadie smiled apologetically at Tom Satville. "I think it's more like one or two."

"She reads a *lot*," confirmed Tal.

"But she reads *everything*," Lil went on. "Books about string theory. William Gaddis. Donna Tartt. Mystery novels. Crazy stuff. John Grisham."

"She loves John Grisham," Sadie agreed. "And British mysteries. Cozies. Elizabeth George. Who's not actually British."

"And *every* magazine," continued Lil.

"*Every* magazine?" asked Tom Satville.

"A lot of magazines," Sadie conceded with a shrug. "She has a lot of time on her hands."

"Like what?" asked Tom Satville.

"*Harper's, The Economist, The Nation, The New Republic*," Sadie told him, ticking the names off on her fingers. "*The American Prospect, The Christian Science Monitor, Mother Jones, The Utne Reader, The Atlantic*, though she won't read their fiction. She hates short stories. Um. A bunch of Jewish magazines, like *Hadassah* and *The Jewish Week*. *Commentary*. Though she doesn't agree at all with their politics. And she's always complaining that they're boring."

"So she's kind of a public intellectual?" Satville asked, sending Tal into a spasm of silent laughter.

"Um, not really," Sadie told him. "She's more of a completionist. She also reads *Ladies' Home Journal* and *Better Homes and Gardens* and all that. She clips recipes for me."

"There are more, Sades," Lil insisted.

"Really?" asked Sadie. She was hungry and if she and Tal were going to go their separate ways this evening, if she wouldn't see him until the following night, then she'd rather get their parting over with. "I suppose *Time*," she added. "And sometimes *Newsweek*. And, of course, the *Times* magazine. And she's probably the only person who reads those local neighborhood magazines. *Quest*. *East Side Spirit* or whatever it's called. And *New York*. She actually loves *New York*."

"*The New Yorker?*" suggested Tom Satville.

"No. Not anymore. She canceled her subscription."

"Really?" Tom Satville appeared shocked. "That seems *odd*."

"She says it became just like *People* after Tina Brown took over. She's really down on the rise of celebrity culture."

"She should talk to Ed Slikowski!" cried Lil, so loudly that Sadie worried that Ed could hear her. "That's his thing, too." The four of them turned to look at Ed, who was still at the front of the loft, cornered by Caitlin Green-Gold. To his left, Sadie spotted Beth walking through the front door, trailed by Dave.

"Hey." Sadie turned to Tal. "Where are they going?"

"Let's go see," he said, taking her hand. "We'll be back," he called to Lil and Tom Satville.

It's time to leave, Sadie thought. She was bored and tired and hungry. *Bean,* Sadie thought, *I'll get Beth and we can go to Bean.* The room, now, was filled with strangers—friends, perhaps, of the band? After several wrong turns, Sadie and Tal arrived at the front of the loft, its door propped open by a cement brick, where Dave and Beth sat on the front step. Dave jumped up as soon as he saw them. "You wanna head?" he asked Tal.

"Sure, if you're ready," said Tal, squeezing Sadie's hand.

"Have fun," she told them. "I'll talk to you tomorrow." Tal nodded and kissed her quickly on the cheek, his gaze already off down the street.

For a moment, she and Beth watched them walk away, Dave lighting a cigarette, their lanky frames oddly similar when lit by the yellow glow of Bushwick's old streetlights.

"What do you say we go get some dinner?" Sadie asked Beth.

"That sounds great," she said. "Let me just run to the bathroom, okay?"

Sadie nodded. "I'll go find Lil and say good-bye."

Inside, the girls fought their way through the crowd, which seemed to grow thicker and wilder by the minute. Midway through, Sadie realized that she'd lost Beth, and that Lil was nowhere in sight. Left alone in the middle of the large room, Sadie surveyed the company. An unusually large number of guests wore glasses. *Is our entire generation going blind?* she wondered, irritated. *What a lazy metaphor.* She, at least, seemed to be. For weeks, she'd been plagued with headaches, like a needle inserted into the back of her head. She'd mentioned it to Tal on Wednesday and he'd suggested she get her eyes checked. "That's how I knew I needed glasses," he'd said. He wore contacts now. "Oh, no, I don't think that's it," she'd said. "I have perfect vision." But the very next day, after work, they'd gone to a French movie on Court Street—she'd insisted on doing *something* to celebrate—and spent the whole two hours scrambling to read the strangely fuzzy subtitles. *Glasses,* she thought, *bleh.* She knew that is was "cool" now to wear glasses—so cool that (could it be?) perhaps some of the glasses that surrounded her were props—but she somehow couldn't rid herself of her mother's Eisenhower-era admonition against them. For women, of course. For men, they posed no threat to desirability. This was Number 367—or perhaps 54—of Rose Peregrine's Rules for the Upkeep of the Modern Female, which began with the obvious (sweaters should only be cashmere; fur coats, mink or sable), delved into the practical (tweezers should always be slant-edged), before devolving into extreme esoterica. Sadie, unlike Lil, had a limited appetite for down-to-the-stitches descriptions of calfskin wallets with brass clasps and leather linings ("Anything else just *falls apart*"), or the appropriate colors—black, brown, bone, or, on occasion, navy blue (provided one owned corresponding shoes)—and styles for handbags, which had to have a strap of at least an inch in width and should never extend below one's waist; legs must never be shaved, only waxed ("it just grows back thicker!"); hair must never be colored at home ("you'll ruin it!"), only at "the hairdresser's"; skirts that ended above the knee and patent-leather shoes were suitable only for prepubescent girls ("you don't want to look like a streetwalker!"); and faces should only—*only!*—be cleansed with cold cream.

The older she grew, the more Sadie found herself unconsciously following Rose's strictures, even as she became increasingly frustrated with Rose's adherence to them, particularly those that veered away from the areas of women's ablutions. Rose would not, for example, eat with her coat on, or while walking down the street, or at any sort of bar, or at a cafeteria-style establishment, or, God forbid, *from a tray.* She had no tolerance for plastic cutlery and refused to drink water from a bottle, much less to *buy* water in a bottle ("We're not in *Mexico!*"), but believed flocked paper luncheon napkins to be a wonderful modern contrivance. Her views on what constituted "food" did not include the cuisines of Thailand, India, Japan, Malaysia, Spain, the islands of the Caribbean (which she also refused to visit, saying this region had "no culture"), or the nations of Latin America, excepting Argentina, which was "European, *actually*" and "has a very large Jewish population, you know." Her mother, she thought lately, was becoming a character.

To her right, Caitlin Green's husband—yet another pale, skinny man, with slitted brown eyes and black hair sticking up in messy, greasy spears—was feverishly explaining the object of some foundation he worked for or with or maybe had started himself (she knew she'd heard about it from Lil but couldn't recall the specifics). He wore an oversized sweatshirt, the hood pulled up over his head, though the loft was quite warm. "There are all these kids who inherit money, you see," he said now to the people assembled around him. Then he caught her eye and smiled. "Trust funds, stocks, property, huge companies, whatever. And they don't know what to do with it. They don't come from a culture of philanthropy. Their parents are these conservative fucks. So they inherit these portfolios with all these completely felonious investments: De Beers, Nike, McDonald's, the Gap, Marriott. We show them how they can take that money and reinvest it in environmentally conscious, nonracist companies with safe and fair business practices. But mostly we show them how to responsibly give it all away."

"Why should they give it all away?" asked a small woman with streaky blonde bangs and penciled-in brows, who Sadie realized was Taylor—the groupie who'd caught the bouquet at Lil's wedding. "It's their money," said Taylor defensively, as though the man were threatening to take away her own fortune. "I don't get it."

"Why should they keep it?" asked Caitlin Green's husband, as Sadie struggled to think of his name. "So they can buy yachts and Gucci bags? So they can widen the gap between the rich and the poor that's *destroying this country*? Why not start a foundation? Or do something cool with it?"

"Are there *really* that many people inheriting millions of dollars?" asked Taylor.

"More than you'd think. I bet you know tons of people who have independent incomes, but you just don't realize it, because they don't flaunt it. Half the artists in Williamsburg—*more* than half—have trust funds. Painting is expensive. The studio space. The supplies."

"Really?" asked Taylor. "Like who? Who has a trust fund? People here? Like Lil?"

"Like her." He jerked his thumb at Sadie, who froze, her mouth automatically forming a polite smile. "She works in publishing, right, but the interest from her trust really pays the rent. No one can actually live on an editorial assistant's salary. Anyone who works in publishing for more than a year has an independent income."

Sadie's face went hot. She tucked her hair behind her ears and tried to avoid the gaze of the small crowd that was now appraising her, scrutinizing her person for signs of immense wealth. Seeing the look on Sadie's face, he grinned. "There's nothing to be embarrassed about. I'm the same as you. You just gotta start giving it away."

"If I gave it away," said Sadie tightly, "I'd have nothing to live on."

Lil, she thought. *What is* wrong *with her?* Why had she ever told her—how did Lil get such things out of a person?—that the interest from her trust "really paid the rent." Meaning, of course, that her salary was tiny and were it not for her small trust, she would have had to either move back home (which was *not* a possibility) or find a different sort of job (working at her dad's hedge fund? My God) or simply never spend any money at all on anything but rent and food, which was impossible, as Lil knew all too well, for without certain strategic checks from Lil's father and Tuck's mother, Sadie knew, she and Tuck would have long been out of this loft. But that sort of help, presumably, wasn't worth mentioning to Caitlin's husband. No, of course not. What Lil, surely, didn't realize—because why would Sadie tell her the banal details?—was that in Sadie's first year, as an assistant, she'd made just $300 per week, after taxes. The rent on her little, unremarkable apartment was $750/month—more than half her salary—and it was one of the cheapest things she could find at the time (though Emily had lucked into that place in Williamsburg for $550, abandoned by a boyfriend, but she had no kitchen sink and the landlord had almost killed her).

Caitlin's husband had departed, thankfully, and been replaced by a troupe of sideburned men in black, chunky glasses discussing a new restaurant on Clinton Street. "The menu is market-driven," said one. *Market-driven,* she thought, *is an* economic *term.* Sighing heavily, she wiggled her toes in her sandals, and pulled a cigarette from a bowl on Lil's little end table, and lit it with a kitchen match. She only smoked in desperate social situations, which this seemed to be turning into. Without Tal, she felt strangely lost, and she'd been waiting for Beth for quite some time now. The band was testing their amps or whatever, which meant it had to be getting late. "Check, check," echoed through the room, followed by a long squawk. The guests, as one, put their hands to their ears and folded their heads into their necks, like turtles. *Time to go,* thought Sadie, and began picking her way to the back of the loft, where she found Beth half crushed against the bedroom door, a panicked expression wrinkling her round face.

"My bags are in there," she whispered.

Sadie looked at her uncomprehendingly. "Is the door locked?" she asked.

Beth shook her head and pointed at the door. "Listen," she said, and Sadie held her ear to the door, feeling, really, a bit ridiculous.

"I don't hear anything," she said.

"They must have just stopped," Beth said, shrugging. "There are people in there. Arguing."

"Are you serious?" asked Sadie, rolling her eyes. Sadie herself never brought a bag to parties, in part to avoid situations like these. She carried money and a MetroCard in the pocket of her dress. On the train over she'd read a manuscript, which she'd stowed on the bookshelf above the couch. "Let's just go in." She was beginning to feel queasy with drink— and, she supposed, cigarette—and almost desperate for food. Perhaps, she thought, they should go somewhere closer than Bean. That Thai place on Metropolitan. Or the old red sauce joint over on Devoe.

But Beth gave her a pleading look. "I feel weird."

"Okay," sighed Sadie, dropping her cigarette into a beer can. "I'll go in. Is it your black bag? With the scalloped edge?"

Beth nodded. "And two shopping bags. One from Daffy's. One from, um, Barneys." Sadie raised her eyebrows.

"Barneys? What did you get at Barney's?"

Beth flushed. "Nothing," she said. "I'll tell you after. Something for the wedding."

The wedding? thought Sadie. *They've been engaged for like five minutes.*

"All right," she told Beth, in a more gentle tone. "I'll be right back."

She opened the door a crack, stuck her face in, and glanced around. The room was lit only by rows of candles in long glass jars, which lined the room's two window ledges, a beautiful effect, really. On the floor lay a jumble of belongings: messenger bags, paperback books, thin summer sweaters, large leather satchels propped up against the baseboard, spilling books, lipsticks, pens and pencils, errant tissues made ghostly in the flickering light. In the far corner, she spotted Beth's bag, its lacy edges outlined against the white wall. Closing the door behind her, she made her way across the room, grabbed the thing and its companions, then headed back out. Midway through the room, she saw them—the lovers or fighters or whoever they were—out of the corner of her eye. They were staring at her, frozen, backed up against the closet doors on the other side of the room, liked trapped animals. Slowly the faces swam into focus: a woman with wide, sleep-starved eyes and long dark hair. Caitlin Green and her awful husband. Of course, Sadie thought sourly, they're just the sort of people to take over a room at a party, without regard for anyone else's needs, and cause some sort of scene. She nodded in their direction, then turned her eyes back to the door. The hesitant glow of the candles suited Caitlin's husband. He looked almost handsome, his hair mussed and falling over his face, the bones and hollows of his cheeks exaggerated by shadows, the sweatshirt no longer hiding his chest, which appeared broader without the heavy folds of cloth covering it. Sadie felt vaguely disappointed. How could a normal man have married the odious Caitlin Green?

"Mission accomplished," she told Beth, grinning, when she emerged into the brightness of the loft's main room.

"Oh my God, thank you," said Beth, with an embarrassed smile. "I was thinking I should just leave it and pick it up tomorrow, but my keys are in there."

"Let's go find Lil and make our excuses," said Sadie. "I'm starving."

"Where's Emily?" Beth shouted as they made their way back through the throng, which was growing by the minute. "Do you think she wants to come along?" But the crowd was so thick now they could barely make their way through it. These were strangers, surely, Sadie thought, for they were treating the loft as if it were a club: throwing cigarettes and beer bottles on the floor, saying "Where's the booze in this place?" and "Whose crib is this?" Sadie grabbed Beth's hand, so as not to lose her, for she could see Lil now, toward the front of the loft, sitting on the back of a sofa, blowing cigarette smoke through the bars of the front window— but she was blocked on all sides by the broad, T-shirted backs of sweaty men, laughing and gesticulating. "Excuse me," Sadie said ineffectually. Behind her Beth murmured, "I hate this."

And then, like a gift, a hand reached out from her left and pulled her through the wall of men. "Hey, hey, Sophie," called the voice attached to the hand. And she turned, uncomfortably, to face it. "Sophie, hey." She found herself peering into a pair of bloodshot eyes, framed by the black hood of a zip-up sweatshirt. Caitlin's husband, holding a cigar—no, no, a giant joint, which he would probably call a "spliff"—in the hand not attached to her arm. Sadie's mind raced. She whipped her head around so as not to lose sight of Beth.

"*Sadie*," she said, her throat closing in on her. She did not want to speak to this person. "I'm afraid my name is Sadie."

"Right, sorry," the man said. "We haven't been introduced, really. I'm Rob."

"It's a pleasure to meet you, Rob," she recited, by rote, shaking his hand.

"Listen, I'm sorry about before," he said. "I hope I didn't embarrass you." She laughed forcibly.

"Oh, please, don't worry at all. It's fine. Very nice to meet you." She gave him a little nod—what Emily called her "bow"—and turned to catch up with Beth. How had that man, the husband, managed to get to the middle of the room before she did? *Because he's a weasel,* she thought. *He tunneled his way out.*

Eventually, she emerged by the loft's front door, where Beth was shaking hands with Tom Satville—she had found another route out, clearly—who smiled at her with a familiarly odious mixture of condescension and attraction. "Hello, again," she said, smiling in a forbidding way, so as to preclude any further conversation. "Lil, it's time for us to make our excuses. This was *lovely.*"

"It was," said Beth.

"You're going to miss the band," cried Lil. "They're so good."

"Next time," said Sadie, hugging Lil.

As she and Beth stepped outside into the cooler air, Sadie remembered. "Shoot," she said. "My manuscript. I left it on the bookshelf. I'll just run in and get it."

"I'll wait here," said Beth. "I can't go back in there." Sadie skipped in, waving at friends and acquaintances, as she pushed her way through them. "You're back," said Lil, with a tired smile. She was nestled in the corner of the couch by the window, alone, her feet tucked under her, like a little girl.

"I forgot my manuscript." Sadie slipped off her sandals, stepped onto the couch, and reached her hand up on top of the tall bookshelf. From her perch, she saw the whole party—like a tableau—the swelling crowd, the little clusters of like-minded sorts within it, girls in bright dresses, their bare arms shimmering. Men bobbing their heads and laughing, handsome, their faces arranged in expressions of intelligence and concern. Their clothing was meant to be ironic—large-collared button-downs from the

1970s, slogan-splattered T-shirts from the 1980s—as though they were holding on to some bits of their childhood as armor against the brash and brutal era in which they'd become adults. The girls, too, wore puff-skirted dresses from the 1950s and 1960s. She felt an urge to draw some sort of attention to herself, to grab one of the glasses that littered the bookshelves and clink it, telling everyone here to . . . what? "Check, check," came at her again, a deep baritone from the back of the loft. She looked over at the band and saw, some feet to their left, the door to the bedroom open. Out of it came a thin, dark-haired girl—Caitlin Green—and a moment later, a dark-haired man. The man's hair was shot through with gray. Tuck Hayes. No, Sadie corrected herself, Tuck *Roth*-Hayes.

six

As a child, Sadie Peregrine hated Sunday afternoons, that languorous period when she was meant to start her homework—the homework she'd been avoiding all weekend—and when she began thinking about the tortures of the week that lay ahead. She much preferred Saturdays, at home with her quiet parents, going to matinees, eating Chinese food, or even Sunday *mornings,* when the entire Peregrine clan—her "immediate extended family," as she thought of it—gathered around her parents' table for breakfast. The best part though, was the early morning, before anyone arrived, when her mother slept in and she and her father had the house to themselves, to read the funny pages aloud and eat contraband doughnuts, before running out to the appetizing store on Lex for sable, whitefish, lox, cream cheese, bialys, bagels, and a half loaf of the thin-sliced black bread favored by Sadie's grandmother, who lived alone in a sprawling apartment off Fifth, tended to by a silent maid named Gretchen, though for as long as Sadie could remember there'd been talk of moving her into the Hebrew Home in Riverdale, if only they could get the lady to agree, which didn't seem likely. ("To the *Bronx,*" she rasped whenever confronted with this idea. "You want me to live in the *Bronx*? With *old people*?")

They would arrive home, lugging brown sacks, and Sadie's father would put on a pot of coffee—even then, the smell was delicious to her—and bring a cup up to Rose, along with the paper, then return to the kitchen, where he and Sadie would slice tomatoes and onions, wrap the bagels in foil, place them in the oven to warm, and set the dining room table with delicate, gold-rimmed china and thick, white cotton napkins. Sunday was Rose Peregrine's day off. She emerged from the bedroom just before the first cousins arrived, clad in her weekend costume of wide-legged wool trousers and a dark cashmere sweater (winter), or wide-legged linen trousers and a pale silk sweater (summer). At exactly eleven, Peregrine after Peregrine arrived, interrupted by the occasional Gold-schlag—usually, Sadie's aunt Minnie, a stout, white-haired woman, her pale, watery eyes magnified by thick-rimmed glasses—come up from the depths of the Lower East Side, a neighborhood feared by the Peregrines, most of whom lived within blocks of Sadie's parents (though in recent years a few had defected to the West Side and even, like Sadie, Brooklyn).

For a few hours, while her family ate and argued, Sadie could forget that the following day she'd be thrust into that den of snakes known as school, where the grown-ups loved her and the children hated her. But the moment the last Peregrine departed—inevitably, her bachelor cousin Bruce, who never had anywhere else to be and was a little in love with Rose—she settled into a funk, sick with anxiety.

Now that she was grown, Sadie rarely managed to get uptown early enough to do the shopping with her father, but she never missed break-fast itself, even when she was out late the previous night, and the mere act of getting out of bed seemed as monumental a task as *flying* up to East Ninety-third Street on the strength of her own arms. Likewise, she still dreaded Sunday afternoons. For she had wound up in a career that car-ried its own form of homework: the reading of manuscripts, on which she was always, terminally, behind, despite her being—sometimes she thought this her only skill—a pretty quick reader. In the midafternoon, feeling full and sleepy and thirsty (and sometimes drunk), she kissed her parents good-bye and headed home to read the latest coming-of-age tale—for that is what they all were, lately, and all of them set in the Mid-west—or memoir of addiction.

Except often the city got the best of her. On sunny days, she might find herself walking down Madison and browsing in the overpriced, awful shops or strolling through the park, eyeing the dogs in the dog run and the families lolling about in the grass. Or her father might suggest a matinee and, well, she had so little time with him lately, how could she refuse? Rainy days, she often wound up at the Met, sitting in an obscure corner and watching the passersby study Chinese pottery or medieval armor or the enormous, frightening canoes of the Pacific Islands, with those grim ancestral faces carved into their prows. Night would fall, all too quickly, and Sadie would hurry home, order a pizza or Chinese, put on her pajamas, and sit on the couch, surrounded by rubber-banded man-uscripts, which seemed, in her absence, to have reproduced themselves, like rabbits. But then, at nine, she'd think *Masterpiece Theatre*—which she and her parents had always watched together, her mother driving her mad with questions ("Is that her fiancé or her brother?")—and turn on her small television, with its clothes-hanger antennae. Or Tal would call and say "Can I come over?" and of course she would say yes.

Come Monday morning, she'd have nothing read. Though the fact of the matter was Delores didn't really care these days. She was in her sixties, a holdover from publishing's slightly less tarnished age, when independent firms, the Knopfs and such, put out serious books and editors didn't need to seek approval on titles from marketing departments or regional salespeople. Her voice could be heard three offices down, and she dressed in peculiar flowing garments—some invented hybrid of hostess dress, tunic, and caftan—and enormous pendants built around monstrous, irregularly shaped pearls that bubbled and flared in a volcanic manner and left pink indentations in her pale, lined neck.

Forty-odd years earlier, when Delores had found herself a job in the typing pool, their firm was a largish literary house, with a host of well-reviewed and popular authors, and a Boston office devoted to books on subjects political and texts for college classes. A sharp-witted, chain-smoking Vassar grad, she'd climbed quickly to the top of the editorial heap, and, in the 1960s, discovered a group of popular and controversial neorealists, heirs to Dreiser's earnest throne, one of whom became her lover. All this Sadie discovered during her first year with Delores, who went to lunch, two or three times a week, with agents or authors (really: old friends) and returned to the office soused (or, at the very least, *relaxed*) and wanting to chat. These lunches were, like Delores, a relic of the company's grand and glorious independent past. A year before Sadie arrived in Delores's outer office, they'd been gobbled up by a British conglomerate (albeit willingly: the company was bankrupt) and forced to move from their book-lined Union Square offices—rooms in which many of the century's greatest writers had fretted over galleys—to the media giant's putty-colored midtown headquarters. ("On the *West Side*," Delores complained—a refrain not unfamiliar to the daughter of Rose Peregrine. "I wouldn't mind so much if we were, at least, on the *East Side*, where things are civilized.") Now Delores held court in a boxy room, with wide Venetian blinds and black halogen lamps. She'd tried to bring her old desk—a beautiful oak thing, with grapes carved along the legs—but the corporation wouldn't have it. No one, they told her, could bring in outside furnishings. Not plants, not lamps, and certainly not desks.

Not surprisingly, Delores—who wore her *cedre* hair in an archaic puff and covered her watery green eyes with saucer-sized lenses of 1970s vintage—was unhappy with her new digs, despite having successfully dismantled the smoke alarm in her office with a mother-of-pearl-handled letter opener, and converted one of her stainless steel file drawers into a makeshift bar. Over the four years of Sadie's employment, Delores began coming into work later and later, swaddled in her enormous whiskey mink, and departing earlier and earlier.

In Sadie's first year, when she'd still been a little nervous around the lady, Delores had greedily insisted on reading most of the submitted manuscripts herself, staying home Fridays to do so, like many editors, and, though she no longer did any serious editing of the few books she took on ("What's the point? It's all crap"), she refused to allow Sadie to try her hand at it. But gradually, the tide had turned, so that now Sadie not only did *all* the reading and editing (drafting letters to authors, in which she outlined changes, which Delores merely signed without so much as glancing at them), but also handled most of the purchasing of manuscripts. It worked like this: A manuscript came in from an agent. Sadie unwrapped it and placed it on Delores's desk. An hour or a day later the manuscript turned up on Sadie's desk, a Post-it note stuck to its top, saying "Looks interesting. Pls. read" in Delores's slanting scrawl. Sadie read the thing—sometimes that night, sometimes weeks later, depending on the urgency surrounding the manuscript in question—and wrote up a report for Delores, leaving manuscript and report on the woman's desk. An hour or a day later, the thing, once again, landed back on Sadie's desk, with another Post-it, saying either "I agree. Terrible. Pls. call Liza and say 'pass.'" or "Yes!!!! Spend up to 50K. Tlk. to Val if nd. more." Sadie would then call the agent, make an offer, and complete the negotiations. Once the book was bought, it was she who went through it, line by line, and it was she who asked the writers in for coffee or lunch, passing off her edits as Delores's own.

The authors, Sadie suspected, understood exactly what was going on. And so, she thought, did the other editors. Every year she received a decent raise and Val often stopped her in the hallway and said, "Hey, great work on such and such." And now, of course, there was this business with Tuck's book and her allegedly imminent promotion, which Delores hopefully wouldn't sabotage in order to keep Sadie permanently installed in her outer office. Delores was prone to fits—temper tantrums of tornadolike proportions—during which she picked on Sadie's every alleged mistake: the time Sadie accidentally sent a manuscript back to the wrong agent or the time she had the flu and didn't read a particular novel in time for Delores to bid on it, and the book—wouldn't you know?—stayed on the bestseller list for two years.

Thus, in the weeks before her promotion was announced—before she at last moved her things quietly out of Delores's court and trained some poor new girl to take her place—she vowed to avoid even the tiniest error. She would read every manuscript carefully and quickly, as soon as they came in, just in case Delores snapped back to life.

And so it was, that the Sunday after Lil's party Sadie woke filled with determination. This particular Sunday—of all Sundays—she would simply run uptown, say hello, grab a bagel, and head back home to read. She would tell Tal that he could come over late or the following day, though she'd been aching for him since the previous night, after he'd run off with Dave without even kissing her good-bye. She'd have an hour on the train, each way, which would be good reading time, and then most of the afternoon and evening (*No PBS,* she told herself sternly). She would not fall prey to her mother's protestations—"Sadie, you haven't seen my new tablecloth!" "Sadie, tell me what you think about this dress," "Sadie, I don't want any leftovers, eat another chub"—nor would she drink any wine, even if her cousin Bruce brought something nice. She was tired enough from the party, or, really, from dinner with Beth. They'd talked for hours, parting with a long hug and a promise to do the same again soon, and Sadie had left convinced that Will Chase was all right, that she would love him, as Beth did. She hated that Beth had felt Sadie needed convincing. Why had she said all that about Will months back? Beth would always think Sadie skeptical of her marriage.

And she *would,* she thought, lying in bed, willing herself to get up and into the shower, she *would* give him a chance, so as not to let some strange distance develop between herself and Beth, as it had between her and Lil—though they wouldn't admit it—because she had never quite warmed to Tuck, though there was, of course, still time. Then, like a shot, her head cleared and the party unfolded before her. *Tuck.* Why *should* she warm to Tuck when he had spent a whole evening—a party thrown for him by his wife, to celebrate his success, which Sadie herself had orchestrated—hidden away in his own bedroom with Caitlin Green, of all people. Was Tuck having an affair with Caitlin Green? No, it didn't seem possible. Caitlin was just so awful. No. No. People just didn't *do* things like that anymore. They were too busy checking their email or what have you. She glanced at the clock. Nine o'clock. If she got out of the house in half an hour, she'd have time to walk by that optician's shop at Eighty-first and Lex and see if it was open for a couple of hours on Sunday, like it used to be. The ache behind her eyes was worse.

Just then the phone rang, and Sadie, without thinking, answered, expecting to hear Tal's voice, or perhaps her mother's, on the line. She found, instead, Caitlin Green. "Sadie?" she said, in an odd, muffled voice. "I need you to come meet me this morning."

Oh, you do, thought Sadie. "Um, I'm afraid I have plans this morning," she said, tucking the phone between her shoulder and her ear, and padding to the kitchen. *And you're the last person I'd break them for.*

"Look, we need to talk," insisted Caitlin, in tones verging on a whine.

"About what?" said Sadie, with a dismayed sigh. If Caitlin was calling her, then nothing good could have happened in that bedroom the previous night.

"You *know,*" said Caitlin. "Listen, I only have a minute. Rob just went to get the paper. Could you come over this morning?"

Sadie quickly calculated that she could leave her parents by one-ish, spend an hour with Caitlin—an *hour* with Caitlin!—and be home by three-thirty. But maybe it would be better to just get it out of the way, then try to make it up to her parents for the end of breakfast.

"Fine," she said, sighing. "I'll meet you at Oznot's in an hour."

"No," said Caitlin. *No?* thought Sadie. *I'm doing what you want!* "Just come here. I don't want anyone to hear us talking."

"Fine," said Sadie, and scribbled down the address in her planner. With dread, she called her parents and told them—they were quite put out—that she'd probably have to miss breakfast. An hour later, she pushed open the door to Caitlin's building, a lobby-less tenement, its floor and stairs covered in split linoleum, patterned to resemble bricks and mortar, curling away at the walls' edges. The air inside this little passageway smelled of oil and cabbage. Sadie, sweat pricking at her underarms, began a slow ascent to the fourth floor.

With much clanking and clacking of locks, Caitlin opened the metal door to the apartment and propped it with her foot. A large black dog with a diamond-shaped head and small piggy eyes snuffled asthmatically at her bare feet, its muscular tail thwacking loudly on some unseen object. Caitlin's toenails were painted a flat metallic blue, the polish flaking slightly at the rims. Such colors—blue, green, smoke gray—were popular that year, but Sadie thought they looked like mold. "Hi," Caitlin said. "Come in. Do you want a cup of coffee? I'm just making some." Sadie squeezed past Caitlin, stepping awkwardly over the hound and into the apartment. "Sure," said Sadie, looking around her, as Caitlin repeated the loud rigmarole with the locks and chains.

The front door led into a nice-sized kitchen, with the sort of flimsy, off-brand stove and fridge you saw in every rental in the city, a gleaming new butcher-block counter, and a few shiny wire shelves screwed into the wall above it. A Soviet propaganda poster hung gloomily above the kitchen table, which appeared to be another piece of butcher block, with legs—of unfinished, jaundiced pine—nailed into its corners. On this table and on the wire shelves sat bottles and bottles of vitamins and herbal tonics, outlines of large capsules just visible behind the amber glass. The shelves also held dozens of boxes of soy milk in different flavors, and cloudy plastic bags of rice and beans. In a far corner, three tall paper canisters of something—Sadie stepped closer to make out the words—called "Spiru-tein." The sort of stuff, Sadie thought, that athletes take to enhance their performances. But Caitlin, with her dark circles and her pallor, didn't quite look the athlete, and a pack of American Spirits sat on the table. The dog came over and shoved his head between Sadie's knees. She reached down and petted the creature, running her hand along its short, coarse fur. "What's his name?" asked Sadie.

"Mumia," Caitlin told her, fiddling with the coffee machine, a German drip.

"Mumia?" Sadie repeated.

"Yeah, you know, Mumia Abu-Jamal?"

"Yes," Sadie said. "I know." She seated herself at the kitchen table, though Caitlin seemed dead intent on letting her stand for the entirety of their interview.

"He was a stray," Caitlin explained. *Of course he was,* thought Sadie acidly, though she herself was against purchasing pets, when there were thousands of unwanted ones in the city's shelters. "We found him tied up under the bridge, *completely* covered in blood, and brought him home."

"But he's okay?" asked Sadie, inspecting the dog, who was sweet, sweeter than he looked, for scars.

"He's fine. But he infested the place with fleas."

Sadie immediately withdrew her hand from the dog, who let out a long whimper and settled, heavily, by her feet. "*Really,*" she said.

"Don't worry," Caitlin told her. "We bombed. There are still some in the bed—they like warm places—but the rest of the house is clean."

"Oh, good," said Sadie.

"He's a great dog," Caitlin continued. "He's in love with the little Chihuahua downstairs. Did you see her?" Sadie shook her head. "Mrs. Jimenez brought her up from Puebla. She was quarantined for, like, three months. Did you meet them when you came in?" Before Sadie could answer, she went on, "They're the nicest family. A mother and father, and eight daughters . . ." Breathlessly—while Sadie irritably wondered whether or not the coffee machine was actually brewing coffee, for it was ominously silent—Caitlin proceeded to provide a comprehensive history of the building's inhabitants, their ailments and financial problems, and the various ways in which Caitlin and Rob had helped them out at one time or another. The third floor housed a Chinese family. The first had, until recently, been the home of a second Mexican family. But this clan had mysteriously—to Caitlin's mind—moved out. Caitlin and Rob suspected the landlord of reporting the family, all here illegally, to the Immigration and Naturalization Service, in order to have them deported, thus leaving the apartment empty and allowing him to rent it for three times the price. Last week he had finished remodeling it and yesterday the new tenants had moved in. "Some hipsters," Caitlin scoffed.

Just two years earlier, this specific section of Williamsburg (east of Bedford, but west of the BQE) had offered deliriously cheap rents: rundown apartments for $300 or $400 per month, nicer ones for $700 or $800. Now, Caitlin said—as if Sadie wasn't aware of this—the area was being gentrified at warp speed. Developers had broken ground on two new apartment complexes, one two doors down, on the site of an old chicken processing plant, the other a block or so down Havemeyer Street, next to Will Chase's building (or, really, Will and *Beth's* building, since Beth had pretty much moved in), which was itself a fairly new structure, home to white professionals. The Latino families—most from Puebla, some from the Dominican Republic—who had occupied the area in recent decades were being pushed out. Landlords who hadn't replaced a sink or stove in years were now hiring laborers—the same Mexicans, Caitlin said, who were being pushed out of their homes—and putting granite counters and steel appliances into the old railroad flats and charging $1,800 for them.

"And how long have you lived here?" asked Sadie, glancing at the gleaming butcher-block counter.

Caitlin paused and wrinkled her brow before responding. "Since last June, so about a year. Which makes us old-timers in the neighborhood." Caitlin gave Sadie a meaningful look. "The place is filled with trust-fund kids who moved here, like, a week ago. All the old Italian ladies are being forced out. It makes me so sad."

In the years since graduating, Caitlin had acquired the raspy, cigarette-tinged voice of a fifty-year-old alcoholic. It was hard to believe that in her early, enthusiastic college days, she'd sung with Nothing But Treble, an all-female a cappella group that wandered around campus, subjecting passersby to high-pitched renditions of Edie Brickell and Suzanne Vega songs. Before long, though, Caitlin had fallen under the spell of Hortense James, the English department's lone radical feminist, and made herself over in her idol's image, lopping her hair into a severe bob, and donning men's shirts and work boots with her long skirts. She stopped singing (too frivolous, presumably), dropped her boyfriend—a short, hirsute person who had no compunctions about publicly displaying his affection for her—and announced that she was bisexual. But the queer contingent on campus—whose circles overlapped with Sadie's—had regarded Caitlin with suspicion, and she generally could be found with the little group of strange, sad-eyed girls she'd gathered together as comrades, presumably because none of them fit into any of the campus's larger social circles. They were timid or angry persons, all underweight or overweight, with out-of-date eyeglass frames and odd nicknames like Kitten or Poodle or Candy and real names that seemed more suited to those in middle age, like Judith or Peggy or Trish. If they took acting classes, they did scenes from *The Glass Menagerie* or *Our Town*. If they took creative writing classes, they turned in stories about old ladies in small Southern towns making horehound candy (famously, the one called "Poodle," had inspired George Wadsworth, Sadie's mentor, to say, "The first sentence of a short story should convey an emotion. *Cute* is not an emotion"). They sat in the nonsmoking section of the snack bar, drank hot chocolate, studied on the library's second floor, among piles of brightly colored cushions and "womb" chairs, attended "Early Eighties Night" at the Disco, obtained their meals from the campus's stale dining halls, and, come weekends, ate pizza at Lombardi's, which served fluffy, buttery pies reminiscent of those available at Pizza Hut. Sadie and *her* friends sat in the smoking section of the snack bar (even if they didn't smoke), drank coffee, studied in the library's basement lounges or in private scholar studies on the third-floor gallery, brought their mentors to the Disco on Friday afternoon for "professor beer," ate their meals at co-ops, and ordered stromboli from Uncle John's, a Chicago-style hole-in-the-wall staffed by aging punks.

"Coffee'll be ready in a sec," said Caitlin, placing a pastel box of soy milk on the table. "We're vegan," she announced. Sadie, of course, had heard all about Caitlin's eating habits from Lil, who thought Caitlin and Rob were pathological about food. Caitlin sat down in the chair next to Sadie, perhaps a little too close.

"Wow. Vegan," said Sadie. *When,* she wondered, *is she going to come to the point?* The coffee machine began to sputter, thankfully, and Caitlin jumped up and grabbed two brown, earthenware mugs from an open rack by the room's lone window.

"You know, meat stays in the colon for up to a week," Caitlin was saying. "It's disgusting, when you think about it, and it explains why you feel so *heavy* after you eat a steak. Here's coffee." She placed a mug in front of Sadie. "Sorry I don't have any sugar. We're trying not to eat it, at all. It's addictive, you know."

Unlike coffee, thought Sadie, taking a sip. It was weak and sour, but she said "Thanks" and poured in some soy milk, which rose to the top in mealy chunks.

"Listen, Caitlin," she began, interrupting an explanation of different types of intestinal flora.

"I know, I know," Caitlin broke in. "Lil's your friend, I'm not. You're on her side." She glanced petulantly at Sadie. "I know you never liked me." *Oh, let's not do this,* thought Sadie. "None of you did," Caitlin continued, staring intently at Sadie over the rim of her mug. "I was too political for you. Too radical. I made you uncomfortable." Sadie struggled not to laugh. Caitlin seemed to believe that reading bell hooks made her a radical.

"Not really," she said, taking a tentative sip of coffee, which the soy milk had done little to improve. "That's kind of . . . extreme, isn't it? I—we—maybe didn't agree with you about everything, but we weren't apolitical."

"Yeah, well, you weren't out protesting the Gulf War either."

"You're wrong," Sadie retorted, a bit too sharply. "Emily, Lil, Dave, and Tal all went to the Washington march. And Beth didn't go because she was glued to the television. She had friends in Israel. She was obviously worried about them." She paused and took a breath. Why was she defending herself when she'd done nothing wrong? Caitlin pursed her lips and nodded her head.

"*Israel,*" she spat. "Of course she was worried about her friends in *Israel.*"

"What's your point?" asked Sadie, then thought better of it. "You know, forget it. The point is—"

The dog raised himself creakily to his feet and began licking Sadie's bare knee with a warm tongue.

"Mumia," shouted Caitlin. "No!" The dog lay down, with another whimper, and placed his head atop his paws. "Sorry," she told Sadie, "he's not really trained."

"Um, that's okay," said Sadie, reaching down to stroke the poor beast's head. She was beginning to feel she had slipped down the rabbit hole. "Listen, Caitlin," she began, again, "this was ages ago. You and Lil are friends now. Why rehash this?"

"Because," Caitlin said slowly, in her careful way. Sadie was now beginning to wonder if she had, indeed, rehearsed all this. "You made me feel terrible about myself. *By existing?* Sadie thought. What had she ever done to this girl? It was true, though, she'd always felt the peculiar heat of Caitlin's resentment, from the first time they'd met, as freshmen in a low-level English class. Each time Sadie spoke in discussion, Caitlin made a self-conscious little noise—a "hrumph" or a "huh"—as though she couldn't believe Sadie was passing off such bullshit as insight and she wanted the class to know that *she,* Caitlin Green, wasn't buying it.

"I'm sorry," said Sadie flatly. "I didn't mean to hurt your feelings—"

"Right, right, right. Because you just didn't think about me at all." Sadie flushed. This was true. But she'd rather Caitlin speak honestly, she thought, than make these grand statements about politics.

"Caitlin—" Sadie began, but the girl cut her off, thrusting her pointy little chin forward.

"No, no," she said, her voice rising, "I thought about *you* all the time. I was so jealous of you. It's funny, right?"

Sadie flushed again, her face—she knew—turning from pink to red. "That's insane," she said, in a voice that was harder than she liked, because she, curiously, had lost all sympathy for Caitlin—which made her realize that she'd actually *had* sympathy for her when the conversation started. "Why would you be jealous of me—of us?"

"Because everything was easy for you. And you had everything: men following you around, the right clothes, the right vocabulary." *Oh, please,* thought Sadie. Caitlin's parents, she knew, were academics of one sort or another. There was nothing wrong with her vocabulary. She was trying to flatter Sadie into friendship, to guilt or shame her into, as she'd said, being "on her side" rather than Lil's. But then she was a bit flattered, wasn't she? How could she not be, she who'd been friendless as a kid? Sadie had not thought herself "popular" or "cool" in college—and she had pretended that Oberlin society was immune to such classifications—but there was something thrilling, wasn't there, about the possibility that she *had* been part of some coveted elite? And there was something shaming about finding this possibility thrilling. All of which, she realized, Caitlin knew. She frowned and pushed her coffee away.

"Why don't we go into the living room?" said Caitlin suddenly, as if she'd just remembered that such a room existed.

"Sure," said Sadie, and followed Caitlin and Mumia down a dark little corridor—past a sunny nook, in which a brand-new iMac sat on a built-in desk, and an alcove, of sorts, that held a double bed, covered with an Indian-print fabric—into a bright, pleasant room, with two large windows overlooking Metropolitan's little commercial strip: a bar, a Thai restaurant, a car service, an ancient hairdresser's shop, and a host of boarded-up storefronts. On one wall stood two tall glass-fronted bookcases filled with political and theoretical tracts: Marx and Engels and Guy Debord and Gramsci and Chomsky. On the opposite sat a large, blond-wood-framed futon, on which rested three enormous cats: one on each end of the seat and a third stretched along the top of the backrest. With their legs tucked under them, their breasts puffed out, and expressions of superiority etched on their round faces, they resembled giant pigeons.

"You're not allergic, are you?" Caitlin asked.

"No," said Sadie, seating herself between a tabby and an orange tom. "I love cats." The large rug below, she saw, was clogged with fur, a pale, fibrous layer thick enough to obscure the carpet's pattern. The dog settled down on it, oblivious to or uninterested in the cats, and Caitlin yawned, folding herself into a metal-framed leather side chair, reflexively pulling a cigarette out of a second crumpled pack, which lay on the chair's arm. The soles of her feet, Sadie saw, were gray with grime.

"*I'm* actually allergic. I get shots every week. And I have an inhaler." The girls looked at each other.

"So," said Caitlin, impotently flicking a small Bic lighter. Her cigarette was still unlit. "Tuck and I are in love."

Sadie hadn't realized she'd been holding her breath—but she had and now she was able to release it, though her heart began to beat faster with anxiety. This was not, of course, good news, but first of all, she doubted its truth, and second, she was relieved that they'd simply arrived at the point. Though Caitlin had not, Sadie noted, come out and said that she and Tuck were sleeping together. Was it possible that they weren't? No, Sadie thought, it wasn't.

"Oh," she said. "Really."

"Mmm-hmmm," said Caitlin. "I mean, Rob is *incredible*. He completely takes care of me. It's like, he even makes sure I take my *medication*. But he has this problem"—she leaned in toward Sadie, suggesting in her demeanor that she and Sadie were of like minds, that Sadie would surely understand what she was about to impart—"because he *worships* me, we can't have that kind of *animal,* rip-each-other's-clothes-off sex. Do you know what I mean?"

"I do," said Sadie, wondering if this was the truth or not. *Did* she? Or had she simply read about it? "And with Tuck—"

"It's *amazing,*" said Caitlin.

"Oh," said Sadie, idly petting the brown cat to her left. She could not, somehow, imagine Caitlin and Tuck in the throes of passion. Perhaps because she didn't want to, or perhaps because every gesture of Caitlin's was so calculated, so measured, that it was difficult to envision her giving herself over to anyone, and particularly not to moody Tuck. Why, why would Tuck do this? With Caitlin? *Lil,* Sadie thought reflexively, *is so much prettier.* She suddenly remembered that line from the end of *The Locusts Have No King,* when Dodo runs off with Larry. "Funny, how often it's the wife who's the good-looking one," the secretary says, or something like that.

"And Rob—" Sadie began, her tongue feeling thick and strange in her mouth.

"He knew I was a feminist when he married me," said Caitlin, impatiently waving a hand. "And he's a feminist, too. He *knows* that marriage is, by definition, a misogynist construct." *Then why did you get married?* thought Sadie. "I mean marriage, historically, is all about keeping 'woman' in a secondary role. Did you know that in traditional Jewish weddings vows the woman says—" Sadie tuned out. She'd heard all this before, as had anyone who'd gone to college in the past three decades. Caitlin's spin on it seemed to be that before birth control, marriage was a way of keeping a woman constant, while men could sleep with whomever they wanted. Now, of course, things were equal, and women could seek pleasure just as men did. "The thing is," said Caitlin, returning to the personal, "no one man is ever going to satisfy a woman. Women are too complicated. They need different men for different occasions."

"Isn't that kind of essentialist?" *Why am I even bothering?* thought Sadie. But before she could think better of it, she said, "And what occasions do you need Tuck for? Funerals? Gallery openings?" This was exactly what Caitlin wanted from her. Dramatic accusations.

"Sadie," Caitlin said. It was the first time, Sadie realized, that Caitlin had uttered her name. She hated the sound of it in Caitlin's mouth, as though the girl was claiming ownership of it, like those overstuffed, unsmiling cats had claimed the couch. "*Life,*" she said, pausing dramatically after this word. "Is. Complicated. You know what my friends and I used to call you in college?" Sadie's heart began to beat faster. It was rare, she'd found, for people to tell you what they truly thought of you, and she'd long ago left off caring. But now, somehow, she found herself anxious, and terrified, to hear what Caitlin had to say, even though she knew this was just another ploy—no more the truth than anything else.

"What?" she asked.

Caitlin smiled. She had been waiting, Sadie saw, for this moment. "Princess White Bread."

Sadie laughed, though she wasn't sure it was funny. "I'm Jewish," she said. "And my family tends toward pumpernickel."

Caitlin cocked her head patronizingly. "You'd never know it. It didn't bother you that Pound was a fascist." Junior year, Sadie remembered, they'd had Wadsworth's British Modernism together and Sadie, yes, had argued that great art transcends the politics and biography of the artist, that such details are parochial and irrelevant. In truth, she didn't care much for Pound. She found his poetry flimsy and pointless. She was more of an Eliot person, but to mention this was to raise the issue of Eliot's anti-Semitism, which she certainly didn't want to do.

"Yes, well," she said, with a smile. "You know, 'every woman adores a fascist.'"

"Funny," said Caitlin, though Sadie wasn't sure she got the reference. "That's actually a really dangerous statement, don't you think? Basically condoning violence against women, right? But I guess from your little white tower everything is a big joke. Life seems very simple and clean, right? But it's not." Her voice was growing shrill. "It's messy and dirty. Things happen. People have needs."

"*Caitlin,*" Sadie snapped, unconsciously falling into her mother's practiced society drawl. She was furious, suddenly, furious with Caitlin for getting a rise out of her, and furious with herself for falling prey to Caitlin's traps. "Is that *really* all sex is to you?" she asked, her heart racing now, adrenaline making her ears hum. "A need. Like scratching an itch. That's *depressing.*"

Caitlin shook her head and sucked in her lips—a carefully arranged look of deep sadness. "No." She smiled broadly, which had the strange effect of making her face appear genuinely sad. "I love him." Perhaps, Sadie thought, Caitlin did truly love Tuck. And why not? He was handsome—though Sadie didn't find him *attractive* per se—and smart. She couldn't quite explain why he irked her so. Sometimes she worried that the problem was hers, that *she* was the difficult one. Then, of course, she remembered why she was there and her sympathies disappeared.

"And I know he won't leave Lil. He loves her, he really does, but he feels like he's failed her, which makes him kind of hate her, you know?" Sadie wished that this was not true, but she feared that it was.

"And I hate to say it," Caitlin continued, "because I love Lil, but it's kind of her fault."

"Oh, *really*," said Sadie, her anger rising again.

"She just has such conventional ideas about marriage. She thinks Tuck isn't supposed to look at another woman, or find anyone else *in the world* attractive, which is just impossible. And she has this, like, Depression-era work ethic. She's totally hung up on productivity. She can never just relax. So, if he's lying on the couch, thinking, she gets furious with him. And he feels castrated. So he acts out, against her, to prove her wrong." She lit her cigarette now and sat back in her chair.

Sadie looked down at her lap and saw that she'd clenched her hands into fists—turning her knuckles yellow and grotesque. The cats stared at her, their yellow eyes still and knowing. Was there—there *was*—the faint smell of cat pee coming from the animals? Or, no, the couch itself. She shifted uncomfortably. There was nowhere else to sit, other than the floor. "So she knows," she said.

Caitlin shook her head, blowing thin trails of smoke through her nose. "No," she said. And for a moment, she appeared to study Sadie, deciding whether to continue. "You know, it's not just me," she said. "For a while, he had a thing with this waitress at a coffee shop by his office. I don't know if he actually did anything with her, but he used to go there, just to see her. And there was this woman he was seeing right before Lil, who he was totally in love with, but she had a boyfriend and wouldn't sleep with him. After he and Lil got married, she broke up with her boyfriend and started calling Tuck." She tapped her ash into her coffee mug. "Women love him."

Sadie considered this, unsure what to say. "You're right," she responded finally. "Life *is* complicated." Caitlin nodded enthusiastically. "But you"— she could feel the anger rising within her and struggled to tamp it down— "are *making* your own life more complicated than it needs to be. I just, I don't understand. Why did you marry Rob if you weren't going to be faithful to him? Why get married at all?"

Caitlin frowned. "I didn't think of it in those terms. Faithful or unfaithful. Those are bourgeois terms. I thought of it in terms of value. Utilitarianism, you know? Marrying me would make Rob really happy.

And it would make me happy, too. And I knew that no man would ever make me *completely* happy, so why not choose one who would make me mostly happy."

Money, Sadie thought suddenly. Rob was wealthy, wasn't he? *Very* wealthy, if his little speech the previous night was any indication: only the very rich spoke disparagingly of the compromised values of the somewhat rich. *Did she marry him for money?* she thought. *Did people do that anymore?* Rose's voice insinuated itself in her head: *Don't be stupid, Sadie. Of course people do that. All the time.*

"I guess I just thought that you would understand all this," said Caitlin, pouting in a manner that, in a different set of circumstances, might have been dubbed flirtatious. Sadie dropped her face into her moist hands. This was too, too much. She thought of her family, drinking dark, thick coffee from her mother's set of mismatched Limoges, of her old cat George, asleep on his tattered red pillow, waiting to be fed scraps of salmon and leftover cream. She should be there now.

"*Caitlin,*" she said, almost choking on the name, "the way I see it, if one is going to devote one's life to social justice—to challenging the status quo and trying to make the world a better place—one needs to start by living an ethical life. By being honest with oneself and trying not to hurt others." Sadie had not quite known that she thought this until she said it, and with a pang she wondered how honest she was with herself—and how many others she'd hurt, if only in small ways.

Caitlin compressed her full lips and nodded. "You think I'm hurting other people?" she said in a small voice that, too, sounded practiced.

Sadie suppressed a laugh. "Well, you're cheating on your husband. I'm assuming he doesn't know. Right?" Caitlin nodded. Suddenly Sadie had a terrible thought: she needed to tell Lil. It was her responsibility, wasn't it? She pushed this thought away.

"And Tuck isn't the first"—as she said this, she knew it to be true—"right?"

Caitlin nodded again.

"So you're cheating on your husband, first of all, with the husband of a person you allegedly *love.*"

Caitlin pursed her lips again. "Your logic only works," she said, "if you buy into the bourgeois approach to marriage, which is *positively medieval.*" A childish rage overtook Sadie. She feared she might burst into tears from frustration.

"What other approach to marriage *is* there?" she said, her voice cracking. "Marriage is *marriage*. It means pledging yourself to one person. If you don't believe in marriage, then you shouldn't have gotten married." She stood up, brushed the cat hair off her skirt—or tried to—and walked to the window. The sky, blue when she arrived, had clouded over. "You know, you're right. Tuck isn't going to leave Lil for you," she said, her voice low and threatening. "He's not."

"I know," said Caitlin coolly.

"Good," replied Sadie. She snatched a cigarette from Caitlin's pack and stuck it in her mouth. "Then stop seeing him. Just drop Lil and Tuck as friends. Move on."

"I can't. Our lives are intertwined. Rob and Tuck are really close. It would be unfair to Rob."

Sadie lit her cigarette. "He'll get over it. You're missing the point. You need to end this." Caitlin started to speak but Sadie raised her voice. "You, you need to listen to me. You need to stop justifying your actions with this political rhetoric. When you get down to brass tacks"—ah, there was Rose, creeping in again—"you're just an *ordinary* woman who's cheating on her husband and deceiving her friend. You're not some *renegade* subverting 'conventional ideas about marriage.' You're not *glamorous*. You're not Erica Jong—who's an idiot, anyway—or Germaine Greer or Simone de Beauvoir. You're not *empowering* yourself, you're *degrading* yourself. It's pathetic. You're *selfish*. You're just *selfish*." Caitlin's olive complexion paled and Sadie felt her skin grow even hotter. Her outburst sprung less out of fealty to Lil, she suspected, than general anger with Caitlin. This embarrassed her, this urge to reform Caitlin, who faintly repulsed her, with her unwashed feet and searching eyes. But there was something attractive about her, something that made Sadie want to help her, however slightly, even as she knew she was being played by her. The girl was clearly unhappy—miserable—caught in some pathetic *mythology* she'd devised for herself. A bit like Lil, Sadie supposed. "If you don't believe in marriage—or if Rob isn't right for you, if you don't love him enough, or *whatever*"—she hated this word, where had it come from?—"then get a divorce and be alone. Learn to take your own medication."

To Sadie's surprise, Caitlin nodded soberly. Her face had returned to its normal color. "You're right," she said. She took a third cigarette. *Smoking*, Sadie realized, *that's how she lost all that weight*. "I guess I read so much theory. I write so much about symbolic actions that I think about my life as a novel, kind of. Like in *Passing*, that Nella Larsen novel? Have you read that?" Sadie nodded. She had. She'd liked it, too.

"That's my period," said Caitlin. "The twenties and thirties. Harlem Renaissance. There are all these novels where the heroine liberates herself by smoking and drinking and having wild sex."

"What happens at the end?" she asked, though she knew the answer. The heroine of *Passing* throws herself out a window.

"Well." Caitlin laughed. "Usually she dies, actually. Society has no place for her."

"Does she get caught?" asked Sadie.

"Hmmm. I'm not sure. I've never thought about it."

I bet, thought Sadie. "The reason I ask is," she said mildly, "I guess I sometimes wonder if people have affairs in order to get caught." Caitlin stared up at her, rapt, her mouth open in a sort of O. "I mean, like last night. Why did you need to go off into the bedroom? Lil could have walked in."

"We had to talk," admitted Caitlin. "And Lil almost did walk in. It was a close call." She smiled. "We keep having them lately. Tuck says it's a sign that we need to stop." Sadie's cigarette had burned down and she had no place to put it. Spent, she sank back into the couch, breathing deeply of cat urine. The cigarette had made her head throb and she needed to use the bathroom. "Last week, we were on the couch, right there—" Caitlin pointed to the ginger cat, who had now gone to sleep, thrumming like a cricket. "Where Shiva's sitting. And we'd just had an argument, actually, about how we needed to stop . . . doing this . . . But then. Well, we can't be in the same room with each other without—"

"Yes, yes," said Sadie, waving her hand to fend off elaboration.

"All of a sudden, we hear these loud footsteps stomping up the stairs. At first, I was confused, because, you know, we're on the top floor. No one comes up here except us. But then it occurred to me that, you know, Rob's not the most popular guy. He has an FBI file like *this* thick." She held her fingers a few inches apart. "He's doing some stuff, like, really advance stuff for this huge thing in November. And his other big project right now, I can't really talk about it, but it's this big protest against one of the biggies."

"The biggies?"

"Top of the Fortune 500. More powerful than the government. Truly evil. Rob is organizing this whole thing with the Rainforest Action Network and the anarchist collective. Protests all over the country, with street theater and all sorts of stuff. They're going to, like, burn an effigy of the CEO."

"Wow," said Sadie, though this didn't sound particularly effective to her.

"So I'm thinking, this is the FBI or something, coming looking for Rob. I'd been half expecting it for a while. And then I start thinking, what if Rob is doing stuff that I don't know about. He's really into guerrilla tactics and he reads obsessively about the Weathermen and Abbie Hoffman and SLA and all that. Some of the people he works with are really hard-core ecowarrior types. They're like chaining themselves to trees and dismantling logging equipment and blowing up generators and all that. Anyway, we're, like, naked and there's this pounding at the door. And two seconds later these guys are shouting, 'Open up. This is the United States government.' You wouldn't believe it. I mean, it was *unbelievable*. And Tuck completely freaked out. He just pulled his . . . pulled himself together and ran into the bathroom. It was *unbelievable*."

Sadie could, rather easily, believe it. The scene unfurled in her mind in the manner Caitlin had suggested: like a movie. Tuck peering at his face in the bathroom mirror, clearing his head, so as to form a smile for the intruders, whoever they might be. Caitlin tumbling off the couch and pulling on a stained kimono, a few strands of hair rising from her head. She wondered how much Caitlin was embellishing.

"It really seemed like they were going to break down the door, but I put my robe on, finally, and opened it and this pig flashed me his badge and said—just like on *Law & Order*"—here Caitlin lowered her voice and approximated a Brooklyn accent—"'Agent Connelly.' *Irish!* How cliched is that? And then the other guy—there were two of them, in normal clothing, *suits*—whips out his badge and says, 'United States —'"

Sadie finished her sentence for her: "Immigration and Naturalization Service."

"Mmm-hmmm." Caitlin said. "How did you know?"

Sadie shrugged. "Just a hunch."

"They were here for the *family downstairs*. Mr. and Mrs. Jimenez. Can you believe it?" Shaking her head—the relief, apparently, was still vivid—she picked another cigarette out of the pack and contemplated it. "The weird thing is: Mr. and Mrs. Jimenez are legal. They have green cards."

"Strange," admitted Sadie. "Could they be fake?"

"Do you think?" asked Caitlin. "I suppose."

"So, what happened?" asked Sadie.

"Well, at first they thought I was Mrs. Jimenez. I mean I have dark hair and I'm kind of tan right now, so it's not *such* a stretch, I guess. I told them that I wasn't, of course, and explained that they had the wrong apartment, but then, as I was talking, I realized that I wasn't going to send these bastards to the Jimenezes' place, either, so they could take them all out to some INS prison—those places are just, like, hotbeds of human rights violations, you know—and ship them back to Mexico. So I said I didn't know of any Jimenez living in the building. And then they got very suspicious and asked to see my ID. I got my wallet and showed them my driver's license, and my ID cards from Cornell and Oberlin, which I still have, and my faculty card from LaGuardia, and they seemed to believe that I was who I said I was." She laughed. "A CUNY prof. Boring as shit."

Yes, Sadie thought, *it would be so much more exciting to be Mrs. Jimenez from Puebla, living in a three-room apartment with nine other people.*

"They asked who else lived here and I said, 'My husband,' and they asked for *his* name, and I was just like, *Why do they need* his *name? He's not here.* So I asked them, and they got all suspicious again and said, 'For the record.' And I didn't know what to do. So I told them. And two seconds later, Tuck came out of the bathroom to make sure everything was okay." She pressed her lips together. Her cigarette, still unlit, was growing moist between her fingers. "He was worried about me."

"I'm sure," said Sadie.

"The first guy, the Irish guy, was such an asshole. He just kind of smirked and said, 'I presume this isn't your husband.' But the other guy— he was black—just looked really uncomfortable, and he was like, 'Let's get out of here.' And they left."

"Wow," said Sadie.

"Yeah," Caitlin sighed. She pawed, bluntly, at her eyes and yawned.

"So what happened?" asked Sadie. "With your neighbors."

"Oh, right." Caitlin sat up and lit her cigarette. "Nothing. They weren't home. But the Feds are clearly watching them. There's always a policeman on the corner now. And look out the window." Sadie looked. In front of the hairdresser's sat a plain, navy blue sedan. "An unmarked car," said Caitlin, raising her brows darkly. "They come every day at noon. And they're there when I go to bed."

"Is it noon?" asked Sadie, alarmed.

"It's one," Caitlin said.

"Oh my God." Sadie sprang up. "I'm sorry. I have to go. I actually have to work today."

"Why don't you stay for lunch?" Caitlin jumped up, too, a caricature of a concerned hostess. "Are you hungry?"

"No, no." Sadie struggled to remember where she'd left her bag.

"I was going to make a big tofu scramble. It's really great. We have fresh coriander, from our roof garden."

"Sorry," said Sadie. She walked to the threshold of the hallway, hoping Caitlin would stand up and follow suit. "I can't eat tofu." She smiled. "Had too much of it in college."

"Oh my God," said Caitlin. "Me, too."

"Then why are you making it?" asked Sadie, unable to contain her impatience. Caitlin shrugged and slunk down in her chair, childlike.

"I need protein." She shrugged. "You have to be really careful, being vegan, you know."

"But"—*Don't,* Sadie told herself, *just don't ask*—"why are you vegan?"

"Rob feels really strongly about it." Caitlin lit the cigarette. "It's political. We're opposed to factory farming and genetically modified food. It's complicated. Though I ate anything before I met him. I knew I shouldn't, but I did. I kind of lack discipline." The ginger cat, just then, jumped off the couch with a loud *thwop* and ran into the kitchen, releasing a larger dose of the ammonia smell. In the spot where she'd sat, Sadie saw a dark, wet stain. She had to get out of this place immediately.

"Couldn't you just tell him that you don't like it?" she snapped. "Has it ever occurred to you that if you tried to make your life with Rob a little more . . . *fun,* you might not need Tuck. Or someone *like* Tuck."

"What do you mean?" asked Caitlin, her brows knitting together.

Sadie looked straight at Caitlin. "Well, it's just, if you make *every* single choice in your life based on how that choice affects the entire world, then you never get to have any fun."

An odd look had taken hold of Caitlin's face, something between an angry pout and a baleful grin. "What do you mean *exactly*?" *She doesn't want Tuck to leave Lil,* Sadie realized. *She likes her life just the way it is.*

"Well, if you don't want to eat tofu, then *don't,*" said Sadie, exasperated. "Go out and eat a cheeseburger." She paused, knowing that she sounded ridiculous, like her own mother. "Take a long bath. Get dressed up. Go out to dinner. Go to Oznot's or go into Manhattan and go somewhere really nice. Take a walk along the river at night. Just do things for the sake of doing them *together.* And read a novel just because you want to. Something not from your period."

Caitlin protested. "The problem is I don't have time. I'm teaching freshman comp and it's, like, all these dead white guys—"

"I know, I know, but I mean you should read something just for pleasure. Before you go to bed at night. *Sentimental Education*. Have you read that?" Caitlin shook her head. "You'd like it. It's about the horrors of the bourgeois. Just go over to the library on Devoe and get a bunch of good novels: Dickens, Austen, the Brontës. The books you loved when you were a kid. Remember when you could just give yourself over to a book?" Sadie sighed. This was why she hadn't gone into academia, so she wouldn't become like Caitlin, dogmatic and weird.

"I do," Caitlin admitted, offering a glimmer of a genuine smile. "I miss that. Don't you?" Sadie nodded. "I get what you're saying. What else would you do if you were me?"

Sadie considered, shrugging back a tiny feeling of satisfaction—perhaps she could master the girl's unhappiness. But a part of her knew she was being baited, knew Caitlin was laying a trap. "Well," she said slowly. "I'd get rid of this futon. It smells of cat urine."

Caitlin laughed again. "It does, doesn't it? We pulled it in off the street. After we got upstairs we realized that it smelled like cat pee, but we thought maybe the smell would fade. But then *because* it smelled like cat pee, the cats kept peeing on it. Mumia won't go near it."

And you let me sit there? thought Sadie, furious. "Caitlin, Rob has money, doesn't he?" she said, a thin stream of poison leaking into her voice. She was breaking the cardinal rule of New York bohemia—just as Rob had done the night before—pointing out a person's financial situation. Nowhere but in New York, Sadie thought, were people so embarrassed to have money. "Why do you need to pull in furniture off the street? Can't you just go out and buy a sofa?"

Shifting her weight uncomfortably from foot to foot, Caitlin considered this. "Rob has money from his family," she said finally. "But he believes—it's kind of an anarchist collective thing—that we should live as close as possible to the poverty level. We have a really strict budget and whatever extra money we have goes into Rob's projects. He's starting this new organization, kind of a support group for wealthy kids who want to live an ethical life." She paused. "You must know a lot of kids like that, right? You went to Dalton, didn't you? Maybe you could talk to the alumni people about bringing him to talk to the students? Or the alums? He's an amazing speaker. He's giving a talk at the New School in a couple of weeks. You should come.

"Mmm," Sadie murmured, glancing around the room. The bathroom, she thought, must be at the rear of the house, off the kitchen. She needed, desperately, to use it, but maybe not as desperately as she needed to leave. "I"—she smiled—"have to get going."

Caitlin, at last, rose and followed Sadie back to the kitchen, where she unlocked the door. Mumia jumped up, placed his paws on Sadie's shoulders, and licked her face. "Hey, sweetie," she said stiffly, thinking again of fleas.

"Down," Caitlin commanded. With a dejected whine, the dog lay back down on the scuffed linoleum floor. Sadie glanced toward a door by the window—the bathroom, surely—but picked up her bag, which was heavy with manuscript, and slung it, purposefully, over her shoulder. "You know, I'm glad you spoke honestly to me," said Caitlin. "No one ever does. I think people are intimidated by me."

"Sure," said Sadie. She could barely concentrate on Caitlin's words, so badly did she need to use the bathroom.

"You're right about some things. It's *such* a cliché, but I guess I keep thinking that none of this will hurt Lil, since she doesn't know about it. Like, maybe it makes things better between her and Tuck, even, because he's happier." Here, she looked up at Sadie, widening her eyes in an attempt to indicate sadness and regret. "I know that this sounds dumb to you," she said, coughing into her hand. "You know, I feel like you just don't know much about real life." *Oh my God,* thought Sadie. *I cannot believe this.* "You've never really been *in love,* have you? You think everything is so clean and easy. That I'll just, like, get a pedicure and go out to dinner and everything will be fine. But it doesn't work like that. Life is *messy.* It's dirty."

"Right," said Sadie, through tight lips. She was not, *was not,* going to play along anymore.

"You're not going to tell Lil anything, are you? About Tuck and me? Or about our talk?"

At last, thought Sadie, *the real point.* "I don't know," she said, her chest tightening with rage. And with that, she slipped out the door, raising her arm in a stiff little wave. She couldn't manage to get out the word "good-bye."

Down the first flight of stairs she walked calmly, taking care not to trip on the curling folds of linoleum, the low heels of her sandals tapping in a way that pleased her. At the landing, the smell of cabbage grew stronger, and she began to skip, then run down the final flights, bursting out the door into the fresh air, which wasn't actually fresh at all, but thick with exhaust fumes from the BQE, and rotting garbage from the Dumpster at the corner, and overused oil from the Chinese takeout shop. Sadie looked around her. To the east lay Lil's apartment. (*Should I go right now and tell her? I should, I should.*) To the south, she caught a glimpse of Will and Beth's building, a ten-story brick box. Several blocks west and a few north she could find Emily. So many friends nearby. Williamsburg always made Sadie feel conscious of being a *type*—all these girls, these *women*, dressed just like she, wandering the streets carrying yoga mats and clear plastic cups of iced coffee and thick books of recent vintage, hair pulled back from thin faces with small, sparkly barrettes. And the men, in their low-slung corduroys and wide-collared shirts, carrying messenger bags, or sitting in the garden at the L reading copies of *McSweeney's* or Philip K. Dick novels, stroking their sideburns.

And yet Metropolitan, today, was devoid of life. Which was just as well. She felt disgusted with humanity, and with herself. Why had she stayed so long? Why had she even *bothered* to try to talk to Caitlin? And why was it, she wondered, that Caitlin—just as in college, she realized—had managed to make her feel bad about herself. That perhaps she did know nothing of life in all its grit and dirt. That she had not given herself over to passion—ugh, that word—as Caitlin had. Was it true? She thought of Tal. Did she love him? She did, she did, and she told him so all the time. But then wasn't there a part of her that wondered, is this all there is? Not that it wasn't good, or that it wasn't enough, or that it wasn't exciting, but that it seemed, somehow, that there should be more. That she couldn't just marry the guy who lived down the hall freshman year, the guy who'd waited patiently until she came around. And this was it, wasn't it? That falling in love with Tal had been less an active choice and more a succumbing to the inevitable. And she could imagine, so easily, their life together, all so easy and good, the shine of approval from their friends and their parents and their steady accumulation of objects and houses and the negotiation of careers (for this was what was bothering him, she knew, that he *knew* he wasn't coming back from L.A., that after this movie there'd be another movie, and then pilot season, and that he wanted her to come, and she also knew, somehow, that she might say she'd come, might visit him for a week in his new studio in Silverlake or wherever, knowing that she couldn't stay, couldn't live there, couldn't even learn to drive, and it all just seemed a bit too much. She just somehow couldn't do it.

Stop it, stop it, stop it, she thought, *stop this. Caitlin's a snake. You love Tal. She's not capable of passion. She just wants what everyone else has.*

The clouds had drifted off and the sun, once again, cast a dusty, yellow light on the streets. It was a beautiful day, a perfect June afternoon. She *should,* of course, go home, make a salad, and read. But she *would,* she decided, walk down to the river, then maybe have lunch alone at Oznot's, while reading. She smiled broadly, goofily. How good it was to be completely *alone.* Putting on her sunglasses, she trotted across Metropolitan, imagining she could see the water in front of her. As she crossed Roebling, she became aware of a voice behind her, growing closer and closer. "Miss, miss, miss," the voice was saying. *Miss what?* she thought. Then a soft hand grabbed her upper arm. She let out a little scream, stopped short, and found herself looking into the round, freckled face of a man not much taller than she. His hair was sandy and thick, with a slanting cowlick above his left eye, and he wore a plain, dark suit, which gave her an idea who this might be. And, somehow, she knew that *he knew* that she knew who he was. "Are you all right?" the man asked. His voice was not deep, but had an appealing rasp.

"Yes, yes, I'm fine," she said. His hand, which was warm and dry, was still on her arm. With a sheepish look, he slowly released his grip.

"You're sure?" he said. "Nothing happened to you inside that house?"

"No, I was just visiting someone," she said, smiling, though she wasn't sure why.

"You looked a little upset when you emerged from the building," he said, furrowing his brow.

Was this some sort of Fed lingo, *emerged from the building,* she wondered, like a state trooper saying *Step away from the vehicle.* "Well," she said, drawing out the word, "I was. It's a long story."

"I have time," said the man, sliding his hands into the pockets of his pants.

"Okay," said Sadie. "But I'm not sure it's going to interest you."

"Try me," he said, with a shrug.

"Okay," repeated Sadie, suddenly nervous. "Well, I found out that this woman—the woman I was visiting, she asked me to come over, I don't really like her, though really, she's just a sad, *sad* person and I should feel sorry for her. Anyway, she's having an affair with my best friend's husband." She smiled again, this time self-consciously. "*Right.* That's more than you needed to know."

A grimace overtook the man's open face. It was his eyes, Sadie thought, that gave him such a—what was it?—*receptive* look. They were a deep, unusual shade of blue, almost turquoise and, this was the thing, spaced wide—too wide, really—on his face. He was older than she by at least ten years, and he'd spent time in the sun. "Eh," he said, shaking his head. "That is *not* good."

"No," Sadie agreed. *Shouldn't he be showing me his badge or something?* she thought. *Aren't there laws about that?* Could it be that he wasn't the INS guy? And she was talking to some random guy in a suit? No one in Williamsburg wore suits.

Cocking his head, he seemed to consider her anew. "Why did you run off down the street?" he asked.

Sadie laughed. "I don't know. I was so happy to be out of that apartment, that building. It smelled like cat pee. It's a long story." She paused. "Why?"

The agent shrugged, then looked Sadie straight in the eye. "There's some bad stuff going on in that building. Your friend should get out of there."

"She's *not* my friend," Sadie told him.

"Yeah, well then, *forget* her." He smiled. "The evil *seductress*."

Sadie laughed. "Vile fornicator," she said.

"Jezebel," he said. He reached into his left-hand jacket pocket and crisply extracted a black leather case, which he flipped open to reveal a large badge. "I'm Agent Michael Connelly," he said, sticking out his right hand and, again, meeting her gaze directly. "Nice to meet you."

"Sadie Peregrine," she said, shaking his hand, a firm, quick grasp. "Just a normal civilian. I don't actually even have a driver's license to show you. Would you like to see my library card?"

"That's okay," he said, flipping his little case closed with a snap and returning it to his pocket. Her vision, she realized, couldn't be so bad, as she'd read the initials on the badge clearly: not INS, as she'd expected, but, in clear black ink, FBI.

seven

The following Sunday, Sadie rose early and gave her father quite a shock by appearing on his doorstep at eight o'clock, just as he was leaving to pick up food for breakfast. Amiably, they walked over to Lex, selected their fish, and returned home to prepare the house for their guests. At ten, as they sat in the kitchen, reading the movie reviews from the Friday paper—having given Rose the Sunday paper—Rose called downstairs in the stentorian voice she reserved for situations she considered emergencies, "Sadie?" Father and daughter shared a frowning glance. It was rare for Rose to emerge before eleven. "Sadie," Rose called again. "Can you hear me?" Sadie skipped up the stairs, by way of responding. Like her father, she was almost constitutionally incapable of raising her voice.

Reaching the third floor, she found the door to her parents' bedroom partially open. "Mom?" she said, rapping on the door and poking her head in the room.

"Oh, Sadie," came Rose's voice. She was in the bathroom, an entirely white chamber, en suite, and nearly unchanged since the 1930s, with a massive pedestal sink, chrome towel bars, matte subway tile, scalloped deco sconces, and an enormous claw-foot tub, in which Rose took her evening bath. As a child, Sadie found this chalky vessel a bit too similar to the Egyptian sarcophagi at the Met and refused to bathe in it, though she'd loved her parents' bedroom, which, too, had changed little over the years: the walls painted Wedgwood blue, the trim white, the floorboards, which were plain and wide as in a country house, stained amber and covered partially with what Rose embarrassingly referred to as "an Oriental," in muted tones of blue and peach and yellow. The room faced the back, looking out over the little garden plot, and through its two tall windows received fragile southern light, mostly blocked by full silk curtains, sweeping from ceiling to floor, in the color Rose called "bone." A chaise longue covered in heavy silk patterned in green and white (or perhaps bone again; Sadie had trouble differentiating between the two) stretched against the far wall, under the windows, and next to a short three-legged table, holding a telephone and a hardback library book (Rose considered new books an unnecessary expense). On the wall by the hall door stood a sweet old sleigh bed, topped with a down coverlet (also in bone) and the many pillows Rose favored (with her predilection for reading while propped up against the headboard). The bed, as yet, was unmade—the coverlet on Rose's side turned down and the paper spread neatly out across it. Sadie picked up the magazine section—bearing a close-up photo of an African boy—and sat down on the chaise.

"I just read the funniest thing in the paper," Rose called. "Lil's husband, he's called Tuck, but his real name is William, isn't it?"

"Yes," confirmed Sadie.

"I thought so. Well, it seems that he's been arrested." Rose appeared delighted by this development.

"William Hayes has got to be a pretty common name," said Sadie. "Are you sure it's him, Mom?" Sadie was sure it was, and sure it had something to do with whatever had transpired at Caitlin and Rob's the previous week. It was too much of a coincidence: Federal officers barge in on a man having sex. Within ten days, he's arrested. Clearly, it was Rob who was under surveillance, right? Not the Jimenez family? She was, perhaps, in a position to find out. Agent Connelly had called her on Monday. She'd blanched when she heard his voice on the line—why, why had she given him her card?—and yet, she'd also been uncomfortably, blush-inducingly thrilled, and stunned into silence, when he'd said, in that resonant voice, his diction oddly precise, without any introductory chatter, "I've been thinking a lot about you." *Oh my God,* she'd thought. "I should tell you," she'd near stammered, curiously choked with emotion (Caitlin's words, and their implication, floating back at her: *You've never really felt anything; You've never really been in love*), "I'm involved with someone right now." And then, as if in a dream, she heard herself say, "But I've been thinking about you, too." She had, as yet, said nothing to Lil about Caitlin and Tuck—nor had she mentioned anything to Tal, though she told herself she would, if only so she wouldn't be the sole bearer of this awful secret—but after this hushed conversation, her arms pricking with sweat as she hung up her heavy office phone, she felt that she couldn't, not yet.

Patting her face with a white hand towel, Rose emerged from the bathroom, still in her nightgown and bathrobe, a peach-colored thing with creamy silk piping. Sadie had an identical one, a gift, of course, from Rose.

"Hi, Dolly," she said, walking over and giving Sadie a quick peck on the cheek. "Let me look at you." She stood back and examined Sadie, who had dressed carefully—as she did every Sunday—in anticipation of this moment.

"What a cute dress!" she said. "Let me see. Stand up." Sighing, Sadie rose and allowed her mother to pluck at the hem of her skirt. "Where is that from?" Rose was extremely interested in young people's costumes and shopping habits. Sadie laughed.

"You gave it to me, Mom."

The older woman scrunched her slender nose. "I *did*?" She made this second word two syllables, suggesting that, perhaps, Sadie was trying to pull off some elaborate ruse.

"Umm-hmmm," said Sadie, nodding.

"Where did I get it?" Rose asked suspiciously. She gestured for Sadie to sit down again, then joined her on the chaise, so that the two might solve this mystery together.

"Bergdorf's," said Sadie. She was already bored with this conversation. "So," she said, picking up the paper and depositing it on the chaise, "Tuck was arrested? You're sure it's him."

"Bergdorf's when?" asked Rose, squinting at the dress.

"Last summer. End-of-season sale. So, Tuck—"

"Didn't I get you a blue dress, too?"

"Yes," said Sadie, with a sigh. She started making up the bed. Her mother could, potentially, stand here for hours, cataloging Sadie's wardrobe. "So, Tuck was—"

"Yes, yes," said Rose. "It's funny, isn't it? Lil didn't say anything?"

"I haven't talked to her."

"Tuck and some other fellow. I can't remember his name. It sounded *vaguely* familiar." She picked the paper off the chaise and riffled through it. "Where is it, where is it. It was a funny sort of article. I read the beginning, then skipped to the end. There's a picture of Tuck." Sadie stacked the pillows and ran her hands over the coverlet. She had, she realized, come up to her parents' early with the vague intention of seeking counsel from her mother—should she tell Lil or stay out of it?—but the subject now seemed unbroachable.

"Ah! Here it is." She extracted the Style section.

Sadie laughed. "The *Style* section? So, I take it, he wasn't arrested for murder?" Rose peered at Sadie distractedly over the tops of her reading glasses, which she'd extracted from the pocket of her robe.

"No, of course not. What makes you say that?"

Sadie gave her a wry smile. "Nothing, Mom. So tell me what happened." Rose cleared her throat. "*Well*. Sadie, I don't know if you know this, but there's been all this trouble with Crown, the hotel company. Your father has been very concerned about it. His firm, you know, has a big account with them. Your father personally owns stock in the company—"

"Yes, yes, but what's the trouble?" As these words came out of Sadie's mouth, she realized exactly what the trouble was. Prisons. Of course. Rob Green-Gold. But it was too late, her mother was going to explain it, in her peculiar, laborious way, taking forever to get to the point.

"Well, it turns out Crown actually makes most of their money off of prisons. It's kind of funny, isn't it? Hotels and prisons. It's kind of like that housing project in Chicago, those big towers that were made into luxury apartments. The apartments were just the same, but some were luxurious—"

"Yeah, Cabrini. They've been torn down now," said Sadie impatiently. "But, yeah, I've read all about Crown. They kind of dominate the prison industry."

"Yes," said Rose, "well, they *made* it an industry and, it seems, they've been building prisons faster than the courts can"—she clicked her tongue—"*drum up prisoners*. They just keep building prison after prison. All on government commission, of course. Some are half empty. Even though there's some ridiculous number of prisoners now, twice as many as ten years ago. Ten million. Or something like that. All from drug crimes, of course. *Reagan*." She shook her sleek head. Reagan was a continual source of trouble for her. Sadie's father had voted for him the first time he ran ("We were in a recession; he had a strong domestic policy; you didn't live through the Depression, Sadie, you don't understand") and, thus, Rose blamed poor James Peregrine for every failure of the administration, as well as the one that followed. "Anyway, people are starting to think that there's some sort of conspiracy: Crown and the government in cahoots to build more prisons and make more money for Crown—and the politicos approving the prisons—imprisoning every black man in the country in the process. I keep reading about it in *The Nation*. Your father thinks it's all a load of bunk, but the company stock is dropping—"

Sadie could stand it no longer. "Mom, Mom, Mom"—Rose stopped talking and shot Sadie a wounded look—"I *know*. What happened with Tuck?"

Rose raised her black eyebrows. "There's no need to be short with me."

"I wasn't being—"

"Just the facts, ma'am, right? If that's the way you want it. Fine by me. I need to get dressed." She stood up, her mouth set in a hard line, and sighed dramatically.

"Please, Mom," said Sadie, struggling not to laugh. "Tell me what happened. Sit down."

Rose complied petulantly. "Well," she said, "it seems that Tuck participated in a, a *theatrical* protest against Crown. The company was having some sort of executive dinner at the St. Allen on Central Park South, which isn't *called* a Crown and everyone thinks it's still an independent hotel. It used to be, when I was your age, but now everything is owned by some big company. Anyway, Tuck and these people crashed the dinner."

"But why is it in the Style section?" Sadie laughed.

"Some designer had something to do with it." Sadie tried, quietly, to peer over her mother's shoulder. "Shall I read it to you?"

"Yes," said Sadie, and Rose smoothed the paper and began:

A FASHIONISTA FINDS HER CAUSE

In the 1960s, countercultural types—protesters of the Vietnam War, back to the landers, hippies, yippies, residents of communes, and other bohemians—could be easily identified by their uniform: raggedy hipster jeans, peasant blouses, fitted leather jackets, Frye boots, small round glasses and, of course, the long, flowing locks memorialized in that summer-stock staple "Hair."

These days, it's a bit harder to tell a bona fide radical—not that there are all that many in this apolitical, apathetic age—from your average college student, with the entire country's twentysomething population clad in standard-issue Gap jeans, Patagonia jackets, and Timberland boots. That is, unless you're talking about the loose network of young people affiliated with überactivist Rob Green-Gold's fledgling organization Wise Wealth, which helps the young and loaded "lead ethical lives," by making "lifestyle choices"—like adopting a vegan diet and refusing to patronize chain stores—and donating part of their inheritance to left-of-center causes. Such causes might include PrisonBreak, another of the energetic Mr. Green-Gold's ventures, this one devoted to dismantling the country's "prison industry," in which—according to Mr. Green-Gold, and a number of other prominent antiglobalization advocates—large corporations make fat profits off the labor of mistreated prisoners. Mr. Green-Gold's innovative ideas and approaches have won him no small measure of fame, and as a result, his organizations have attracted the fiscal and personal attention of any number of Hollywood's left-wing elite. Sean Penn, Susan Sarandon and Tim Robbins, Uma Thurman and Ethan Hawke, Debra Winger and Leonardo DiCaprio have all pledged money to PrisonBreak, as have rock stars (Kim Gordon and David Byrne), literary luminaries (David Foster Wallace, Junot Diaz) and technomoguls like Steve Jobs and Ed Slikowski.

But perhaps the most interesting adherent of Mr. Green-Gold's ideas is a person generally not associated with radical causes: Soho dress designer Susanna Chang. Known for her charming, retro frocks—rendered in lush silks, adorned with ribbons and bows and beads—Ms. Chang has "never had any interest in politics." "For ten years, I had tunnel vision," she explained, speaking over the phone from her Greene Street atelier. "I didn't think about anything but building my business." All that changed six months ago when Mr. Slikowski—a former beau of Ms. Chang—introduced the designer, a petite brunette habitually clad in kitten heels and knife-pleated skirts ("I run them up myself on my old Singer . . ."), to Mr. Green-Gold. The activist—a self-described "anarchist" who "doesn't know anything about fashion"—and the fashionista immediately hit it off.

Rose cast her eyes down the page. "All this is about the designer. Okay, here we go."

Upon their initial meeting, Ms. Chang told Mr. Green-Gold that she'd love to help out PrisonBreak in whatever way she could. The two stayed in touch, but it wasn't until last week that Mr. Green-Gold called Ms. Chang into action.

And so it was that on Friday evening, sixty attractive young people marched into the Grand Ballroom at the St. Allen, clad in sumptuous evening clothes designed by Ms. Chang and constructed by her Brooklyn seamstresses over a feverish five-day period. Though the styles of the women's dresses differed—from a full-skirted strapless gown that called to mind Dior's New Look, to a close-cut, curve-hugging number with a plunging V-neck—they were all cut from the same cloth: bold black and white stripes, the sort that once adorned prison uniforms. The men's tuxedos used this same cloth, to alarming effect.

These well-dressed young people were not exactly invited to the event they attended: Crown's annual executive dinner, attended by 200 of the company's top executives and big investors. Crown operates most of the nation's prisons—as well as many of its top hotels, including the St. Allen—and, as such, is the leading target of the PrisonBreak campaign. "Crown has a direct interest in keeping our prisons filled, which means they have a direct interest in perpetuating the racist, classist inequities of contemporary American society," said Mr. Green-Gold. Ms. Chang's costumes were meant to show Crown exactly how "fine the line is between prisoner and hotel guest."

At 7:00 p.m., Crown executives and investors arrived in the Grand Ballroom for cocktails and hors d'oeuvres. At 7:30, Mr. Green-Gold's "operatives"—as he jokingly refers to them—began to filter into the crowd, a few at a time. At 8:00 p.m., when the group moved into the seating area for the banquet, the rest of the prison activists—including Mr. Green-Gold, his wife, Ms. Chang, Mr. Slikowski, and Ms. Gordon—joined them. Slowly, the protesters formed a human chain around the curtained edge of the ballroom. The first speakers stepped up to the podium, the guests wondering exactly what the silent young people, in their matching outfits, were doing. At 8:45, Charles Harris, the company's chief financial officer, strode over to one of the protesters—journalist William Hayes—and asked, sotto voce, what was going on. "I didn't want to make a scene, call security, that kind of thing," said Mr. Harris, speaking from his midtown office yesterday. "There were a lot of very pretty girls. And they were all very quiet and well behaved."

Initially, perhaps. After Mr. Harris approached Mr. Hayes, the protesters began milling through the banquet hall, passing out leaflets emblazoned with the phrase, "Stop Building Prisons." After a brief period of confusion, Mr. Harris and a group of executives tried to force the protesters out of the ballroom. Hotel security was called. But before in-house officers arrived, a skirmish broke out involving Mr. Harris, Mr. Hayes, Mr. Green-Gold, and several unidentified protesters and Crown employees. Hotel security officers broke up the fight and turned Mr. Green-Gold and Mr. Hayes over to the city police officers who arrived soon after. Several other protesters were detained for questioning, but their names have not yet been released, for reasons of security. The matter has been turned over to the Federal Bureau of Investigation, which has been monitoring Mr. Green-Gold's activities for "at least a year," according to a source who spoke on the condition of anonymity.

As Mr. Green-Gold was led out of the hotel, into the waiting police car, he cried, "I've already got my uniform" and "A thousand more bucks for Crown." And he looked great as he did it.

Rose stopped. "The rest is about the designer," she said. "She avoided the fracas, it seems." Sadie nodded, then met her mother's eyes. Suddenly, the two women burst out laughing. "He looked *great* as he got into that police car," said Sadie, through giggles. "Actually, he does look pretty swell," said Rose. Sadie took the paper from her hand. On the first page, bottom left, was a color photo of Rob Green-Gold, smiling broadly and clad in what would indeed have been a smart tuxedo were it not for the white stripes. His eyes, she saw now, were a bright, appealing green. Off to one side, she saw Caitlin, in a floor-length, tailored gown, her hair pulled to the top of her head in what looked to be an elaborate chignon. Long gloves covered her arms. And—was that . . . yes!—a small tiara glittered atop her head.

"So do you know this boy?" asked Rose. "Is he a friend of Tuck's?" Sadie nodded.

"A very old friend, from childhood. I don't know him, really. He married a woman named Caitlin Green, who was in our class at Oberlin. She and Lil are friendly, and the four of them hang around together. Partly because of proximity, I think. They live right down the street from each other." Sadie pointed to Caitlin. "That's his wife." Rose laughed.

"The glamour puss? With the long gloves? She's bad news." Sadie stared at her mother.

"What makes you say that, Mom? Just from a picture?"

"*Look* at her," Rose cried. "The gloves! The *tiara*! She's completely ruined that lovely dress by piling on all that junk. Where did she even *get* a tiara?" Sadie laughed. "I bet this whole thing was her idea. I mean, the girl's married to this boy who probably walks around in jeans and a Save the Whales *T-shirt* all the time. And he's some kind of vegetarian. He's devoted his life to this *cause*." Rose Peregrine had no patience for people who devoted their lives to "causes," placing them in the same camp as born-again Christians and devotees of avant-garde theater. "She probably dreamed up this whole thing just so she'd have a chance to get dressed up, poor thing." *And there I was,* Sadie thought, smiling, *telling her to get dressed up.* Then a phrase came floating out at her—"*constructed over a feverish five-day period.*" Had she had a hand in this? It could be. The thought, strangely, pleased her.

"You're probably right, Mom," she said.

"Of course I'm right, Sadie. Give me a little credit. I've been around the block. That girl set this whole thing up and roped Tuck into it, too, no doubt. There's a certain type of girl who wants to have men fighting over her all the time."

"You really think Caitlin set up this whole elaborate protest to get *attention* for herself?" Sadie asked.

Rose considered. "No. The boy was probably planning the protest. The costumes were probably her idea. No straight man would think of something like that, right?" She took the paper back from Sadie and opened it to the middle page, where the story continued. "Look, there's another picture." She ran one manicured finger along a large black-and-white shot of the protesters lined up against the back of the hall. It *was* a rather remarkable sight—the row of young people in identical stripes, the women beautiful and dewy, the men handsome and stalwart. Ed Slikowski, Sadie thought, could stand to wear a suit more often. In person, he'd seemed much more slight, boyish. "There's Tuck," said Sadie, tapping her finger on the page.

"Yes, yes, I saw Tuck," said Rose, taking off her glasses and rubbing her eyes. "But where," she asked, "is Lil?"

•

That same day, Beth took the train up to Scarsdale to spend the day with her mother. She and Will had set a date for their wedding (the third Saturday in September) and chosen a site (her family's place in Maine), but she had yet to begin looking for a dress or to select invitations or to register for gifts. They'd only been engaged for two weeks, of course, but, according to her mother, September was just around the corner: the invites needed to go out within four weeks ("You *have* to give people eight weeks notice"), and if she didn't pick a dress *immediately,* she wouldn't have enough time to order the thing and have it fitted ("three months is the standard, Bethie"). And so Beth had agreed to come to Scarsdale for the day to look at card stock and gowns, even though she didn't care much about either—she didn't see why she needed an actual bridal gown, rather than simply a nice dress (and did it *have* to be white? She hated white), but her mother had simply, somehow (she tried to trace the thread back through their daily conversations but couldn't), assumed that Beth would want a real wedding dress and everything that went along with it, and Beth was too tired—or too *something*—to correct this assumption, in part because she didn't know exactly *what* she wanted.

Will was still in San José. She'd spoken to him in the early morning—five o'clock his time—and he'd said, "Choose whatever you like for the invites. Just no flowers or birds." After she hung up she realized that she'd forgotten to ask him about the wording on the invitation, as she'd promised her mother she would. There were, Mrs. Bernstein had explained, two approaches to a wedding invitation: the traditional, in which the bride's parents were named first ("Dr. and Mrs. Donald Bernstein request the honor of your presence as their daughter Elizabeth Anna is joined in matrimony with William Henry Chase), or the modern, in which both sets of parents are listed at the top ("Dr. and Mrs. Donald Bernstein and Mr. and Mrs. Harold Chase request the honor of your presence at the wedding of their children Elizabeth Anna and William Henry"). The latter was more egalitarian, but Beth thought it would seem weird, seeing as Will not only had been married before but also had a *child*—and presumably did not need his parents' permission to marry. Beth herself favored simple things and wondered why they couldn't just have a plain white (or cream?) card that said, in plain black (or brown?) letters, "Please join Beth Bernstein and Will Chase as they start their lives together." Okay, well, maybe not "start their lives together." But some simple, clear statement. Lil and Tuck's invitations were very modern and elegant—a designer friend of Tuck's had done them—but then Lil had planned her wedding in defiance of her mother, rather than with respect for her wishes.

Beth adored her mother—secretly, she considered her mother her best friend, though she knew how deeply uncool this was—and didn't want to argue with her about small things, like invitations, which didn't matter much to her, but seemed, like everything else about the wedding, very important to her mom, who was already asking questions like "Do you think you'll wear your hair up or down?" and "Would you like to have those little disposable cameras on the tables?" Which was strange, since Beth's mother wasn't one of *those* mothers, the Scarsdale mothers, though in certain, superficial ways she resembled them: blonde pageboy, tailored slacks, Tod's driving mocs. But the details betrayed her hippie past: embroidered Chinese jacket, "ethnic" jewelry, ancient Subaru (she refused to trade it in for a new model), and unwavering affection for *The Moosewood Cookbook*. She'd married Beth's father, then a bearded dental student intent on opening up a free clinic in the Bronx, at his family's house in Maine— just where Beth planned to do it—with as little pomp as possible, barefoot and clad in a gauze sundress, potluck-style meal, surrounded by close family and a few friends.

There weren't many pictures of this humble event, but Beth, as a dreamy little girl, had studied them all, trying to fit them to the images of weddings she saw on television or in books: princesslike women in enormous dresses, slowly gliding toward an elderly robed figure. In those embarrassing days before adolescence, she'd wished fervently that her parents' wedding had been the fairy-tale sort, particularly when she visited friends' houses and looked at leather-bound albums filled with photos of grand ceremonies and grander receptions at the Pierre or the St. Regis or the Scarsdale Country Club. Of course, in college, it was cool to be able to say, "My parents were total hippies. My mom got married barefoot in a Mexican dress."

Now, as she sat on the train, sipping hastily bought coffee from Zaro's and staring at the passing trees, the paper unread on her lap, she wondered what her children would say about their parents' wedding. She smiled and pressed her forehead into the chill window. *Children,* she thought, *I'm going to have children. I'll give them something to talk about,* she thought, closing her eyes. *But what?*

•

Beth was coming in on the 8:34 train, which meant Mrs. Bernstein needed to be at the station at 9:20 in order to catch her daughter as she disembarked at 9:22, provided there were no problems, as there so often were, with Metro-North. Beth had wanted to come later—"Mom, it's *Sunday*"—but they simply had too much to do. There was no way around it. They needed the whole day. Mrs. Bernstein, who was used to rising early for school, woke at seven (*late,* she thought), skipped down to the kitchen, tamped some grounds into her little moka pot, and leafed through the *Times* magazine, which contained an article about how kids of Beth's generation lived in a state of perpetual adolescence, stowing their belongings in Hello Kitty backpacks and playing video games. *It's true,* thought Mrs. Bernstein. Beth—who had been such a good, mature child, neat and reasonable and temperate in her moods—had lately been behaving like an infant: insisting on moving to New York (signing a lease on an apartment, even!) without a firm job (though that, thankfully, seemed to be resolving itself), rushing headlong into this romance with Will, and, now that it appeared to be working out (Mrs. Bernstein had been, honestly, doubtful), refusing to get started on planning the wedding. She *refused* to think about even the most basic things—buying a dress, booking a caterer—the things other girls looked forward to doing. It was as though she expected Mrs. Bernstein to simply take care of the details for her. And that absolutely was *not* going to happen. Though, of course, Mrs. Bernstein was happy—truly happy, what mother wouldn't be?—to assist Beth in any way she could.

And that, in the end, was exactly what Mrs. Bernstein had come to realize: Beth needed her assistance. The girl simply didn't know where to begin, and thus, her mother must take her in hand and show her what to do. The irony of this was, of course, that Susan Bernstein—back when she was Susan Gilman, of Shaker Heights, Ohio—had insisted on planning her own wedding in the most unconventional manner possible, despite the fact that she knew *exactly* how a proper person planned such an event, as her own mother thought of little other than balls and fundraisers and luncheons and, of course, weddings. When Beth announced that she was getting married—to this man the Bernsteins had only met once or twice (but then, how often had her parents met Donald before she married him?)—a vast reservoir of knowledge came rushing back to Mrs. Bernstein: invitations mailed no less than eight weeks in advance, seating charts, veil lengths and levels of fullness (elbow length, fingertip length, cathedral length), and so on.

Over the two weeks that had passed since Beth and Will's announcement—as Beth avoided even talking about the wedding—Mrs. Bernstein had found it more and more difficult to refrain from asking: "Are you thinking passed hors d'oeuvres for the cocktail hour? Or just crudités?" and "How many bridesmaids do you plan on?" Just to get the girl's mind going. There was also the temptation to burst out with passive-aggressive statements like "If you don't register soon, you won't get any engagement presents, because none of Daddy's family will know what to get you." To which—when she finally *did* give in to the urge and say it—Beth, unsurprisingly, said simply, "Mom, we're not getting married for the gifts! We're getting married because we love each other. I don't think we want to register, anyway." And Mrs. Bernstein, querulously, had replied, "Everyone gets married for the gifts. Otherwise you'd just shack up together *forever*." Of course, she didn't believe this at all. She hadn't thought of gifts either when she'd married Donald. Why had she said it? She couldn't say.

Earlier in the week, she'd finally gathered herself together and given Beth a quiet ultimatum: they needed to get the basic wedding stuff done as soon as possible, otherwise they'd be in deep water. "I've looked at the calendar and the invitations absolutely have to go out by July fifth," she told her daughter, using the voice she reserved for talented but lazy students. "They need to get to guests by the tenth, otherwise people won't have time to make travel arrangements. And we *must* figure out the food. And your dress."

"Okay, Mom," Beth had said amiably, to Mrs. Bernstein's surprise, and agreed to come out to Scarsdale over the weekend. It would be both easier and cheaper, Mrs. Bernstein thought, to obtain most of the wedding things in Westchester. They could simply go to the stationers in town, or to Neiman's or Saks, where they could also take a look at dresses for both Beth and her bridesmaids (though she hadn't yet said anything about bridesmaids; was it possible there would *be* no bridesmaids?). It was too bad Altman's had closed, she thought for the thousandth time.

She couldn't help but wonder if Beth's procrastination had something to do with second thoughts about this man, Will; or, rather, about the fact that he'd been married before (unhappily, but still) and had a little boy, who would be coming to live with them once they were married (and, Mrs. Bernstein hoped, installed in a bigger apartment). Apparently, the little boy was precious and sweet and well adjusted despite the tragic circumstances of his birth. But Beth herself had only met the child a handful of times and a kid who seems charming during an afternoon at the park inevitably becomes a little less so when it's time for dinner and bath and bed. Or when tired or sick. "You won't be able to sleep in on Sundays, you know," she'd warned Beth. "And sit around all day reading the paper. You can't do that with a kid." Beth had said she knew that, she understood, she loved Will and she loved Sam. But Mrs. Bernstein worried.

Standing at the counter, she waited for the coffee to bubble up to the top section of the little pot and went over, again, what they needed to do: invitations (choose paper, envelopes, inserts, figure out the wording), dress for Beth (ideally they'd simply choose one today), dresses for bridesmaids and a suit or tux for the little boy, Sam (Mrs. Bernstein could buy her own dress later, coordinating with Will's mother), food (Beth *must* look at the menus Mrs. Bernstein had sent for from the few caterers who did events on Vinalhaven), cake (she had photos from various bakeries), and, well, that was probably enough for one day. Steam began to escape the top of the steel pot. Mrs. Bernstein turned off the heat and poured the thick liquid into a squat white mug. A year earlier, she'd replaced the house's ancient, crumbling kitchen. All the surfaces were now a glittering white. When she'd selected the cabinetry and countertops (poured concrete, very much the *thing* these days), she'd imagined the room transformed into a rustic hideaway, the kitchen of a Cotswolds cottage, with roses tapping at the windows, and sun lying in patches on the floor's pale tiles. Now she wasn't sure she liked it. The effect was a bit sterile.

She brought her coffee to the table and riffled through the paper until she found the Style section, which she habitually read first, in order to ease herself into the harder news. She skimmed the wedding announcements for former students, then turned back to the front page and began an interesting story about a group of radical young people who'd protested the practices of some huge, evil-seeming corporation. Turning to the story's second page, she saw a familiar face in the line of protesters dressed in clever simulations of prison garb (what a great idea!). A handsome man in, perhaps, his middle thirties. Was he a student of hers? She looked at the caption. "Journalist William Hayes (far right, foreground) was arrested on Friday, along with Robert Green-Gold, following a skirmish with Crown executive vice president Charles Harris. Mr. Hayes is currently writing a much-anticipated biography of tech guru Ed Slikowski, who also participated in the protest (third from left)."

William Hayes. Why was that name familiar to her? She'd finished the story and moved on to a piece about spas for dogs before the name and the face coalesced—Lil's husband, who had, *of course,* introduced Beth to Will in the first place. *Wow,* she thought, *that's so neat!* She felt an impish desire to wake Don and tell him that one of Beth's brainy, apathetic friends was in fact—could you believe it?—some sort of radical, who'd been arrested. All of Beth's Oberlin chums—the girls, that is; the boys were a whole different story, which she didn't even want to think about now—reminded Mrs. Bernstein of little girls dolled up for a party, in their ladylike dresses and ringlets. When she was their age, she'd run around braless, in raggedy jeans and leotards, Beth propped on her hip, her hair hanging down her back in thick clumps. But they were sweet girls, definitely, and all very smart. And that was the way, wasn't it? The rebellious parent begets the dutiful child. Perhaps Beth was more political than she knew. For all Mrs. Bernstein knew, Beth could have been at this protest, along with Lil and Tuck. She looked at the photos again. What fun! And how creative! This young man, Green-Gold, sounded really interesting. Perhaps he'd want to come speak at the high school? She'd have to ask Beth about it.

•

Beth's train got in on time—miracle—and mother and daughter had time for a quick breakfast at the diner, after which they walked a block to the stationers in town, where they priced a simple cream card, with matching envelope and response card, and to the small bridal shop a block over, which was packed to the gills with high school girls being fitted for prom dresses. Beth wouldn't look at anything with lace or beads and snapped at the saleslady, who was, Mrs. Bernstein admitted, a bit of a dolt, hovering over Beth and bringing her poofy, frilly things, with leg-of-mutton sleeves, or rhinestone cuffs. "We can go, sweetie," whispered Mrs. Bernstein, as they sat wearily on a fake Louis XIV love seat, plastic-wrapped sample dresses on their laps, waiting to get into one of the four dressing rooms. Squeals rushed at them from behind the flimsy white doors. "You're not crazy about any of these dresses, are you?" Beth shook her head. "Then, let's go to Saks." They got up and slipped the dresses back on the overstuffed racks.

Outside, Beth raised her hands over her head and stretched. "That was awful," she said, letting out a little laugh.

"I know. I didn't think they'd have anything that was right for you, but I didn't think it would *hurt* to take a look. Boy, was I wrong!" She glanced at her watch. "Is it time for lunch? Should we eat in town? Or we can just go to Saks and eat there."

Beth considered. "Let's go to Saks. I'm not really hungry."

"Okay," said Mrs. Bernstein, resolving to give in to any and all of Beth's wishes for the entirety of the day. "So is Sam excited about the wedding? You loved being a flower girl at Aunt Margo's wedding. Do you remember?"

"Just barely," said Beth. In fact, she did not remember at all, but she wished she did.

"You wore the most adorable dress. I still have it—in the cedar closet. It was pink cotton, with a layer of thick lace over it, and a wide black satin ribbon around the waist. And you had little black shoes with straps."

"Mary Janes?"

"Yes, yes. You looked so cute. You loved to get dressed up. Other kids hate it, you know. But you loved it."

"Really?"

"Yes." Mrs. Bernstein slowed her gait, distracted. "Beth, I just remembered. Did you read the paper today?"

Beth hadn't. It still sat unopened in her bag. "Why?" she asked.

Her mother smiled mischievously. "Well," she said. "Let's put it this way. A friend of yours has been arrested." Beth looked at her mother blankly. None of her friends were very likely to be arrested, unless it was for some sort of benign negligence, like unpaid parking tickets. Then, of course, she knew. *Of course.* There was only one person it could be. One person with a temper, who would, perhaps, get into a fight at a bar, or leave a restaurant without paying, or break into a friend's apartment through the window and get mistaken for a burglar. Her sinuses prickled. "Maybe you know all about it already," Mrs. Bernstein said. Beth shook her head. "No?" cried Mrs. Bernstein, her blue eyes twinkling. "Okay, if you had to choose one friend who might be arrested, who might it be?"

"I don't know, Mom," said Beth. "I have no idea."

Frowning, Mrs. Bernstein reached up one small hand and smoothed her daughter's fine hair. This moodiness was just too much. "I'm sorry, honey. What's bothering you?" Beth clicked her tongue on the roof of her mouth and jerked her head away.

"*Nothing,* Mom. Nothing is bothering me. I'm fine."

Mrs. Bernstein shrugged. Why were children like this? "Okay," she said.

They began walking, in silence, down Chase Road, toward Mrs. Bernstein's red Subaru. In silence still, they drove out of the town center and got on the Bronx River Parkway going north, toward Saks. "So," Mrs. Bernstein said finally. "I'm thinking we can stop in at the stationery department and quickly price invitations, then head directly to the bridal salon, the fun part! We want as much time there as possible, right?" She flashed Beth a broad smile. "They're having a sample sale, so it may be mobbed, though the sale started on Thursday, so everything may be gone, but that's fine. You should choose the dress you like. Don't worry about whether it's on sale or not. Daddy and I are paying for this, okay?" Beth nodded nervously. She hated talking about money. "You only get married once," Mrs. Bernstein rambled on. "And then we can go to Neiman's and take a look at the dishes and stuff. I don't remember if they do bridal or not. But it could be a good place for you to register." Beth nodded, avoiding her mother's sidelong gaze. A familiar feeling took root in her chest, like warm needles. If she spoke, the tears would start. In the months since she'd met Will, she'd barely cried in the old way, as she had, embarrassingly, at Lil's party the previous week. She'd thought herself reborn, reinvented, with a new sort of confidence, a new toughness, which was strange, ironic, really, considering the uncertainty of those first days. She smiled now, the warmth in her chest abating, as she remembered how nervous she'd been, thinking he was interested in Sadie. She knew now—he'd confessed, much later, maybe in January—that he'd asked about Sadie merely as a way of speaking to Beth without seeming as though he was hitting on her. "An age-old tactic," he'd said. "Really," she'd asked. "It seems kind of weird." "Well," he replied, "it worked, didn't it?"

After that first date followed a week of terrible anxiety—Beth wondering what exactly had passed between them—during which she heard nothing from Will; and then another week, during which she wondered why exactly she agreed to go out again with this man. But she'd gone, of course she'd gone, as she'd thought of little but him—her mind, returning eternally to him, the feel of his hands on her, the set of his jaw—and she felt she had to see what came next, as though their fates were ordained, their story already written, and she needed merely to show up to catch the ending. And so she'd gone, rather than running away, as some little voice inside her kept suggesting, so that even, at the last minute, as she walked in the door of a dark Italian place in the West Village—a relic from a more mannered era, with silent, nodding waiters and dark booths and brass fixtures—she'd thought, *Should I just go? I could just go home right now.*

Part of her thought that he mightn't show up, that she'd be left alone, sipping Chianti, for hours. But then, no, he was there, waiting for her at the table, a bottle of wine in front of him. He stood when she came in and kissed her gently, on the cheek. Some level of reserve had vanished, though all his pretensions and weird turns of phrase and banter remained. He was so—she struggled to find the word—*unbridled* in his opinions, and somehow this—she saw now—forced her to figure out her own thoughts about all sorts of things, rather than simply blandly agreeing or saying "I don't know much about it." That night his problem—this was how Beth thought of it now—seemed to have disappeared. He never mentioned it again and she'd not asked, though she liked to think that she'd cured him. Soon they were spending every Wednesday and Saturday together—Will arranged for Sam to spend the latter night with his mother. They always ended at his apartment, rather than her sublet, which still felt more like a hotel than a home and was, after all, in Queens. He

showed her pictures of Sam—a saucer-eyed waif, with blond curls sticking out all over his head, and rosy lips—but refused to allow Beth to meet
the boy. "Doesn't it bother you?" Lil asked her constantly. "Not really,"
said Beth, though it did, of course. "It would drive me crazy," Lil told
her. "He's keeping the most important part of his life from you."

One day in April—a week or so after Will signed his divorce papers—
Beth finally cracked. "Are you ever going to let me meet Sam?" she asked
as they sat at his small table, sipping the dregs of an after-dinner coffee
(Nescafé, Will's secret shame). "No," he responded. "I'm not." Beth was
so shocked she didn't know what to say. "Not until I know you're going
to be in his life permanently," he went on. "So you need to think about
whether you want that." She'd nodded numbly. *Permanently,* she thought,
egads. The ongoing fact of his marriage had neatly allowed her to avoid
questions of permanence. But now it was over. Nothing in her life felt
even close to permanent, not her apartment, nor her work, which
involved, of course, her dissertation, which was seeming more and more
distant and irrelevant in the face of the job she'd finally managed to wrangle for the spring semester, teaching two 200-level English classes at
Baruch—for so little money, she'd been using her credit card to buy food,
which made her burn with shame—with no real indication that they'd
give her a real contract, though she seemed to be making inroads with
both Gail Bronfman and NYU, where she'd start teaching summer session in a week. It was just one class, but in her field, at least, and for a
thousand dollars more than at Baruch, where the students had barely spoken English. Will kept telling her to pitch stories to magazines, now that
her piece had come out on *Salon* (to little fanfare, though it had thrilled
her to see her name on the site, her words below it).

A month later, on a Saturday evening in May, as they once again
sipped their after-dinner coffee—he could cook, she'd discovered—he
called from the little kitchen, "So, tomorrow, I thought you might want
to come along with Sam and me. We're going to the Central Park Zoo."

"Um, okay," said Beth, heart pounding.

"Here's something to wear," he added offhandedly, coming out of the
kitchen and handing her a small black box, the sort of small box people
were always being handed in movies and television shows, the sort of
small box that could only contain one thing. Beth had never wanted such
a box or the thing in it; nor had she ever dreamed of being presented
with one of these objects, not in any sort of romantic, traditional way.
She'd been annoyed—deeply annoyed—by the way Lil behaved in the

months before her wedding, and surprised that Lil wore that enormous, *suburban* ring. She'd said it was out of duty to Tuck's mom, but Beth knew better. Lil liked it.

But then Lil also liked (*loved*) being the center of attention, while Beth hated it. Her bat mitzvah had been, incontrovertibly, the most painful day of her life. But all that aside, when she got right down to it, she'd simply never imagined one of those little boxes in her future. Nor had she envisioned a ring, engraved invitations, a big dress. But now here she was, racing toward Saks, a "rock" (as Emily put it) sending shards of light through the car's interior, to buy a white dress for her wedding, her *real,* big, catered wedding, to a man she'd known less than a year, a man who had—there was no getting around it—started their relationship *very* strangely and then, even when it achieved a level of normalcy, kept her at arm's length. It was, she thought, the way things were done in some hazy, nebulous past—the 1950s?—or in the books she'd read growing up: a girl ventured out into public places with a man—movies, dinner, plays—and eventually he proposed.

She glanced at her mother, who was humming softly, and, adopting a cheerful tone, asked, "So, who was arrested?" She forced a laugh, which quickly mutated into a cough, for she knew the answer to this question— Dave, of course, always *Dave*—and dreaded hearing her mother's commentary on the person in question. Her mother had never liked Dave, though she'd tried her best to hide it.

Mrs. Bernstein smiled. "You're sure you don't want to guess?" Beth nodded. "Okay, then I'll tell you." She paused for drama, as she did in class when reading aloud from Poe or Lovecraft. "*Tuck.* Lil's husband."

Beth exhaled deeply. "*What*? You're *kidding.* What was Tuck arrested for? He's, like, a writer. What for?"

Mrs. Bernstein laughed. "Protesting. He was part of some big demonstration against Crown, you know, that big hotel company. Apparently, they also run prisons, and exploit the prisoners. Horrible stuff! It was very clever. The demonstrators dressed up like prisoners, sort of. Lil really didn't mention it?"

"No, she didn't," said Beth, frowning. "I haven't spoken to her in a few days, though."

The mall loomed ahead of them and Mrs. Bernstein's mind clouded, again, with font sizes, response cards (postcard or matching envelope?), thread count (or should they not bother to register for sheets? Nobody ever bought them anyway; it felt somehow too intimate), and shades of white (would Beth look best in pure white or a cream? Probably the former). In one practiced motion, she swung the Subaru into a spot—far from the entrance, but you couldn't hope for better on a Sunday—grabbed her purse, and hopped out of the car. Slowly, Beth followed. Mrs. Bernstein squeezed her daughter's shoulders and kissed her loudly on the cheek. "Oooooh, we're going to have fun," she said. Beth smiled. "Yes," she said. "You're feeling okay?" Beth nodded. "I'm fine, really, maybe a little tired." Mrs. Bernstein studied her daughter's face. She did look tired, puffy under the eyes. She was teaching summer session at NYU—"It's a big deal," she'd squealed, "they hardly ever use adjuncts at Tisch!"—and maybe it was all too much for her, all that prep time, plus her dissertation (which Mrs. Bernstein feared was getting a bit *lost*), and the wedding to plan, all these decisions to make. "Okay, we won't tire you out too much today." She pulled open the heavy glass door that led into the men's department and gestured grandly for Beth to step inside.

The familiar aisles of Saks had a calming effect on her and she felt, suddenly, that she might ask the question that had been plaguing her. "Sweetie, have you thought about bridesmaids?" Without warning, Beth heaved a great, gulping sob and burst into tears, just as they arrived in the cosmetics department, with its hot, white lights. Mrs. Bernstein, shocked, reached up automatically and put her arms around Beth, who stood frozen in the middle of the aisle. A gray-haired Clinique salesperson approached them tentatively, tissues in hand. "She can come over here and sit down if she likes," she said. "Thanks," said Mrs. Bernstein. "I think we'll go to the women's room." The saleswoman nodded and pursed her lips. "Second floor," she whispered. "Through lingerie." Mrs. Bernstein gave her a conspiratorial smile. "Okay, Bethie, let's take a little walk." Beth nodded and clung to her mother. "I'm sorry," she mumbled. "I feel so stupid."

"Shhhhhhhh. It's okay," Mrs. Bernstein murmured, guiding her toward the escalator.

By the time they reached the lounge, Beth's sobs had subsided into hiccups. Mrs. Bernstein deposited her on a beige couch, walked over to the cooler, and siphoned off a little paper cone of water, then sat down beside her daughter and placed it in her hands. Beth drank it, meekly, glancing at her mother over the rim of the cup. "Honey, what's going on?" This set off a new avalanche of tears. "I . . . don't . . . know," Beth choked out. Mrs. Bernstein was beginning to grow frightened. Beth's problems had always been easily resolved by a trip to the doctor or a week of rest. Her tears were frequent, yes, but generally passed quickly. She was sensitive, Mrs. Bernstein thought, but not particularly complicated. "Okay, okay," Mrs. Bernstein said, pushing Beth's damp bangs off her forehead. "You don't have to tell your old mother. We can just go home. Is that what you want?" Again, the tears. Mrs. Bernstein wondered, disloyally, if this was a passive-aggressive attempt to wiggle out of planning the wedding. Perhaps she should tell Beth that it needn't be some big affair? A pang of disappointment shot through her. No. *Everyone* wanted a real wedding. It was already decided. It would be a grand, old-fashioned thing, at the Vinalhaven house, with a lobster dinner, and fresh oysters and champagne. *So* much fun.

"No," Beth sobbed, to Mrs. Bernstein's relief. "No. We can stay. It was just—" Her voice broke. She took a deep breath and buried her face into her freckled hands. "It was just that. I thought you meant—" Her voice became a whisper. "*Dave*." Mrs. Bernstein was baffled. "Sweetheart, what do you mean? What about Dave? Dave your old boyfriend?" Beth sat up and shook her head from side to side, like a dog. She snuffled into the tissue. "When you asked me to guess who'd been arrested," she said slowly. Mrs. Bernstein nodded encouragingly. "Well, at first, I thought, none of my friends would ever be arrested. And then I realized, Dave. He's the only one who would do something like that. I mean, not get arrested for protesting. I was thinking it was something like getting into a fight. Or breaking into some *illegal* place. Dave is always doing things like that. Sneaking into places. And he has an awful temper. Remember the barbecue?"

Mrs. Bernstein laughed. The summer after Beth's graduation Dave had taken the train out—somewhat grudgingly—for the Bernsteins' July Fourth barbecue. After sulking away most of the afternoon, he ended up deep in conversation with an older male cousin of Dr. Bernstein's, a psychiatrist who had recently adopted Buddhism (after stints with Hinduism, Unitarianism, Confucianism, Scientology, and various strains of Socialism). Mrs. Bernstein tended to describe this cousin as a "condescending jerk" and on this particular day he was loudly yammering on about Buddhism. Somehow (it wasn't hard to imagine how), he and Dave got into an argument, which began with the cousin suggesting that Dave didn't really understand the "underlying principles" of Eastern religions and ended with Dave clutching a lawn chair in one hand, a steak knife in the other, saying, absurdly, "There's an easy way to solve this. You want to go around the corner? Stand up, you pussy." The cousin—a fattish sort, with a fey beard—cowered behind a potted ficus and told Beth that her boyfriend appeared to have sociopathic tendencies. Had he harmed animals as a child? Dave stormed out without saying good-bye, and presumably (he and Beth had never spoken of the incident) walked to the train station and skulked home to Brooklyn. Mrs. Bernstein had thought it all pretty funny. That cousin was just awful. He told *everyone* that they didn't understand the "underlying principles" of this or that. But Beth was distraught afterward, feeling that she had failed Dave in some way. Now, however, she joined Mrs. Bernstein in a chortle.

"So you were afraid Dave had been arrested?" Mrs. Bernstein asked softly. "You were afraid for him?" Beth's face went slack. "No, no. I wasn't afraid. It was just . . . I try not to think about him. I can't stand to think about him. He makes me so mad." Mrs. Bernstein nodded sympathetically. "I know, I know. And you thought I was going to make you have some silly little chat about him. That I was acting like he was just another of your friends, like Lil or Sadie." Beth furrowed her brow. "Something like that." Mrs. Bernstein bobbed her blonde head. "But sweetie, what's the trouble with him? Is he upset about your wedding? I mean, that you're getting married? Is he making things difficult for you?" Beth shook her head. "No, no, he . . . he hasn't said anything about it." Before she could think about it, a little laugh escaped Mrs. Bernstein. "And I suppose that's the problem." Beth looked at her miserably and said nothing. "Do you see him? In the city?" Beth shrugged. "I see him sometimes. At parties." "Your friends invite you two to the same parties?" Beth let out a guffaw. "Mom! He's *their* friend, too. He's known all of them as long as I have. What are they supposed to do? It's not like they're *your* friends, having little sit-down dinner parties. These are party-parties, with, like, a hundred people or something. It would be weird if they only invited one of us." Mrs. Bernstein nodded. "I guess, it's just now that you're *engaged,* I thought—" "Mom, it's not, like, *1950*. The world hasn't changed because I'm engaged."

Mrs. Bernstein struggled to stay calm. Beth rarely spoke to her this way, as though she were some sort of fossilized relic, incapable of understanding a young person's mores or woes. But since she'd returned last fall, she'd been increasingly impatient and irritated with her parents, as though she was going through a delayed adolescence. Mrs. Bernstein had no idea why, unless, well, the Bernsteins had been in California when Beth arrived—visiting Jason at Stanford, over his fall break—and maybe Beth resented their not having been home to greet her and help her settle in to her new place. Perhaps she'd felt alone—abandoned—and fallen in with Will too quickly? But she'd *insisted* she would be fine. And she was twenty-seven years old, after all. At twenty-seven, Mrs. Bernstein had Beth, and a job, and a house, and Jason on the way.

No doubt, Lil's wedding in and of itself had come as a bit of a blow. It's always hard, Mrs. Bernstein thought, when the first of your friends marries. One of *her* friends had got married right out of school, to some man she'd met in the Village, and moved to a vegetarian commune in Maine. The rest of them thought it kind of a lark, as they were all going off on their single-girl adventures: Mrs. Bernstein to Morocco with the Peace Corps; her other friends to canvass for labor unions or environmental groups or to teach at public high schools in the Bronx or Brooklyn (where one, Marcy Goodman, had a gun pulled on her, long before they'd all started to worry about such things), or to internships at magazines or publishers. Now that friend—the first to marry—taught poetry at Colby and was married for the second time, to a doctor. The first husband moved back to New York and was never heard from again.

Why had she thought of that—Judy Horowitz and her communard? Yes, because of the difficulty when one's first girlfriend marries. One feels betrayed. Was that why Beth had rushed into this engagement—and set the date for the wedding so soon? Because she felt abandoned by Lil? Until this point, Mrs. Bernstein had thought the exact opposite: that Lil's happy marriage had made Beth see that Beth herself was also worthy of happiness in love. That Beth, too, might date a handsome, successful man—and even marry him—rather than the dissolute, self-important *slackers* (to use the kids' lingo, which was quite apt in this case) she'd preferred since high school. Mrs. Bernstein also suspected that Lil and Tuck had made her see that marriage was not some archaic institution (as Beth had, no doubt, been taught at Oberlin, just as Mrs. Bernstein had before her), but a real and eventual part of life. Some of Mrs. Bernstein's friends called it a "necessary evil," but Mrs. Bernstein didn't feel this way. She believed that some people were *made* for marriage. Beth, for example, had a nurturing personality and blossomed when she had someone to take care of; and yet, by the same token, she was also a fragile girl and needed someone to look out for her, to remind her to rest and take her vitamins. In May, when she and Will had come home to tell the Bernsteins about their engagement, she'd already seemed worlds happier and healthier, with a bloom in her cheeks and a sparkle in her eye. Remembering this, Mrs. Bernstein brightened. Until today, Beth had seemed over the moon about her wedding. She couldn't *really* be thinking of Dave. She sighed again.

Beth, in some ways, resembled her father, a quiet, bookish man, prone to grand gestures (elaborate pieces of jewelry left on the toaster for Mrs. Bernstein to discover upon waking) and fits of melancholy (entire weeks spent in silence, reading and rereading *Sophie's Choice*). During Beth's long illness in high school, Dr. Bernstein had spent every free minute sitting on the couch with the girl, watching old tearjerkers—*Now, Voyager; An Affair to Remember*—and eating pumpkin seeds, his X-ray-filled briefcase open on his lap. It was during this same period, Mrs. Bernstein remembered, that Beth had read *Sense and Sensibility*—or, actually, all of Austen's novels, in a two-volume set, brought home from the library—and favored the foolish and romantic Marianne over the wise and practical Elinor. At the time, Mrs. Bernstein had ascribed this bizarre proclivity—*everyone* preferred Elinor, that was the whole point of the novel, wasn't it?—to illness: Marianne, like Beth, was prone to sickness. But had that early sympathy led to this exact moment? Perhaps. For Marianne was hung up on what were then called "first attachments," believing a girl could never truly devote herself to anyone but her first love. Was this what was plaguing Beth? This girlish idea? That character learned, the hard way, that first loves didn't work out so well, generally. Did Beth not remember the ending of the novel?

"Bethie, do you think you're still in love with Dave?" Mrs. Bernstein heard herself asking, though she truly didn't want to hear the answer. Already, her mind was starting to turn to the practical: how they might cancel the wedding, if it came to that. Thank *God* they hadn't ordered the invitations yet (or sent them out!). Beth dropped her head to her mother's shoulder. "*I don't know,*" she cried, lapsing, yet again, into sobs. Mrs. Bernstein released the breath she had been holding. "Okay, okay," she said, though she was growing weary of all this drama and mystery. She steeled herself and took a firmer tone. "Sweetie, let's try and talk about this. Tell your old mother what's going on." Gently, she pulled Beth's head up. Tears still leaked from the girl's eyes. A pair of middle-aged women walked in the door, murmuring quietly to each other and shooting Mrs. Bernstein quick, sympathetic glances. Beth pulled a clean tissue from the miniature box and pressed it to her face. "I'm sorry, Mom. This is so embarrassing." She smiled a small smile and looked around her at the lounge's pale walls. "Crying at the Clinique counter at Saks." Mrs. Bernstein smiled broadly. "Well, kiddo, we all have to cry somewhere. It could have been worse, right? It could have been at the Prescriptives counter. Those Prescriptives women are *mean*." Beth smiled. Mrs. Bernstein decided to press her luck. "And I'm sure plenty of women cry in the dressing rooms." She raised her pale eyebrows knowingly. "That's true," said Beth.

"So," Mrs. Bernstein began. "So," Beth sighed. Mrs. Bernstein smiled encouragingly. "Nothing has happened," Beth began. "Except in my head. It's just, well, you know." She fumbled for the words. "Last fall, when I saw Dave at Lil's wedding, I felt kind of *affected* by him, but I thought it was just because I was nervous. Because, you know, things were never resolved between us." Mrs. Bernstein noted Beth's use of the passive voice. What the girl meant was: *Dave* left things unresolved. She narrowed her blue eyes. Beth continued. "A few days later, I suddenly realized that I was mad at him, *really* mad at him. And *that* was why it was hard to see him. Because I thought I was over it—what had happened after college—but I wasn't. I was still mad." She laughed and shook her head. "I told Lil about it and she said, 'Duh, Beth. We all knew that. Everyone except Dave.' And then she told me that Dave felt like *I* dumped him. Can you believe that?" Mrs. Bernstein scrunched up her face. "Well, I don't know. You never told me, exactly, what happened between you two." Beth rubbed her eyes with the heels of her hands. "Honey, don't. You'll give yourself wrinkles," said Mrs. Bernstein, drawing Beth's hands down to her lap.

Chastised, Beth pulled her shoulders back and gathered strength to tell the story. "Well, he said he wanted to see other people," she said shakily, "when we went to grad school. But all summer, before we left, it seemed like things were the same. Then we went away and he was always just, like, weird and tense. And I was always the one who would call. He never called me, not really. One day I just decided to stop calling—" Mrs. Bernstein could restrain herself no longer. "Beth, that was the *right* thing to do!" she cried, grabbing her daughter's hands. "He was treating you badly! Of course you stopped calling. And now he's sulking, saying you 'dumped' him. Come *on!*" She leveled her eyes with Beth's. "Sweetheart, you know what's going on here, right? He thought that you would go off to Milwaukee and"—she rolled her round eyes—"*pine* for him. And he would cat around for a few years. Then you'd come back and still be in love with him. But instead, you started seeing Will and now you're marrying him." Beth shook her head. "I don't know if that's it, Mom." "Beth, why do you think he told Lil that he felt rejected by you? Because he knew she'd tell you." Beth nodded. "He's playing games with you. Just like he did in college." "No, Mom, he's not that calculating. He's not manipulating me." Mrs. Bernstein considered. "There are different ways of manipulating people," she said carefully. "Sweetie, Dave is a wonderful guy, in many ways. He's smart and funny—" Where was she going with this? She willed herself not to say too much and upset Beth. "But he has very serious problems. He's immature. He was your first real, serious boyfriend, I know that, but I don't know if marrying him would make you happy." She restrained herself from adding that age-old mother's lament, *Does he even have a job?* Of course, she knew the answer: yes, he had a job. Waiting tables.

Beth pressed her lips together. Mrs. Bernstein could see she was trying not to cry again. "It's just—" She stopped. Maybe, Mrs. Bernstein thought, it would be better to stop talking about this and head directly to the bridal salon. Sometimes talking about things made them worse, rather than better. Beth opened her mouth. "It's just— Well, what I was going to say was just that we avoided each other, mostly, in the fall and the winter. But once Will proposed—once we got engaged—I guess I kind of *wanted* to see him, to show him my ring and how happy I was. So I went to Lil and Tuck's party last week. Will is in San José. And . . ." Mrs. Bernstein's mind raced frantically. Had she slept with him? If so, she must be told that it's *okay*. Mistakes happen. The wedding could go on. She must simply forget about it and move on. Sex was just sex. A choked sound emerged from Beth's throat. "I got to the party and, at first, I didn't see him and I sort of panicked, thinking he wasn't coming, but I was kind of relieved at the same time, you know? But then I went to the back room to get something to eat and there he was. My heart just went crazy when I saw him. I know that sounds dumb, but that's how it felt. And he just walked over to me and said, 'Have you tried the dates wrapped in bacon? They're amazing.' And we just started talking like no time had passed. It was just like it was when we first met, in college, when we were first friends." She laughed, a bit bitterly.

"All those months—when we were first apart—I called him every night and we had *nothing* to say to each other. And then, last week, it was like, we couldn't stop talking. It was like that horrible time never happened." Mrs. Bernstein waited for more, but Beth was fiddling with her tissue, coiling it into a rope. "It was such a *relief* to talk to him. Mom, I felt like for the first time in years, like, like I could say *anything*. Like I was talking to the only person who really and truly *knows* me. Who completely understands me." Mrs. Bernstein's face contorted in sympathy. "But what about Will?" she asked. "Is it not the same with him?" "No, it's different." She pressed the pads of her fingers into her eye sockets. "How?" Mrs. Bernstein pressed. "Well," Beth sighed. "I don't know. I guess, well, Will likes to joke around more. And he's, he's, just different. I don't feel like he *knows* me the way Dave does." "Well, sweetie, you've known Dave a long time. You only met Will last fall. You can't really compare the two." As she said this, she realized that it was *she,* of course, who'd asked Beth to compare the two men. "You know what? I think you need time to sort all this out, to think things through. It sounds like maybe we should postpone"— she couldn't bring herself to utter the word "cancel"—"the wedding for a month or two." Beth nodded dully. Another pair of women walked into the lounge—mother and daughter—smiling at Mrs. Bernstein and Beth. "Why don't we get washed up and go have some lunch and then we can talk more?"

"Okay," said Beth.

Ten minutes later they were seated at a small table at the café with fresh cups of coffee in front of them. Beth's face, pink from the cold water, had gone slack and impassive. "So we can go home and see Dad, if you want. Or we can just poke around here a bit, maybe get you some new shoes. Is there anything you need?" Beth shook her head and took a sip of coffee. "We can look at wedding dresses," she said in a low voice, her eyes fixed firmly, *childishly,* on her place mat. "Oh, honey, no," cried Mrs. Bernstein, who now, unaccountably and much to her distress, felt like *she* might cry. *Why, why, why,* she asked herself. "This isn't the right day. You need to figure out what you want. If you're still in love with Dave, you can't marry Will. It's unfair to you, but it's more unfair to Will and to Sam, too. Beth, he's been married before, to someone who treated him badly. When he asked you to marry him, he meant it for keeps. Honey, think about it. He wouldn't even let you meet that poor child until he knew you were going to be his stepmother."

"I know all that, Mom," Beth said, in a cold, distant tone. "And I know I want to marry him. We can get the dress today and order the invitations. I forgot to ask him about the wording, though." Annoyance overtook Mrs. Bernstein and she struggled to tamp it down. What was wrong with Beth? She pitches some sort of fit, about how Dave—a person with the emotional development of a sixteen-year-old—*understands* her. And now, when Mrs. Bernstein takes her concerns seriously—rather than dismissing them, as *most* mothers would have—she insists that everything is fine and they carry on planning the wedding. Did she think her mother would be disappointed in her if she *didn't* marry Will, with his blue-chip job and his natty suits? She and Don had tried—in every possible way—to make their children independent thinkers, to let them know that their parents would love them no matter *what* path they chose in life. She had not—not *ever*—suggested to Beth that she marry for any reason other than love. (And she had shuddered, some months back, when Beth told her an awful story about Sadie's mom dismissing Tal, such a great kid, because he was an actor and would "never make a real living.")

But the trouble with Dave—who was from a very nice family, and Jewish (which Will, of course, was not, a fact that would cause some problems with the ceremony, but she wouldn't think about that now)—wasn't simply that he had neither money nor the impetus to make it. The trouble was Dave himself. He just didn't have it in him, to take care of Beth, in *any way*. Instead, Beth would end up taking care of Dave, catering to his every mood and whim. What Dave needed was not a dreamy kid like Beth but someone like Lil, a forthright go-getter who would shake him out of his stupor, who would refuse to tolerate his selfishness. He was nothing but a spoiled little boy. But then, that was exactly the type that made women cry in public restrooms, wasn't it? She'd met her share of such types. In college, of course. And later, too.

Some years back, when Beth was just a little girl in overalls and braids (and Jason not yet born), a tall, curly-haired substitute began appearing at the high school, clad in a black turtleneck and a tweed blazer, like Hollywood's version of an English professor. As it turned out, he *was* a professor, of sorts: a Yale Ph.D. who'd failed to get tenure at some small New England college and returned home to his parents' house on Larchmont Avenue. The students had worshipped him—his dark, wounded eyes, his unsettling habit of answering a question with a question—and the female teachers (married and single) quivered whenever he entered the staff lounge. In the end, he'd run off to Oregon with a precocious seventeen-year-old from Mrs. Bernstein's Honors class. The girl's parents—the Goldbergs of Christie Street—eventually went to the police, who put out a warrant for the man's arrest. Though by the time the Portland cops found him—in some squat or something—the girl had sensibly put herself on a bus back to New York.

The man returned, too, some years later. He'd tapped Mrs. Bernstein on the shoulder one day, not so long ago, at the MOMA—a traveling exhibit of Picasso's paintings of women, aptly enough—and said,

"Scarsdale High School, right?" Though her hair was shorter—trimmed to her shoulders—Mrs. Bernstein knew she looked much the same as she had twenty years prior. The man, however, bore no resemblance to his younger self; he'd had to recount his biography (Yale, Oregon, young Jodi Goldberg, police) before she could place him. Time had not been kind to him, though his eyes still glimmered, darkly, with the provocative charisma of a tragic hero. She was, she realized, a good deal younger than he, though she hadn't thought so during their brief period as colleagues (she with a little girl and a husband and a large house). Then, she'd resisted his attempts at banter; she'd not been one of the women who'd gathered around the whorl of his pipe smoke, waiting to be favored with a sliver of attention. And she was surprised that he'd even remembered her; in fact, if she was honest with herself, she was *flattered* to be plucked out of a crowd, her face remembered from two decades before. But she'd simply said "Hello, hello" and "How are you?" and "Nice to see you" and gone on her way. Later, she heard, through the grapevine of old Scarsdale families—to which she now belonged, having married into one—that the man had been hospitalized, repeatedly, for some sort of drug problem. His parents had bought him an apartment in Chelsea and were "helping out" while he started up a tutoring business and wrote a novel about a working-class family on Martha's Vineyard, where his own family summered.

But she herself had never, not really, been attracted to that sort of man: the desolate loner, the misunderstood genius. In her youth, these boys had been jargon-spitting hippies or self-serious radicals or hard-drinking painters. Today, it seemed, they were would-be rock stars or postmodern novelists or overeducated malcontents. Regardless, she always went more for the quiet, slow-and-steady-wins-the-race types—like Donald, whom she'd thought she might marry from the minute she met him, at the Hungarian Pastry Shop, on a blind date. She'd never really, truly loved anyone before him—not in the way Beth loved Dave—and it was the easiest thing in the world to say yes, when he'd said, casually, "Why don't we get married?"

Now she wondered, as the waitress deposited a tarragon chicken sandwich in front of her: if that yes was causing Beth such anguish, then perhaps she oughtn't make good on it, Dave or no Dave. "Beth," she began, carefully. "You don't have to marry Will just because you said you would. You can change your mind." Perhaps she shouldn't push the issue, she thought before continuing. "You don't have to marry *anyone*. It doesn't have to be a choice between Will and Dave. If Will isn't the one, and Dave is maybe the one but not ready to commit to you right now, then you could just be alone for a while. You could get a new apartment. Your dad and I could help you find your own place." Beth had sublet her sublet for the summer. As of July first, she'd be living with Will. "And I'd have to talk to your father, but I bet we could help with the rent."

"No, Mom, no," said Beth, her expression growing grim. Mrs. Bernstein ignored her. "You could just *see* Dave and figure out if it's going to work. And maybe see some other people, too. You know, honey, lots of my friends didn't get married until they were in their thirties and they were very happy. They had a lot of fun, living in the city on their own. It's *good* to be on your own."

With uncharacteristic violence, Beth pushed away her plate, her sandwich untouched. "No, Mom, it's not. It's *not*. You don't know what it's like. It's *horrible*." Mrs. Bernstein could say nothing. Her mouth felt fused together. "It's *supposed* to be *good* to be on your own," Beth continued angrily. "Everybody says that. But it's not. It's not fun. I don't want to be alone anymore." "But, Beth, you can't just marry the first man who asks you because you don't want to be on your own anymore." Beth put her hands to her temples. "I *know* that!" Her voice was rising to levels inappropriate to the third-floor café at Saks. "Mom, I'm not an idiot. I wouldn't marry Will if I didn't love him. It's just, I'm afraid—" Her voice cracked and Mrs. Bernstein prayed no tears would come. It was too much, just too much. "I'm afraid I love Dave, too." Her head sank low toward the table. Miserably, she looked up through her bangs at her mother.

Before Mrs. Bernstein could formulate a response, Beth had pulled herself up straight in her little wire bistro chair. "I guess, I just don't think 'the one' exists. I think we make choices. We decide who 'the one' is, but we don't realize we're *deciding* because our, I don't know, conscious minds are saying, 'This is the one.' But there are all these other people out there, who we could just as easily fall in love with and make a life with. It would just be a different life, a different sort of being in love. I don't know why I've chosen Will. I don't, really. Maybe because it makes more *sense*. I can *imagine* our life together. But when I imagine life with Dave, I see a blank screen. Or, I see him, in an apartment, alone." She laughed. "I've been thinking about it all week. And, it's like, I can see us talking and laughing at dinner. Or walking around. But when I get to an apartment, I see him, alone."

Mrs. Bernstein nodded and picked up half of her sandwich. Beth's dilemma was clear to her now: in marrying Will, she'd finally have to relinquish her fantasy of Dave, the little notion she'd kept tucked away as she went about the business of her life, knowing, perhaps, that it would never come true, that he would never be the person she'd wanted him to be, or even the person she'd met all those years back, when she was really just a teenager, and he an attractive, sarcastic boy, with immense talent (a piano prodigy, a winner of awards) and brains, destined for greatness. He wouldn't be that boy again, no, certainly not. And he hadn't become the man they'd all expected. Perhaps he would, with time, and some other woman would reap the benefits. But Beth would be happy then, with a career (with any luck, NYU would keep her on for the fall) and a successful, handsome husband and children of her own (along with Sam, of course). Her daughter was right: people simply made choices.

Beth was eating her own sandwich now—grilled cheese and tomato, always her favorite—with good appetite. The color had returned to her face, though her nose and eyes were still red from the tears. Mrs. Bernstein made a note to take Beth back to the lounge for a quick powder; otherwise, she'd hate the way she looked in all the dresses. The girl dabbed at her lip with her large cloth napkin. *Pure white,* Mrs. Bernstein thought. *With her freckles, the dress has to be pure white.* She looked around the room at the tables and tables of women picking at salads or sipping spoonfuls of soup, sharing small slices of pie or Danish cut in quarters, just as she and Beth used to do. All of these women, she thought, had chosen—at some point—propriety, security . . . over *what,* though? What was the other option? An *amour fou?* For a grand passion to be grand, need it come with danger? Hadn't she loved Donald madly—and didn't she still—despite him being exactly the sort of person her parents might have chosen for her, with the house in Scarsdale, the inheritance, the dental degree, the practice he'd taken over from his father? Her eye settled on an important-looking lady, with a thick sheath of white hair and a scarf fastened by a large cameo. Had that matron, one day in the distant past, given up a Dave for a Will? If she hadn't, where might she now be? A memory languished along the fringes of Mrs. Bernstein's brain—some choice not taken, a dashing lover promising excitement and *understanding.* Whom could she be thinking of? That sad man with his dark, loamy eyes? No. There was no one, no one at all.

eight

Dave Kohane lived in a pleasant, three-room garden-level apartment on Bergen Street, which he'd purchased earlier that year with the bit of money he'd come into following the death of his grandmother. This lady—his father's mother—had been a tiny, churlish person with great mounds of white hair, who, until the very end, cooked massive *Mitteleuropean* dinners, beginning with hot borscht and ending with plum tart, a roast chicken or pot roast arriving somewhere in between. She had not been rich—at least, not by New York standards—but had, it turned out, been far richer than her two sons knew. She ate brown bread and cottage cheese for breakfast every day, dressed herself in boiled wool suits purchased during the Kennedy administration, and sent Dave and his cousin Evelyn, her only grandchildren, twenty-five-dollar checks twice each year, for Hanukkah and their respective birthdays in November and May. Dave's uncle Steve, Evelyn's father, was a corporate lawyer and devoted considerable effort to wresting control of his mother's assets, thinking he could invest them for her—or, better yet, turn them over to another Kohane cousin, a crackerjack CFP who had cut his teeth in analysis at Goldman, Sachs—but the woman refused, saying Dave's grandfather had arranged everything "very nicely" before his death. She had a "nice young man" at T. Rowe Price with whom she spoke once each month.

As it turned out, this nice young man did very well by her. "Jeez," Uncle Steve had said, sipping beer in Dave's parents' tiny kitchen, two weeks after the funeral. "Who knew Mom was loaded? Those twenty-five-dollar checks. God." Dave's father nodded sympathetically. He was a lawyer, too, but did labor work, having met Dave's mom when they were both canvassing for the AFL-CIO after college. Dave's mom made documentaries about migrant workers and African wars. They didn't think about money much. Or rather, they thought about it all the time, having rarely had enough of it, but—as they explained to Dave when he was old enough to understand—they'd decided to make compromises. They could have the life they wanted—working for the common good and so on—and live in a small apartment, with carefully chosen luxuries (his father had an overhealthy and, Dave thought, clichéd interest in wine); or they could live a different sort of life—devoted to the acquisition of goods and property—and be less happy in their work. Dave's father, at various points, had considered going corporate. And Dave's mom had, on several occasions, been offered jobs at commercial production companies (particularly after a documentary she produced won an Emmy). But they'd stuck to their guns—scrambling and scraping to send Dave to St. Ann's with Evelyn—and now, in their middle years, they were doing rather well. Their small apartment—one floor of a Baltic Street brownstone that went co-op in the eighties—was now worth twenty times what they'd paid for it. And thanks to that Emmy, Dave's mom now ran her own production company, out of a little town house on West Ninety-third, with an endless succession of contracts from PBS. The previous year, after she'd finished a six-part series on DNA, they'd bought a small house up near Woodstock, then flown off to Paris and Provence. Next year, they'd go to Italy. And now that they had this surprising influx of cash, from Dave's grandmother, they could do so in a bit more style.

Dave and Evelyn's share of the money was small in comparison to the sums received by their parents, but large by their own meager standards, as both had been impoverished since leaving college. Evelyn, who was always making Dave look bad, had handed the entire sum over to her father to invest. Dave had originally assumed he'd just live off the money, seeing as he was barely employed at the time of his grandmother's death, having just dropped out of Eastman. But then his father sat him down after dinner one night and suggested that the cash would disappear pretty quickly, much more quickly than Dave could imagine, and Dave should think seriously about making some big, practical sort of purchase, like an apartment. Since moving back to the city from Rochester, Dave had been sharing a place down the block from his parents, on an unsavory stretch of Baltic, across from a loud, crime-riddled school, with an actor named Jake Martin—one of Tal's less fortunate friends—whom he rarely saw in person but caught glimpses of on *Law & Order,* on which he'd played an organic fruit vendor, a stabbing victim, and a distraught single dad. Dave didn't love cohabitation, but *buying* a place seemed so grown-up. He hadn't the slightest idea how one might go about completing such a task. He was afraid, however, to display his ignorance in front of his father and mother and Uncle Steve (who was, again, drinking beer at his parents' kitchen table when this suggestion was made), and so he said, "Yeah, that's a good idea. I'll think about it."

A few weeks later, he paused outside the window of a Court Street Realtor, studying the photographs of available apartments. He recalled the phrase "twenty percent down"—or was it "twenty-five percent down"?—and suddenly realized what this formerly nonsensical term meant: You paid twenty percent of the price of the apartment in cash. Then you took out a mortgage for the rest. Armed with this rudimentary knowledge, he calculated that he could afford to spend about $200,000—that was, presuming he could pay the mortgage and maintenance—and scanned the posted photos for properties within his budget. The next day, he was filling out piles of paperwork—mortgage preapproval and so on—and before he knew it, he'd made a bid on this apartment, the first he saw, with its little garden and strange, dark middle room. It was, the Realtor told him, "priced to sell," because the owners had already bought a new place, a loft space in a newly renovated building two doors down, and needed the cash.

He'd been back in New York for ten months now, cobbling together his mortgage payments from teaching piano (which he hated), accompanying (which he hated even more), copying scores for composers (which he vacillated between hating and loving), and various sorts of menial labor, like temping or waiting tables (which, strangely, he enjoyed). The trouble was that while he had very strong feelings about what he *didn't* want to do, he possessed only an extremely vague idea of what he did want to do. This being that he would like to work on music that people actually listened to, rather than classical music, which, really, no one cared about anymore. Or only the people who played it and wrote it and taught it. Normal people simply weren't interested. Maybe they listened to the Brandenburg Concertos or "Appalachian Spring" or kept WNYC on as background music or attended a concert once a year so they could feel *cultured,* but that was it. This was exactly why he'd given up piano. Or this was what he'd told himself when he decided to drop out of Eastman: that he didn't want to be part of the absurd, archaic institution that classical music had become. He wanted to make *real* music, music that possessed some sort of relevance to the dominant culture, music that meant something.

But the truth was that over four unhappy years of grad school, he'd come to the sad realization that he was not a genius or a prodigy, as he'd been told throughout his life, and that he would not have a career as a soloist, but would be lucky to get a seat with a second- or third-tier orchestra in a provincial city or a teaching post at a Bible college, also in some unappealing place like Kansas or Missouri, teaching talentless undergrads. Both possibilities fell into the don't-want-to-do category. In theory, he wanted (he thought) to compose music, to do something really revolutionary, something that would garner the respect of critics *and* a popular audience, something that would transcend current notions of genre. In practice, however, he was only just now figuring out what such music would be, now that he was in this band, this kind of *good* band, and there was the remote chance of people playing it. Very remote, though, as the band was really a one-man outfit: the lead singer, Curtis, wrote all the songs and refused to entertain the notion of any other members contributing, though the other guys didn't seem to care at all. It was just Dave who minded, who would have liked to write his own songs, with a lead piano line, and maybe even sing lead vocals from time to time (he had, he thought, a pleasant tenor).

Lying in his bed, mornings, on Bergen Street—thinking he should really get up and write down the snippet of melody drifting in and out of his brain—he comforted himself with the thought that he was destined for higher sorts of things than pop songs, for this hybrid music he imagined, this *relevant* classical music. But there wasn't really any such thing. He would have to invent it. Otherwise, what were his non-pop options? Scoring films (*romantic swell as the spaceship hurtles into the dark heart of the unknown galaxy*)? Drafting minimalist pieces that called for the players to bang on sheets of metal or pluck violin strings with their teeth? Or shuffling together neoromantic motifs from the pantheon of canonical symphonies, like all the bright-eyed composers at Oberlin, with their tweed jackets and college scarves? He'd hated them all. What would they do, anyway? Get Ph.D.'s at Berkeley or Stanford. (The money was all out west, for reasons he didn't understand. It wasn't like people on the far coast listened to classical music any more than people in New York or Boston.) Live off grants and sad little commissions from Bang on a Can or Kronos? Yes, that's exactly what they'd do. Then settle into dull teaching gigs and fuck the cute violinists. A life of perpetual irrelevance, like a character in a Philip Roth novel or a Woody Allen movie. Or Herzog, fucking Herzog. No way. No, fucking way.

The irony was, of course, that in college—not to mention in the many years that preceded college—while his friends flailed about, taking classes in performance art or the history of Christian utopian movements, wondering exactly what they wanted to do with their lives, his future had, essentially, been set. *Not* worrying about career and so on had freed up a lot of his time at Oberlin, allowing him ample hours to fret over other things, like girls or existential matters. During the three years he'd lived with Tal—first in Keep, then in a shabby house off North Professor Street—Tal had patiently listened to Dave ramble on about such things, while they ate cold fried chicken from Convenient Food Mart and sipped cans of Pabst Blue Ribbon.

Now, with the clear vision provided by hindsight, Dave saw that Tal might have found Dave annoying or whiny or, as Sadie would say, "a bit tiresome," and maybe this was why Dave rarely heard from him anymore. In those days, he'd had a lot more to complain about than did Dave: Tal's parents were Boston conservatives who scrutinized Tal's grades each semester and expected him to go to law school, like a good Brookline boy, never mind that Tal had no interest in law (or medicine or business or the other professions deemed acceptable by his dad), had, in fact, never expressed interest in doing anything other than acting, and, more to the point, was not some stupid, deluded sucker, like half—no, *more* than half—the losers in the theater department (Emily excluded, of course), but seriously, hugely, freakishly talented and in possession of that certain something that makes people, if not stars, then at least compulsively *watchable*. Everyone thought so, *everyone*. One of his professors had encouraged him to apply to Yale; another had suggested he leave school and simply find an agent.

"Tell your parents that Peter Carson thinks you can get into Yale," Sadie had encouraged him (had she loved Tal even then? Did she *really* love Tal now? He'd always half thought *he'd* been the one she wanted, not that he'd ever admit that to anyone). "My parents," Tal told her, "don't care about Peter Carson or what he thinks." They were so reluctant to encourage his acting that his senior year at Concord they'd refused to attend any and every play in which he was cast—from *Midsummer* to *Six Characters in Search of an Author* to the play that Tal himself *wrote*—which would have been enough to make Dave fucking burn their house down, but not Tal, he loved them, the Morgenthals—"They're great, really"— and he couldn't stand the thought of disappointing them, even in the smallest way, which just made no sense to Dave. *Poor Tal,* Dave had thought, again and again in college, watching his friend take these *deadly* poli-sci classes to pacify his hard-ass father, who was under the impression that his only son, his only *child,* would be Harvard Law, class of '97, not that Tal did anything to disabuse him of this notion.

"He's wearing himself out," Dave told Sadie early in their senior year.

"It's moronic. He rehearses until, like, midnight, then he hangs out with me and when I go to bed, he, like, *studies*."

"Dave, there's a difference between wearing yourself out and *working*," retorted Sadie. "We all can't live Dave Kohane's life of leisure."

But Sadie, for once, didn't get it: that Tal might give it all up, give *everything* up, might become this *waste of a life,* this suburban nothing, that he might become one of those people who do the "right" thing, the *expected* thing, that he might go to fucking law school and get married and live in fucking Newton and listen to public radio in his Volvo and Dave would be left alone, alone with himself.

As it turned out, Dave was the waste, the one who disappointed everyone. Nine months after commencement, there was Tal, hawking Clearasil between segments of *90210* (which Dave watched ironically— or so he told himself). There was a Snickers ad, a play at the Atlantic, then a little spot in a skit on *Conan,* then *regular* spots in skits on *Conan,* then— almost simultaneously—the secondary role in a truly awful Robin Williams movie, a tertiary role in a short-lived sitcom, and the sale of a screenplay, to the producers behind *There's Something About Mary,* which Tal had decided was "subversive" rather than stupid (Tal, who, in college, had watched *La Dolce Vita* so many times he'd worn out the tape), and now this bigger movie, this movie that seemed like it wasn't actually going to *suck*. Suddenly, he was out of town half the time and when he wasn't, he was with Sadie, or he was working on screenplays with his writing partner, some cocky comedy guy who could never remember Dave's name, and beyond that he always had things to do, people to see, and he never invited Dave along with him, almost as if he was afraid Dave was going to hit up his shiny, successful friends for—what?—a part in their next asshole movie? Money?

He wasn't famous, Tal, not even close, but that could change at any second. A few months ago, the alumni magazine had run a little story about Tal and two other alums working in film, an older, famous screenwriter and an even older director of art-house features. Tal, at twenty-six, was the youngest. He was twenty-seven now, as Dave would be in November, which made them four years older than Curtis Lang, the frontman for Dave's band, a scruffy-haired kid with a long, serious face, class of '98, who wrote strange, meandering tunes with even stranger lyrics, studded, though, with moments of freaky insight, which Dave wished he'd come up with himself. "How selfish of you, to believe in me," went one.

In the mornings, as Dave lay in bed thinking, his new neighbors stomped across the floor—he hadn't considered this problem before purchasing a garden-level flat (which was, of course, just a nice name for a fucking *basement*)—occasionally shouting to each other from one end of their apartment to the other. These cries permeated Dave's ceiling, the materials of which—wood, plaster—translated the English words spoken nine feet above him into a muffled hum, like the incomprehensible mumblings of the unseen adult characters in Peanuts cartoons. The female part of the couple was strange and sexy, with a broad, mannish face and wide-set hazel eyes. He saw her sometimes at the Met Foods, buying limp stalks of broccoli and flower-imprinted luncheon napkins or large quantities of limes for the parties this couple regularly held, loud affairs to which he was usually invited and occasionally attended, returning to his own apartment after a dull conversation with an aspiring journalist or web designer, only to hear the noise of the gathering—hoots and crashes and stomps and laughs—in his own apartment, nearly as loud as it had been moments before, when he'd wandered the center of it, wine glass in hand.

The building was made of limestone and sounds echoed strangely, select tones amplified. Sometimes, Dave thought of recording them and using them for something. More often, he thought of how the town house was once home to a single family, before being carved up into little apartments, the detail stripped out of them, narrow halls carved in to make way for tiny baby rooms and closets. When Dave was little, his aunt Judy—Uncle Steve's wife and Evelyn's mother—had died, and his father and uncle had talked endlessly of leaving their apartments—Dave's family in Cobble Hill, though it was just called "Brooklyn" then, and Evelyn's in Brooklyn Heights—buying such a house, and restoring it to its former grandeur, for their two small families to share, the unstoppable Kohane brothers, no longer separated by the twenty-odd blocks between Joralemon Street and Baltic. They'd grown up in such a house, a few miles east in Midwood, chasing each other up and down the stairs (and profited nicely from its sale after their mother's death). As kids, Dave and Evelyn paid weekly visits to this ancestral home. They, too, chased each other up and down the carpeted stairs, but with much less vigor than their fathers, both of them quiet children, always collapsing onto the nearest sofa with a book and a cookie, dark circles ringing their almond-shaped Kohane eyes. Dave, even skinnier then, could never quite work himself into the frenzy of teasing that came so naturally to the other little boys. He would try, pouncing on Evelyn as she sat reading, and pulling her hair or tickling her until she screamed "Stop, stop, stop, I hate you" in a hoarse voice and ran up the stairs to lock herself in her father's old room, where she kept a cache of worn stuffed animals and dog-eared mystery novels. Dave would trail her, reach out a long, bony hand to grab her sneakered foot, and drag her down the stairs, booming "You must come vith me," like his father imitating Bela Lugosi, but his heart wasn't in it, and eventually he'd let her go.

Adolescence morphed him into one of those wan kids you see near Lincoln Center on Saturdays, heading off to Juilliard with a black nylon bag full of music, his skin cast green from the fluorescent light of the practice room. He did a double degree at Oberlin, piano performance and philosophy, which he finished in just four years, though—he frequently reminded his parents—most double degree students took five. And he had headed off to Eastman after graduation, full of hope and excitement. Or that's what he'd thought at the time. Now he saw that maybe this wasn't the case. Maybe he'd headed off to Eastman already defeated and full of fear. That if he'd really wanted that life—the solo career, the record deal, whatever—he wouldn't have gone to Eastman at all, but would have entered the big contests, sought out the agent, done the things you do to become a sort of star. The whole *point* of going to Eastman was to wind up with a job at some sad, loser college.

In truth, he hated to think about that time—four years of his life spent in fucking *Rochester*—and tried to steel his mind against it. But, of course, the more he tried to turn himself to other subjects, the more he played over the injustices and embarrassments and disappointments of those years at grad school, which seemed, in a way, to have all blended into one long winter. He had arrived on campus—in a weird, unpopulated section of Rochester (which was itself a weird, unpopulated city, all too reminiscent of Cleveland)—full of swagger, certain that he was the department's show pony. At Oberlin, he'd been a star, a coveted player—he and Tal equals then—respected by the composition students for his knowledge of new music, which was unusual in a pianist (or any sort of classical musician, for that matter). In fact, as an undergrad, he'd had his choice of schools—Juilliard, Peabody, and, yes, Eastman—but he'd chosen Oberlin for reasons both practical (they'd offered him a full ride) and sentimental (his father was '67). As a freshman, he'd been given an orchestra seat, a rare honor for so young a pianist. And though he was perpetually behind on his practicing—endlessly playing catch-up, scrambling to learn pieces at the last minute, hours before a concert—it always worked out in the end.

He'd held his senior concert in Finney Chapel—just a few weeks after Liz Phair played there—and included some unusual stuff on the program, Xenakis, Satie, whatever. At least a hundred people came, a huge turnout for a recital: most were held in the Conservatory's tiny auditoriums, attended only by professors, close friends, and bewildered, bored family. But Dave was not, as he often mused with satisfaction, a normal Con student. He pulled beer at the bar in the student union—the Disco, or the 'Sco, as the freshmen dorkily called it—along with Tal and Sadie, and had a large following among the grunge contingent, the flannel-clad guys who played in bands and the long-haired girls who worshipped them. He dated the girls (before Beth, of course, though there was a fling or two *during*) and hung around with the guys—a bunch of whom lived in a shambling pile of wood called "Slack House" or "House of Slack"—drinking bad beer, watching kung fu movies, and engaging in ironic discussions of popular culture. And he played in some of their bands, including an outfit called Quizmaster Quest (after an obscure video game) that became legendary on campus, due less to their sound, which was largely cribbed from fIREHOSE and the Minutemen, and more to the emaciated good looks of the lead singer, a hollow-eyed Minnesotan named Jan Jensen.

By comparison, Rochester was cold and wretched, both meteorologically and socially. All the other piano students were Asian and silent, or blowsy and schoolmarmish and headed for teaching jobs at Lower Arkansas Community College, or old and male and balding and terminally flustered, or outrageous flaming queens, who smoked cigarette after cigarette in the little courtyard outside the practice rooms. And he the lone straight male, wandering angry and disheveled around the dull, deserted streets, wondering if he should ask out the pretty flautist in his theory class, the one who always wore prim round-necked sweaters, like a coed from the 1950s. But her thin, childlike body disturbed him. He lay in bed at night, envisioning her next to him, her tiny hands running up and down his chest like spiders, and felt like a lech. He started practicing at weird hours and sleeping at even weirder ones, having no friends and no responsibilities other than the few classes he needed to attend and teach, all of them easier than his hardest at Oberlin. By October, it was freezing. He wore thermals under his jeans and sat by a bracingly ugly man-made waterfall that had been mysteriously set into the town's creepy industrial landscape, feeling sorry for himself and allowing the crashing water—pouring off great slabs of smooth, dun-colored cement—to clear some of the detritus in his head, or, at the very least, to allow him to stop hearing his students' imprecise notes, and Beth's whispery voice on his answering machine.

He'd spent the previous summer at home, in Brooklyn, cramming four years of *stuff* into his tiny childhood room, the back abutment of his parents' floor-through. At night, he drank beer with his friends from St. Ann's, all of them staying in New York and starting jobs at publishing companies or design houses or theater troupes. He planned on practicing—planned on practicing *every day* and reading *In Search of Lost Time*. Instead he sat on the stoop of his building, smoking and skimming the arts section of the *Times*. He slept until noon, or sometimes one or two, then padded into the apartment's tiny kitchen, unchanged since the mid-1970s, and made himself a cup of coffee in the smallest of his mother's three French presses (his mother was *insane* about coffee).

All that summer he attempted to avoid speaking to Beth, who was holed up at her parents' house, thirty miles north, reading Victorian novels and swimming in her neighbor's pool. Once a week or so, she'd train into the city on some errand and call him from Soho, where she was having her hair cut, or midtown, at a matinee with her grandmother. "Come over," he always found himself saying. And she always agreed to, with studied nonchalance, and made her way, hesitantly, to Brooklyn. He'd throw on stained khakis, stained T-shirt, and flip-flops and meet her at the Bergen Street F stop, as she had a suburbanite's sense of distance and always got turned around on the way to his parents' apartment, thinking she'd gone too far when she wasn't even halfway there. Through the station's wrought-iron bars, Dave watched the smatterings of people getting off the trains—mostly studenty types, like himself, for who else would be at liberty to wander the city at three in the afternoon?—mesmerized by the flow of the metal cars, sleepy with heat, longing for a cigarette. Just when he was beginning to worry that she was lost, Beth would appear, hair lank around her soft, pliant cheeks. Her eyes were the exact same shade as her hair—the color of weak tea—which lent her the look of a forest creature, perhaps a fawn. She was such a *Beth,* he thought. What if her mother had named her Jo?

As they sat drinking iced coffee at the new bistro on Smith Street (three months earlier it had been a crack bodega that his mother crossed the street to avoid), the sweat slowly drying under their arms and along the sides of their spines, Beth detailing the horror of a Scarsdale summer ("I think every guy I went to high school with is going to medical school in the fall") and the advances made upon her person by the manager of the local Banana Republic, where she'd recently bought a maroon dress that her mother *hated,* Dave would be thinking of the moment when they would walk the three blocks back to his childhood room and he would give her a glass of his dad's white wine, and Beth would stop her nervous chatter. He would put his arms around her—her body soft and white, smooth and unmuscled, like fabric—and lead her to his small bed, the fan blowing on them as they sweated and sweated the already damp sheets. Afterward, Beth would sleep, thick from wine, and he'd wake her for dinner with his parents, an event she loved and hated. She knew—she *certainly* knew—that it was over, that he didn't love her enough, or that he did, but she wasn't quite the person he wanted to love, and that he invited her to Brooklyn because she loved him—for her, he was the one, the end, the thing in itself—and he knew, he *knew,* he should love her with equal devotion, should embrace some semblance of their future, their contributions to the Oberlin scholarship fund, but he couldn't, he just couldn't. And neither could he say "No, don't come" when she called and said "I'm here." At dinner, she told funny stories, complimented his mother's chicken paillard, and laughed at his father's stupid jokes. Dave sat silently, in a semisulk, avoiding his mother's serious blue gaze. She knew, too, of course, that Dave had closed himself off to Beth, who was pretty rather than beautiful, sweet rather than dangerous, devoted rather than confused, and she tried to avoid saying "You're making a mistake," though she didn't need to, really, which annoyed him, as everything seemed to annoy him that summer.

Even Tal. Who, at that point, wasn't faring much better. Over commencement weekend, he'd confessed to his parents that not only had he not been accepted at any of the law schools—Harvard, Yale, Columbia— they'd simply assumed he'd attend, but he hadn't actually even sent in any of the applications. "But you've always wanted to be a lawyer," his mother kept saying, "ever since you were a little boy." If Dave were in Tal's place, he would have said, "No, Mom, *you* wanted me to be a lawyer. *I* wanted to be an actor." But Tal was Tal and he just smiled and shook his head.

Still, when the Morgenthals got back to Brookline, he and his father had it out. Tal called Dave a few days after commencement. "Things are pretty dire here," he said, in a sharp, ironic tone that did little to mask his very real anguish. "My mother won't come out of their bedroom. My father says I've broken her heart." To add insult to injury, they'd transformed his childhood room into a blank, Formica-filled office for his mother's kosher-style catering company—Ella's Edibles—which had expanded tremendously in the four years since Tal left home, the Jews of Brookline (not to mention Newton) having entered into a Renaissance period and being in need of an endless supply of salmon puffs and mock sushi.

"Oh, man, I'm sorry," Dave told him. "What are you going to do?"

"I'm leaving," he said, to Dave's surprise. "I'm just going to come to New York. Carson said he'd put me in touch with agents." There was a brief silence. "Do you think your parents would mind if I stayed with you for a few days?"

"Um, no," said Dave, who was sure his parents wouldn't mind, but suddenly, confusingly, felt that *he* might.

"It'll just be a few days," Tal said. "I've just got to get out of here."

"Do you have a job?" asked Dave, feeling like an asshole.

"No," said Tal, his voice ragged, "I don't have a fucking *job,* Dave. How could I have a fucking job? Who are you, my fucking *dad*?"

"It's just, you know," said Dave sullenly. Why was he annoyed by the idea of Tal moving to New York? Because he would be going to Rochester in two months and Tal would stay and at Christmas, when Dave came home to visit, Tal would be wanting to take Dave to his favorite Chinese place and his favorite coffee shop and it would all just be too much for Dave. Or because Tal was actually doing the thing he wanted to do, rather than hiding in some dumb graduate program where he'd learn nothing he hadn't learned already. "It's expensive here. It's, you know, there are broker's fees and stuff. Sorry. I was just, you know—" Dave heard a sharp intake of breath: Tal willing himself to be calm. Dave had heard him do it a thousand times while on the phone with his dad.

"I *know,*" he told Dave. "I have bar mitzvah money. It'll float me for a while. I just need a place to stay while I find an apartment, but I can ask Sadie if I can stay with—"

"No, man, that sounds great." A strange sensation had overtaken Dave, which he quickly recognized as relief. Tal was coming. He loved Tal. "Come whenever. You can stay as long as you need to. My mom loves you."

He arrived the next day, Sunday, on the Chinatown bus, his fraying army duffel slung over one shoulder. Dave met him on East Broadway, under the Manhattan Bridge overpass, and took him to the dim sum place in the mall built into the bridge's northern buttress. "Did you tell them you were going?" Dave asked. Tal gave him an odd look.

"Of course I told them."

"And your dad didn't go ballistic?"

Tal shook his shaggy head and laughed. "No," he said, "it was weird. He was completely calm." Dave thought, but did not say, that this was not, somehow, all that weird. Tal's father, like Tal, could be torturous in his restraint.

"What did he say?" asked Dave. Tal smirked and adopted the posture of his father—spine flat against the back of his chair, mouth turned down at the corners, glasses dangling from one hand. "'Tal, I don't understand why you're being so irrational,'" he intoned. "'If you don't want to go to law school, fine. But renting a place in New York? It doesn't make any sense. When you pay rent, you're just throwing money down the toilet.'" Dave laughed.

"So what does he want you to do? Live there with them forever?"

"Yup," said Tal.

"No," said Dave.

"Oh, yes," said Tal, his grin growing wild. "He has it all planned out. I'll live with them for three years and work at his firm"—Tal's father did something mysterious having to do with the mergers of enormous companies—"and save enough money to buy a place. In Boston, of course."

"Not Brookline," Dave said.

"Of course Brookline. Or Newton. Or Cambridge. Though Cambridge"—he smirked—"isn't really cost-efficient."

Chewing on shumai and shreds of bean-curd skin, Dave began to pick out the threads of the restaurant's din: individual voices gabbing in Mandarin, the plates clattering against each other or the sides of rubber bussing tubs, the hiss of steam from the dumpling carts that traversed the aisles. "I don't get it," Dave said finally. "They turned your room into an office. He's not even speaking to you. But he wants you to live with him? For *years*?"

Tal laughed, a sad, hollow sound. He was tired. Dave should have taken him right home, let him get settled in. "It's normal, right," he asked Dave, who started nodding even before Tal had finished the question. "I mean, it's normal for grown children to find their own apartments. I'm not doing something weird, right?"

"Um, *yeah*," Dave said, with a grimace. "Tal, *come on*. It's totally normal. You know that."

Tal shrugged and gulped his Tsing Tao. "I don't know," he said. "He said I'm breaking her heart."

"By not going to law school? By not living with them until you're like thirty?" Dave rolled his eyes. "Trust me," he said. "They'll get over it."

"I guess," agreed Tal. "I went to synagogue with them yesterday—"

"Wait, they go to synagogue?" asked Dave.

"Yeah," Tal told him. "Not so much when I was growing up, but now they've become weirdly religious. They go every Saturday. It's good for Mom's business."

"Ohhhh, right," said Dave.

"It all comes down to the bottom line with the family Morgenthal," he said, raising his eyebrows, which were dark and thick and extraordinarily straight. "But, yeah, it was really weird to be back there. I don't think I've been since my bar mitzvah. And, you know there's that part where they, where you, you know, stand up and recite the mourner's kaddish, if you've lost someone in the last year." Dave nodded. He and Evelyn had been forced to attend daily services at their Zionist summer camp, albeit of the stapled-together-hippie-prayer-book variety. "Well, my dad stood, because, you know, Grandpa Harry—" Dave nodded again. Tal's grandfather, a chain-smoking garmento, had died in December, during finals week, which meant Tal had missed the funeral. "And I couldn't remember the prayer, so I tried to read it in Hebrew, and I couldn't—I'd forgotten everything, so I just sort of pretended, but I just felt like such a loser." Dave looked at him, unsure of his point. "*My own grandfather* and I can't even say this little prayer for him."

"Well, you *could* have—" Dave started, but Tal waved his words away. "What?" asked Dave. "What?"

"I don't know," said Tal. "I just, I don't know."

•

In Rochester, Dave's plans for hard-core dating—not to mention any semblance of a normal social life—were quickly thwarted. There was no one even remotely datable. He spent nights on the phone with Beth, listening to tales of Milwaukee, a town that seemed vaguely more exciting than Rochester, which bothered him. In mid-December Beth obtained a "best friend," named Glyn, a Brit who'd actually crossed the pond to write his dissertation on *Gilligan's Island* or some other such absurdity. Suddenly Glyn's name came up every five minutes—"Glyn's mom came to visit and brought us Marmite. *Marmite,* Dave!"—and Dave decided it was over, Beth could no longer call him at four in the morning to tell him she was lonely. He was always wondering if Glyn was in the other room, sleeping, incapable of properly quelling the particular loneliness of a Jewish girl from Scarsdale. And he could not call her either. No, he most certainly could not. Dave's mother worked for PBS, after all, so what was he doing mooning over a girl who sought meaning in, like, *Hollywood Squares*?

He started hanging around with the queens—who were, he saw, just like his Oberlin friends, cynical and bitter and frighteningly smart—and spent his weekends at Rochester's gay clubs, of which there were surprisingly many. He took up smoking for real, buying cartons of Basics, and he ignored the messages that piled up on his machine, from his mother, from Tal, from Beth, and from Evelyn, who always managed to make him feel like an ass. "Dave, did you get my email," she'd say, modulating her voice so as not to seem irritated. "I'm wondering if you're coming home for Grandma's eightieth birthday party in March."

That summer—and the three that followed—he stayed at Tal's place in Williamsburg and waited tables at a Southern restaurant on Cornelia Street. He tried to pretend his parents lived in a different city—half ashamed, half proud that he'd ignored them all year—and spent most of his time alone, actively not doing what he *should* have been doing, which was, of course, practicing. Some nights, half drunk from the staff round that commenced at midnight, after the kitchen closed, he'd walk home, across Houston, then Delancey, and up and over the Williamsburg Bridge, a fat roll of cash bulging in his pocket. At the dead center of the bridge, he'd stop and rest, his buzz worn off, and peer out over the railing at the tall buildings that lined the Manhattan bank of the East River, inside one of which lived Sadie's aunt Minnie, an ancient, balding schoolteacher, fiercely devoted to Sadie, having never had any children of her own. He'd gone with Sadie to visit her a few times—she loved young people—in her boxy apartment, overfilled with Judaica and peeling, dark-veneered furniture, and left feeling virtuous and terribly, horribly alone. Later, when his grandmother died, he wondered why he'd never thought to bring Sadie out to visit her, or even to visit her at all, unaccompanied by his parents. And why *hadn't* he gone home for her birthday in March?

Each August, his coffers replenished, he'd return to Rochester, sick with excitement and anxiety, certain the next semester would mark his triumph, his ascendance. Instead, he fell further and further behind, racking up record numbers of incompletes and incurring the wrath and, even worse, disappointment of his professors. After the fourth year of this, he drove back, once again, to Rochester, and instead of unloading his summer stuff, he silently packed up his winter stuff and his books and drove back to New York, steering his car to his parents' apartment, rather than Tal's, for this year, he knew, Tal had been glad to see him go, though their paths had barely crossed: Tal had been out of town half the time, on location in Vermont, and when he was in town, he was always making plans with Sadie, plans that didn't include Dave, though, of course, they always said "Come along" as they headed out the door. It was the fall of 1998, a month before Lil's wedding. His mother happened to be at the front window when he pulled up, and ran downstairs, he thought, to greet him. Instead, he received a look of cold fury, her thin lips pressed into an even thinner line. She knew. "This is just like you!" she said grimly. "To *quit* right before you're finished. What is *wrong* with you?" He shouted something back—trying to ignore the fact that she was crying—something about never having wanted to go to Eastman, having done it for her and Dad, because everyone expected him to, though he didn't know if this was true or not, he just knew it would hurt her. And, of course, it *had*. "Well, you're not staying here," she'd shouted. He'd gone around the corner to Sadie's, though she didn't seem particularly happy to see him either. A week later, he'd moved into Jake Martin's dusty apartment, selling his car to cover the security deposit. Three months later, in January, he'd bought his place. Which meant, he supposed, that he was back for good. This was his life.

Over his ten months in New York, he'd settled into a dissolute routine of sorts. The piecemeal way in which he earned money meant that each day was markedly different from the next: On Sundays, he spent most of the day practicing with the band—they were calling themselves Anhedonia, though they worried that was too much of a cliché—in the space they rented in DUMBO, a cement-floored room in a warehouse that had been converted into studios. On Mondays, he attempted to lay out the principles of music theory for a small but terrifying bunch of students at Queens Community College. Though he only taught one two-hour class, the task generally consumed his entire day, as it took him a good ninety minutes to get out to the college, which was only accessible via a chain of obscure city buses. After class, he stayed and fooled around on the piano in his classroom, access to a half-decent instrument being the one perk of this awful job. (He'd hated practicing at Eastman, when it had mattered, but now he looked forward to it, if only because it was preferable to getting on the bus and making the slow journey back to Brooklyn.) Tuesdays and Wednesdays he stayed at home, recovering from his trip to Queens, and doing whatever copying work he had at the time. This was a tedious, detail-oriented business—often done by composition students desperate for extra cash—which entailed taking a large piece of music (a symphonic score or some such thing) and copying out, by hand, the parts for separate instruments (anywhere from four to sixty). One major score could take him months. In a bizarre, masochistic way, Dave enjoyed the coolie labor of copying, even though the scores he was copying were usually the worst derivative sort of crap. He loved the sight of the fresh black ink on the clean white page, and it was pleasurable to pattern out the beautiful, curving notes. He'd generally memorized parts of the pieces by the end, crappy though they were.

Thursdays, Fridays, and Saturdays, he worked at a popular restaurant on Smith Street called Madame Woo's, a cross between a traditional bistro—white tile floor, cloudy gilt-framed mirrors, Parisian street signs, black-and-white photos—and a Midwestern Chinese joint, with purposefully tacky red vinyl booths, a kitschy drinks menu, and a weird assortment of pan-Asian antiques. Thursdays and Fridays, he worked the main dining room, which was filled with older couples eating multi-course meals and moaning about real estate. Saturdays, he covered the front bar, in which girls of his own age perched on bamboo stools at the high tables by the front doors, watching the passersby or perhaps desiring to be watched themselves, in their sundresses and capri pants and tank tops. In the room's dark interior, similar girls clustered around small tables, talking animatedly to one another over watermelon margaritas and square plates of Vietnamese ravioli. These women inevitably flirted with him, often in an adorable, sweet, shy manner, as though they were simply bowled over by Dave's particular charms and didn't make a habit of throwing themselves at waiters. Among them, sometimes, was his upstairs neighbor, Katherine, flanked by two pretty friends, who always insisted on shouting something that managed to be both offensive and flattering, "I can't *believe* you really work here! You just don't *seem* like a waiter." "Well, I am," Dave would say. "Which makes me uniquely qualified to tell you about our specials. We have a nice roast duck in red curry sauce . . ." And the girls at the neighboring tables would lean in to hear what he was saying to these lucky friends of his, to see if he was somehow giving them preferential treatment.

Sometimes, he thought he saw Beth among this crowd of women and a little shiver went through him. But the tall girl sipping lemonade alone, making marks on a thick manuscript, was not Beth, nor was the fair-haired girl smiling calmly at a short, fat, freckled man. He would not admit that he was looking for her, that he was hoping to find her in his section, nor would he admit that he missed her—for he wasn't even sure that he did—but he had no trouble confessing a less savory desire: he did not want her to marry Will Chase. Or anyone, for that matter. And yet, he did not want to marry her himself. And so he did nothing, nothing other than disparage Will to his friends—"Isn't he kind of *stiff*?"—and take home the endless rounds of women who, like Katherine, made themselves strangely available to him when he approached their table, notepad in hand: a wholesome-looking yoga instructor who liked to go to foreign films at the Quad (not French films, as would be Dave's choice, but tragic Chinese and Indian social realist flicks about child prostitution and such); a sunburned blonde who had played guitar for Their Own Devices, a Chapel Hill band that had been famous for a moment in the mid-1990s, though, the girl explained, they'd made no money, really, despite having toured the world with Neil Young and Sonic Youth; a boyish French girl who drank wine by herself at the bar, scribbling in a little notebook, and whom he'd shocked with his decent French. He was particularly fond of a lawyer, an earnest lefty like his dad, who'd been in his class at Oberlin, tiny and vivacious, with bright black eyes and shiny black hair. He hadn't known her at school, but she recognized him the moment he approached her table.

As of late, these girls were feeling rather neglected, for Dave's free nights were becoming increasingly rare. The Reynold Marks shows were coming up, and nearly every night, he found himself walking over to DUMBO, trying to ward off the pangs of anxiety that this whole endeavor instilled in him. "You've got to just get over yourself," Sadie kept telling him, and he knew she was right, but he still felt stupid and awkward around the band's other four members, mostly because of the enormous—or, okay, *big*—discrepancy in their ages. The drummer, a spoiled kid named Marco LaRoue, was only nineteen, nearly ten years Dave's junior. He'd been kicked out of Bard his freshman year for drug trafficking. Which sounded hard-core, but in reality he'd just received a packet of pot through the mail (a campus mailroom clerk had detected the scent and called the cops). Like Dave, he'd gone to St. Ann's, but he was one of the rich kids. His father was some sort of big art dealer and the kid now had his own place, a loft in a mixed-use DUMBO building, not far from the practice space. His father, he said, had bought it as an investment, thinking he might want to open a satellite gallery in

DUMBO and since it was just sitting there empty, well, why not move in, right? ("Yeah, man. Totally," Dave had responded.) He was obnoxiously handsome in the manner of an Italian movie star: full lips, olive skin, dark curly hair, the sort of large, hooded eyes that celebrity journalists inevitably describe as "soulful."

When the band went to Pedro's for a beer after practice, girls stared at him, openmouthed, or whispered to one another, perhaps wondering if he *was* a movie star. Some nights, he sulked and ignored them. Others, he played up this attention, sending over drinks to a table of pretty girls and bowing in their direction, like James Bond or a Korean gangster, which made Dave want to puke, even as he wished he could pull off such suavity without seeming like a complete asshole. He treated Dave in a similar manner: Sometimes, he jumped off the ratty plaid couch they'd installed in the practice room and gave Dave a manly hug, kissing him on both cheeks (his mother was from Milan, his father a Brooklyn Jew who had spun LaRoue from Lazarowitzky), and offering him a beer. Other times, for no discernible reason, he simply glared at Dave, responding with extreme sarcasm to any words that emerged from Dave's mouth. Sadie suggested that he was intimidated, owing to Dave's advanced age and musical pedigree. Quizmaster Quest, after all, was the stuff of Oberlin legend—their tapes on rotation at WOBC—particularly now that Jan Jensen's postcollege band, Ladderback, was getting some serious play. But Dave suspected it was the exact opposite: the guy thought Dave some sort of fogy, with his Cure and Smiths references, and his classical repertoire. He remembered, quite clearly, what it was like to be nineteen: twenty-seven had seemed impossibly old, an age he'd never reach.

Sundays and evenings, when Dave arrived at the DUMBO space, they were generally all there already, sitting around smoking pot and drinking beer, talking and laughing. Sometimes they stopped abruptly when he walked in the door, which terrified him (were they discussing *him*?). Just as often, they simply ignored his arrival, the reedy Curtis continuing on whatever stream of thought he'd been following before Dave's arrival. Had they all decided to meet early purposefully, in order to exclude him? Had they told Dave to come at eight, knowing they'd arrive at six thirty to share a pizza and perhaps trade stories about Dave's lameness? Thinking about this possibility, he'd grow furious, for he was so utterly and decidedly *not* lame. He had not sold out. He hadn't gone to law school or become a web designer or a day trader. And he knew more about music than the four of them put together. Not just classical or whatever—*all* of it, Beethoven, Schopenhauer, the Carter family, Bill Monroe, Gershwin, Elvis Costello, Hüsker Dü, the Sex Pistols, David Bowie, Bauhaus, Bob Dylan, Django Reinhardt, every *fucking* thing.

And the fact was that they *were* wasting him, wasting his talent and skill (playing these piddly little parts, not letting him write songs), not to mention his knowledge, his experience, even his Jan Jensen connections. He kept thinking he would quit, but then he would think better of it, mostly because of one incontrovertible fact: they were good. Really good. Curtis's songs—which somehow managed to be both ironic and romantic—were lovely and true. It was a pleasure to play them. And yet, he wanted to play his *own* songs, which had, since his joining the band, begun to materialize. They were different from Curtis's, of course, but in the dark of his apartment, at the ancient upright he'd pulled in off the street, or the too-expensive keyboard his uncle Steve had given him his first year at Eastman, they sounded just as good. Darker, plainer, more plaintive, and with, he thought, more humor. They were piano songs, of course, not guitar songs, though the guitar would come in, on most of them. And he wanted a violin—a fiddle, really—on some, a sort of Weimar sound on others.

"Does he even know you're writing songs?" suggested Sadie, when he complained about Curtis and his lack of interest in Dave's work for the millionth time. Dave was trying, really, to not be irritated by the fact that he now only saw her alone when Tal was out of town. Though he supposed he saw her more often than he saw Tal. "Why don't you just tell him? Play them for him."

"Trust me," Dave told her. "He does *not* care. He knows I did comp at Eastman. He *knows* I'm writing stuff."

"So, then why don't you just quit and start your own band?" asked Sadie, in an overly patient way, as if to indicate that they had *had* this conversation before, hadn't they, which, of course, made him furious.

"I don't *want* to quit," he told her. "I *like* the band. You don't understand."

But she had a point, and the real truth was that he was afraid to quit, afraid that without actual physical people—people he knew and could touch and whine about in their absence—for whom to write songs, he would cease to write them, as he had after leaving Eastman and before joining up with Curtis. Each time he worked up the nerve to quit, something happened that disallowed him from doing so. First, they booked that show at Mercury Lounge (Marco's dad knew the owner). So he decided to stay on for that. And now this Reynold Marks gig, which was, really, a huge fucking deal, even though Reynold Marks was, yes, *lame*. He'd been vaguely cool at one point—a college radio staple—but then there'd been that big single, some shitty ballad, and—bam—the baseball-capped morons at Syracuse and SUNY-Binghamton and wherever had stopped listening to Hootie and the Blowfish or Dave Matthews or whoever long enough to buy a million copies of Reynold Marks's second album and go all apoplectic when he appeared on Letterman.

The thing about Reynold Marks, though, was that he was a *pianist* (like Dave) rather than a guitarist (like Curtis), and for this reason alone Dave felt a strange affection for the guy—though he would never admit it to anyone—and wondered if the presence of a pianist, not just a keyboard player, wasn't what attracted Marks to Anhedonia (if that *was* what they were going to call themselves), now that it mattered, for the show was almost upon them, and Curtis et al. were going kind of nuts about it. Actually, it was two shows—two *sold-out* shows—a Thursday and Friday night at the end of the month. Dave had found subs for his shifts at Madame Woo's and carefully laundered his favorite T-shirts, a faded black relic from the first Pixies tour ("Death to the Pixies") and a tattered navy thing with the Oberlin seal on it, in cracked white ink, passed down from his father. They sat on his dresser, sending out faint beams of promise in advance of their wearing. He had secured VIP passes for all of his friends, except Beth, who wouldn't want to come anyway. They were rehearsing nearly all night, every night, and Dave was behind on a huge copying project for some big-deal Juilliard guy. He'd have to work night and day in August to catch up.

Curtis had prepared the set list, of course, without input from anyone else. He'd chosen mostly newer songs, which was sort of stupid, Dave thought, and kind of stressful, as they now had to rush to learn them all. And as soon as they'd mastered one, Curtis decided it sucked and swapped in something newer. The guy was incredibly prolific, churning out a few songs a week, and always thinking the newest stuff was better. And even the new stuff, he couldn't leave alone. "What if we try it really slow?" he'd say, about a fast, anthem sort of thing that was, Dave thought, *meant* to be fast. Or "What if we change the key?" *Then why did you write it in this key,* Dave wanted to ask, but never did, of course. And Curtis, of course, never asked what Dave thought of anything. He seemed to regard Dave as something akin to an animated piece of furniture. "*Why* don't you just *talk* to him?" Sadie had moaned a few days prior, dropping her head heavily onto her right hand. Tal had left for L.A., his big-deal film, so suddenly Sadie was free for drinks whenever Dave wanted. "You're killing me."

"You don't understand what this guy is like," Dave told her.

"He seems perfectly nice," she insisted. "Play him the stuff you're working on."

"*Seems* nice," Dave explained, "but has the icy heart of a hired assassin."

The closer they got to the show, the more quiet and impassive Curtis became, gesturing with his long hands to indicate "louder" or "softer" or "faster" or "slower" instead of speaking the words. He was living in the practice space now, in a pup tent, having given up his apartment (and the unfriendly girl installed in it) and quit his job at a coffee shop in order to devote every waking minute to the band. Dave had started biting his cuticles again, after years on the wagon. He awoke in the early morning, breathless and anxious, with the feeling that he had somehow boarded a train that refused to stop. This was his chance, his shot—things were going, somehow, to change, would change irrevocably, so that his life would be divided into "before" and "after" the show—and yet, somehow he had, he felt, already missed it, already messed it up.

Exactly a week before the show they broke early—they were sniping and snarling at one another, anyway, and fumbling, now, even on songs they knew well—and went to sit at Pedro's short, cruddy bar. Marco and the others sipped Maker's Mark while the bass player recounted some long story about a member of Sleater-Kinney, who had been married to some indie rock guy, but they were now divorced and had formed a band together, which was much better than Sleater-Kinney. *Quasi,* thought Dave, *yes, tell me something I don't know.* But he pretended the bass player, whose name also happened to be Dave, was providing him with new and fascinating information and drained his beer. *I should go home,* he thought, *I hate these people.*

But he hated even more the thought of being left out of anything, *anything,* they did, and so he ordered another beer and before he could finish it Curtis slid onto the stool next to him, mumbling "Hey" to Dave and gesturing to the bartender for another round. Several days' worth of patchy beard covered his pale cheeks and a sharp smell wafted from parts of his long body that Dave didn't want to think about. There was no bathroom in the practice space—just a grimy shared toilet down the hall—and he was showering, presumably not very often, at Marco's. "So," said Dave, already weary of the conversation, already hating whatever was going to come out of his mouth next. He turned into a moron when left alone with Curtis. "So, we sound pretty good, huh." Curtis nodded.

"Yeah, I guess," he said. *It speaks,* thought Dave. "I'm just really stressed out about . . ." His voice trailed off and he raised his hand, making an incomprehensible gesture, a sort of circular wave.

"I know, I know," said Dave, shaking his head. "It's rough. It's a lot of pressure."

"Exactly," Curtis replied, sighing deeply. "I didn't think it would be like this. I didn't think it would happen this way. That we'd have something so . . ." He waved his hands again.

"Big?" Dave offered.

"Yeah! Something so big, so quick. You know?" Dave nodded. He'd not expected this either—no, that was a lie, in a strange way, he *had,* that's why he'd stayed on. Though he wasn't entirely sure what the gig would mean for them. A deal? With a small label? Or a big one? (Didn't big labels stick to bland pop acts these days? But then, didn't big labels own all the small labels now anyway? Though Merge was still independent, he supposed, and maybe Kill Rock Stars.) And, if so, how would their lives change? Would they suddenly have money? He knew—having dated the girl from Their Own Devices (she'd be at the Thursday night show)— that a band could become kind of famous without actually making any money. But he also knew that sometimes—who knew why?—particular bands became instantly popular. First, you'd see them written up in the *Voice* or *New York Press,* a small blurb, maybe, explaining the group's merits and urging you to go to their show Wednesday at the Knitting Factory or Arlene Grocery or Luna. Then there'd be a little something in *Time Out,* with a big photo (five guys against a red wall, disheveled in old cords) and a coolly sycophantic profile, dubbing them as, maybe, "the best band you've never heard of" or "Brooklyn's best-kept secret." Next, flipping through *The New Yorker,* you'd see a little sketch of the band (Buddy Holly glasses, vintage Converse, shaggy hair) in the "Goings On About Town" section (Saturday at Mercury Lounge or Northsix), and you'd think, *Oh, I heard they were good. Where did I hear that?* At the dentist, you'd find a photo in the "Cue" section of *New York.* And then, before you knew it, there they'd be, on the *cover* of *Time Out,* for the annual music issue or whatever, in which they promote five new bands as The Next Big Thing. Days later, the cover of their album would appear in the window of the Virgin Megastore, magnified a hundredfold, in between the latest horrors from Janet Jackson and Celine Dion. Presumably, their single would be getting some serious airplay (Dave didn't listen to the radio), the corollary video in heavy rotation on MTV, and they would be appearing on *Saturday Night Live* and *Letterman* and *Conan*. And your friends, who saw them months ago at the Knitting Factory, would be saying, "No, they're *really* good. I know they're everywhere, but they're *actually* really good." And sometimes, they were. *It could happen,* Dave thought, *to us. It could.* He glanced at the other guys, who were now talking about some girl they knew who was dating Stephen Malkmus. They lived and breathed this stuff. Were they lying awake at night, Schlitz buzz going sour, imagining the moment the Sub Pop A&R guy approached them backstage? Or, what? Dave couldn't get past that point, the offer, the approach. He didn't know what would happen after. It was, for him, like sex: when he fantasized about it, he never got past the seduction.

A crumpled pack of Basics had materialized on the bar. Curtis pulled two out and handed one to Dave as if they were old friends. "You really think we sound good?" he asked. Dave shrugged. "Yeah, yeah," Curtis muttered, shaking his head slowly, indicating neither yes nor no, but some sort of befuddlement. His lips were full, the sort described as bee-stung when possessed by women, and looked out of place with his otherwise sparse features. "'Cause I have this weird feeling that we're getting worse."

"No, no, man, no way," said Dave, though he knew, as he said it, that it was a lie, that the shows—the thought, the *threat,* of the shows—were, it was true, having some sort of pernicious, soul-draining effect on Curtis, who seemed to be losing his Buddha-like countenance, his flannel-shirted imperviousness to—no, *disregard* for—the treats and temptations of the normal, lucre-propelled world. All of a sudden it dawned on him: Curtis *wanted* it. That's why he was rattled. He wanted it all. The record deal, the European tour, the *Rolling Stone* cover. He had wanted it all along, wanted it *rabidly,* wanted it so badly he *couldn't even speak.* And suddenly Dave liked him.

"Well," Dave said, "it's probably for the best, right? Nobody'd sign us if we were too good. Right? It's all about mediocrity." To his surprise, Curtis laughed—a true, honest-to-God, fully formed *laugh,* which gave Dave an embarrassing sense of satisfaction. *He likes me,* he thought, and the thrill this gave him immediately dissolved into shame. He was drunk, he realized.

"Seriously," said Curtis, scrutinizing the still-pristine filter of his cigarette. His voice had dropped down to its normal whisper. "I don't think it's working. It's like, we sound too much *the same,* you know. I keep"—

he waved his hands and shook his head—"futzing with it, but it's still not right. We need something else, you know?"

"I don't know," Dave answered. But then, all of a sudden, he *did* know and blood began to pound at the delicate centers of his ears and through the rigid veins at his wrists and temples. Even the smallest fibers of his being seemed to stand on end, screeching at him to speak plainly, for once, to scrape off this stupid mask of ironic indifference, because what good had it ever done him, anyway, and his mouth opened, the words already formed and spilling out of it, for they had been lying dormant now for weeks, lined up and ready to march out along his tongue, to crawl out into the world and pierce the heart of his no-longer enemy. "Yes, Curtis," he would say, "I completely comprehend your meaning, despite your utter and complete inability to speak in normal English sentences, which everyone apparently finds charming and indicative of your superior intelligence and freakish musical talent, but which I happen to find annoying, *but all that aside,* I have that something else you think we need. If you would proceed with me to the piano, I will play you the three songs that will, I believe, win us fame and fortune and ass-licking reviews in the *New York* fucking *Times* and the love of that loser Reynold Marks, which is maybe a sellout, asshole thing to want, but I want it, and you know you want it, too, because he can help us, and I need some help right now, and so do you, since you're living in a *fucking pup tent* and you clearly haven't bathed in weeks. So come with me to the piano, my friend, come with me *right now.* Curtis, my friend, *I am your man.*"

But he didn't say this or anything like it. He said, casually, "I think we sound good," even as Sadie's voice somehow, in his head, morphed with his mother's voice into a chorus of "*Dave, what is wrong with you?*" And for them he had no answer, other than that there was some perversity of spirit, some untraceable, possibly archaic, pretty definitely misguided—he knew, he knew!—idea that true genius, or even just a good pop song, should be discovered by accident, by fate, rather than by canny maneuvering or self-promotion or mere suggestion. If he asked for it and received it, the resultant triumph would be cheapened, tainted, by his efforts. Or maybe it was that he was afraid to fail. Again. "Seriously, man, we sound good," he said again, because an unfamiliar expression was distorting the calm sea of Curtis's face, an expression Dave slowly recognized—with shock—as anger.

"Don't lie to me, okay," said this new, unfamiliar Curtis, his voice rising in volume. "I'm trying to *talk* to you." And then, as if in a dream, he heard Sadie's—and his mother's!—words come out of Curtis's mouth. "What's wrong with you, man?" Dave looked at him, speechless. "I mean, what's your problem with me. Or with us. You act like we're a bunch of stupid kids. I just don't get it. I am so *sick* of your attitude." Bending low over the bar, Curtis at last lit his cigarette, his face growing increasingly red and taut, as if someone had turned a crank and tightened the flesh that covered it. "We're a band, *man*. We're supposed to be like a family." He took a sharp breath. "You think we're too"—again, the wave of his bony hand—"for your songs."

Dave had gone from speechless to stunned. Accused, he almost found himself issuing denials: *Songs? What songs?* But even he was not this perverse. A strange calm settled over him in the face of Curtis's fury. Instead, he said, "What do you mean?" Curtis sighed heavily, took off his thick-rimmed glasses, and placed them carefully on the bar. His eyes looked small and vulnerable without them.

"I'm really tired," he told Dave.

"Me, too," said Dave. "We should get some sleep."

"Yeah," said Curtis. "So, you're starting your own project? That's it, right?"

"What?" Dave asked. "Oh. No. I don't have"—he smiled, for as he said it, he knew it was true—"the necessary leadership skills."

"Then what're the songs for. What're you gonna do with them?"

Dave blinked. "I don't know," he said. "How—"

"Sadie Peregrine told me," said Curtis. "She said they're, like, the best thing ever." The blood returned to Dave's ears and resumed its infernal crashing, washing out the sounds of the bar, the clanking of glasses, the hiss of the soda nozzle, the clack of balls on the pool table behind him. Sadie? Curtis and Sadie had met once, maybe twice, in passing. When? At Lil's party, a month or two ago? Yes. Why had they been discussing him—not just him, but his most private, crazy-making pursuits. Curtis was moving his mouth again, but Dave could hear nothing of his words for the cacophony in his ears and the hot flush that had crept into his cheeks, which seemed to emit a sound, a buzz or hum, of its own. He was furious. And he felt, without willing them to, his legs pulling his body down off the bar stool and readying for flight. "She's really cool," he heard Curtis say from a million miles away.

"No," said Dave, slinging his bag over his shoulder, already loathing himself for this small betrayal. "She's not."

nine

Curtis Lang met Emily Kaplan at a party given by Dave Kohane the following summer. It was Labor Day, in the year 2000, and the entire group was in town for the holiday weekend. All except Tal, who was in Israel shooting some sort of thriller. "It's 110 degrees here," he'd emailed Dave the week before. "But it's amazing." They'd all agreed to come to Dave's little thing, just twenty people or so, the first gathering he'd held at his apartment, though he'd been living in it for a year and a half now. The previous owners had left a small barbecue, which he'd never used, so he decided to serve up a big batch of ribs. On the Saturday before the party, he went to his parents' place and obtained a recipe that called for brining and marinating the ribs, which were supposed to be the large beef kind, but (according to his father) could possibly be the small pig kind, then walked over to the butcher on Smith Street to pick up the meat, only to find that the store—operated by a portly Italian man who owned half the buildings in the area—was closed. Back at home, he called Emily, who was still at her dodgy place in Williamsburg (the rent *still* $500 per month), and explained the situation. "Do you think any of the Polish butchers on Bedford are open?" he asked. "Would you want to buy a few pounds of ribs and bring them over here?"

"Um, sure," said Emily, warily.

"You're sure? I'm not ruining your day?" he said.

"No," she said, with a bit more enthusiasm. "We could go to a movie after, maybe."

A couple of hours later, she rapped at his door, red hair frizzing in the late summer heat, a slightly pissy look on her face, which was flushed from exertion. He opened the wrought iron gate and grabbed the white plastic bags from her. They were incredibly heavy. "Em, whoa, how did you carry these?" Emily was five foot two, almost a full foot shorter than Dave.

"Well," she considered, "let's just say it wasn't *fun*. I got pork ribs. The guy said you need a pound per person, because there isn't much meat on them. So I got twenty pounds. It ended up being, like, sixty bucks."

"Okay," said Dave, quelling a mild panic. Sixty bucks was way more than he'd expected to spend. It was just like Emily to agree to do him a favor, he thought, then mess it up (twenty pounds of ribs? What was he going to do with twenty pounds of ribs?) *and* make him feel guilty. But then, she was sweet to do it, and so at the last minute, and those bags were *really* heavy. And the money was fine, *fine,* he told himself. He had more cash than usual, from band stuff: they'd signed a small deal with Merge in the end. Over the summer, they'd flown to Lincoln, Nebraska, of all places, and recorded an album. In late September, they were supposed to go back to mix the thing. "I'll stop at the cash machine when we go out."

"Okay," said Emily, walking past him toward the kitchen, which was really just the back wall of his living room. "I also got some stuff for ceviche." She began unpacking thin bundles of green, frondy things and clear plastic bags of fish. "I can make my dad's recipe. It's really easy. Do you have any white wine?" Emily's family had lived in South America— Chile or someplace—for a few years, her mom on a Fulbright, and picked up all sorts of interesting recipes, which Emily would occasionally deploy. The whole lot of them spoke Spanish as a result, even Emily's sister, Clara, who was crazy and lived in a halfway house in Durham. None of the group had ever met her. Emily hardly ever spoke of the girl and they constantly forgot that she *had* a sister. From time to time, she'd mention Clara in passing and they'd think, *Who?*

"All right," she said now, washing her hands. "You can squeeze the limes. I'll cut up the fish." A moment later, she'd found a cutting board Dave hadn't even known he owned and the blue bowl his mother had given him when he'd moved in. She pulled out another bag, filled with small, pastel creatures. "Octopus," she said. "In Peru, they use black clams." She looked at him. "The limes are right there."

"Right," he said. There seemed to be way too many limes. At least a dozen. "Tell me again what you want me to do with them?"

"Forget it," she said, rolling her eyes. "I'll do it."

"Okay," he said, and sat back down on the couch, watching as she poured salt on the fish, set it to soak in water, then sliced and squeezed the beautiful green limes. "You know how this works, right?" she said, briskly slicing the white slabs of fish into squares and piling them in the blue bowl. "The lime cooks the fish."

"Wait," Dave asked, "you don't actually *cook* it at all? Don't you have to boil it or something first?"

"No, Dave." Emily laughed. "I just said. The marinade cooks the fish. It's a chemical reaction. It, you know, alters the molecular structure of the fish."

"Is that safe to do at home?" he pressed. "I don't want to poison everyone with day-old raw fish."

"It won't *be* raw," Emily told him, grabbing a large pot for the ribs, which would be brined overnight, then marinated. "Didn't you work in a restaurant?"

She was, Dave thought, amazingly efficient. It would have taken him hours to put all that together, and he would have cut corners in a disastrous way, deciding not to peel the shrimp or something. Who else would come over and help him like this? Not Sadie, not since she'd dumped Tal for Agent Mulder—as Dave liked to think of him—and effectively disappeared. "So he has, like, *a gun*?" Dave had asked Sadie too many times to mention. But then, he had to ask dumb questions like that, because he couldn't ask the real question, which was, "Um, Sadie, you're, like, seeing someone who works in *law enforcement*?" Dave had only met the guy a few times, though they'd been dating—*oh my God*, he thought, as he calculated the months—a year now. No. More. Which, in a way, made things easier for Dave, as he didn't have to worry about *liking* the guy, or even becoming friends with him, and then feeling weird about Tal, who asked about Sadie in his emails, always, and Dave always said the same thing. "She's okay." Not, "She's still dating that Fed she dumped you for."

"He works weird hours," Sadie explained, when her friends complained that she never brought him around. "And he's always away." But they suspected otherwise. Or, at least, Dave did. He was an *FBI agent*, which was just insane. He wore, like, *suits*. He would not mix. "He did philosophy at Brown," Sadie told them. *Yeah, like a million years ago*. The guy had to be at least thirty-five, probably more like forty. "He's not some sort of freak." In truth, Dave's few encounters with him had been relatively pleasant. He had a sort of craggy, Peter Coyote thing going on, and he listened intently—even *intensely*—when Dave explained the minutiae of copying out scores, which he was still doing, though less frequently, and said, "That sounds so satisfying. I love the way music looks on the page," which was exactly—*too* exactly—how Dave felt. And yet, he was an *FBI agent*. He'd been investigating their friends. Okay, not their friends, but people *like* them. People they all sort of hated, but still. Though he wasn't anymore. He'd had himself taken off Rob Green-Gold when he started seeing Sadie. Which, Sadie said, was why he was out of town all the time. Apparently, all the anarchist activity—his specialty—was elsewhere, in Seattle, and Albuquerque, and Florida.

"Is Sadie bringing Agent Mulder?" he asked Emily. "She said she might."

"I'm not sure," said Emily, dropping the rib bones into Dave's big pot. "I think she's afraid that Lil will bring Caitlin and Rob, and it would be weird for him."

"Oh, right," said Dave, with a smirk. "Why doesn't she just ask Lil not to?

"I don't know," said Emily. She smiled faintly. "I think maybe she thinks"—she smiled broadly at this construction—"Lil is still mad about Tal. She doesn't want to talk to her about Michael. And stuff."

"Hmmm." Dave shrugged. If he thought about it, *he* was possibly still mad at Sadie for dumping Tal. He tried not to think about the fact that he'd been nearly as annoyed when Tal and Sadie had *started* dating as when they broke up. At least that had made sense. This new guy—okay, not so new—made no sense at all. And Tal had pretty much stayed out of town since. Dave pushed all this from his mind and turned to Emily. "What's up with your play?" he asked. It had been a year or so since a team of producers, *serious* producers, had picked up the play for a small Broadway house (Broadway proper, not off-Broadway, as she'd initially been told). Every once in a while, she'd mention that she'd been in a showcase for backers or some such thing, but otherwise the production didn't seem to be moving forward at all, which sucked, really, since her career, if it could be called that, didn't seem to be moving forward at all either.

She'd been in New York for six years now and worked steadily—doing the terrible stuff, like dinner theater in Connecticut, and the weird, experimental stuff, like Brechtian productions at La Mama—but still couldn't make enough money off acting to leave her day job. And despite Lil and Sadie's urging, she refused to ask Tal for help. And he, maddeningly, refused to offer. ("Maybe he just doesn't think she's good enough," Lil had recently suggested. "Maybe he just doesn't *think*," Sadie corrected.) On her lunch break, she ran to auditions. Evenings and weekends, she rehearsed or took dance and voice lessons or toiled at the gym. When she landed a part in some long run or tour, her company allowed her an unpaid leave and in the event of such an occurrence, she saved nearly every penny she earned. That is, what she had left after paying her rent and utilities and student loans. Unlike the others', her parents hadn't been able to pay for even a fraction of her tuition. Every penny *they* earned went to Clara, who was always in and out of some expensive mental hospital, or needing money for bail or lawyers or rent or psychiatrist's fees or who knows what. Rent, probably. And food.

Emily, meanwhile, lived a spartan sort of existence: though the walls of her apartment were covered, dorm room–style, with all sorts of colorful, kitschy prints, she owned no furniture save for a sagging bed, a small, battered couch that they pulled off the street, a child's white dresser, and a matching desk, brought up from her parents' house in Greensboro. In fact, it was kind to call her apartment such, for it was really a small, sloping room along the back wall of which the landlady had installed a two-burner stove and tiny fridge. This space represented one entire floor of a doll-sized back house on North Eighth Street, a block from the Bedford Avenue L stop. To get to the apartment, you had to walk through the front door of the building it backed (a four-story town house, long converted into dismal flats), out the back door, down a splintered wooden staircase, through a sad little cement courtyard, then up another staircase to the back-house's front door. A surly Polish man lived above her, a jovial Mexican man below. Emily was friendly with both, as well as with a few of the tenants in the front house, a disproportionate number of whom were unemployed. As the girls often lamented, Emily's kitchen had no sink— the landlady had been promising to install one for years—and her lone kitchen cabinet, a strange, ancient metal contraption, contained one ruined Teflon pan, one large tin pot for cooking pasta, a few chipped pieces of Pfaltzgraff picked up at the Salvy on Bedford, and four black mugs, bearing the name of her firm. She rarely spent money on herself, the way the other girls did, getting manicures and stupidly expensive haircuts.

Not that she needed to worry about the latter. Her red hair—once the same carroty shade as Dave's—had darkened a bit in the years since college, to a streaky auburn, but it was still head-turningly beautiful, no matter that she'd cut it to her shoulders, which the girls thought made her look a bit *boring,* like the worker bees whose cubicles adjoined hers. In her off-hours, she still wore the sorts of clothes she'd worn in college— minidresses from the 1960s and enormous wedge-heeled shoes—and she arrived at the Labor Day party thusly clad, in an alarmingly short dress, printed all over with palm trees and men on surfboards. The top of the dress tied around her neck, leaving bare her bluish white shoulders and her back and arms. She'd planned on arriving early, to help Dave get the grill started and mix up some margaritas, but instead she showed up nearly an hour late.

"Clara called just as I was leaving the house," she explained breathlessly, as she clomped through the threshold of Dave's apartment and dropped her big straw bag on the sofa. "I could *not* get her off the phone. She was coked up. Have you ever been around people on coke?" Dave shook his head. He knew more pot-smoking types. "It's the worst. They can't stop talking. They think everyone is their best friend." *It's good,* Dave thought, *that she can take this stuff in stride.*

The party swelled, unaccountably, to unexpected proportions. By the late afternoon, Dave's garden was filled with people—a full third of them, by Dave's count, strangers—seated on the stacked railroad ties that lined the grassy area, sipping beer from bottles and gnawing happily on rib bones. The ribs and ceviche disappeared quickly, and Dave had to run out and buy hot dogs and tofu pups and potato chips at the fancy bodega on Court Street. Everyone seemed more excited by the hot dogs—blistered and bubbling—than the ribs, which was a bit annoying, after all that brining and marinating. Dave's "date" for the party was Meredith Weiss, the dark-haired lawyer he'd been seeing, on and off, for more than a year— nearly two years, actually. His other girls had mostly moved on: the blonde poet now lived with a semifamous novelist, in a brownstone on Wyckoff (though she and Dave were still friendly); the yoga teacher was studying anthropology at Columbia and had moved up to Morningside Heights; the French girl had returned to France; and so on. Only Meredith remained.

He wondered if she might now be considered his girlfriend, if only by default; it had been at least six months since he'd seen anyone else. The idea kind of appealed to him, partly because—and he could admit this— he was lonely, with Sadie absorbed in her weird romance, and Tal pretty much gone, off playing poker with Philip Seymour Hoffman or whatever the fuck he was doing. Meredith was great, too, *really* great. Occasionally, he found himself saving up funny stories to tell her or reading things in the paper and thinking of her. He had a feeling that the evening would serve as a turning point; that, in bringing Meredith into his fold, he might now be able to settle in with her, to leave off the callow restlessness of his youth, exemplified by the Beth debacle, an episode that increasingly unnerved him; he still didn't quite understand his behavior and preferred not to think about it.

In the garden, Meredith sat in a little circle with Lil, Beth, and Sadie, who had come without Agent Mulder, just as Emily had predicted. They all sat cross-legged on the grass, drinking the champagne Sadie had brought (typical Sadie; champagne for a barbecue) from plastic cups. They hadn't been friends, per se, at Oberlin, but they knew enough people in common, he supposed. From across the garden he waved, and Meredith caught his eye with her own dark one and smiled, her little brown arms emerging from a plain black sundress, her shiny hair, almost as black as the dress, curling to her shoulders. Proximity to those pretty women, all of them laughing and waving their arms, somehow made her more lovely. How, he asked himself, could he have ever considered her simply one of many? How could he have taken her so lightly?

As the sky began to darken, Dave—who hadn't eaten a thing, between manning the barbecue, mixing drinks, and introducing strangers—realized that he was, as was so often the case, on the verge of inebriation. He slipped inside the house to grab a glass of water and found there, to his surprise, Emily sitting on his couch with Curtis Lang, engaged in some sort of quiet, intense discussion. Emily appeared to be picking bits of apple out of a glass of sangria and feeding them to Dave's cat, Thermos, who had a bizarre predilection for fruit (cantaloupe, in particular), but who would, no doubt, throw up all over the place later. Dave sighed and cracked his knuckles. Not trusting his voice, he nodded in their direction, grabbed a glass, filled it, quickly, with lukewarm tap water, and walked back out to the patio. Lil and Sadie waved their hands at him, gesturing for him to come over, but he was too tired to walk the ten feet between them. He sat down, heavily, in a chair, and grabbed a handful of tortilla chips (where had they come from? Had he bought them?).

"Dave," Lil shouted, cupping her hands around her mouth. "Dave, c'mere." Wearily, he rose to obey her, clutching his water glass for stability. He wound his way to the back of the patio, where the previous owners had planted grass and bulbs, which had surprised him, his first spring, by sprouting into little purple and yellow and white flowers. Tuck was now manning the barbecue, smiling as he flipped hot dogs into the buns he'd neatly lined up on a plate. He would, Dave thought, do anything to avoid Sadie: his book was now three full months late. "He's *got* to get it in," Sadie had told Dave back in July, the last time he'd seen her. "They'll make me cancel his contract. They will. This isn't the kind of book that they can publish in five years. Ed's not really in the news anymore." He'd left the magazine and, was now, apparently, making a film. "A documentary?" Dave asked. Sadie shook her head. "A feature. A dot-com satire. Set in San Francisco. They start filming in the fall, I think." Sadie, too, had moved on to bigger things. A novel of hers had unexpectedly made it onto the bestseller list and she'd been promoted again. Though she didn't, Dave thought, seem particularly happy about it. "I'm just a little tired of tending to other people," she'd told him. "I read these manuscripts and I think, 'I can write a better book than this.'"

"You should," he'd said, but she'd just shrugged and sipped her drink.

"Dave," Lil called again. *I'm coming,* he thought, somehow unable to gather the energy to say it aloud. It seemed to be taking him forever to walk across the garden. There were all these *people* in the way, more and more of them, continually stepping directly into his path. "Hey," he said to the girls when he finally reached them. Lil pulled on his pant leg, indicating that he should sit down. "Is Emily still in there with the rock star?" she asked, raising her arched black brows.

"Yeah," he said. "Why?" The girls laughed.

"They've been in there for hours," Sadie informed him solemnly. "For the whole party, really."

"You're kidding," Dave said.

"Nope," Lil insisted, raising her eyebrows in a knowing way that set Dave's teeth on edge.

"That's weird. What are they talking about?" he asked peevishly.

"Musical theater," suggested Sadie. "Curtis is really into Sondheim, right?"

"No," cried Lil. "Andrew Lloyd Webber!"

"Oh, right," said Sadie. "He always wears that *Phantom* T-shirt." Dave tried to laugh along with them, but his stomach had begun to turn in on itself and his head felt like it might explode. He was hungry and tired and annoyed. How could Emily have spent the whole party talking to Curtis? Making conversation with Curtis was like slowly pulling out the hairs on one's head.

"Seriously," he said, pouring a slug of champagne into a dirty cup. "They have nothing in common. It's weird."

Sadie tilted her head to one side. "I don't know. He looks kind of like Ken Posa . . ." This was Emily's college love.

"Yeah," said Lil. "He doesn't actually look like Ken, but he sort of has the same *look,* you know? That shy schoolboy look."

"Yes, yes, you're right!" cried Meredith, nodding vigorously. "With the hair that kind of sticks up like a baby chicken. And the big eyes. Like it's *painful* for him to speak." Across the patio, as if they knew they were the subject of discussion, Emily and Curtis emerged from the back door, her bright head followed by his dull one. They walked to the barbecue, where Curtis obtained hot dogs for them, daintily handing Emily a paper plate and a fresh beer, then sat down at Dave's wrought-iron table (it, too, had come with the apartment) and resumed their conversation.

"He's really young, right?" asked Lil in a dramatic stage whisper, though there was no way that Curtis might hear her, being a good twenty feet away, with a wall of bodies between them. Dave nodded. "Class of '98." The girls emitted cries of shock and, Dave thought, delight. They stared at him, rapt, waiting for more information.

"He's a good guy," he said. "His parents are both psychiatrists. They're kind of freakishly nice. They, like, come to our shows."

"Oh, no," moaned Lil. "Shrinks' kids are always fucked up."

"Um, Emily's father is a therapist," Sadie reminded her. She cocked her head at Dave. "We know you don't love him."

"He's cool," said Dave. "He's great." Then he remembered something. "You know, he's married."

"Wait," said Sadie. "He's *married*. He's, like, *twelve*. How is he married?"

"I know!" agreed Meredith.

"He got married in college—" Dave began.

"In *college*—" cried Beth.

"—sophomore year, so that he could live off campus—"

"*Ohhhhh*." This was not so strange. Oberlin's housing regulations were draconian: no student could live off campus—in a house, rather than a college-owned dorm or co-op—until junior year, and even then, one had to luck into a high number in the housing lottery. That is, unless one happened to be married, which no one was, of course. But every year a few students—those with older, cooler friends or those whose nicotine habit had grown too heavy to tolerate what the brochures called "a nonsmoking environment"—lined up potential spouses and begged rides to Cleveland's city hall in order to get around this ridiculous rule. Junior or senior year, they'd have the marriage annulled. Or so they said, at the outset. Their friend Josh Weissman, who was gay, was still officially married to a quiet girl named Jill Bialystock. He lived in San Francisco, she in Ithaca. Presumably, when Jill wanted to marry someone else (or Josh, if gay marriage became legal), they'd fill out all the requisite paperwork.

"So he's not *really* married," said Lil, with a little sigh of relief. They were all so worried about Emily—poor, single Emily—like a tribe of mother hens. Why, Dave thought, was no one worried about *him*?

"Not *really,*" Dave admitted. "But sort of. He and his wife—it's really weird to say that—ended up getting involved." The girls, in silence, exchanged a dark glance. "Their senior year, I think. They'd been living together for a while—in Blue House, remember?" They smiled, for they did—a big, rambling house on North Professor. Their friend Erin had lived there senior year, in an attic room with a slanted ceiling. "And they got really close. They moved to New York together."

"Weird," said Meredith.

"But kind of charming," said Sadie, "right? It's like a romantic comedy."

"*Green Card,*" said Beth. "Meets *Reality Bites.*"

"Exactly," said Dave, who suddenly realized that he was still standing, and sat, too hard, down on the grass beside her.

"But they broke up," suggested Lil, anxious to get to the point.

"Yeah," said Dave. This was why, it turned out, Curtis had moved into the practice space. His wife, Amy—who had, in Dave's first weeks with the band, shown up occasionally at rehearsals bearing bags of vegetable chips and soy jerky—now lived in Park Slope, Dave explained, in some sort of collective, and worked at the food co-op. In November, she'd be going to Seattle with a rainforest group, to protest the WTO's regulation on something to do with an endangered species of turtle. "She says Curtis lives irresponsibly."

"She must know Caitlin and Rob," Lil said excitedly. "They're going, too."

Dave shrugged. "She seems like kind of a freak," he said. "So maybe she and Caitlin are friends."

"*Dave,*" said Lil.

"A child bride!" cried Sadie. The girls nodded. They looked, he realized, vaguely impressed, which only served to further darken Dave's mood.

"So, they're getting divorced, right?" asked Lil.

"Yeah," Dave told her. "They haven't been together in a while. She has a boyfriend, some anarchist guy. That's how all this started. She met this guy." The girls looked at one another, skeptically. They were wondering, he knew, if they should go over and rescue Emily from the clutches of this Married Man. "It's definitely over," he told them confidently, though he wasn't entirely sure this was true. "I mean, they were teenagers. It wasn't a *real* marriage. It's like if Beth and I had gotten married." Immediately, he regretted this last part, though it was certainly true. All the girls looked down into their cups, stealing furtive, embarrassed glances at Beth, who had gone all red, and Meredith, who was nodding, oblivious to Dave's gaffe.

"Hey," came a voice across the garden, and they all turned to see Ed Slikowski making his way toward them, pushing his dark hair out of his eyes. "I put some beer in the fridge, man," he told Dave, shaking his hand. "This is a great place."

"Thanks, man." Ed Slikowski flummoxed Dave. He was always just a little too *nice*. From Dave's experience, someone like Ed—for whom doors seemed to open as he walked by (he was making a *movie? How?*)—should be a complete ass.

"Ed!" cried Lil, rising up to kiss his cheek.

"Ed!" called Tuck, putting down his tongs and striding over to them. He handed Lil a hot dog and shook Ed's hand. *Great,* thought Dave, *now I've gotta cook again.* A small crowd had formed around Ed, including Will Chase—it killed Dave, the way he glanced at Beth proprietarily—and those odious Green-Golds, whom Lil had indeed brought along. *Um, this is* my *party,* he thought sullenly. *Fuck it,* he thought. *The hot dogs can burn.*

But then, across the garden, Curtis and Emily moved from the table to the grill, where they stood companionably, shoulder to shoulder, prodding the hot dogs. Emily's breasts were rather in evidence, pooching out of the low neck of her dress, and it made Dave a little embarrassed to see it. The girls all thought Emily's problem was that she wasn't willing to give anyone a chance. She'd go out on one or two dates, then decide the guy was wrong for her. But Dave—who spent a lot of time at parties with Emily and who was, after all, a *guy*—thought that the trouble was, in fact, the exact opposite. That she tried *too* hard. Introduce her to some guy she might really like and suddenly she became coy and flirtatious, pouting her lips and putting on what Lil called her "stage face," which meant that she arranged her features in such a way as to indicate "happy" and "upbeat" and "sexy." But when she spoke to men she didn't care about she was her sweet, cool self. And of course these men pursued her, to no avail.

Which category would Curtis fall into? It didn't really matter, because there was no way Curtis would be interested in Emily. Dave knew guys like Curtis. They dated androgynous elfin girls who worked in record stores and could spout music trivia on command, or tall, skinny, model types, with long, sleek hair and overly visible midriffs. And sure enough, as Dave watched, Curtis strode across the stone patio, and kissed Marco's sister Paola—a smiling sylph, with shiny black hair to her waist—on both cheeks, holding her thin shoulders in his hands rather intimately. He heard a faint echo of her hoarse "Ciao." The crowd had thinned a bit and sounds were starting to float across the patio, snatches of conversation. His upstairs neighbors—Katherine and Matt—walked out the back door, grabbed beers from the ice bucket, and waved at him.

Just then, Emily snuck up behind him and proffered a hot dog. "I grabbed the last one for you," she said. He took the thing, not sure if he should eat it now—he feared dribbling food on himself, in his inebriated state—or make his way to someplace private before he wolfed it down.

"Thanks," he told Emily.

"*De nada,*" she replied, crouching down beside him and fidgeting with the ties of her dress. "Listen, I'm gonna take off. Is it okay if I grab some of the ceviche? I told Mr. Gonzalez I'd bring him some. He has his own recipe and he's curious about my dad's." Dave's ears turned hot. This was *so like* Emily, to offer him something, then take it away. She barely knew Mr. Gonzalez. He was just her neighbor—an old man, dwarflike, with a brown wrinkled face—not a real friend. Why should she bring food to him, Dave's food, particularly when Dave himself was *fucking starving,* and, more important, too fucking tired to go rummaging through his messy kitchen cupboards for a piece of Tupperware.

"There isn't any left," he said.

"There's a whole bowl in the fridge that you didn't put out. I wasn't sure if you were saving it for something or what." Scratching his head, Dave looked around, then remembered the hot dog, cooling in his hand. There were still a lot of people around, showing no signs of leaving. He wanted, more than anything, to go inside his cool, dark apartment and shove the entire hot dog in his mouth, *alone.*

"It's not going to keep," offered Lil, annoyingly. She was in some sort of mood today.

"You know what?" said Emily, standing up. "Forget it. It's too much trouble. Listen, I'm going to head." Her voice had a wounded tone that Dave thought just too much. He hoisted himself up.

"No, no," he said, "let me grab something for you to put it in." Emily shrugged.

"Okay," she said, "thanks," and followed Dave to the kitchen. Without too much trouble, he found a wobbly cottage cheese container and handed it silently to Emily, who grabbed the blue mixing bowl and spooned ceviche from the large container to the small, purple octopus arms waving in the air. Dave grabbed a cigarette from a pack somebody had left on the counter and lit it with a kitchen match. "The G is running weird after six, isn't it?" Dave asked her. "Do you have money for a cab? You don't want to wait for Lil and Tuck? You could split one?" Emily put the blue bowl back in the fridge and shook her head.

From the dark little hallway stepped Curtis, brown eyes blinking owlishly behind his glasses. "I'm going to take her home," he said. "I brought Carmen. I was heading that way anyway. We can grab some dinner. All I've eaten today is that hot dog." Carmen was Curtis's highly impractical vehicle, an orange Karmann Ghia convertible, courtesy of his father, who bought and restored old cars. Dave took an odd pleasure in the absurdity of Curtis's existence: he didn't have an apartment, was still living in the practice space (in a tent and a sleeping bag, no less), but he did have a restored-to-mint collector's car, which he parked on Front Street, apparently unworried about someone stealing it, or stripping it, or bashing in its front window with a tire iron, as had been the fate of every car ever owned by Dave's parents.

"Cool," Dave said, holding out the found pack—Marlboro Lights—to Curtis, who pulled out a cigarette and lit it with his old Zippo, cupping his hand protectively around the flame as though caught in a heavy wind.

"I'll be right back," Emily said, disappearing around the corner, presumably to the bathroom.

"Excuse me for one sec," Dave said to Curtis, and, without waiting for a response, trailed Emily down the hall, placing his foot in the bathroom door as she shut it.

"What the—" she said, then opened the door. "What's up?" she asked him. He slid past her and sat down on the toilet. Slitting her eyes at him, she closed the door with a firm click. "Dave, what's the deal?" *I don't know what the fucking deal is,* he wanted to say. *How do you expect me to know what the fucking deal is?* A peculiar feeling was spreading through his abdomen, as though some particular organ—stomach? intestine?—were dropping into a deep pit. Like those dreams he had—maybe everyone had them—just as he slid into sleep, dreams in which he fell into a black void, rousing himself (suddenly, frighteningly) by pressing down on the mattress with an arm or a leg to break the imagined fall.

"So where are you guys going for dinner?" he asked, his words slurring just as he'd feared. He was still, to his surprise, clutching a lit cigarette in his left hand. How nice. He took a long, invigorating drag and watched, through a haze of smoke, as Emily splashed water on her face. She was so fresh and clean. For a moment, he felt the urge to bury his hot head in the cool, white stretch of her neck, to put his arms around her and fall asleep. Then he wondered where he'd put his hot dog. He hadn't eaten it, that much he knew. "Bean, I guess, if it's open and we can get a table." Bean did a nice shitake and spinach burrito, which sounded pretty good to Dave at the moment, and he had the fleeting thought that he should join them for dinner and simply let his party continue on without him. Only his close friends would notice if he left, really, and he doubted they'd mind. But Carmen only seated two. And, of course, they didn't want him to come along. There was that.

Emily patted her face dry and dug around in her bag, extracting a couple of tubes. With two small fingers, she dabbed a red, eerily blood-like liquid onto her cheeks, then rubbed it in. "Em, don't get upset, but I just wanted to say, you know, I have to see Curtis almost every day, so if you don't, if you're not . . ." He drifted off, unsure of what he wanted to say. "What were you guys talking about?" he asked.

"Musical theater," Emily told him. Dave guffawed, sending ash flying onto his bath mat. "No, really."

"Really," Emily insisted.

"Musical theater," Dave repeated, trying to catch Emily's eye in the mirror. If he and Emily could share a little look, a little glance, it would mean that they were in this together, that this was all some big joke, that Emily and Dave would continue to band together against the Curtis Langs of the world. But Emily avoided his gaze, deeply involved in spreading some sort of flesh-colored ointment under her eyes and along the sides of her nose. "Among other things," she finally said, with a smile.

Dave's head, he realized, had begun to faintly throb, syncopated beats that fought for dominance with a rushing, whirring sound in his ears. *Champagne,* he thought, he shouldn't drink it, not ever. *Fucking Sadie,* he thought, *and her stupid champagne.* Emily ran the faucet again, sprinkling water on her hair and twisting a few fuzzing ringlets around her index finger. He tried to picture her coming by the practice space to pick Curtis up, coming out for drinks after practice, transforming herself from his friend to Curtis's girlfriend. He did not want this. And yet, he thought, as the cacophony in his head grew more chaotic, he did not—*definitely* not—want Emily to be his own girlfriend, either, though her neck still looked almost unbearably inviting, like a slab of vanilla ice cream. Then what did he want? Separation. *Boundaries,* he thought, *that's the word. I want boundaries.* He breathed in deeply, inhaling the peppermintish scent with which she was spritzing herself. She pointed the bottle at him and grinned. "Em, if you could just keep in mind that I work with Curtis," he started again, hating his words as they came out of his mouth. "I kind of work *for* him." Emily nodded. She was running a little wand over her lips, leaving a trail of clear gloss.

"Aye, aye, sir," she said curtly, giving him a little salute, and with a sigh, she began returning the various pieces of her toilette to her large straw bag.

Suddenly, Dave realized what he wanted. It was very simple: for Emily to stay in his cool, minty bathroom; for Emily to *not* get into Carmen and go to Williamsburg and have dinner with Curtis at Bean. If she left the bathroom, he would lose her to Curtis—he knew it, he could see it from the way they bent their heads together on the patio—Curtis, who already had everything, the band, the stupid orange Kharmann Ghia, the perfect, irritating family in their big, stupid house in Montclair, the supreme and unshakable confidence in his own talent. It wasn't fair. He shouldn't have Emily, too. It disgusted him, just thinking about Emily crossing over into the World of We: "We went to the best wine bar last night!" and "We can't make it to your birthday party, Dave, we have to go to Curtis's cousin's engagement party." And worst of all: "Have you seen *Being John Malkovich*? We loved it."

He had already lost so many: not just Beth and Lil and Sadie, but Tal, who had put the first chink between him and Sadie, if he really thought about it, and, moreover, was gone, always gone, in the wilds of somewhere, off shooting something, not "filming," but always "shooting," such an annoying, pretentious term, it made Dave want to slam his head through the bathroom's plaster wall. He was gone so often and for so long that Dave had stopped keeping track of the particulars of his work and was perpetually surprised to see that familiar angular face appear in a Yahoo! commercial or a trailer for a downmarket teen comedy, the sort of thing he and Tal would have lavished with ridicule just a few years earlier (only to sheepishly rent it a few months later, telling themselves it would be fun to watch stoned). Tal had dumped him, just as Beth had dumped him, just as everyone had dumped him—everyone but Emily, cool, beautiful Emily.

Before he could think any better of it, he'd stood up, threaded the long, aching fingers of his left hand through her hair, turned her face toward him, and begun kissing her, the scents of her various lotions sending him into a sort of swoon. Her neck was as cool as it looked and her lips were the sort of lips he liked—like Beth's, actually, full and swollen, like a child's—and they slid against his own with an almost unbearable softness, the gloss that coated them leaking into his mouth (its taste a cloying ersatz strawberry) and onto his chin. She held one hand, her left, awkwardly in the air, like someone halfheartedly trying to hail a cab, but otherwise seemed to be lost in the same spell that had overtaken him. Through his nose, he breathed deeply and shuddered a little, which only deepened the roaring in his ears. And then, just like that, she pulled away, pushing his hands off her. "Dave," she said sadly, and shook her head from side to side. "Dave." Wiping the remnants of her lip gloss on the back of her hand, she strode out of the bathroom.

Dave followed her out. In the kitchen, they found Curtis, just as they'd left him, leaning against the counter, cigarette in hand, and reading a stained, tattered copy of *The Moosewood Cookbook*. He grinned broadly at Dave. "I hate this fucking book," he said, ruffling the book's stained pages. "I ate at Harkness for three years. We had that gado-gado once a week. I want to *burn* these stupid hippie recipes."

"Go ahead," Dave told him. "I stole it from Keep." *Go*, he thought, *leave. Get out of my house. Let me eat my hot dog in peace.* (He had spotted it on the counter, blessedly untouched.) But a moment later, as he watched them climb into Carmen (parked illegally in front of his building, but then Curtis was the sort of person who never got a ticket, it was like he had a fucking force field around him), an overwhelming sadness settled around him. He wished they were still there. He wished he were not standing alone in his living room, with a headache and a garden full of guests to attend to on his own, without Emily. Or even Curtis. Sadie was wrong. He did love the guy.

Back on the patio, the party, thankfully, appeared to be winding down. Katherine and Matt were heading upstairs to their own apartment; they'd come straight from a weekend away, at his parents' place in the Berkshires, without even dropping their bags off. "We knew," moaned Katherine, "that if we went upstairs we'd just *collapse* and never make it down here. The traffic was *unbelievable*. It took us forever just to get down here from the bridge. Like, six hours."

"Three hours," said Matt, shaking Dave's hand. "Thanks, man. Great party. Everyone was really nice." Lil, Tuck, Beth, and Will approached, the girls flitting around, gathering their sweaters and bags and who knows what. "Well, see you soon," said Tuck, slipping an arm around Lil. "Yeah," said Dave, thinking, *Go, leave. I'm tired.* He kissed the girls good-bye, shook their husbands' hands, then sat down heavily in his favorite chair, an overstuffed piece of Victoriana he'd rescued from the street, and closed his eyes, before, through a boozy haze, he remembered Meredith. Where was she?

He'd barely seen her all summer because of their colliding schedules—he in Lincoln, recording; she working night shifts at the prosecutor's office, traveling to the ends of Brooklyn to look at murder victims, *corpses.* And it had been some time, too long, since they'd slept together. He looked around the patio, inventorying the remaining guests: Marco and his sister, their bass player, some of Dave's friends from St. Ann's (fucking trust-fund drug addicts, all of them), a pair of pianists (one Eastman, the other Juilliard), three veterans of Madame Woo's, and a number of people Dave didn't recognize. The sky had gone dark by now, though the lights from the nearby houses—and perhaps the collective glow of the city—kept the patio bright.

At last he found Meredith, sitting with Sadie and Ed Slikowski on the railroad ties, the girls swinging their bare legs and holding to their lips pale cups, which glowed pearlescent in the moonlight. "We're playing the name game," Sadie informed him. "Meredith went to Riverdale."

"She did," Dave confirmed. But his presence, who knew why, put an end to the game. The four of them sat, in silence, watching the party go on, the guests talking, the tips of their cigarettes circling the air like fireflies. He'd lost his hot dog again. He would, he decided, take Meredith out to eat, once everyone left. Why, why would they not leave? And then, as if she'd read his mind, Sadie stood up. "I think it's time for me to make my excuses," she said, flashing Dave a lopsided grin.

"I'll head out with you," said Ed.

What about Agent Mulder? thought Dave. *Agent Mulder, where are you? Did you really need to go off on your secret mission this weekend?* "Thanks so much for coming," he said, and they walked out, their laughter flowing back at him in waves. The rest of the guests followed. Dave saw them all to the door, Meredith trailing behind him, gathering her things: a thin, lacy sweater; a large black tote; a hardback book she'd put down when she came in, splayed on the coffee table, some sort of history thing.

Finally, Dave closed the door. The laughter of the guests grew progressively softer and softer as they made their way down Bergen Street. "Hey," he said awkwardly. His throat didn't seem to be functioning properly. And though he felt like he was shouting at her through a long tunnel, the word came out as almost a squeak. "Can I take you to dinner?"

"I guess," she said, dropping her bag with a closemouthed smile. "We should talk, at least. This summer has just been crazy. That case, the drive-by, has taken over my life."

"I know, I know," Dave told her. "Let me just wash up and drink a glass of water."

"Sure," said Meredith, sitting down on the edge of the couch and flipping open her book. "Are you sure you're not too tired?" she called as he slunk back down the hallway to the bathroom. He couldn't summon the energy to answer, which clearly meant that he *was* too tired—but then wasn't he *always* too tired? Clicking the door shut, he ran the tap and scooped cold water over his face, just as Emily had done earlier. In the mirror, his face appeared ominously gray, the whites of his eyes bloodshot, the skin around them scaly and bluish. His towel still carried Emily's peppermint scent. He raked his damp hands through his hair, strode out to the living room, and sat down beside Meredith. "So," he said, running his hand down her narrow arm, though any attraction he'd felt for her had vanished—and yet she was here, on his couch, just as he'd expected, so he felt compelled to go on, to carry out his plan. She was as pretty as Emily, as Sadie; prettier, really, than Beth, from an objective standpoint. "How are you?" he asked. She shrugged, lifting her arm to her dark head.

"I'm good. A little tired. I don't mind working nights, but it takes its toll on your body, you know? It's not natural."

"Yeah," he said, and thought about kissing her, if only so they wouldn't have to talk anymore. She was tired? *He* was tired. Too tired to talk—and there, *yes,* he felt a brief stirring in his groin, but as an image, an exciting image, began to come into focus in the depths of his brain, Meredith's pixieish features were supplanted by Emily's stranger ones and he felt, for a moment, *oh God,* that he might cry. "I know," he said quietly. "I'm tired, too." And he put his arm around her shoulders, then reached up and stroked her hair, which felt much as it looked—nearly slick in its softness, like a wet road at night—and thought, *Well, this is nice. It is. It is.*

"Listen, Dave," she was saying and twisting out of his grasp, "I need to tell you something." The throbbing in his head had returned. Or maybe—yes, definitely—it had never left; he had simply stopped paying attention to it, momentarily. He had a feeling that he knew what was coming. Generally, when women said they needed to talk to him, they had just one subject in mind: Dave's inadequacies, the ambiguous nature of their relationship. Nearly a year ago, the girl from Their Own Devices approached him on this topic, seated on this same brown canvas couch, her knees tucked into her chest. The earnest, plaintive look on her sunburned face had been too much for Dave and he spewed forth a stream of half-truths—which he believed to be whole truths at the time—which led to crying, followed by the slow sex of reconciliation, followed by no modification of Dave's behaviors. A month later, she went to Yaddo to write poems, met that novelist—older, Indian, *New Yorker* editor—and now she was married, pregnant, ensconced in her brownstone.

In truth, he had suspected for a while that Meredith wanted to get married, purchase some sort of couple-appropriate piece of property, and do the things people did (not people he knew, just *people*), much as he had suspected similar things of Beth, and he'd been right, hadn't he? But Meredith was an Upper East Sider, after all—like Sadie, he supposed, and yet not like Sadie at all—and occasionally returned from trips to her parents' classic six on Seventy-second with words about how nice it was up there, how *clean,* how she *totally* understood why people move uptown once they have kids (Sadie, by contrast, liked to say, "Why not just move to Westchester?"). After college, and before Dave, she'd dated some superboring guy—Dockers, polo shirt, Topsiders, puffy face—from her class at Fordham Law. He now made an astronomical salary doing corporate stuff for a huge firm. They'd run into him on Smith Street once: twenty-eight going on forty. Prematurely bald, a dead expression in his pale blue eyes, jowls slopping over the collar of his shirt, cell phone clipped to his belt. As they parted he'd said, "Catch you later." "What a loser," Dave had moaned, too loudly. Meredith shrugged and said, "He's nice." That was the sort of person she was, he thought now. Boring. That was why they hadn't been friends in college, wasn't it? But boring, in a way, was good, he thought. He liked the little structures and demands she imposed on her life—she ate dinner, for example, at her little kitchen table every night, even when she was alone. That was good, he thought. That was healthy.

"So," she said, standing up and walking toward the kitchen sink. "I'm getting married." Dave felt his jaw drop. He willed it shut.

"You are?" he asked stupidly. "But how?" Meredith tossed her head back and laughed.

"Well, it's not as complicated as you think. You hire an officiant, send out some invitations, buy a dress." The blood rushed to Dave's face.

"That's not what I meant," he heard himself say, nearly shouting. "You know that's not what I meant. Don't fucking make fun of me." Now he *was* shouting. He sounded, he knew, like a cornered child, whiny and on the brink of tears. And the worst of it was, *he didn't care.* Not a bit. He really, truly didn't care at all. He felt, if anything, relieved. And yet: the little men inside his head were beating their mallets even harder and faster, and now their compatriots inside his ears were sending tidal waves of hot blood from one section of their home into another. "What I meant was, *how* are you getting married when I didn't even know you were seeing anyone else. Who's this *asshole* that's marrying you, when you've been seeing me at the same time you were seeing *him.*"

"Dave, come on," said Meredith, shaking her head. "We haven't seen each other in months. Or did you not notice?" She laughed. Dave was having trouble following her words. "I mean," she went on. There was more! "Dave, we just went to parties and had fun. You were never serious about me. We never really talked."

Dave glared at her, folding his arms across his chest. The hammer, so distant before, now beat inside his skull. "You never wanted to talk," he said. "All you wanted to do was go out. And we *were* serious. We were . . ." He searched for a word, which increased the force with which the small men beat their mallets. Not "lovers," yech. "We were *dating.* We were moving toward something." Meredith laughed again. Dave shifted miserably on the couch.

"No, we were moving *away* from something. Dave, do you think I'm an idiot? You see, like, a different girl every night. And besides, you're not the sort of guy I'd ever marry." Now the blood was swishing in his ears, thick and hot. A near-physical urge to grab Meredith and shake her, forcing her to speak to him sensibly, overtook him. He folded his arms more tightly around his chest.

"What," he said, his voice sounding strange and trembly, "what do you mean by that?" She shrugged. Her nonchalance was awful.

"I don't know. I've thought about it a lot. I suppose—"

"Forget it," he said, "fucking forget it. I know the answer. I'm not some loser like that Tim asshole, some guy you can push around, some corporate drone." She shook her head, sadly, *pityingly,* Dave realized with a sick feeling.

"Do you mean *Phil?* You know, Dave, see, this is it. This is the problem. You don't know anything about Phil. Do you know what he did before he went to Fordham? He was in a band, just like you. A kind of big band, in Seattle, Red Scare." Dave bit the inside of his lip to keep from screaming. Red Scare *was* big. They'd come to Oberlin, played at the Disco, in '91, opened for the Pixies. He'd worked that night. The lead singer, he remembered, had OD'd, many years ago. "You just have these *ideas* about people, who they are, what they're like, but none of it is real, none of it is based on the actual people or the things they do or say." She was angry, too, now, and he was glad of it. "You're *delusional*. You just *decide* things are true—you and I are 'going out' even though we haven't seen each other in months? Come *on*. And you just seem *incapable* of worrying about anyone's happiness other than your own."

This was unbelievable. Truly unbelievable. This boring woman was in his house telling him what was wrong with *him*. A woman who owned Bananarama albums and went through Oberlin without taking a single English class, a woman who was so dull and status quo that he couldn't even be bothered to speak to her in college. But then, as suddenly as it had arrived, his anger left.

Why, if he was so terrible, had she spent so much time with him? And why was she wasting her breath yelling at him, if she didn't care about him at all? Resting his head on the back of the futon—he was so tired, so tired, and *hot*—he asked her these questions. She smiled at him. Pityingly. Again.

"I *do* care about you. I didn't plan on saying any of this. I just wanted to let you know that I'm, you know, engaged. So there was no ambiguity. I figured we'd stay friends. Because that's really all we are, all we've been." She held out her left hand and he saw, for the first time, that it held a rather large diamond in a plain silvery setting. Platinum, he supposed. That seemed to be the material for such rings.

"I don't understand," he said miserably, knowing he should stop, "what you mean when you say I'm not the sort of guy you'd marry." Before she could answer, Dave let out a strange little croak and—he stretched out this part of the story when he told Sadie about it a few days later—slumped sideways on the couch, odd-colored lights flashing on the insides of his eyelids, then blackness and that awful sensation of falling, falling, into a bottomless cavern, but this time he couldn't rouse himself. He'd passed out, dead away.

Later, when Meredith talked to Sadie about it—they became great friends after the party—she said that Dave's arm felt hot on her shoulder, terribly hot, but she didn't think anything of it. His face, too, was red, bright red, but she figured the color came from anger, not—as the paramedics informed her—from severe heat prostration (he'd been in the hot sun all day, drinking, his fair, fragile skin unprotected). She thought, at first, that he was joking around, pretending to be stricken with grief over her announcement or slain by her harsh assessment of him. "Dave, I've gotta go," she told him, and washed her wineglass, before realizing that he hadn't moved, not an inch. When she tried to rouse him, she found his skin burning—"I've never felt anything like it," she told Sadie at Robin des Bois the following weekend, "it was like touching an electric stove"— and strangely dry, like the leather seat of a car. Even more alarming, he wouldn't wake. She called 911, asked for an ambulance, wondered where the nearest hospital was (Long Island College Hospital on Atlantic?), then ran upstairs and got Katherine and Matt, to see if they might drive Dave (and her) to the hospital. By the time they'd figured out which was the nearest (it *was* Long Island College), the ambulance had arrived, its sirens audible five minutes before it pulled up in front of the brownstone, where Curtis's Karmann Ghia had been parked just an hour before. Burbling into walkie-talkies, the paramedics lifted Dave onto a stretcher, hooked a scary web of tubes and masks and things onto him, hoisted Meredith into the vehicle, and zoomed off. Dave came to as they lifted him out of the ambulance, rolling his head from side to side and moaning. They'd strapped his arms down to the stretcher with small cloth ties, which Meredith thought barbaric, but apparently people often awoke hysterical and pulled their IVs out, spurting the paramedics with blood, and undoing all the good the drips had done. "I'm sorry," he told Meredith in the solemn voice of the terminally ill (as portrayed on film, at least). "If I hadn't been so scared, I would have laughed," she told Sadie. "He might have been dying, for all I knew."

He was in the hospital three days, rehydrating and having bloodwork done, just in case. Meredith visited him each evening, plagued by a vague worry that she'd caused his illness by speaking her mind. Her fiancé came along on the third day, a jowly guy in Adidas track shoes—not so dissimilar from Phil in appearance. As it turned out, he wasn't a corporate type at all, but a writer for *Rolling Stone*. He'd seen Anhedonia twice, once at Mercury Lounge and once when they'd opened for Reynold Marks. They were friends now, too, the three of them, and Sadie and even Beth (and Will, if he was in town) sometimes joined them for drinks or dinner in the neighborhood. "It's stupid," Meredith told Sadie (who told Lil, who told Dave). "We were meant to be friends, but we couldn't really become friends until I was married and we could kind of *relax* about all the sex stuff. If we were both women, none of this would have happened. We would have just become friends, with no complications, no pressure to sleep with each other, no wondering whether we were 'in love.' None of that stupid shit."

"Unless you were both lesbians," Sadie responded. "Or bi."

"Right," Meredith said, "but you know what I mean."

"I do indeed," Sadie told her, twisting her mouth to one side. "Except, well, I don't mean to be querulous, but Dave has lots of close female friends. Emily, Lil. Me. And we've never had anything like this happen. No weird ambiguity."

"Right," said Meredith, in her clear, reedy voice. "Except that's a whole different pair of gloves." Sadie laughed. This was one of Rose Peregrine's pet expressions. Sadie'd taught it to the group. And now Meredith. "Nothing like this would ever happen with you," Meredith went on, swishing the dregs of her coffee. The stuffed alligator on the wall of the café stared down at the girls with his dusty glass eyes.

"Why not?" asked Sadie. Meredith rolled her eyes.

"Haven't you seen the movie?" she asked. "He's in love with you."

ten

Sadie Peregrine was pregnant. This was big news. For many reasons, not the least of which being that she wasn't yet married—*Rose Peregrine was going to lose her shit,* the group said—or that the father, as it turned out, wasn't her boyfriend, Agent Mulder, but Ed Slikowski, whom they hadn't even realized she was seeing, though they'd certainly been a bit suspicious of the frequency with which his name began showing up in conversation.

It was January of 2001, a bleak, cold winter, the sort that unfailingly led Rose to cry, "Don't you wonder how the settlers survived? I could barely make it home from Bendel's!" But the weather gave Sadie a convenient excuse to stay home ("It's cold, Lil, I'm not schlepping all the way to Williamsburg"), so that she might avoid her friends and family for as long as possible, until she figured out what to do. There was a chance, she knew, that the pregnancy wouldn't stick, and she could put it behind her and think through this mess she'd gotten herself into with Michael and Ed. And Tal, too, she supposed, for it was he that she wanted to call, he that she wanted to ask for help, but she couldn't, of course. But she also knew, somehow, that it *would* stick, that this was it, that she needed to be a grown-up and rise to the occasion, make some decisions. And though, rationally, she knew the best thing would be for her to wake up bleeding one morning, the mere thought of this possibility, as the weeks went on, became enough to crowd her eyes with tears.

At the end of the month, she made an appointment with an obstetrician in Soho, randomly selected from her insurance plan's directory—she certainly wasn't going to old Dr. Moss, up on Park, whom her mother saw—and told her assistant she might be gone for a few hours. "I'll hold down the fort," he said, with a tight smile. She'd been arriving late and leaving early in recent weeks—waking sick and headachey, and growing so again by the end of the day, so that she couldn't wait to get home, take off her too-tight dress, and lie down—and she could feel the hot force of his resentment as she breezed by his desk and closed the door to her office with a satisfying click. She'd harbored the same during her years with Delores.

"So, you're ten weeks," said the doctor, a pert young woman with a blonde pageboy, running a wand over Sadie's stomach, her eyes fixed on the screen of a creaky sonogram machine. "Everything looks great." She pointed to a tiny, pulsing bean. "Nice, strong heartbeat." She pressed a button and, with a whir, the machine emitted a small paper version of the image on the screen. "Here's a picture to show your husband," she said, meeting Sadie's eyes for the first time. She was visibly pregnant herself, Sadie realized. Everyone seemed to be pregnant lately. In her neighborhood and Lil's, she couldn't walk a block without coming across some hipster, heavy with child, or a grinning new mother, baby strapped to her chest in a carrier or peeking out of a sling. "I probably won't be able to deliver you," she went on, gesturing toward her abdomen. "But the other doctors in the practice are excellent."

"Great," said Sadie. She'd been half expecting the doctor to tell her that it was a hysterical pregnancy and send her off to a shrink. Barring this, her intention had been, she supposed, to ask about her "options"—she couldn't utter the word "abortion," even silently—but she could not bring herself to do so, whether it was because of the doctor's own pregnancy or her cheerful assumption that Sadie, like the doctor herself, was a settled matron, anxious to call her husband with the good news.

"And you're feeling okay? Any bleeding? Cramping?"

Sadie shook her head.

"Nausea? And you can keep food down?" She picked up Sadie's chart.

"Mostly. I *do* get pretty nauseated. When I wake up. And then again around five or six."

"But you can keep food down?" Impatience was creeping into the doctor's voice. *How long have I been in here?* thought Sadie. *Five minutes?*

"I can."

"Excellent. Just try not to let your stomach be completely empty or too full. Eat small meals. The nausea comes from having no food in your stomach. Or from eating too much. Carry saltines around with you."

"Okay," said Sadie, thinking, *Saltines? That's your advice? Eat saltines?*

"Do you have any questions?" The doctor had already repositioned herself closer to the door.

"I shouldn't tell anyone until twelve weeks, right?" she asked hopefully.

"That's the rule," said the doctor, moving closer to Sadie. "But I'd say it's fine. Once we get a heartbeat, it's usually fine. Most miscarriages happen around six or seven weeks."

"Oh, okay."

She looked down at the chart again. "So you'll go up to the hospital in two weeks for the nuchal. Call and make the appointment today." She smiled and made for the door. "You can bring your husband. It's pretty cool. Anything else?" Her hand reached for the doorknob.

Sadie sat up on the table. "Um, I'm so tired all the time. That's normal, right?"

The doctor smiled. "Completely normal. Just make sure to listen to your body. Sleep when you're tired."

But Sadie couldn't sleep when she was tired. She had a job. She'd been slogging through her days like a somnambulist, missing her stop on the train, forgetting to buy milk, unable to make it past a few pages of a manuscript. And so it was that she dressed herself, handed over thirty dollars for her copayment, and fought her way up Broadway, a sharp wind lashing her face, to Lil's new office, on the twelfth floor of a small building between Prince and Houston. At the end of the last semester, Lil had suddenly—and without consulting with Sadie—taken a leave from school and accepted a full-time job at the poetry foundation where she'd interned the past few summers. She'd started after the New Year, editing the foundation's little magazine, really a glorified newsletter. "The last editor became a staff writer at *New York* magazine," Lil told Sadie as she showed her around the office, a large loft cordoned off into columns of offices. Lil's was doorless, a sort of pen, but beautifully situated by the back window, which looked out over the low buildings and water towers of Little Italy, Chinatown, and the Lower East Side.

"There's my aunt Minnie's building," cried Sadie, pointing to a brick tower by the water. "I can't believe you can see that far east."

"How is she?" asked Lil, pursing her lips. In college, Sadie had dragged Lil—and Dave, and Beth, anyone who would come—to see her aunt, who served as a sort of surrogate maternal grandmother, Rose's parents having died long before Sadie's birth.

"Okay. All her friends are dying. I think she's pretty lonely."

"I'd love to see her," said Lil. Sadie did not, lately, want to bring Lil round to her family. Lil's interest in them made all too stark Sadie's own neglect (it had been months since she'd visited Minnie; she resolved to go that weekend).

"Sure," she said. "We'll make a plan."

Outside, the sun had come out and the wind had picked up, blowing the ends of Sadie's scarf around her face. Light flakes swirled around them. At Kelley and Ping, they were greeted with a welcome gust of warm air.

Steam rose from the grills of the open kitchen, where white-coated cooks tossed noodles in pans. Lil and Sadie sat at a low table by the bar and surveyed the plates in front of them: pad thai, pad see yew, Chinese broccoli, all glistening with oil, the sight of which made Sadie's stomach lurch. *I should have ordered soup,* she thought. But all the soup involved meat, which she was definitely off, chicken in particular. She was also, however, off vegetables, particularly strong-tasting vegetables, and so she pushed the broccoli toward Lil and spooned a few noodles onto her plate.

"So are you thinking you want to go into journalism?" she asked Lil. *Like Tuck,* she almost said. "Is that why you took this job?"

"I don't know." Lil shrugged happily. "Maybe. Sort of. They offered it to me and it just seemed like a good opportunity. I've never had a *job* job before." From the pile of noodles, she plucked a shrimp with her chopsticks and contemplated it. "It's so *easy,* compared to grad school. It's weird. We have these meetings and people argue about, like, what hors d'oeuvres to serve at the Jorie Graham reading." She bit the top off the shrimp. "And I just go home and I'm *done.* No papers to grade."

"Do you think you'll go back to school?" The previous semester her dissertation proposal had at last been approved, after three revisions. It seemed, to Sadie, such a waste to leave now. Why not just write the thing and be done with it? But she supposed that was easy for her to say. She wouldn't want to spend three years reading through jargon-heavy essays on Mina Loy.

"I don't know. I mean, what's the point? What am I going to do when I finish? Go teach at, like, a junior college in Wyoming? Tuck *won't* move to someplace like that. And anyplace he *would* move, I won't be able to get a job, because everyone else wants to move there, too."

"But isn't it possible you'd find something here? I know it's a different field"—Lil began shaking her head, an irritated expression taking over her face, for she knew what Sadie was going to say—"but Beth seems to be doing okay . . ." In the fall, she'd become *Slate's* television critic—which was exciting and much deserved, since she'd been writing for them for a year, making, she said, pretty much nothing (though Sadie wondered if anyone actually *read* Slate, or if they just *talked* about reading it)—and had promptly been offered classes at NYU's J school, which she'd taken, despite having already signed on to teach Television and History, two sections, to undergrads at Steinhardt. They'd barely seen her all fall. And when they did, she looked drawn and tired, eternally curling herself into Will's arms and yawning. Will, for his part, seemed almost too proud of her. "Did you read her *Sopranos* piece?" he was always asking. "Did you read that piece she did on *Gilmore Girls*?" The Svengali thing, in Beth's case, had worked, Lil said.

"It's *totally* different. English is just impossible." Her voice began rising. Sadie protested silently. She knew all this, but still, somehow, thought Lil should finish the degree just on principle. She'd come this far. "You have to be so, so good. Or ethnic. I'm, like, this white girl writing on Modernism. No one cares." She gulped down a slug of water. "And what's the point? I'd just get a job like this once I was done."

"Hmmm." Sadie kept her lips pressed together. She could hear Tuck in this defeatism and it bothered her. It was fine for Tuck to generally fuck everything up—his manuscript was now nearly eight months late, and unless it was *brilliant,* she mightn't be able to push it through—but not to bring Lil down with him. She was sure that he was behind all this. Probably, they needed the money. *Leave him,* Sadie felt a sudden urge to scream. *Just go. Now.* But how could she, when she'd withheld the major evidence in her case? If she had told Lil about Tuck and Caitlin right away, immediately, before she could think better of it, would Lil have left him, or merely been furious with Sadie? She truly didn't know. She tried not to think about the more difficult question: whether Tuck and Caitlin were still sleeping together.

"You should eat some of this," said Lil, sighing, spent. She poked, desultorily, at the remains of the pad thai. "Or I'm going to eat it all. I'm *starving.*"

"I'm not so hungry," said Sadie. "I'm a little sick to my stomach." And then, before she could think better of it, she said those words, relics of so many movies, with the ability to silence a room. "Actually, I'm pregnant."

Lil swallowed, her chopsticks frozen in the air. "Oh my God. How?"

Sadie smiled. "Well—"

"Was this planned?"

"*No.*" Sadie laughed, but Lil just stared at her, stricken. *Could* she *be pregnant, too,* Sadie wondered for a moment, *and she's upset that I've stolen her thunder?* Then, she realized, no, Lil *wanted* to be pregnant. Of course. And Tuck was probably saying no. He was one of those guys who would say no, no, no, then once the baby arrived go on and on about how perfect it was.

"How far along are you?"

"Ten weeks."

"Aren't you supposed to wait until twelve to tell people?" The unmistakable edge of schadenfreude was creeping into Lil's voice. *I was right,* thought Sadie. But there was something else, too: like the doctor, Lil just assumed she was happy, she was going to keep it.

"The doctor said it was okay." She wasn't sure where to go, what else to tell her. It was all too messy, too embarrassing, to discuss. Why *had* she told her? Because it was messy, embarrassing, because she didn't know what to do. "I just went, actually."

"Oh my God," said Lil again. "Wow." She shook her head. "So, what does Michael think?"

"Nothing. I—" Sadie sighed and bit her top lip, a habit her mother was always on her about. "You know I've been spending a lot of time with Ed—"

"*Oh my God,*" Lil repeated, her jaw flopping open. "Is it?"

Sadie nodded. "Definitely. Michael's been in Florida most of the fall."

"Yeah. What is he doing there again?"

"I don't know." It was true. He told her almost nothing about his assignments, though Lil and Dave refused to believe this. Beth had read enough spy novels to know it was true. Sadie took a tentative bite of noodles. Telling Lil was a relief. She was no longer completely alone.

"Doesn't matter," said Lil, waving a hand in the air. "Oh my God," she said again. "Ed Slikowski. Have you told him?"

Sadie shook her head.

"What are you going to do?"

"I don't know."

"Will he be happy?"

"I don't know." Sadie ate another bite. Suddenly, the gates had opened. She was ravenous. "I *think* so. He's been, you know, saying, 'Hey, let's just get married—'"

Lil snorted. "Have you ever dated anyone who hasn't said that to you?"

"*Yes*—"

Lil again waved her hand dismissively. "Whatever. So you're going to tell him and get married?"

"I guess."

"And what are you going to tell Michael?" Lil seemed, now, to be angry at her, as if Sadie's problem was one she envied.

"I don't know. He thinks everything's fine. Or, I don't know. Maybe he doesn't."

"*Sadie,*" said Lil. Her mouth settled into an odd smile. "Oh my God. This is crazy." Sadie nodded. "You and Ed barely know each other—"

"That's not really true—"

"He's been gone since October. How much could you have seen him?"

"He came in a lot," Sadie protested.

"He didn't call us—"

"Well . . ." He'd come in, specifically, to see her. Four times. Taking the red-eye on some no-name airline. Though it had started before he'd left—for San Francisco, to shoot this film he'd written with his friend Jonathan, and then somehow gotten backing for—in much the same way it had started with Michael: a phone call to her office, a few days after Dave's party. "I kind of want to talk about Tuck's book," he'd said. "I'm getting a little nervous about it. I just sort of want to put that all behind me, not have it all dragged out again." *Well, don't worry,* she'd almost said, *since it looks like Tuck's never going to turn it in.* "I could take you to lunch. As compensation for listening to me whine." And so she had found herself at the sushi place on Fiftieth, over by the McGraw-Hill building— Ed with his beard and his faded T-shirt ("Watertown Little League") pleasantly out of place among the suits—talking about everything but Tuck's stupid book, which had already taken up way too much of her time and emotional reserves, and thinking, *You're the one who should be writing a book.* His pale, pale gaze unsettled her even more so than had Michael's darker, softer one a year or so before, when they'd met in a similar midtown restaurant; and even as she told herself, *Oh no, oh no, he's not interested in me, this is about the book,* she knew that there would be more, that she would follow this where it went (though she hadn't thought it would go *here*). The next night, he'd taken her to an opening, crowded and loud, impossible even to see the small photographs that lined the walls. "This is dumb," he'd said after a minute, putting his arm around her and guiding her out of the gallery, to a dark restaurant down the street. "I have a boyfriend," she'd told him suddenly. "Right," he'd said, smiling. "Me."

"Where would you guys live?" Lil asked now. This question had, of course, crossed Sadie's mind, but she'd banished it as too advanced for her current position. Her own apartment, which she loved, was small, the parlor floor of a narrow brownstone, divided into two rooms and a tiny kitchen. And Ed was homeless. During his tenure in New York— three-odd years—he'd sublet a friend's place on Wyckoff Street, a garret-like chain of slope-ceilinged rooms, just a few blocks from her own place. ("I can't believe I never ran into you," she'd said when she discovered this.) There was room in that apartment for a baby, she supposed, but the friend had reclaimed it and Ed had put his few possessions in storage before he left for San Francisco. All fall, he'd stayed with friends in Oakland. Now he was in L.A., at his mom's in Pasadena—"It's death"—directing another video, for a band she'd never heard of. He'd be back in two weeks to start editing and was planning, she knew, on staying with her. "We could manage in my place for a while." She sighed. "I definitely can't afford something bigger in my neighborhood."

"But Ed has money, right?"

Sadie shook her head. He'd made nothing off of *Boom Time,* in the end, nothing but his salary. And he'd dipped into his own funds for the movie. How deeply, she didn't know. But—and this was the thing about Ed—he didn't care, at all. He just seemed to trust that all would be fine.

"I guess, my point is, it just seems like a lot, all at once. Like you guys need to see if you're right for each other, before you have a *baby*." Lil was leaning in toward Sadie now, her eyes widened to dramatic proportions. Sadie knew this face. Lil's serious face. Her I-know-what's-best-for-you face. Sadie hated this face.

"I completely agree. But I don't know if we have a choice."

"You *do*. I mean—" Lil lowered her voice. "You don't have to have it."

Sadie nodded. "I know." Tears, unbidden, were rising into her eyes. It was all a bit impossible. She didn't have to have it, she knew. And yet she couldn't not have it. "I just. I feel like I do."

"You *don't*"—Lil grabbed her hand—"it's just societal pressure. We're in the middle of a baby boom. Everyone's having kids. I feel like *I* want one, even though I know we're not ready—"

"Who's ever ready?" Sadie truly believed this.

"People who are married." Lil's voice had regained its previous sharpness. She gripped Sadie's fingers harder and rested her elbows on the table. "Settled. Who have enough money."

Sadie shook her head. "That's not what I mean. I don't feel pressured to have it. *I* feel like I should have it." She wiped the tears from her eyes and, with a shudder, caught her breath. "It feels like the right thing. Like the right thing to be happening to me now. Like, it's good." Lil looked at her, nodding. "Like, I needed something. I'm just"—the tears came again, sending a hot ache through her sinuses—"so sick of everything." She fumbled in her bag for a handkerchief. "I told Ed, months ago, that I broke up with Michael."

"*Sadie*—"

"I tried to do it and then I just couldn't. I kept thinking I'd wait until he was in town, then he'd come in for a day and I just *couldn't*."

"*Sadie*—" She held her hand up to Lil and shook her head no. She couldn't stand to hear Lil's recriminations, nor could she justify herself. She didn't know why she'd done it, done any of this. Though the usual psychobabble had occurred to her: She'd been an unpopular child, an undesired teen. She'd come into her beauty late. She hated, more than anything, to disappoint those who loved her. But there was, wasn't there, the possibility that she was morally bankrupt? Or a monster of narcissism, who needed everyone to be in love with her? (She, who'd been so stalwartly alone through college, while her friends twittered over this guy or that one.) She'd done the same thing to Tal, hadn't she? But then there was simply Michael, that even as she found herself withdrawing from him, saving her thoughts, her stories, for Ed, she still, somehow, desired him: the broad expanse of his chest, the low rasp of his voice, even the way he held himself remote from her. Was this why she'd not told Lil about Tuck's affair? Because who was she to judge him? Had she not done the same thing? Twice? Was it different because she wasn't married? Because Tal and Michael had both been out of town? She'd told herself that it was, but she knew, really, that there was no difference. Dishonesty was dishonesty. Cowardice was cowardice. "Everything just feels so pointless," she heard herself saying, though she'd not actually thought anything like this until the words began coming out of her mouth. "It's all, like, where are we going to eat for dinner? What movie are we going to see? Do we publish this in the fall or the spring?" She looked down at her plate. "There's no urgency to anything. No reason for anything."

"Until now." Lil dropped Sadie's hand and peered, sadly, into her face. "Until now."

•

She'd been gone nearly three and a half hours by the time she got back to the blank towers of Rock Center, and her assistant, Shelby, gave her a smug grin. Earlier in the month there had been a round of layoffs—the company had been bought, once again, by an even larger conglomerate— and while the other remaining assistants still appeared shell-shocked and submissive, wandering the hallways like schoolchildren, with manuscripts clutched to their chests, Shelby seemed to take his exemption from the executioner as further proof of his genius. He was a good assistant, Sadie

told herself for the millionth time, but a bit of a jerk. "Val's been looking for you," he said, handing her a sheaf of pink message slips.

"Okay," said Sadie. "I'll go find her." This meant the rest of her afternoon would be lost. Once Val pulled you into her office, there was no
getting out. There would be no returning the thousand phone calls that
needed returning (more now), no looking over the new chapters of that
farm book, nor sitting on her small, hard couch and reading the new
Peter Koren manuscript (why had Little, Brown not bought it at option?
Or had their offer been too low?). She would take it home, as usual. What
she wanted, really, was to lie down on that couch and take a nap.

Shelby shook his head. "She's in a meeting. She'll come find you when
she's done." *Ooooh, you're in trouble,* he seemed to be saying. Though this
was not necessarily the case. Val sometimes came by to ask Sadie's advice
about yoga classes—she spoke often of her athletic pursuits, though no evidence of such could be seen in her physique—and gifts for her daughter.

A few minutes later, as Sadie began sifting through the rows and rows
of email that had arrived in her absence, Val rapped at her half-open door,
her plump face flushed with anxiety. She was dressed, as usual, in a
pantsuit, the sleeves of her jacket pulling tightly over her upper arms, and
her hair was freshly shaped into dated layers and waves, which crested
stiffly above her shoulders. "You have a minute?" she said.

"Absolutely." Sadie swiveled her screen toward the wall, so her eye
wouldn't be drawn to the flow into her inbox, and gestured toward the
chairs in front of her desk. But Val ignored her and stood, rubbing one
leg against the other.

"What's going on with that New Economy book?" For a moment,
Sadie had no idea what this could be. She did fiction, mainly; the occasional memoir. "Has the guy delivered?" Then, she realized: *Tuck.* Of
course. She'd been expecting this conversation for months. *Oh, God, not
today,* Sadie thought. She calculated the risks of lying, saying he'd turned
in the first two chapters (as she'd been begging him to do for months and
months). It was unlikely Val would ask to read it—she read nothing—but
you never knew.

"No," she said, inwardly flinching.

"Shoot." Val dropped heavily into one of the two chairs facing Sadie's
desk and crossed her ankle over her thigh, a masculine pose. "Have you
read the business section today?"

"Not yet." Sadie never read the business section, though she knew
she was expected to.

"First Media sold the magazine." Val waved her hands around questioningly, then snapped her fingers. "*Boom Time*. To a private investor."

"A private investor?" Sadie was Peregrine enough to know that this was highly unusual.

"Sort of. That Irina Walker person. Have you read about her?" Sadie shook her head, worried—as always with Val—that she should have. "She's a socialite." Val grimaced. "She bought a couple of art magazines last year and now it's looking like she's building a little conglomerate. She hired James Stewart as her editorial director."

"Wow."

"She's starting a travel magazine. A *smart* travel magazine." She tipped her head to her left shoulder and raised her eyebrows, as if to say *We both know that's an oxymoron*. "So have you seen any chapters?"

"No," said Sadie decisively. She had made her decision—honesty!—and she would stick with it. "But I have the samples."

Val shook her head. "It's late, isn't it? A year?"

"No, no, no, no. Much less. It was due in June."

"Seven months." She picked a proposal off Sadie's desk, glanced at it, and tossed it back. "Eight. Do you think he's really writing it?"

"I do." Sadie hoped this was true.

"Do you think he's almost done?"

"I do." This, she suspected, was *not* true.

"We gotta get this in now. We should be publishing this *now*."

"You're right." To Sadie, a story in the business section didn't constitute a major peg, but there was no point arguing with Val on this. Particularly since when last they'd spoken of the book, back in July, Val had said, "Do we really need this? That Yahoo! book is tanking. Maybe we should just cancel the contract."

"Put some pressure on. See if he can deliver this week." It was Thursday, so this seemed unlikely. "We can rush it through. They're relaunching in June. Jim Lewis is editing. Walker's got deep pockets." She nodded significantly. "We can time it to coincide. In September, no one's gonna care."

"Okay." Sadie nodded. "I'll call him right now. From what I know of it, he's really close."

"Even if he's not happy with it. He just needs to turn it in."

"Right."

Val looked at her watch and uncrossed her legs. "You doing okay?" she asked. "You seem a little tired."

"I've just been a little overwhelmed. I've got a lot on the spring list."

"Yeah, there's a lot going on." Sadie watched, with relief, as Val stood and started toward the door. "Ed Slikowski?" she said suddenly, turning back toward Sadie, whose heart began to beat sickly in her chest. *She knows,* she thought. Though how could she? "He's on board with this? We're not going to have any legal stuff?"

"He's fine with it. He and Tuck are friends. Friendly. Yeah, he's fine."

"What's he doing now? Did he start another magazine?"

Sadie shook her head. "He's making a film. With Jonathan Davis. From the *Times.*"

"A *film*?" Val sometimes had trouble believing in the existence of media other than print. "How did that happen?"

"It kind of makes sense," said Sadie, congratulating herself on her patience. "It's based on a story he did a few years ago—"

"A documentary?"

Sadie shook her head. "A feature. Set in Silicon Valley. Sort of social satire. About a software company—a little company, you know, where all the employees are twenty—that's taken over by a big multinational." She paused. "He directed a Lotion video last year."

Val shrugged. "Who's backing it?"

"I'm not sure." Sadie knew exactly. She feared appearing to know *too* much about Ed. And, yet, she also wanted Val to understand that he wasn't, say, tooling around in his backyard with a video camera.

"Hmmm." Val leaned against the doorjamb and folded her arms across her chest. "You think something's going to happen with it?"

Sadie nodded. "It's likely."

"Good. I was thinking for a while we were going to have to cancel this one." She laughed. "'Cause no one cares about Ed Slikowski anymore, right?"

Sadie sighed. "In a certain *realm,* they do. Tech people. And they buy books."

"Do they?" She tipped her head to the left again and yawned. "Don't they just buy video games?" Then, with one brisk movement, she stood upright. "Well, let's just get it in." *Trust me,* Sadie thought, *no one wants this book done more than me.*

After Val left, Sadie shut the door, settled into her phone posture—chair swiveled to face the window, arm leaning on the short wooden bookcase that adjoined her desk—and began dialing. Tuck didn't pick up at home, nor did he pick up his cell. On the first, she left a calm, firm message—"I need you to call me back when you get this"—but on the second she abandoned her reserve. "Listen, my boss wants to publish this *now*. I need to show her some chapters or she's going to cancel your contract. Which would mean you'd have to pay back the first third of your advance. I need to see something right away. Whatever you have." Kapklein wasn't at his desk, either, and his assistant, maddeningly, wouldn't put her through to his voice mail. "I need to talk to him *today, okay?*" "Well, I don't know if he'll be back—" Sadie slammed down the phone before the girl could finish. This was Kapklein's fault, too. He was too busy writing his own book—some idiot thing about training to ride the rodeo, which never would have sold if he hadn't been an agent—to pay any attention to Tuck.

The question now was whether she should talk to Lil. She'd tried—and largely succeeded—to avoid the subject with her, though Lil, of course, would have been happy to spend hours, days, discussing it. If she told Lil what was going on, Lil would certainly (happily) put pressure on Tuck—even if only to get him to call her back, which would be a start—but Lil would call her every five minutes asking for updates, and weigh in on edits and all sorts of other things that she didn't know enough about (which was a possibility even if Sadie didn't bring her in at this particular juncture), and grow bitchy and morose if all didn't proceed exactly as Lil thought it should, which it most likely would not, since she seemed to think the book would shoot up the bestseller list and make a million dollars and so on. And perhaps it would (though probably not), but Sadie wouldn't know until she *read* it.

Before she could come to a decision, the phone rang and she snatched it up. "Hey," came Lil's voice. "What are you doing tonight?"

"Um, nothing," said Sadie, before she could think better of it. "I've got to get some reading done. I'm swamped."

"Do you want to meet Beth and Emily for a drink?" She laughed. "And me. Maybe Dave. Emily called him."

"Sure," said Sadie hesitantly, glancing at her couch. It was four o'clock. Could she manage to nap for an hour without Shelby walking in on her?

"Is six okay?"

"Six is great."

"We were thinking Von."

"Von is great." No, she would say nothing about Tuck. Not now, not later.

"And I haven't told them."

"Great. Thank you. So, I'll see you at six."

"Okay." Lil made a clicking, hesitant sound. "Also, I have a question for you. What would you think about—"

"What?" Sadie was beginning to lose patience.

"Nothing."

"Okay." Sadie laughed. "Listen, I'd better go. I'll see you soon, okay?"

•

At four thirty, Sadie grabbed her bag and coat and fled, with barely a nod to Shelby—*Fuck it,* she thought, *I'm his boss; if I need to leave, I'll leave*—with a half-formed plan to call Michael from her cell phone—and say *what?*—then sit down somewhere and read before meeting up with the others. In the elevator, as she wrestled her coat on, she realized she'd left the Koren manuscript sitting on her desk. No, no, she wouldn't go back. Definitely not. It could wait until the weekend.

The trains, already, were mobbed and overheated, moisture condensing on the windows. She emerged, sweating through her sweater and coat, at the corner of Houston and Broadway for the second time that day. A horrible corner, where tourists crossed the street in thick, shuffling swarms, headed for the gigantic shoe stores that lined the blocks above and below Houston, or the even *more* gigantic chain stores between them, the same as those in the suburbs, but somehow made more glamorous, *better,* by their location. She was surprised—as she always was in the winter months—to find that it was already fully dark, though the air, she thought, was slightly warmer than it had been. Or at least the wind had slowed. It felt good, actually, against her hot cheeks. She unwrapped her scarf and headed south, weaving between the stalled tourists, who lingered in groups, consulting maps or lighting cigarettes.

At Prince, she headed east, combing the familiar shop windows: the Tibet shop, the shop that sold Tintin paraphernalia, Sigerson Morrison, and the designer consignment shop where all the salesgirls were bored and fussy. When she was a kid, these streets had been filled with bakeries and cheese shops and pizza places and private clubs where men in undershirts played billiard and indoor bocce ball and pinochle. But now everything was chic and spare, all the storefronts lined with steel and glass, their interiors filled with wispy chiffon dresses and slender-heeled shoes, the first signs of spring. At each one, she paused and considered going in, throwing off her heavy coat and pinching skirt and slipping on the layers of pale silk, though they weren't really her style—too form-less, too muddy in color (Rose always cautioned her away from neutrals). And come spring, she might be wearing maternity dresses anyway.

And on she walked, down Mulberry, past the bakery that kept odd, mysterious hours and the new, overpriced kitchen supply shop, then west on Spring, and south again on Mott. In the window of a shop on Broome, a mannequin stood clad in a long-sleeved maroon dress with a deep V-neck, a broad belt, and a soft, fluttering skirt. *That would look good on me,* she thought. Then, to her inexplicable dismay, she saw it: a tiny bump protruding below the wide sash. A maternity shop. Cleverly dis-guised as an elegant little boutique, with exposed brick walls and wide oak plank floors, but a maternity shop nonetheless. *Why not,* she thought, and sucking in a little breath, she pushed open the heavy door and stepped inside, the heels of her boots clacking ominously on the wood floor.

Gingerly, she fingered the silks and cottons on the sparse racks that lined the western wall. Opposite, a very pregnant blonde modeled a red sleeveless dress, running her hands up and down her stomach, which was frighteningly vast. "Do you think it's too big?" she asked the salesperson in an imperious tone that Sadie immediately pegged as uptown.

"No, definitely not," came the response. "You want it to be a little loose in the belly. You've got three more months."

The woman clucked her tongue. "Yeah, I just can't imagine that I'm going to get any bigger than this. But I guess I will."

"You will," said the salesgirl, in a firm, low voice. She was young and pretty, her dark hair pulled back into a thick ponytail, and slender in the way all New York shopgirls were slender. Sadie somehow couldn't imag-ine that she'd experienced pregnancy firsthand. "Hello," she called out to Sadie, as if sensing her skepticism. "All that stuff's on sale. It's all samples. There are some amazing deals."

"Right," she said, a self-consciousness creeping up on her. Were they—customer and clerk—wondering what she was doing here, with her near-flat (though not as flat as it had been) stomach? She held up a dress of blue silk charmeuse, a knot of fabric between the breasts from which folds of fabric fell in a sort of ripple. If it weren't a maternity dress, she would definitely consider it for her cousin Jenny's wedding in May. But then—*Of course,* she thought, for the second time that day—by the time that wedding came around she might need a maternity dress. And what about her own wedding? Would she and Ed marry—*if* she went through with this, the baby? And before or after the baby? Surely, that would be the first question out of her mother's mouth. Somehow, getting married seemed more terrifying than having a baby. The monstrous planning involved. Her mother's checklists.

Across the room, the blonde had changed into a black version of the dress in Sadie's hands. "That looks great," said the clerk, tugging at the hem. It did, in fact, with her pale hair and freckly skin.

"You think?" the woman asked, glancing at Sadie. "It's so hard for me to tell. I feel *huge*. My face is all puffy." She patted her thin cheeks and twisted her torso to see the back of the dress.

"It looks great," Sadie confirmed.

"Thanks." The woman pulled up the sides of the skirt and watched them float back down. "It's so hard to tell. It's like it's not my body." Reluctantly, she took her eyes from her own reflection and faced Sadie. "How far along are you? Three months, right?"

"Yes," said Sadie, thinking, *Close enough*.

"I was totally like you," the woman said. "I was looking at maternity clothes when I was, like, *a day* pregnant." Sadie found herself nodding. She *did* know, didn't she, in some weird way? Yes. "I guess it's like that for a lot of people. Especially when you've been trying for a while, like we were."

"Yeh," Sadie agreed.

"Well, before you know it you'll look like this," the woman offered, running her hands over her silk-covered stomach. "And, p.s., all that clothing I bought at first? It's all too small on me now. It's like, you have to buy new stuff every six weeks."

"You do," confirmed the salesgirl.

"Wow," said Sadie. She was strangely reluctant to end this conversation. *Tell me more,* she wanted to ask the woman. *Who's your doctor? What's a nuchal? Did you feel this sick and tired at first? Did you feel like nothing else in the world mattered? Like you could leave your job—your job that you loved—and never come back again? Like you could think of nothing else but this person inside you? Were you afraid that this person would eclipse you, would occlude your very being, that your life would become the baby and nothing else, and that— and this is the most important thing—you wouldn't mind?*

"Good luck," the woman chirped, padding back into the dressing room.

"You, too," said Sadie.

Outside, the sky had turned a deeper black. Sadie pulled her coat around her and glanced at her watch. Five thirty. She should start heading up to Bleecker. Suddenly, she wanted nothing more than to go home and get into her warm bed, never mind that getting there involved the horrible, hot train, with its sickening lurch, never mind the various thoughts and worries that would crowd her head the minute she stepped over the threshold. Sighing, she pulled her gloves back on. She could call Lil back and say she was too tired. No, no, she would go. It would be fun. She had seen no one, really, in months. It would be good.

She turned back up Mott. At Cafe Gitane, she bought a paper cup of coffee, decaf, and sipped it carefully as she crossed Houston. In the near distance, where Mott came to a dead end, intersecting with Bleecker—the street on which Von lay to the east—she saw figures carrying signs and shouting; among them wandered large persons in fluorescent vests. A protest or strike. With orange-vested cops to keep the peace. There were demonstrations all over lately, as the economy slowed and slowed. So as not to get caught up in the proceedings—her body, now that it was a vessel, struck her as frail—she crossed to the other side of the street. But as she approached Bleecker she saw that the signs were emblazoned with images rather than words, fuzzy red-tinted photographs of large-headed alien-type creatures. "Oh my God," she said aloud, stopping cold. "No." And then she started to laugh. The creatures were not, of course, aliens. They were babies. Or, no, fetuses. The protesters were shouting, over and over, "Murderer," rendering the word nonsensical. This was an antiabortion rally. *Antichoice,* she corrected herself. *In New York?* she thought. *In the village?* Bleecker, at its eastern end, was a posh block lined with quiet, elegant restaurants. As she rounded the corner, she found her answer: Planned Parenthood, the words imprinted in discreet teal script, several feet above the building's glass doors. Somehow—how?—she'd never noticed.

A whoop went up from the crowd and she saw a flash of orange pass through the door and barrel its way through the crowd. *Escorts,* Sadie realized, *not cops. Escorts for the women who need to go inside.* "Murderer!" a lone female voice screamed. "You're an evil *murderer!*" Sadie started. This was too much. The escort, she saw, was emerging from the crowd, a thin, black-haired girl held tight in her large arms. "That's enough," the escort shouted. "Enough already." She hailed a cab and put the girl quickly inside it. Sadie watched as the cab sped away, east, toward the river, the girl's face—pale, round, sleepy, above a puffy black jacket—staring out the back window.

Oh God, thought Sadie. *This is crazy.* Lil, she knew, would say that "fate" had brought her here for a reason. But *what* reason. To frighten her? Or the opposite? In a movie, a novel, the meaning would be clear. Wind crept icily down the collar of her coat and she tucked her scarf deeper inside, against the heat of her neck, then turned her head up to the sky, which was starless, a faint slice of a moon glinting faintly in the distance, so slim she nearly missed it. *Even the moon has deserted me,* she thought, smiling at herself. *God, Sadie,* no one *has deserted you. Stop it.*

A moment later, she reached the bar—the voices of the protesters still all too audible—only to find the doors locked. She waved at the bartender, who stood behind the counter, wiping glasses. He waved back and held up six fingers, shouting, "We open at six!" She looked at her watch. Twenty till. "Okay," mouthed Sadie, flummoxed. She couldn't stand out here in the cold for twenty minutes, listening to the pro-life fanatics chant their stupid lies—though, in a strange way, she wasn't sure now that they *were* actually lies—nor could she walk past them again, out to the shops on Broadway. *Okay,* she thought, *fine,* and turned abruptly east, away from the protesters, toward the Bowery, nearly colliding with Tal, who, for a brief moment, looked nearly as surprised as she, his face open and kind, the face she remembered from freshman orientation, when she'd sat next to him at a rap session. But then his features hardened into—there was no denying it—something akin to hatred, revulsion, disgust. He wanted, she could see, to walk right past her, to pretend she didn't exist, to make her understand that for him, she *didn't* exist. And *she* wanted—it was an almost animal urge—to take him into her arms and make him love her again. How could she go on with Tal—*Tal*—hating her? She could not.

"Tal Morgenthal," she said, forcing herself to smile. This, of course, was what Lil was going to tell her—Tal was in town. Did she mind if he came along? Would she have said *No problem*? Or, *You know, I think I'd better go straight home*? "Or, sorry, Tal *Morgan.*"

"Just according to SAG," he said, with a shrug. He wore a blue duffel coat, like a schoolboy. "Would you believe there's another Tal Morgenthal?"

"No." She laughed. This had been an old joke between them. "I wouldn't."

"It's true," he said. "How are you?"

She nodded, unsure how to answer this question. "Okay," she finally said. "I'm okay."

"Great," he said flatly. "You look . . . beautiful. But then"—his tone grew impossibly cool here, and a needle threaded through her stomach—"what else is new, right?"

"How are *you*?" she asked. She did not look beautiful, she knew. Her hair was frizzy and her face splotchy from the cold.

"I'm well," he told her, with great force, as though he meant it, as though he wasn't simply making chatter. "I am. Well. I'm doing this play at Circle in the Square. So I'll be around for a while. Which is great. I've been doing all this crap. And you know, I've been in Israel."

"I heard," she said. "You were doing a film?"

"A couple. Then I stayed on and did an ulpan."

"You learned Hebrew?" she asked, though of course she knew what an ulpan was. "How was it? Were you there in the fall? Wasn't it dangerous?"

He smiled, hugely, and shook his head. "No, it was completely fine. I think the newspapers give you a skewed impression." The familiar slope of his nose, his straight black brows, struck her now as strangely delicate, as *young*. But then, he was, compared with Michael, or Ed. "It was amazing. You really get why people believe. Jerusalem, it's like"—he held up his hands, fingers wide—"you feel fully human. You just want to *lick* the ground." Her skin tingled at this description. She'd had much the same experience, at sixteen, when she'd spent a summer there. She hadn't thought of that trip in years. "There's *so* much. I got back to L.A. and it was just—I couldn't cope. It's like all the clichés are true. Everyone is empty, shallow, and stupid."

"*Really?*" Ed had said much the same thing to her, repeatedly.

"No," Tal conceded. "It's just all anyone talks about is business. Everyone's trying to *make it*. It gets kind of sad." Lately, Sadie had been feeling this way about New York. But she just nodded. "So, I'll be here through March. Maybe we could get coffee sometime. If you have time. It's really good to see you."

"Sure," she said. "Are you still at your place on Union?"

"Yeah," he said. "I'm excited to be back. I met this guy in Jerusalem who's from South Williamsburg. Isn't that weird? He's, like, Satmer, though he kind of doesn't fit in." Sadie nodded. Tal had always collected people like this: rebels, outcasts, loners. She supposed he felt like one himself, though you wouldn't think it to look at him. "Anyway, he's going to take me all around there. It's ridiculous that it's like ten blocks away, but I've never been."

"Me either," said Sadie. "That's cool. What play are you doing?" Her heart had started thudding, though, thudding so heavily that her throat seemed to vibrate, turning Tal's voice into a weird, wordless buzz. She was hot. Too hot. *Oh God,* she thought. She knew what this meant. *Please no,* she thought. *I am not,* she told herself sternly, as she had at lunch, *I am not going to throw up.*

"—Daniel Sullivan, you know, who directed *Proof,* so . . ."

"Wow," she whispered. Sweat was beginning to bead her forehead.

"How are you?" asked Tal, blinking behind his small, square glasses. He looked, she saw, different, though she couldn't say how. "I feel like I've become this L.A. guy. I'm just like 'my play blah blah blah and don't you want to hear more about me.'" Scratching his head, he seemed to notice the protesters for the first time. "Weird," he said, with a frown. "Anyway, how are you?"

Before she could answer, her phone began to bleat. "Sorry," she said, unsnapping the front pocket of her bag. Her phone, the beast, was flashing red, its bleat now squawking. "Lil," she said, trying to smile, though her bile was rising. "I'm sure she's late."

She snapped open the silver clamshell. "Hey," she said.

"Hey is for horses," came Ed's low voice.

"*Hey.*"

"How's my baby?" he asked, and her heart leapt—how did he know?—then, of course, she realized he was talking about *her.*

"I'm well," she said breathlessly, clumsily trying to unbutton her coat. "I'm *quite* well."

But she wasn't, she wasn't at all. Another wave of nausea was rolling over her, saliva filling her mouth, her limbs turning liquid. Her stomach flipped over and seemed to throb in on itself, as though, well, as though something was moving inside her. *Something* is *moving,* she thought, and an image of the baby came to her—some crossbreed of the aliens on the signs across the street and the fresh pink newborns she'd seen in Brooklyn. Sadie could see her—a girl, it was definitely a girl—curled up in a blue pool, a round blue pool suspended inside her. Another wave arrived and she knew, without a doubt, that she was going to throw up. *Coffee,* she thought. Without thinking, she ran down the block, her gorge rising sickly, ducked between two cars, and vomited heavily onto the pavement. "Oh my God," she said, her voice raw, rasping. "Oh my God." To her right was a shiny black SUV, its tire splattered with her lunch, looking much as it had on the plate. She sat on its front fender, praying she wouldn't set off the alarm. "Sadie," she heard Tal shout, through a fog. "Sadie?" Ed called, his voice tinny and distant.

Morning sickness, Lil had told her, was once taken as a sign of a pregnancy's strength: if you had it, you knew you wouldn't lose the baby. Her doctor, however, had already told her this wasn't true. "Old wives' tale," she'd scoffed. In Sadie's right hand, her phone sat limply, moist from sweat, Ed's voice still emanating faintly from the earpiece. She wiped her mouth with the back of her left hand and fumbled in her old, battered bag for a bottle of water. "Sadie," called Ed, louder now. "Are you there?" She sighed heavily and shook her head, her curls falling back into place on her collar.

"I'm here," she said. "I'm here." Her stomach twisted again, a jerk like a kick, her throat convulsing. *The baby,* she thought, *the baby is already doing what babies do. She's asking for her father.*

eleven

For a year now, Emily Kaplan and Curtis Lang had been having an affair. Of course, it wasn't actually an *affair* per se since Curtis and his legal wife, Amy, had been separated for more than a year. But Emily, who liked to make everything a big joke, had taken to calling herself "the other woman" and, lately, "Mrs. Robinson." Amy, apparently, had made some derogatory comment about Emily's age when Curtis mentioned that he was seeing someone new, and Curtis had repeated this comment to Emily (unwisely, her friends thought), as evidence of Amy's hypocrisy—she considered herself such a radical, and yet she wasn't above common pettiness. "She's ridiculous," he said, smiling with just his upper lip. If she's so ridiculous, Emily thought sourly, then why haven't you divorced her yet?

A year earlier—even a few months earlier—such thoughts wouldn't have occurred to her. Things had changed for Emily. When she'd met Curtis, she'd been a working actress—with roles, back-to-back, for years—on the brink, she was sure, of breaking through into some sort of success. The play she'd made a splash in the previous year, at a little theater on East Fourth Street, was still headed for Broadway and the director had sworn, and continued to swear as the transfer was endlessly delayed, that he was taking the original cast with him. "This is as much about you as it is about us," he'd told them, gesturing to the playwright. And it was true. The critics had raved about the "energetic young cast" and Ben Brantley had singled out Emily herself, as "an irresistible redhead with a deadly combination of spot-on comic timing and screen-siren looks." *New York* and the *Voice* had pictured her in a flattering close-up. But none of that mattered in the end. The delays were over, at last, the final backers in place—and they'd decided to recast with "box-office draws." Emily's role, the second lead, had gone to a well-known sitcom actress, a redhead like Emily, of anorexic proportions.

It was Labor Day again; or the day before, to be exact, Sunday. Alone in her increasingly decrepit apartment, Emily folded her laundry. In the bathroom, five plain knee-length shifts—her summer work clothes—hung damply from plastic hangers slung over the curtain rod. The fol-

lowing day, Dave was hosting what he now referred to as his annual barbecue. The following week, her play—and it *was* still *her* play, though she
was no longer in it—would start previews. Ads were appearing on buses,
the redhead's grinning face popping out of the lower left corner. In a
misguided gesture of apology, the director had sent Emily tickets for
opening night and invited her—along with the other members of the
original cast—to the big party that would follow it, at some cheesy pan-
Asian place in Chelsea.

For eighteen months, believing this role awaited her ("another
month," the director kept telling them, "we just need one more producer
to sign on"), she'd gone on hiatus from auditioning. Which meant that
she hadn't worked—hadn't had a role—in over a year and she was, now,
fucked. Truly and completely fucked. Her friends had warned her—"Is
it really definite?" Sadie and Lil kept asking—but she had not listened,
no, because, the truth was—she could see this now, all too clearly—she
had been looking for an excuse to stop auditioning. She was tired. For
years, she'd run around the city, from audition to audition, eternally late,
eternally lugging a mammoth backpack stuffed with dance clothes, yoga
clothes, book to read while she waited, manila envelope of headshots,
protein bars, huge bottles of water, and sacks of cosmetics. For years she
had dieted and fasted; had risen at five thirty to go to the gym; had spent
every lunch hour at yoga or dance or an audition or memorizing lines or
reading sides or researching agents or doing something else *productive,*
while the rest of New York milled around her, chatting and laughing and
shopping and eating sandwiches made from triple-cream brie and drinking wine and spending the money they made doing who knows what.

The promise of this role—*her* role—had allowed her to live, at last,
like a normal person. At lunch, she sat on a bench and ate a sandwich,
watching the tourists lope around Rockefeller Center. Sometimes she
met up with her actor friends, still picking, carefully, at their sad little salads, and their horror stories filled her with incredible relief. She had
moved on and up in the world. No longer would she suffer through cat-
tle calls, through the nonunion productions of *Midsummer* set on Mars,
through the West Radish Playhouse take on *Brigadoon*. Her career, she
imagined, would play out in the way it often did with indie actresses, the
ones who were attractive in a quirky way, too tall or too short, big nosed
or small eyed, or, like Emily, redheaded: the play would be one of the hits
of the season and would lead Emily to some sort of interesting television
drama, which would, in turn, win her a cult following of devoted fans,

who would tell the uninitiated, "You know, she's *really* a stage actress." Movie roles would follow and she'd return to Broadway triumphant, in a revival of *Burn This* or, maybe, playing Portia in the park.

In truth, she'd expected some of that stuff to happen after the *Times* review, after the photo in *New York,* and so on. And she did get calls from talent managers and agents. She'd signed with one, a young, aggressive-seeming guy who sent her on auditions for commercials—Trident, Ford, Allegra—and suggested she start doing voice-over work (he could recommend a great coach, who would help her make a demo tape). But within a few months, after the guy's initial rabidity wore off, he stopped sending her out. She wasn't sure why. Because she hadn't landed any of the parts? Because she didn't want to do voice-overs (and certainly didn't want to pay for a coach)? Maybe he'd simply taken on another young redhead—younger than Emily, cuter than Emily, thinner than Emily—who might be an easier sell? Or was it just like *everything* in theater—inexplicable?

Regardless, she hadn't worried about it at the time, because *she had her play* and soon enough she'd sign on with someone great, someone at ICM or wherever. But no. Sadie had been right. Lil had been right. Everyone had been right. And now it was over. She was fucked. She had nothing. She had never, not ever in the entirety of her life, wanted anything other than the theater. Broadway. The whole sad cliché of it. But still, she'd wanted it, wanted it badly enough to waste her days, her expensive degree, her everything, answering phones for a soulless banker. This play had been her shot, her chance, her break—if she couldn't count on going to Broadway in a play for which she'd won raves, then what *could* she count on? Nothing. Nothing but Curtis. Curtis, who was eternally baffled by the reams of paperwork he needed to file in order to divorce Amy and, of course, marry Emily. Which was similar to nothing. She was a secretary now. Nothing but a secretary.

Nowadays, when she walked around at lunch, she made little lists in her head—the sort that women's magazines often instruct girls to make—of all the good things in her life: She had a cheap apartment in a popular neighborhood, which she could sublet for three times her rent. She had a stable job. She had her friends, though they were all busy with their husbands and careers and, in Sadie's case, baby. But still. She had great parents, too, she told herself—supportive, kind, cool, easy to talk to—though she'd barely spoken to them lately. She just couldn't, *couldn't,* bear to tell them about her recent travails. Their disappointment—not to mention her mother's disapproval, the I-told-you-so's registering in her thin, nasal voice—was more than Emily could bear. She'd also told them nothing of Curtis, for she knew that once she told them something, *anything,* about him, she would end up telling them *everything* about him and be subjected to her mother's hysterics on the subject of his marriage. "It doesn't matter if he's only married on paper," her mother would say. "You can't have a real relationship with a man who still has ties to someone else. It's not *honest.*" Her mother was hung up on honesty. "Just give him an ultimatum. Tell him: 'Divorce her next week, or it's over.'"

The fact was, though, that she was never quite sure if such measures were necessary, for she was happy, really, and she and Curtis lived rather like the married couples Emily knew. Happier, actually. Curtis had finally moved out of the practice space and into a massive loft around the corner from her, on Wythe, which he shared with a group of scruffy, Curtis-like guys. On weeknights, after Emily came home from work, he walked over to her place and poured himself a beer—or, well, he had done before he gave up drinking, back in April. Now he made himself a cranberry spritzer—thick, sludgy, unsweetened cranberry juice from the health food store, seltzer, a wedge of lime. But he still opened a bottle of wine for Emily and poured her a glass. He was a better cook than she—he'd learned at the elbow of his father, a great gourmand in the baby boomer style, who'd worked his way through Julia Child—and, after drinks, could often be coerced into cooking chicken pounded paper thin and covered with chopped tomatoes, or steaks with peppery, seared crusts and melting pink interiors, which Emily ate in small, tentative bites, a vestige of her collegiate vegetarianism. Other nights, Emily made her way to the tiny two-burner stove and made pasta with pesto or vegetables or tomatoes and garlic, swatting Curtis away when he tried to add great knobs of butter or glugs of oil to her pots. He liked to pretend they were a couple of a different era, drinking their highballs while dinner bubbled away on the stove. "Salisbury steak? Hmmm, my favorite," he'd say, with a close-mouthed smile and a swat at her ass.

The band practiced during the day now—now that being in a band was their actual job—but some nights he had a show, usually opening for someone else, and Emily went and listened, sipping a pale beer in the VIP section of Irving Plaza or Bowery Ballroom. During the week, he went back home to sleep. He could only write in the morning, he said, and he preferred to wake up in his own bed so he could get right to work. Emily didn't love this arrangement, but neither did she hate it. She, too, preferred to be alone in the morning, actually, to drink her coffee in silence. And there was something pleasant about Curtis's leave-takings, as well, something that pleased her in the way she half woke as he kissed her good-bye, then fell back into a hot, dark slumber.

On Friday nights, they went to dinner at Bean or Planet Thailand or one of the new places in the neighborhood. Saturdays, they slept in, ate a late breakfast at Oznot's, then wandered around the neighborhood— poking in shops, watching the dogs run around McCarren Park—or they got on the L and went to a movie or the Whitney or the Cloisters. Curtis was passionate about photography and abstract expressionism and, oddly, Renaissance art. He loved the gloomy symbolism, all those doomed maidens and dying animals and bloody saints. Sometimes, they walked across the Williamsburg Bridge and wandered around the Lower East Side, looking for the Henry Street building in which Curtis's great-grandfather had practiced medicine at the turn of the last century. They bought nuts and red licorice and candied ginger from the spice shops on Hester Street and ate dim sum from carts at the big Chinese palace on Elizabeth Street. And sometimes, they woke up early and went to the flea markets in Chelsea, looking for the old cameras that Curtis collected, or the rotting furs that Emily loved to try on, Curtis snapping her photo as she made faces in the mirror.

In the evening, they went to parties or to hear his friends' bands play or hung around at Curtis's loft, which inevitably became, on Saturday nights, the site of an impromptu party, the air thick with the woodsy scent of ganja, which Emily would not smoke, ostensibly because she feared damaging her voice, but really because she had a mortal fear—a phobia, almost—of drugs in general, having seen the effects of them on her sister. But she was happy to pass the joint to Curtis—who appeared to be smoking more and more, now that he'd given up drinking, but that was fine—and his roommates and their girlfriends and, often, dozens of other cheerful persons, their friends, all younger than Emily and *her* friends, but somehow easier to talk to for this very reason. They didn't want to know why Emily wasn't married or how she *felt* about being tossed out of her play or why she stayed, endlessly, at her asinine job, or why she stayed with Curtis, for that matter. And for this, she was grateful, so grateful that she could overlook the fact that they were the sort of people—the sort of *girls*—she'd avoided in college: the girls who attached themselves to boys in bands. Their names were Meadow and Melody and Rain and Phoenix and Blue and they wanted to know if she'd known Karen O at Oberlin, if she did yoga, if she'd seen them filming *The Real World* on the North Side a few years back. They thought Curtis was cool, the coolest, and Emily cool by extension, though she suspected that they wondered why Curtis wasn't dating someone *cooler,* someone who had an opinion about Interpol and Cat Power and Pavement versus Stephen Malkmus and the Jicks.

On Saturday nights, Emily slipped into Curtis's bed—it was the one night of the week she usually stayed there—alive with contentment and optimism, and awoke the next morning, sun snaking in through the gaps in Curtis's ratty bamboo blinds, feeling much the same, relieved to be far from the blinking light of her answering machine (her mother, Lil, Sadie, even Tal, once, asking about the play), from the sad piles of unopened bills on her small white desk, from the dust under the gray couch, the dirty refrigerator, the sheets that needed changing, the piles of laundry waiting to be carted to the Laundromat on Bedford. Curtis made coffee in a dented aluminum percolator and brought it to her in bed, inky black in a white mug that said "Mom" in brown pseudocolonial script. She sat, naked, propped up against pillows, and drank it, feeling pleasantly debauched and slightly hungover, while he went for breakfast and the papers. After they'd quibbled over who got the magazine first and eaten Danish or doughnuts or egg sandwiches or grapefruits halved and sprinkled with sugar, and just as Emily was beginning to feel that this was all she ever wanted, that she needed nothing other than this man—this expansive, wonderful man who rested his soft brown head on her hip and read "The Ethicist" aloud to her—Curtis would begin to get antsy and irritable. He wanted, she knew, to play his guitar, to walk around by the water and work out songs in his head, or to lie on his bed in silence. He wanted, she knew, to be alone. It was time, she knew, to go.

For Sundays were, they had agreed, the day on which they took a break from each other. Lying in Curtis's bed—really just a futon pad laid out on the floor—with the gray Williamsburg light sliding in through the windows, she couldn't bear the thought of leaving him. But leave him she did, growing peevish and querulous as she gathered her clothes and dressed and made her way through the hallways, to the loft's massive steel door. Arriving home to her dismal little flat, she thrust herself into some sort of activity to fend off despair. In truth, she *needed* Sundays to herself—when else would she wash her clothes, pay those bills, do her shopping, straighten her drawers, read books and, of course, see her friends. And some Sundays, the plodding nature of her chores satisfied her, and she felt sure that all would be okay. Come Monday, Curtis would arrive at her spotless apartment, find Emily radiant—hair shiny, skin dewy—and immediately divorce Amy. And Emily would morph back into the girl she was a year prior—vivacious, original, headed for stardom, at the start of a brilliant romance.

The girl she was now would fall away like a bad dream. She hated that second girl, despised her, even as she felt herself becoming her, more and more. Even worse, though, was the way she felt her friends thinking of her as this second girl, as though she were a hapless victim, wittingly brutalized by the theater world (in general), the producers of her play (in specific), and, of course, moody, immature, rock-star Curtis, who was never going to marry Emily. She'd overheard Lil saying she'd "had such a hard time" and become "obsessed with that stupid play." Even in conversation with her, they let little remarks slip, unable to resist the impulse to improve her life.

"Have you ever thought about going into publicity?" Sadie asked. "You'd be, I think, really good at it."

"Curtis just seems so *different* from you," Lil opined. "Isn't it hard being with someone so quiet?"

"You don't want to do TV?" asked Beth. "Just theater?"

"Maybe you just need a change, any change," Sadie suggested. "Something new."

But she didn't. She didn't want to go work in PR or advertising or marketing, or any of the subliterate, pointless fields that might hire an almost-thirty-year-old failed actress with "people skills." She also didn't want a shiny new boyfriend, some chatty egoist like Tuck or Will. Over the years, before she'd met Curtis, her friends had tried, continually, to set her up with men, all of them awful. Lately, her mother had become aware of JDate and emailed her the registration page. ("Look how easy it is! You can use that nice picture from Lara's bat mitzvah.") But JDate—and all those other online personal services—were the same, in spirit, as setups. The man she married was not going to be someone who posted his digitally altered picture online under the handle "DramaGeek," in the hopes of finding a woman who could talk Sondheim with him (even *if* that guy was straight).

"So then who *is* the guy? How do you find him?" Sadie had asked when Emily explained this theory to her. "I don't know," Emily admitted, feeling her face grow hot, her anger rise. "But he's not going to be the person you'd expect. And definitely not an *actor*." This was when she still thought she was going to Broadway. She'd felt bold and brash and happy alone. A month later, she'd met Curtis. Which was how it always happened, wasn't it? You had to be completely satisfied with yourself, certain that you could live forever alone—she saw herself like Katharine Hepburn, in slacks and turtleneck, rattling around her cluttered apartment—before you could attract others. But once you settled on someone—settled *in* with someone—you lost the contentment and confidence that attracted him in the first place. You began worrying about *his* happiness, and his goals and wants, so that you internalized them, and your own happiness and goals and wants were banished to some dark and musty part of yourself. She'd seen it happen with Lil, who had clearly dropped out of Columbia so she wouldn't be a threat to Tuck's precious intellect, and with Beth, who always seemed exhausted lately, running herself ragged teaching adjunct, still—at NYU, but *still*—and writing for anyone who would have her (Will kept telling her to give up the teaching, but she couldn't let it go, the idea of herself as an academic), her dissertation still unfinished, and schlepping Sam to soccer and gymnastics and swimming, as if she could make up for not being his actual, biological mother by sheer calories spent. Emily could barely stand to see either of them. They were, she supposed, the Ghosts of Marriage Future, with their glib, superficial chatter; they seemed positively terrified that she might engage them in some sort of real conversation and pierce the fragile bubble of their unions. And yet—*and yet*—she was jealous, stupidly, embarrassingly jealous of their clichéd resentments ("Tuck stayed out until *four* last night") and their domestic squabbles ("Will just *won't* do the dishes") and even their boredom ("I feel like we have nothing to talk about"). Marriage, with all its flaws, had to be better than her current state, a sort of limbo.

There was Sadie, too, of course. She and Ed seemed happy—though Emily still couldn't believe that Sadie had ended up with someone other than Tal—and even happier now that they had Jack, who at two weeks struck Emily as preternaturally alert, with his enormous blue eyes, and vast, drooping cheeks. But then, they had things better than the others, in a way. They were—*Why, why,* Emily often wondered—the sort of people for whom everything came easily. In April, Sadie's ancient aunt had died, leaving Sadie her apartment in the old union co-ops on Grand, unnervingly close to the Williamsburg Bridge. They'd moved in just a few weeks back, right before Jack was born. She'd visited them the day before, in the new apartment—boxy but pleasant—and been struck by the *effortlessness* of their interactions, Sadie resting against Ed on her old velvet couch, Jack sleeping on her lap. Was it because they were still sort of new? Or was it simply that they were *right*? Regardless, she was dismayed to find that it made her a little sick. "I think you're the most calm new mother I've ever seen," she told Sadie, trying not to grit her teeth.

"Well, you should come back next week." Sadie had laughed, giving Ed a wry smile. "I might not be so calm."

"I'm going to Toronto," Ed explained. "The film festival."

"Oh, right!" Emily had completely forgotten about this. "So exciting!"

"Yeah, well, we'll see what people think."

"People are going to think it's brilliant," said Sadie.

"Are you nervous about being alone?" Emily asked her.

"Mmm-hmmm," said Sadie.

"You don't want to go?"

"I do," said Sadie. "I was planning on going. But what would I do with Jack. He has to nurse every five minutes. I don't know if I could leave him with a sitter." She smiled down at him. "He's so little. And how would we even find a sitter?" Leaning over, she kissed Ed's cheek, a gesture so intimate that Emily had to look away. "And I think it's probably better for Ed to go alone. He has to *network*."

When Jack woke, Sadie handed him to Emily. She'd been startled by the warm heft of him—his breath hot on her shoulder, his eyes meeting her own—and she'd walked out the door limp with yearning, though she didn't understand why. She'd never particularly wanted a baby. Or even marriage. Was it the world, changing around her? Everyone seemed to be getting married these days, and everyone in Williamsburg seemed to be having babies. Or was it all, yes, because she had nothing, *nothing*?

Meanwhile, Curtis was on the verge of having everything. As was, of course, Dave, which was particularly irritating, since he was, by far, the laziest person she knew. The band's first album, recorded over a year ago, would finally be coming out the following week. There had been some uncertainty eight-odd months back, when their label was bought by another, larger label, which fired the original staff (who used their buyout cash to start another label). The new people—the marketing execs, the producers, the other nameless, uncategorizable middle managers with whom Curtis and Dave and the other guys met in glassy midtown conference rooms—didn't know exactly what to do with them and admitted as much. For a while there was talk of dropping them ("The market's saturated with this Elliott Smith kind of stuff"); for a while there was radio silence—no word, nothing, no calls answered; but finally, in the end, things had turned out surprisingly, strangely well. In May, a younger producer actually *listened* to the Lincoln recordings—during all those months of grumbling and silence, no one, it turned out, had bothered to listen to the band's stuff—and decided the band had a "unique sound" and "next-big-thing potential," terms that made Curtis more nervous than elated. "Now is when I'd really like a beer," he said after hanging up the phone with the producer. "So have a beer," Emily said. "I can't," he told her, with a flash of anger. "You know I can't."

But then money—not huge amounts of it, but money nonetheless—began to arrive, money for them to live on while they mixed the album. Money to hire a famous, crazy photographer to take moody, retro shots for the album cover; money to plaster the city—or at least the East Village—with posters of that cover; money to send them on tour (they left on Thursday; Emily had been trying not to think about it); money to pay a shrill publicist with streaked blonde hair and a Five Towns twang, who called almost daily with reports of her success on their behalf: a piece in *Time Out*, a piece in *New York* to coincide with their show at Hammerstein Ballroom (back of the book, but still); reviews here, interviews there, *Saturday Night Live* was maybe interested. "Big things are *HA-pen-ING*," she liked to say. And then the biggest: an off-puttingly cool magazine—its text printed in mod sans serif, its models clad in rags—selected them as one of its "five bands to watch." Or something like that. The issue would be out on Tuesday—Curtis had been promised an advance copy, which never arrived—and it was possible, the publicist kept bleating, that the band would be on the cover ("They've told me the cover is a POS-si-BIL-ity. Fingers crossed!"). A couple months back, Curtis and Dave and the others had been styled and photographed and interviewed. Afterward, they'd talked about how silly it all was, but Emily could see they all loved it. All except Curtis, who seemed even more fidgety and quiet than usual. When Emily asked him about it—Was he not excited? Worried? Anxious?—he shrugged his shoulders, which were narrow, and blinked behind his round glasses. "I don't really want to talk about it," he told her. "I'm trying not to think too much about it. I don't want to be disappointed. This could all turn out to be nothing."

Emily tried not to take such statements as a reproach of her own, more optimistic mode, which had led to such extreme disappointment. But there *was* reproach in his voice, she could feel it, whether Curtis intended it or not, and she told herself not to be bothered by it, for if she allowed herself to be offended on this count there was no turning back, the gates would open and it would all be over. At work, over the long, dull day, she found herself dwelling on this small injury. It was one thing, she thought, for her friends, who had known her for so long, to express anxiety over her future or her well-being (though, of course, it annoyed her when they did so). It was quite another for Curtis—who was younger than she, who had barely struggled—to criticize her, to act as though she was to blame for everything that had happened, when she had been cheated, wronged, taken for a ride, and when he didn't know the first thing about theater, anyway, about how things worked, how promises were made.

This line of thinking troubled her, for it smacked of Clara, who eternally believed herself cheated, wronged, taken for a ride by anyone who'd crossed her wayward path. And lately a new worry had crept into Emily's tired brain: that she would end up like her sister, talking to her demons on a street corner. Clara was on her mind, as she seemed to be all Emily and her parents spoke of these days. Back in May, Clara had been found in a roadside motel off 70, ranting about a patient of their father's, a skinny high school student who, she said, had broken into the room, raped her, and stolen her "meds." Indeed, there were no meds on the premises, but this appeared to be because she'd taken them all herself and, as a result, entered into what the ER doctor called a "drug-induced psychosis." Emily's father, for the most part, concurred and a day later, the Kaplans drove Clara up to a facility in Vermont. Now, every afternoon around four, Emily picked up her line at work and heard Clara's low, cigarette-scarred voice complaining about the food, the know-it-all psychiatrist, and the crazy people in her group sessions. "They're all *crazy*-crazy, know what I mean? Not like me."

Meanwhile, Emily knew, from talking to her parents, that the institute was on the verge of kicking Clara out for refusal to cooperate. "She lies," her mom explained. "She simply will *not* tell the truth about anything in her sessions. She lies to her psychiatrist. She lies to the nurses, to the other patients in group. And she refuses to take blame for anything. It's all part of the disease." Emily asked why, then, they were planning on letting Clara leave. Shouldn't she stay until they'd cured the disease? "Yes and no," her mom said, clicking her tongue impatiently. "Hasn't your father explained this to you? They used to think Clara had a mood disorder. Mood disorders are stabilized pretty easily with medication. You know this, Emily, you took psych"—Emily's parents were fond of reminding her of this, by way of suggesting that she had other skills, that she could leave this ridiculous acting business anytime and become a therapist, like her father—"but

Clara never responded well to any of the medications. They never really worked. *You* know." Emily did know. What she didn't know was why her mother felt the need to rehash Clara's sad history each time Emily asked a question about her sister's current situation.

"So now, this new doctor says the other doctors were wrong. She has borderline personality disorder—"

"Mom, I *know*. But I don't get why the doctor is trying to send her home for lying, if lying is a symptom of her disorder."

"It's because of *money,* Emily. Personality disorders take *time*—months, years—to treat. You can't just give someone like Clara a pill and send them on their way. The doctor thinks Clara would need to stay at Brattleboro for *a year* in order to make some real progress. And there is absolutely no way we can afford a year at that place. The well has run dry, my dear." She let out a brittle laugh. "Since she can't stay long enough to be treated properly, there's no point in keeping her there for much longer, unless she has some sort of breakthrough."

"What does that mean?" Emily asked.

Her mother sighed. "She needs to start talking. Or show some sign of progress. Like that she's in touch with reality." For the time being, she told Emily, they were giving Clara "coping classes," which would help her develop techniques for managing her anger, for keeping the various elements of her life in check. She was learning to draw up lists of pros and cons, which would help her make decisions (she would often become paralyzed at, say, the grocery store, unable to choose between Raisin Bran and Special K), to balance her checkbook, to keep a calendar on which she would write down the due date for her rent and credit card bills and shifts at work, and other seemingly basic human activities that Clara had never mastered.

"Isn't there anything else they can do?" Emily asked her mother. "A different type of therapy? Behavior modification?"

Again, her mother let out a heavy sigh. "Well, I guess that's what the coping classes are. And they *are* trying some other things. We'll see."

To Emily, Clara actually sounded better. And yet Emily herself seemed, somehow, worse. Each day, her emotions snuck closer and closer to the surface of her skin, threatening to interfere with even the most minor components of her daily life. A week earlier, she'd completely lost her temper when the guy at the post office had refused to accept her credit card without ID, even though she'd been buying stamps from him for years. She'd run home to Curtis, taut with anxiety.

"You're not mentally ill, okay," Curtis said, with a shrug, when she told him what happened. "If that's what you're asking."

"I know," she said. "But, Curtis, I just went *crazy*. I started screaming at the guy. It was exactly the kind of thing Clara would do."

Curtis twisted his puffy lips into a smile. "It's the kind of thing *everyone* does. Postal workers are assholes."

"I know," she said again, looking down at her feet.

"Do you want to talk to my mom about it?" he asked.

"No, no," Emily said quickly. His parents were both psychiatrists at New York Hospital, on Sixty-eighth Street. He met them for lunch every couple of weeks, and sometimes Emily accompanied him, trying to keep up with the Drs. Lang as they trotted through the building, dropping off papers, conferring with their residents, armies of clean-shaven, short-haired, vaguely pompous young white men in dark suits covered over with lab coats, who eyed Emily and Curtis suspiciously.

Mr. Lang specialized in sexual dysfunction. Mrs. Lang in eating disorders, which, Emily had recently discovered, through rampant Googling, were a type of borderline personality disorder. The Langs made Emily a little nervous, though she knew they didn't mean to and she should just *chill*. If anything, Curtis's parents were overly familiar: Peace Corps vets, like her own parents, who lived in a renovated Victorian—white, with black shutters—in a quaint, lushly landscaped town, with an overabundance of antique shops and bistros. They'd met at Harvard Med and still seemed appropriately fond of each other, both of them tall and thin and long faced, and clad in the sorts of garments worn by affluent suburbanites who wish to broadcast their interest in nature and the various activities one might partake in by way of communing with it.

Now that Curtis and his sister Cordelia were grown, the Langs spent part of each year in Africa, volunteering at an AIDS clinic. Their house was filled with tribal masks and fetishes, which frightened Emily, with their empty eyes. She knew it was politically incorrect of her to feel this way. She also knew that Sadie would have said that Emily's fear of the masks was really a manifestation of—"a *mask* for, if you will," she could hear Sadie saying, with a laugh—her fear of the Langs, Curtis included. For in a way, the problem with her visits to Montclair lay less with the Drs. Lang and more with the way a different Curtis emerged the minute he set foot on their plush lawn: the suburban overachiever, the yearbook photographer, political activist, track star. She didn't *mind* this Curtis, but she knew, somehow, that if Curtis were to betray her, to renege the promises he'd made to her, to leave her, that this second Curtis—the Montclair Curtis—would be responsible. For this Curtis—who sweetly brought up the subjects on which he knew his father loved to expound, like T. S. Eliot and North Fork wines—was first and foremost a Lang, and secondarily everything else.

It had taken her some time to realize that Curtis was, despite appearances, still under the thrall of his parents' expectations. When she'd met him, a year prior, she'd thought him the exact opposite, some sort of pure being, like a bodhisattva, shot down from a higher plane to bless mortals with his unusual wisdom. He didn't want to talk about any of the things other people talked about at parties: new restaurants, rents, movies. He hadn't read a magazine since 1984, when his subscription to *Highlights* expired, and he hadn't read a book published since around that same date, other than *Vineland* (he was mad about Pynchon, the only person she knew who'd made it through *Gravity's Rainbow*). He didn't go to movies and didn't own a television. He hadn't asked her what she did or where she lived or how she found her apartment. What *did* they talk about? she wondered now, padding around her clean apartment. Family, she supposed. Art.

On her second visit to Montclair, in March, Mr. Lang served a cassoulet—"French peasant food!" he cried in such a way that Emily knew he shouted this whenever he served the dish—and a big salad, and talked at length about the wine, which came from a grape that had fallen out of vogue but was now being revived by artisanal vintners in Virginia ("Turns out the soil has *the exact same pH level* as the Loire"). After dinner, Mrs. Lang shooed Emily and Mr. Lang into the study—they'd eaten at the big plank table in the Langs' sleek open kitchen—and summoned Curtis to help her with the dishes. "How about some port?" asked Mr. Lang, raising one bony finger, and slipped through the study's second doorway, which led to a funny little passageway under the stairs. Emily was left alone in the Lang study, a dark, book-lined room straight out of Martha Stewart, though presumably the room's design and decoration predated Martha Stewart's invention of herself as the arbiter of things domestic. Emily ran her finger over the books in the cases: medical and psychological texts, British mysteries, short stories by Cheever and Carver and McCullers, paperback thrillers, a shelf of yellowing editions of poetry, presumably dating to the Langs' undergraduate days. One section of a bookcase was covered with a massive door, behind which, Emily suspected, was a television. She imagined Curtis as a towheaded kid, lying on the flat kilim, watching cartoons.

From the kitchen came the low murmur of Curtis's voice, punctuated by the higher, sharper inflections of Mrs. Lang. Emily tried not to listen, until she heard Mrs. Lang say, unmistakably, "What's Amy up to these days?" Curtis's response—or the parts of it she could make out, from where she sat frozen in an oversized leather club chair—had something to do with Amy's continuing legal problems, following her arrest in Seattle at the WTO the previous year, and the fallout from a massive protest against Crown: a mock New Orleans funeral for the company, with an effigy of its CEO in a coffin, and a fifteen-piece brass band ("It was really cool"). Emily had read about the protest in the paper—and heard a bit about it from Lil, as Caitlin Green-Gold and her husband were, of course, involved—and wasn't surprised to hear that Amy the Anarchist had been in attendance. But she *was* surprised that Curtis could outline Amy's activities for his mother. She'd been under the impression they were barely in touch. *Just calm down,* she told herself. *It's not a big deal.*

But a few days later, she flew into a rage—"You still love her!" etc.—and Curtis confessed that part of the time he didn't spend with Emily—Sundays, his time, he'd said, for solitude—was spent at Amy's place, visiting Dudley, the grayish, wiry-haired dog they'd adopted in college. Curtis kept a photo of Dudley in his wallet and looked longingly at every dog they passed on the street. "I miss him," he told her. "He's an old guy. He's not going to be around much longer." Emily's fury—tamped down, briefly, by thoughts of Dudley—leapt into her throat again.

"Well, I'm sure it's good to see Amy, too," she said, in a clipped, formal tone. "You guys have known each other for so long. It would be terrible if you just, you know, never spoke." Curtis nodded slowly. He appeared to be slightly afraid of her, which only made her more angry.

"Yeah, you're right," he said carefully, after a while. "I was a terrible husband to her and I feel like I can kind of make it up to her by being a good friend. She can't really take care of herself. It's hard for her, being alone."

Emily refrained from pointing out that Amy had a boyfriend who lived on her block—whom she'd started sleeping with while she and Curtis were still living together—and so she wasn't *alone,* was she? She also managed to restrain herself from mentioning this development to her friends, since she knew they would make too big a deal out of it. But she added a third Curtis to the list: the Curtis who spent time with Amy on Sundays. She would never meet this Curtis and that was absolutely fine with her. She wondered whether he and Amy talked about politics or their mutual friends or the weather or what, and whether, in doing so, he studiously avoided mentioning Emily, as he avoided mentioning Amy to Emily.

Not that it mattered. On Sunday afternoons she went about her chores with the specter of Amy trailing her, like some kind of hovering, bewinged Disney witch. Come Sunday night she often felt that she'd rid herself of this ghost, so content was she in her small, neat home, her three plants watered, her hair freshly washed, her bed lined with clean sheets, her laundry folded and put away, her face pink and exfoliated, a pot of tomato sauce bubbling on the stove. Some Sundays, she even found herself dreading Curtis's Monday invasion. Maybe, really, she was meant to be alone. Maybe she *preferred* being alone and she'd simply been conditioned by the media—or society in general—to think she had to partner off with someone and start a family and so on.

This was how she felt on some Sundays. On other Sundays—like this one, the day before their anniversary—Amy remained unvanquished, a convenient repository for all Emily's fears and anxieties. As the evening wore on, she practically had to sit on her hands in order to keep herself from picking up the phone and calling Curtis. This was another thing she'd sworn she wouldn't do: call him on Sundays. She didn't want to seem incapable of going a day (less, really!) without speaking to him. Nor did she want to appear to be checking up on him, making sure he actually came home from Amy's place, though of course she *did* want to make sure, particularly since the Monday, back in April, when Curtis walked in the door, kissed the top of her head, and announced, quietly, that he was going to quit drinking.

"Quit drinking," Emily parroted, shocked. Curtis loved to drink. More than anyone she knew. She put down the bottle of wine in her hand. "Quit *drinking*," she repeated. The phrase sounded strange and false to her, like something from a Jimmy Stewart movie or an Arthur Miller play, as though drinking were Curtis's occupation and he'd decided to leave it and pursue something more lucrative, like selling aluminum siding. "Why?" she asked, hearing a whine creep into her voice. Curtis shrugged and smiled, sitting down on Emily's gray couch. He picked up that week's *New Yorker,* which lay open to the movie reviews, the section Emily read first. "Curtis, *why?*" she asked again, sitting down next to him and taking one of his hands in her own. Instead of looking at her, he glanced blankly at the bottle of wine on the counter.

"Emily, I mean, come on. Why does anyone quit drinking?" She pursed her lips together so as not to ask him to please stop using that ridiculous phrase.

"I don't *know* anyone who's 'quit drinking,'" she told him primly.

"Sure, you do," Curtis said. "Clara." Emily recoiled at the mention of her sister's name.

"*Clara* stopped drinking," she told him, feeling that now-familiar switch click on, unleashing an electric jolt of anger; there was something strangely exciting, even *sexy* about it, that odd, off-kilter feeling that anything, *anything,* might fly out of her mouth, "because she's *crazy*. You're nothing like Clara. Are you"—she was on the verge of screaming, the muscles in her arms strangely taut, her temple pounding—"are you saying that you're an *alcoholic*? Is *that* what you're saying? Because you're *not*. You don't know anything about it, Curtis. You're *not* an alcoholic."

"I could be," he said, his eyes still on the magazine. "And I am like Clara in some ways. I have a problem with addiction. I smoke. I drink too much coffee."

Emily threw up her small hands. "Curtis, this is crazy! My sister has serious problems. It's offensive to say that you, your, I don't know"—her voice sputtered—"the fact that you smoke, like, a pack of American Spirit Lights every two days is in some way the same as my sister being an unreformed junkie who can't function in normal society." She was screaming now, her voice ragged, and Curtis had put down the magazine and dropped his head into his hands. His legs were so long that his knees poked up in sharp angles from the low couch.

"Please calm down," he said, in such a quiet, heartbreaking way that Emily burst into tears.

"This is Amy, isn't it?" she said. "This has something to do with Amy."

"No, no," he told her. He'd been thinking, a lot, he said—with the album coming out and the tour and all that—and realized that everything he and Emily did together involved drinking. They never sat and talked without a glass of wine in their hands. "You just have one, but I always want another. I get a taste for it." And he thought, just as an experiment, that he'd stop and see how things progressed without alcohol as a "lubricant." *Amy,* she thought. *That sounds like Amy.* And sure enough, when pressed, Curtis confessed that Amy had planted the idea in his head: she'd been insisting, lately, that Curtis's drinking had driven them apart. And she was concerned, sweet girl, that it would do the same to him and Emily. Alcohol was a depressant and Curtis had depressive tendencies anyway, she said. He should really think about Prozac or Zoloft or something.

"Curtis, that's just stupid," Emily said. "You don't need to be on anti-depressants." But she was remembering that in college he'd gone through an amphetamine phase ("It helped me focus") and an LSD phase ("It helped me write"), and she was counting the number of his lyrics that had something to do with one drug or another. Or self-loathing. Or suicide. *Okay,* Emily thought, *maybe I'll give her this one.*

"According to Pfizer, we all need to be on antidepressants," he said, smiling, but she would not, *no, she would not,* let all this go with a laugh.

"Oh," she said, folding her arms against her chest. "Well. Then. Why don't we hook up the IV right now." Curtis shrugged again, maddeningly, then let the real bomb drop: Amy had decided that they shouldn't divorce until Curtis "sobered up." Not, he insisted, because she didn't want the divorce—she *did,* he said—but for Curtis's own welfare. She didn't want him to go through with the divorce in some sort of alcohol-induced fog only to regret it later.

"Why would you regret it?" asked Emily. "And why does it matter? If *she* wants the divorce, too, then why should she care if *you* regret it." Curtis sighed and gave her a look of great tolerance, as though Amy's logic was flawless and Emily a dolt for not understanding, but he would be kind enough to explain it one more time.

"She wants us both to be in the same place." This was not Curtis-speak either, this "same place" talk. "Emily, listen, I don't know why I'm defending her. This is crazy. I'm making you miserable with all this. I want to be with you—you're my girl." He grinned and shot her an embarrassed look. "I don't want to be with Amy. I, I don't even want to *talk* about Amy." He moved his long hands around, formlessly, helplessly. "All this stuff with the band," he said, his voice growing smaller. "I'm nervous."

"But isn't that normal?" Emily asked angrily. Suddenly, as though a camera inside her were shuffling its lens around, bringing everything into sharp focus, she understood what bothered her, what made her anxious about the way Curtis engaged with the world: he viewed every feeling, every fear, as aberrant, as necessitating a cure. Is this what came of having psychiatrists for parents? Or was this what he meant when he said he had an "addictive personality": that he was always seeking to soften the edges of his emotions.

"Curtis," she began. If she didn't force herself to talk, she was, she was sure, going to start screaming. "You don't have to do something just because she wants you to—" And then she stopped herself. Another thing she'd sworn: no negative words about Amy. They would only make Emily look bad and Amy wronged. Somehow, she saw, she and Amy had shifted positions. When she'd met Curtis, Amy had been the villain—she had cheated on Curtis; she had belittled him and abused him—and Emily his savior. Now, somehow, Emily had become the evil temptress who had seduced Curtis away from his *wife*. How had this happened?

"She's just asking me to do this one thing," he said firmly. "And it's something I've been thinking about doing anyway. It's the truth."

Emily nodded. "Okay," she said. "No drinking. For how long? Did she give you a time?"

"Three months."

"Okay. Three months."

All summer Curtis avoided drink, seemingly without any trouble. The guys had long stopped bringing beer to rehearsals anyway, now that they had a proper practice space in a nice, finished loft building a few blocks down on Bedford. She stopped drinking, too—at least when she was with him—and was delighted when she found that she'd lost a few pounds without even trying: the simple caloric difference between having a glass of wine with dinner each night and not. Each evening he went to a meeting at a church on North Eighth Street—two blocks from Emily's apartment and she'd never taken note of it—and conferred with his sponsor, a thirty-year-old legal proofreader, whom he hated at first, then grew to like. "If we hadn't met through AA, I bet we would have become friends anyway," he told Emily. The sponsor was alarmed to hear that Curtis was about to start (or restart, as the case was) divorce proceedings. Apparently, you weren't supposed to make major life changes when you were in "recovery."

"It's not a 'major life change,'" Sadie cried when Emily explained this to her, over a much-needed glass of wine at Black Betty, back in May. "He and Amy haven't lived together for two years. Getting *back together* with her would be a 'major life change.'"

"I know," said Emily. "I know."

She came home from such outings with friends, hoping she didn't smell like a bar, to find Curtis sitting on the couch tensely reading a paperback, resentful, it seemed to her, that she was not required—or willing—to participate in his experiment with abstention. But the nights she stayed in were no more comfortable: he arrived at her place reeking of smoke, his large, round eyes lowered with shame. What, she wondered, had he been talking about at the meeting? "How was it?" she'd asked the first night. But he'd just shrugged and flung himself down on the couch. "We're not supposed to talk about it," he mumbled, hours later, into her hair. "The meeting. It's private." "Okay," Emily said, and thereafter tried, brightly, to talk around the subject, chatting about her day at the office or her friends, or silently crawling on top of him and burying her head in his neck, until the discomfort abated and he became *her* Curtis again. Still, she realized, she now had a *fourth* Curtis to contend with: the Curtis who went to meetings at a dingy, Italianate church and talked to strangers about deeply personal things—things he wouldn't (okay, *couldn't*) tell her. Three private selves was, she thought, verging on too many.

During the day, at work, she read about alcoholism and depression. There were, she found, hundreds of websites devoted to each and twice that many message boards where people conversed about their own struggles or those of their husbands, mothers, brothers, and so on. There was a large group, Al-Anon, for family and friends of alcoholics, which had meetings of its own all over the city. Briefly, she considered going, to show her support for Curtis's endeavors—but then dismissed the idea as overzealous and more likely to annoy or embarrass Curtis than to impress him with the extent of her devotion. Instead, she kept reading, tracking the cycle of addiction—and depression, for the two seemed interlinked—from start to finish. She read about genetics—the importance of family history—in both diseases ("Alcoholism is a disease," the AA sites shouted). She memorized the signs of alcoholism—Do you drink alone? In the mornings? Do you have blackouts? Do you frequently drink to excess?—and the signs of depression. Curtis, she decided, had none of the former, and some of the latter. She read about codependency—which seemed, clearly, to be what was going on with Curtis and Amy—and "addictive personality," the existence of which, she discovered, was currently in debate among psychologists and neurobiologists, though it made a sort of sense to her, for she saw Clara in the profiles she read, and Curtis, too, and most troublingly, herself, the way she *had* to have her first cup of coffee—made precisely the way she liked it, in a tiny French press, with a half teaspoon of sugar—at precisely 8:00 a.m., and her first glass of wine at 7:00 p.m. Now that Curtis had given up *his* glass, she found herself, during her lonely Sundays, counting the minutes until she could allow herself this pleasure. On the good Sundays, when she was content with her own company, she sat, lazily drinking, through the evening, then fell into bed early, her head pleasantly fuzzed. On the bad Sundays, though, she tried to resist the urge, for wouldn't it be slightly disloyal to Curtis to drink in his absence? Wouldn't she somehow jinx their whole affair if she took so much as a sip of pinot noir?

But on this Sunday—this bad, bad Sunday, which should have been a good, better-than-good Sunday, for the next day was a holiday and they would be happy, they would be celebrating, they would be among their friends!—as she cooked her sad solo meal (spaghetti with jarred sauce), a spot of rage broke through and she brought out the bottle and the corkscrew, ensuring, in her private schema, that Curtis wouldn't call that night—as he sometimes did on Sundays—just to say good night and that he loved her and was thinking of her.

"Fuck him," she said aloud. "I'll see him tomorrow. I don't need to talk to him tonight." At that, the pins of the top lock thunked heavily in their steel casings. Emily jumped and put down the bottle with a heavy thud, just as Curtis's long head poked through the door.

"Hey," he said, loping across the room and kissing her.

"Hey," she said warily. He had never, ever broken their Sunday rule. "What are you doing here?"

Curtis shrugged. "I just thought I'd stop over and see you." He looked at the bottle of wine on the counter. "Were you just about to have a glass of wine?" She nodded. "Go ahead," he said. "I'll have one, too."

"But what about—" she asked.

"My three months are up," he said, grinning. "I saw Amy today and she talked to my sponsor. He told her that I've been clean for the whole summer."

Emily began to laugh. "Oh my God, *Curtis,* I got so wrapped up in all this that I guess I thought it was forever." She wrapped her arms around him and squeezed. She felt giddy, lighter than she had in months, since this whole business had started. "So, if you're having a drink, does that mean you're not an alcoholic?"

"Yep," he said. "Just like you said. I've done a lot of thinking."

Emily ran her hands over his long arms, with their fine brown hairs, and wrapped them around her. "Oh my God, Curtis, it's been so hard. I've been trying so hard not to ask you about it, but I feel like there's nothing else to talk about." She looked up into his face. "So this means, right, that you'll get the divorce soon? Right after Labor Day?"

Curtis nodded. "Not *right* after Labor Day, because of the tour. But right when I get back."

Say nothing, she counseled herself, but her pulse had already sped up, the words rushing out in venomous spurts. "But you're not leaving until

Thursday. Couldn't you get started on the paperwork on Tuesday? You know, Meredith Weiss said she'd help." Curtis sighed and took off his glasses. Without them he looked young, so young that she wanted to grab him and hold him and run her fingers through his hair. She wanted to say, *I'm sorry. I hate myself for being this way, but I can't stop.* But her mouth had turned hard. She couldn't open it to speak.

"We have the show on Wednesday night, at Hammerstein, and Alana"—this was the publicist—"has some interview for us, some NPR thing, and some other stuff. It's gonna be crazy."

He sounded, she thought, as tired as she felt. *Good,* she thought, *he deserves it.* And suddenly she knew what she wanted: she wanted to punish him. "She won't do it," she said. "Why don't you just tell me the truth?"

Curtis held up his hand to her and gave her a look so sad she knew she was right. She pulled her legs from his and planted them on the floor. "Okay," he said, nodding. "She just wants to wait a bit. A few months. It's no big deal."

"Oh my God." Emily dropped her head in her hands. She'd expected him to deny this, to say no, no, no, everything was fine. "A few *months.* No. No. *No.*" Before he could answer, she'd sprung up from the couch and was shouting, "I am so *sick* of her shit. If I ever have to hear her name again, I'm going to fucking *slit my wrists.* She's a stupid, manipulative, selfish bitch. I just don't get it. I don't fucking get it." She had moved from shouting to screaming, her hands shaking with rage (*adrenaline,* she thought, from some rational corner of her brain). "What the fuck is *wrong* with you? Why don't you see it? She does this *shit* to you, Curtis, she *manipulates* you." At this word, she began to cry, which only made her more angry, for Amy, *fucking Amy,* didn't deserve her tears. "Everything goes right for you and she does this stupid *shit* to cut you down, telling you you're an alcoholic—it's fucking *ridiculous.* And you *believed* her." Curtis was staring at her, lips parted, from his perch on the couch, the skin around his eyes white and shiny with fatigue.

"Emily, come on," he said, in a whisper. "Don't say these things. This isn't you."

A hoarse sob escaped her throat, then turned into a scream. "This is me. I want to get married and have kids and do . . . do normal things, *just like everyone else.* Just like fucking Amy, the fucking *anarchist,* with her fucking apartment in *Park fucking Slope,* that her fucking *parents* bought her." Her breath was coming in big ragged gulps and her eyes burned, but the storm was passing. All she wanted now was for him to leave, to leave her alone. "I'm just like everyone else," she said, pressing her hands into the sockets of her eyes. "I want the same things. I want a normal life."

"No, no, you're not," he said, wrapping his arms around her. "You're *not*." He smoothed her hair back from her hot forehead and she allowed herself to relax, to melt into him for a moment before she remembered what he'd said—there would be no divorce, not now, *not ever,* she knew. She shook his hand off.

"She manipulates you. She manipulates you," she whispered into his chest. "Why do you let her? Why, Curtis? Why?" And then, plain as day, she saw the answer to her own question. She pulled away from him and wiped her hand across her nose.

"Hey, hey," he said softly, and reached out a hand to gather her back into him, but she twisted away.

"You're going to go back to her. You don't think you are, but you are. Otherwise, you wouldn't put up with this." Curtis's face went white.

"No," he said. "Emily, how can you say that? That's crazy. How many times have I told you that I love *you*. I want to be with you. You're my special girl." For a long moment he looked at her, almost as if he were seeing her for the first time. Then he ran his hand over his face. "Could I have a glass of that wine now?"

Emily nodded, stepped back to the counter, uncorked the bottle, and poured them each a glass. Drinks in hand, they sat side by side on the sofa, in silence. Finally, Curtis drained his glass in one draught and took Emily's hand in his own. "It's been hard," he said. "She's been a part of my life for so long—a part of my family, too—that I can't imagine life without her."

"I know," said Emily.

"And she just can't seem to manage on her own." He looked at her sadly, his brows sliding closer together, and Emily saw that she was right—she hadn't been sure of it until she said it—that he was going back to Amy. Already, he was looking at Emily like someone he used to love, something he'd sacrificed to the greater good. Amy was wrong about him after all. He wasn't motivated by selfishness, but by a desire to set the world right that was as strong, stronger, than Amy the Anarchist's. The thought made her ill—a great gob of something rising sickly in her throat, sweat prickling out all over her back—and she stole her hand back from Curtis.

"Why a few months?" she asked.

"What?" he asked.

"You said before that she wanted you to wait a few months. Why?" Curtis blinked, slowly, behind his glasses.

"Health insurance. I have it through my parents, still. She's on my plan." Emily nodded, worrying her lip—the tears were coming back. She hadn't known that Curtis even had insurance, much less that he was responsible for Amy's.

"Why," she asked, "didn't she bring this up in May?"

"Because," he said, turning to face her, "in May she wasn't pregnant."

"Okay," said Emily. A calm had come over her, giving her the peculiar feeling that she was watching someone else have this conversation with Curtis, rather than engaging with him herself. "Okay. I get it. I understand." Curtis slid over and pulled her to him. This time, she didn't resist.

"It's not what you think," he said. "It's not mine. I never—"

"I don't care," she said. "I just don't care anymore. Please. I don't want to hear anything about it. I don't want to know." The tears, at last, made their slow, itchy march down her face, but they came with something like relief: these were the last tears she would cry over Amy, because it was *over*. She and Curtis were through. They were breaking up, to use the high school parlance. The thing she'd dreaded was now, finally, happening. "Leave me alone," she said. "Please just leave me alone." And, to her surprise, he obeyed, pulling his warm arms away from her.

"You're going to be fine," he said. "You're not like her. You're strong."

"*I know,*" she said, but he didn't seem to hear her.

"Better than fine. You're going to find someone better than me, someone who deserves you." *Can't he, at least, spare me the clichés,* she thought. But then he kissed the top of her head and she loved him all over again. And then, somehow, he was walking out the door.

In the dark courtyard, he turned and looked back at her, a black, stringy figure, like a rendering of Ichabod Crane she'd seen once, at the little museum in Sleepy Hollow. She raised a hand to him—a royal wave—and he to her. In a moment, he was gone and Emily's tears stopped. She rose, creakily, from the couch, found a tissue and blew her nose. It was unimaginable that Curtis wouldn't simply walk back in the door, smiling his closemouthed grin, and crawl into bed with her. They wouldn't make love again. Not ever. At this thought, her mind fell into a tailspin of sorts. She cupped her hands around her mouth, afraid she might scream, then drank down her goblet of wine and fell into a deep, restless sleep, splayed out on the small couch, still clad in her blue sundress with the apple print. At four, she woke and had a moment of warm, sleepy bliss before remembering what had happened. Her mind began to race. Dave's party was tomorrow—no, today. Would Curtis go? Should she go alone? But then she'd have to explain what happened with Curtis. No, she couldn't do it. She couldn't tell them that Curtis had left her—Dave's smug face materialized before her—and she certainly couldn't do it at the party. She wouldn't go. And perhaps she should call Curtis to let him know that she wasn't going, so that he might go without her. No, no, God, what was wrong with her. Why was she worrying about denying Curtis the pleasure of *her* friend's party?

And so her mind went, in circles and circles, until well past dawn, when she took off her dress, slid between her cool, clean sheets, and fell into a dreamless sleep. When she woke, the second time, it was after one; she was relieved, at least, that she'd slept through half the day—only eight more hours to get through before she could sleep again. She stayed in bed for as long as she could stand it, flipping through magazines she'd already read, ignoring the ringing of the phone. Eventually, sleep came again, then morning, and she rose and went to work, where she took great pleasure in doing everything absolutely perfectly: faxing and filing and photocopying with the utmost precision, answering the phone in exactly the way her boss preferred. At six, she raced to the train, as she always did, to get to her apartment before Curtis and, thus, have time to change her clothes, take a shower, smear on lip gloss. But as she pushed through the turnstile, she realized that Curtis, of course, wouldn't be coming. There was no reason to rush home. She was free to do whatever she wanted: run errands, window-shop, meet friends, see a movie. A movie. A dumb, soppy, girly movie at the huge, awful multiplex by Union Square. Yes.

The 6 train rolled into the tiled station and she rose with the crowd and pushed her way onto it, but at Union Square, where she normally switched to the L, she walked up the stairs and into the park, crossed from the north to the south side of Fourteenth Street amid another, younger throng, and bought a ticket for the seven fifteen showing of a romantic comedy that Curtis had refused to see with her ("You should go with your girlfriends"). The theater was deserted, it being Tuesday, and she stood, bewildered, in the foyer for a moment, sick with regret. Going to the movies alone suddenly seemed pathetic. *I should go home,* she thought. *I can't sit through a movie. I should go home and lie down.* But her home was haunted now, not by Amy, as on those gloomy Sundays, but by Curtis. "Okay," she said aloud, glancing around to see if anyone had heard her, then strode out the glass doors onto Broadway, forcing her shoulders back, as she did in yoga class, her head high, and turned herself back north. She had forty-five minutes to kill and she would sit in Union Square, alone, and read the fat book that Sadie had given her, about a Midwestern family, a satire.

But the street was as crowded as the theater deserted. "Excuse me," she said to the tourists in their polo shirts and khakis. "Sorry," she said. "Can I just sneak by here," she said to the clumps of hard, angry-looking teens awkwardly smoking menthol cigarettes and laughing so loudly she wanted to scream at them to shut up. "Ex*cuse* me," she said, and edged by them, flattening herself against the window of the Virgin Megastore, where she found herself face-to-face with Curtis. Or, not Curtis himself, but his likeness: a blown-up image of the band's album cover hung in the store's southmost window. It took her a moment—more than a moment—to realize that this was indeed Curtis, her boyfriend until less than twenty-four hours before, staring at her from a piece of foam board, his name imprinted in white script, like handwriting, above his head, the other bandmembers standing slightly behind him, receding into the background as the label wanted them to (though Dave's red hair flamed like a beacon). The teens kept laughing and laughing, until Emily began to wonder if they were laughing at her—if her skirt was tucked into her underwear or her face streaked with mascara—but, no, they were shouting, "Shaneekwa said *what?*" and "She is *stupid*." Emily was nothing to them, they hadn't even noticed her, a small, sad girl—no, *woman*. To them, she was old, in her dull, gray shift. A nonentity, in the same negligible adult category as guidance counselors and youth ministers.

She squeezed past them and stared, glassy-eyed, at Curtis. With his long, sad face, his large, watery eyes, airbrushed and exploded 300 percent—literally larger than life—she saw what she'd never seen in the flesh-and-blood Curtis: a strange ferocity. She had been such a fool. She had believed it all, this romantic crap. She had really believed it, some mystical system of cause and effect, in which Curtis had no desire or need for material, earthly success—wanted only to be able to do what he loved to do, even if it meant living in a pup tent and eating beans—and was rewarded for his *lack* of ambition, while she, she had wanted it all too badly, and thus would never have it. It was all just *bullshit*. Curtis had wanted it more than anything. And she hadn't wanted it enough. That was the truth. The real, actual truth. She had jumped at the chance to give up auditioning. She had freed Curtis from keeping his promises to her, freed him to go back to Amy. And Amy? Well, she'd fought for him—and won. Perhaps she really did love him more than Emily did. Or perhaps Emily wasn't capable of loving anyone or anything enough to fight for it. Sadie, she knew, would say that Curtis shouldn't have made her fight for him in the first place. That he didn't love *her* enough. That he was weak. But then what did Sadie know, Sadie, who'd never had to fight for anyone, anything, in her life. ("What would she do," Lil had asked Emily years back, "if men didn't just fall in love with her on sight?")

Across Broadway beckoned the maroon interior of a Starbucks knockoff that had recently joined forces with an overpriced sandwich shop. Hiking her bag on her shoulder, she crossed the street and strode inside, squeezing through the maze of small tables, and found a seat near the south window. All around her, tourists gabbled in French and Spanish and German, and NYU students in faded jeans and pastel lip gloss chatted about their boyfriends ("He'll only give me his *cell* number!" "Okay, so he's *totally* married!"). At the next table, two dark-haired women spoke in low, husky voices, taking large sips of red wine and fumbling with their packets of cigarettes. "Cabernet," Emily mumbled, to her surprise, when the waiter came to take her order. *Maybe I am an alcoholic,* she thought.

When the wine came, she drank deeply. The warmth that spread through her head and limbs was thrilling—she was strong, invincible, she could do anything, fight anyone for anything, she *could*. The room slowly came into sharp focus and she saw that she was the only lone woman. The only lone woman and there she sat, drinking, *alone*. "Oh my God," she said, shaking her head as if to clear it of thoughts. She pulled out her wallet, extracted a ten, slipped it under the wineglass, got back on the subway, and went directly home, where she found her apartment a bit less haunted than she'd imagined. The red light on her answering machine blinked angrily. Suddenly, she was tired, exhausted, but she would not go to bed, not without doing something, something to show she was not defeated, so she watered her plants—the African violet in the north window (a gift from her boss), the ivy in the bedroom, the spider plant in the south window—and knelt by the bathtub to wash the dishes. She made the bed, put her clothing away, changed out of her work dress and into her kimono, then sat down cross-legged on the floor in front of her answering machine, which itself sat on a small tile table, a gift from Curtis, who had given it to her soon after they met, when he noticed that she kept the machine on the floor. This was the sort of person Curtis was, she thought, biting her lip again: he didn't mind living in a pup tent and eating beans, but he thought it barbaric that she didn't own a phone table.

Gathering a pad and pen, she pressed play and listened to Sadie, Lil, Dave, and Beth ask her if she wanted to head to Dave's place together (Sadie, Lil), what time she might arrive (Dave, Beth), and why she wasn't there (Dave again). The sixth, seventh, and eighth messages were from her mother, pinched and impatient ("Emily, if you're there, pick up—Please, Emily—*now*"), increasingly angry ("Emily, where are you? your cell is off; call me *back*"). The ninth caller she couldn't place at first: "Hi, Em, just calling to say hello and, um, see how you're doing. I guess you're out." The voice was high, sweet, female, slightly nervous, slightly shy, hesitant, apologetic. Her stomach twitched: Clara. She stopped the message midway and replayed it.

"Hi, Emily, just calling to say hello, and um, see how you're doing. I guess you're out. I kind of need to talk to you and there's no way for you to call me here, really, so I guess I'll try you later. Or maybe, well, I guess I'll just tell you why I'm calling. I don't know if Mom told you or not, but they're letting me out of here on the tenth. Um, next Monday. And I—" Here her voice wavered. "I don't really have anywhere to go. I can't go back and stay with Mom and Dad. I just can't. I thought, well, I talked about it with Mom and with my doctor, and I thought, well, I'm really okay now. I feel like, I think, I finally understand things. You're going to be amazed, Em. For the first time, I feel like I can think clearly. And if it's okay, I thought, well, I thought I would come live with you."

twelve

Bad luck came in threes, Emily supposed. Her play, Curtis, and now Clara. If everything went well with Clara, Emily thought herself surely due for a dramatic change of fate. Yet, all these things—the play, Curtis, Clara—struck her as thoroughly interlinked, incapable of existing without the others. Had she not been tossed out of the play, and subsequently sunk into a depression or crisis of identity or whatever it was, then things with Curtis might not have fallen apart. And had she not freed Curtis to return to Amy, then Emily might not have allowed Clara to come stay with her.

Her friends were appalled by this latest turn of events. "How long is she going to stay?" asked Lil. "Is she going to sleep on the couch? What if you *meet* someone? You'll have no privacy." This was true; Emily's small bedroom had no door, just an archway that led directly into the living room. "Is she going to get a job?" Sadie, ever practical, wanted to know. "You *can't* support her forever. It'll kill you. You *can't*."

But she wouldn't have to. While Clara was at Brattleboro, her parents had completed the paperwork—mountains of it, according to her mom—necessary to get Clara on SSI, which was, Emily found out, disability for crazy people. The payments, her mom said, should start soon after Clara's arrival, along with a lump sum representing compensation from the date the Kaplans had filed. Emily thought they could use the money to find a larger apartment. "It's *not* going to be that much," Sadie told her. "There's no way. She's going to have to get a job."

"Yeah," said Emily doubtfully. "I guess so."

"You know, you don't *have* to do this, Em," Sadie insisted, her straight brows moving closer together, Jack sleeping on her chest in a pale blue sling. Ed had left for Toronto the previous day but she still, to Emily, seemed perfectly at ease, as if she'd *always* had an infant curled up on her like a pea pod. They were sitting in the new café on Bedford, where a mall, of sorts, had been installed in the shell of the old girdle factory, and everyone around them seemed younger and in pursuit of a level of hipness that made Emily deeply anxious. On their faces, aviator glasses. On their feet, brightly colored Pumas, Nikes, Adidas. On their legs, shredded jeans of recent vintage. On their heads, the sorts of billed caps worn by truckers and convenience-store attendants, emblazoned with embroidered patches advertising obsolete products or brands of interest to the ironically inclined: CAT, John Deere, U-Haul, Pabst Blue Ribbon, Caldor. The guy sitting next to Sadie wore his whiskers in an elaborate handlebar shape. "He's styling the Marc Jacobs show," he told his companion, an overweight girl with a bowl cut. "I'm *so* jealous."

"I *do,*" said Emily.

"Why?" asked Sadie, sighing with exasperation.

"She's my sister," said Emily. Sadie, Lil, and Dave were all only children. Which, Emily thought, explained a lot. Tal would have understood, but Tal was gone. She hadn't heard from him in almost a year.

"She's mentally ill," countered Sadie.

Now that Clara was coming, she regretted ever telling her friends the extent of her sister's woes. They looked at Clara's situation too clinically, as though she were a character in an after-school special: the shaggy-haired girl getting high in her elementary school bathroom; the cinematic junkie, gorgeous and emaciated, lying comatose in a squat, dirty needles stuck in her arm. They didn't understand that Clara was just a normal person, like any of them. At Chapel Hill, before her first big breakdown, she'd studied painting. After she came out of Holly Hill, with a fat prescription for Prozac, which no one had heard of at that point, she refused to go back to school, saying she was embarrassed ("I just can't face them"). And so she stayed home and took classes at Greensboro, but something was changed, broken, *wrong.* She couldn't finish a painting—her little studio in Gatewood was filled with eerie portraits, complete except for the subjects' blank, flat faces—much less a class. And yet somehow, despite the drugs and the feuds with professors and the classes failed due to lack of attendance, she managed, after eight-odd years, to put on a cap and gown, march across the sneaker-scarred floor of the Coliseum, and snatch her degree from Dean Garfield, known to Emily and Clara as Uncle Bo (he'd been a new history hire the same year their mother started in women's studies). Along the way, she'd learned to weld and solder and build things with wood and sew and weave fabric and rewire a lamp and knit, the result of trading painting for sculpture. And she'd learned to cook, too, and bake bread, during the years she'd waitressed at Liberty Oak. Those were good years, as were the ones in which she'd worked at a local architecture firm—she'd talked about going back to school, becoming an architect herself—but they were outnumbered by the bad ones. And they had been long ago. The Clara of recent memory had flung a heavy ball of dough at Emily when she'd argued that no, their parents didn't actually favor her, and no, she didn't think Clara's ex-husband was sneaking into her apartment and adding rat poison to her coffee.

But the Clara who emerged from the Trailways bus into the bleak bowels of the Port Authority seemed positively sane—happy, even. She carried a large tote bag imprinted with the words "Nurses are better lovers"—given to her by Jolene, her favorite nurse, she told Emily (who reflexively wondered if she'd stolen it)—and a bouquet of wilted purple irises, which she'd picked up during her layover in Burlington. "They're for you," she told Emily. "I saw them and I thought, 'Those are the flowers for my sister.' Because I know you love purple." Emily thanked her and took the cellophane cone of blossoms, laying them across her arms like Miss America. Purple had been her favorite color approximately twenty-six years earlier, following a stray comment from a stranger that lavender brought out the red of her hair. At the time, she'd also been fond of stuffed unicorns, stylized images of rainbows, and the original cast recording of *Annie*.

Arm in arm, the sisters made their way up and out of the bus station, Clara nearly skipping with excitement. Years later, Emily would say that Clara's arrival was the best thing that could have happened to her, for it allowed her to put her own problems—the play, Curtis, her career—behind her and focus her energies on rehabilitating her sister: occupational therapy, just like the little sweaters Clara knitted at Brattleboro, destined for the tiny shoulders of crack babies in New Haven. Perhaps more important, there was the fact of September eleventh, the day before which Clara arrived. Emily didn't quite see how she could have faced the terrifying—and terrified—city all alone, *newly* alone. As it was, she had Clara, who reacted to the tragedy with somber, tearful shock—an appropriate response and, Emily told her mother, a measure of the extent of Clara's recovery. "It's amazing, Mom," she'd said. "She's like a different person. They must have found the right meds for her. I mean, it's incredible. It's like she can *see* other people, you know."

The Old Clara would have looked at the planes, the hijackers, the legions dead or missing, the vigils and shrines, through a purely solipsistic lens, insisting, maddeningly, on some personal connection, like "My sister used to work in the Trade Center"—this was true; years back, Emily had temped there—"Can you believe it? She could have been there." The

New Clara sat on the couch, hands pressed to her cheeks, saying, "Oh God, Emily, those people, those poor people. We've got to do something. Is there anything we can do?" There wasn't really, they found out when they called the various numbers for volunteers. Only people with medical training were needed, though Emily and Clara could go to the Javits Center and see if there were any tasks for them. But they were in Brooklyn and the train wasn't running and Emily had already walked all the way home from midtown in her least comfortable shoes—crossing the bridge with legions of refugees from the Financial District, their suits and hair covered in an odd white ash, their eyes grimy and red—and so they stayed in the apartment, listening to the radio in silence, periodically trying to call their parents and Sadie (alone with Jack, *my God*) and Beth (Will's office was down there, wasn't it?) and the others (*Curtis,* Emily kept thinking, *I really should call Curtis*), but the phone was dead, endlessly dead, the network of Emily's cell phone permanently busy.

In the afternoon, they walked over to Lil and Tuck's and watched their television, gulping beer as the towers collapsed over and over on the screen before them. Lil was uncharacteristically silent, Tuck unusually chatty. "We knew," he kept saying. "We knew this was fucking going to happen. It's bin Laden. They've been fucking monitoring him for years." Clara and Emily, from their respective chairs, nodded. "Did you read that piece about him in *The New Yorker?*" They had not. "It was, like, a *year* ago. In *The New Yorker.* Lawrence Wright or one of those guys—I can't remember—anyway, whoever, he, essentially, said bin Laden was going to do something like this. And fucking Bush paid no attention."

"I don't think Bush reads *The New Yorker,*" said Clara, with a smile.

"*You know what I mean,*" said Tuck, his arm wrapped around Lil, who sat limply on their sprung green couch, still dressed in her work clothing—a smart wrap dress, black, with blue flowers, that gaped slightly at the center of her chest. Diane von Furstenberg, Emily thought, though she didn't know how Lil could afford it. There was no way she was making more than thirty grand working at that nonprofit.

"You have to finish," Lil said a few minutes later, after so long a silence that Emily didn't know to whom she was speaking or in response to what. Her voice was low and hoarse, her eyes cast down in her lap.

Sullenly, Tuck extracted his arm from her shoulders. "I'm *going* to finish," he said.

Oh, thought Emily. They were talking about Tuck's book, of course, which was now a year late—maybe more. Back in July, under extreme duress, he'd turned in the first three chapters, which Sadie had pronounced "pretty good" ("overwritten," she told Emily and Beth privately, "I should have never mentioned Gay Talese"). By August, as Sadie's due date approached, the famous Val had resumed her ominous questioning, and Sadie began a phone campaign ("Tuck, *please* just give me whatever you have before I go on leave"), this time to no avail. Jack had come, a week early, and Tuck had been passed on to her former assistant, who could not be counted on to shelter Tuck from Val's bottom line.

"This could be *it,*" said Lil, finally, looking up from her lap and into Tuck's pale, oblong eyes, glowing flintily above the knobs of his cheekbones. "This could be the end. We all could have died today. We *could* have." Emily nodded encouragingly. "We have to *do* something. I just feel like we have to *make* something, to *do* something. Like, we have to stop wasting our time, watching television"—she gestured toward the muted set, on which a firefighter stood talking, tears rolling down his face, smoke and ash and who knows what roiling in the air around him—"and reading *magazines,* and just, you know, going to movies. Do you know what I mean?" She turned to Emily, who nodded. "I feel like all we do is go out to dinner. We don't *do* anything. We're just *consumers* of culture. We need to be *manufacturers* of it. Like Ed. He's doing something. He's *making* something. We're just *sitting here*. This isn't—" Her eyes, now, were bright and shiny and wide open, a brilliant, pupil-less brown. All remnants of tears or anger or sadness had left her voice, which rang out clear and high, her diction exaggerated, overly precise. As a freshman, Emily remembered—how long ago that was—Lil, too, had thought herself an actor. This was how they'd met. In Peter Carson's Acting 101. "This isn't what we were going to do. We have to *do* something."

Rising, slightly, from the low, square chair in which she sat, Clara took a deep breath. "We *do*—" she said.

"We *are* doing things—" said Tuck, his wide mouth swollen with anger.

"I know what you mean," Emily jumped in. But Lil wasn't paying attention to her, or to Tuck—she was staring, openmouthed, at the television. Emily, Clara, and Tuck followed her gaze and saw people—miniaturized in relation to the huge building—jumping out of the windows of the top floor of one of the towers.

"Oh my God," said Lil, her hand rising to cover her mouth. "Why would they show that? Oh my God."

"Because," said Tuck, drawing his wife back into his arms, a gesture that filled Emily, on the one hand, with relief, and on the other with a sort of knee-jerk revulsion, which she was helpless to explain. "Because," he said, his cheek against her glossy hair, "it's the truth."

●

Her company called her—called everyone—back to work on Thursday the thirteenth, which she thought callous and strange. Even in midtown, the air had an awful, poisonous scent and the few people she passed on the street had the appearance of ghosts, their eyes empty and lost, unsure where to look. Half her coworkers didn't show—including Emily's boss, who lived on Long Island—and she found herself wandering around the chilly, fluorescent-lit warren of empty cubicles and dark offices, looking for someone, anyone, with whom she might speak in some sort of normal, human manner. But everyone had their heads down, earphones in, fingers flying across the keyboard, mouths moving against the dull black plastic of the phone's receiver. Business as usual. She knew, then, that she must quit, soon, not because she was ill-treated (though, if she thought about it, she was) or the company shamed her (though it did), but because Lil was right: it was time—time to stop spinning her wheels and find something to do with herself, something that meant something, that contributed *something* to the world, even if only in the smallest way, something that mattered to her, something that was vaguely in accordance with the moral, the political, the ethical stakes she'd once felt so integral to her person. She would quit, she decided, by the end of the year, which gave her nearly three months to figure out a new course of action.

But as the days passed, her resolve weakened, because she was, for the first time in ages, *happy*. As promised, Clara was tending to the housekeeping in exchange for staying with Emily, rent free, and living off Emily's salary, since the SSI money had not yet come. She went to Tops every afternoon and came home with food Emily knew nothing about— baccalà, kielbasa, lamb shank—and made elaborate stews and puddings and casseroles, then explained them to Emily as they ate, or told stories Emily had never heard, how she'd jumped off the roof of the art building and landed on the college president's beloved Mercedes; or how she'd snuck into the local post office and stole a stanchion. ("Isn't that a federal offense?" Emily asked. "Probably!" cried Clara.) She cleaned, too, with the kind of manic fury and focus Emily remembered from high school, when she'd often happened on Clara in the basement, painting with such intensity that she didn't hear the door open. The apartment looked better than it had when Emily moved in: the stove shone, the counter glistened, the windows sparkled.

Mornings, when Emily rose to go to work, Clara still lay on the sofa, in a deep, stonelike sleep; and at night, when Emily went off to bed, Clara waved good-bye and picked up her sketchpad. "It's *so* good that she's drawing," she told her mother, who called Emily's office each afternoon for updates on Clara's state of mind. "I suppose," Mrs. Kaplan said sourly. "But she shouldn't be staying up so late. She should be keeping normal hours. The doctors all said so. And Daddy agrees." Some nights, after dinner, Emily tried to help Clara go through her finances—she was in terrible debt—and sort through the stacks and stacks of mail—three months' worth—that the post office had delivered soon after her arrival. "We'll do it slowly," Emily coaxed. "We'll just look at a little bit every night until we're done." "Okay," Clara agreed, but after five minutes, she picked up a magazine. In the end, Emily sorted through it herself and, from her cubicle, called credit card companies and Verizon and various Southern department stores and explained that her sister had lost her mind and would be resuming her payments in a short while, and could they please reduce the interest and so on.

These negotiations proved, not surprisingly, more satisfying to Emily than to Clara, and Clara's lack of enthusiasm for Emily's little triumphs began to grate on her. "I wish you wouldn't spend so much time on this," Clara told her, one evening toward the beginning of October, as they sat on Emily's small gray couch.

"It's not that much time," Emily countered. "And your credit is completely ruined. We have to restore it."

"Why?" asked Clara.

And Emily realized she wasn't sure *why,* which annoyed her, though not as much as Clara's question. Clara was older than she, she should know why it was important to have good credit. At such moments, she felt cheated. Why could she not have a normal older sister, who bossily offered advice, rather than staring at her, openmouthed—as Clara was now—seeking explanation for the basic tenets of modern life. "Because we *do,* Clara," she whined, unable to suppress this little surge of anger. Rising from the couch, leaving behind her half-eaten bowl of pesto-coated spaghetti, she flounced through the arched doorway into her bedroom and threw herself facedown on her bed. "That's what *normal* people *do,*" she called, wishing that Clara might somehow disappear for an hour or so, leaving Emily completely alone. Lil and Sadie and Beth were right. The apartment was too small for two people. Once the back payments came in from Social Security—it should be, Mrs. Kaplan promised, any day now—they could look for a new apartment, with two bedrooms, bedrooms with actual doors.

As it turned out, Emily was spared this particular agony, for Clara made friends with the landlady—a peroxide-blonde Pole, Krystyna, who'd never uttered a kind word to Emily—and discovered that she was evicting the upstairs tenant, Mr. Kisliewski. "He's a drunk," explained Clara gleefully. "Em, you wouldn't believe it. He completely trashed the apartment! It'll cost thousands for Krystyna to fix it up!" Clara convinced the landlady not only to give the sisters the second apartment—"You are good girls; nice girls," she said, "You pay your rent on time, no trouble, like the Poles"—but also to keep the same rent Mr. Kisliewski had paid, a rent even lower than Emily's.

"But—" Emily stammered. "How?"

"September eleventh." Clara nodded grimly. "Everyone's going home to, like, Kansas. She says she'd rather have reliable tenants—and make less."

"Oh, right," said Emily. "Right."

The trade-off, Clara revealed triumphantly, was that she, Clara, would renovate both apartments, making them into a duplex. Which, she said, shouldn't be difficult, considering the house had originally been a single unit, the conversion cheap and shabby.

"Okay, imagine this, Em," she said, standing at the center of the tiny living room, her round little arms raised conductor-style. "We knock down that wall." She pointed to the flimsy back wall, behind which lay the ugly, carpeted stair to Mr. Kisliewski's place. "We take the carpet off the stairs—it's wood underneath, I checked—and put up a banister. It'll open the whole place up. Then we build out the counter so that the kitchen extends across the room, under the window . . ." And so on.

"Clara, I don't know how to do any of this stuff," Emily told her peevishly. She was, again, feeling that same sense of truculence. People just *didn't* renovate rental apartments. "I don't have time to take on this kind of project."

"Em," Clara said, sitting down on the couch next to her. "You won't have to do *anything*. I'll do it all. Everything."

"How can you do everything?" Emily asked, her voice growing louder. "You're not a contractor. Or a carpenter." She knew she should shut up or risk triggering one of Clara's tantrums. But Clara remained stunningly calm.

"Emily, I know what I'm doing," she said. "At Klopfeld Morgan"—this was the Greensboro architecture firm—"I was actually *working* on plans for interiors. I wasn't just an admin. And, you know, any idiot can knock down a wall."

A week later, Emily arrived home from work to find her belongings swathed in a fine white dust. The back wall was gone, revealing the staircase—its covering of brown-gray shag removed—and Clara was running a floor sander ("the guy at the hardware store just loaned it to me!") up and down the living room floor.

"Shouldn't you be wearing a mask or something?" shouted Emily, looking for a dust-free spot to drop the mail.

Clara shrugged. "It can't be worse than smoking, right?" The sun from the stairwell window was turning her wiry hair an odd shade of yellow. "Isn't this great?"

And it was, in the end. Bright and open, just as Clara had promised, with wide, gleaming, caramel-colored plank floorboards, pale aqua walls, and sweet, white kitchen cabinets that they purchased from the salvage yard by the Williamsburg Bridge and repainted. They found a red dinette set at a junk shop on Wythe and made the area adjoining the new kitchen—previously Emily's living room—their eating place. Emily's battered couch they pushed a few feet east, into what had recently been Emily's bedroom—they would sleep upstairs now, in two square, sunny rooms, separated by a generous hallway—and Clara sewed a slipcover out of some red fabric she found in a bin at the Salvation Army shop on Bedford.

It was a dream apartment, really, particularly when compared with the squalid rooms from which it had sprung. Emily's friends were amazed by the transformation—and told Clara she ought to work in interior design or architecture—but no more so than by Clara herself. "She's so *normal*," Lil told Emily. "I mean, she's really nice and doesn't seem crazy at all. She looks like she lives in the suburbs or something. Like someone's mom." This was true. In high school, Clara had dyed her long chestnut hair—shiny, shampoo-commercial hair that Emily had envied—pink and purple and green and blue, and worn short black skirts over black tights and high boots with thick soles, and Emily thought she was the coolest person in the world. Now she was plump and puffy, from years of medication and the starchy sanatorium food, and appeared to own no clothing other than the faded sweatpants and stained green tunic she wore every day. Her hair had turned an odd beige color, somewhere between mud and straw, and had taken on the coarse texture that comes from too many color changes in too short a time, and her face, which was round and small, had gone even rounder, with the peaked Kaplan chin jutting out from her jaw, like an afterthought. Like Emily, she had blue eyes. "Her best feature," Emily's mother carped, "now that she's ruined her hair." It was amazing, Emily thought, that this woman had been instrumental in the creation of women's studies departments at Emory and Chapel Hill. But Emily, too, hated to think about Clara's poor hair, once so extraordinary and luminous.

"Do you have to color it?" she asked Clara one Saturday, as they walked toward the shops on Wythe, chairs in mind.

"I'm so gray," said her sister. "It makes me look old."

And so, toward the end of October, the renovations done, she took Clara to a small salon, suggested by Sadie, for "corrective color" and a new cut. "What's your natural color," the hairdresser asked. "Damned if I know," Clara told her, with a loud, *too loud,* laugh. One of Clara's canine teeth was turning a dull gray color, Emily noticed, a sign that the tooth was dying. Could it be saved? No, probably not. And besides, Clara, at the moment, had no insurance. Perhaps Beth's dad could see her pro bono, or at a reduced rate? Emily kept meaning to see whether she could put Clara on her own policy, as a dependent, but it was unlikely, until the SSI kicked in, certifying that, yes, Clara was officially *dependent,* in the truest sense of the term, but by that time the point would be moot, for she would be eligible for Medicaid (or was it Medicare?). Though, did Medicaid (Medicare?) cover dental? Had her mother mentioned this? She probably had. Why would Clara have a dying tooth? Had she stopped brushing her teeth? Of all Clara's missteps, this one somehow seemed the most tragic, for it was so permanent, so unignorable. Teeth, once wrecked, could never be saved.

Three hours later—after Emily had read through a half dozen back issues of *In Style*—Clara emerged with a sleek brown pixie cut, which made her eyes look huge. "You look gorgeous," Emily told her, though she worried that the new style also made Clara's body look huge. Silently, the tiny blonde behind the salon's register handed Clara a printout, which Clara immediately passed to Emily, who tried not to blanch when she saw the sum owed: $300—though the sign said a cut was only $65 and color was "from $85." "Thanks so much," she said to the blonde—who had done nothing, really, and didn't need to be thanked, but it was either that or start screaming—and handed over her credit card, generally reserved for emergencies. It was worth it, she told herself, to see Clara smile at herself in the mirror and, later, when they met for dinner, to hear Lil and Beth tell her how great she looked. Clara needed to feel good about herself, to gain confidence, if she was going to fully piece herself back together.

Though the fact was that in some ways Clara appeared to be somewhat more together than Emily herself, an occurrence that after more than two months of living together, Emily was still unable to explain. There was new medication, she knew—she watched Clara take it each night, an antianxiety drug—but there had been new medication before. Her mother eventually supplied the answer.

"You need to promise not to get upset, Em."

"Okay," Emily agreed nervously.

"Clara had electrical treatments at Brattleboro. It was kind of a last resort—"

"You mean, like, electroshock therapy?" Emily asked, certain she had misheard her mother.

"They don't actually use that term anymore—"

"Oh my *God*, Mom. You're kidding." Her mother sighed, which only served to infuriate Emily, as if she'd known that Emily would be prickly and uncompromising and judgmental, when that was *not at all what was going on.* "Didn't that go out with, like, lobotomies and padded cells?"

"Okay, *enough*, Emily." Her mother's voice had gone sharp. "That's enough, *okay*. Yes, you're right, they didn't use it for ages, but now it's making a comeback. Apparently, it's useful in treating certain types of cases—like Clara's—in which the disease is preventing the patient from making progress. They were desperate, Emily. *We* were desperate."

"But it's the same thing," Emily pressed. "Electroshock therapy. They're just calling it something else."

Again, her mother sighed. "Yes, Emily, that's what it is. But it's different than it was in the sixties, Em. It's very high tech."

"Mmm-hmmm." She pictured the apparatus described in *The Bell Jar*: electrodes, wires, a leather pad that disallows a person from biting off her own tongue.

"We're losing sight of the point here," her mother said. "The point is that it worked, right? She seems good to you, right?"

"Yes," Emily admitted. "Like a different person."

This new Clara began venturing out into the neighborhood, making daily rounds of the neighborhood's junk shops: Ugly Luggage, the Salvation Army on Bedford, the unnamed place on Driggs operated by a moody Hasid, the dingy furniture outfits over on Wythe with higher prices but better stuff, and various church shops on the south side that Emily had never noticed but Clara quickly discovered. She brought home an endless stream of treasures: mismatched Fiesta ware in the muted, sallow palette of the 1960s; a crystal chandelier, which she deftly installed in their entryway, previously lit by a bare bulb protruding from a chipped, grime-streaked socket; two overstuffed chairs; a new desk for Emily; a green enamel teakettle; vases of different shapes and colors and sizes ("You know how you never have the right size when someone brings you flowers?"); eight balloon wineglasses in Czech crystal; and new clothing for herself, none of it exactly right—a pair of stretch-velvet leggings, those awful rayon dresses, imprinted all over with tiny flowers, that everyone had worn in the early 1990s—but all of it better than her previous uniform. So clad and coiffed, she installed herself, afternoons, at the L, where she drank coffee and smoked Marlboro Light 100s (which she considered more elegant than their shorter brethren) with the regulars, among them the proprietors of not one but two radical book publishers (one socialist, the other anarchist), a tattooed couple who ran a local circus, a yoga teacher, a massage therapist, and a gay performance artist who sang show tunes in a bunny suit.

Now, in the evenings, Emily found an assortment of these local characters sitting on her couch or her glossy new floor, engaged in heated discussions of matters political ("Bush knew about the attacks; he and bin Laden are in cahoots") or religious ("Buddhist meditation actually *alters* the *chemistry* of your *brain*") or personal ("Clara, you just need to tell your mother to *butt out* of your life"), while smoking cigarettes, the ashes from which they deposited in Clara's new collection of vintage ashtrays, culled from her daily junk rounds. "Hey, Red," the socialist publisher called, annoyingly, the first time Emily walked in and discovered him sitting on her couch, eating a tofurkey sandwich from the health food store on the corner. "I've seen you around for years. How come we never became friends?" *Because you're creepy,* Emily thought. But slowly, he grew on her, as did the others. The yoga teacher gave her a pass for a free class and clasped Emily's hand warmly when she took her leave. The Ugly Luggage woman brought Emily a pair of kelly green cowboy boots—picked up on a buying trip in Dayton ("the vintage clothing capital of the country")— which Emily adored. And the manager of the Salvation Army baked them muffins, studded with mysterious fruits, lopsided but delicious.

But the second publisher—the anarchist publisher—was the most frequent and friendly guest, inviting Emily to book parties and asking her gross, too-intimate questions ("What do you think is the most erogenous part of the male body?"). Soon, he'd made Clara an "intern" at his publishing house, which operated out of a giant loft down on South Eleventh Street. In exchange for lunch and cartons of cigarettes, she stuffed envelopes and sorted mail and read through the manuscripts and letters that poured into the office lately. "There's so much stuff I didn't know about the government. Like, do you remember in the eighties, all that stuff in Nicaragua, with the Sandinistas? Did you know that the CIA was really training the rebels?" Emily did indeed know. She'd gone to Oberlin, after all. But she said nothing. "I was so gullible before. It's like I've opened my eyes and I see all this corruption around me. I guess I was so focused on my own problems that I couldn't see what was going on in the world."

Clara, it seemed, had become an anarchist. Emily knew she should be alarmed, or at least annoyed by the irony of it—boyfriend leaves her for an anarchist; sister comes to take his place, then becomes an anarchist, too—but, in truth, she found it both amusing and heartening, another sign that Clara, as she herself acknowledged, was awakening to the world. Each evening, her sister presented Emily with some new revelation and Emily nodded dutifully, trying not to argue or to correct her misconceptions, for, she thought, Clara would parse it all out in time, as Emily had herself, years and years ago, in her teens. Contemporary anarchists were not, Emily discovered, as she'd previously thought, a united, organized body, like Democrats or the Green Party. There were many different factions, though these factions didn't think of themselves as holistic factions, per se, because anarchism is, by definition, against organization. The publisher, and, thus, Clara, believed in a rather different set of tenets than did Amy, it turned out.

"She's one of those ecowarrior types," Clara scoffed, when Emily mentioned that she had a "friend" who was also an anarchist and described some of the "friend's" activities and beliefs and affiliations. She hadn't told Clara anything about Curtis—she knew Clara to be incapable of keeping anything from their parents—but she couldn't resist getting Clara's take on Amy. "I mean, I bet she's doing good stuff, but people like that are focused on the *micro*—keeping Citibank from destroying the rainforest or saving the whatever rare bird. You know what I mean?"

"Hmmm." This dismissal somehow comforted Emily. "And what are you—your group—what are you focused on?"

282 · *Joanna Smith Rakoff*

"Well, we're not a group, you know. We're a network of like-minded individuals with a common goal."

"Right."

"But, anyway, we're focused on the macro. Total revolution."

Emily laughed. "What? You mean you want to overthrow the government."

"Yeah, sort of," said Clara, with a pained look that made Emily feel like a cretin. She could see that Emily wasn't taking her seriously (though, okay, how *could* she?). But this, too, was a sign of her recovery, wasn't it? She was somehow sharper, more aware of the minutiae of other's reactions and emotions. And, Emily thought, maybe she was giving her sister the short shrift. She had become so cynical, so conservative. At sixteen, would she have responded to all this anarchy stuff with excitement? Maybe. "I mean, it's like, permanent, *systemic* change. Clearly, democracy isn't working. I mean, not that this *is* a democracy. Bush is essentially a dictator."

The internship cut into Clara's shopping time, which was just as well, since the apartment was now coming to resemble the junk shops from which all the stuff had originated, so much so that Emily, on a cool Sunday evening, after Clara's friends had departed for their various homes, and the two sisters sat on the couch contentedly, drinking cooling mugs of cocoa, gently suggested getting rid of some of it. Did they really need three Fiesta ware pitchers? Maybe they could sell a couple on eBay? Clara balked, saying the stuff was valuable and she and Emily could pass it on to their daughters when the time came. "I'm about as far as you can get from marrying, Clara." Emily laughed. "I can't really think about my hypothetical daughter's legacy."

"Well, you should," said Clara, puffing out her lower lip and snatching a Milky Way from a bowl on the coffee table. Over Halloween, she'd stocked the house with sweets, but not one trick-or-treater had come by. "You really *should*," she repeated, in a tone that alarmed Emily, a glint in her bright eyes that Emily hadn't seen since Clara's arrival. "You *really* should. Since, you know, we're not going to get anything from Mom and Dad. We have to make our own heirlooms."

"What do you mean?" asked Emily, her heart racing. She knew, she knew that nothing good was going to come of this conversation, for she was angry, angry at Clara for speaking of their parents in such a mercenary way, when they'd supported Clara for ages and ages, and when—this was it, really—Clara had played such a vital role in wrecking their finances.

Was it possible she didn't realize the latter? No, no, it wasn't. Clara was smart.

"Mom sold Nana Dorrie's crystal," said Clara, compressing her mouth into a grim line, which gave her, strangely, the aspect of a lizard.

"Crystal *what*?" There had been, hadn't there, a massive chandelier in the foyer of their paternal grandmother's house in Beaumont. Their uncle Darren lived there now with his horrible second wife and the unremarkable fruits of both marriages.

"Crystal *everything*. Nana's set of crystal. Service for eighteen. Water goblets. Wineglasses. Cordial glasses. Three decanters. A punch bowl and ladle and glasses—"

"You mean the stuff we used at Passover? Those big glasses?"

Clara nodded vigorously. "She got something like fifteen thousand dollars for them."

"Fifteen thousand!" This was more money than Emily could imagine receiving all at once. "For glasses?"

"Yeah. They're Baccarat."

Baccarat. Emily had often walked by that shop on Madison without slowing her pace—one of a zillion stupidly expensive shops for who knew who: tourists, the future wives of bankers, social strivers—without thinking its icy, boring goods had any significance for her, just as she'd gulped water from those huge, medieval goblets, with their rows of bulbous drops striping from base to rim, countless times, laughing over-heartily at her pink-faced cousins' repellent jokes, without considering the value of the heavy glass in her hand. But Clara had.

But this was not the most pressing thing, the most dire thing, was it? Their parents were dismantling their house to pay for Clara's care. When her mother said the well had run dry, Emily had not thought she'd meant it, not really.

"Why?" she asked Clara, as though they were normal sisters and she, the younger, could ask Clara, the older, for explanations of the mystifying adults around them, instead of vice versa. She knew the answer to the question, of course. They'd sold the glasses to pay for Brattleboro.

"Because she hates me," said Clara, her face turning grotesque, witch-like, the point of her chin thrusting forward, her mouth curling into a grim scythe, the bright points of her eyes nearly eclipsed by the swelling folds of skin above and below them.

"No, no, Clara, that's not true and—"

"No, it *is* true," she insisted, in the singsongy tone of a wounded child.

Emily had been right. The storm was rising. She braced herself. "*I* was supposed to inherit the crystal. And she couldn't stand the thought of me having it. She thought I would wreck it and that *you* should have it, because you take care of things. But she knew she couldn't give you *everything*." Emily turned her face away sharply, as if she'd been hit. She had forgotten—How had she forgotten, or allowed herself to forget?—how much Clara, when it came down to it, seemed to hate her. She had, if she thought about it, spent her whole life trying to make up for whatever injury—her existence?—had caused this strange, groundless resentment, through the murk of which she still managed (why, why?) to love her sister.

"Clara," she said softly. "They need money. Things have been hard for them for a long time." She couldn't bring herself to say *because of you,* though she knew Sadie, and Lil, too, probably, would have told her that she should have, that Clara needed to understand the consequences of her behavior; but they didn't understand that Clara couldn't control her behavior.

"What kind of person does that?" Clara was saying now, spittle rising to the corners of her lips. "What kind of person sells a family heirloom? It didn't even really belong to her. It was from *Dad's* family." Though it was really all the same: her parents were second cousins.

"I'm sure Dad was okay with it—"

"No, you never let me be angry about anything, Emily," she screamed, fumbling furiously for her packet of cigarettes, which, once secured, she clutched to her chest like a doll. "You always tell me to calm down. I don't *want* to *calm down.* I'm sorry I can't be fucking *perfect* like you."

And then, as suddenly as it had come, the storm broke. Tears popped into Clara's eyes and her face went slack with sadness. "I'm so sorry, Em," she said, leaning over and pulling Emily to her. "It's not your fault. I've just made such a mess of my life."

"No, you haven't," said Emily, though this was so patently untrue that she loathed herself for saying it. "You haven't." She could go no further, could not embellish the lie, so she walked over to the stove and put the kettle on. They would have tea, no matter that their cocoa mugs still sat on the table, not even half empty.

"I'm so selfish, I'm so selfish," she moaned, and Emily felt her heart crack open inside her chest, leaving a dark wound, worse than anything inflicted by Curtis, worse because the things Clara said were true. Clara *was* selfish. She *was* manipulative. And cruel, even. And Emily, just maybe, had not loved her enough, because of it, even as she'd told herself—as did her parents—that the illness, not Clara, was to blame for her behaviors.

But now Clara was better, wasn't she? The volts—who knew how many—had altered her brain chemistry, allowing her to smile and laugh, to knock down walls and sand floors, to cook dinner and make new friends, to care about Nicaragua (albeit Nicaragua of twenty years prior) and the families of the victims of the World Trade Center attacks and the world in general, to say "I'm selfish" and understand that she should not be. All of the things Emily had proudly (why proudly? What had she done to facilitate such progress?) related to her mother.

But she had been a fool—again—for Clara was clearly still ill and she had known it, hadn't she? It was, Emily thought, as though Clara wore a veneer, a *thin* veneer, of health that was beginning, slowly, to crack.

The next morning at work, Emily Googled "borderline personality disorder" and found, really, too much, some of which she remembered, dimly, from her undergrad years, and all of which both corresponded to her mother's laments—"does not respond to medication"; "needs long-term treatment"—and described Clara almost too perfectly. "These individuals may suddenly change from the role of needy supplicant," intoned the *DSM-IV,* "to righteous avenger of past mistreatment."

After lunch, she picked up the phone and, before she could think better of it, dialed the number of the Payne Whitney clinic, the website of which had come up repeatedly in her morning's search. "Judith Lang," she told the operator, who connected her without a word. "Dr. Lang, hello," she said, as her voice was converted into ones and zeros by the hospital's voice mail system. "This is Emily, Emily Kaplan. I hope you're doing well. And I hope you won't think this is too weird, but I'm calling because I have a, a bit of a problem that, um, lies within your area of expertise—" Inwardly, she cringed; why was she speaking like this? "And, I guess, I don't really have anyone else to consult about it, so I was hoping you might have just a few minutes to talk to me. I'm so sorry to trouble you. You can reach me at work . . ."

The following day, Emily found herself navigating the familiar corridors of the Payne Whitney pavilion, curiously filled with emotion. She had not thought she would return to this place without Curtis. Mrs. Lang—*Dr.* Lang—sat inside her sanctum on the second floor, conversing intently with one of her interchangeable residents—or interns, Emily couldn't remember which was which—and waved Emily in without slowing her monologue. "We'll just be a minute," she called. "We've had a slight emergency this morning." Emily smiled uncomfortably and walked over to the window, studying the small, tree-rimmed square below with great concentration so as not to appear overly interested in the discussion they'd foisted upon her, which had to do with a patient refusing medication. "Okay, that's it. You're all set with this?" she asked the resident.

"Good to go," he said, a phrase Emily disliked.

"This is Emily Kaplan, by the way," she told the man, swiveling back on her vast leather chair and reaching one arm in Emily's direction. "A friend of Curtis's. Her father runs the postpartum depression clinic at UNC."

"Interesting," said the resident, with a stiff grin that made it clear that it wasn't.

"Okay, well, we need to grab some lunch," Dr. Lang told him, waving a long hand at him and turning to Emily. "I'll see you on rounds at three." Tripping slightly over the doorjamb, the resident rushed out, and Mrs. Lang gave Emily a small, awkward hug. "Is everything okay?" she asked.

"No," Emily said, though she'd meant, actually, to say yes. "Not really."

"Hmmm," Dr. Lang murmured half an hour later, chewing thoughtfully on a bite of roast beef. "Your sister *does* sound like a classic borderline. The paranoia, the chain of broken relationships, the life lived in chaos, always making herself out to be the victim. Though I can see why they were thinking manic depression. She clearly has the periods of intense focus—"

"Yes!"

"—followed by periods of despair, but that's pretty typical." Electroconvulsive therapy, she said, was being used lately to treat severe depression or manic depression when drugs weren't working. Dr. Lang herself occasionally prescribed it for patients. They were just starting to use it on "borderlines." "The ECT, you understand, doesn't do anything for the borderline personality disorder, most likely. It just treats your sister's depression. And mania. It treats the symptoms, rather than curing the disease itself." Emily nodded. "Did they do unilateral or bilateral?" Emily confessed that she didn't know. "How many treatments did you say she had?" Emily didn't know this either. "Hmmm. Well, how long was she at Brattleboro?"

"About three months. But I don't think they started them right away."

"Criminal." Popping the last bit of sandwich into her mouth, Dr.

Lang vigorously wiped crumbs from her lap, glanced crisply at her watch, and stood up, towering over Emily, who sat before the remains of her salad, unsure if she should follow. She decided to stand. "It's just criminal. Releasing a patient like that. Midway through treatment. *If* that." She began walking toward the elevator. Emily followed, two steps to every one of the doctor's. "I'll call Jay Fleming, get her records. Can you make me a list of the other hospitals she's been at?"

"Ye—"

"And does she have a doctor in Chapel Hill? Or someone at Duke?"

"Yes. I think so. I can find out."

"Email it to me today."

"Okay—"

"Generally patients with problems as severe as your sister's do ECT every two weeks for about a year. Not once or twice, then never again. And they're monitored closely for years afterward." She pressed, with great precision, on the elevator's up button. "So we'll need to get her started again. Do you want to bring her in tomorrow?"

Emily shook her head and grimaced. "No, no, I don't think she'd come. She thinks she's well now and if I suggest she see a psychiatrist she'd . . . freak out." Dr. Lang gave her a stern look.

"Well," she said, her tone, Emily thought, slightly colder, "would you want me to come meet her in a casual way? We could all have lunch at that nice Thai place? Or I could stop by your apartment?" Emily considered. How would she explain a lunch date with someone their mom's age? She could say Dr. Lang was a former professor, in town for a conference. "Or, would you rather I sent a resident? Someone closer to your own age?" She grinned. "They don't let anyone over forty into Williamsburg, do they?"

"That might be better," said Emily, laughing. Dr. Lang had never joked with her before. "He—or she—could come for Sunday brunch, if that's good. We always have a big crowd. Clara won't even notice one extra person."

That Sunday, a sandy-haired young man rapped on her door, clad in neat garments that might have appeared in the dictionary under the term "casual attire": faded jeans of no particular style or brand, flannel shirt of nondescript color, bulky wool sweater striated with cables and loops, one creamy strand of wool unraveling at the joint between collar and shoulder seam, all of which appeared to have been pressed, down to the loose thread. "I'm Dr. Gitter," he said, glancing nervously around. "Josh Gitter."

He may or may not have been the resident she'd met earlier in the week on her visit to Dr. Lang's office, for he was pale, blinking, bespectacled, mildly Jewish, moderately preppy, like the rest of Dr. Lang's minions.

"Come in," said Emily, leading him into the apartment. "It's a little smoky in here. I hope that's okay." The doctor smiled a quick, tight smile—as if to say that it wasn't okay, but he was happy to suffer for the sake of the common good—sizing up the various bearded and tattooed persons before him, taking pulls off their cigarettes and swills of Clara's dark, thick coffee.

"Hey," shouted the anarchist publisher. His son was racing madly around the room, chasing a stray cat that had climbed in through the window, lured by the platters of lox. "Hey," the others shouted, waving ringed fingers holding half-eaten bagels. "Welcome!" Clara called. Dr. Gitter raised his hand, said "Thanks," and smiled at Emily. "Have some coffee," she said quickly, leading him to Clara's latest recovery project: a gold velvet chair with a tufted, buttoned back.

And there he remained, silent and unmoving but for the occasional bite of bagel—garlic, without butter or cream cheese—for an hour, while Clara's throng rose and fell, in waves of chatter and laughter, around him. At one, he rose from the chair—a quick, Dr. Lang–style movement—and gestured toward the door with his head. Emily followed him into the vestibule. "Can we talk outside?" he asked, in a quiet voice that wasn't exactly a whisper.

"Sure." The gravity of his tone caused her, stupidly, to giggle. "I'll walk you to the subway." She grabbed her coat and keys and slipped out the door.

"Listen," he said the minute they hit the street, "your sister isn't doing well. She's in a sort of manic state and I suspect she's going to crash. But it's definitely going to get worse first."

"Are you saying she's manic-depressive?" she asked. "We were told that was a misdiagnosis. That she's actually—"

Dr. Gitter waved his hand impatiently. "Borderline. I know. Brattleboro sent her records. From what I can see, that's pretty accurate. What I mean is: I suspect there's a psychotic break around the corner. She's flying. Which could mean she's abusing her meds. You need to take them and mete them out to her."

Emily knew she could not do this—and, really, did she need to? She saw Clara take her pill each evening. "She's an adult. I can't really—"

Again he waved his hands, cutting her off. "You *can.*" He pursed his lips, which were wide and dark, and shook his head. "She has a serious history of abuse." He sucked his lips for a moment, then whistled. "I can't believe they gave her Klonopin. You know, right, that it's like the thing now. K-pin. King Pin. All the kids do it. It's cheaper than coke. Cheaper than crack."

"No, I had no idea, so you think—"

"Yes—"

"But it seems to be working," said Emily, aware that she was flailing, that she, somewhere in the back of her mind, *did* have an inkling that Klonopin was one of those drugs—Ritalin, Vicodin, OxyContin—that was always showing up in the paper, found in the bloodstream of some Choate suicide, or in the glossies ("Confessions of a K-head") or whatever, and that, yes, okay, maybe she'd suspected Clara's newfound focus verged on the manic, on the potentially—but just potentially—chemically induced.

"Maybe." The doctor shrugged. He wasn't wearing a coat, she noticed, despite the cold wind that surged up around them, blowing dried leaves in a little circle at their feet. They were still outside the door to the building that fronted Emily's little back-house. "But it could just as easily be the Prozac and Tegretol. Now, *that* I get—" And on he went, talking, Emily thought, largely to himself, about various drug protocols and combinations, and the difficulties of medicating borderlines, who are famous for overdoing or ignoring their drugs, until Emily could stand it no longer.

"I don't think she's on Prozac—"

"*I saw her file,*" he said, almost angrily, as though Emily were responsible for all this—but then, she supposed, she was. "They have her on Prozac and Tegretol, which is pretty standard. The Klonopin is just as needed, for anxiety."

"Okay, okay," said Emily, raising her hands in a gesture of surrender. "I'm sorry," she added, uncertain what she was apologizing for.

"It's okay," said the doctor, shoving his hands deeply into the pockets of his jeans. He was cold. She should walk him to the subway, send him back to wherever he came from—uptown, most likely—but he kept talking. "This is serious stuff. The bottom line is: she needs to be hospitalized, long-term. For starters, let's get her to the clinic tomorrow morning. We'll start up the ECT again—she definitely needs to finish the first course of treatment—"

"No," she said. "Wait. This is too much. I mean, I mean . . ." Her voice drifted off and he looked at her patiently as he'd no doubt been taught to do in medical school. She wasn't sure where to begin. "I mean, presuming I can actually get her there—she thinks she's all better, you know—I, *we*, don't have any money. We can't pay for a minute at Payne Whitney. She doesn't even have insurance."

He shook his head, a gesture of impatience. "Dr. Lang will figure it out. Don't even think about that."

Emily thought this doubtful, but was tired of quibbling. "Okay, but I have to talk to my parents—"

"Your parents," he said, "released her to *your* care. *You're* in charge."

"Yes, that's true," she said, but her own patience was tapping out. Who was this guy to tell her what to do? He'd spent an *hour* with Clara and thought he knew exactly how to cure her.

"Well, then," she said, slowly, icily, "*I* need to think before I commit my sister to a mental institution."

The anger on his face mirrored hers. "Oh, come on. Don't be melodramatic. You're not *committing* her. Your sister is ill. She's not going to get better with intermittent therapy. She needs a consistent course of treatment. She needs to start up the ECT again and start working with one doctor, over a long period of time. Months. A year. Or more. She needs analysis and behavior modification and closely monitored meds." He ticked these last three off on the fingers of his left hand—fingers that had gone red from the cold.

Emily was so furious she couldn't speak. Her mouth, against her will, hung open. "Why don't I walk you to the subway," she said finally, swallowing to bring some moisture back to her mouth.

Dr. Gitter ran his hands through his hair, so that it stuck up in peaked tufts, and nodded.

In silence, they turned down Bedford, where the sidewalks were suddenly full of people talking and laughing, pleasantly lit from brunchtime Bloody Marys, the girls of Williamsburg in their scuffed boots and jeans and beaded cardigans beneath vintage coats with Bakelite buttons, their arms twined round the narrow waists of shaggy-haired boys, who moved along the avenue as if they owned it, boys like Curtis.

"Listen, think about all this and we'll talk on Monday. But seriously, this is *serious*. You don't want to play around, okay?"

"Okay." And then he was gone, trotting down the grayish steps that led to the train. Emily leaned against the chipped iron fence that encased the entrance, staring down into the dark maw of the station, the muted roar of an arriving train just audible from below. This had not gone quite as she'd expected, though she wasn't sure now *what* she'd expected, but certainly not bring your sister in tomorrow. *Like, seriously,* she thought, watching the crowd emerge from underground, a surge of volatile, chattering bodies. *This is serious. Okay, dude.*

She returned to an empty apartment. Clara had retired to Sweetwater, no doubt, with her friends, to play pool and sip a postbrunch beer (though, should she be drinking? Why had Emily not asked this before? Why had her mother—or Clara's doctor—given her no instruction? She should have asked Dr. Gitter). Relieved, Emily collapsed in a heap on her bed, as she tended to on Sundays lately, now that Clara's weeknight gatherings were bleeding over into the weekends. The crowd, the food, the smoke all conspired to exhaust her, though, in truth, she didn't mind so much, losing her one day of solitude—the less time to reflect on things the better. What troubled her was the expense of all the nice food Clara insisted on serving. Braised lamb shanks over couscous. Chili with three different kinds of sausages and sirloin that she ground herself in the Cuisinart. Lox and sable on Sunday mornings. Every night she cooked enough for a dozen, saying, "We'll put the leftovers in the freezer." But there were never any leftovers. The constant stream of visitors—each offered a bowl of whatever was on the stove—made sure of that.

Meanwhile, the SSI money had *still* not arrived, and Emily was beginning to think it never would. She'd read up on the subject—online, at work, as usual—and discovered that it could take *years* to kick in. The previous week, she'd taken out a cash advance on her credit card, which she'd used only three or four times in eight years, as she knew she couldn't afford to keep a balance, not with her student loans, her newly doubled rent, and so on. Still, when the crisp twenty-dollar bills shot out of the cash machine—just as they did when she withdrew money, her own money, from her account—she felt a keen icy relief, that dissolved an hour later when she got home and looked up the interest rate. *Twenty-five percent.* Plus a four percent fee.

What she needed, she knew, was to find a way to make Clara spend less money, without causing her to panic. Every Monday, she gave Clara cash for groceries—seventy-five dollars, which seemed enough for two smallish women—and every Wednesday Clara asked for more: for cigarettes, for coffee, for this *great* painting she'd seen at the Salvy, which she was sure was valuable. And so Emily handed over a twenty or two, so as not to seem stingy. But by Friday Clara was asking for more again, for supplies for her Sunday brunch, which always ran at least sixty bucks in and of itself. That seemed the obvious place to economize. She couldn't ask Clara to stop inviting her friends over, so she instead suggested serving eggs and potatoes instead of lox and bagels. For two weeks, Clara obliged. The third week, Emily looked in the fridge and saw the familiar Russ & Daughters carrier bags, but opted to say nothing. Clara hadn't asked her for money, and Emily presumed she must have saved grocery money from the past few weeks to pay for the nice fish and cream cheese, which was good. She couldn't, no, couldn't even consider the possibility of Clara taking cash from her though she had been feeling that her wallet seemed to empty more rapidly lately. And even if this was the case, was it really so bad, stealing a ten every now and then? In a way, the trouble, really, wasn't that they were overspending but that they needed more income—just a little more, another thousand a month, and they'd be fine. Not rich, but fine.

Since Clara could not, reliably, be taught to economize, Emily tried to cut corners for the both of them. She drank two cups of coffee at home before leaving for work, rather than buying her second at the L before she got on the subway. She skipped breakfast and brought her lunch—salad, in a square Tupperware container—instead of buying it. She let her gym membership lapse and began running, though she hated it, and using the vouchers given to her by the yoga instructor. But these small economies made little difference and all day, as Emily sat at her dreary desk, she devised moneymaking schemes. They could knit hats and scarves and mittens and sell them to one of the overpriced gift shops on Bedford. She could write a story for a women's magazine about taking care of her mentally ill sister, or proofread for Sadie's company.

But nothing panned out: the gift shops all had suppliers of fancy hand knits; she'd need "clips," according to Will, to write for magazines; and Sadie's company kept proofreaders on staff. And so she sank lower: she began buying a lottery ticket once a week, though she knew this was a waste of a precious dollar. She carefully, painfully, withdrew her most pristine vintage—the sixties cocktail dress of deep turquoise satin that she'd worn to Lil and Tuck's wedding; a crocheted halter dress, very *Charlie's Angels;* a car coat of emerald and gold brocade—and sold them to a shop on West Broadway, but she got so little money that, on the train home, she trembled with regret. She answered a posting on the bulletin board at the L for an art model, but when the artist called her back—his voice thick and phlegmy on her machine—she didn't pick up the phone, in fear that it was some sort of scam and the guy was really a pornographer, which led her to think about stripping. Between their sophomore and junior years of college, her friend Tova had worked at a club downtown called Goldstring. Just one night a week, all summer, and she'd earned more than enough to pay her room and board for the year. But Emily had neither Tova's body—lush, brown, firm—nor her larky brain ("It's funny," she'd told Emily, "the guys are so excited; it's *hilarious,* and empowering, too—you feel really hot"), and she just couldn't bring herself even to investigate. She thought more seriously about phone sex, which you could do from your home, or at least Jennifer Jason Leigh had in *Short Cuts.* But that was impossible, too, since Clara would surely hear her holed up in her room moaning, "Oh, you're making me hot. Oh, you're such a bad boy. Fuck me, fuck me."

On and on she went: She thought she could teach yoga classes, but it took time and money to get certified. Or she could teach after-school acting classes for kids, but where? In what space? When she passed a wig shop, she realized she might sell her crowning glory—her hair—but even that avenue proved closed. Her hair was too short now. "Grow it out and come back in a year," the owner told her. *You don't understand. I need money now,* she wanted to say, but she nodded mutely and left, without even a thank-you. Finally, she called her pseudo-agent and told him she was interested now in doing voice-over work and she was sorry she'd been out of touch. But he didn't call back. And so she began going on auditions again, on the off chance that she'd be cast in something with night rehearsals, as even the measly income for a show would help. But nothing, nothing was offered to her; all the parts seemed to be for actors older or younger, or other types: perky blondes, or wispy blondes, or statuesque blondes, or angry Latinas, or angry black women.

Then one night, she was sitting at Von with Lil and Sadie—Sadie's first outing after having Jack—trying to make her nine-dollar glass of wine last as long as possible, when she saw the bartender—tall, black-haired, beautiful, in clothing far more fashionable than anything she or her friends owned—pocket a tip. Sadie and Dave and Tal had all worked as bartenders in college, not just because it was a cool job in terms of the campus hierarchy, but because it paid more than working in the dining hall or the student union or the library, because of *tips.* A cute girl could, she knew, clean up. Three days later, she had a job at a simple, pub-style place on First Avenue, all the way up at Seventy-second Street, safely north of her friends' orbit. Not that her friends would ever go into this sort of bar, with its brass rails and banker clientele, its televisions tuned to football. She told Clara she'd been cast in a play that rehearsed nights and she'd be out late Mondays, Wednesdays, and Fridays for the next few weeks. Clara, as expected, didn't ask for any details. "Congratulations," she cried, and flung her arms around Emily. "That's so great! You're gonna be a star. I always said it."

Her first night, a Wednesday, Emily arrived at the pub in what she thought was ideal bartender attire: black leather pants, a low-cut black T-shirt emblazoned with the word "Angel" in red rhinestones, and her green cowboy boots. The manager, a portly guy named Declan, looked her over approvingly. "You're an actress, right," he said, lighting up a Winston. Emily had forgotten about the smoke. She hated smoke, but perhaps she would get used to it. And her own apartment wasn't all that much better than a bar.

"It's true," she said, grinning. "I am."

"Well, you're gonna be a star, I can tell you that."

Emily laughed to slake off the smarminess of this exchange. "That's what my sister says."

"Yep. All our girls are actresses. They leave when they get a break. Go to L.A. for pilot season. The last one, Kirsty, she's on this new sitcom about lawyers."

Emily learned how to work the taps, how to change a keg, how to pour a drink, and how to work the dishwasher. At eight, the bar began to fill with short-haired men in suits, their ties loosened or stuffed in pockets. Business, Declan told her, had been "booming" since September eleventh. The men drank beer after beer after beer, and the occasional shot of whiskey or bourbon or scotch on ice, and began leaving fives and tens for her instead of singles, smiling slyly as they slid the bills across the bar.

By midnight, her feet were aching and she hopped miserably from foot to foot. By two o'clock, closing time, they'd gone numb and her exhaustion had given way to exhilaration; she wiped down the bar and glanced around to see what else she might do. Declan was seated at a small table, settling the till. "Go home," he told her, waving a meaty hand in her direction. "You're done. Good work." Outside, she closed her coat against the chill air and walked up and over a block to wait for the Second Avenue bus. She could take it to Fourteenth Street and transfer to the L train. The bus, usually so unreliable, came right away and zoomed off down the deserted avenue. She was the only passenger. At this time of night, she thought, rich people took taxis and poor people were asleep or at work. Furtively, she unzipped her backpack and leafed through the bills she'd collected, which amounted—she was shocked to see—to almost two hundred dollars! And this was a *Wednesday!*

On Friday, she made even more, and the following Monday somewhat less, but still enough to make it worth the effort. That Tuesday, at work, she was tired, but not all that much more than usual, and her job—her *day* job—definitely didn't require any particular level of alertness. At this rate, she could work for a few more weeks—say, until after New Year's—and make enough to catch up and get them through the holidays.

•

After Thanksgiving, business at the bar picked up and Emily's tip take-home increased, but it still wasn't enough. She'd managed to cover the holiday meal—Clara had, typically, invited the whole neighborhood—and the various expenses of the weekend, and pay back a bit of her accruing debt, but then December rent came due, and with it the bills. And the holidays were rapidly approaching. She'd told Clara, firmly, that things were a bit tight and they should skip gifts this year. "Okay," Clara said, but the look on her face suggested that she would not obey this edict and Emily, in a state of panic, asked Declan if she could take on another shift or two. As it turned out, the other "girl" was going home early for Christmas. Emily could work Tuesdays and Thursdays, if she wanted. "You can have Saturdays, too," he said, keeping his gaze on the till. "We can always use an extra hand. But I wouldn't necessarily recommend it. These guys can get pretty rowdy on Saturday night. And five nights a week is enough, anyway. You don't want to exhaust yourself." Emily nodded. Those rowdy men would tip well, she thought, especially near Christmas.

"Maybe I'll try it this Saturday and see how it goes?"

"Okay. We'll see how it goes. If you're wiped out by Friday, let's forget about it."

"Okay," Emily said, but she knew she would come in.

Come Friday, she understood his reservations. Working every night until two—getting home close to three—was pretty different than working every *other* night. Saturday morning she slept very late. In the bathroom, she had to turn away from her reflection in the mirror. The thin skin under her eyes had swelled in the night and turned a dull shade of gray. Her eyes themselves were red and itchy from the smoke and lack of sleep. Faint creases ran from the sides of her nose to the corners of her mouth. Had they always been there? All day her bed seemed, quite audibly, to be calling to her, asking her to please, please come back and lie down, just for a minute; but she did her laundry and straightened her room and read a novel until it was time to go uptown to work. Walking to the train, she could barely lift her feet, and kept tripping on jutting bits of sidewalk and stumbling into people. But once she arrived at the pub, she felt better; for a few hours, she needn't think of anything but beer. For a few hours, others would tell her exactly what they needed from her: pint of Guinness, bottle of Sam Smith, vodka tonic.

At seven—when her shift started—the bar was already half full. Short-haired men in sweaters sat at the small tables and laughed loudly, far more loudly than usual. In fact, all the sounds in the bar—the music of the jukebox, the clink of glasses, the crunching of pretzels—were decidedly amplified today. She stashed her stuff in the back room, applied some fresh lip gloss, and took her place behind the bar. Men—and even a few women, in low-rise jeans and little sweaters and high-heeled boots—poured in, all of them wanting Sam Adams special Christmas ale, which was good, because they had too much of it—the distributor had made a mistake—and, Declan said, come December twenty-sixth no one would touch the stuff. "It's really good," she told the endless stream of men, though she hadn't tried it herself. "It's brewed with nutmeg."

Around ten, as her eyes began to droop with exhaustion, she heard, among the clamoring voices, one that sounded discomfortingly familiar. Scanning the room, she was confronted with the sloping profile of Dr. Gitter—truly the last person she wanted to see. In the three-odd weeks since his visit he'd left six, maybe seven—more, actually, but Emily didn't like to think about it—messages on Emily's cell phone, first simply asking her to give him a call, then informing her, in brisk, efficient tones, that he'd arranged for Clara to be admitted to the clinic, gratis, but that Emily needed to call him immediately so they could "get things going"; then imploring her to call him, as he was "seriously concerned about the Clara situation"; and finally chastising her for ignoring his previous messages and warning her that if she didn't call back soon, he and Dr. Lang might not be able to help her ("I don't understand this, Emily. Dr. Lang is very concerned. Please just give us a call back.").

Each day at work, Emily added "Call Dr. Gitter" to her list of things to do. Each day, however, six o'clock rolled around and she hadn't made the call. By now she'd waited so long that she was embarrassed—by her own rudeness, her ingratitude, and by the knowledge that this man thought her dilemma so dire. That he viewed Clara with the cold eye of a clinician made sense to her. That he viewed Emily herself in a similar way made her furious. Her face flamed just thinking about it, and she slunk to the corner nearest the storage closet and farthest from where he stood, near the bar's front window, drinking what appeared to be some sort of scotch, in the company of three similarly dressed (faded jeans, sweaters) and bespectacled (small, wire-framed) men who she presumed to be other members of the Lang team. *He won't recognize me,* she thought, sloshing gin over ice for a stocky guy in a football jersey.

But a sort of panic—exacerbated, she knew, by her exhaustion—had set in: her heart thumped wildly, so wildly that her eyeballs seemed to rattle in their orbs. She knew what Sadie would say—that she couldn't face Dr. Gitter because she knew he was right—even though she'd not given her the opportunity to say it. She'd been so wrapped up in Clara, and now work, that she'd barely seen her friends all fall. *Maybe I should tell Declan that I'm too tired and need to go home,* she thought, whipping her head toward the back wall just as Dr. Gitter turned slightly toward her, futilely scanning for an empty table. *What is he* doing *here,* she screamed inwardly. The answer came to her a moment later, so obvious that she started to laugh at her own stupidity: the hospital. The hospital was down the street. It seemed a private enclave—removed from the towers and brownstones of the Upper East Side—but it was, in reality, a relatively short walk away. Chances were, Dr. Gitter—and all his cronies—lived nearby. Once they coupled, they'd move to Scarsdale or Greenwich or Tenafly, like the Drs. Lang and *their* cronies. She pulled three more pints for a trio of sniggering guys with gelled hair. "Here you go," she said, pushing the glasses of beer toward the rim of the bar with a satisfying clink. "Um, miss . . ." said the fat one, pointing toward his glass. And Emily saw her escape: the glass was filled with foam, which meant the keg was killed and needed to be changed.

"Declan," she called, "cover for me. I need to change the keg." Declan grimaced. She suspected he didn't think "the girls" should be doing man's work like lifting the heavy kegs.

She pulled the storeroom keys out of her pocket, unhooked the empty keg, scooted under the bar's back exit, keg in hand—she was short enough that she didn't bother to unhook the heavy counter flap—and pushed her way through the crowd, into the back room, where she sat down on a stack of boxes and let her head fall heavily to her knees. For a moment, she thought she might allow herself to fall asleep, right there on the fat brown boxes of Sam Smith Oatmeal Stout. But there was no way she could sleep, for real, with her brain having transformed into a repository for little else but anxiety. Slowly, she ran the wand of her lip gloss over her dry lips, and when she could delay it no longer, she shimmied the new, heavy keg onto its little metal cart. Hopefully, Dr. Gitter had finished his scotch and headed off to his boxy one bedroom in some blank residential tower, where he would recline on his beige couch and watch—what? football? *Friends?*—on an oversized television.

Outside, in the bar's main room, the crowd had thickened. "Coming through! Lady with the beer!" she shouted. The tricky part was maneuvering the cart behind the bar, which meant either lifting the counter flap with one hand—balancing the keg with the other—or ducking *under* the bar while pushing the keg, in a sort of crab walk. The floor sloped up and, regardless of which option she chose, it took strength and control to keep the cart from wobbling. Tonight, she decided to duck under, but the keg resisted her attempts to wrangle it, refusing to roll up the incline. For a bleak minute, she thought she could hold it no longer, that it was going to roll back onto her, over her, and into the small crowd clustered around the opening in the bar. But then, at the last second, grinding her teeth together, she regained her grip and pushed it, with a final jolt of strength, up and into the space behind the bar; stupidly pleased, she ducked down and followed it, emerging on the other side to clapping. A group of spiky-haired soldiers had been watching her. "Good job, Red," one of them yelled. She smiled weakly—and did a quick check for Dr. Gitter, who appeared, thankfully, to have left—then began rolling the cart toward the taps, at the center of the long bar. But something was wrong, the wheels wouldn't turn. She gave the right one a push with her sneakered foot and the cart released momentarily, then stopped again as a sharp pressure, hot and metallic, spread across her foot, turning, slowly, to pain. "Oh my God," she whispered, afraid to look down.

"Oh, shit, oh shit, oh shit," she heard Declan say, though she couldn't see him. "I knew it, I fucking knew it. I *told* you. You shouldn't have come in tonight. It's too much." She nodded mutely. And then the pressure was half gone, but her foot throbbed horribly, like a beating heart, like, she thought, the heart of the frog she'd dissected in tenth-grade biology, the frog that was still alive, its brain killed by a pith, so they could slice it open and note the functions of its valves.

"Oh my God," she said again, for her legs were turning to something like gelatin and buckling beneath her. But someone—Declan—had anticipated this and was placing a chair under her and pressed her firmly into it, propping her foot on another.

"Is she okay?" another voice asked. Emily's head had dropped down again, into the palms of her hands.

"I know her," called yet another voice, "I know her and I'm a doctor. Can you let me through? Let me through." In a rush, her stomach seized up and her ears began to ring. *Oh shit, oh shit, oh shit,* she thought, her brain echoing Declan's cry. *No, no, no, no, no, no. Not him, anyone but him.* And then a hand—Dr. Gitter's hand—was lifting her foot off the chair— "No, no, no, no," she heard herself moan, like a child—and then placing it down again on something softer, more pliant, and decidedly more comfortable: a lap. "Okay, I'm just going to take your shoe off," he said. Quickly, he pulled the laces out of her sneaker—was it good or bad that she had worn sneakers?—and pried the thing off, sending a hot needle of pain through her foot. Wordlessly—as if they were a seasoned pair of EMTs—Declan handed him a bag of ice wrapped in a towel, which he draped over Emily's foot. She winced. "It's okay," Dr. Gitter said, in the same practiced voice he'd used a few weeks earlier as they'd walked down Bedford. She was no less irritated by it now. "You're fine. I think you've probably broken a bone in your foot, but you're going to be just fine. We just need to get you to the hospital for an X-ray, okay?" *What do* you *know about broken bones,* she thought. *You're a shrink.* But the foot—it didn't feel like *her* foot but like an inanimate object, maybe a football attached to her with glue and string—felt a little better now, cooler, and the stars, she found, were no longer whirling around her. Nervously, she pulled herself upright, but rather than facing Dr. Gitter, she turned to survey the crowd, mostly silent now, hypnotized by the Drama of the Keg and the Foot.

"She's okay?" called one of the soldiers. *I'm not dead,* she thought. *You can ask* me *that question.*

"Yeah, she's fine," Dr. Gitter replied. "We just need to get her to the hospital. Can you guys clear a path?" The soldiers immediately flew into action. And Emily, reluctantly, turned to face Dr. Gitter, who was, to her annoyance, grinning. *This is funny to you,* she thought. *What an ass.* But she said nothing and thankfully, neither did he. He looked, absurdly, like a doctor on a hospital drama, with his short, light hair and his dark, round eyes and his long nose with its wide nostrils.

"Okay, Emily," he said finally. "I'm going to put your foot down for a second, so I can come around and lift you up." And before she knew what was what, she was being carried outside into the cold, cold air, the odd sensation of a stranger's arms around her. Declan ran after, awkwardly holding out her bag and coat. Dr. Gitter slung them over his shoulder—

again, he himself didn't have a coat; what was wrong with him?—and slid her into the cab that had pulled up, seemingly without being hailed.

"We can walk," she said, "it's only a few blocks." But he just raised his eyebrows at her, his face too white in the cab's reflected light, and in a moment they'd arrived at the hospital's emergency entrance. Dr. Gitter carried her past the dozens of people waiting, directly to the nurse's station at the front. "I'm really okay to walk," she said.

"No, you're not, honey," said the nurse, padded, Filipino, her hair a funny maroon color. "You can take her right back if you want," she told Dr. Gitter. "Saul's on. And Ashwari."

"Thanks, Lucy," he said, depositing Emily on a stretcher and covering her with a pile of itchy blankets. Wouldn't, she wondered, a wheelchair do? A stretcher seemed a bit over the top, but she was, suddenly, too tired to speak. And it felt so good to lie down, even on the cold, hard stretcher. If only she could roll over and go to sleep. "Are you cold?" he asked. Emily nodded. "You're in shock." She nodded again. "We're going to go right up to X-ray," he told her. She felt strange, lying prone on her back like that, and looking up into his face from below. "This is one of the few benefits of working in this place. No waiting in line at the ER. Those people have been sitting there all night. But you get to cut straight to the chase."

"Good," replied Emily, trying to smile, but her eyes would no longer stay open.

She drifted in and out of sleep for what seemed like hours, as her beleaguered foot was X-rayed, injected with a local anesthetic, and operated on, the broken bone—the metatarsal, the doctor told her—snapped and pinned back into place. She was propped on pillows in a high hospital bed, her foot in a plaster cast. A different Filipino nurse fed her pills ("for swelling and pain"), handed her a baggie of the same to take home with her, and ushered Dr. Gitter into the room. Seeing the clear set of his face, remorse immediately washed over her; she'd dragged some nice person into her troubles, exactly the sort of thing she wanted to avoid— exactly the sort of thing that Clara did, that borderlines, she knew, did— and, worse, she'd been a bitch to him, if not in action then in thought. It must, she knew, be almost two in the morning, and here this man—this stranger—was forced into having to take care of her. "I'm sorry," she said, discovering that her throat ached. Why? Instinctually, she reached a hand up to her neck.

"The anesthetic," he said. "It can do that. It's weird." Emily nodded. "Dr. Gitter. You don't have to stay here with me. It's late." And yet, as she uttered these words, she realized she was almost desperate for him to stay. What would she do without him? How would she get home? She had no cash on her. (*My tips,* she thought suddenly. *Will Declan hold my tips for me?*) She couldn't walk. Who could she call? Not Beth or Sadie, not at this hour, not anymore; and not Lil, who could barely take care of herself, much less Emily, and whom she hadn't spoken to in at least a month. There was Dave, she supposed. And Clara. Clara, of course, would come in a second; she was probably still up. But she didn't want Clara. Which left Tal, who wasn't even around, as far as she knew. Dave had told her he was in Israel again, despite the dire situation there, not filming but on some sort of retreat. "Maybe kabbalah?" Dave had said, grimacing. But she herself had heard nothing from him since last spring, when he'd given her passes to that show at Circle in the Square—a new play, with Holly Hunter, whom Emily loved, but kind of boring and Gurney-ish. They'd had a drink after, she and Curtis and Tal, making stiff, awkward conversation, Tal gingerly asking about *her* play (she could see now that he, too, was skeptical of her hopes, but too politic to say any-thing). Lately, she wondered if he'd pulled away from her because it was all too strange: the contrast between his success and her failure. She still didn't understand why he'd never offered her any help during all her years of struggle. Could he not have put her in touch with his agent? Could he not have suggested her for roles? Did he think so little of her talents? In college, he'd been her biggest fan. They'd played opposite each other in *The Rehearsal,* her favorite production from undergrad. "You really can go," she told the doctor.

But he ignored her. "Cool cast," he said, smiling. "Can I sign it?"

"I guess." She laughed, struggling to contain her annoyance that he hadn't *listened* to her. The thought of him pitying her or staying out of obligation was too much. "Listen, you *really* don't need to stay. I can get home okay myself. I'm completely fine."

Abruptly, he sat down in the chair beside her bed. "Let's drop the tough-girl act for a second," he said. Taken aback, she pushed herself up on her elbows—she'd never thought of herself as anything remotely sim-ilar to a "tough girl"—but pain shot through her foot and up her leg, and she lost, for a moment, her ability to breathe. Dr. Gitter slid his arm behind her shoulders and lowered her down against the high bed. "Okay," he said, puffing out his cheeks and blowing out a stream of air. "Okay, okay. Try to lie still, okay? Try to rest. You really did a number on your foot, okay." Sitting down in the chair, he inched it closer to her bed. "Now, listen, we need to talk." She crossed her arms and looked at him. It was two in the morning. She had a broken foot. She did not want to talk. "What are you doing at McKinney's? I thought you worked at a bank."

How did he know this? *Oh,* she realized. *Dr. Lang.* She smiled. "I do. I just needed a little Christmas money. You know."

He looked at her strangely. "No, I don't know. Why don't you tell me?"

"Well, things are kind of tight and the holidays are coming up." She reached up and touched her hair, which felt wiry and stiff. She must look awful. "So I thought I'd get a, you know, temporary job, just until things even out a bit." He shook his head sadly, and shame flooded through her, though she wasn't sure why.

"Emily, I need to explain to you how things look from my perspective. Will you listen to me for a minute?" She nodded, though she really, truly didn't want to hear what he had to say.

"Okay, I meet a young woman whose sister has a history of serious mental illness, substance abuse, and even occasional violence, not to mention a substantial criminal record—"

"*No*—"

He held up his hand. "I've seen her records, Emily. You signed the releases. Brattleboro, Holly Hill, Chestnut Ridge, Duke. So, I *know,* okay. I know everything—"

"But—"

"Let me finish. So this young woman's sister has now come to live with her, basically because their parents have washed their hands of the sister. They've been supporting her for years and it's killing them, which is common, actually. This young woman loves her sister and her parents, and she wants to do right by them. It seems like the sister is in better shape. Even the parents are starting to think she's okay and cut her a bit of slack. But she still should be under a psychiatrist's care." He slowed down on these words, for emphasis. "Her medication definitely needs to be monitored. And so does her lifestyle. She can't be drinking alcohol or taking any other meds—which she very well might, since she's done so in the past. And there are little signs—little glimmers of a psychotic break—that this nice young woman has noticed, which is why she came to my colleague for help in the first place. And I meet the sister and I see why this nice young woman is afraid. The sister is out of control. She's going to crash. There's no doubt." He pressed his fingertips together and shook his head.

"I tell the young woman that I could, very possibly, arrange for her sister to come to one of the best clinics in the country for *free,* but she would need to stay at the hospital, as an inpatient. And this nice young woman says no, no, that her sister is getting better, really, and it would make things worse for her to be put into *another* hospital, because part of the sister's problem—which is, by the way, common to borderlines—is that she hates that people think she's crazy, and she's just found a group of friends and is settling into some sort of new life—"

"Dr. Gitter," Emily cut in wearily. "I'm so tired. Do we really need to do this now? Could you maybe just tell me your point?"

"My point?" he asked, shaking his head, as if he couldn't believe she'd asked such a ludicrous question. "My point is that I *told* you to rein her in. I told you to keep her on a fixed budget, to mete out her meds, to *watch her*—"

"I did. I *did*—"

"Then why, tell me *why*—the next thing I know, I see the young woman—"

"Could we stop with 'the young woman'—"

"—pulling beers at the crappy bar in my neighborhood, waiting on the asshole frat guys." His hands, she saw, were gripping the rail at the side of her bed. "And she looks like she's lost twenty pounds in the last three weeks and she has dark circles the size of the Grand Canyon under her eyes, which are beautiful, by the way." Emily squirmed. Had he really just said that? A man she barely knew? Did men do things like that—tell women they had beautiful eyes? Wasn't that kind of creepy? Or had her year with Curtis—and her years alone—made her jaded? "Now, what exactly am I supposed to think?"

"I—"

"That she didn't listen to anything I said. That she's just letting her sister wreck both their lives."

Oh, don't be a drama queen, she thought, but she said, "She's not—"

"No," the doctor retorted. "She *is*. Clearly, she's burning through your cash. You're working yourself to the bone. You can't control her. This is big trouble, Emily."

Emily shook her head. "I'm not," she insisted. "It's just a difficult time. We've had so many expenses. Our rent doubled. And—" Her hands fluttered uselessly on the blanket. She was too tired to explain. Why couldn't he simply understand, without her having to utter the words? But then that was the problem, wasn't it: he *did* understand, despite everything she said. "We took this larger apartment and I didn't realize how the utilities would go up. And we needed stuff for it. I didn't have anything. I could live with just a plate and a saucepan and a mug." She laughed and shrugged. "And I did. Clara wanted to live like normal people."

Dr. Gitter looked at her sternly. "Normal people don't work—what—sixteen hours a day. And I live just fine with a plate, a saucepan, and a mug. And a coffeemaker."

Emily smiled gratefully. "Yes, definitely a coffeemaker."

"Emily," he said, softly now. "Your sister is ill. She needs to be hospitalized."

"No," Emily said. "It's not an option."

He leaned in closer. "It's the *only* option. You can't take care of her. Your parents can't take care of her. She can't take care of herself. If you just cut her off and try to let her manage on her own, she's going to wind up dead or in jail—"

"She's *fine* now."

With a sort of groan, he stood up and let his head fall into his hand. "You know that's not true."

The kindness in his voice was too much for her. It had been so long, months, since she'd spoken, really spoken with her friends—since she'd really talked to anyone honestly—and the force of his attention made her nervous, as nervous as his million messages on her voice mail. When she opened her mouth to speak, a dry, weak sound came out. She closed her lips, swallowed, hugged her arms close around her, and then, embarrassingly, began to cry, in great, huge, pitiful sobs, burrowing her face into her hands, snot streaming from her nose. The doctor stood stiffly for a moment, looking down on her, then moved to the side of the bed and twined his arms around her, causing her body to shudder and collapse. "It's okay," he whispered.

"*No, no, it's not, it's not,*" Emily sobbed, her face pressed against his sweater. "Everything is *wrong*. I was in a play and it went to *Broadway* without me. And it was my *one* chance. And I wasted a year with this stupid guy and . . ." She broke into a loud, hiccuping sob. "And then Clara said she was coming and I was so *glad* to have my sister with me. I always wanted to be *close* to her, like in *Little Women,* you know?" He nodded. "But she always hated me. She always, always hated me and I thought now we could be *real* sisters. We could have fun. And I thought she was getting better, but I made a mess of that, too. I'm a *failure*. And I hate her, too. I hate her."

Again she began to cry, which felt good, too good, to admit all this, the truth, the actual truth—or a version of it, the darkest slant on it—which she could not, somehow, have told any of her friends, and certainly not her parents. And good, too, to give in to the impulse to cry and scream and say *No, no, no, no, everything is* not *all right*—to *not* be the girl who showed up for work on time, no matter that three miles from her house there's a mass grave, burning and smoking, no matter that the world appears to be ending and that her work is pointless and soulless—and this, really, was what felt good, to simply not care, not care that she was burdening this man with herself, her sister, her troubles, that she had forced him, awkwardly, to comfort her, and that she had done so, very possibly, because she was utterly, pathetically alone, so alone that the arms of a stranger, wrapped firmly around her, felt, like her tears, better than anything she had felt in a long time.

"It's okay," he said again, and this time she didn't contradict him. "This is crazy talk. You're not a failure, not at all. You've been doing a great job taking care of her. It's hard. Look, I know how hard it is. And that stuff with Curtis—" At this, she abruptly pulled away. How strange to hear his name from another man's mouth. "That's who we're talking about, right?" She nodded glumly. "He's an idiot." And then, with a gulp, she was laughing. Because he was, wasn't he? "That whole slacker thing. I mean, come on." He was laughing, too, but then he wasn't. "Listen," he said, "none of this is your fault."

"No, it *is*. You're right. I didn't even try to keep her under control. I just wanted her to be happy. Sometimes"—she lowered her voice, and the sobs came again, like hiccups—"sometimes I think I'm just like her." He pulled her close again and her breath began to come in something less than gulps.

"Why would you think that?"

She pulled herself out of his arms and looked straight up into his eyes, which were, she saw, not as dark as she'd thought: a pleasant brown. Hazel, really. "Because of my genes. It's in our family. Everyone's crazy. My grandfather killed himself." His face crumpled and for a moment she thought, strangely, he was going to kiss her. "I keep thinking—it's like there's a bomb inside me, ticking, and one day it's going to go off and I'm going to be like Clara. Every time I lose my temper or can't sleep or eat chocolate cake for breakfast—"

"Okay, okay." He laid a cool hand across her forehead, as if he was trying to gauge her temperature. "I get it. But you're not like Clara. Or your grandfather."

"It's not just my grandfather. It's my whole family. And my parents are second cousins, so I've got a double dose of it. All the Kaplans marry each other. They're freaks."

"But not you?" he asked. "You didn't marry a Kaplan?"

"No." She laughed. "Oh my God, if you'd met my cousins, you'd never have asked that. They're like these Range Rover–driving idiots."

"Well, if that's not an option," he began, twisting his mouth into a broad grin, "why don't you marry me?"

"What?" A tissue had found its way into her hands and she was, she suddenly saw, worrying it into moist shreds.

"I'm serious," he said. "Marry me."

"You don't even know me," she said slowly. "We just *met*."

"No, we met last year, when you came in with Curtis. I remember the day. You were wearing a blue dress. I thought you were the most beautiful woman I'd ever seen." Emily flushed. Curtis, in the whole year they'd been together, had only ever told her she looked "nice." Out of the sides of her eyes—she simply couldn't look him in the face; this was all too strange and embarrassing—she glanced at Dr. Gitter. "You used to come in and have lunch under the skylights, and I could see your hair from across the atrium. I thought, 'That's the girl for me.' And you always asked Dr. Lang the most intelligent questions." He looked directly into her face. "I loved the sound of your voice. I thought, 'There's no way she's going to stay with that loser.' When Dr. Lang told me that you and Curtis had split up, I almost said, 'I knew it!' And then, a couple months later, there you were, knocking on the door of her office. I thought, 'It's fate!'"

"I thought," she said, happy to seize on this small point, "that scientists don't believe in fate."

"Doctors have to believe in fate, otherwise they go crazy." He sighed and stood up, brushing invisible crumbs off his jeans. "So, whaddaya say? You want to get married? My dad's a rabbi. He can marry us if you want. Or we can just go to city hall."

Again, Emily shook her head. "I don't"—she was unsure how to respond to all this, where to begin her objections; he had to be kidding and if he wasn't, well, that was just as strange—"know anything about you. Though you seem to know something about me."

He grinned. "Dr. Lang talks a lot. What do you want to know about me?"

"Have you ever been married?" Emily asked.

"No." He laughed. "I've pretty much been working night and day since I started med school. And I did everything the hard way: two residencies instead of one. I thought I wanted the excitement of the ER, saving lives and all that. Turned out I was wrong."

"I'm not sure I can marry a workaholic," said Emily, half laughing at the absurdity of this conversation. She knew, of course, that he wasn't really asking her to marry him, and yet, somehow, she was arguing over the fine points of their arrangement. "Well, you won't be. It's all over. As of January, I'm no longer Dr. Lang's chief resident. You're looking at plain old Dr. Gitter, assistant professor of psychiatry, Cornell School of Medicine. From now on, it's banker's hours for me." Flummoxed, Emily gnawed a hangnail. "Except," he added, "when I have late patients."

"Right," she said, laughing. "I'll miss you. But I can have dinner with friends."

"Exactly." He smiled at her. "I'll miss you, too. But we can have a glass of wine when I get home, talk about our day."

"This is all very, I don't know, nineteenth century."

"Yes," he nodded. "There were some good marriages in the nineteenth century. I'm way into the Victorians. Dickens, Austen, Trollope. George Eliot. Mrs. Gaskell."

"Yeh, me too," said Emily, though she hadn't read Trollope or Mrs. Gaskell. She was relieved, for clearly he was dropping the joke, and now she could turn over, go to sleep, and, maybe, never see him again—or maybe not. But then, slowly, he placed her hand on top of his.

"You know, I'm serious," he said, still smiling. "And I know you like me."

"I—" Emily began, feeling the blood rush again to her face—unattractive red spots would be appearing on her cheeks and forehead within moments—because, *oh my God,* it was true, so clearly, stupidly, obscenely true that she wasn't sure how she'd kept herself from admitting it. And hadn't she known, all along, that he'd had his eye on her? That *he* would be the resident Dr. Lang would send to her apartment? And the worst was: Hadn't she, maybe, maybe, *pushed* things—allowed herself to start crying—because she knew he'd take her into his arms; wasn't *this* what shamed her?

"Why did you think I kept calling you?"

"I—" But she could offer no answer.

"Admit it. I'm not so bad." But Emily, somehow, had lost the ability to speak. She thought she might cry again if she so much as moved her head. "Look, I don't want you to think I'm some kind of weirdo—"

"I don't—" Emily managed, before her throat closed with tears. She swallowed, hard, and smiled. "I don't. But you're not really serious." Her voice sounded hollowed out, a husk of a voice.

"You know I'm serious," he told her, sliding her hand on top of one of his. And she did, she supposed, but it was just too strange to contemplate. It was just *unfathomable*. Not, she suddenly realized, that he really, actually wanted her to marry him, but that her life could change in an instant, that the grim routines of the past few years—her whole adult life—could be erased in a moment, simply by saying yes. And her heart began to beat faster because she knew, she knew that she was going to do this, that anything was possible. And then, with a start, she realized that no, nothing was possible.

"What about Clara?" she asked. "I can't just leave her on her own."

His face crumpled. "Emily," he said, "you know she has to be hospitalized. She's got to finish the ECT. She needs daily therapy."

"No," said Emily. "Not now. She's doing so well. And she won't go. She won't even talk about it."

Dr. Gitter shrugged and smiled. "Well, then she can come live with us. I can monitor her—"

"Oh my God," Emily broke in, laughing. "You can't be serious. You want my crazy sister to come live with us? That's like the plot of a sitcom."

"You're not going to scare me off," he said. "I'm not afraid. We can find a big enough place—"

Emily thought of something. "Wait," she said. "Where? Where do you live? Do you live around *here*?"

He nodded. "All the residents do. To maximize sleep. You roll out of bed ten minutes before your shift starts."

Grinning, she shook her head gravely. "Well, there's our problem. I don't think I can marry someone who lives uptown."

"Good," he said. "I hate it here. My lease is up in January. We'll move wherever you want."

"Brooklyn?"

"Sure," he said. "Brooklyn is great."

•

For two weeks, Emily held court on the living room couch. Her friends brought her flowers and cookies and ice cream and containers of noodles from Planet Thailand. One by one, she told them what had transpired. None were surprised to hear she was engaged. She'd always been one to keep things close to the bone. And, after all, none of them had seen her all fall, since Clara's arrival. They'd assumed she was dating someone new. But they were appalled that she'd been in such dire straits and not let on, even a smidge. "Oh, Emily," said Sadie, jostling Jack on her lap. Ed was away again, in L.A. doing some retracking. They'd just found out that his film was going to Sundance and Sadie seemed almost manic with excitement. She'd extended her maternity leave for another month, unpaid, but after the New Year she'd have to go back. "Let's not talk about it," she told Emily. "I'm pretending it's not happening." She kissed Jack on top of his head. "Why didn't you ask me for help?" she asked. "I wish I could have done something."

"Weren't you exhausted?" asked Beth, who came bearing the not surprising news that she was pregnant, and began crying before Emily even got to the part about dropping the keg. "It's not fair," she said, tears rolling out of her large brown eyes. "You shouldn't always have to carry other people's burdens."

Dave brought a television and a DVD player—"I just got new ones," he insisted, "they're really cheap now"—and sat watching John Hughes movies with her all afternoon, gnawing on Twizzlers and shouting "Kiss her! Kiss her already!" at Eric Stoltz and Andrew McCarthy.

Lil wanted only to talk about Josh and the wedding. Where would it be? And when? Where would they live? Was she really going to quit her job? What would she do? "And what's going to happen to Clara?" she asked in a low voice. Emily shook her head. "I don't know. I guess she could come live with us." Lil looked horrified. "Live with *you*. You're kidding."

They planned the wedding for the spring, the ceremony at his father's synagogue, the reception in the backyard of his parents' house. On the twenty-ninth, they put a down payment on a plain, brick house on Dean Street, cheaply divided into two apartments—Clara could live in the smaller place upstairs, they in the duplex below—a few blocks from Dave in one direction, and Beth and Will and Sam, in the other. "I wish Sadie hadn't moved," Emily lamented. "She's just a few stops away," said Josh. "And maybe she'll move back." Emily worried that Clara would be resistant to leaving Williamsburg, but instead she was excited about the prospect of another renovation. On the thirtieth, Emily's cast came off and was replaced by a pneumatic shoe. "Let's celebrate," Josh said as the hospital's glass doors parted, silently, and they stepped onto Sixty-eighth Street, Emily leaning on her new cane, which made her feel, really, rather jaunty.

"Okay, but no dancing, I guess."

"Right, no dancing," he said, hailing a cab. "City hall," he told the driver. Emily opened her mouth questioningly. "What?" he said. "We can still have the wedding. We need the gifts, right? You get great gifts when you're the rabbi's son."

Emily laughed. "What's going on?" He took her hand.

"We're going to go get married now, so we can start our life."

"But we don't have rings. Or witnesses. And don't we have to have blood tests?"

"No blood tests, not in New York. And we don't *really* need rings."

At the clerk's office, they discovered that they did really need rings, as well as a license, after the acquisition of which they would have to wait twenty-four hours before the clerk would perform the actual marriage itself.

"Should we forget it?" asked Emily. "Just wait until May?"

"We're here," said Josh. "Let's get the license."

The next morning they returned to the clerk's bereft little antechamber, where Sadie met them, with Jack in his carrier, laughing and drooling, and Dave trailing after them. "Lil and Beth are on their way," she explained, handing Emily a little bouquet of freesias. "Ed's stuck at the airport. But he said to call him so he can hear it on the cell." After, they took a cab to Chinatown and ate soup dumplings and sesame balls, toasting with scratched glasses of Tsing Tao. At three, Josh became all business. "We're off," he said. He'd arranged, it seemed, for them to borrow a friend's cabin up near Great Barrington.

"Do you think they'll still have a real wedding?" Lil asked sadly, pulling her coat tight around her. "I think Emily really wanted one."

"You mean *you* really wanted one," said Sadie, laughing. Jack, perched on her lap, squawked, releasing a fat stream of drool, which Beth reached over and mopped with the restaurant's stiff napkins.

"*No,*" bristled Lil. "Em does."

Josh's friend Craig, a tall oncologist with wire-rimmed glasses and bristly black hair nodded sagely. "They will, they will. Josh's mom would die if they didn't."

"Hmmm," Lil murmured, punching buttons on her cell phone. "Tal," she said, "you missed out big-time. You need to get back to New York."

"Where is he?" asked Sadie as they clambered east on Pell Street, stepping around the clumps of already drunk tourists in oversized parkas.

"Jerusalem," Lil told her. "I think."

"Again?" asked Sadie.

"Have you spoken to him?" asked Dave, his jaw tensing.

Lil shook her head. "Just email. I got a long note"—she grinned—"long for *him*—a couple of weeks ago. He said he's taking a break from film stuff. And TV, I guess. It was kind of interesting. He said he doesn't want to do crap anymore, basically. That he only wants to work on things that he loves, or that are, like, making the world *better*. Sort of."

"What does that mean?" said Dave, though he understood, really. Why, though, had Tal written to Lil about all this, rather than him?

Lil shrugged. "No more serial-killer films?"

"No more Robin Williams movies," said Dave.

"But, you know, I saw him on an AOL commercial last night," said Lil. "How can he not have an ethical problem with AOL?"

"Yeah," said Dave. "I saw it, too. Fucking sellout."

"He shot that years ago," said Sadie, a slight tremor in her voice. The situation in Israel was so bad right now, though better, maybe, than in the spring, when there'd been that terrible disco bombing, all those students killed. "They're just recycling it."

At the Bowery, they turned north, not yet ready to part ways. It was nearly dark already and they needed to get home, to change for the evening ahead. They had reservations at Oznot's, a set menu with oysters and steak that struck them all as wonderfully old-fashioned. Four hours later, they sat at a large table across from the bar, the girls in glittering, shining dresses, not warm enough for the weather, the boys in their usual, drinking some sort of champagne cocktail. They were due, *over*due, at a big party in DUMBO, but no one felt much like going.

"I'm so tired," said Beth. She was three months along, her stomach protruding already from her pale yellow dress. "It's driving me crazy. I can't get anything done."

"It gets better," Sadie told her. "Soon."

"Maybe we should get you home," said Will, pulling her close to him.

"We could just go back to our place," Lil suggested, "and drink champagne." Her friends looked at one another uncomfortably.

Craig had come along with them, filling Emily's empty seat, and brought a friend, a short, pleasant-faced surgeon, who filled the seat meant for Josh. "A year ago," Sadie blurted, "Lil would have been trying to set you up with Emily."

"*I* would have?" Lil shouted. "*You* would have."

Tuck took her arm. "*Okay.*" He laughed. "Enough champagne for you."

"What?" said Lil. "I'm fine."

"Me, too," said Sadie, threading her fingers through Ed's. It was their first night out together since Jack's birth. They'd left him, nervously, with a neighbor, a college girl studying early childhood development at Hunter.

"Let's toast," said Ed, raising his glass. His plane had landed just an hour before and he couldn't stop yawning. "To new friends and old. To their happiness and health."

"To Sundance!" cried Sadie.

"*Sadie,*" said Ed, ducking his head and tucking her arm under his.

"Here, here!" the group cried, tinking their glasses. "Here, here!"

Dave kept his arm raised. "To Emily," he cried, his voice hard and bright. "Who deserves happiness more than anyone."

"To Emily!" they cried. "To Emily!" their voices echoing throughout the small, dark room, tiled, as it was, in glittering shards of mirror, in which they saw themselves reflected a thousand times over, and broken into as many parts.

thirteen

After her foot healed, Emily applied to a premed program at Columbia—to the shock of all her friends but Sadie, who said, "Of course!"—and took a job down the hall from Josh, at the clinic, assisting a neuropsychiatrist who was trying to determine whether men and women possessed different brain chemistries. For five years, she'd been observing the frontal lobes of songbirds and was on the verge, she explained to Emily, of publishing a paper stating that yes, definitely, men's and women's brains are completely different. Emily had to sign a confidentiality agreement, which struck her as hilarious.

Each morning, she and Josh took the subway uptown, carrying warm cups of coffee in their cold hands and sharing the paper. In the sunny atrium of the pavilion—which she had so recently considered purely the Langs' territory—they parted ways, Emily heading west toward her boss's office and Josh heading east toward his own. At lunch, they ate sandwiches in the atrium, before Josh walked up to his new office on Eightieth Street to see private patients. Emily met him at home, on Dean Street, where they sat on the couch and ate omelets or at restaurants on Smith Street or Court Street, where they joined Clara, who was occupied with making slipcovers for the chairs in her new apartment, or her friends, who insisted that they wanted to "get to know him." "He's so *nice,*" they whispered to her, as they sat side by side along the banquettes of the various Spanish or French or Italian bistros, with their tiled floors and distressed mirrors and black-and-white photos of French bulldogs and saucer-sized medallions of Chilean sea bass. Josh scanned the menus of these places, then signaled for the waiter with an upraised hand, while Emily and Beth were still debating the safety of ordering moules frites on a Sunday.

One cool Monday in April, Emily arrived at the clinic alone—Josh had departed early for Eightieth Street to meet with a new patient. Siphoning herself a cup of coffee in the lobby's small café, she nearly bumped into a dark-haired man, his cheeks rough with beard, who on closer inspection appeared to be Tuck Hayes. Tuck *Roth*-Hayes, Emily corrected herself. It had been—how long?—four months, perhaps, since she'd seen him and he looked worse for the wear. Increasingly, Lil had been appearing alone—when she had appeared at all, as she regularly canceled lunch dates—and speaking little of Tuck's flaws and virtues, his ambitions and efforts (or lack thereof), the subjects that had consumed her in their first years of marriage. "My nagging him doesn't do anything except make him annoyed with me," she'd told Emily and Beth some months back. "I have to let him do what he wants to do, at his own pace."

What Tuck wanted to do wasn't exactly clear. In November, he'd finally turned in his book, just as things were getting really bad: magazines shutting down (*Lingua Franca*, which was depressing; *Talk*, which was inevitable), dot-coms shouting bankruptcy, and all the pundits intoning doom, doom, doom for everything: the economy, the American two-party system, the air-travel industry. The age of irony, they were told, was over. Yet, no one wanted tragedy, because things were already tragic enough. And no one wanted comedy, real, straight comedy, because laughter—or at least the absence of tears—was an affront to the newly sober state of the nation. Readers, according to Sadie's publisher, wanted books on Islam and terrorism and fundamentalism and the Middle East and globalization and germ warfare. They wanted books about America's place in world culture, books that would explain why "they" all hate us so much and books about Afghanistan and Osama bin Laden and the oil industry and the intense corruption of the Bush family and the crimes allegedly perpetrated by Hillary Rodham Clinton, books by *Times* and *Washington Post* reporters, books by foreign correspondents who posed for their author photos in camouflage vests, against a backdrop of sand and blue, blue sky. They did not—at least, according to Val—want to part with thirty dollars to read about Internet impresarios and dot-com bazillionaires, and particularly not about Ed, who wasn't exactly one or the other, who hadn't invented anything or made a sick amount of money or, when you really thought about it, done much of anything, other than start a magazine. *Boom Time* had relaunched as planned, the previous June, and no one, really, had cared very much. Times had changed. A magazine was now just a magazine, not an instrument of cultural revolution. And Ed, well, no one cared about him either, according to Val, at least. Val, who was so nonplussed that Sadie had coupled with her subject—apparently it wasn't such an uncommon occurrence—that she didn't feel the need to mince words.

"Didn't we cancel the contract on that one?" Val asked when Sadie called to tell her the manuscript had come in (hoping Val would conveniently forget how late Tuck had delivered). She was still out on maternity leave, of course, and Tuck had been instructed to send it to her old assistant, but Tuck, being Tuck, just gave it to Sadie at home. "I'm thinking we should write this one off, Sadie. That Amazon book bombed. The one by that fat guy. Remember?"

"I think," Sadie responded, carefully measuring out her words, "you might want to *read* it first. The writing is great—" This had become her mantra with regard to Tuck's book. "It's not really a book about Ed. It's more of a memoir. Sort of social satire. A commentary on the times. The dot-com bubble."

"Does it need work?" Val had asked her. Sadie had admitted that it did—"just a little"—and Val instructed her to send Tuck edits; she'd read the revise. Her edits, however, did not strike Tuck as "little."

"She doesn't get what he's trying to do," Lil fumed to their friends. "It could take him another year to make these changes."

"That's absurd," Sadie insisted coolly. "It's a month's work." She and Lil were barely speaking. But then, Lil rarely—or never, actually—called Emily either, though she kept in touch with Caitlin Green, as did Tuck, apparently. Emily had run into the girl on Atlantic in March and been the recipient of a breathless monologue about her divorce ("Rob just didn't understand me"), her move to Carroll Gardens ("It's so *warm* here! Like Paris"), and the rather too intimate specifics of Lil's marriage: Tuck, according to Caitlin, hadn't started in on his rewrites yet—he was still smarting that Sadie hadn't accepted the book wholesale—and was instead spending his afternoons at Belmont, under the tutelage of a local celebrity, the editor of a trust-fund-financed Williamsburg magazine, the sort with fashion spreads that looked like stills from seventies porn films. As a result, he'd lost sums of money equivalent to the next installment of his book advance, which he'd figured he'd have in hand by now. So they were back to square one, Lil and Tuck, living off Lil's small salary. Even if Lil didn't yet know it. *God,* thought Emily. *I hate him.* "Don't say anything to Lil," Caitlin told Emily. "I shouldn't have said anything. I'm sort of his confidante."

"Don't worry," Emily told her, more bitterly than she intended. "I haven't even spoken to her in a month or two."

It had been longer than that since she'd seen Tuck—since New Year's Eve—and he'd lost weight, the flat hollows of his cheeks cast blue under the bright overheads of the hospital cafeteria. For a moment she contemplated pretending she hadn't noticed him—turning on her heel and heading up to her office—but then he caught her eye and she forced a smile. "Tuck," she said. "What are you doing here?"

"Emily Kaplan," he said in his deep, rasping voice, running a hand over his face. "Boy, am I glad to see you."

"What's up?" asked Emily. Nothing good, she knew. "What are you doing here?"

"Lil's here," said Tuck, waving his hand toward the elevators. "Upstairs."

"Oh my God," said Emily. Upstairs meant the clinic. "Is she okay?" She thrust a few bills at the glowering cashier.

"Can we sit down? I've been up all night."

"Um, sure."

They carried their coffee to a small table by the terrarium, where Tuck took a long gulp, then shook his head from side to side, like a dog, his hair, which he'd let grow long, flopping around his ears.

"Lil had a miscarriage," he said at last.

"Oh, no," Emily cried. "Oh, Tuck."

But he was looking away from her, up at the ceiling, then across the room, where a long-legged resident, Anne-Marie, was cleaning her glasses on the hem of her lab coat.

"Is she okay?"

"She's fine. The bleeding got kind of scary, so the doctor said to bring her in. To the ER." A shudder of relief skipped across Emily's shoulders. She had been wrong. Lil wasn't in the clinic. She was next door—"upstairs," in the next building over—in the regular hospital, recovering from a normal physical ailment. "They did a D and C and she just kind of freaked out. She was just, like, *crying*—" He waved his hand in the air, unable or unwilling to explain what else Lil had done.

"It can be painful."

"I guess."

"How far along was she?" It couldn't have been very far. Emily would have known. "They're keeping her for tests? Or she lost too much blood?"

Tuck shook his head. "She wouldn't stop crying. They brought in a psychiatrist. He said she seemed depressed and they decided to admit her—which took fucking all night."

Emily drew in a breath. So it was as she'd initially thought. "There's a lot of paperwork. Insurance companies."

"Yeah, and we had to wait for a bed." She nodded, but her mind had left Tuck. She needed to call Josh immediately and get his take on this.

And she needed to find Lil. It was all she could do not to run toward the elevator bank, leaving Tuck alone at the table without so much as a good-bye. But she was due at her desk in ten minutes. The bird lady was big on punctuality. She also wasn't sure they'd let her in to see Lil, unaccompanied by Josh.

"You should go home and get some sleep," she said, more sharply than she intended.

"Yeah," he said, his voice cracking on this one small word. "I have to bring Lil some things. She doesn't have anything to wear. Her clothes are all a mess." Suddenly, Emily felt sorry for him. Was it his fault he was broken? If she were Lil, would she have stayed with him? Probably. Yes, probably. "I may have some stuff in my office. An extra sweater, at least. I'll go up and see her. Do you know what room she's in?"

"I can't remember."

"Doesn't matter. I can find out." Emily stood and glanced at her watch. "I'll go up to her as soon as I can."

From her desk, in the antechamber of the neuropsychiatrist's mahogany-lined office, she left a message on Josh's voice mail, explaining the situation sotto voce, so as not to alert the nosy receptionist whose desk adjoined hers. Twenty long minutes later, as she halfheartedly fiddled with spreadsheets on brain activity, he called her back. "She's probably fine," he said, against a backdrop of blaring horns. "Just overwrought and exhausted. Do you want to go up and see her now? Will Barbara let you out for a sec?"

The door to the bird lady's office was closed. "I could probably sneak out for a few minutes."

"Okay," said Josh, his voice breaking up slightly in the wind. "I should be there in about ten minutes. We'll go up. Or do you want to go right this second? I can call and let them know you're coming."

"No, no, I'll wait for you," said Emily.

•

At the front desk, they found a plump nurse talking intently to a tall, bald doctor, "The patient is recalcitrant. She keeps insisting we let her out. Says she's here by mistake. Usual stuff." Emily was continually amazed by the eerie manner in which the hospital staff's conversations exactly mirrored those on hospital dramas.

"Bob," Josh called to the doctor, who took his eyes off his clipboard at the sound of his name.

"Hey, what's up?" said the doctor. His plastic name tag read "Dr. Robert Goldstein."

"You know my wife, Emily, right? She's working with Barbara."

Bob held out his hand. "I've seen you around, I know. How do you like the bird lady?"

"She's great," said Emily, through gritted teeth—her stomach had started flopping the minute they entered the clinic. She remembered visiting Clara after her first breakdown, Clara, hollow eyed and furious, screaming at Emily, at her parents, that they'd ruined her life.

"We've got a situation," said Josh, with another grin, mimicking the clipped tones of a cinematic cop. "A friend of Emily's was admitted last night. From the ER."

"Right, right," he said, pulling out his cell phone and scrolling through messages. "The miscarriage. Lillian Roth."

"Lillian Roth-*Hayes*," Emily piped in.

The doctor gave her an irritated glance. "A bit paranoid, possibly delusional, hostile to the nurses. Generally friendly to me. Eager to please. She's seriously not happy to be here, though."

Josh nodded. "What are you thinking?" Bob puffed out his cheeks and blew out a gust of air. "Well, I just did the intake interview—we're swamped today—so these are just preliminary ideas." He gave Emily an appraising glance, as if trying to gauge how many words to mince in her presence. "You know, I can see why they sent her over—couldn't stop crying, was screaming about it all being the husband's fault, all that—but she doesn't seem depressed to me, just upset about the miscarriage."

"So you're thinking acute problem, few days' rest, send her home?" asked Josh.

"Actually, I'm tossing around narcissistic personality disorder." He raised his eyebrows at them, as if to say, *How do you like them apples.* "Maybe dependency disorder," he added, glancing back down at his cell phone, which he held flat in his palm, like a detonator.

"Dependency disorder?" said Emily. "Lil is"—her voice began to fail her—"*so* independent."

Bob turned to her again, this time more kindly, his voice taking on the formal tone she knew he must use with patients. "I'm sure she is," he said. "And she certainly seems very opinionated and able to speak her mind. But dependency disorder is more about an emotional dependence on another person, or people, that"—he moved his hands in circles—"is so strong that you lose yourself, literally, in that other person. You're so dependent on that other person's moods and desires that you can't determine your own. You seek approval constantly."

"Oh," said Emily. She hadn't realized that such a thing qualified as mental illness. How, in all her reading on psychological complaints, had she not come across this particular malady? It sounded fake, like something spoofed on *Saturday Night Live*.

"Your friend Lillian's relationship with her husband seems to indicate possible dependency disorder," Bob went on, sliding his phone back into a holster on his belt and picking his clipboard off the counter. "But. Well. These are just preliminary thoughts. I need to talk to her more. Talk to the husband, too, get some background."

"Tuck! You're going to talk to Tuck?"

"Yes, we generally talk to the person responsible for the patient, so we can get a sense of history. Behavior patterns." She thought he might ask if there was a reason why he should *not* speak to Tuck, but instead he turned to Josh and said, "It's also possible there's nothing wrong with her. Emotional strain. Difficulties in the marriage. Normal stuff." Josh pushed his lips together. "Okay if we stop in and see her?" Bob nodded. "She's in 406-B. Alone for now."

Inside room 406-B, they found Lil lying on her side in the bed nearest the window, her face turned away from them, several layers of thin white blankets pulled up around her shoulders, which were covered in the pale green of the hospital's standard surgical gown. Splayed out on the pillow, her hair looked fuzzy and dull, preternaturally black, and her skin yellow and raw under the room's cruel fluorescents. On a rolling table beside the bed sat an untouched lunch tray, containing pale blobs of food, vaguely recognizable as pudding, mashed potatoes, and some sort of poultry. Tonight, Emily knew, Lil would have to eat dinner in the cafeteria, with the rest of the patients, presuming Tuck arrived with her clothes. From the pocket of her lab coat, Emily extracted her glasses— she wore them only for distance, but now she felt she might need a shield between Lil and herself—and watched as her friend stirred. "Who is it?" she called, her voice thick with sleep. Emily rushed to the far side of the bed and sat down in the chair beside it. "Emily!" Lil cried, bolting up and embracing her friend. "I was hoping you'd come! I wasn't sure if you'd find out that I was here, like, automatically. Like if a list of patients gets circulated to the whole staff or something? I asked Tuck to call you but I didn't think he really would. He asked me for your number. Isn't that crazy? I'm lying there on a gurney, bleeding, and he wants me to find him a phone number—which he *has* anyway, in his phone." She swallowed, hard, and Emily handed her the cup of water that sat on her tray. "Thanks," she said. "I'm so thirsty." She drank again, with a loud gulp. "I'm so glad you're here!"

Emily smiled. Lil seemed exactly like herself. "Josh is here, too," she said, gesturing toward the door.

"And I'm glad you're here, too," Lil told him, rather grandly.

"Actually, I'm going to head out for a minute, " he told them, with a smile. "I'll be back in a bit." And then he was gone, the door shut, and Emily alone with Lil, a prospect that, she realized, rather frightened her.

But before she had time to contemplate this, Lil had thrown her arms around her again. "You look *amazing*!" she said. "I love your glasses. Why do you never wear them?"

"Well, they're really only for distance—"

"God, I *love* them. The color of the frames really makes your eyes look really blue."

"Thanks. But—" She paused, unsure how to ask Lil what happened. "How are you? Tuck told me—"

"I'm okay," snapped Lil, as if it was strange of Emily to ask the question. Emily nodded and said nothing. "I'm much better than last night. Emily, it was such a *nightmare*. Would you believe they just left me in this, like, weird *room* alone after the D and C?" She paused and gave Emily a questioning look. "Tuck told you what happened?" Emily nodded. "It's just been so awful. I kept thinking it was a mistake, that I wasn't *really* miscarrying. You know, we've been trying for so long."

"I know," said Emily. Actually, Lil had never told her this, though Emily had guessed it; they had all guessed it. "I'm so sorry about all this."

"I just don't see why it all had to be so awful." She shook her head sadly. "My doctor was supposed to meet us here. That's why we came all the way up here. But she got stuck in traffic, so they made us wait forever. And then, finally, they were like, 'We can't wait any longer. We have to do it *right* now! You're running the risk of infection! You could die!' And so I was completely terrified."

"Why do doctors *do* that?" asked Emily.

"I don't know," said Lil. "I guess they're thinking of the worst-case scenario. I mean, maybe they were right. Maybe I could have died."

"I guess," said Emily.

"It was scary," Lil told her. "All of it. I was half awake—they give you this twilight sleep stuff—and I could kind of feel it, like a tugging. And afterward, they put me in this room—I guess it was the recovery room—and they just left me. I sort of fell asleep and when I woke up, my entire body was in *spasms*. It was just unbelievable. I've never experienced anything like it. It was like"—she closed her eyes for a moment, searching for the right words—"a pair of jaws inside me snapping open and shut. I really, *literally,* thought I was going to die."

"Oh, Lil! How awful!"

"I felt like an animal. I heard this horrible moaning and was thinking, 'Make it stop'—and then I realized it was *me*."

"But someone eventually came in to check on you, right? And brought you painkillers?"

Lil nodded. "And I was still in sort of a daze, like half asleep, and couldn't figure out how to signal a nurse or a doctor or how to get Tuck. Eventually, a nurse heard me and came in. She asked me what was wrong and all I could say was, 'It hurts. It hurts.' And would you believe, she said, 'Most people are fine after a D and C.'"

"Oh my God," said Emily. "That's insane."

"I know! I've never had one before! How am I supposed to know how *most people* react afterward? And why should it matter to me? Then she said, 'The doctor has to see you before I can give you anything.' It was almost as though she thought I was lying! I'm writhing in pain and she's *yelling* at me. She left for a while longer and then a man came in—the doctor, I guess—and had me sit up. I was actually feeling a little better—until I sat up. And I couldn't help myself, I started moaning again—it was so embarrassing. And he just said, 'Your uterus is contracting. That's all it is. There's nothing wrong. Sometimes it hurts for a while afterward.'"

"And he gave you pain medication?" Emily could and could not believe this. Some of the doctors she'd met through Josh were shockingly callous. And the nurses were worse. Bitter. Resentful. Some of them, at least.

"Yeah. He gave me a pill. And I fell asleep again. But this is the worst part." She bit her lip from the inside and furrowed her brow. "When I woke up, there was somebody else in the room, a woman. She was asleep and this man was standing there stro—" Her voice broke and tears began to creep into her eyes. "He was stroking her hair and whispering to her and holding her hand. And all this time I'd thought Tuck hadn't come in because he wasn't allowed to. But he *was,* he *was,* and he just didn't want to."

A sob escaped her throat—a small, defeated sound—and she laid her head in her hands, her back hunched into a *C* shape. "Maybe he didn't know," Emily suggested, in a soft voice. It was very possible, actually. "The doctors in the ER are so busy. They might not have even told him where you were."

Lil looked up. The whites of her eyes were a terrifying, mottled red. "He could have asked."

"Yes," said Emily, and sat down beside her friend on the bed, smoothing stray tentacles of her hair, which, she saw, was threaded with gray.

But Lil squirmed in her grasp. "I'm fine," she said, twisting her neck as if to crack it. "I guess he didn't tell you that it was his idea for me to come here."

"To New York Hospital?"

"No!" Lil shook her head impatiently. "*Here*. He told the doctor that I was hysterical. And that I refused to come home with him. He said I'd been acting strange and depressed for days, since I started to miscarry. And that he'd been worried about me since September eleventh. And that he thought I was going to try to kill myself. Me!"

"Oh my God." This was worse than she'd thought. But then, maybe he really *had* been worried about her. Hadn't Lil retreated from all of them in recent months? Wasn't that, in and of itself, a sign of depression? "And he *told* you he told the doctor that?"

Lil let out a little snort. "The *doctor* told me!" *That seems weird,* thought Emily, resolving to ask Josh about it. "He asked if it was true and I said sort of, in a way, that I'd been very sad, but I didn't think I was *depressed*. But then I said—and this was probably a mistake—that maybe I *was* depressed. That I didn't actually know because I wasn't sure what depression meant anyway and I thought it was all a bogus term invented by Pfizer and Eli Lilly." Emily laughed. She could just see one of the humorless residents dutifully scribbling Lil's comment on her chart. "Later, when he brought the psychiatrist in, I heard him say that I was hostile and paranoid. He had, like, woken me up to talk to me—and he wanted me to be, you know, *friendly*?"

"I know," Emily told her. "I know. It's ridiculous." The two women sat there for a moment, looking out the window, which faced the spare brick buildings of Seventieth Street. This was, Emily realized, the first time she'd been inside a patient's room at the clinic. It didn't look quite as she expected. There were, for example, no bars on the windows. She supposed they were fused shut and made of some sort of dense, unbreakable glass. A fat pigeon warbled and thrummed on the stone sill, swelling his gray chest. "That looks like Thermos," said Lil, sitting up to get a better look.

"Dave's, um, cat?"

"Yes, look." Lil pointed to the pigeon and smiled. "The way it's all puffy."

With her face in repose, Emily was alarmed to see that Lil looked old. Her bright beauty—black hair, fair skin, large eyes, like an Italian film star—appeared to be hardening into a *caricature* of beauty: containing all the proper elements, but lacking the harmony to fuse them into a lovely whole. For years now, ever since college or marrying Tuck or leaving Columbia or *something,* she'd been in a state of constant movement, running glibly in conversation from one thing to another, eternally thrusting the focus of her attention on some minute detail of another person. She was a perfect, devoted, obsessively attentive friend, who could spend hours dissecting Emily's or Sadie's or Dave's problems; who always remembered birthdays and bought too many perfectly chosen gifts; who would meet for coffee at the drop of a hat—and yet over the years somehow those virtues had hardened into something akin to flaws. The light of her affection shined too brightly for any one friend to bear, and she demanded too much in return, more than anyone could give. It was not that she wanted the same—the birthday surprises, the days of rapid-fire conversation—all of that would have been bearable and easily, if not agreeably, accomplished. No, Emily thought sickly, what she wanted was complicity. She wanted her friends to swallow her own willful misconceptions about her life: that Tuck was a genius and she his happy muse. Or, in a different mood, that Tuck was a monster and she his unwilling victim.

"What happened with the psychiatrist?" Emily asked.

"Oh." Lil waved her hand dismissively. "He was really nice, actually. Indian. Skinny. Kind of good-looking."

"Dr. Mukherjee," Emily said.

"Yes! You know him!"

Emily nodded. "Just a little. Josh used to supervise him."

"He was great. He just sat and talked with me for a while. And then he said it seemed like I'd been through a lot and asked if I would want to have a rest for a day or two. And I said that sounded okay to me. I figured they'd move me to the OB-GYN floor. I thought I could just sleep a lot—I'm so tired—and maybe Dr. Mukherjee would come by and talk to me. I've just had so much going on." Lil sighed gravely. "Well, he said he'd make some arrangements and I should try to sleep. I thought I wouldn't be able to fall back asleep, but I did. And when I woke up I actually felt much better. Tuck finally came in and sat with me for a while and I told him I thought I was okay to go home. But then when I sat up, I had those spasms again. I stupidly told Tuck and he said, 'Well, then don't sit up.' And I just burst into tears, because why did he have to say that? I mean he could have *thought* it, but he didn't have to say it."

"Of course!" assented Emily, who thought he didn't necessarily have to *think* it either.

"I don't know what's wrong with him," said Lil quietly, and Emily braced herself for more tears.

Just then, an awful shriek came from somewhere in the corridor, followed by a metallic crash. "Nooooooo, nooooo," sounded the voice. The girls looked at each other, eyes wide. Rubber soles squeaked quickly by, followed by an electronic bleep and buzz. "Yikes," said Lil, with an ironic smile, but Emily could tell she was scared. "It's probably just an anorexic. They cause most of the scenes. They'll, you know, pretend to eat for a while, then just sort of lose it." Lil nodded warily. "It's kind of interesting, actually, they're—the anorexics—well, they actually have borderline personality disorder, like Clara. It's a personality disorder—not a mood disorder, like depression—which is why it's so hard to cure." Lil, she saw, had begun to shiver. She stared out the window, an odd, unreadable expression on her pale face. "Are you cold?" asked Emily, snapping herself back to attention. Lil nodded, her eyes still wide with fear, her mouth a grim, rigid line. True, honest fear, Emily thought, with a sudden clarity, was not something with which she and her friends had ever had to cope. They lived in such comfort, such luxury. In college, they'd been aware of their position of relative privilege. But now, well, now they got annoyed when their cappuccinos arrived without the requisite amount of foam. *Oh, shut up,* she told herself. *That's not true.*

"Take my sweater," she instructed Lil, taking off her lab coat and unbuttoning her cardigan. She had forgotten the extra sweater she kept in her desk. "Tuck is coming this afternoon with some clothes for you. They told you, right, that the patients in the clinic wear their own clothes. They—you—have to get dressed every day." Lil nodded again and slipped the black sweater over her hospital gown. "Lil, there's really nothing to be afraid of," Emily started. "This isn't like *The Bell Jar* or *Girl, Interrupted* or whatever." She smiled a little and, before she could correct her expression, was pleased to see Lil smile back at her.

"Or *The Snake Pit?*" offered Lil, with a weak smile.

"Definitely not *The Snake Pit.* It's really small and private and everyone is here voluntarily. And short-term. The longest stay is maybe six months. Most people are here for a few weeks or a month or two. And it's *totally* normal people. A lot of depression. A lot of bipolar disorder. A *lot* of anorexics." There were also, she knew, a number of schizophrenics, but she thought it better to leave them out for the time being.

"But I'm *not* depressed. I don't want to take Prozac or Zoloft or whatever—"

"You won't have to—"

"They gave me some pills when I got in this morning. I don't know what they were."

"They were probably just sleeping pills or—"

"I didn't need them. There's *nothing* wrong with me." Lil's voice had started to rise in volume. "Tuck just put me in here so he'd have something to hold over me for the rest of our lives. So we wouldn't have to have a baby. He doesn't wa—" Here she began to cry. "—want one. He doesn't. He *always* says that I'm crazy. Whenever we get into a fight about something, he says I'm crazy, that I need *help.* But I'm not *crazy.* I just get *upset,* because he doesn't *listen* to me. It's like, he can't have anyone be *upset.* We all just have to be happy all the time and accept whatever he says, even when he's *wrong.*"

"I know, I know," said Emily, taking Lil's cold hand.

"He wanted to get rid of me. He doesn't care about me. What kind of person would do this to his wife? I should be at home and he should be taking care of me."

"Maybe he thought that they'd take better care of you here," said Emily, when her friend had lapsed into small, calm sobs. "Maybe he was really worried about you." She ran her hand over Lil's thin back, the knobs of her spine protruding from Emily's sweater. "Lil," she said tentatively, unsure if the information she had to impart would make Lil feel better or worse. You know, this is—" She paused. "This is a voluntary facility. Tuck didn't put you here. He couldn't make you stay here without your consent."

She had thought that, hearing this statement, Lil would utter a sigh of relief and brighten a bit. Instead, her face turned wooden. "Voluntary," she said dully.

"Yes. You don't remember signing any forms?"

"No."

"Well, it was late and you were tired and scared and in pain."

"Yes," Lil said, but now she was looking at Emily as if she was the enemy. *Oh, God,* Emily thought, *I'm an idiot. Why didn't I see it? She wants to blame Tuck. She wants this to be his fault.*

"So I can leave whenever I want?" Lil asked. If she was excited about this prospect, her voice showed no evidence of it.

"Not exactly," Emily told her. "Now that you're here—and you've signed yourself over to the clinic's care—you can't leave until they make sure you're not a danger to yourself. Or, I guess, others. But that doesn't really apply in your case."

Lil laughed. "Actually, it does. Tuck told them that I attacked him with a pair of scissors."

Emily tried to smile. "That's crazy. You didn't, right?"

Lil shook her head, still laughing a little. "No, I mean, yes." Emily's mouth fell open. "I didn't *attack* him! I just held them up to him. I was *so* mad, Emily. He went out last night. He knew I was miscarrying. It started on Friday. I'd been in bed all weekend. I told him I felt weird and dizzy, that the bleeding seemed heavier. I said I wanted to call the doctor. But he said I was 'wallowing' and I should get up and come out with him. Can you believe it? While he was out, I started to get scared. Everything started to hurt. I was afraid if I got up I was going to fall down."

"Where did he go?" asked Emily, not sure why it mattered.

"A screening of Ed's movie. He said he needed to go for the book."

Emily had received an invite to the press screenings, too. She and Josh had RSVP'd for one the following week. Surely Tuck could have postponed.

"He said he'd come home right after, but he didn't. And I was so tired, but I was afraid to go to sleep—like, I wouldn't wake up or something. He got home at, like, two and he acted like nothing was wrong. He tried to hug me and I just couldn't—couldn't let him touch me. And he kept coming at me. And then, I don't know how, there were scissors in the night stand. And I just picked them up and said, 'Stay away from me. Leave me alone.'" She stopped talking suddenly, as if someone had flipped a switch at the base of her skull. "Oh God, Emily. Maybe I am crazy. Only crazy people have fights like that."

"No, you're not," Emily said firmly. "Plenty of people have fights like that. You've just been going through a rough time. The doctors will see that immediately."

Out of the corner of her eye, she glanced down at her watch. More than half an hour had passed. She half rose from the bed. "Listen, Lil, I'm sorry but I'm going to have to go in a minute—"

Lil grabbed her arm, panicked. "Are you going to talk to the doctors? Will you tell them I'm not crazy? Or out of control or suicidal or something. You'll tell them right? Can you explain that to them?"

Emily sat back down again beside her friend. "Of course, of course," she said, though she wasn't sure if she could do this or not. "And Josh will be here to see you in a minute, I think. He'll talk to the other doctors and find out what's going on."

"And what about Tuck?" Lil asked forlornly.

"He should be back soon—with some clothes and things for you. I'll call him and check in." She tried another smile. Lil wanly smiled back. Her mirth about the scissors had vanished.

"Do you think I could get something to read?" she asked in a small voice.

"I'm sure the nurses can bring you some magazines. I'll ask them." Emily hoped this was true. There could well be some sort of ban on outside reading material. "And I have a book in my bag. I'll bring it to you as soon as I can. I've got to go back to my office for a bit, then I'll come back and bring you some things."

"What is it?" asked Lil, skeptically. Emily knew her friends doubted her taste in literature. She was the only one of them who hadn't been an English major, and the only one who'd read *Bridget Jones's Diary* and *The Girls' Guide to Hunting and Fishing*.

"You'll like it." She was reading a novel given to her by Lil herself, years earlier. Josh loved it, too, and had suggested Emily pick it up. "*The Forsyte Saga*."

Like a child, Lil clapped her hands together and smiled. A real smile. What was it Tuck used to say about Lil? That she was born in a bookshop? Within the belled sleeves of the green gown, her arms looked pale and wooden and miniaturized—like the limbs of a doll or a mannequin. "Oh! The Forsytes! If only I'd married Young Jolyon instead of Soames."

Emily laughed and kissed Lil on one cheek. "No spoilers!" she said, holding a hand up to Lil. "I'm not even through the first chapter." She took off her glasses and slid them into her pocket. "Okay, I'll be back. Try to relax, okay? Sleep if you can. And I'll ask the nurses about sending in some magazines."

Rubbing her arms, she walked back down the hall toward Maria, the gossiping receptionist, and Barbara, the bird lady. They were both brisk and resourceful—the sorts of people who made to-do lists each morning, then spent the day dutifully ticking off items. Rumor had it Barbara had delivered a paper at the NIH while in labor with her first child. That paper—on the gene mutation that causes pseudohermaphroditism—had made her career, as a twenty-seven-year-old resident. In May, Emily would be thirty. Her moment for greatness—or, that particular sort of greatness—had passed, hadn't it?

But that moment *had* existed. She was sure of it. There had been a window, a brief exhilarating time, when something might have happened—when she might have become (so painful to think of it now) if not a *star,* per se, a—what? Whatever Tal was. A working actor. But that wasn't *all* she'd wanted—the supporting parts in crappy movies—she'd wanted more. Clichéd phrases swam into her head. A "leading light of Broadway." Inwardly, she cringed, not simply because the term was so twee, but because such creatures simply didn't exist anymore. Well-reviewed stage actors went on to roles on well-reviewed television shows (or, just as often, *bad* televsion shows)—or were plucked by Hollywood—and in this way secured their measure of fame. But, she hadn't wanted fame. She had simply wanted to *work,* to play Phoebe, Nora, maybe one of Shepard's foul-mouthed, haunted women.

And now here she was, in her lab coat, tending to Barbara's hummingbirds. And here, too, was Lil—who had become a scholar of poetry because she couldn't find the wherewithal to write her own verse, only to let go of even those safer, secondary aspirations—in a faded green gown and a borrowed sweater, stoking the ashes of Tuck's ambitions. It was unkind, Emily thought, to compare herself to Lil right at this moment, when poor Lil was so clearly at a disadvantage. But the events of the morning had put her in a strange humor, jumbled together, as they were, with some distasteful memories of Lil lecturing her, through the years, on how to find a man.

It was later, hours later, when she realized she'd walked right by the nurses' station without asking about magazines for Lil—or making a case, as Lil had bid her, for her friend's sanity.

•

As soon as Lil heard the door click shut, she flopped over onto her back and stretched her body to its full length, reaching her toes down to the footboard and her arms overhead. Her body ached and throbbed, as though she'd been beaten by a thousand tiny bats, and there was a peculiar tightness in her abdomen—the residue of the previous night's pain. Then again, maybe the pain was still there, lurking, muted by the drugs they'd given her. In a way, she hoped this was so, as it better justified her stay in this creepy room with its faux homey touches (a putrid border of flowers, a Chagall print), staffed by plump, worn-faced nurses in ugly crepe-soled shoes. It was midafternoon already—she'd been in this place for a good twelve hours—and she'd barely yet caught sight of a doctor. Just the tall, bald one who'd come in this morning, fired a few questions at her as though he were reading them off a questionnaire, and abruptly left, saying Dr. So-and-So would be in later. She couldn't tell if he was referring to himself in the third person or if he was speaking about an actual third person, the doctor who would oversee her case. Regardless, no doctor had so much as peeped in the small window set into the door of her room. Just an endless parade of nurses, bustling around and bringing this or that, refilling her water jug, giving her more forms to sign, asking to see her insurance card again and again, and on and on until she wanted to scream or, at the very least, lock the door so she might sit undisturbed for a few minutes and try to sort through the various competing threads in her mind.

Earlier, she had, in fact, tried to do exactly this, only to find that the door, of course, wouldn't lock from the inside (nor, she later discovered, would the bathroom door). And her fiddling had summoned the attention of yet another sour nurse. "Is something wrong?" she'd asked.

"Everything's fine, thanks," Lil told her impatiently.

But the woman lingered, maddeningly. "Are you sure?"

"Yes," Lil said. "I'm *fine*. I don't need *anything*." And slammed the door right in the nurse's face. Later, when this same nurse—a short, plain-faced woman of indeterminate ethnicity, with a greasy gray braid—brought her lunch, she'd refused it just to spite her. "I don't want it," she'd complained, in a whiny voice that now embarrassed her (why had she made such a fuss, particularly since she was actually hungry?).

"Well, I'll just leave it right here, okay?" the nurse said calmly, as if she were talking to a child. "In case you get hungry."

"I don't *want* it," Lil insisted. "The smell is making me sick. I'm *not* going to eat it. Please just take it away."

"I need to leave it, hon," the nurse said calmly. "We can't have people saying we starve them, can we?"

Now the tray sat beside her bed, gravy congealed into a gelatinous mass, reminding her of her rashness and stupidity. What she really wanted was to stand up and stretch. To move her legs a bit and hang straight over from the waist, as she did in yoga class. But she was afraid that the nurses might barge in and find her in this position, her body revealed by the flapping gown. And so she stayed in bed and picked at the skin that had formed on the pudding. It was good, she found, in a terrible way—the appealing metallic of artificial vanilla—and sweetly reminded her of her childhood, which had been punctuated with lime Jell-O and pudding from a box and other such toxic, processed foods, which people simply didn't feed their kids anymore. Normal people, that is.

Earlier, Lil had thought she might call her mother—which showed how desperate she was feeling—but there was no phone in her room and the nurses had confiscated her cell phone when she was admitted, along with a host of other things from her purse: pens, cuticle scissors, lip gloss, keys. She'd asked one of the nurses if she might have the cell phone back, just for a minute, to call her mother. But the woman had told her no, that her husband would take care of all that, and she shouldn't worry. Lil had argued, but now she saw that she wouldn't have made the call anyway. She couldn't tell her mother that she was in a mental hospital. It had been hard enough to tell her, for the third time, that she was miscarrying. "We're all so fertile in my family," her mother had said with typical callousness. "I can't imagine what the problem is!" The implication, of course, was that there was something defective about Lil or perhaps Tuck or the two of them together, and that if Lil had married a nice doctor, someone like her father, and bought a ranch in the Palisades—rather than staying in the dirty, expensive, outmoded East and forcing her parents to send her checks every month or two so that she and her bohemian husband wouldn't starve—none of this would be happening. Well. Perhaps it wouldn't. But she could never have gone back— could never go back—to L.A., to that stultifying sort of life. The blondes in their huge, beastly cars. The kids who'd made fun of her. They were all still there, working in film or television as midlevel producers or agents or entertainment lawyers; taking meetings with their frat brothers from UCLA; stocking their glass houses with kids; meeting their parents for brunch on Sunday. Their lives unfolded before her all too vividly. "Yech," she said aloud, and polished off the pudding, just as Josh walked in the door.

"Not bad, right?" he said.

"No," she agreed, "it's pretty good."

"You should try the rest," he told her. "It's really much better than it looks. And I can guarantee you'll feel better after you eat something. They taught me that in medical school." Lil laughed. This was just the sort of joke her father often made. Perhaps *that's* what they were taught in medical school—a barrage of self-deprecating witticisms. "I'd bring you something from outside, but it's strictly against the rules. We could be putting a file in the cake. You know." Lil smiled at him. She felt, instinctively, that he was on her side—that he believed, perhaps also instinctively, in the force of her sanity and the extent of Tuck's villainy even more so than did Emily, who knew her better, like a sister, and was slightly prone to disbelieving Lil. Men had always liked Lil better than did women. "I don't need a file," she told Josh now, with a smile. The pudding *had* made her feel better and she shot an inquiring glance down at the mashed potatoes. "There are no bars on the windows."

"True," he said. "So no file for you. But listen, how are you doing?"

She wasn't sure how to answer this question. "Emily told you . . ." she began tentatively.

He nodded. "Emily gave me the gist of it. And I got the rest from Dr. Goldstein—the doctor who spoke with you this morning—and Dr. Mukherjee, who spoke with you last night."

"So you know I was kind of tricked into coming here," she said.

"Well," he said briskly, "I'm not sure I'd put it that way. I'm thinking you *feel* you were tricked. But it sounds more like you might have misunderstood—maybe you didn't want to understand—some of what Dr. Mukherjee told you last night. Maybe the painkillers and the anesthetic and the pain and lack of sleep and the general stress of the situation impaired your judgment, but—" Lil began to speak but he held up his hand. "I was going to say that you're a very intelligent person and my take on the situation is: You understood, if only partly, that you would be brought here to the clinic, a psychiatric hospital. But later, after you agreed, you regretted your choice."

His voice maintained its original gentle, friendly tone, but his words now took on a scientific efficiency that, like his joke, reminded her of her father, lecturing her about 401(k)s and filing her taxes on time. How could Emily—*Emily,* of all people—have married a *doctor?*

"Does that sound at all right to you?" he asked, squaring his eye with hers. It did and it didn't. Instead of answering, she found herself beginning to cry, the knowledge, inescapable, that these tears weren't exactly genuine making them come all the faster.

"I guess you think I'm crazy and I belong here," she sobbed.

He shook his head. "People belong here if they need help."

She rolled her eyes. "So do you think I need help?"

"From what I've heard and seen in the last few minutes?" he said, raising his finger pedantically.

"Yes—"

Again, he held her off with a small gesture. "Do I think you're mentally ill? No." Lil let loose a stream of air. She'd been holding her breath, she realized, while she awaited his verdict. *Why do you care?* she thought. *Why do you always need everyone's fucking approval?*

"Really?" she said. "You don't think there's anything wrong with me?"

"No more than the next person. I'd say that, from what I know of it, you've had a big shock. A miscarriage can be devastating, especially if there's no specific cause. And especially if you've been trying to conceive for a significant period of time. That aside, I'd say maybe circumstances have contrived to make you feel like your life is no longer within your control."

"Yes," she said, amazed, relieved. How did he know? "That's exactly how I feel!"

"And I also think that you may have lost a bit of perspective on certain things. Spending a few days—or maybe a week—here can help you figure out how to put things back in order. And regain that perspective."

This was starting to sound a bit like something out of a manual or maybe the clinic's promotional brochure, and Lil's mouth twitched with disappointment. Josh was not, as she'd thought for a fleeting moment, brilliant. He was boring, safe, conventional, perhaps not even all that smart, just like her parents, her family, wondering why, oh, Lillian, *why* would you want to marry that man or move to that apartment or wear that dress or raise your voice at dinner? He was, Josh *was,* advocating for her to stay in the hospital, just as her father would do in the same situation. She could hear him now, the words he said a thousand times a day, to patients unhappy with their noses or ears or chins, "If there's a problem, you may as well fix it." Everything, in her parents' world, could be remedied by this drug or that procedure. And everything that wasn't perfect needed remedying.

"You're talking about Tuck, right?" she said sullenly. Josh nodded. "You think I should leave him."

"I don't know," he said, and she could see he was being truthful. "But I think you'll benefit from being away from him for a few days. In a neutral place."

"But couldn't I just go to the Bahamas by myself?"

"Yes," he said, "but you're here. And Aetna doesn't pay for trips to the Bahamas."

She nodded. "And I guess that would be running away from things, rather than confronting them," she said, supposing that was what he was going to say next.

"Depends," he answered. "But that's beside the point."

The truth was, she liked the idea of a few days, even a week away from the endless cycle of work, dinner, laundry, shower, errands, away from the pressure of having to talk to Tuck, from the arguments, sparked by who knew what (an appreciation of the dinner salad, a refusal to pick up the phone), from the awful creep of his hands on her, which she craved and dreaded. In the hospital, she could lie in bed and read novels all day, like she did when she was a kid, and watch movies on television, and write in her journal, if Tuck would bring it, that is, if she was willing to *ask* him to bring it, running the risk of him reading it. She could talk to the doctors about all the things that were bothering her—Tuck's lethargy, his inflated ego, his inability to finish rewriting his book, his strangely chauvinistic ways (why did *she* have to cook dinner and do the dishes every night?), at odds with his liberal persona. It would be like a vacation.

What she *didn't* like was the idea of Josh trying to convince her to stay—which did indeed seem to be the case, and which made her wonder if he was keeping something from her, if he thought she was worse off than he was letting on. "If I said I wanted to leave now," she asked tentatively, "would you let me go?" Josh cocked his head to the side, apparently gathering his thoughts, and Lil's stomach dropped. Her suspicions had been correct. "Because you said that you thought I was fine, right?" she said, to fill the silence.

"Yes," he replied, "and yes, if you want to go home, you can go home, but it might take a day or two. You'll need to be evaluated by Dr. Goldstein and a couple of others. They need to make sure that you're stable. Because if they release you and something happens, they could be held accountable. You get that, right?"

"But isn't it obvious that I'm stable?" she asked, mostly because she wanted Josh to say "Yes, of course."

Again, he took too long to answer. "Honestly? In psychiatry, you learn to never take anything for granted. The obvious answer is not always the right answer. The person who seems perfectly well-adjusted could jump off a roof tomorrow."

"*I'm not going to jump off a roof!*" Lil cried. "My *God*."

"Okay," said Josh, nonplussed, which only served to further Lil's annoyance.

"I don't need a fucking lecture on psychiatry," she said before she thought better of it. "Why don't you just tell me? Just tell me what you think. *Obviously,* you're thinking things about me, things that you're not saying. Just *tell* me." Even as these words were forming in her mouth, she knew she'd taken the wrong tack; she was pushing him away, literally, for now he was unfolding himself from the ugly vinyl chair and walking over to the window, his back, in its white coat, facing her. It was a nice back, broad and tapering, and for a brief, mad moment, she thought she might get up and put her arms around his waist, breathe in his clean, doctor scent, of orange antibacterial soap and powdered latex gloves and bay rum and Pepto-Bismol tablets, and he would turn in her arms and tell her she was the one he really loved, the one he wanted, and kiss her and grab her hair with his clean fingers, and tell her that he would take care of her, as he had taken care of Emily, and Tuck would just disappear, as if he'd never existed. And then he turned, a sharp movement, and gave her a look of such blank pity that she thought she would scream. "*Tell* me," she shrieked. "Stop treating me like a child. Just *tell* me."

"I will not," he told her, hitting each word, the way she'd been taught to do in acting class, "be bullied into saying things I don't want to say or don't think you're ready to hear."

"Bullied," screamed Lil. "*Bullied*. I'm not bullying you—"

"*Yes,* you are," he said. "Now, listen. I'm in a strange position here. I'm trying to talk to you as a doctor, but also as a friend. You want me to talk to you just as a friend? Okay, well, then I'll give you some advice. You're in a destructive relationship and you should get out of it. You're extremely bright and I can't imagine how or why you can't see it. But clearly your husband is doing you no good." Lil stared at him, shocked. "But," she said, her voice still, she knew, too loud, "but you hardly know Tuck."

Josh waved his hand dismissively. "I know him well enough." With the formal air of a man waiting for a train, he held his wrist up, checked the time, and walked back over to her bed. "I need to get going. If you want to leave, talk to Dr. Goldstein and he'll, I'm sure, get the release process going. If you have any problems, just tell Emily and I'll intervene. Tuck should be by with clothes for you. You can eat dinner in the cafeteria tonight, with the other patients. If Tuck doesn't come, Emily and I can go over and grab some stuff for you. She still has your extra key, right?"

"Yes," said Lil, sullenly avoiding his gaze.

"Okay," he said, more gently now. Why had she yelled at him? He had been her ally and she had alienated him. She was left alone, as usual. "Okay, Dr. Goldstein should be in soon." He paused by the door. "And try to get some food down. You'll feel much better. Really."

When the door clicked shut, she took a quick look at her lunch, now thoroughly chilled, and found her appetite gone. The nurse had not come by with magazines and Emily had not returned with her book. There was no clock in the room and Lil had no watch, but she guessed it was midafternoon. How would she pass the time until dinner? A twinge of despair passed through her. More than anything, Lil feared boredom. She slunk down in the bed, wrapped the covers tight around her, and pressed her hands to her eyes, sending bright sparks across her lids. It would be nice to sleep, she thought, but she knew sleep wouldn't come, not now. She could no longer ignore the brightness of the room or the nasty truths crashing around inside her head. Had Tuck always been such a cold creature? To leave her alone in the recovery room? To leave her alone on Friday, as she bled and bled? To have advocated for her staying on at the hospital? So he wouldn't have to take care of her? To see her suffering? Would the man she'd married have done such things? No, she didn't think so. But then would she, four years earlier, have held scissors to him, just so that he mightn't touch her? No, no. Tears arrived in her eyes with a sting. On the wall in front of her, just then, she noticed tiny spots of light, striped red, yellow, green, blue. She sat up to look more closely— where were they coming from?—and they disappeared. When she slunk down again, they reappeared. Maybe she *was* crazy. But then she saw their source: her ring, her engagement ring reflecting the late afternoon sun. *How stupid,* she thought, *stupid, stupid simple irony. Like something from a Julia Roberts movie.*

But here she was sobbing again, and yet, she almost felt like it was someone else, some other girl, sobbing into her pillow, thinking these childish, petty thoughts that had somehow become her own: that she didn't want to give back her ring, or her married name, or the handsome man she'd married, or his friends who had become her friends. She didn't want to go back to being alone in the world and having no one to care for but herself—she had never really been good at taking care of herself anyway. And if she left Tuck, what would keep her here, in New York.

Her job, her friends, yes, but what were such things compared to a *marriage*? She'd thought friendship so important before she married, but now she felt that her friends didn't really know her—couldn't really know her—as well as Tuck did, even if that knowledge made him hate her. There was no point, she'd realized lately, in trying to talk to most of them about anything important. If she complained about Tuck, they offered her quick solutions, the kinds of things you read in stupid women's magazines. If she spoke of him positively, they glanced at one another nervously. They understood nothing. They hadn't seen her at her most base, screaming until her chest ached, sobbing in bed and bleeding; nor had they ever made her happy the way Tuck did, made her feel that she could do anything, *be* anything. She had known she wanted him—and only him—from the first moment she saw him, striding up the steps in front of Low Library. And still, now, when he walked into the room, she forgot that the rest of the world existed. But perhaps this was the problem. Each time he walked into the room, she greeted him like a drowning woman clutching a life raft. And each time he walked out the door, her heart seized with panic that he was never, ever coming back.

As the afternoon wore on, her eyes drooped and closed. The noises of the clinic—the squeak of the nurses' rubber shoes, the clang of metal carts, the shouts and cries and chatter of patients—receded into a sort of background chorus, much like the traffic outside her apartment, which had kept her awake for one night, years back, when she and Tuck first moved in, then never again. Curled inside Emily's soft sweater, the hospital blankets heavy against her legs, she slept a thick, dreamless sleep. When she woke, the sky pressed black against her window. The pigeons were gone. Someone had removed her lunch tray and replaced it with a dinner tray, the food still giving off faint wisps of steam. On the table beside her bed lay a copy of *The Forsyte Saga*—the copy she'd given Emily a few months back, after Emily had asked "What should I read next?" though Lil had never expected Emily would really read it. Lil had the same edition at home, a wan Sargent on its cover. She looked around the room. There was no suitcase, no shopping bag filled with clothes, no signs that Tuck had come by. She shivered a little in her sweater—she'd already begun to think of it as hers, rather than Emily's—and realized that she felt something akin to relief. He was gone, finally. She snapped on the bedside light and ran her finger over the reproduced Sargent, a blushing girl, of about Lil's own age, with red-gold hair and dark, serious eyes, who was, Lil supposed, meant to represent the doomed Irene Forsyte.

Inside the book she found a note from Emily, saying that she hadn't wanted to wake her, that she'd bring clothes and things for Lil early tomorrow. Which meant, Lil thought, that it was true, it was true: Tuck was gone. She stretched her arms over her head, plumped her pillows, and opened the novel, flipping past the introduction and the table of contents to the front page of the first book, "The Man of Property." The epigraph, which she'd somehow never noticed, though she'd read the book twice, read: "You will say . . . 'The slaves are ours.'"

It was Shakespeare, apparently, *The Merchant of Venice*. One of her favorite plays, yet she couldn't recall the line, nor who spoke it. She turned the page and began reading of the Forsytes "at home"—a party for the engagement of young June Forsyte to Philip Bosinney, an architect. The marriage, Lil knew, would never take place. Phil would fall in love with Irene, the unhappy wife of June's uncle Soames, and then he would die, crushed under a carriage wheel. June would become a spinster, a bit of a kook. Irene, having tasted real love and passion, would leave Soames. Many years later, she would marry again—this time happily—to Soames's cousin Young Jolyon, an amiable, left-leaning artist.

All this knowledge was, suddenly, too much for her. She could not read of June's engagement, not right now, knowing what the future held for the girl, fictive though she was. She could hear the crunch of bones as the carriage wheel bore into Phil Bosinney.

Slowly, Lil closed the book, curled back on herself, and drew the covers up around her shoulders. She was tired again. Very tired. And her head ached. Why had she said that to Emily, earlier, that she should have married Young Jolyon instead of Soames? The metaphor was untrue, imprecise, sloppy. Since leaving Columbia, she'd let her mind go. She no longer thought about things with the rigor of a scholar. *I want to be that person again,* she thought. Tears, genuine ones, came to her eyes again, and she shook her head against the pillow, as if to ward them off. *How can I be that person again?* She closed her eyes and pressed her cool palms to them. Jolyon instead of Soames. Ridiculous. Irene had married Soames for money, not for love. The opposite of Lil, really, and a mistake of truly tragic proportions, as Galsworthy made all too clear. Though nothing, Lil supposed, compared to marrying for *love,* only to wake one morning and find it vanished. Or, she thought, to wake and find it had never existed.

fourteen

One morning in June, Sadie Peregrine wheeled her son, Jack, west on Grand Street to the new Seward Park playground, and took her accustomed seat under the shade of the young, vulnerable fig trees that shaded the southern rim of the main play area, with its thick rubber matting and developmentally appropriate jungle gym. At five that morning, Ed had kissed her good-bye, grabbed his orange gym bag, and headed to JFK. By nightfall he would be in Sarajevo, shooting his and Jonathan's next film, about journalists who hunt down a war criminal. This time their little fledgling company—just he and Jonathan and a bunch of interns—was producing, in conjunction with Miramax. "Out!" said Jack, thrusting his body in the direction of the swings. "Out! Out!" To their left, a group of young mothers—well, mothers of roughly her own age—were engaged in hushed, fervid conversation, their eyes flicking ominously toward Sadie, their ringed hands clutching tall pink paper cups bearing the black, retro logo of the coffee shop just west of the park. Their toddlers waddled up the fat lacquered steps that led to the baby slide, gripping the shiny red handrails with small, chubby fingers, shrieking and squawking and shouting "*Mama!*" and "Mah-*mee!*" as they made their precarious ascent.

On the other side of the park, to Sadie's right, a fleet of spring-mounted metal ducks wobbled atop shiny round bases, their long beaks set in expressions of exaggerated forbearance. In the three months she'd been coming to this park, she'd never seen a child go near them, perhaps because a clique of wool-clad Orthodox women had staked this area for *their* kaffeeklatsch. Today, as always, they chattered loudly in Yiddish, arms folded across their chests, eyes tracking their multitudinous broods as they ran in circles around the perimeter of the playground, just inside the edges of the safety mat, shrieking and squawking in their own, slightly more guttural style, their dark, smocked dresses and sweater vests oddly pristine and charmingly outmoded, the clothing of storybook children. Every so often, they reversed directions and shouted out the name of one of their numbers: Shlomo, Hudl, Chani, Tzippo-rah, Shoshana, Gitl, the names of Sadie's Goldschlag ancestors, who had, like so many of their kind, lived in this neighborhood a hundred years prior, straight off the boat from Russia. They'd all left—for Brooklyn, the Bronx, Long Island. All but her childless aunt Minnie, her grandfather's sister, who had married the neighborhood dentist and taught school at P.S. 110 on Cannon Street and bought her apartment in the union co-ops. The few remaining Goldschlags—cousins of her mothers, out on the Island—were still furious that she'd left the place to Sadie ("What does she need it for? With all that money from the father's side?"), never mind that she and Rose had been Minnie's most frequent—sometimes *only*—visitors in recent years, that they'd brought her uptown for lunch every Sunday.

"Mama, *out*," said Jack.

"Okay, sweetie," said Sadie, depositing her own pink cup of coffee on the bench. She knelt in front of him, doubled the knots on his red canvas sneakers, and unbuckled the stroller's belt.

"Ga," shouted Jack, taking her hand and pulling her past the toddler slide, toward the swings.

"You don't want to go down the slide?" she asked, pausing.

"No. *Gah*." This was, for some reason, his word for swing. It had taken Sadie several weeks to figure this out.

"You're sure?" It worried her, just slightly, that he preferred to play with her—or with other adults, or alone—than with other children, not because she feared he was missing some sort of developmental milestone, but because she suspected, at times, that in her own quest for solitude, her own refusal or inability to make nice with the neighborhood mothers, she was, in some way, thwarting Jack's burgeoning need for the company of kids his own age. And yet, the very term "playdate" made her want to slit her wrists. "Maude and Sophia and Ava look like they're having a lot of fun."

On cue, Maude's and Sophia's and Ava's mothers muted their chatter and turned to look at Sadie and Jack. "Oh, hi," called one, waving. "I didn't see you there."

Yes, you did, thought Sadie. "Hey," she called, raising a hand to shield her eyes from the sun.

"Minga," said Jack, raising his arms to be picked up. "Mommy. *Minga*." This word was still a mystery.

"Swing?"

"*Minga!*" *Good enough*, she thought, and hoisted him up onto her hip, then headed toward the empty row of black bucket swings, the eyes of the three mothers heavy on her. They were dressed alike, in jeans and T-shirts and Birkenstocks. One was fat and taciturn, with a low, ironic voice, and a frown permanently etched onto her chubby doll's face. Another, freckled and painfully thin, radiated an anxious energy that set Sadie's teeth on edge. The third woman—she who had deemed Sadie worthy of a hello—had the small, drooping eyes of a basset hound, a pink, robust complexion, and a tendency toward cheerful, exuberant gestures. Her name was Vicky. She'd moved into Sadie's building at the same time as Sadie, just before Jack was born, found her henchwomen, and launched a neighborhood "mommies' group," which met each Wednesday afternoon at various pet-free, peanut-free apartments, to drink watery decaf, debate the merits of Huggies versus Pampers (versus the sleeper, Seventh Generation), and compare notes about the various tradespeople they employed to renovate and clean their apartments.

In the foggy months of Jack's infancy—those final, sepia-toned weeks before September eleventh, and the wretched ones immediately following—Sadie had attended on occasion, thinking these women would become her friends. Instead, she found a scene reminiscent of junior high: the mothers discreetly sniping at one another and forging hard alliances from which Sadie was excluded. She had, perhaps, arrived too late to the party—their children were all a bit older than Jack—but more likely she was just constitutionally unfit for these sorts of situations. She tried gamely to keep up her end of the conversation—"Huggies seem to work better for Jack"—but she knew they could sense her irritation and boredom, she knew they considered her prickly and superior, and she knew that perhaps she *was,* and that she shouldn't be, because they were all in this together, weren't they? Still, she found herself sighing and rolling her eyes, as Vicky slyly denigrated a neighbor who'd placed her daughter in daycare at four months. And still she went to the meetings, bearing cake or cookies or flimsy plastic containers of strawberries, because she was, frankly, desperate for the company. *They're not so bad,* she told herself. *They're nice.* And they were, indeed, better than nothing, better than being completely and entirely alone with a mysterious infant and despairing for one's city, one's world, oneself. Ed had been in Toronto on the eleventh, had finally come home at the end of the week, not for lack of trying, but he was gone often after that, at the office late, or in L.A., or on location. Sadie insisting that she would be fine, fine, then bursting into tears when he called home. "I'm so tired," she'd say. "I'm just so tired. But I'm okay."

"I'm calling your mother," Ed kept saying, his voice low and tight. "She needs to get down there and help you. I don't know what's wrong with her."

Her mother, of course, thought that a new baby was no cause for any special treatment. "I wore my regular clothes home from the hospital," she told Sadie three hours after Jack's prolonged entry into the world, while Sadie lay, stunned and starving, in a high bed at Roosevelt Hospital. "And a week later I was back at my League of Women Voters meeting. I was the chair then, you see." Still, at Ed's behest—her mother *loved* Ed, despite constant complaints about his proclivity for "raggedy sneakers"—Rose came down on weekday afternoons to "help," crowing loudly about the neighborhood, which she still viewed as the teeming ghetto of her youth. Her concept of help, however, was generally limited to expounding on the myriad ways in which the care and upkeep of babies had degenerated in the modern era. "Whole landfills are *devoted* to disposable diapers," she said, as she sat on the couch eating the babka she'd picked up at the East Broadway Bakery, and observing Sadie as she emptied and cleaned out the diaper bin. "I can't believe you're not using cloth." Sadie reminded her mother that she'd had a full-time nanny—the blonde, glamorous Michelle, who'd cared for Sadie until she started first grade—to change and launder those cloth diapers.

"She walks in the door," Sadie complained to the mothers, from the depths of Vicky's faux-Stickley couch, Jack splayed out in her arms, a stream of milk drying on his jowl, "and says, 'A cup of coffee would be nice.'" The mothers clucked with disapproval but offered no sympathy. All of *their* mothers, it seemed, supplied them with weekly casseroles and babysat on demand and paid for sessions with postpartum doulas, the very notion of which would have made Rose Peregrine choke with scorn. "I think you need to explain your needs to her," Vicky counseled. "She doesn't understand that you need help. You can't expect her to be a mind reader." The others nodded in agreement. "Maybe," Sadie replied skeptically. The problem with these women, she was beginning to see, was that the insularity of their concerns made them strangely self-centered, which in turn left them strangely immune to compassion. In devoting their every thought to their children and their households, they had become like children themselves, utterly convinced that ultimate justice lay in the firm rules that governed their days—the cry-it-out and no-dairy-until-age-five and siblings-should-be-spaced-two-years-apart—and that anyone who veered from these laws was doomed, if not to misery, then at least *difficulty*. She could feel herself being pulled under, pulled into the narrow confines of their world: the playground politics ("We invited Ella to Ava's birthday party and then we weren't invited to Ella's party!"), the inane competitiveness ("Sophia was holding her head up by the time she was a week old, but that's *very unusual*"), the crippling anxiety ("The doctor said to give her soft cheese, but what does that mean? How soft? What kind of cheese *exactly*?").

Sometimes she saw them solo, at the candy shop on Hester, buying organic, unsulfured dried fruit or single-estate, sustainably grown baking chocolate, or at the coffee shop, sipping cappuccinos and plying their babies with scones, and they were always perfectly nice, causing Sadie to ease up on her previous judgment and to wonder what exactly was wrong with her, what defect Rose had somehow inflicted on her that led her now, as a supposedly mature adult—a wife, a *mother*—to forcibly isolate herself and her child from the social fabric of her new neighborhood. They were fine people, they just weren't *her* people.

But her people—her *real* friends, of whom she now seemed to have dispiritingly few—were all still in Brooklyn. Just a few stops away on the F or the J, but somehow they were all so *busy*. Beth had Emma—almost a year now, a sweet, chubby girl with wispy blonde hair like her half brother, Sam—and her writing, with its endless deadlines, and had found friends in her neighborhood (Sadie's *old* neighborhood, it pained her to think). Emily had work and school and Josh, with whom she was still in the early, obsessive stage of romance, and Clara, too, whom Josh had gotten into a special, intensive outpatient treatment program at the clinic's Westchester campus, which was great but required a *lot* of time. And Lil, well, Lil had stopped speaking to Sadie after everything went wrong with Tuck's book, though the truth was, she'd pulled away the minute Sadie announced she was pregnant. Tal, of course, was no longer her friend and she tried not to think of him (though sometimes—even after all these years—she found herself noting a song or a book or an idea to mention to him, before remembering, *Oh, I can't*). Dave was often away—touring, recording—and when he wasn't, he was fully occupied with his music friends, many of whom had babies of their own, babies they toted with them to dinner, to midnight shows at M Shanghai and Galapagos, babies they dressed in miniature *Star Wars* and Clash T-shirts and took to "Rock-a-Baby" classes at the Brooklyn Brewery, where they tossed Shakey Eggs in time to "Ziggy Stardust" and "(The Angels Wanna Wear My) Red Shoes" and the first track from the new Radiohead album. But these were not Sadie's people either, not exactly, much as Dave—and, perhaps, Sadie herself—would have liked them to be.

Usually, though, Sadie was content on her own. The rhythms of motherhood—the regularity, the structure of it, the dinner at six and bath at seven and bed at eight—suited her. And then there was Jack himself, with his hooded Peregrine eyes and his fair Peregrine hair and Ed's pale eyes and long legs and arms, who had emerged from her, fully formed, the sort of child whom Rose described as "easy": a decent sleeper, an infrequent crier, an eater of brussels sprouts, in possession of a broad, ready smile that charmed the proprietors of the local bakery and dry cleaner and pizza shop. In the night, when he woke and clung to her, his hot face in her shoulder, she felt the individual muscles of her heart slowly ripping into their isolate strands. She loved him so. No one had warned her of this, this furious, frightening animal love that turned her into a strange, senseless being, who had given up a job she loved—though she supposed she was already loving it less well before Jack came along; she supposed she had been perhaps looking for a reason to give it up— because she couldn't bear the thought of leaving her infant with an underpaid West Indian woman who had abandoned her own children to take care of Sadie's. It had turned her—a fearless traveler—into an anxious, twittering freak who had yet, in the two years since Jack's birth, to board a plane, for what if it were to explode on takeoff, or, more likely, fall prey to box cutter–wielding madmen, causing her life to end, and preventing her from ever again watching Jake's prodigious cheeks burst into a smile or slacken into sleep. It had happened two weeks after Jack's birth. It would happen again.

And yet there were days. Sometimes, Jack's very easiness—his warmth, his attachment to her—made him *difficult*. He still, at nearly two, often wanted to sleep on her lap for naps, rather than in his crib, so that the process of putting him down took hours and left her senseless with exhaustion. And though he was happy to sit for half an hour, loading and unloading blocks into the back of his plastic dump truck, he didn't want her to read while he did so. "Mama, *guck*," he cried, and snatched the paper from her hands. And then there were nights: when he woke, sobbing, frightened by some shadow in his room or corner of his developing psyche (or, as Ed said, simply thirsty), and refused to return to sleep, making her feel heartless for, in her exhaustion, desiring that he do so. Even when Ed was home, it was Sadie he wanted in those terrible hours, and Sadie he wanted before he went to sleep in the evening, and before his naps, and when he woke up in the morning. For he was, somehow, still nursing. This great big boy, who barely fit on her lap, with his head of wild curls. A year ago, she'd offered him milk, just as the doctor told her to, and he'd puckered his lips and said "No. Bad." She'd tried everything: soy, goat, sheep, rice, which was supposed to most resemble breast milk. But he refused them all—just as he'd refused the bottle (filled, then, with breast milk, pumped, painfully, in dribs and drabs, at the kitchen table, after he went to sleep) at two months, then three, then four.

"He's not *still* nursing?" Rose asked each time they visited. On this one point Rose and Ed happily agreed. "You've *got* to wean him," Ed had said the night before. "You're wearing yourself out."

"*How?*" Sadie snapped. "I'm trying." But the truth was: she wasn't. Not because she didn't want to—she did. In a way. Sometimes, while he nursed, he rested a fat, proprietary hand on her breast, occasionally giving it a hard squeeze. "No," she said, prying his fingers off her, fighting a wave of irritation. But why? She had shared her body with him this long, hadn't she? Was it fair to suddenly demand it back? No. And yet, she was tired. So tired. Too tired to be groped by a three-foot-tall toddler. And yet, too tired to figure out a way to get him into his crib that didn't involve pawing her.

Exhaustion had become a defining principle for her, guiding every choice she made, leading her, increasingly, on a lazy and lonely track: emails and phone calls went unreturned for months; the dry cleaning lingered in the shop; her hair grew flat and fuzzed with dirt; the paper collected on the coffee table, crisp and unfingered, for she could not bear to read about the endless war, the latest foibles of the absurd regime that had launched it, the murders and fires in the Bronx and Queens and far-out Brooklyn. This exhaustion, she knew, was far from a new story, so far that she could barely bring herself to mention it when Beth or Emily, on the rare occasions she spoke with them, asked how she was. And *yet* she thought she *did* have it harder than, say, *Vicky,* whose husband was a social worker at a school in the East Village and arrived home promptly at four in the afternoon every day, as Vicky never failed to remind her. "You should do what Noah and I do," she'd advised months back, when Sadie, in a weak moment, admitted that she was having trouble coping. "He has half an hour to settle in after work. Then at four thirty it's *my* time." She smiled meaningfully. "Ava goes to bed at six, you know, and then we have *our* time." But Ed did not get home at four o'clock—ever. He was gone for days, sometimes weeks, in L.A. for meetings, or, lately, directing videos or commercials, because, though she told neither her parents nor her friends this, they needed money, badly.

"Why don't you go with him?" Vicky had asked a few days ago as they loaded laundry into their building's industrial washers, Jack and Ava pushing around the heavy wire carts. It was a question she'd heard before: from Beth, from Dave, from Emily, from her mother, who thought it was Sadie's *duty* to accompany Ed wherever business took him, or hey, who could blame him for finding "a little something on the side" (Rose had really used this phrase). They didn't seem to understand that Ed wasn't on vacation, lounging by the pool at Chateau Marmont. "He's going to *Bosnia,*" she reminded them. "But it's safe there now, isn't it?" they asked. She supposed it was. But still, it just seemed a bit *much.* What would she do with Jack all day—Ed was often on set for twenty hours in a row—in a place where she didn't speak the language, where she knew no one. "It's actually kind of nice being alone," she told everyone.

There was truth to this. In the evenings, after she put Jack to bed, she felt almost giddy with freedom: She could take a bath! Eat cookies for dinner! Get into bed at eight o'clock and read, just as she'd done when she was single, in her little apartment on Baltic Street, but *better,* for then she'd always been consumed with work, with the endless piles of manuscripts to edit.

But on this June morning, as she deposited Jack in a swing and gave him a push, the evening and its small luxuries seemed very far away. Ed would be gone for four months, an inconceivable amount of time. She'd slept badly, anxious about Ed's travel, anxious about the months without him, months of picking up the milk and purchasing birthday gifts, and doing the laundry, the endless laundry, and generally managing everything alone, and as she lifted Jack into the swing and gave him a push, she found herself prey to self-pity, an increasingly common phenomenon. The older Jack got, the more she realized that the difficulties of being alone with him for such long stretches were larger than just the everyday hassles: each day, she faced a million tiny choices—choices that would affect who Jack would become and how he regarded the world—and each day the repercussions of those choices grew larger and larger, swelling inside her head like a sponge, absorbing the material around it. Would she let him watch television? Eat candy? Drink juice? Wear the obnoxiously boyish clothing—with plasticky renderings of basketballs and trucks—purchased for him by her mother? Take a bath with her, now that he was more a boy and less a baby? And the smaller, more subtle things, too: if she grew impatient with him, if she snapped at Ed on the phone, if she seemed sad or angry or depressed. All of these things could somehow damage her son's psyche. Or had she absorbed too much of the rhetoric of the mommies' group? She should, perhaps, have gone with Ed.

"Down," Jack said now, thrusting one sturdy arm out in front of him, like a little commandant. "Ga!" He'd barely been in the swing five minutes.

"You want to come out?" she asked doubtfully.

"*Yes*," he said, tossing his arm out again. "Mama! Ga!" His eyes, she saw, were rimmed with red. Like her, he'd slept badly the night before. Today, she'd put him down for his nap early, before noon. "Mama, *ga!*" he said a third time, as an enormous blue pram materialized in front of the gate that led into the baby swings. At the helm of this outsized device stood a short young woman, her eyes covered in trendily large sunglasses, her diminutive form dwarfed by the girth of her haul, which she was having trouble maneuvering through the narrow entryway.

"Let me help you," said Sadie, striding over and holding the door open.

"Mama!" Jack called.

"Mama will be right back, sweetie." Awkwardly, the small woman attempted to guide the stroller past Sadie.

"Thanks," she said irritably. "Could you hold my coffee?" She pulled off her sunglasses with a noisy clack—revealing the small, sharp face of Caitlin Green-Gold. Caitlin had changed. Her hair was blonde and her arms, which were bare, were sheathed in ropy muscles and tanned to fine cocoa. She wore a plain black dress, of matte jersey, in the wraparound style. On her left hand sat a disarmingly huge diamond embedded in the chunky platinum confines of a Tiffany Etoile band, much disparaged by Rose ("It's *masculine*"), who had been known to while away an afternoon expounding on the hideousness of Tiffany's recent inventions.

"Caitlin," said Sadie. "Do you live down here now? Wait, sorry"— she jogged a few steps back toward Jack, who was trying to fling himself out of the swing—"let me get this boy down." Freed, Jack ran through the gate and off toward the slide, now abandoned by Ava, Sophia, and

Maude. "Sorry," she said to Caitlin. She was unsettled to find that she was glad to see her. "Do you mind chasing after him with me?"

"No," said Caitlin. "We can sit down over there."

"We can try."

"So, that's Jack, right?" said Caitlin, once they were installed on the bench under the fig trees, Jack occupied—if only momentarily—with the captain's wheel atop the play structure.

"Yes," said Sadie. "And this is . . ."

"Oh," rasped Caitlin distractedly, as if she'd forgotten the contents of her stroller. "Ismael." By rote, she pushed back the canopy to reveal the infant's sleeping face, which was a lovely pale brown color.

"He's beautiful," said Sadie honestly. He had a long, attractive nose, rather than the usual infant gumdrop, and a head of wispy black ringlets. "How old is he?"

"Eight weeks. And Jack's two?" Sadie nodded. "I heard about it from Lil. She was so jealous."

"He'll be two in August," said Sadie, deciding that she would not be baited into talking about Lil.

"Is he going to school in the fall?" asked Caitlin. Sadie sighed. She'd been getting this question a lot lately. The mothers in the neighborhood—like the mothers of middle-class New York, in general—were single-minded in their pursuit of the perfect preschool, and the process of getting their Zoes and Maxes into it. Ava and Maude and Sophia, of course, were all going to school in the fall, and Sadie had listened wearily as their mothers detailed the chosen institutions' educational philosophies and the celebrities with kids on the rosters.

"I don't think so," said Sadie. "I think we're not going to send him until he's four, when he can go to public pre-K. But we haven't really talked about it much." It was true. Somehow, they never had time.

"*Four,*" rasped Caitlin.

"Yeah, we just felt like he has the rest of his life to be in school. He can spend a few years at home with his parents." There was also the fact that they couldn't quite afford it.

"Oh," said Caitlin, in such a way that it was clear she felt this to be utter nonsense. "So you both work at home now?"

Sadie sighed. Caitlin had *not* changed. She still traded on forced intimacies. As always, she'd proceeded right to the heart of the matter—that is, asked a leading question. For surely she knew, from Lil—who knew from Emily and Beth and Dave—that Ed was often away. "No, I stay at home with Jack. Ed's a filmmaker, a producer." She still felt odd, pretentious, saying this. It sounded so glamorous, so West Coast, though the reality was ludicrously far from it.

"I know," said Caitlin. "I saw *Command Enter*." She did not say whether she liked it or not, which, Sadie thought, was either an indication that she hadn't or a Caitlin-style calculation, meant to keep Sadie on her guard. "What's he doing now?"

"Actually, he just left this morning on a big shoot."

"Where?"

"Bosnia. He'll be gone for a few months."

This seemed, strangely, to impress Caitlin. "Wow, but that's rough. I start losing my mind if I'm alone with Ish for more than a few hours. But I guess it gets more fun when they're older."

"It does," said Sadie, though she'd found those early months enjoyable, too, in a very different way. "Sorry, hold on—" She ran over to the play structure, where Jack stood at the edge of a too-high drop. "Jack, come to Mama," she said, positioning herself by the toddler slide, which he promptly shot himself down, landing at her feet.

"Do you miss your job?" asked Caitlin. And though this question followed the line of their conversation, Sadie still felt somewhat startled by it. None of her friends had asked her this, not directly, nor had they questioned her when she'd decided that she couldn't go back—or, rather, that she couldn't stay. For she *had* gone back, when Jack was four months old, and stayed for three days, weeping into the phone, as the nanny—pretty, devout, with the lilting tones of the Caribbean—complained that Jack wouldn't take the bottle ("I'll just give him the formula, okay? Maybe he like that better"; "No!") and Jack himself screamed. "Do you think you'll go back?"

"I don't know," said Sadie, though the truth was, she did know. She was done. Done with the whole corporate thing. Done with ushering through other people's books. The debacle with Tuck's book—Val had canceled his contract after Sadie left, without so much as a glance at his rewrites—had been the final nail in the coffin. She needed to stop wasting time, to write her own. And she had started, however hesitantly, in the dark hours before Jack woke, while she drank dark coffee with sugar, the only time of the day when she felt keenly focused, able to think. But she would not discuss this with Caitlin. Or with anyone, really, but Ed, who thought she should think about screenplays. "A publishing satire," he suggested. "Or a Whit Stillman kind of thing." Maybe, she told him.

"Have you been to the mommies' group?" Caitlin asked, jerking her head toward Vicky and her cohorts, who stood huddled by the sprinkler, which was shaped like a rainbow.

"Yes," said Sadie. "Horrible."

"Oh. My. God," agreed Caitlin. "*So* horrible. They, like, think that they're liberal because they feed their kids organic baby food, but they're like Betty Friedan's worst nightmare."

For the first time that day, Sadie smiled. "It's true," she said.

"Mama," Jack cried suddenly, grabbing her finger and pulling her toward the bench. "Baby. *Baby.*" As they approached the bench—Caitlin trailing desultorily behind Sadie and Jack—a faint cooing noise began emanating from the big pram.

"He's awake," said Caitlin flatly. And he was. Kicking his thin arms and legs against his soft white blanket and gazing, alarmed, at Sadie and Jack, who arrived at his side first. A moment later, when Caitlin stepped into his line of vision, he let out a frantic wail. "Okay, okay," said Caitlin, her face turning a bright scarlet. "Hold on a second." She began rooting in the bottom of the pram. *Pick him up,* thought Sadie, her blood pressure rising perceptibly. Across the park, Vicky whispered urgently in the ear of her skinny friend, while the fat one shook her head from side to side, setting her jowls aquiver.

"Baby," said Jack nervously. "Baby."

"Would you like me to pick him up?" asked Sadie.

"That would be great," said Caitlin, through gritted teeth.

In her arms, Ismael felt impossibly light and springy—had Jack ever been this small?—his hot tears soaking the shoulder of her dress. "It's okay, little sweetie," she said, kissing his head, soft black curls flattening under her lips. His smell was different than Jack's—muskier, more herbal. A different soap, that was all it was, and yet it was enough to make him seem almost a different species. "It's okay," she said. But he was already calming, breathing in great, huge, shuddering gulps.

"Baby," said Jack, staring solemnly up at her, his blue eyes darkening with confusion. "Baby." This was what he called himself. "Baby!" he shouted when he found photos of himself floating around the apartment. "Jack baby do it," he said when he wanted to climb onto a chair or eat applesauce unassisted. But he was really a boy now, hitting his Spaldeen against the wall and racing his Little People airplane across the floor and demanding to be read *Mike Mulligan and His Steam Shovel* ten times in a row.

"Okay," said Caitlin, who had emerged from behind the stroller holding a short, fat bottle filled with the thick, supernaturally white weight of formula. Sadie was almost afraid to look in the direction of Vicky. Breast-feeding was, of course, one of the key points of her ideology. Breast-feeding, that is, for a prescribed amount of time: no less than one year, no more than a year and a half. "After that it's bad for their development," she'd told Sadie numerous times, clucking her tongue in the direction of one of their neighbors, who still boldly nursed her three-year-old in the park. Sadie had said nothing, telling herself, *Forget it, Jack. It's Chinatown.* Jack, at least, generally confined his habit to the home.

Sadie handed Ismael to his mother, with some reluctance, and sat down on the bench beside her. His eyes now fully lined with red, Jack scrambled up beside her and watched as Ismael sucked rhythmically at his bottle. "Nurse," he whispered to Sadie, with his most impish smile. "Nurse."

"No, sweetie," she said gently. "It's not the nursing time. We only nurse before we go to sleep."

"Nurse," he said more urgently, reaching an exploratory hand toward her left breast. It was time, she thought, to get him home, to bed.

"He's still nursing?" asked Caitlin, her composure regained.

Sadie nodded. "I'm trying to wean him, but I can't quite figure out how. He's always been a big nurser. He wouldn't even take a bottle. It's part of the reason I didn't go back to work."

"He'll stop when he goes to school, right? And I guess it keeps him tethered to you," said Caitlin, sending an acid jolt into Sadie's mouth. *Fuck you,* she thought, wishing she could summon a more intelligent response. "I couldn't do it," Caitlin said, with a shrug. "I felt like a cow. There's so much pressure to breast-feed now. It's like your baby is going to die if you don't. They scare you with all this stuff about breast-fed babies being smarter."

"But it *is* supposed to be better for the baby," said Sadie, ever aware that she didn't want to play the role of Vicky, arbiter of all things maternal. And yet who was Caitlin to judge her? Caitlin Green-Gold, of all people?

"Actually, there's a lot of contention over that." In Caitlin's arms, Ismael's eyes were drooping shut. "Because of toxins in breast milk, from plastics and pesticides and all that. We have all these toxins stored up in our fat cells—just sitting there, like, *forever*—and they're released into our breast milk. So some people are saying that formula is actually better, in certain ways."

"*Really.*" Jack had clambered into her lap and dropped his head sweetly on her shoulder. "*Nurse,*" he whispered. "*Nurse.*"

"Yeah, there was a big thing about it in *Nature* last year. But none of the mainstream media picked it up."

"*Really?*" said Sadie, pulling Jack's hand out from the neck of her dress. Why had Caitlin been reading *Nature*? "That's surprising. It sounds like *just* the sort of story the mainstream media would pick up. Or, at least, NPR."

Caitlin rolled her eyes. "*NPR?*" she snorted. "Are you serious? The mouthpiece of the pseudoliberal hegemony? Like they're going to run a story that would question the status quo."

"That breast-feeding is better—"

"The upper-middle-class postfeminist baby-worship *bullshit,*" spat Caitlin. "Where, it's like, if we don't spend *every* minute with our kids, if they're not attached to our tits twenty-four hours a day, we're guilty of child abuse. I mean, I totally get the cultural imperative behind it, but I just think it's bullshit."

"What's the cultural imperative behind it?" asked Sadie, as she knew Caitlin wanted her to, though she suspected she knew the answer.

"We're the kids of fucking baby boomers," cried Caitlin. "Our moms either waited too long to get pregnant, then went back to work right away, or had kids early, then got pissed about it and went to encounter groups to get in touch with their rage." She sighed. "Either way, we were all parked in front of the TV after school, eating Doritos. So now we have this, like, collective desire to return to a simpler age, when gender roles were more clearly defined: Mom stayed home and baked cookies. Dad went to work."

"Which means," Sadie carried on, quelling uneasiness at her own hypocrisy, though it was apparently Caitlin's hypocrisy, too, "that all these women with Ph.D.'s are standing around the playground talking about diapers."

"Right," said Caitlin, rubbing Ismael's back in wide circles. "Like your friend Beth."

Sadie laughed. "Beth is a staff writer for *Slate.* And teaches at NYU."

"Whatever." Caitlin shrugged. "The mommy group culture. It's a waste. And a formula for unhappiness. Not that what our mothers did made them—or us—happy."

"So, what do you think we should do?" Sadie asked. What she meant, she knew, was, *What do you think* I *should do?* It was a question she had been afraid to ask herself in recent months—a question she had been afraid to raise with any of her friends. "If we shouldn't stay home and we shouldn't go back to work—"

"See, I think that's the wrong way of looking at it," Caitlin responded, shaking her head. In her arms, Ismael had fallen back asleep, his head turned toward Sadie, snoring lightly through his tiny, elegant nostrils. "*Nurse, nurse, nurse,*" Jack moaned softly as she stroked his curls, so much softer than her own. He was exhausted, poor boy. "It's not about going back to work or staying home. It's about cultural concepts of what constitutes a woman's identity. It's about whether a woman, when she becomes a mother, has to give up every other part of her identity. That's *really* what all the second-wave feminists wanted."

"I thought they wanted help washing dirty diapers and control of the family finances." She grinned. "What does Marilyn French say? 'Shit and string beans.'"

Caitlin waved her hands dismissively. "That was just window dressing. What they wanted was to not just be"—she affected a child's high whine—"'mommy, mommy, mommy.'" In her arms, Ismael shuddered, deep and contented, and turned his face into Caitlin's chest. "Hey," Caitlin said in a soft voice. "Hey, little man."

"And now?" Sadie contemplated transferring Jack to his stroller. He would be reluctant. There would be tears. But he was too heavy to carry all the way home. Ed could do it, but not she.

"Now it's like the Eisenhower era all over again. They all *want* to be 'mommies.'" Her mouth slack with disgust, she gestured toward Vicky and her clan. "And, of course, big business likes it that way, 'cause they can sell them more stuff. There's, like, the whole mommy industry. You're not a *real* mom unless you have a four-hundred-dollar diaper bag and you go to Mommy and Me yoga at Jivamukti and you read 'mommy lit' and nurse your kid in a two-thousand-dollar ersatz midcentury modern rocking chair. You've seen all this, right?" Caitlin gave her a challenging look.

"Hmmm," said Sadie, rising and depositing Jack in the stroller. He immediately began to wail. "You know," she called to Caitlin, before she could think better of it, as she handed Jack his favorite toy, a wooden figurine of a Victorian policeman, found in the basement of their building and washed in hot water. "You should write a book."

"I should," said Caitlin, with such an air of entitlement—*Of course*

I should write a book, seeing as my thoughts are so profoundly original and penetrating—that Sadie immediately regretted giving her mouth over to the still-active editorial section of her brain.

"Read book," Jack called now, calmer. "Take nap."

"I've really got to get him home," said Sadie, turning to Caitlin, who sat, still, on the bench. "He's exhausted."

"We'll walk with you. Where do you guys live?"

"In Hillman," Sadie told her. "On Columbia Street."

"You're kidding." Caitlin stood and fell in step beside Sadie. "I'm right across the street. In the Amalgamated."

"*Really?* How funny that we've never seen each other before!"

"I usually walk up to Tompkins Square Park," Caitlin explained.

Ahead of Sadie and Caitlin, on the winding concrete path, the Orthodox mothers streamed out through the gate, their kids skipping alongside them, and turned east on Grand.

"How long have you lived here?" Caitlin asked as the gate clanged shut behind them. From the corner of her eye, Sadie could see Vicky waving. She was nice, really. Sadie waved back.

"Two years. A little less."

"We just got here in January. It's cheaper than Brooklyn now." Sadie was not sure that this was true, but she said nothing. "Do you have a two-bedroom? Or a three?" The layouts of the apartments in the area's buildings were all roughly the same—having been built by the same cooperative organization immediately before and after the war.

"Two," Sadie told her, again having the feeling that Caitlin already possessed this information, through Lil, and that these banal questions were leading somewhere, somewhere Sadie might not want to go. "What about you?"

"Our place is, like, a combined space. It's four one-bedrooms."

"That sounds great," said Sadie, fighting a discomfiting wave of jealousy.

"Yeah, it's a lot of space. And, you know, the apartments in the Amalgamated are so much nicer than in the other buildings—"

"*Really*," said Sadie. No, Caitlin had not changed.

"Yeah, I mean, because it's prewar. So the ceilings are higher and the windows are larger and we have great moldings. The other buildings, the apartments are so boxy. We looked at some when we were trying to buy."

"We like to think of it as Modernist," said Sadie, with a smile. She, of course, lived in one of those boxy apartments.

"But the guy who combined the places had the *worst* taste. It was like Boca, circa 1983. White leather couches. Pink tile floor. Mirrored doors on the closets."

"Bleh." Such decor was common in their buildings.

"*Yeah,*" said Caitlin. "*Really* bad. We're ripping everything out. Knocking down all the walls. It's been going on for*ever*."

Their apartment, Sadie realized, must be the one she'd heard everyone talking about: it was the first in the neighborhood to sell for more than a million dollars. The real estate section had done a story on it.

"Do you miss Williamsburg?" she asked suddenly. She herself still missed Brooklyn even after two years, though her old neighborhood was rapidly being invaded by hedge fund managers and suchlike, exactly the sort of people she'd moved there to avoid. Still, Dave and Emily and Beth were all there, and it would be nice to be around the corner from them again, especially now that Beth had Emma. But they couldn't afford it, not now, not yet. Everything that came in seemed to flow right back out again. They were still making huge payments each month on the credit cards Ed had used, in part, to finance his film. The money from the distribution deal—which had not been insubstantial—had gone right into his company, into the new film. The thing was: it didn't have to be this way. After Sundance, he'd been offered development deals with Fox and Paramount, but he'd—to Sadie's shock—turned them down. He didn't want, he explained, another *Boom Time* scenario. "That was a bad, bad time," he told her. "I woke up feeling like shit and it just got worse as the day went on." *I know,* she told him. *I understand.* And she did. He wanted control over his work. "I don't care about the money," he said. "If you do things right, the money will come." Thinking of this—his earnestness, the sound of his voice—she felt, suddenly, the weight of his absence. *Maybe,* she thought suddenly, *I should just pack us up and meet him in Sarajevo.*

Caitlin was talking about Williamsburg. Sadie had missed the answer to her own question. "But I was also glad to get out. By the time I left it had changed so much. It used to be a *real* neighborhood. Everyone was an artist. Now it's, like, filled with trust-fund kids and lawyers. Starbucks is trying to open a branch on Bedford."

"*No!*" Sadie shouted.

"Seriously," Caitlin nodded. "A Starbucks on Bedford." She sighed. "And the new people in the neighborhood are excited about it. That's the thing."

"But I'm sure the old-timers are protesting. Rob must be planning something, right?" Sadie was pleased she remembered the name of Caitlin's husband, though he hadn't ever bothered to remember hers.

"*Rob,*" Caitlin scoffed, rolling her eyes, "is in North Carolina solving the problems of displaced migrant farmworkers."

"North Carolina!" said Sadie, stunned—and strangely pleased—that she and Caitlin had somehow wound up in this same corner of Manhattan, their husbands off in distant regions, their babies cleaving to them alone. "But what about his prison project? What was it called?"

"PrisonBreak," Caitlin told her. "His old assistant took over for him. It's huge now. They have a staff of, like, twenty. And they're running Crown into the ground." She paused. "Lil didn't tell you? We're divorced."

"Oh," said Sadie, glancing down at Ismael, who, she saw, looked nothing, *of course,* like the pale, wormy Rob. She had heard this news, hadn't she, maybe? From Emily? Perhaps. "I'm so sorry."

"Ismael's not his," she said, following Sadie's glance. "He's Osman's. My partner."

"Oh," said Sadie, who had stopped short when she realized that— miracle of miracles—Jack had fallen asleep in his stroller.

"It's so funny," Caitlin went on. "When I married Rob I *thought* I was rebelling against my parents' bourgeois values, marrying an activist, you know? But I was really just buying into them. Marrying a rich Jew, just like they wanted. Not that they'd ever said so."

"Hmmm," said Sadie. She had grown tired of Caitlin and was unsure of what to do now that Jack was suddenly—and without any effort on Sadie's part—asleep. He hadn't fallen asleep in his stroller in months. Could she move him into his crib without waking him? Could she even stop walking? If so, she could buy a second cup of coffee and sit in the park and read.

"It all came out when I married Osman. They were furious. I'm so out of touch with them that I thought they'd be thrilled. He's a programmer. He works for, like, Google. Totally solid. But he's Pakistani." She pulled her sunglasses out of her stroller bag and clumsily slid them onto her face. "He worships Ed, you know. All those guys do."

"Wow," said Sadie, uncomfortably. "So what did his parents think?" She was interested against her will. "Were they okay with you?"

Caitlin nodded. "They're professors, just like my parents. Class is the great equalizer, right?"

"I suppose."

In silence, the women walked past Moishe's Bakery, gazing at the black-and-white cookies and prune hamantaschen in the window.

"So you're still in touch with Lil?" asked Caitlin as they reached the corner of Columbia Street, where they'd soon part ways.

Sadie shook her head. "No, not really. Not since she left Tuck."

"Me, too," she said, nodding her head solemnly. "We weren't as close after she got out of the hospital. She was really in a bad way."

"I was under the impression that there wasn't really anything wrong with her," said Sadie, keeping her gaze fixed ahead of her. "Emily saw her right after she was admitted and said she seemed fine. She was just upset about the miscarriage. And angry with Tuck." She could not prevent herself from narrowing her eyes at Caitlin. "Emily said she got worse in the hospital."

They had reached the entrance to Caitlin's building and stopped. "That's not how it seemed to me," she told Sadie, with a shrug. "And remember, I saw her a lot more than all of you did right before she got sick."

She wasn't sick, Sadie started to say, but before she could, Caitlin had cocked her head toward the archway leading into her building. "Do you want to come in?" she asked.

"Oh, no," said Sadie. "I really should get him home and try to put him in his crib." Caitlin pushed a lock of yellow hair behind her ear. "He can sleep in Ismael's crib." She gestured toward her son. "And you and I can have some coffee." A broad, almost loony smile suddenly sliced across her face. "Oh, and we have kittens! We just brought them home from the shelter. Do you remember our old cats? Those fat things." Sadie smiled faintly. She did indeed. "They died a year ago. All three within a month. It was like they had a pact." For a moment, her jaw softened. "I miss them. But the kittens are cute. If Jack wakes up, he can play with them!"

Sadie sighed and succumbed, as she'd known she would. She was too tired to argue. "That sounds great," she said, and followed Caitlin down the ramp, through the brick archway, across the pretty courtyard, with its oblong fountain, and into the small foyer of the building.

"The contractor's not here today," Caitlin explained as they trundled themselves into the small, clunky elevator. "So it shouldn't be too loud. The kitchen guy might be taking measurements or something, but he shouldn't bother us too much." The door closed loudly and Caitlin pressed the cracked black Bakelite button, the "4" long rubbed off its face. With a jolt, the ropes and pullies and gears started up their low thrum. The truth was, Sadie loved these buildings. Caitlin was right. They were the most beautiful in the neighborhood, modeled on a Parisian complex of the 1920s. Her own building, constructed some seven or eight years later, was a brute.

"Have you guys renovated?" Caitlin was asking her. "It's total hell. We have, like, twenty *guys*. The architect. The contractor." She began ticking them off her fingers. "The soundproofing guy. The cabinet guy. The stone guy. The concrete guy. The tile guy. The floor guy. The electrician. The plumber." Sadie nodded sympathetically, though her apartment still had the original 1948 kitchen, complete with a monstrous white BiltRite stove and painted oak cabinets that leaked sawdust onto her pots and pans. She had to wash everything before she used it. "It's not functional," Rose had cried two years earlier, when they'd cleaned out the apartment after Minnie's death, Sadie so pregnant she could barely bend over, and still with a month to go.

"I like it," Sadie had insisted. It seemed barbaric, somehow, to just come into the apartment in which Minnie had lived for fifty years, nearly half her life, and start ripping things up. But then there was also, again, the money. They didn't have forty grand on hand.

"No," she told Caitlin as they landed, with a jolt, on the fourth floor. "We haven't had any work done."

"It's such a pain dealing with all these people roaming around your house." Woefully, she jangled her key ring in the direction of the green metal door to the right of the elevator. "Osman leaves for work before they arrive and I'm supposed to tell them what to do—and I have *no idea*. He's used to ordering people around. He grew up with servants. But I just have no idea." A couple of short bangs and the low murmur of voices issued forth from the apartment. "Steve is here," Caitlin sighed, selecting a gold Medeco key, similar to Sadie's own, and inserted it into the dull brass lock. With a thwack the tumblers fell—and Jack's eyes popped open. For a moment it seemed as if he might close them again. Then his face contorted into a familiar expression—the silent scream, Ed called it—and it was clear things would not end so easily. The wail that followed seemed magnified a thousandfold by the hallway's stucco walls; and yet, somehow, Ismael slept on.

"Oh, baby," Sadie cried, as she struggled to unlatch the straps of the stroller. "You're so tired. My poor baby. We should have gone home." Jack in her arms, sobbing in great gulps, she followed Caitlin into a loftlike room of jaw-dropping size. Even Jack seemed stunned by the expanse of the space in which he found himself, for he immediately stopped crying, pointed to a wide floating staircase that presumably led to a second, lower floor, turned his face to Sadie, and said, "Oooooooh!" Large windows lined three walls. In one corner, the makings of a kitchen surrounded a short, whiskered man in paint-covered clothes, wrestling with a piece of wood.

"Hey, Steve," Caitlin called.

"Hey," he called back.

"We're just home for lunch. We won't get in your way."

Steve laughed. "I'm starving," he shouted. "What are we having?"

Caitlin shot Sadie a panicked look. "Well, actually, we're just going to have coffee, but Meera can find you something."

He laughed again. "I'm playing with you," he said, and returned to the obstinate slat of wood.

In another corner sat a long, rustic table, lined with austere metal chairs, and overhung with three small crystal chandeliers all in a row, the spindly, deconstructed sort they sold at ABC. On the far side of the staircase, south of the kitchen, two long, spare sofas faced each other. A pelt of some sort lay between them, cow or gazelle or perhaps some unidentifiable Western sort of beast. Near its head—or where its head would have been—a sole, uncomfortable-looking chair, seemingly made of twigs, presided over the room with a certain hauteur, as if daring anyone to sit on it. The rest of the space was bare, as were the windows. And the floor was not oak plank, like all the other apartments in the building, but a flat, uniform red. "Colored concrete," Caitlin told her. "It's the 'latest thing.'" She smirked, so Sadie might understand that she didn't care at all—of course—about the latest thing in interior design, but was, rather, making fun of herself for installing a trendy floor. "People are using it for kitchen counters, mostly, but our architect convinced us to do the floor. It was a fortune. I can't believe we did it."

"Down, down," said Jack, and ran off the minute his feet touched the ground, with which he seemed to be transfixed. He stared down at it, turning in circles, and trying to catch the eye of Steve, who was affixing a hinge to a cabinet door. From the bowels of the apartment came, quickly, the sound of flip-flopping sandals, followed by the emergence from the lower level of a dark, glossy, bowed head and a slender body, encased in faded jeans and a gauzy cotton tunic of the palest aqua.

"Hey," Caitlin said to the woman, who was very pretty, with large, dark eyes and a small, dimpled chin. Her thick black hair fell past her shoulders in heavy waves. "We're back." She gestured to Sadie. "This is my friend Sadie"—without meaning to, Sadie flinched at this description—"and her son, Jack. Do we have something for him to eat for lunch?"

"Sure," said the woman, with almost off-putting grace. "Meera," she said to Sadie, holding out a neatly made hand, which Sadie took in her own.

"Hi," she said. "Jack will eat anything, really. And if it's any trouble, we can—"

"It's no trouble at all," said Meera. With one swift move, she lifted Ismael out of his stroller and onto her shoulder, where his fat cheek slouched against the soft fabric of her shirt. "Come, Jack," she said, "do you want to help me put the baby in his crib? Then we'll have some nice stew?"

"Yes!" Jack cried, clambering down the stairs alongside her. "Baby!"

"So," said Caitlin, spreading her arms widely. "Grand tour. This is the upstairs. The kitchen, you can see, isn't completely functioning yet. We can go downstairs and have some coffee."

"Great," said Sadie, following her down the stairs, just as Jack trailed Meera up them, whispering "baby" and "sleep" to her as he passed. The lower floor was as close and cluttered as the first was spare and empty: a replica of a 1970s-style rec room, with two ship-sized couches, slunk low to the ground and clad in orange velveteen, a white woolen shag rug, built-in Danish-modern cabinets lined with books and CDs. One held a nook with a small bar sink, a drip coffeemaker, an electric kettle, and shelves of mugs, brandy glasses, and highballs. At the center of another was a large door, which she presumed hid a television. Caitlin, she thought, was the sort of person who would buy the largest television possible—then hide it. The room, long and narrow, divided in half by the staircase, and lined with doors that presumably led to bedrooms, was much less sunny than the great room upstairs, but far more cozy, and Caitlin seemed to relax once installed on an orange couch. Suddenly, Sadie felt sorry for her, padding around on her cold concrete floors. "Osman's a programmer?" she said, for lack of any other subject.

"Yeah," Caitlin told her, filling the coffeepot with water. "Back in, like, '95 he started this company with his friend Sal. He went to Reed. Everyone was doing things like that out there." From the refrigerator, she extracted a small brown bag of ground coffee and haphazardly dumped some into the filter. "No one I knew had even heard of the Internet." Sadie nodded. It was true. In 1995, all her friends had been in grad school or trying to be actors or writers or painters or directors. She'd worked in an office—a professional office, with fifty-plus employees—without a single computer, typing letters on an IBM Selectric. How strange all that seemed now.

"They developed these message-board-type things. You know, the software that makes them work. Eventually, Yahoo! bought the company for I don't know how much." She widened her eyes. "A *lot*."

"Hmmm," said Sadie. *If it was that much,* she wondered, *then why does he have a job?* But then, who knew? Maybe he'd lost it all in 2001. Maybe he liked to work.

"Sit," Caitlin instructed, as if she'd suddenly remembered that Sadie was there, that she wasn't just talking aloud to herself. She kicked off her sandals, grabbed a stray pencil from the bookshelf, twisted her hair into a knot, and settled back down on the couch. Obediently, Sadie seated herself on the opposite couch. "Do you mind if I smoke?" Caitlin asked.

"No, of course not," said Sadie, though she did.

"Good." Caitlin grinned. "That's one of the things about South Asians. They smoke their lungs out and drink like fiends. Americans are so puritanical. People give me the worst looks when I'm out with Ismael and I light up. I want to say to them, *Give me a break. I smoke like one cigarette a day.*" From the bookshelf above her head she extracted a yellow packet of American Spirits, pulled a cigarette out, lit it with a kitchen match, and inhaled deeply. The coffee machine let out a deep burble.

"Shall I pour?" Sadie asked, gratefully rising from the couch.

"Would you? That would be great."

The coffee, Sadie could see, was too weak—an amber color, almost like tea.

"Is it okay?" Caitlin called.

"Yes, fine," Sadie lied, pouring the stuff into two of the little mugs.

"It's good coffee, so you can drink it black," Caitlin informed her.

"Great," said Sadie, and passed her a mug.

"So where did you deliver?" Caitlin asked.

Sadie had been waiting for this question. Normally, when she met new mothers, this was the first thing they wanted to talk about. "Roosevelt."

"New York Hospital," Caitlin told her. "How was Roosevelt? I almost went there. I wanted to do the Birthing Center, at first."

Sadie shrugged. "It was okay. I had kind of a hard labor. Back labor—"

"Me, too!"

"It's awful, isn't it?"

Caitlin nodded. "Did you do the epidural?" This seemed to be the second question all new mothers asked her.

"I did." She wished she hadn't. But it was all so far in the past now—the vivid reality of Jack trumping the twelve hours in which he'd fought his way out of her body—that she didn't feel like explaining how it had stopped her labor, so that she'd then had to be given Pitocin, and on and on.

"Me, too," said Caitlin. "I'd always thought I wanted to give birth at home, in a tub, with a midwife. And then, you know, I was going to do the Birthing Center. But then I thought if I was going to deliver in a hospital, I might as well go the whole medical route. Demerol. Epidural. Whatever they could give me."

Sadie supposed Caitlin thought natural childbirth part and parcel of the Plot Against Women. *Why should we suffer when we don't have to? It's not natural, it's medieval.* She'd heard these arguments before, from her mother.

"I kept thinking about Lil," said Caitlin, "as I was lying there, waiting to push."

Enough, thought Sadie. "Why?" she asked.

"Well, it just seemed so ironic. I'm in New York Hospital, having a baby, and, like, a year before, Lil was in the exact same place having a miscarriage. It just seemed so unfair. She wanted kids more than anything." She shook her head in a cinematic gesture of sadness and took a sip of coffee. "This needs cream," she whispered, and sprung, catlike, from the sofa. "I suppose you know how it turned out," she said, striving to sound casual, as she strode across the room. "With Tuck. And me."

Unconsciously, Sadie let loose a deep breath. That's where all this had been leading. Of course. Who thought about a friend's miscarriage on the delivery table? No one. Caitlin simply wanted someone with whom she could talk about Tuck. "Cream?" Caitlin asked, holding out a carton of organic half-and-half.

"Sure," she said, though the coffee was beyond hope.

Caitlin sat back down, sipped loudly, then gave Sadie a serious look. "He was the love of my life," she said. *Oh God,* thought Sadie. *Why today?* "I know you think it was just about sex." Sadie did not correct this notion. "I think, at first, it may have been purely sexual, for Tuck, at least. But it never was for me. From the minute I met him, I *knew*." This was all sounding a bit too Danielle Steel for Sadie's tastes. *Knew what?* she wanted to ask, not because she actually cared but because she couldn't stand Caitlin presuming that she understood what she meant, that Sadie, too, had had some moment, with some man, probably not her husband, when she "knew"; when, in fact, her life—contrary to her adolescent expectations—had been a series of accumulated moments, of knowing bits and pieces at different times and hoping they would add up to some knowledge that would be useful to her, and feeling different conflicting things, and trying to suss out the difference between love and friendship, between trouble and desire, and between love and desire (that was the tricky one, as everyone *knew*). She did not believe, most certainly did not believe in the one moment of "I knew." Moreover, she didn't—did she?—want to hear about whatever had happened between Caitlin and Tuck.

"It was never going to work, of course. Even if he hadn't had Lil and I hadn't had Rob. Tuck's one of those guys who's afraid of happiness, you know? Who feels like he can't be happy, like he doesn't deserve it, so he always has to do something to wreck it. He *always* has to fuck things up." She lit another cigarette from the first and took a loud sip of coffee. "And it didn't last that long, the sex part. It was just too *agonizing,* doing that to Lil. He loved her, really, but he loved her *intellectually*. And he was incredibly protective of her. But he still craved women who were *different*. Wilder."

Oh, please, thought Sadie. *Wilder*. Which meant what, exactly? That she'd cheat on her husband? Watch porn? Take it up the ass? *What?* That she bought into his overblown ideas of his own coolness? But then this was Caitlin talking, not Tuck. She was speaking, of course, of *her* overblown ideas of her own coolness.

"Lil probably told you. I know she knew. It was so obvious. When he and Lil would go to parties, he would play this game with her where she'd have to pick out the woman he'd most like to sleep with, *other than her,* of course. He always said *other than her*. If she guessed wrong, he'd go and talk to the right woman. If she guessed right, he wouldn't."

"*Really,*" said Sadie. Was this true? Lil had never told her anything like this, anything of cruelty on this level, though she'd heard certain things from Emily, things Lil had said in the hospital, but she'd discounted them as exaggerations, as the product of depression and grief. Just as she'd struggled to forget her knowledge of his affair with Caitlin, so that she might forge on with her friendship with Lil. She should have told her. She should have. Their friendship had died anyway. She took a sip of coffee and found herself unable to swallow it.

"It's not a big deal," said Caitlin. "He didn't sleep with them. After me, he decided he couldn't do that anymore." *Right,* thought Sadie. "Sex made him feel too vulnerable." The sour smell of the coffee was making Sadie slightly ill. She had to get rid of it—immediately—and nearly ran to the little sink beside Caitlin to dump it out.

"Oh, don't do that!" Caitlin cried. "Meera will do it."

On cue, the girl's feet, in their slim, silvery sandals, appeared on the stairs. "Hello," she called. "We've come to see the kittens."

"Mama, Mama, Mama," called Jack, appearing behind her. "Cat. Cat. See kitty cat."

Sadie had forgotten about the kittens. Where were they, exactly? Locked in some special kittenproof room?

"Hi, sweetie," she said, pulling Jack into her arms. "Did you have a good lunch?"

"Yes," he said, wriggling free from her grasp and grabbing Meera's slender fingers. "Meera." He gave her a mischievous look, then collapsed into giggles. "*Mee*-rah." In his right hand he held a squat, creamy plastic ring rattle, filched from Ismael.

"So," Sadie said, clapping her hands together, "let's see these kittens."

"All *right,*" said Meera, with a smile. "They're just in here." She opened a door at the back of the rec room and let them into a small, bright laundry room.

"They were living in the courtyard," Caitlin explained. "This group of cats. One day, I rounded them up and brought them all over to the animal shelter in Williamsburg." *Oh God,* thought Sadie. Those cats had been in the courtyard her whole life. An old man who lived on Bialystoker Place left food out for them. When it got cold, they squeezed into the basement of the Amalgamated through an exhaust pipe and the janitors took care of them.

Meera nodded approvingly. "It's a no-kill shelter," she added.

"Yes," said Caitlin. "I was filling out the paperwork and one of them started making strange noises."

"She was giving birth," said Sadie. She'd read enough *Little House on the Prairie* to know what happens when an animal starts making strange noises.

"Yes," Caitlin cried. "There were six just like this. All spotted. They were so small, like mice. I wanted to take them home, but the woman at the shelter said they had to stay with their mom for at least two weeks. We brought these two home last week. The rest have been adopted." She snorted. "Two weeks! Imagine if we let these guys"—she gestured to Jack and, Sadie thought, Meera—"out into the world at two weeks."

These words, somehow, caused a sob to lodge in Sadie's throat. *Two weeks*. She turned to Jack, to see if he had registered Caitlin's meaning, if her words had frightened him, but he was engrossed in the kittens, his blond head level with theirs. He was good with animals, she thought proudly. "You have cats, right, Jack," she said. She turned to Meera and Caitlin. "We have two. When we adopted them they were as small as these guys. Now they're huge. Fat." In Rose's view, the cats were "morbidly obese," but Sadie couldn't worry too much about this. They were sweet cats, friendly and good with people, more like dogs, really. They flopped down on the floor and begged to be petted. And they never scratched. *I'm good,* she thought, the unexpected swell of emotion still lodged somewhere in her chest. *I'm a good person. I am,* she thought. *I am.* She had made them gentle, all three of them, the cats and Jack. She had done—was doing—something.

"Cat," said Jack, attempting to pet all the kittens at once. "Cat."

"One at a time, sweetie." Sadie turned to Caitlin. "What are their names?"

"Actually, we haven't decided yet. So he can just call them 'cat' if he wants to."

"*Cat,*" said Jack, laughing. "Cat cat."

"Mama, look." He turned to face her, but the white toy obscured his face; it was not a toy, of course, but a bottle, filled with something thick and white.

"Is that?" she asked, pointing.

"I hope it's okay," said Meera. Her accent was British, precise, soothing. "It's one percent milk. Organic. He's not allergic? He seemed to—" She patted herself on the chest. "He was—"

Sadie nodded. "I know."

"But I thought that couldn't be right, because American children, I know, are off the breast before a year, usually. But he was just kind of *grabbing*—" She pressed her lips into a polite little smile.

"I know, I know," said Sadie again. "It's fine, really. He needs to drink milk. He's not wanted to. It's good."

"Oh, good," said Meera. "He actually didn't know what to do with it when I first gave it to him. But I think he likes it." Jack nodded, the bottle still in his mouth. "I know he's too old for a bottle, but we don't have any sippy cups yet."

"It's fine. Really, it's fine," Sadie told her. "He'd never take it from me. A bottle. Or milk, either. I actually lied to the doctor at his last checkup, said he drank it. So it's good, really. He's growing up." She knelt beside him and gave him a kiss on the cheek—and he threw his free hand around her neck. "Good," he said. "Good."

"Yes, it's good, right?" she asked him.

"Yes," he said. "Good."

And so it was.

fifteen

S adie stopped visiting the new playground after that day. Instead, she took Jack to the play area in her own building's courtyard, which was older and smaller, but closer and, she discovered, friendlier. As such, it was more than a year before she saw Caitlin again. By that time Lil was dead and the world had, slowly and irrevocably, become a darker place than any of them could have imagined.

Each day some fresh horror arose: The train bombings in Madrid. The endless car bombings and suicide bombings in Iraq and Pakistan and Israel and Afghanistan, with their roster of civilian victims (children; always children). The Vietnam-style rapes and massacres of Iraqi families—and the accompanying photos of the sweet-faced Virginia boys who'd perpetrated them. The kidnappings, all over the Middle East and North Africa, of journalists and contractors and translators. The beheadings— videotaped, aired on television—in Iraq. Everywhere, everything was wrong, wrong, wrong.

And then the prison scandals broke, in the spring, as Sadie waddled uneasily around Grand Street, waiting for her water to break, Jack impatient with her slow gait. In the hospital—her wide window overlooking the Hudson, Mina asleep in a clear bassinet beside the bed—she flipped open *The New Yorker* and found a photo that made her breath stop: a man, barely recognizable as such, balanced precariously on a brown carton, his head covered with a black, conelike hood, his body draped in a black blanket, his arms spread wide, wires sprouting from his fingers. "Oh my God," she said aloud, and slammed the magazine shut, her heart racing. But she read the article—after a bracing cup of coffee—and all those that followed, forcing herself (why? why?) not to skip over the details of the acts of torture ("sodomizing a detainee with a chemical light") or the leering, abhorrent faces of the officers, their thumbs jubilantly raised, like frat boys after a beer run.

Back home, in their still-unrenovated apartment, lead paint chipping off the cabinets, ancient stove chugging ever on, Mina sleeping with her and Ed, Jack waking at five and crawling in with them, too, Sadie found herself unable to sleep past dawn. Each day she rose and shuffled wearily to the kitchen, put on the water for her coffee, and snapped on the news. She needed, now, to know, just as, in those first years of Jack's life, she'd needed *not* to know, left the paper to yellow on the coffee table. "The world is a dark, horrifying place," Ed told her. "You're totally right. But you've got to try to *filter* a little. Or you're going to go crazy."

"I know," she said. She had been thinking the same thing herself. "I just feel like it's only a matter of time before something else happens." Something big, something bad, something *close*. "And I just feel like I have to pay attention."

Come August, the Republican convention arrived—and the security-alert level for the city was raised to "orange." Ed's offices, in Chelsea, were dangerously close to the Garden, where the convention was being held. "Stay home," she said, the first day of the convention, trying not to let her tone belie the extent to which she truly *needed* him to heed her.

"I can't," he said. "I'm swamped." He was once again going to Toronto—with a little DV thing he'd produced, sort of postapocalyptic—and frantically making final cuts to the Bosnia film in order to make the Sundance deadline. There were a million other projects, too, so many she could no longer keep track.

"I know," she said, wrapping her arms around him. He was no longer the skinny guy she'd met—strange to think—six years ago at Lil's wedding. She'd thought him so old then—thirty. Younger than she was now. After they'd moved in together, she'd discovered that he primarily subsisted on breakfast cereal. "I'm sorry. I'm crazy."

And perhaps she was: by lunchtime, the pundits had issued an all-clear. October, they said, was the time to worry about, the month when everything Sadie feared might start up: suicide bombings (why *hadn't* they happened here yet, she often wondered), train and bus and car bombings, September eleventh–style attacks, the scope of which would be impossible to envision or foresee or *stop*.

"Why October?" she asked, the next day, as she and Ed sat on the couch, trying to wake up, Mina nursing, Jack dropping his blocks, one by one, into Sadie's chipped Dutch oven. From the kitchen, their old radio, one of Aunt Minnie's relics, droned. "It seems so random."

"The elections," said Ed. "It's right before the elections."

"But we're not going to *cancel* the elections. And why would they care who wins? We're all imperialist scum to them, right?"

"Yep," said Ed, scanning the Metro section. "Godless pornographers."

"Do you think it's still okay for Jack to go to school?" asked Sadie.

They had decided, in light of Mina's arrival, to send him to a new preschool on Avenue A two mornings per week. Ed would drop him off on his way to the office.

"Why wouldn't it be?" His tone annoyed her. He knew why. Of course he did.

"I don't know. In case something happens." She knew she sounded foolish. "Remember on September eleventh, how difficult it was for families to find each other." She still, she suspected, harbored a bit of unfair resentment that she'd been alone on that day, alone with Jack, her friends across the river in Brooklyn, her parents uptown, all of them unreachable, that she'd been reduced to knocking on Vicky's door and collapsing, shocked, into one of her dining room chairs, Jack in her arms.

"Nothing's going to happen," said Ed, smoothing the hair off her forehead.

But something *had* happened, she discovered when she put Mina in her crib and went back to the kitchen. In Russia, Chechen separatists—with possible links to al-Qaeda, but then they said that about shoplifters these days—had taken hold of a school. Hundreds of parents and children had been herded into a gym, trip wired with homemade bombs. Already, they'd killed twenty men—the strongest, the youngest—and thrown their bodies out the windows. It was hot and the terrorists refused to allow the hostages any water. Children, Russian authorities worried, might be dying of dehydration.

"There are babies in there," she told Ed, her voice cracking. "Babies Mina's age."

"Okay, we're going to turn off the radio now," he said, striding into the kitchen and doing exactly that. "I'm staying home today." He came back into the living room and took Sadie in his arms.

"No, you—"

"And we're going to get dressed and get some breakfast and go to the park."

"Can we go to *Seward* Park?" asked Jack, hugging her legs. He'd become incredibly possessive of her lately. "Don't kiss Mommy," he told Ed. "Don't talk to Mommy."

"Sure, we can go to Seward Park," said Ed.

"Why does this keep happening? It's going to happen here."

"What, Mommy?" asked Jack.

"It's not going to happen here," said Ed, though she knew he didn't believe that.

"It *has* happened here. Columbine."

"That was different," said Ed. He stood and stretched, revealing the black hairs on his stomach. "You know that." He pulled her back against him and lowered his voice, speaking into her hair. "Terrorists are not going to storm the My Little Village preschool on Avenue A." Something prevented her from admitting that this was true. "I think you guys should come to Toronto with me."

"Okay," she agreed, though she didn't want to. It would be she running around after Jack and endlessly nursing Mina, she calling strangers to see if they could babysit.

"And I'm going to put the paper on hold. I read it online anyway."

"Okay," she said, trying to inject a bit of lightness into her voice.

But in the end it didn't matter. When the bad news arrived, it came the way bad news always does: with a phone call at an odd hour. It had been so long since Sadie had spoken to Emily that, for a moment, in her pleasure, she forgot that five in the morning was a bit too early for a catch-up call.

"So, I have some really strange news," came her friend's voice, unquavering. "It's hard to believe."

And somehow—in the sort of flash she'd read about in countless hackneyed novels, novels she'd rejected without a further thought—she knew that it was Lil, that something had happened to Lil, that it was over, there would be no tense reunion, there would be no triumph over Tuck, that this was the end. *No,* she told herself. *Don't be stupid, Sadie.* "Okay," she said, her voice still hoarse with sleep. Emily's, she realized, was not. "What happened? What is it?"

"Lil," said Emily, and Sadie's heart began to thrum like a machine. She'd known, she'd known, she'd known, and this was, somehow, her fault, for *she had known,* even before the call came. All this worry she'd been extending toward her family, her city, the world. It should have been focused on Lil. Lil was the doomed one, the one she needed to watch. If she'd been more tolerant, more forgiving. If she'd paid more attention, if she hadn't canceled the paper, if she'd made more allowances for Tuck and his book, if her obligation had been, first, to Lil, and second to her company, her position, her idea of herself as an arbiter of culture, if she had been less *hard,* hard and unforgiving and inflexible, just like her mother. She'd missed Lil, missed her terribly—the energy and vitality she brought to even the smallest of things; her *sharp*ness, or whatever it was, *her,* she'd missed *her*—though she wouldn't admit it, and couldn't reconcile with her. Why? Why? Because she had been afraid of Lil, she remembered, afraid of Lil's capacity to swallow her friends whole, to suck them into the vortex of her life.

No, no, no—what was the truth?—that she had been increasingly vexed by the complications of Lil's life, the endless dramas and intrigues, the scrutiny of every interaction, the constant threat of histrionics, the narcissism. At the end, the months in which their friendship faded to black, Lil had contemplated an affair with a supposed friend of Tuck's, some guy from the neighborhood, a would-be screenwriter with a soul patch and trucker hat. It had all been too much for Sadie, all this talk of lust, "connection," of Lil's boredom and frustration with Tuck. *Just deal with it,* Sadie had longed to say, *we're* all *bored and frustrated*. Who was Lil to think that her life could be perfect, that she was exempt from the compromises her friends—everyone in the world—had been forced to make in order to maintain some semblance of happiness, of sanity, in order to live a productive life, a meaningful life? How had Sadie been so hard? How, and why? Lil had been so unhappy. And it had—she had forced herself not to think of this—been her fault, in part. If she had said something about Caitlin and Tuck, the affair, those years ago, could she have prevented everything that ensued? No, Ed would say, *had* said, when she'd told him about it. But it was easy for him to say.

"This is hard to believe," said Emily, exhaling heavily, "but Lil has"—she paused—"Lil died. This morning. Lil is dead."

"What?" said Sadie, trying, she realized, to sound as though she were surprised. "What happened?"

"I'm not actually sure," said Emily. "It seems like she had the flu."

"The *flu*?" said Sadie. She'd expected the back-alley assault, the drunken car wreck, the hijacked plane. "She died of *the flu*? What happened? That seems impossible."

"I know," said Emily impatiently. "They're doing an autopsy." She paused. "Can we talk more later? We took her to the hospital and I've been up all night. I've got to call Beth and Dave. They don't know yet."

"I can call everyone. Go to bed."

"I think we should really try to get in touch with Tal. He would want to know."

"I can call Tal."

"And Tuck." Emily sucked in her breath, then made an odd sound, like a bark. "Oh my God, Tuck doesn't know. Tuck."

"I can call Tuck. Go to bed."

"I don't know if I can sleep," admitted Emily. "I just can't believe this."

"Lie down," Sadie instructed her. "I'll call everyone." A terrible thought struck her. "Do her parents know?"

Emily sighed. "Yeah. They're flying in. They knew she was sick. Her dad told her to go the hospital. I thought he was overreacting." The sound—strangled, guttural—came again and Sadie realized that Emily was crying. "Imagine how they feel. I keep looking at Sarah and thinking what it would be like to lose her."

"Oh my God, Emily, *stop*," said Sadie, though she'd certainly thought such things about Jack and Mina. "Stop thinking about it. Get into bed and try to get some sleep. I'll call everyone."

That afternoon Sadie met Emily and Beth—and their children—at her parents' house, just as (they all tried not to say) they had six years earlier, before Lil and Tuck's wedding. How long ago that seemed, how impervious they'd thought themselves to the pedestrian dangers of adult life. It had seemed a game to them, Lil's marriage, a lark. How stupid they had been.

"Is Dave coming?" Beth asked.

"I don't think so," said Sadie. "He had studio time booked. You know, he's recording this solo EP."

"He couldn't cancel?" asked Rose.

"He thought it might make him feel better not to miss it."

"*God*," said Beth, her face growing red. "What is *wrong* with him?" Her voice was rising. "He's such an asshole. Lil is *dead*."

Rose shook her head. "What about Tal?" she asked. "I always liked Tal."

"*Tal*," Emily scoffed.

"He's flying in," said Sadie. "He said he'll call when he gets in."

"Well, it's good he's coming," said Rose. "Lil was so fond of him."

"Lil was *in love* with him," said Emily.

"No, she wasn't," said Sadie.

"I always liked Tal," said Rose.

"No, you *didn't*," moaned Sadie. She had no patience for her mother today. Mina had been up all night, nursing every hour. She was teething, most likely, which meant that she wouldn't sleep tonight either.

"Well," said Rose, shooting her daughter a warning look. "I can't imagine what her parents are going through right now." With a sigh, she poured chamomile tea from her large white pot into the thin, flowered cups she'd laid out on the coffee table, never mind the three kids toddling along its edge, wooden peg people clutched in their hands.

"Are they here?" Beth asked.

Emily nodded. "They're staying out on the Island. With Lil's uncle. Remember? The religious one?" They looked round at one another, from their seats on the Peregrines' worn brown couches, their eyes bleary and slitted with shock. Yes, they nodded, they remembered Lil's stories about Passover at this uncle's house, the eight-hour seders.

"We offered them a room," Rose explained, "and said they could have the house for shiva. But they said they wanted to stay with family. She's going to be buried on the Island."

"They're bitter," said Sadie, picking up her cup.

"Of course they are, dear," Rose replied. "They just lost their only child." But, as usual, her mother had missed her point: that the Roths thought New York had killed their daughter. If Lil had stayed home and gone to UCLA, none of this would have happened. Lil would be piddling around the kitchen of a hacienda-style ranch in the Palisades, marinating chicken for fajitas, a Honduran nanny minding her baby, while she waited for her husband to pull up in his glossy BMW, bright silk tie loosened around his neck.

"They blame *us*," Sadie said to her mother, her voice rising more than she wanted it to.

"No, they don't," said Rose. "Trust me. They have enough on their minds. They're not thinking about you."

"Mom," said Sadie, throwing her hands up in the air, causing Mina, balanced upright on her lap, to laugh, Buddha-like. She was a chubby baby, a better sleeper than Jack—until recently, at least—with thick dark hair just starting to curl. Already, Sadie could see that Rose preferred her. Rose had no use for boys. "They're not even letting us come to the funeral."

"What?" said Beth. "What are you talking about?"

Rose nodded. "Dr. Roth has decided the funeral is just for family."

"You're kidding," said Beth. "But we loved her. We took care of her."

"They're letting us plan a service for her," said Sadie, her throat tightening. "Here, in the city. For her friends. I was just about to tell you."

"Letting us?" said Emily. In the room's far corner, her daughter, Sarah, red hair in wispy pigtails at the top of her head, haphazardly loaded squat plastic figurines into Jack's plastic pirate ship, which Jack then silently resituated. "Do we need their permission to have a memorial service for our friend?"

"No," Rose told her sharply, and with a tsking sound. "But she's their child and you need to respect their wishes. They're devastated. You need to have some sympathy. My *God*."

"We *do*, Mom," said Sadie, chastened.

Rose took a loud sip of tea. "Honestly, if they blame anyone, it's Tuck." The girls looked at one another. They blamed Tuck, too, but they wouldn't say so aloud. "And why shouldn't they? A girl like Lil, with that sort of high-strung personality, should have married someone who was willing to take care of her. Someone like Will or Ed." *If only you knew,* thought Sadie. "Someone solid and responsible. Tuck wasn't that sort of person. Tuck only thinks about Tuck."

The girls nodded, their faces tilted toward their teacups, for there was blame in Rose's words, as though Lil's death was the result of her poor judgment all those years ago. And, yet, somehow, it *was,* wasn't it?

"But wasn't it all a question of timing?" asked Beth suddenly. Emma swiveled her neck and looked at her mother questioningly. "If he'd sold his book earlier—"

"And turned it in on time," muttered Sadie.

"And turned it in on time," conceded Beth, "before the bubble burst. Then it might have been really big. And they would have had more money and there wouldn't have been such a strain on their marriage."

"Maybe," said Rose Peregrine. "Maybe not. Nobody ever has enough money."

"If they'd met *now*," said Beth, ignoring her, "everything would have been different." The girls nodded uneasily. Tuck had finally made a name for himself by breaking a big story about forced labor in the South— something he'd uncovered while, irony of ironies, attending Rob Green-Gold's second wedding in remotest Georgia. He was writing a book on the subject, for a good deal more money than he had the first.

Or maybe he's just an asshole, Sadie thought, but said, instead, "We should talk about the service."

"Yes," said Rose. She was anxious, Sadie knew, to get down to the cool labor of planning, the ticking off of items on her list. Sadie hadn't asked for her help, but she was grateful for it. "I've called Emanu-El and we can do it there, if you girls want. In the chapel."

"Okay," said Sadie. "Thanks."

"That's perfect," said Beth.

"I think, first, we need to make a list of everyone who should know about this and then, from that, who might want to speak. I assume you girls. And Dave. Maybe one of her professors?"

"George Wadsworth," said Beth. "If he can fly in."

"Whoever," said Rose. "Just keep it short. And then we need to think about food." This was what really interested Rose. "We'll lay it out in the library. Do you want to do lox and bagels? Or you can just have cold cuts. And people can make sandwiches. And do you want to have wine?"

"Isn't it kind of strange to have food?" asked Sadie. "Are people really going to want to eat?"

"Sadie, it's just what's *done*," sighed Rose. "Grief makes people hungry."

"Lox and bagels," said Emily, putting her hand on top of Sadie's. "Let's do that."

"All right." Rose smiled. "I'll call Russ & Daughters and order platters. You girls start on your list."

But there were children to attend to, children getting bored and fussy and tired and wanting to be taken to the park or home for dinner and a bath and bed, and so they wrestled them into sweaters and jackets and strapped them into strollers and carriers, and kissed Rose good-bye, promising they would return tomorrow, list in hand, and start making phone calls. Rose's housekeeper, Olga, could watch the kids.

"I would really think about making those calls tonight," Rose said as the girls maneuvered their charges down the front steps.

"Okay, okay, Mom, we'll make them tonight," said Sadie, over Mina's rising wail. "I've got to walk," she told the others crossly, the minute the door clicked shut. "This child is exhausted."

"Let's walk," agreed Emily. "We can go down to Sixty-third and get the F."

Slowly, they made their way across Ninety-second Street, three women and four children, past the narrow wooden houses that Sadie had loved so as a child—the only such in Manhattan—and around the streams of other young mothers, their blonde heads arced over thin cell phones, and diminutive matrons walking small, fluffy dogs, and children, flocks of children, gray and blue and scarlet uniforms visible beneath their open coats. It was four o'clock, but it felt, Beth said, much later, for the sky had grown dark and thick with clouds, just as it had six years earlier, when Lil had married. On Sadie's chest, Mina had fallen asleep, her dark head lolling onto her small shoulder. "The autopsy should be done by now, right?" Sadie asked quietly, turning her head toward Emily.

"Should be," Emily agreed. "They'll call the Roths."

"Not you? Because you were there with her?"

Emily shook her head. "Next of kin."

"So what exactly happened?" asked Beth, in a thin, strangled voice. She did not, Sadie thought, really want to know the answer. Typical Beth.

"I don't know," Emily told her. "She had the flu—you know, fever, chills, bad cough. And it didn't go away. She called me and asked if we knew a clinic she could go to—you know, she didn't have insurance. And we gave her a couple of names, doctors who have a sliding scale. But we weren't worried. People always get sick when the seasons change, and there's a really bad flu going around this year. They're saying everyone should get vaccinated."

"Yeah, I already did," said Beth.

"Yeah, so, I guess she decided to ask a neighbor of hers, who's, I think, a doctor at a homeless shelter, for advice—"

"Oh, no," groaned Sadie.

"And she told Lil that she just had the flu, that she didn't need antibiotics. She should take echinacea and vitamin C and rest. And then she started having trouble breathing and she got scared. She called us and we took her to the hospital. They said it was pneumonia—"

"Of course!" said Sadie furiously.

"—and they started giving her antibiotics and fluid, but she still just looked awful, and a few hours later—" Her voice, all of a sudden, became something akin to a choke and she stopped dead, in front of an optician's shop, the window filled with glittering frames. "I don't know," she said. "I don't know what happened. I don't understand. They're saying maybe the hantavirus. She's been sick so much this year. But I just—" She began, quietly, to cry. "How could she have died? She had the *flu*." Beth grabbed her sobbing friend and began sobbing herself, her tears forming a dark spot on Emily's blue coat. Bewildered, their daughters stared at them, eyes wide, then, as one, burst into tears themselves. Sadie quickly put the brake on Jack's stroller, thinking, *We're blocking the sidewalk,* and knelt before the two little girls, Mina's head bobbing against her chest, and kissed their soft, rosy cheeks and held their small, cold hands and stroked their silky heads, until Jack called, "Mama, Mama," and she turned him to face the girls, arranging the strollers in a little huddle. "It's okay," she told the children. "Everything is fine. We're just a little sad. But it's nothing for you to worry about." They looked at her silently, their eyes huge as only children's eyes can be. "It's nothing to do with you," she told them, wishing she could tell herself the same thing.

In the chapel, they decided, they would have seasonal bouquets with blush roses, which were Lil's favorite, and large daisies and hydrangeas. Nothing funereal, like calla lilies, which Lil had hated. As a child, she'd been a flower girl in a stylish Los Angeles wedding, in which all the attendants wore black and carried a single stem of the white, waxy flower. "Very eighties," she'd told them in college, when they'd talked about the awful weddings they'd attended—and what their own weddings might be like, *if* they ever married, which Lil insisted she would not. They'd spoken of funerals, too, after reading *The Loved One* in their British Modernism class. They'd all agreed that the American way of death—to use Jessica Mitford's term, for they'd all read that book, too, and *loved* it—was appalling: pumping the body full of embalming fluid and caking the face with makeup. Being Jewish, they had a particular dread of wakes, which none except Sadie had ever actually attended. "It's creepy," Lil had said. "Why would you want to look at a dead body. The *person* is gone."

"It's a primitive ritual." Sadie had shrugged. "Kind of barbarian. But it gives people a sense of closure. That's why they do it. They feel like they've had the chance to say good-bye." Lil had rejected this notion as thoroughly bourgeois, based on a misguided attachment to the material. She was all for cremation.

"I'd want my ashes scattered, too," she said.

"Where?" asked Tal.

She considered. "I'm not sure. Someplace that had some sort of significance in my life. But I don't know where."

"Not going to happen," Tal had said. "You're Jewish. You have to be buried intact, wrapped in a cotton shroud, in a plain pine box."

And this was exactly how she would be buried, on Monday afternoon, following the service. The body had arrived that morning and was sitting in a funeral parlor in Roslyn. The funeral would not, Mrs. Roth had explained, take place within the two days specified by Jewish law, because of the autopsy and because of the large number of family and friends traveling in for the service and funeral. Sadie, who had somehow become the Roths' contact, had refrained from mentioning that Lil would have preferred cremation. "What does it matter, right?" Emily said. "It's horrible, but the funeral, all this, it's for the living, isn't it?"

Monday morning came quickly, as gray as the days that preceded it. The group rose early, dressing carefully in their most sober garments—

"navy, gray, dark brown," Rose had instructed them tersely, "black is just for the family"—and hurrying up to the synagogue to get things ready. Emily and Beth brought their little girls over to Sadie's this time, where the neighbor's nanny would tend to them, for a king's ransom. Jack would go home with a friend after school. "Can we get coffee?" Emily asked, as they rode the long escalator up from the Sixty-third Street subway stop. "I feel like I'm about to fall apart." And so they stopped at a bakery and bought tall cups of coffee and oversized, sticky Danish, which they ate in big, greedy bites in the synagogue's downstairs function room, while they waited for the platters of fish and bagels to arrive. Rose was right, grief made them hungry. When the trays arrived, at nine forty-five—after the florist had installed her bouquets in the chapel, and the wine and beer and soda had been arranged to Rose's liking, the bartender Rose had insisted on hiring installed at his perch—they gazed at them longingly. "It's okay to pick," said Rose, folding a piece of sable into her mouth. "But we need to slice the bagels." Like sleepwalkers, the girls obeyed, wondering where Dave might be—he had promised to arrive at nine—and why, it seemed, men were excused from all the nasty bits of life. Their husbands, all three, had gone to work, promising to meet them at the service.

At ten thirty Dave materialized, in a rumpled gray suit, at the back of the chapel as Emily tested the microphone. "My God," she boomed. "Where have you been?" He walked toward her. "What can I do?" he asked. "Nothing," she said, with, she was surprised to find, a laugh. "It's all done."

"Okay," he said. "I'm going to run outside then," which meant, she knew, that he was going to have a cigarette; he was the only one who still smoked, though Lil had taken the habit up again after she separated from Tuck. "Is Tal here?" She shook her head. "I'll come with you," she said. In the foyer, they found Beth and Sadie, hopping from foot to foot on their black heels.

"We're trying to figure out if we're supposed to greet everyone as they arrive," said Sadie, by way of a greeting. "Or just let them come in and find their seats."

"That sounds like a problem for Mrs. Rose Peregrine," said Dave.

"It might be better," came a voice behind them, "to just let everyone sit down."

And there, lit from behind by the pale sun that leaked in through the synagogue's glass doors, stood Tal, though it took them all a moment before they recognized him. He'd grown a beard, long and full, and his hair fell to his shoulders, curling around and over his collar. He was dressed, to use Rose's term, like a Bible salesman, in black wool trousers and a white dress shirt, his jacket flung over his arm. "Someone from the shul can stand out here and direct people. You guys—we all—can just go in and sit down."

His friends looked at one another.

"Hey, man," Dave called, grabbing his arm as if they'd seen each other three days and not three years earlier.

"Oh my *God,*" said Emily, running over and embracing him. "Tal, you freak. Oh my God. I can't believe it's you. The famous Tal Morgenthal. When did you get in?"

But before he could answer—before he could say hello to Dave or Beth or Sadie, who could barely bring herself to look at him—the door opened again, and a cadre of low voices interrupted them. "I guess we should get in there," said Dave. Sadie nodded. She had, the girls saw, gone almost green. "I don't want to talk to anyone until after," she said, almost, they thought, *hysterically.* "I just don't."

Quickly, the pews began to fill. They had thought they would only need a few rows of the space, but it seemed now that they might fill it. Lil *had* been loved. There was Abe Housman and Maya Decker and Meredith Weiss and a whole band of Oberlin people. Curtis Lang arrived, with Amy, who looked like she'd been dragged along, and Marco LaRoue and his sister Paola, the men slapping Dave on the shoulder and kissing Emily's cheek. "You look nice," Curtis told her, sliding into the pew behind her. "Thanks," she said tightly, worried that she was going to be stuck in conversation forever. But then the husbands arrived, all at once, as if they'd planned it: Josh, then Will, coattails flying, and Ed. Behind them trailed Dave's parents and Beth's parents, with her little brother, Jason, followed by a knot of older persons, with dark hair and wild brows, whom they vaguely recognized from Lil's wedding as Roths. Lil's boss from the poetry association—a short, barrel-chested man, with enormous eyebrows—strode in, dressed like an English gentleman about to embark on a hearty walk on the moors, with his minions: the pretty young women who staffed his office and had been Lil's coworkers for years. The group had met them all, over the years, at Christmas parties and such.

"Who's that?" Emily whispered to Sadie, cocking her head toward a short, pear-shaped woman with spiky blonde hair and enormous earrings of oxidized metal. "Oh," Sadie said. "Heidi Kass. She was Lil's advisor at

Columbia." Professor Kass was followed by a troupe that could only be academics: A tall, white-haired man in a sweater vest and Wallabees. Two elderly women in shapeless dirndls, their thin hair pulled back in wispy buns. A young, angry-looking fellow—"Joyce scholar," said Sadie impishly, "I'm sure of it"—accompanied by a short, bald man in red, round plastic spectacles and matching suede Hush Puppies, and a bone-thin creature, grayish hair falling past her waist, clad in a puff-sleeved blouse—a pirate shirt, Lil would have called it—and a tight velvet vest. "And who's Stevie Nicks over there?" Emily asked. "Andrea Simmons Smith," Sadie told her, raising her dark brows. "She's a poet. Kind of famous. Her last book was a series of poems based on Dorothy Wordsworth's letters. Sort of wonderful, but sort of cringy."

In the middle of the central aisle, then, appeared an old man in a baggy suit, with pale, thinning hair, who Emily abruptly realized was Sadie's father. She hadn't seen him in years, but she remembered him as tall, hale, athletic. Without Rose on his arm, he looked lost. "Dad," Sadie called, in a voice that made Emily want to cry—would her brisk, efficient parents ever be this frail?—but the Roths came up behind him and he turned and embraced them. Sadie, overcome, turned away.

In the back row, Rob Green-Gold—he'd kept the married name, even after his divorce, so as to avoid confusing his many followers—seated himself and his latest wife, a Johnson heiress who had parted with half her income under his tutelage, next to a group of tousle-headed young men: the Slikowskers of yore. And there was that cheerful Texan Lil dated in college—what was his name?—flanked by their professors, whom they hadn't seen since graduation, all those years ago: George Wadsworth, tall and thin and severe; Joan Silver, clad, just as they remembered her, in a jumpsuit; Martin Donahue, white-haired and rabbity.

A new wave of mourners rushed in, scanning the pews for blocks of seats. Beth recognized the band guys from Lil and Tuck's wedding, and a tiny elderly person, escorted by an attractive young man in a dark suit. "Who's that?" Sadie asked Emily. "I *think* that's Althea Gibbon." Sadie blinked. "She started the poetry foundation?" Emily nodded. "She loved Lil." She was followed by a clump of underdressed young people. "Poets," Sadie suggested. Emily nodded. "Interns."

The mourners kept coming. Lil's friends from Columbia. Dave's neighbors Katherine and Matt. Lil's childhood friend Daniel, who was now a reconstructionist rabbi in Philadelphia, and his pleasant-faced wife. A tall, bald man, accompanied by a stout woman, her face set in a frown.

"Emily, oh my God," Josh said. "It's your friend Bob Goldstein." "Dr. Bob," she cried. "Wow. And Nurse Hopkins. And isn't that Paj Mukherjee?" Josh nodded and waved at the doctors, until Emily tugged his arm down. "We'll talk to them later," she whispered, then flashed him a smile to counteract her wifely tones.

The clock moved past eleven, but the stream of people kept flowing. Lil and Tuck's neighbors in Williamsburg: the British waiter from the L café, the owner of the yoga studio, nearly unrecognizable in a brown wool dress (none of them had ever seen her in anything but knit pants and tank tops), the redheaded woman who ran Ugly Luggage, the slender bartender at Oznot's, and, as Rose stage-whispered, "Girls, let's get this started," and the rabbi strode across the front of the sanctuary, Clara and her anarchist publisher, waving at the group and sitting down a few rows behind them.

Sobered by the sight of the cleric, in his neat suit and shiny shoes, the group settled down, until a blonde apparition emerged at the base of the aisle, paused dramatically, hands sculpturally aloft, and surveyed the crowd: Caitlin Green-Gold—now Caitlin Shamsie—in a smart black shift, vividly pregnant. Ismael's small, noble face peeped over her shoulder, suspended in some sort of sling or cloth backpack, which looped around her shoulders. "Oh, no," Sadie moaned.

Rose leaned over—she and Mr. Peregrine were behind them, with the Roths—and tapped her daughter's shoulder. "What in the devil is that?" she asked.

"I don't know, mom," Sadie intoned.

"*You don't bring a child to a funeral,*" said Rose, in a clipped tone. "What is that girl thinking?"

Sadie shrugged.

"I hope she's going to take him out if he starts crying."

"I'm sure she will," said Ed, patting Rose's hand.

Rose made a noise, something between a grunt and a snort, and settled back in her seat. Caitlin was still standing, ostensibly looking for a seat. Many eyes had turned to her, including those of the rabbi. "This is *just* like her," Emily whispered.

"I know," said Sadie, instantly regretting it. But soon Caitlin had seated herself next to George Wadsworth—Sadie remembering how she'd spoken so disparagingly of him all those years back—forcing everyone in the row to slide down, and making a big show of untying Ismael from his red baby sack.

"Sadie, I think we should get started," said Rose, leaning over Sadie's shoulder.

"*Okay,*" snapped Sadie, and slipped out of her seat.

From the bima, she could see that the chapel was, indeed, nearly full. The flowers drooped heavily in their vases, emitting a pale, vegetal scent, and the skies had cleared, sun slanting through the high stained-glass windows, sending slats of light across the heads of those gathered and along the stone floor. "Thank you all for coming," she said into the small, silver microphone. Her voice reverberated around the room, shocking her, briefly, into silence. *What am I doing,* she thought. *I should have practiced. I should have written something out.* But then she surveyed the rows of stunned faces, all looking to her, if just for a moment, for relief, for answers, for comfort. And she found herself speaking of meeting Lil during freshman orientation: she had been walking through the lobby of Talcott, unsure of which parlor (north or south?) her "rap group" was meeting in, when a voice called down to her, asking, "Hey, do you know Stephie Eichel?" Startled, she looked up and saw Lil, whose dark hair then hung nearly down to her waist, in a black crepe dress from the 1940s, shortened to midthigh, and a pair of cherry red Doc Martens. (The Oberlin folk tittered at this description, as she'd known they would, for this was how they'd all looked then.)

"She's my best friend," Sadie told her. "How do you know Steph? You're from New York? Have we met?"

"Not exactly," Lil had said. "Steph was my roommate at Bennington last summer. She had a photo of you above her desk." Then she gave Sadie a huge smile. "I walked by you every time I went to the bathroom." The crowd dissolved, too readily, into laughter. They could all, Sadie knew, hear Lil saying those words, or something like them. And she had, of course, told this story for exactly this reason, to lighten things up, as Rose had instructed her to, but as the noise—a guffaw, a small clap, a series of whispers—grew to fill the room, a surge of anger shot through Sadie, and she found herself on the verge of shouting *Shut up, shut up, shut up, it's not funny, none of this is funny*. "But that was the sort of person Lil was," she heard herself say, her mouth slumping too close to the microphone. "It doesn't at all feel right to say *was*—" Her voice was cracking now, her fingers twitchy with adrenaline, but she barreled on. "When she loved people—and she loved so many people, so fiercely—she memorized everything about them, even the snapshots they pinned to the wall. She remembered every piece of clothing you wore, every meal you ate, every word you ever said. Her friends were so important to her. Lillian was a true extrovert, in the best sense of the term: she needed people to invigorate and inspire and challenge her. And she, in turn, invigorated and inspired and challenged everyone she knew."

She had diverged from her plan, her plan to keep things calm and brief, to avoid lionizing Lil in death, to not indulge in sleek exegesis on Lil's life; she had diverged from the notes she'd scrawled early that morning on the blank sides of a pile of yellowed index cards, relics of Aunt Minnie, and she stared, then, blankly, at the crowd gathered before her, unsure of where to go from there. And then it occurred to her that it was okay, that her friend, her dear friend, had died and she needn't maintain her composure so completely, needn't pretend that she'd memorized a perfect, glib speech. "Excuse me," she said, and pressed her hands, which were cold, to her hot eyes for a moment, stopping herself from moaning with relief. How nice, she thought, it would be if she could simply stay in this pose until it was all over, until Lil was in the ground, six feet of dirt mounded on top of her. How nice it would be if she could just sit down right then, right up there, on the bima. She was so tired, so very tired.

"Is she okay?" she heard Rose whisper, too loudly, of course. *I'm fine,* she snapped silently, and arranged her face into a practiced smile. When she dropped her hands, the first thing she saw was Tuck—standing at the back of the room, his thick hands messily shoved into the pockets of his gray pants, a satiric smile on his face. How much of her little speech had he heard? Suddenly, her girlish remembrances seemed foolish and sentimental—like set pieces from a movie—and her assessments of Lil like the aphorisms you read on an herbal tea bag ("True friends inspire and challenge you"). Why had he come? They had tried to make everything so nice, to make everything just as Lil would have wanted it, and he had come and ruined everything.

"Thank you for coming," she said, her voice sounding choked and far away, and made her way, shakily, back to her seat between Ed and Emily. Jumpily, she listened as Dave played his song (spare and beautiful; how Lil would have loved, in life, to have him write a song for her) and Beth read a Millay poem. Would Tuck realize the impropriety of his attendance? No. Each time she darted her head toward the back, there he stood, slouched against the wall, like a man in pain, burying his broad, angular cheeks in his hands, as if a particular phrase or reminiscence had moved him beyond control, a pantomime of a grieving man. "Why is he here?" she whispered to Ed, as Emily made her way up to the bima.

"He loved her," he whispered back. "He did, Sadie. Don't be so hard on him." He pulled his hands from hers.

"He didn't," she said, too loudly. But then she remembered their wedding—the rustle and shadow of Lil's parchment-colored gown as she'd walked over these stone floors, the vast, greedy grin on Tuck's face, the vows they'd made to each other, in their clear, young voices. *He did,* she thought, almost against her will. For this made it all more difficult to understand. Had he stopped? Why? She wanted it to be one way or the other: he had never loved her or he loved her still and everything bad that happened had been some sort of mix-up or misunderstanding, as in Shakespeare or Austen.

Emily spoke with a smile and a twinkle, telling of the escapades she and Lil had embarked on during their single days. Lil, she said, had an "inability to compromise—when she wanted something she wanted it." And it was this fierce engagement with the world that made her, "at times, a pain in the ass. She was the person who would tell you if your new haircut was all wrong or if your boyfriend was a jerk—but also the most deliriously fun person to be around. She could make going out for a cup of coffee seem like a big adventure."

This was all Sadie had planned—because she'd not known whether Tal was coming, she'd not factored him in—but when Emily stepped down, George Wadsworth jumped up—"May I have the floor, please?"— and spoke, in his neat, clipped way, of Lil's intellectual curiosity; and then Lil's young cousins, giggling with discomfort; and a sweet aunt, with Lil's large eyes and dark hair; and Heidi Kass from Columbia; and Lil's boss from the poetry organization; and Lil's freshman-year roommate, Robin something, an elfin creature with a smooth cap of black hair, who taught school in Ohio. The group had forgotten about her—though she and Lil had stayed friends until the end—and felt terrible when she began sobbing midway through her words. How thoughtless of them not to include her in the planning—not to make sure she had a place to stay in the city. On and on they came; just when it seemed there was nothing more to say, someone else stepped forward. Meredith Weiss, a young poet, a Columbia classmate, and finally, to Sadie's shock, Rose Peregrine gingerly made her way to the aisle and took hold of the microphone.

"I've always said that Sadie, my daughter, has the most marvelous friends," she began, in what Sadie liked to think of as her Katharine Hepburn voice, with the exaggerated emphasis on verbs, the hard i's and r's and a's. Sadie had never heard her say any such thing, but, strangely, rather than her feeling annoyed, the tears she'd fought off earlier rushed into her eyes, sending a hot flash of pain across her brow. "As some of you know, I was always *particularly* partial to Lillian," she went on, with a grand smile. "Sadie and Lillian became friends *really* as soon as they arrived at school and their freshman year Lil came to our house for Thanksgiving. It was immediately clear that Lillian was a *special* girl, marked for a *glorious* future. She was a person who listened during conversation, who truly wanted to know about others' experiences, who wanted to *learn*. Over the years, she spent many weekends at our house and we had many *remarkable* conversations. Mr. Peregrine and I have always regarded her as a second daughter, of sorts, and we tried to take care of her, as parents would, because her own parents were so far away." Here she smiled, grandiloquently, at the Roths. "But I fear we didn't do a good enough job." She paused and Sadie thought, for a moment, that her mother might loose a few tears herself. But instead Rose's voice hardened and she moved to a different subject. "We were thrilled when Lillian moved to New York. Not just because we were fond of her and glad that Sadie would have a good friend in the city—though all of that was true—but because it was rare to meet a person who loved New York more than Lillian. It was impossible to imagine her living anywhere else." Behind Sadie, Dr. Roth issued a wet cough. "And for an old lady like me—I was born in Brooklyn, you know—it was positively thrilling to watch Lillian discovering New York for the first time. It makes you see everything anew. I miss her so much."

Rose seemed to have worked out a plan with Mrs. Roth, without having notified the girls. She gave the woman a nod as she finished and Mrs. Roth slowly made her way to the front of the room, propelling her tiny frame forward with great difficulty, like a character in a dream who finds the air around her suddenly turned to Jell-O or chocolate pudding. Was she drugged? Sadie wondered. Probably. Her black suit was a near replica of Rose Peregrine's navy one and Sadie, for a moment, wondered if her mother had taken Mrs. Roth to Bergdorf's on Saturday. On either side of Sadie, Beth and Emily emitted small sounds of distress. "I want to thank you all," Mrs. Roth said, her voice thick and low. "You loved her. And she loved all of you. I've never seen a girl who loved her friends so much." And then she collapsed, sobbing. "Oh God," Beth whispered. "Oh God." And Sadie jumped up and embraced the woman. Together, she and Rose guided her downstairs, sat her at a table with a glass of white wine and a bagel, and held her thin hands together, in silence. "I wanted to have another," she told them finally. "But we couldn't." With a shudder, she dropped her wet face into her hands. "Yes," murmured Rose, inexplicably, rubbing the woman's thin back. From the hallway, Sadie heard the faint sounds of footsteps, the low thrum of voices.

"We'd like you to come," Mrs. Roth said finally. "To the funeral. Please. All of you. I don't know what Barry was thinking."

"Oh," said Sadie, feeling herself on the verge of tears. "Thank you." She swallowed the wetness that had gathered in her throat. "We loved her."

"Barry's ordered cars," said Mrs. Roth, pulling a compact out of her bag and staring at it uncomprehendingly. "There's room."

"Okay," said Rose. "Let's have a little drink now."

A moment later, they were invaded. All around them, people talked and, strangely, laughed in little groups, their hands obscured by bagels striped pink by salmon. Dave stood with Meredith Weiss and her husband, the two men making movements with their hands, as if playing a guitar. The husbands—Ed, Josh, and Will—sat together at a small table drinking what appeared to be—but could not be, since Sadie and Rose had not provided it—scotch, the Slikowskers gathered around them like groupies. At a large table, the Roths talked loudly with each other, while Sadie's parents nodded and sipped glasses of white wine. At another, Dave's parents flipped through a yellowing Hebrew songbook, singing snatches of tunes Sadie remembered from camp. Curtis Lang and his bunch positioned themselves by the bar—*of course,* Sadie thought—as did the band guys from the wedding and their respective spouses, and Rob Green-Gold and his girl. The bartender they'd hired to pour wine and Calistoga water, a tall kid with spiky hair, appeared a bit stagestruck.

Beth and Emily stood, in silence, by the tray of bagels, scanning the crowd. Eventually, Sadie left Elaine Roth in the care of her husband and made her way over to them. "I was just going to talk to George Wadsworth," said Beth.

"Okay," said Sadie, through what felt like a layer of cotton wool. It was hot in the room, way too hot, and her breasts, she was realizing too late, were quickly becoming engorged, hard as rocks and painful at the tips. This was the longest she'd left Mina, more than four hours, and she had, she calculated, missed two feedings, before and after Mina's morning nap. She'd brought her hand pump in her bag. Or—*oh no*—she hadn't. Had she? She'd left it out—she could see on the kitchen table, freshly sterilized, in a Ziploc bag—but had she actually grabbed it on the way out? "I'm going to go wash my face," she told Emily. "Will you be okay?"

"Sure," said Emily. Sadie could tell she didn't want to be abandoned, but she slid off anyway, past clusters of Roths in animated discussion, to the little cabinet in the north corner, in which she'd stashed her bag. The room, she thought, was growing hotter and hotter. Why had she worn wool, wool that was now stretching uncomfortably over her breasts? Hadn't she attended a thousand oversubscribed luncheons in this very room, with its nonfunctioning windows? "Excuse me," she said to a man's gray flannel back. But instead of allowing her to pass, he turned and handed her a glass of wine. Tuck. "Sadie Peregrine," he said. "I was just coming to find you. Thought you might need a drink."

"Oh," said Sadie, dumbly. Her breasts, now, were pricking. In a moment, she knew, she'd begin to leak. She had not—*what was wrong with her?*—worn pads. They'd ruined the line of her dress.

"I loved what you said about Lil," said Tuck, his voice ragged and cracking. "You planned all this? You and your mother?"

Sadie compressed her lips into a thin line, an expression her mother had told her, time and again, was unattractive. "Actually, we all planned it together," she told him truthfully.

"Oh, right," he replied, nodding his broad head. "The *group*." He took a long sip of wine and raised his eyebrows at her. He hadn't, she saw, even bothered to shave.

"We tried to figure out what Lil would have wanted," she added, feeling herself somehow—why? why?—becoming the person he thought her to be: girlish, silly, false. She gulped down her wine, as if it were water, for she was thirsty, suddenly, unbearably thirsty.

"That's really *nice* of you," he said.

"I'm sorry," she said, then stopped and closed her eyes. Why would he not go away? What was she sorry for? He looked at her, guilelessly, for the first time in—how long? Years? Ever? It had been at least a year since she'd last seen him, probably more, and the lines that ran from his nose to the corners of his mouth had deepened, exaggerating the hard slant of his cheekbones, and lending his face a peculiar plasticity, as if he were not human but a marionette. His mouth went slack, in expectation of kindness, and Sadie found herself reaching up and embracing him. For a moment, he stiffened and then, with a small sob, he wrapped his arms around her and dropped his head to the top of hers. He was hot, too, and he smelled of sweat and tobacco and alcohol, though not unpleasantly so, and she wanted to tell him it was okay, everything was all right, it wasn't his fault, none of this was his fault, and if it *was* his fault, then it was hers, too, for she could have fought harder for him, for his book, though that wasn't really the point, the point was that she had abandoned Lil, too—so wonderful, but so exhausting, and Sadie had grown so tired, had felt that she didn't have time for difficulty anymore, not once Jack came, and the world changed, and she was so depleted and afraid—and they were two of a kind, in a way, weren't they, now? And she was sorry, she *was,* she was so sorry. But before she could say a word, there it was, yes, the hot, prickling spurt of milk, soaking the slick fabric of her bra and the rougher one of her dress—hopefully not Tuck's suit—and cooling immediately, a sensation she loathed. She pulled away from his embrace and folded her arms across her chest to hide the stains. "I'm afraid," she said hoarsely, "I have to make my way to the ladies' room." He looked directly, disconcertingly, into her eyes, as if daring her to leave. What was it? What did he want from her? She could not say what he perhaps wanted her to say. A moment ago, in his arms, she had thought she could absolve him. But now her empathy had disappeared. Her mind had gone blank. "I—" she said. "I was wondering, do you have the time?" Still, he stared at her, his face strangely immobile, and she thought that he might kiss her, for he looked, rather literally, like a drowning man, battered by waves and wind, scouting for a lifeboat. He held up his wrist to her. "Thanks," she said. "If you'll excuse me," and she turned on her heel and galloped up the stairs, sloshing wine out of her plastic cup with each step, soothed by the efficient click of her heels on the stone steps, a sound she'd relished in childhood, when she'd sat in the synagogue's coatroom reading novels, the edges of minks and sables tickling her arms, listening to the distant voices and music from the bar mitzvahs or weddings or fund-raisers at which her parents danced.

At the ladies' room she found a line—older women in suits, Lil's aunts and cousins—and she walked on, without hesitating, into the foyer, then pushed open the synagogue's heavy metal doors. Outside, the sun shone heavily, pricking her arms through the weave of her dress, and the sky was a brilliant, deep cloudless blue. The cars Dr. Roth had ordered to drive the mourners out to the Island had not yet arrived. Shading her eyes with one hand, she peered up Fifth, to see if they were on their way. European tourists, brightly and tightly clad, in groups of two and three and four, strolled gamely along the sidewalk, dispatched from the St. Regis and the Plaza and the Sherry-Netherland, and bound for Barneys or Bergdorf's or the park. Suddenly, an odd thought possessed

Sadie: What if *she* were to cross the street and enter the park? She had a fat book in her bag—a galley of the new Zadie Smith, which she hadn't yet opened—and the arts section of the paper. She could buy a bottle of water and lie under some big tree—how good it would feel to lie down without Jack jumping on top of her or Mina nursing beside her—and read, just as she and Steph had in high school. Would anyone really miss her?

Just then the glossy nose of a town car glided silently up to the curb. With a low hum, one dark window slid down and the driver, in a cap, called out to her: "Roth?" he asked. "Um, yes," she said, pulling her arms back over the stains on her dress. He nodded. "The other cars'll be here in a second. There was some traffic on the bridge."

"Okay," she said, "do we need to get on the road soon?"

The driver pulled back a crisp white sleeve and studied the enormous face of his watch. "The funeral's at three? I'd say, we leave in fifteen minutes, we'll be in good shape." A second car was already rolling up behind the first.

"Great, thank you. I'll start rounding people up."

Some sort of herding instinct—or perhaps Rose Peregrine—had propelled the crowd upstairs before Sadie had made it past the foyer, much less back to the ladies' room, and she unexpectedly found herself within a mass of people, many of them hugging her and kissing her cheeks. Dr. Roth began guiding his family into the waiting cars, which drove off, one by one, like an army of beetles. When just he and Mrs. Roth remained, he walked quickly over to Sadie. "We've ordered extra cars," he said. "For you"—he waved his arms in a circle—"for the group, the friends."

"Oh," she said, "thank you. Thank you." He nodded, by way of an answer, and helped his wife into a car. Sadie's mother and father climbed into the car behind them. "See you there," Rose called. "Yes," said Sadie weakly, wondering where her friends had got to, where her husband was—but then there they were, Beth and Emily and Dave, and, yes, *Tal,* bringing with them a gust of the synagogue's stale air. Ed put his arms around her. "Hey," he said. "How are you holding up?"

"They ordered cars," she told him, told all of them. "We can go. The Roths said so."

"You don't have to go," said Ed, pulling back and inspecting her face, a gesture she hated, actually. "If you're tired."

"I want to go," she said. She did. And yet the thought of driving out to Long Island made her want to go back inside the synagogue and crawl under a bench.

"I don't mean to intrude," the driver called. "But we should get going. Traffic's bad today."

Beth and Will and Emily and Dave climbed into the car, followed, before they could stop her, by Caitlin and Ismael, and Meredith Weiss, whose husband had gone back to work, as had Josh.

"Um," Sadie said, looking at Ed.

"They can make room for you," he said.

"You're not going to come?"

He looked at her uncomfortably. "I was thinking I'd go back to the office." She folded herself into his chest, stiffly, stupidly, conscious of Tal nearby.

"Okay," she said. "That's fine."

"No, I'm going to come," he said, resting his head on hers. "I'm sorry I said anything." He pulled her closer. "It's just because we're leaving tomorrow." Toronto, she'd forgotten about it. "But I can go into the office tonight." He pulled back from her. "I just thought, you know, we weren't supposed to go to the burial, so I'd planned to go back—"

"It's okay," she said, pulling away from him, irritated. She wished that he'd just go and leave her alone with her friends. "I'm okay to go alone."

"No, I can come," he said, pulling her close again and pressing his face into her hair.

"No, I forgot we were leaving. Maybe Jack and Mina and I should stay here."

"*No.*"

"We can make room," Beth called, glancing angrily at Caitlin.

"We should really get on the road," the driver said.

"I have a car here," said Tal, whom Sadie had sort of forgotten about. His thin shoulders had grown thicker with age, pulling at his white dress shirt, but he otherwise looked eerily the same, his wide slash of mouth sloppy, like a child's drawing, red against his new beard. "I can take you."

Ed looked at her. "Sure," she said. "I'll go with Tal. You go to the office."

"You're sure," he said, inspecting her face.

"I'm *sure,*" she said.

"We've met," said Ed, holding out his hand to Tal. "At Lil and Tuck's. A few times. I'm Ed Slikowski."

"I know," said Tal. "Tal Morgenthal." He turned to Sadie. "I'm parked around the corner.

"Can I have a ride?" came a hoarse voice. Tuck.

"Sure," said Tal, with a heavy exhale. "Let's go."

•

They sat in silence over the glistening ribbon of the East River, but once the grim houses of Queens gave way to the strip malls of western Long Island, Tuck leaned in toward the driver's seat.

"So you found God?" he asked Tal.

"*What?*" said Sadie.

Tal smiled, keeping his eyes fixed on the road ahead of him, and said, "I wouldn't put it like that."

"What?" asked Sadie again. "What are you talking about?"

Tuck nodded, ignoring her. "I can understand that." He nodded again and lolled his head lightly against the window. For a moment, Sadie thought that they might continue in silence, as befit the occasion, but then he sat up again. "I just never saw you as the religious type."

Tal shrugged.

"Tal?" said Sadie, unsure, even, of what to ask him.

"So what are you?" Tuck pressed. "Lubovitch?"

"Tuck, *what* are you talking about?" Sadie swiveled fully around to face Tuck, but he refused to meet her eye. He'd pulled off his jacket, she saw, and rolled up the sleeves of his white shirt. The hair on his forearms was turning gray. And his face had lost all of the softness she'd seen after the service.

For a moment, Tal turned from the road and looked back, wearily, at his companion on this bleak journey. "No," he said. "Not Lubovitch. Not even close. The opposite."

"But you're religious, right?" Tuck pressed, with a slight guffaw. "Was it like, one of those guys stopped you on the street and asked if you were Jewish—and next thing you know you're in the mitzvah mobile? Didn't they, like, recognize you from that Robin Williams movie?"

Tal said nothing.

"Sorry," Tuck offered. "I'm an asshole."

"You are," Tal agreed.

"Tal?" said Sadie. He had not, she saw, taken off his yarmulke when they left the synagogue, but then neither had Dr. Roth or many of the other men. "We all thought—"

"Oh, come on, Sadie," said Tuck. "Are you blind?"

"You don't need to take that tone with her, okay?" said Tal, turning his head sharply toward Tuck.

"Tal, what—" Sadie began, then stopped herself. Did she really need to ask? When she thought about it, it all made sense. He had always questioned the purpose of everything. She thought back over the years, trying to piece the story together: the ulpan, the retreat, back when she was pregnant with Jack. The note Lil had told them about, saying he'd nearly given up acting. And then mostly silence. Back in college, she thought, he'd railed against his parents' materialism, their hypocrisy. But they all had, hadn't they? "We thought," she said, not knowing where these words would lead. "We thought you were taking a break. From acting. What have—"

"We can talk about it later," he said. "After."

"Sadie will have to get home to her *children* later," said Tuck, with such venom that the tears she'd been suppressing all afternoon finally rushed into her eyes and down her face. Why did he hate her so?

"Oh my God," she said, wiping her eyes with a fist. "I can't believe this. Tuck, don't do this."

"What?" said Tuck. "I'm telling the truth."

"It's not a big deal," said Tal. "I'll give you the sixty-second version, okay?" He glanced in the rearview mirror at Tuck. "I'd been unhappy. I wanted all these things that seemed unattainable, that everyone, my parents, told me I could never have—"

"Fame," said Tuck

"No," said Tal. "Not *fame*."

"He just wanted to be an actor," said Sadie loyally, though she wasn't sure she believed this; there had been something more rapacious in Tal, the thing that had allowed him to succeed where Emily failed.

"Yeh." Tal shrugged. "And it turned out that I could be. That it *was* attainable. I'd wanted it for so long, my whole life, and then when I had it, it wasn't so exciting. You know?"

"Yes," said Tuck, in a small voice that made Sadie, again, feel sorry for him.

"That's the rational part," said Tal, who seemed to be warming to the task of revealing himself. And now, suddenly, she wanted to know, wanted to know everything, every minute he'd spent apart from her. Her mind began racing. Was there a wife somewhere—in Israel? In L.A.?—wearing a wig and a long, heavy skirt? Was there a baby with Tal's angular face and long arms? And how did he make a living? The Orthodox couldn't act, could they? *Was* he Orthodox? What did he mean, the opposite of Lubovitch? Had he just thrown everything away? *Oh God, oh God,* she thought, *I hope not.* But then, what difference would it make?

"The irrational part is just that I felt this longing to *know*," Tal was saying.

"To know what?" asked Tuck, leaning forward into the space between the two front seats. "Can I smoke in here?"

"*No,*" said Sadie.

"The prayers that my grandfather knew. Things like that. The truth."

Ahead of them, on the LIE, traffic had come to a standstill and Sadie groaned.

"Please stop," she said. She was succumbing, she knew, to temper. As she did more and more these days, though poor Ed bore the brunt of it. "Please just stop talking. Please. I have a headache. I just, I can't listen anymore." Her breasts, stuffed inside the wool dress, had turned to rocks. Why had she not simply asked Tal if she could run to the bathroom before they left? The pump, no, was not in her bag, but she could have hand pumped, like the chipper hippies in the Dr. Sears book. "Please," she said. "Just for a minute."

Both men wore a similar—and familiar—expression of befuddlement, one she'd seen, occasionally, on Ed's face lately. *Okay, crazy person,* they seemed to be saying. But she wasn't crazy, she was tired, and she didn't want to hear about Tal's conversations with God *or whatever.* This was why she'd cheated on him, why she'd left him, wasn't it? This hokey earnestness. It was too much. She wanted Tal back the way he was in college, when they'd walked around campus at midnight, the trees a looming canopy above them, and she'd felt so happy and lucky it was all she could do not to hug him with joy, when they were friends, such good friends, and she could talk with him about anything, without fear of judgment, before things had become complicated, before she'd succumbed. She wanted him the way he'd been the summer before Lil's wedding, when they'd laughed at Dave's sulks and moods, and spent their evenings drinking wine in one café or another, when he'd been on the verge of breaking through, the two of them giddy with possibility. Was this why she'd fallen, crashingly, in love with him? And had she really left him because she knew him too well, loved him too much, because she'd needed him so terribly? Such an old story. An ancient story. A cliché. Did she love Ed less? Or Michael, whose very name still made her flush with guilt, yes, but also desire? No, probably no. But falling in love at thirty was different, so different, than falling in love at eighteen. It was never the same, was it?

"Please stop," she said again, almost without thinking, dropping her head into her hands. "Please. I think I'm a little carsick."

"We're not getting anywhere anyway," said Tuck. Off the exit to their right, a neon sign in the shape of a martini blinked erratically. "We could have a drink." Around them, cars were frantically trying to get across traffic and over to the exit.

To Sadie's surprise, Tal said, "Sure. Why not," and scooted the car over a lane, up the exit, and onto some downtown byway that looked as though it had seen better days. Where were they? Babylon? Great Neck? Someplace that had once been a real town, with a barbershop and a grocer and a pharmacy, but was now just a conglomeration of oversized houses on undersized plots serviced by a series of malls and car dealerships. Tal coasted the car down the street until they arrived at the tall sign that had beckoned to Tuck, parking in the decrepit lot beneath it, weeds sprouting from cracks in the gray, pebbly asphalt.

The bar, too, had seen better days. But it was cool and dark, its wood-paneled walls covered with aged photos of smiling celebrities, its chairs filled with florid-faced old men. "Jameson with a soda back," Tuck told the bartender, a young man with slick, dark hair and the sort of mustache that had gone out of style thirty years prior. "Same," said Tal.

"Will you, um—" Sadie asked. "Can you—" Tal nodded.

"Okay," she said nervously. "Could you order me a cup of decaf, if they have it? I'm going to run to the bathroom."

When she emerged—mildly less uncomfortable—Tuck and Tal had taken their drinks to a small Formica table lit by the red glare of a Budweiser sign and adorned with a set of Heineken coasters. Tuck held a short, unfiltered cigarette between his fingers. "Isn't that illegal?" Sadie asked, nodding at it.

Tuck shrugged and lit a match. "I thought outside of the city you could smoke."

"No. Statewide ban."

"That guy's smoking." At a table in the corner, an ancient man sat hunched over a hand-rolled cigarette and a beer.

"Oh." Sadie looked balefully at her white mug of coffee, which smelled burned, then turned her attention to the faux-wood bowl of miniature pretzels, but could not bring herself to eat even one. They should not be here. They should have waited, patiently, in the punishing traffic, or figured out a new route along the city streets. Now she knew, in a flash, they would never make it to the funeral. Tuck would order scotch after scotch, growing more and more belligerent, until they had to carry him home.

"The *truth*," he said now to Tal. "Don't you feel weird saying that?"

Tal looked at Sadie for the first time, she realized, since his arrival, and stretched his long hand out toward her on the table. Did he mean for her to take it?

"Tal," she said. "The bartender might be able to give us directions to the cemetery that bypass the LIE."

"I just don't get that you could think that the world offers *one* truth," Tuck said. "You went to *Oberlin*."

Tal turned from Sadie, taking a quick gulp of his drink. "So?" he said finally.

Tuck stared at him. "Well, it's just so archaic. It's, like, premodern. Our generation, we're *post*modern. There is no one truth. The truth isn't a fixed thing. It's subjective."

Suddenly, Tal began to laugh. Tuck let out a little chuckle, too, either out of sympathy or confusion. "I loved Kierkegaard in college, too. But it doesn't really hold up, you know. Life just isn't like that. Things are much more black-and-white. She loves you or she doesn't. You have a job or you don't. Your parents are alive or dead." Sadie started at this. Had his parents died without any of them knowing it? Surely he would have told Dave, at least. "The truth is the truth. Incontrovertible facts. How it makes you feel, *that's* subjective." He paused, gauging the length of Tuck's fuse. "You're a journalist, right? Isn't it your job to present the truth?"

Tuck snorted, downed his drink, and waved his hand at the bartender, signaling for another round. "Please. You don't really believe that Woodward and Bernstein bullshit." The drink arrived and Tuck looked at it suspiciously, as though it had come unbidden. "You can drink?" he asked Tal.

"I'm not Mormon." Tal laughed.

But Tuck did not smile. He wrapped his hand around the tumbler of scotch and raised it eagerly to his mouth, flicking his eyes from Sadie to Tal.

"So you had a thing for Lil, right?" he asked suddenly, his tone becoming brisk and efficient.

"No," said Tal, before Tuck had even got the words out. Still, he was too late. Tuck's face was already twisting into a closemouthed smirk.

"Not even in college?" He raised an eyebrow. "All those late nights at the radio station?"

"No," said Tal, smiling and tilting his chair onto its back legs.

"I knew it." Tuck laughed, clapping his hands. "I'm a very good judge of character. She used to say you were in love with Dave. And you fell in love with Sadie because she was a version of him that you could actually have."

Sadie sighed. She'd heard this from Lil, too, a zillion times, and now, hearing it from Tuck, she felt deeply bored. She supposed Tuck wanted to shock them.

"But I always thought it was because she was a version of *Lil* you could actually have."

Was this true? Sadie wondered. No, certainly not. In college, they'd been close, Lil and Tal, and at one point the rest of them had speculated, but they'd speculated about everyone. Though there was that night—which year? junior or senior?—when she, Sadie, had asked him about Lil—why? Had she wanted him, way back then? Had she wanted proof that he didn't want Lil more than her? Was she such a monster of vanity, unable to imagine a world in which men and women didn't trample one another vying for her friendship? No, no, of course not, on all accounts. They'd just been talking—they were *friends*—and he'd told her, without hesitation, something that had made no sense to her at the time. "If Lil became my girlfriend," he'd said, "she wouldn't be Lil anymore."

"What do you mean?" Sadie had asked him querulously. "How could she not be herself? She *is* herself."

"No," Tal insisted. "She'd be *diminished*."

Now, a decade later, she finally understood what he meant: marriage had, certainly, diminished Lil—made her petty and sad and afraid and certainly *less* than the sum of her parts. And this was because of Tuck, yes, but it was also Lil—she had, somehow, allowed it.

"Sadie," Tal said to her now, but she would not look at him, no, she would not.

"I'm going to talk to the bartender," she said. Five minutes later she had directions, in blue ink, on a plush cocktail napkin. "Let's go," she said, hoisting her bag on her shoulder.

They left the small parking lot, with its cluster of dinged, dated cars, and continued through the low, gray town and onto the sort of artery that gave Sadie a chill: mile after mile of auto dealerships and strip malls and gas stations and Bennigan's and Applebee's, streams of people inexplicably filing into their depths.

"We're in hell," Tuck droned, his large forehead pressed to the window, and Sadie, for once, was inclined to agree with him. "This is what Atlanta looks like now. Hell. The fucking Roths *would* make us come out here."

There was traffic on this road, too—presumably other travelers trying to bypass the expressway—and they missed every light. Tuck slowly began to beat his head against the window.

"I bet everyone else is stuck, too," said Sadie. Tuck shrugged, his face still turned to the window, in the posture of a sullen twelve-year-old. But as the road narrowed and the shopping centers grew farther and farther apart—they were getting closer, Sadie was sure—he sat up straight and folded his hands tensely in his lap.

"I know you all think this is my fault," he said. "Everything that happened."

"No," said Sadie. "We don't."

"No," said Tal. "None of us think that."

"See," Tuck nearly shouted. "That's what I just *couldn't stand*. The 'we.'" He mimicked Sadie: "'Oh no, *we* don't blame you.' I got so sick of hearing about your little *group*. Your perfect, *interesting* little lives. Your *interesting* jobs. Your *stupid* perfect families."

"If you knew my father," said Tal, grinning at Sadie. "You wouldn't say that."

"*No*," said Sadie, staring sadly out the window. They were passing by a set of enormous mirrored cubes—a brand-new office park—in which she saw Tal's silver rental reflected a thousandfold, her dark head a small point within it. Her breasts still chafed and itched. The milk she'd expelled into the bar's rancid sink had just barely taken the edge off. Mina was a hungry girl and, already, more milk was coming in. And yet, now, her children, Ed, felt very far away. She could imagine, for a moment, casting herself into Tal's arms and leaving everything behind, telling him to just drive. "Tuck, I don't get it. Were we ever anything but nice to you? We tried *so hard*. We wanted Lil to be happy."

Tuck snorted. "Happy? Lil? How could she be when she was always comparing herself—and me—to all of you?"

"What?" said Tal. "That's crazy."

"Wait, wait, wait," cried Sadie. "Was that—" She grabbed the napkin off the dashboard. "I think we should have turned left at that light. By the first office building." She held the napkin up and tried to make out the bartender's slanted, half-formed cursive.

Tuck was still talking. "All of you went on with your lives, but she still wanted to be the center of all of your attention, like in college, when she was *special*. I could never make her feel as *special* as you all did."

"Please stop," she said, "let me just look at this." They were deep inside the complex now, the too-bright sun glinting off the endless rows of mirrored cubes. It was odd, Sadie thought, to think of the workers inside them, thousands of them, invisible to passersby, typing memos and inventing numerical codes for dental procedures and answering the calls of those defeated by the instructions supplied with their DSL modems.

Tuck was still speaking, but his words were clumping together in Sadie's mind, a haze of sound. They were, she realized, with a sudden twist of the gut, the only car on the road. In order to get directions, they would have to stop at one of the menacing buildings—or drive back toward civilization. The bar's burned coffee—she'd taken just a sip or two—sat acidly in her stomach. She should have eaten after the service. Her mother had said so.

And then, just as suddenly as they'd come upon them, they left behind the silver buildings and found themselves on a bare stretch of asphalt, fields of new grass extending as far as they could see on either side of them. This area must have been clear-cut by the developers, Sadie thought, who'd run out of money. Or tenants. Long Island, she thought, was terribly flat. A terminal moraine. The road here stretched endlessly, infinitely into the distance, a thread of inky black, with the lush sheen of new tar. There was nowhere, nowhere at all, to inquire about the cemetery.

But then—miraculously—they were upon it. First, from the distance, they saw a clump of . . . something—they knew not what. As they grew closer, they made out the forms of trees and a low stone fence. And soon they were driving past mile after mile of graves, low stones engraved with Stars of David—on both sides of the road—and scanning the area for an entrance. "So many dead Jews," Tuck marveled, trying for a satiric tone but managing to sound merely sad. Sadie had a grim thought: *Soon, we'll be among them.*

"I don't know if I want to do this," Tuck said suddenly. "I feel kind of sick. Does it smell like carbon monoxide in here?"

"Not really," said Sadie. "We'll be there in a second. We just have to find the right entrance."

Furiously, Tuck fumbled with his door. "No," he said. "I want to get out, okay? *Now*. How do you get the fucking window down? I need a fucking cigarette. *Open the fucking window. I need to get out.*" From his side, Tal pressed the appropriate button, but Tuck was pulling at the handle of the door, his face flushed and sweaty.

"Whoa," said Tal. "Don't jump out of the car, okay? I'll stop."

"No," said Sadie. "Tal, don't stop. We're almost there. Let's just get there. We're going to miss the funeral."

"*No,*" said Tuck. "I can't do this. Pull the fucking car over. I'm getting out. I can't go. I—"

"You *have* to go," said Sadie. "You've come this far. She was your *wife.*" But Tal pulled off the road onto a mound of dark, soft earth, just as Tuck wrestled the door open. "I can't do this," he shouted, stumbling out of the car, his shoes kicking up sprays of black dirt and clumps of new grass. "*Any* of this."

"Okay," said Sadie, stepping out of the car. "Okay."

From afar, a loud humming eclipsed the sounds of Tuck's raspy breathing. Moments later, a sleek black car sped past them—the first they'd seen in who knew how long.

"That must be them," said Sadie. "Or some of them." She raised one hand to her eyes and watched to see where the car would turn. Tuck would be fine in a moment and they would go on to the funeral, though perhaps they would be the first to arrive, the only ones to get off the clogged highway. But the car didn't turn—it kept going, straight and fast along the spookily straight road, until it disappeared from sight. Tal put his hand in his pocket and gazed questioningly at Sadie, who shrugged. "I guess it wasn't them," she said.

"Tuck," she said. "We really should go."

"No," he said. "I'm not going. I'm going home."

"Home?" she asked. This was too much, this childishness. "How are you going to get home?"

"I don't fucking know," he shouted, loosening and pulling off his tie with a violent tug.

"Tuck, come on," she said, aware that she was using the tone she employed to coax Jack into the bath. "Let's go. It's going to be fine."

But he was already walking off along the shoulder of the road, lighting a cigarette in cupped hands, stumbling with every other step, his shoes sinking into the rich soil. "Fuck you," he shouted, though it wasn't clear whether he was addressing Sadie and Tal or the world or the Roths or the mirrored buildings with their hives of drones.

Tal shook his head and looked at Sadie. "Okay," said Sadie, with a shrug. "Bye." For a long time they stood, watching his slow progress, then they stepped back into the car, the crack of closing doors impossibly loud on the dead stretch of road, and drove off, west, in the direction of an ocean they couldn't see. "He'll be fine," Tal said, reaching a hand toward her. "He won't miss it."

"Okay," she said again. Tal was right, she knew, and she forced herself to keep her eyes facing forward. But still, she saw him, in the rearview mirror: a small, dark figure, hobbling along the side of the darker road, east toward Queens, and then home to Brooklyn. And for a moment she wished that she could join him.

acknowledgments

My most profound thanks to my husband, Evan, and my son, Coleman, for their tremendous patience, kindness, and enthusiasm, and, of course, to Tina Bennett, Alexis Gargagliano, Svetlana Katz, and Stephanie Koven for the same. I'm also hugely grateful to Amy Rosenberg, who read numerous drafts of this novel and offered invaluable edits and insight, and to Andrea Crawford, Ellen Umansky, Kate Bolick, and Rachel Scobie for help in various areas along the way, and to my parents, Stan and Phyllis Rakoff. Much of this novel was written at the MacDowell Colony and with support from its generous, smart staff; at the Writer's Room; and at the beautiful home of Raina Kattelson and Bob, Maeve, and Romi Butscher. Last, it's strange to thank those who can't say "you're welcome" in return, but I'm profoundly indebted to three writers: Sylvia Plath, Dawn Powell, and, of course, Mary McCarthy, to whose marvelous novel, *The Group,* my own is, of course, an homage.